THE ESSENTIAL H.G. WELLS | MANIFESTOS FOR A NEW WORLD ORDER

THE ESSENTIAL H.G. WELLS | MANIFESTOS FOR A NEW WORLD ORDER

H.G. WELLS

Contents

1

Introduction

Few figures in modern history have shaped the intellectual landscape of the 20th century as profoundly as H.G. Wells. While often celebrated for his contributions to science fiction—The War of the Worlds, The Time Machine, The Invisible Man—Wells' true ambition stretched far beyond storytelling. He was a thinker, a social reformer, and a self-proclaimed architect of the future. In his later years, Wells turned his focus toward the pressing challenges of civilization, advocating for a planned world order that could steer humanity away from self-destruction.

This collection, The Essential H.G. Wells: Manifestos for a New World, brings together some of his most radical and influential works on the future of governance, the organization of knowledge, and the fate of mankind. Through these writings, Wells envisioned a scientifically managed society, free from the constraints of nationalism, war, and economic instability. He saw the potential for a World State, a global government led by enlightened elites who would guide civilization toward rational progress.

A Blueprint for Tomorrow?

Wells was writing in a time of political turmoil, war, and rapid technological change—circumstances eerily similar to those of the present day. His belief in a rationally planned society was not merely theoretical; it was a call to action. He envisioned a world in which education, media, and governance were centralized and optimized to create a stable, intelligent, and forward-thinking global civilization.

Many of Wells' ideas were controversial in his time and remain so today. Was he a utopian idealist, striving for peace and order in an unpredictable world? Or was he a proto-technocrat, advocating for a system that, in practice, could lead to centralized control and loss of individual freedoms? Some saw his vision as a roadmap to a better future; others viewed it as a warning of elite-driven control disguised as progress.

The Works in This Collection

This book compiles Wells' most important works on global governance and the future of civilization, including:

The Open Conspiracy – His boldest manifesto for a new world order, calling for a movement of intellectuals and scientists to reshape society.

The New World Order – A detailed exploration of how a global government could function and what obstacles stood in its way.
The Fate of Man – An examination of the existential threats facing humanity and the urgency of a coordinated global response.
World Brain – His proposal for a worldwide knowledge network, a precursor to modern ideas about global information systems.
Why This Collection Matters Today
H.G. Wells' vision may have been ambitious, but many of the ideas he championed have either come to fruition or remain active topics of debate. The concept of a global government, a centralized knowledge system, and a ruling class of experts continues to be discussed by world leaders, economists, and technologists. His work is essential reading not just for historians but for anyone seeking to understand the roots of modern globalist thought.

Was Wells predicting the future, shaping it, or warning against it? That is for the reader to decide.

The Open Conspiracy

THE OPEN CONSPIRACY

Published in 1928, The Open Conspiracy is one of H.G. Wells' most direct calls for a global transformation led by an intellectual elite. Unlike his earlier fiction, this book serves as a manifesto for world governance, advocating for a gradual, non-violent overthrow of existing nation-states in favor of a scientifically managed society.

Core Ideas of The Open Conspiracy

A New Revolutionary Class – Wells envisions a movement composed of scientists, educators, business leaders, and rational thinkers who reject nationalism and work toward a unified world order.

The End of Sovereign Nation-States – The book argues that separate countries, with their competing interests and military conflicts, are obstacles to human progress.

A World State Governed by Reason – Wells proposes that society should be centrally organized by a scientific elite, who would ensure peace, economic stability, and intellectual advancement.

Education and Propaganda as Tools for Change – Unlike traditional revolutions, which rely on violence, The Open Conspiracy suggests gradual ideological shifts through education, the media, and strategic influence.

A Technocratic Society – The book envisions a world run by technocrats, where expertise and rational planning replace political struggle and emotional decision-making.

A "Soft" Revolution Toward Global Control

Wells acknowledges that many will resist such a radical transformation, but he insists that the Open Conspiracy must not be a secret movement—it should function in the open, influencing institutions from within until the idea of world government becomes inevitable.

Rather than a sudden coup, Wells describes a gradual infiltration of existing power structures: universities, businesses, scientific organizations, and governments. Over time, these institutions would shift public opinion and policy toward a unified world order.

Historical Impact & Relevance

At the time of its publication, The Open Conspiracy was viewed by some as utopian idealism and by others as a roadmap for elite global control. Many of its themes—global governance, elite technocracy, controlled education, and internationalism—resonate today in discussions about the World Economic Forum, transnational organizations, and the influence of scientific and corporate elites in politics.

Some interpret The Open Conspiracy as a well-intentioned attempt to prevent future wars after World War I, while others see it as a prototype for modern globalist agendas that threaten national sovereignty and individual freedoms.

Regardless of perspective, The Open Conspiracy remains one of the most explicit and unapologetic blueprints for global transformation in modern history.

2

INTRODUCTION

The Open Conspiracy was Wells' Blue Print for A World Revolution; he regarded this book as his finished statement on the way the world ought to be ordered. Possibly he underestimated, or ignored, the fact that it is often in the interest of subsets of the human race to act against other subsets. Moreover the emphasis on religion seems odd, from a rationalist.

After the First World War, observing the lack of knowledge of most people about most things, he turned to history, starting, in 1918, his Outline of History first published in parts with 'gorgeous' covers, then in 1920 as a two-volume work including colour plates of a lavish nature for the time. In effect it was jointly authored—his chapters were sent to collaborators, and the resulting multiple corrections reassembled by the duly-chastened Wells. A 'popular' one-volume edition appeared in 1930. By the standards of its time this was a best-seller. It was praised decades later by A.J.P. Taylor as 'still the best introduction to history'. Toynbee had a favourable opinion of it. During the 1920s it sparked a controversy with Hilaire Belloc, who believed in such things as the 'Fall of Man'. It was also attacked by a teacher of Greek. Wells' hopes that school history could be taught in an international sense still, of course, have not come to fruition.

He planned and collaborated a hefty set of volumes on biology, The Science of Life, with his own son, and with Julian Huxley; the theme was largely evolutionary (The Origin of Species was published only a few years before his birth). Huxley, a descendant of T.H. Huxley, regarded Wells as something of a Cockney upstart.

And he wrote a descriptive, rather than analytical, book on economics, which includes many ingenious observations but was eclipsed by Keynes' General Theory of four years later.

Some of his books were filmed; his Invisible Man was turned into a filmscript by Preston Sturges, who however regarded his books as not very filmable and infuriated Wells by making the invisible man mad. Another media incident was Orson Welles' radio broadcast of War of the Worlds in 1938, involving aggressive Martians landing in a location Americanised from its original Surrey, and which was reported to have cause mass panic among less educated Americans on the eastern seaboard.

C.P. Snow wrote of Wells that he could 'throw out a phrase that crystallised a whole argument', and that he 'never heard anyone remotely in the same class.' Among these phrases were 'the War that will end War', coined when he worked with the Ministry of Propaganda under Northcliffe during the First World War, which he supported, and 'the New World Order', which he seemed to be the first to use, or popularise, in a 1940 book of that title. His less successful phrases included the 'competent receiver'. He said of himself that he 'worked all the time'.

He was a socialist of an empirical, rather vague, rationalist type, disliking Marx and unenthusiastic about the managerial socialism of the Webbs.

His book The Open Conspiracy was published in 1928, subtitled Blue Prints for a World Revolution. Bertrand Russell said of this book '...I do not know of anything with which I agree more entirely' though since this was in a begging letter perhaps he was just being polite. It was revised and republished as What Are We to Do with Our Lives? in 1931.

In this short book, Wells attempts to answer the question: What should socialists actually do?—to which he confessed several times to having no very clear idea. It's a counter to Marx: why shouldn't non-proletarians unite to change the world?

3

I. — THE PRESENT CRISIS IN HUMAN AFFAIRS

THE world is undergoing immense changes. Never before have the conditions of life changed so swiftly and enormously as they have changed for mankind in the last fifty years. We have been carried along—with no means of measuring the increasing swiftness in the succession of events. We are only now beginning to realize the force and strength of the storm of change that has come upon us.

These changes have not come upon our world from without. No meteorite from outer space has struck our planet; there have been no overwhelming outbreaks of volcanic violence or strange epidemic diseases; the sun has not flared up to excessive heat or suddenly shrunken to plunge us into Arctic winter. The changes have come through men themselves. Quite a small number of people, heedless of the ultimate consequence of what they did, one man here and a group there, have made discoveries and produced and adopted inventions that have changed all the condition, of social life.

We are now just beginning to realize the nature of these changes, to find words and phrases for them and put them down. First they began to happen, and then we began to see that they were happening. And now we are beginning to see how these changes are connected together and to get the measure of their consequences. We are getting our minds so clear about them that soon we shall be able to demonstrate them and explain them to our children in our schools. We do not do so at present. We do not give our children a chance of discovering that they live in a world of universal change.

What are the broad lines upon which these alterations of condition are proceeding?

It will be most convenient to deal with them in the order in which they came to be realized and seen clearly, rather than by the order in which they came about or by their logical order. They are more or less interdependent changes; they overlap and interact.

It was only in the beginning of the twentieth century that people began to realize the real significance of that aspect of our changing conditions to which the phrase "the abolition of distance" has been applied. For a whole century before that there had been a continual increase in the speed and safety of travel and transport and the ease and swiftness with which messages could be transmitted, but this increase had not seemed to be a matter of primary importance. Various results of railway, steamship, and telegraph became manifest; towns grew larger, spreading into the countryside, once inaccessible lands became areas of rapid settlement and cultivation, industrial centres began to live on imported food, news from remote parts lost its time-lag and tended to become contemporary, but no one hailed these things as being more than "improvements" in existing conditions. They are not observed to be the beginnings of a profound revolution in the life of mankind. The attention of young people was not drawn to them; no attempt was made, or considered necessary, to adapt political and social institutions to this creeping enlargement of scale.

Until the closing years of the nineteenth century there was no recognition of the real state of affairs. Then a few observant people began, in a rather tentative, commentary sort of way, to call attention to what was happening. They did not seem to be moved by the idea that something had to be done about it; they merely remarked, brightly and intelligently, that it was going on. And then they went on to the realization that this "abolition of distance" was only one aspect of much more far-reaching advances.

Men were travelling about so much faster and flashing their communications instantly about the world because a progressive conquest of force and substance was going on. Improved transport was only one of a number of portentous consequences of that conquest; the first to be conspicuous and set men thinking; but not perhaps the first in importance. It dawned upon them that in the last hundred years there had been a stupendous progress in obtaining and utilizing mechanical power, a vast increase in the efficiency of mechanism, and associated with that an enormous increase in the substances available for man's purposes, from vulcanized rubber to the modern steels, and from petroleum and margarine to tungsten and aluminium. At first the general intelligence was disposed to regard these things as lucky "finds," happy chance discoveries. It was not apprehended that the shower of finds was systematic and continuous. Popular writers told about these things but they told of them at first as "Wonders"—"Wonders" like the Pyramids, the Colossus of Rhodes, and the Great Wall of China. Few realized how much more they were than any "Wonders." The "Seven Wonders of the World" left men free to go on living, toiling, marrying, and dying as they had been accustomed to for immemorial ages. If the "Seven Wonders" had vanished or been multiplied three score it would not have changed the lives of any large proportion of human beings. But these new powers and substances were modifying and transforming—unobtrusively, surely, and relentlessly—very particular of the normal life of mankind.

They increased the amount of production and the methods of production. They made possible "Big-Business," to drive the small producer and the small distributor out of the market. They swept away factories and evoked new ones. They changed the face of the fields. They brought into the normal life, thing by thing and day by day, electric light and heating, bright cities at night, better aeration, new types of clothing, a fresh cleanliness. They changed a world where there had never been enough into a world of potential plenty, into a world of excessive plenty. It dawned upon their minds after their realization of the "abolition of distance" that shortage of supplier had also been abolished and that irksome toil was no longer necessary to produce everything material that man might require. It is only in the last dozen years that this broader and profounder fact has come through to the intelligence of any considerable number of people. Most of them have still to carry their realization a step farther and see how complete is the revolution in the character of the daily life these things involve.

But there are still other changes outside this vast advance in the pace and power of material life. The biological sciences have undergone a corresponding extension. Medical art has attained a new level of efficiency, so that in all the modernizing societies of the world the average life is prolonged, and there is, in spite of a great fall in the birth rate, a steady, alarming increase in the world's population. The proportion of adults alive is greater than it has ever been before. Fewer and fewer human beings die young This has changed the social atmosphere about us. The tragedy of lives cut short and ended prematurely is passing out of general experience. Health becomes prevalent. The continual toothaches, headaches, rheumatism, neuralgias, coughs, colds, indigestions that made up so large a part of the briefer lives of our grandfathers and grandmothers fade out of experience. We may all live now, we discover, without any great burthen of fear, wholesomely and abundantly, for as long as the desire to live is in us.

But we do not do so. All this possible freedom of movement, this power and abundance, remains for most of us no more than possibility. There is a sense of profound instability about these achievements of our race. Even those who enjoy, enjoy without security, and for the great multitude of mankind there is neither ease, plenty, nor freedom. Hard tasks, insufficiency, and unending money worries are still the ordinary stuff of life. Over everything human hangs the threat of such war as man has never known before, were armed and reinforced by all the powers and discoveries of modern science.

When we demand why the achievement of power turns to distress and danger in our hands, we get some very unsatisfactory replies. The favourite platitude of the politician excusing himself for the futilities of his business, is that "moral progress has not kept pace with material advance." That seems to satisfy him completely, but it can satisfy no other intelligent person. He says "moral." He leaves that word unexplained. Apparently he wants to shift the responsibility to our religious teachers. At the most he has made but the vaguest gesture towards a reply. And yet, when we consider it, charitably and sympathetically, there does seem to be a germ of reality in that phrase of his.

What does moral mean? Mores means manners and customs. Morality is the conduct of life. It is what we do with our social lives. It is how we deal with ourselves in relation to our fellow creatures. And there does seem to be a much greater discord now than there was (say) a couple of hundred years ago between the prevailing ideas of how to carry on life and the opportunities and dangers of the time. We are coming to see more and more plainly that certain established traditions which have made up the frame of human relationships for ages are not merely no longer as convenient as they were, but are positively injurious and dangerous. And yet at present we do not know how to shake off these traditions, these habits of social behaviour which rule us. Still less are we able to state, and still less bring into operation, the new conceptions of conduct and obligation that must replace them.

For example, the general government of human affairs has hitherto been distributed among a number of sovereign states—there are about seventy of them now—and until recently that was a quite tolerable system of frame-works into which a general way of living could be fitted. The standard of living may not have been as high as our present standards, but the social stability and assurance were greater. The young were trained to be loyal, law-regarding, patriotic, and a defined system of crimes and misdemeanours with properly associated pains, penalties, and repressions, kept the social body together. Everyone was taught a history glorifying his own state, and patriotism was chief among the Virtues. Now, with great rapidity, there has been that "abolition of distance," and everyone has become next-door neighbour to everyone else. States once separate, social and economic systems formerly remote from one another, now jostle each other exasperatingly. Commerce under the new conditions is perpetually breaking nationalist bounds and making militant raids upon the economic life of other countries. This exacerbates patriotism in which we have all been trained and with which we are all, with scarcely an exception, saturated. And meanwhile war, which was once a comparative slow bickering upon a front, has become war in three dimensions; it gets at the "non-combatant" almost as searchingly as at the combatant, and has acquired weapons of a stupendous cruelty and destructiveness. At present there exists no solution to this paradoxical situation. We are continually being urged by our training and traditions to antagonisms and conflicts that will impoverish, starve, and destroy both our antagonists and ourselves. We are all trained to distrust and hate foreigners, salute our flag, stiffen up in a wooden obedient way at our national anthem, and prepare to follow the little fellows in spurs and feathers who pose as the heads of our states into the most horrible common destruction. Our political and economic ideas of living are out of date, and we find great difficulty in adjusting them and reconstructing them to meet the huge and strenuous demands of the new times. That is really what our gramophone politicians have in mind—in the vague way in which they have anything in mind—when they put on that well-worn record about moral progress not having kept pace with material inventions.

Socially and politically we want a revised system of ideas about conduct, a view of social and political life brought up to date. We are not doing the effective thing with our lives, we are drifting, we are being hoodwinked and bamboozled and misled by those who trade upon the old traditions. It is preposterous that we should still be followed about and pestered by war, taxed for war preparations, and threatened bodily and in our liberties by this unnecessary and exaggerated and distorted survival of the disunited world of the pre-scientific era. And it is not simply that our political way of living is now no better than an inherited defect and malformation, but that our everyday life, our eating and drinking and clothing and housing and going about, is also cramped, thwarted, and impoverished, because we do not know how to set about shaking off the old ways and fitting the general life to our new opportunities. The strain takes the form of increased unemployment and a dislocation of spending power. We do not know whether to spend or save. Great swarms of us find ourselves unaccountably thrown out of work. Unjustly, irrationally. Colossal business reconstructions are made to increase production and accumulate profits, and meanwhile the customers with purchasing power dwindle in numbers and fade away. The economic machine creaks and makes every sign of stopping—and its stopping means universal want and starvation. It must not stop. There must be a reconstruction, a change-over. But what sort of a change-over?

Though none of us are yet clear as to the precise way in which this great change-over is to be effected, there is a world-wide feeling now that change- over or a vast catastrophe is before us. Increasing multitudes participate in that uneasy sense of insecure transition. In the course of one lifetime mankind has passed from a state of affairs that seems to us now to have been slow, dull, ill-provided, and limited, but at least picturesque and tranquil-minded, to a new phase of excitement, provocation, menace, urgency, and actual or potential distresses. Our lives are part of one another. We cannot get away from it. We are items in a social mass. What are we to do with our lives?

4

II. — THE IDEA OF THE OPEN CONSPIRACY

I AM a writer upon social and political matters. Essentially I am a very ordinary, undistinguished person. I have a mediocre brain, a very average brain, and the way in which my mind reacts to these problems is therefore very much the way in which most brains will react to them. But because it is my business to write and think about these questions, because on that account I am able to give more time and attention to them than most people, I am able to get rather ahead of my equals and to write articles and books just a little before the ideas I experience become plain to scores of thousands, and then to hundreds of thousands, and at last to millions of other people. And so it happened that a few years ago (round about 1927) I became very anxious to clear up and give form to a knot of suggestions that seemed to me to have in them the solution of this riddle of adapting our lives to the immense new possibilities and the immense new dangers that confront mankind.

It seemed to me that all over the world intelligent people were waking up to the indignity and absurdity of being endangered, restrained, and impoverished, by a mere uncritical adhesion to traditional governments, traditional ideas of economic life, and traditional forms of behaviour, and that these awaking intelligent people must constitute first a protest and then a creative resistance to the inertia that was stifling and threatening us. These people I imagined would say first, "We are drifting; we are doing nothing worth while with our lives. Our lives are dull and stupid and not good enough."

Then they would say, "What are we to do with our lives?"

And then, "Let us get together with other people of our sort and make over the world into a great world-civilization that will enable us to realize the promises and avoid the dangers of this new time."

It seemed to me that as, one after another, we woke up, that is what we should be saying. It amounted to a protest, first mental and then practical, it amounted to a sort of unpremeditated and unorganized conspiracy, against the fragmentary and insufficient governments and the widespread greed, appropriation, clumsiness, and waste that are now going on. But unlike conspiracies in general this widening protest and conspiracy against established things would, by its very nature, go on in the daylight, and it would be willing to accept participation and help from every quarter. It would, in fact, become an "Open Conspiracy," a necessary, naturally evolved conspiracy, to adjust our dislocated world.

I made various attempts to develop this idea. I published a little book called The Open Conspiracy as early as 1928, into which I put what I had in my mind at that time. It was an unsatisfactory little book even when I published it, not quite plain enough and not quite confident enough, and evidently unsure of its readers. I could not find out how to do it better at the time, and it seemed in its way to say something of living and current interest, and so I published it—but I arranged things so that I could withdraw it in a year or so. That I did, and this present book is a largely rewritten version, much clearer and more explicit. Since that first publication we have all got forward surprisingly. Events have hustled thought along and have been hustled along by thought. The idea of reorganizing the affairs of the world on quite a big scale, which was "Utopian," and so forth, in 1926 and 1927, and still "bold" in 1928, has now spread about the world until nearly everybody has it. It has broken out all over the place, thanks largely to the mental stimulation of the Russian Five Year Plan. Hundreds of thousands of people everywhere are now thinking upon the lines foreshadowed by my Open Conspiracy, not because they had ever heard of the book or phrase, but because that was the way thought was going.

The first Open Conspiracy conveyed the general idea of a world reconstructed, but it was very vague about the particular way in which this or that individual life could be lived in relation to that general idea. It gave a general answer to the question, "What are we to do with our lives?" It said, "Help to make over the New World amidst the confusions of the Old." But when the question was asked, "What am I to do with my life?" the reply was much less satisfactory.

The intervening years of thought and experience make it possible, now, to bring this general idea of a reconstructive effort, an attempt to build up a new world within the dangers and disharmonies of our present state, into a much closer and more explicit relation to the individual "Open Conspirator." We can present the thing in a better light and handle it with a surer touch.

5

III. — WE HAVE TO CLEAR AND CLEAN UP OUR MINDS

Now, one thing is fairly plain to most of us who are waking up to the need of living our lives in a new way and of making over the state, which is the framework of our lives, to meet the new demands upon it, and that is, that we have to put our own minds in order. Why have we only awakened now to the crisis in human affairs. The changes in progress have been going on with a steady acceleration for a couple of centuries. Clearly we must all have been very unobservant, our knowledge as it came to us must have been very badly arranged in our minds, and our way of dealing with it must have been cloudy and muddled, or else we should surely have awakened long ago to the immense necessities that now challenge us. And if that is so, if it has taken decades to rouse us, then quite probably we are not yet completely awake. Even now we may not have realized the job before us in its completeness. We may still have much to get plain in our minds, and we certainly have much more to learn. One primary and permanent duty therefore is to go on with our thinking and to think as well as we can about the way in which we think and about the ways in which we get and use knowledge.

Fundamentally the Open Conspiracy must be an intellectual rebirth.

Human thought is still very much confused by the imperfection of the words and other symbols it employs and the consequences of this confused thinking are much more serious and extensive than is commonly realized. We still see the world through a mist of words; it is only the things immediately about us that are plain fact. Through symbols, and especially through words, man has raised himself above the level of the ape and come to a considerable mastery over his universe. But every step in his mental ascent has involved entanglement with these symbols and words he was using; they were at once helpful and very dangerous and misleading. A great part of our affairs, social, political, intellectual, is in a perplexing and dangerous state to-day because of our loose, uncritical, slovenly use of words.

All through the later Middle Ages there were great disputes among the schoolmen about the use of words and symbols. There is a queer disposition in the human mind to think that symbols and words and logical deductions are truer than actual experiences, and these great controversies were due to the struggle of the human intelligence against that disposition. On the one side were the Realists, who were so called because they believed, in effect, that names were more real than facts, and on the other side were the Nominalists, who from the first were pervaded by a suspicion about names and words generally; who thought there might be some sort of catch in verbal processes, and who gradually worked their way towards verification by experiment which is the fundamental thing about experimental science—experimental science which has given our human world all these immense powers and possibilities that tempt and threaten it to-day. These controversies of the schoolmen were of the utmost importance to mankind. The modern world could not begin to come into existence until the human mind had broken away from the narrow-minded verbalist way of thinking which the Realists followed.

But all through my education I never had this matter explained to me. The University of London intimated that I was a soundly educated young man by giving me a degree in first-class honours and the liberty to acquire and wear an elegant gown and hood, and the London College of Preceptors gave me and the world its highest assurances that I was fit to educate and train the minds of my fellow creatures, and yet I had still to discover that a Realist was not a novelist who put rather too highly flavoured sex appeal into his books, and a Nominalist, nothing in particular. But it had crept into my mind as I learnt about individuality in my biological work and about logic and psychology in my preparation as the perfect preceptor, that something very important and essential was being left out and that I wasn't at all as well equipped as my diplomas presently said I was, and in the next few years I found the time to clean up this matter pretty thoroughly. I made no marvellous discoveries, everything I found out was known already; nevertheless, I had to find out some of this stuff for myself quite over again, as though it had never been done; so inaccessible was any complete account of human thinking to an ordinary man who wanted to get his mind into proper working condition. And this was not that I had missed some recondite, precious refinements of philosophy; it was that my fundamental thinking, at the very root of my political and social conduct, was wrong. I was in a human community, and that community, and I with it, was thinking of phantoms and fantasies as though they were real and living things, was in a reverie of unrealities, was blind, slovenly, hypnotized, base and ineffective, blundering about in an extremely beautiful and an extremely dangerous world.

I set myself to re-educate myself, and after the practice of writers wrote it in various trial pamphlets, essays, and books. There is no need to refer to these books here. The gist of the matter is set out in three compilations, to which I shall refer again almost immediately. They are The Outline of History (Ch. XXI, § 6, and Ch. XXXIII, § 6), The Science of Life (Book VIII, on Thought and Behaviour) and The Work, Wealth, and Happiness of Mankind (Ch. II, § § 1-4). In the last, it is shown quite plainly how man has had to struggle for the mastery of his mind, has discovered only after great controversies the proper and effective use of his intellectual tools, and has had to learn to avoid certain widespread traps and pitfalls before he could achieve his present mastery over matter. Thinking clearly and effectively does not come by nature. Hunting the truth is an art. We blunder naturally into a thousand misleading generalizations and false processes. Yet there is hardly any intelligent mental training done in the schools of the world to-day. We have to learn this art, if we are to practise it at all. Our schoolteachers have had no proper training themselves, they miseducate by example and precept, and so it is that our press and current discussions are more like an impromptu riot of crippled and deaf and blind minds than an intelligent interchange of ideas. What bosh one reads! What rash and impudent assumptions! What imbecile inferences!

But re-educating oneself, getting one's mind into health and exercising it and training it to think properly, is only the beginning of the task before the awakening Open Conspirator. He has not only to think clearly, but he has to see that his mind is equipped with the proper general ideas to form a true framework for his everyday judgments and decisions.

It was the Great War first brought home to me how ignorant I was, and how ill-finished and untidy my mind, about the most important things of life. That disastrous waste of life, material and happiness, since it was practically world wide, was manifestly the outcome of the processes that constitute the bulk of history, and yet I found I did not know—and nobody else seemed to know—history in such a fashion as to be able to explain how the Great War came about or what ought to come out of it. "Versailles," we all seem to be agreed nowadays, was silly, but how could Versailles be anything else than what it was in view of the imperfect, lopsided, historical knowledge and the consequent suspicion, emotion, and prejudice of those who assembled there. They did not know any better than the rest of us what the war was, and so how could they know what the peace ought to be? I perceived that I was in the same case with everyone else, and I set myself first of all for my own guidance to make a summary if all history and get some sort of map to more serviceable conclusions about the political state of mankind. This summary I made was The Outline of History, a shameless compilation and arrangement of the main facts of the world story, written without a touch of art or elegance, written indeed in a considerable hurry and excitement, and its sale, which is now in the third million, showed how much I had in common with a great dispersed crowd of ordinary people, all wanting to know, all disgusted with the patriotic, litigious twaddling gossipy stuff given them as history by their schoolmasters and schoolmistresses which had led them into the disaster of the war.

The Outline of History is not a whole history of life. Its main theme is the growth of human intercommunication and human communities and their rulers and conflicts, the story of how and why the myriads of little tribal systems of ten thousand years ago have fought and coalesced into the sixty- or seventy-odd governments of to-day and are now straining and labouring in the grip of forces that must presently accomplish their final unison. And even as I completed The Outline, I realized that there remained outside its scope wider and more fundamental, and closer, more immediate fields of knowledge which I still had to get in order for my own practical ends and the ends of like-minded people who wanted to use their lives effectively, if my existence was to escape futility.

I realized that I did not know enough about the life in my body and its relations to the world of life and matter outside it to come to proper decisions about a number of urgent matters—from race conflicts, birth control, and my private life, to the public control of health and the conservation of natural resources. And also, I found, I was astonishingly ignorant about the everyday business of life, the how and why of the miner who provided the coal to cook my dinner, and the banker who took my money in return for a cheque-book, and the shopkeeper from whom I bought things, and the policeman who kept the streets in order for me. Yet I was voting for laws affecting my relations with these people, paying them directly or indirectly, airing my ignorant opinions about them, and generally contributing by my behaviour to sustain and affect their lives.

So with the aid and direction of two very competent biologists I set to work to get out as plain and clear a statement as possible of what was known about the sources and nature of life and the relation of species to individuals and to other species, and the processes of consciousness and thought. This I published as The Science of Life. And while this was going on I set myself to the task of making a review of all human activities in relation to each other, the work of people and the needs of people, cultivation, manufacture, trade, direction, government, and all. This was the most difficult part of this attempt to get a rational account of the modern world, and it called for the help and counsel of a great variety of people. I had to ask and find some general answer to the question, "What are the nineteen hundred-odd million human beings who are alive to-day doing, and how and why are they doing it?" It was, in fact, an outline of economic, social, and political science, but since, after The Outline of History, the word "outline" has been a good deal cheapened by various enterprising publishers, I have called it, The Work, Wealth, and Happiness of Mankind.

Now, I find, by getting these three correlated compilations into existence, I have at last, in however rough a fashion, brought together a complete system of ideas upon which an Open Conspirator can go. Before anyone could hope to get on to anything like a practical working directive answer to "What are we to do with our lives?" it was necessary to know what our lives were—The Science of Life; what had led up to their present pattern—The Outline of History; and this third book, to tell what we were actually doing and supposed to be doing with our working lives, day by day, at the present time. By the time I was through with these books I felt I had really something sound and comprehensive to go upon, an "ideology," as people say, on which it was possible to think of building a new world without fundamental surprises, and, moreover, that I had got my mind stripped down and cleaned of many illusions and bad habits, so that it could handle life with an assurance it had never known before.

There is nothing marvellous about these compilations of mine. Any steady writer of average intelligence with the same will and the same resources, who could devote about nine or ten years to the task and get the Proper sort of help, could have made them. It can be done, it is no doubt being done, all over again by other people, for themselves and perhaps for others, much more beautifully and adequately. But to get that amount of vision and knowledge, to achieve that general arrangement and understanding, was a necessary condition that had to be satisfied before any answer to the question, "What are we to do with our lives?" could even be attempted, and before one could become in any effective way an Open Conspirator.

There is nothing indispensable even now, I repeat, about these three particular books. I know about them and refer to them because I put them together myself and so they are handy for me to explain myself. But most of what they contain can be extracted from any good encyclopædia. Any number of people have made similar outlines of history for themselves, have read widely, grasped the leading principles of biology and grappled with the current literature of business science and do not in the least need my particular summary. So far as history and biology are concerned there are parallel books, that are as good and serviceable. Van Loon's books for example. Yet even for highly-educated people these summaries may be useful in bringing things known with different degrees of thoroughness, into a general scheme. They correlate, and they fill up gaps. Between them they cover the ground; and in some fashion that ground has to be covered before the mind of a modern citizen is prepared to tackle the problems that confront it. Otherwise he is an incapable citizen, he does not know where he is and where the world is, and if he is rich or influential he may be a very dangerous citizen indeed. Presently there will be far better compilations to meet this need, or perhaps the gist of all the three divisions of knowledge, concentrated and made more lucid and attractive, may be available as the intellectual frame of modern education throughout the world, as a "General Account of Life" that should be given to everyone.

But certainly no one can possibly set about living properly and satisfactorily unless he knows what he is, where he is, and how he stands to the people and things about him.

6

IV. — THE REVOLUTION IN EDUCATION

SOME sort of reckoning therefore between people awakened to the new world that dawns about us and the schools, colleges, and machinery of formal education is overdue. As a body the educated are getting nothing like that Account of Life which is needed to direct our conduct in this modern world.

It is the crowning absurdity in the world to-day that these institutions should go through a solemn parade of preparing the new generation for life and that then, afterwards, a minority of their victims, finding this preparation has left them almost totally unprepared, should have of their own accord to struggle out of our world heap of starved and distorted minds to some sort of real education. The world cannot be run by such a minority of escaped and re-educated minds alone, with all the rest of the heap against them. Our necessities demand the intelligence and services of everyone who can be trained to give them. The new world demands new schools, therefore, to give everyone a sound and thorough mental training and equip everyone with clear ideas about history, about life, and about political and economic relationships instead of the rubbishy head-content at present prevalent. The old-world teachers and schools have to be reformed or replaced. A vigorous educational reform movement arises as a natural and necessary expression of the awakening Open Conspirator. A revolution in education is the most imperative and fundamental part of the adaptation of life to its new conditions.

These various compendia of knowledge constituting a Modern Account of Life, on which we have laid stress in the previous section, these supplements to teaching, which are now produced and read outside the established formal educational world and in the teeth of its manifest hostility) arise because of the backwardness of that world, and as that world yields slowly but surely to the pressure of the new spirit, so they will permeate and replace its text-books and disappear as a separate class of book. The education these new dangerous times in which we are now living demands, must start right, from the beginning and there must be nothing to replace and nothing to relearn in it. Before we can talk politics, finance, business, or morals, we must see that we have got the right mental habits and the right foundation of realized facts. There is nothing much to be done with our lives until we have seen to that.

7

V. — RELIGION IN THE NEW WORLD

"YES," objects a reader, "but does not our religion tell us what we are to do with our lives?"

We have to bring religion, as its fundamental matter, into this discussion. From our present point of view, religion is that central essential part of education which determines conduct. Religion certainly should tell us what to do with our lives. But in the vast stir and occasions of modern life, so much of what we call religion remains irrelevant or dumb. Religion does not seem to "join on" to the main parts of the general problem of living. It has lost touch.

Let us try and bring this problem of the Open Conspiracy to meet and make the new world, into relation with the traditions of religion. The clear-minded Open Conspirator who has got his modern ideology, his lucidly arranged account of the universe in order, is obliged to believe that only by giving his life to the great processes of social reconstruction, and shaping his conduct with reference to that, can he do well with his life. But that merely launches him into the most subtle and unending of struggles, the struggle against the incessant gravitation of our interests to ourselves. He has to live the broad life and escape from the close narrow life. We all try to attain the dignity and happiness of magnanimity and escape from the tormenting urgencies of personal desire. In the past that struggle has generally assumed the form of a religious struggle. Religion is the antagonist of self.

In their completeness, in the life that was professionally religious, religions have always demanded great subordinations of self. Therein lay their creative force. They demanded devotion and gave reasons for that demand. They disentangled the will from the egotistical preoccupations, often very completely. There is no such thing as a self-contained religion, a private religious solo. Certain forms of Protestantism and some mystical types come near to making religion secluded duet between the individual and his divinity, but here that may be regarded as a perversion of the religious impulse. Just as the normal sexual complex excites and stirs the individual out of his egotism to serve the ends of the race, so the normal religious process takes the individual out of his egotism for the service of the community. It is not a bargain, a "social contract," between the individual and the community; it is a subordination of both the existing individual and the existing community in relation to something, a divinity, a divine order, a standard, a righteousness, more important than either. What is called in the phraseology of certain religions "conviction of sin" and "the flight from the City of Destruction" are familiar instances of this reference of the self-centred individual and the current social life to something far better than either the one or the other.

This is the third element in the religious relationship, a hope, a promise, an objective which turns the convert not only from himself but from the "world," as it is, towards better things. First comes self disregard then service, and then this reconstructive creative urgency.

For the finer sort of mind this aspect of religion seems always to have been its primary attraction. One has to remember that there is a real will for religion scattered throughout mankind—a real desire to get away from self. Religion has never pursued its distinctive votaries; they have come to meet it. The desire to give oneself to greater ends than the everyday life affords, and to give oneself freely, is clearly dominant in that minority, and traceable in an incalculable proportion of the majority.

But hitherto religion has never been presented simply as a devotion to a universal cause. The devotion has always been in it, but it has been complicated by other considerations. The leaders in every great religious movement have considered it necessary that it should explain itself in the form of history and a cosmogony. It has been felt necessary to say Why? and To what end? Every religion therefore has had to adopt the physical conceptions, and usually also to assume many of the moral and social values, current at the time of its formation. It could not transcend the philosophical phrases and attitudes that seemed then to supply the natural frame for a faith, nor draw upon anything beyond the store of scientific knowledge of its time. In this lurked the seeds of the ultimate decay and supersession of every successive religion.

But as the idea of continual change, going farther and farther from existing realities and never returning to them, is a new one, as nobody until very recently has grasped the fact that the knowledge of today is the ignorance of to-morrow, each fresh development of religion in the world so far has been proclaimed in perfect good faith as the culminating and final truth.

This finality of statement has considerable immediate practical value. The suggestion of the possibility of further restatement is an unsettling suggestion; it undermines conviction and breaks the ranks of the believers, because there are enormous variations in the capacities of men to recognize the same spirit under a changing shape. These variations cause endless difficulties today. While some intelligences can recognize the same God under a variety of names and symbols without any severe strain, others cannot even detect the most contrasted Gods one from the other provided they wear the same mask and title It appears a perfectly natural and reasonable thing to many minds to restate religion now in terms of biological and psychological necessity, while to others any variation whatever in the phrasing of the faith seems to be nothing less than atheistical misrepresentations of the most damnable kind. For these latter God a God still anthropomorphic enough to have a will and purpose to display preferences and reciprocate emotions, to be indeed in person, must be retained until the end of time. For others, God can be thought of as a Great First Cause, as impersonal and inhuman as atomic structure.

It is because of the historical and philosophical commitments they have undertaken, and because of concessions made to common human weaknesses in regard to such once apparently minor but now vital moral issues as property, mental activity, and public veracity—rather than of any inadequacy in their adaptation to psychological needs—that the present wide discredit of organized religions has come about. They no longer seem even roughly truthful upon issues of fact, and they give no imperatives over large fields of conduct in which perplexity is prevalent. People will say, "I could be perfectly happy leading the life of a Catholic devotee if only I could believe." But most of the framework of religious explanation upon which that life is sustained is too old-fashioned and too irrelevant to admit of that thoroughness of belief which is necessary for the devotion of intelligent people.

Great ingenuity has been shown by modern writers and thinkers in the adaptation of venerated religious expressions to new ideas. Peccavi. [Usu. translated 'I have sinned'—RW] Have I not written of the creative will in humanity as "God the Invisible King" and presented it in the figure of a youthful and adventurous finite god?

The word "God" is in most minds so associated with the concept of religion that it is abandoned only with the greatest reluctance. The word remains, though the idea is continually attenuated. Respect for Him demands that He should have no limitations. He is pushed farther and farther from actuality, therefore, and His definition becomes increasingly a bundle of negations, until at last, in His rôle of The Absolute, He becomes an entirely negative expression. While we can speak of good, say some, can speak of God. God is the possibility of goodness, the good side of things. If phrases in which the name of God is used are to be abandoned, they argue, religion will be left speechless before many occasions.

Certainly there is something beyond the individual that is and the world that is; on that we have already insisted as a characteristic of all religions; that persuasion is the essence of faith and the key to courage. But whether that is to be considered, even after the most strenuous exercises in personification, as a greater person or a comprehensive person, is another matter. Personality is the last vestige of anthropomorphism. The modern urge to a precise veracity is against such concessions to traditional expression.

On the other hand there is in many fine religious minds a desire amounting almost to a necessity for an object of devotion so individualized as to be capable at least of a receptive consciousness even if no definite response is conceded. One type of mind can accept a reality in itself which another must project and dramatize before it can comprehend it and react to it. The human soul is an intricate thing which will not endure elucidation when that passes beyond a certain degree of harshness and roughness. The human spirit has learnt love, devotion, obedience and humility in relation to other personalities, and with difficulty it takes the final step to a transcendent subordination, from which the last shred of personality has stripped.

In matters not immediately material, language has to work by metaphors, and though every metaphor carries its own peculiar risks of confusion, we cannot do without them. Great intellectual tolerance is necessary, therefore --a cultivated disposition --to translate and retranslate from one metaphysical or emotional idiom to another—if there is not to be a deplorable wastage of moral force in our world. Just now I wrote Peccavi because I had written God the Invisible King, but after all I do not think it was so much a sin to use that phrase, God the Invisible King, as an error in expression. If there is no sympathetic personal leader outside us, there is at least in us the attitude we should adopt towards a sympathetic personal leader.

Three profound differences between the new mental dispositions of the present time and those of preceding ages have to be realized if current developments of the religious impulse are to be seen in their correct relationship to the religious life of the past. There has been a great advance in the analysis of psychic processes and the courage with which men have probed into the origins of human thought and feeling. Following upon the biological advances that have made us recognize fish and amphibian in the bodily structure of man, have come these parallel developments in which we see elemental fear and lust and self-love moulded, modified, and exalted, under the stress of social progress, into intricate human motives. Our conception of sin and our treatment of sin have been profoundly modified by this analysis. Our former sins are seen as ignorances, inadequacies and bad habits, and the moral conflict is robbed of three-fourths of its ego-centred melodramatic quality. We are no longer moved to be less wicked; we are moved to organize our conditioned reflexes and lead a life less fragmentary and silly.

Secondly, the conception of individuality has been influenced and relaxed by biological thought, so that we do not think so readily of the individual contra mundum as our fathers did. We begin to realize that we are egotists by misapprehension. Nature cheats the self to serve the purposes of the species by filling it with wants that war against its private interests. As our eyes are opened to these things, we see ourselves as beings greater or less than the definitive self. Man's soul is no longer his own. It is, he discovers, part of a greater being which lived before he was born and will survive him. The idea of a survival of the definite individual with all the accidents and idiosyncrasies of his temporal nature upon him dissolves to nothing in this new view of immortality.

The third of the main contrasts between modern and former thought which have rendered the general shapes of established religion old-fashioned and unserviceable is a reorientation of current ideas about time. The powerful disposition of the human mind to explain everything as the inevitable unfolding of a past event which, so to speak, sweeps the future helplessly before it, has been checked by a mass of subtle criticisms. The conception of progress as a broadening and increasing purpose, a conception which is taking hold of the human imagination more and more firmly, turns religious life towards the future. We think no longer of submission to the irrevocable decrees of absolute dominion, but of participation in an adventure on behalf of a power that gains strength and establishes itself. The history of our world, which has been unfolded to us by science, runs counter to all the histories on which religions have been based. There was no Creation in the past, we begin to realize, but eternally there is creation; there was no Fall to account for the conflict of good and evil, but a stormy ascent. Life as we know it is a mere beginning.

It seems unavoidable that if religion is to develop unifying and directive power in the present confusion of human affairs it must adapt itself to this forward-looking, individuality-analyzing turn of mind; it must divest itself of its sacred histories, its gross preoccupations, its posthumous prolongation of personal ends. The desire for service, for subordination, for permanent effect, for an escape from the distressful pettiness and mortality of the individual life, is the undying element in every religious system.

The time has come to strip religion right down to that, to strip it for greater tasks than it has ever faced before. The histories and symbols that served our fathers encumber and divide us.

Sacraments and rituals harbour disputes and waste our scanty emotions. The explanation of why things are is an unnecessary effort in religion. The essential fact in religion is the desire for religion and not how it came about. If you do not want religion, no persuasions, no convictions about your place in the universe can give it to you. The first sentence in the modern creed must be, not "I believe," but "I give myself."

To what? And how? To these questions we will now address ourselves.

8

VI. — MODERN RELIGION IS OBJECTIVE

To give oneself religiously is a continuing operation expressed in a series of acts. It can be nothing else. You cannot dedicate yourself and then go away to live just as you have lived before. It is a poor travesty of religion that does not produce an essential change in the life which embraces it. But in the established and older religions of our race, this change of conduct has involved much self-abasement merely to the God or Gods, or much self-mortification merely with a view to the moral perfecting of self. Christian devotion, for example, in these early stages, before the hermit life gave place to organized monastic life, did not to any extent direct itself to service except the spiritual service of other human beings. But as Christianity became a definite social organizing force, it took on a great series of healing, comforting, helping, and educational activities.

The modern tendency has been and is all in the direction of minimizing what one might call self-centred devotion and self-subjugation, and of expanding and developing external service. The idea of inner perfectibility dwindles with the diminishing importance attached to individuality. We cease to think of mortifying or exalting or perfecting ourselves and seek to lose ourselves in a greater life. We think less and less of "conquering" self and more and more of escaping from self. If we attempt to perfect ourselves in any respect it is only as a soldier sharpens and polishes an essential weapon.

Our quickened apprehension of continuing change, our broader and fuller vision of the history of life, disabuse our minds of many limitations set to the imaginations of our predecessors. Much that they saw as fixed and determinate, we see as transitory and controllable. They saw life fixed in its species and subjected to irrevocable laws. We see life struggling insecurely but with a gathering successfulness for freedom and power against restriction and death. We see life coming at last to our tragic and hopeful human level. Unprecedented possibilities, mighty problems, we realize, confront mankind to-day. They frame our existences. The practical aspect, the material form, the embodiment of the modernized religious impulse is the direction of the whole life to the solution of these problems and the realization of their possibilities. The alternative before man now is either magnificence of spirit and magnificence of achievement, or disaster.

The modern religious life, like all forms of religious life, must needs have its own subtle and deep inner activities, its meditations, its self- confrontations, its phases of stress and search and appeal, its serene and prayerful moods, but these inward aspects do not come into the scope of this present inquiry, which is concerned entirely with the outward shape, the direction, and the organization of modern religious effort, with the question of what, given religious devotion, we have to do and how that has to be done.

Now, in the new and greater universe to which we are awakening, its immense possibilities furnish an entirely new frame and setting for the moral life. In the fixed and limited outlook of the past, practical good works took the form mainly of palliative measures against evils that were conceived of as incurable; the religious community nursed the sick, fed the hungry, provided sanctuary for the fugitive, pleaded with the powerful for mercy. It did not dream of preventing sickness, famine, or tyranny. Other-worldliness was its ready refuge from the invincible evil and confusion of the existing scheme of things.

But it is possible now to imagine an order in human affairs from which these evils have been largely or entirely eliminated. More and more people are coming to realize that such an order is a material possibility. And with the realization that this is a material possibility, we can no longer be content with a field of "good deeds" and right action restricted to palliative and consolatory activities. Such things are merely "first aid." The religious mind grows bolder than it has ever been before. It pushes through the curtain it once imagined was a barrier. It apprehends its larger obligations. The way in which our activities conduce to the realization of that conceivable better order in human affairs, becomes the new criterion of conduct. Other-worldliness has become unnecessary.

The realization of this possible better order brings us at once to certain definite lines of conduct. We have to make an end to war, and to make an end to war we must be cosmopolitan in our politics. It is impossible for any clear-headed person to suppose that the ever more destructive stupidities of war can be eliminated from human affairs until some common political control dominates the earth, and unless certain pressures due to the growth of population, due to the enlarging scope of economic operations or due to conflicting standards and traditions of life, are disposed of.

To avoid the positive evils of war and to attain the new levels of prosperity and power that now come into view, an effective world control, not merely of armed force, but of the production and main movements of staple commodities and the drift and expansion of population is required. It is absurd to dream of peace and world-wide progress without that much control. These things assured the abilities and energies of a greatly increased proportion of human beings could be diverted to the happy activities of scientific research and creative work, with an ever-increasing release and enlargement of human possibility. On the political side it is plain that our lives must be given to the advancement of that union.

Such a forward stride in human life, the first stride in a mighty continuing advance, an advance to which no limit appears, is now not simply materially possible. It is urgent. The opportunity is plain before mankind. It is the alternative to social decay. But there is no certainty, no material necessity, that it should ever be taken. It will not be taken by mankind inadvertently.

It can only be taken through such an organization of will and energy to take it as this world has never seen before.

These are the new imperatives that unfold themselves before the more alert minds of our generation. They will presently become the general mental background, as the modern interpretations of the history of life and of the material and mental possibilities about us establish themselves. Evil political, social, and economic usages and arrangements may seem obdurate and huge, but they are neither permanent nor uncontrollable. They can be controlled, however, only by an effort more powerful and determined than the instincts and inertias that sustain them. Religion, modern and disillusioned, has for its outward task to set itself to the control and direction of political, social, and economic life. If it does not do that, then it is no more than a drug for easing discomfort, "the opium of the peoples."

Can religion, or can it not, synthesize the needed effort to lift mankind out of our present disorders, dangers, baseness, frustrations, and futilities to a phase of relative security, accumulating knowledge, systematic and continuing growth in power and the widespread, deep happiness of hopeful and increasing life?

Our answer here is that the religious spirit, in the light of modern knowledge, can do this thing, and our subject now is to enquire what are the necessary opening stages in the synthesis of that effort. We write, from this point onward, for those who believe that it can, and who do already grasp the implications of world history and contemporary scientific achievement.

9

VII. — WHAT MANKIND HAS TO DO

BEFORE we can consider the forms and methods of attacking this inevitable task of reconstruction it will be well to draw the main lines and to attempt some measure of the magnitude of that task. What are the new forms that it is thus proposed to impose upon human life, and how are they to be evolved from or imposed upon the current forms? And against what passive and active resistances has this to be done?

There can be no pause for replacement in the affairs of life. Day must follow day, and the common activities continue. The new world as a going concern must arise out of the old as a going concern.

Now the most comprehensive conception of this new world is of one politically, socially, and economically unified. Within that frame fall all the other ideas of our progressive ambition. To this end we set our faces and seek to direct our lives. Many there are at present who apprehend it as a possibility but do not dare, it seems, to desire it, because of the enormous difficulties that intervene, and because they see as yet no intimations of a way through or round these difficulties. They do not see a way of escape from the patchwork of governments that grips them and divides mankind. The great majority of human beings have still to see the human adventure as one whole; they are obsessed by the air of permanence and finality in established things; they accept current reality as ultimate reality. As the saying goes, they take the world as they find it.

But here we are writing for the modern-minded, and for them it is impossible to think of the world as secure and satisfactory until there exists a single world commonweal, preventing war and controlling those moral, biological, and economic forces and wastages that would otherwise lead to wars. And controlling them in the sense that science and man's realization and control of his powers and possibilities continually increase.

Let us make clear what sort of government we are trying to substitute for the patchwork of to-day. It will be a new sort of direction with a new psychology. The method of direction of such a world commonweal is not likely to imitate the methods of existing sovereign states. It will be something new and altogether different.

This point is not yet generally realized. It is too often assumed that the world commonweal will be, as it were, just the one heir and survivor of existing states, and that it will be a sort of megatherium of the same form and anatomy as its predecessors.

But a little reflection will show that this is a mistake. Existing states are primarily militant states, and a world state cannot be militant. There will be little need for president or king to lead the marshalled hosts of humanity, for where there is no war there is no need of any leader to lead hosts anywhere, and in a polyglot world a parliament of mankind or any sort of council that meets and talks is an inconceivable instrument of government. The voice will cease to be a suitable vehicle. World government, like scientific process, will be conducted by statement, criticism, and publication that will be capable of efficient translation.

The fundamental organization of contemporary states is plainly still military, and that is exactly what a world organization cannot be. Flags, uniforms, national anthems, patriotism sedulously cultivated in church and school, the brag, blare, and bluster of our competing sovereignties, belong to the phase of development the Open Conspiracy will supersede. We have to get clear of that clutter. The reasonable desire of all of us is that we should have the collective affairs of the world managed by suitably equipped groups of the most interested, intelligent, and devoted people, and that their activities should be subjected to a free, open, watchful criticism, restrained from making spasmodic interruptions but powerful enough to modify or supersede without haste or delay whatever is weakening or unsatisfactory in the general direction.

A number of readers will be disposed to say that this is a very vague, undefined, and complicated conception of world government. But indeed it is a simplification. Not only are the present governments of the world a fragmentary competitive confusion, but none of them is as simple as it appears. They seem to be simple because they have formal heads and definite forms, councils, voting assemblies, and so forth, for arriving at decisions. But the formal heads, the kings, presidents, and so forth, are really not the directive heads. They are merely the figure heads. They do not decide. They merely make gestures of potent and dignified acquiescence when decisions are put to them. They are complicating shams. Nor do the councils and assemblies really decide. They record, often very imperfectly and exasperatingly, the accumulating purpose of outer forces. These outer really directive forces are no doubt very intricate in their operation; they depend finally on religious and educational forms and upon waves of gregarious feeling, but it does not in the least simplify the process of collective human activity to pretend that it is simple and to set up symbols and dummies in the guise of rulers and dictators to embody that pretence. To recognize the incurable intricacy of collective action is a mental simplification; to remain satisfied with the pretensions of existing governmental institutions, and to bring in all the problems of their procedure and interaction is to complicate the question.

The present rudimentary development of collective psychology obliges us to be vague and provisional about the way in which the collective mind may best define its will for the purpose of administrative action. We may know that a thing is possible and still be unable to do it as yet, just as we knew that aviation was possible in 1900. Some method of decision there must certainly be and a definite administrative machinery. But it may turn out to be a much slighter, less elaborate organization than a consideration of existing methods might lead us to imagine. It may never become one single interlocking administrative system. We may have systems of world control rather than a single world state. The practical regulations, enforcements, and officials needed to keep the world in good health, for example may be only very loosely related to the system of controls that will maintain its communications in a state of efficiency. Enforcement and legal decisions, as we know them now, may be found to be enormously and needlessly cumbrous by our descendants. As the reasonableness of a thing is made plain, the need for its enforcement is diminished, and the necessity for litigation disappears.

The Open Conspiracy, the world movement for the supercession or enlargement or fusion of existing political, economic, and social institutions must necessarily, as it grows, draw closer and closer to questions of practical control. It is likely in its growth to incorporate many active public servants and many industrial and financial leaders and directors. It may assimilate great masses of intelligent workers. As its activities spread it will work out a whole system of special methods of co-operation. As it grows, and by growing, it will learn the business of general direction and how to develop its critical function. A lucid, dispassionate, and immanent criticism is the primary necessity, the living spirit of a world civilization. The Open Conspiracy is essentially such a criticism, and the carrying out of such a criticism into working reality is the task of the Open Conspiracy. It will by its very nature be aiming not so much to set up a world direction, as to become itself a world direction, and the educational and militant forms of its opening phase will evoke, step by step, as experience is gained and power and responsibility acquired, forms of administration and research and correlation.

The differences in nature and function between the world controls of the future and the state governments of the present age which we have just pointed out favours a hope that the Open Conspiracy may come to its own in many cases rather by the fading out of these state governments through the inhibition and paralysis of their destructive militant and competitive activities than by a direct conflict to overthrow them. As new world controls develop, it becomes the supreme business of the Open Conspiracy to keep them world wide and impartial, to save them by an incessant critical educational and propagandist activity from entanglement with the old traditional rivalries and feuds of states and nations. It is quite possible that such world controls should be able to develop independently, but it is highly probable, on the other hand, that they will continue to be entangled as they are to-day, and that they will need to be disengaged with a struggle. We repeat, the new directive organizations of men's affairs will not be of the same nature as old-fashioned governments. They will be in their nature biological, financial, and generally economic, and the old governments were primarily nothing of the sort. Their directive force will be (1) an effective criticism having the quality of science, and (2) the growing will in men to have things right. The directive force of the older governments was the uncriticized fantasies and wilfulness of an individual, a class, a tribe, or a majority.

The modernization of the religious impulse leads us straight to this effort for the establishment of the world state as a duty, and the close consideration of the necessary organization of that effort will bring the reader to the conclusion that a movement aiming at the establishment of a world directorate, however restricted that movement may be at first in numbers and power, must either contemplate the prospect of itself developing into a world directorate, and by the digestion and assimilation of superseded factors into an entire modern world community, or admit from the outset the futility, the spare-time amateurishness, of its gestures.

10

VIII. — BROAD CHARACTERISTICS OF A SCIENTIFIC WORL

CONTINUING our examination of the practical task before the modern mind, we may next note the main lines of contemporary aspiration within this comprehensive outline of a world commonweal. Any sort of unification of human affairs will not serve the ends we seek. We aim at a particular sort of unification; a world Caesar is hardly better from the progressive viewpoint than world chaos; the unity we seek must mean a world-wide liberation of thought, experiment and creative effort.

A successful Open Conspiracy merely to seize governments and wield and retain world power would be at best only the empty frame of success. It might be the exact reverse of success. Release from the threat of war and from the waste of international economic conflicts is a poor release if it demands as its price the loss of all other liberties.

It is because we desire a unification of human direction, not simply for the sake of unity, but as a means of release to happiness and power, that it is necessary, at any cost—in delay, in loss of effective force, in strategic or tactical disadvantage—that the light of free, abundant criticism should play upon that direction and upon the movements and unifying organizations leading to the establishment of that unifying direction.

Man is an imperfect animal and never quite trustworthy in the dark. Neither morally nor intellectually is he safe from lapses. Most of us who are past our first youth know how little we can trust ourselves and glad to have our activities checked and guarded by a sense of helpful inspection. It is for this reason that a movement to realize the conceivable better state of the world must deny itself the advantages of secret methods and tactical insincerities. It must leave that to its adversaries. We must declare our end plainly from the outset and risk no misunderstandings of our procedure.

The Open Conspiracy against the traditional and now cramping and dangerous institutions of the world must be an Open Conspiracy and cannot remain righteous otherwise. It is lost if it goes underground. Every step to world unity must be taken in the daylight with the understanding sympathy of as many people as possible, or the sort of unity that will be won will be found to be scarcely worth the winning. The essential task would have to be recommenced again within the mere frame of unity thus attained.

This candid attempt to take possession of the whole world, this Open Conspiracy of ours, must be made in the name of and for the sake of science and creative activity. Its aim is to release science and creative activity and every stage in the struggle must be watched and criticized, lest there be any sacrifice of these ends to the exigencies of conflict.

The security of creative progress and creative activity implies a competent regulation of the economic life in the collective interest. There must be food, shelter and leisure for all. The fundamental needs of the animal life must be assured before human life can have free play. Man does not live by bread alone; he eats that he may learn and adventure creatively, but unless he eats he cannot adventure. His life is primarily economic, as a house is primarily a foundation, and economic justice and efficiency must underlie all other activities; but to judge human society and organize political and social activities entirely on economic grounds is to forget the objectives of life's campaign in a preoccupation with supply.

It is true that man, like the animal world in general from which he has risen, is the creature of a struggle for sustenance, but unlike the animals, man can resort to methods of escape from that competitive pressure upon the means of subsistence, which has been the lot of every other animal species. He can restrain the increase in his numbers, and he seems capable of still quite undefined expansions of his productivity per head of population. He can escape therefore from the struggle for subsistence altogether with a surplus of energy such as no other kind of animal species has ever possessed. Intelligent control of population is a possibility which puts man outside competitive processes that have hitherto ruled the modification of species, and he can be released from these processes in no other way.

There is a clear hope that, later, directed breeding will come within his scope, but that goes beyond his present range of practical achievement, and we need not discuss it further here. Suffice it for us here that the world community of our desires, the organized world community conducting and ensuring its own progress, requires a deliberate collective control of population as a primary condition.

There is no strong instinctive desire for multitudinous offspring, as such, in the feminine make-up. The reproductive impulses operate indirectly. Nature ensures a pressure of population through passions and instincts that, given sufficient knowledge, intelligence, and freedom on the part of women, can be satisfactorily gratified and tranquillized, if need be, without the production of numerous children. Very slight adjustments in social and economic arrangements will, in a world of clear available knowledge and straightforward practice in these matters, supply sufficient inducement or discouragement to affect the general birth rate or the birth rate of specific types as the directive sense of the community may consider desirable. So long as the majority of human beings are begotten involuntarily in lust and ignorance so long does man remain like any other animal under the moulding pressure of competition for subsistence. Social and political processes change entirely in their character when we recognize the possibility and practicability of this fundamental revolution in human biology.

In a world so relieved, the production of staple necessities presents a series of problems altogether less distressful than those of the present scramble for possessions and self-indulgence on the part of the successful, and for work and a bare living on the part of the masses. With the increase of population unrestrained, there was, as the end of the economic process, no practical alternative to a multitudinous equality at the level of bare subsistence, except through such an inequality of economic arrangements as allowed a minority to maintain a higher standard of life by withholding whatever surplus of production it could grasp, from consumption in mere proletarian breeding. In the past and at present, what is called the capitalist system, that is to say the unsystematic exploitation of production by private owners under the protection of the law, has, on the whole, in spite of much waste and conflict, worked beneficially by checking that gravitation to a universal low-grade consumption which would have been the inevitable outcome of a socialism oblivious of biological processes. With effective restraint upon the increase of population, however, entirely new possibilities open out before mankind.

The besetting vice of economic science, orthodox and unorthodox alike, has been the vice of beginning in the air, with current practice and current convictions, with questions of wages, prices, values, and possession, when the profounder issues of human association are really not to be found at all on these levels. The primary issues of human association are biological and psychological, and the essentials of economics are problems in applied physics and chemistry. The first thing we should examine is what we want to do with natural resources, and the next, how to get men to do what has to be done as pleasurably and effectively as possible. Then we should have a standard by which to judge the methods of to-day.

But the academic economists, and still more so Marx and his followers, refuse to deal with these fundamentals, and, with a stupid pose of sound practical wisdom, insist on opening up their case with an uncritical acceptance of the common antagonism of employers and employed and a long rigmarole about profits and wages. Ownership and expropriated labour are only one set of many possible sets of economic method.

The economists, however, will attend seriously only to the current set; the rest they ignore; and the Marxists, with their uncontrollable disposition to use nicknames in the place of judgments, condemn all others as "Utopian"—a word as final in its dismissal from the minds of the elect as that other pet counter in the Communist substitute for thought, "Bourgeois." If they can persuade themselves that an idea or a statement is "Utopian" or "Bourgeois," it does not seem to matter in the least to them whether it is right or wrong. It is disposed of. Just as in genteeler circles anything is disposed of that can be labelled "atheistical", "subversive" or "disloyal."

If a century and a half ago the world had submitted its problems of transport to the economists, they would have put aside, with as little wasted breath and ink as possible, all talk about railways, motorcars, steamships, and aeroplanes, and, with a fine sense of extravagance rebuked, set themselves to long neuralgic dissertations, disputations, and treatises upon highroads and the methods of connecting them, turnpike gates, canals, influence of lock fees on bargemen, tidal landing places, anchorages, surplus carrying capacity, carriers, caravans, hand-barrows, and the pedestrianariat. There would have been a rapid and easy differentiation in feeling and requirements between the horse-owning minority and the walking majority; the wrongs of the latter would have tortured the mind of every philosopher who could not ride, and been minimized by every philosopher who could; and there would have been a broad rift between the narrow-footpath school, the no-footpath school, and the school which would look forward to a time when every horse would have to be led along one universal footpath under the dictatorship of the pedestrianariat. All with the profoundest gravity and dignity. These things, footpaths and roads and canals with their traffic, were "real," and "Utopian" projects for getting along at thirty or forty miles an hour or more uphill and against wind and tide, let alone the still more incredible suggestion of air transport, would have been smiled and sneered out of court. Life went about on its with a certain assistance from wheels, or floated, rowed and was blown about on water; so it had been—and so it would always be.

The psychology of economic co-operation is still only dawning, and so the economists and the doctrinaire socialists have had the freest range for pedantry and authoritative pomp. For a hundred years they have argued and argued about "rent," about "surplus value," and so on, and have produced a literature ten thousand times as bulky, dreary, and foolish as the worst outpourings of the mediaeval schoolmen.

But as soon as this time-honoured preoccupation with the allotment of the shares of originators, organizers, workers, owners of material, credit dealers, and tax collectors in the total product, ceases to be dealt with as the primary question in economics; as soon as we liberate our minds from a preoccupation which from the outset necessarily makes that science a squabble rather than a science, and begin our attack upon the subject with a survey of the machinery and other productive material required in order that the staple needs of mankind should be satisfied, if we go on from that to consider the way in which all this material and machinery can be worked and the product distributed with the least labour and the greatest possible satisfaction, we shift our treatment of economic questions towards standards by which all current methods of exploitation, employment, and finance can be judged rather than wrangled over. We can dismiss the question of the claims of this sort of participant or that, for later and subordinate consideration, and view each variety of human assistance in the general effort entirely from the standpoint of what makes that assistance least onerous and most effective.

The germs of such really scientific economics exist already in the study of industrial organization and industrial psychology. As the science of industrial psychology in particular develops, we shall find all this discussion of ownership, profit, wages, finance, and accumulation, which has been treated hitherto as the primary issues of economics, falling into place under the larger enquiry of what conventions in these matters, what system of money and what conceptions of property, yield the greatest stimulus and the least friction in that world-wide system of co-operation which must constitute the general economic basis to the activities of a unified mankind.

Manifestly the supreme direction of the complex of human economic activities in such a world must centre upon a bureau of information and advice, which will take account of all the resources of the planet, estimate current needs, apportion productive activities and control distribution. The topographical and geological surveys of modern civilized communities, their government maps, their periodic issue of agricultural and industrial statistics, are the first crude and unco-ordinated beginnings of such an economic world intelligence. In the propaganda work of David

Lubin, a pioneer whom mankind must not forget, and in his International Institute of Agriculture in Rome, there were the beginnings of an impartial review month by month and year by year of world production, world needs and world transport. Such a great central organization of economic science would necessarily produce direction; it would indicate what had best be done here, there, and everywhere, solve general tangles, examine, approve and initiate fresh methods and arrange the transitional process from old to new. It would not be an organization of will, imposing its will upon a reluctant or recalcitrant race; it would be a direction, just as a map is a direction.

A map imposes no will on anyone, breaks no one in to its "policy." And yet we obey our maps.

The will to have the map full, accurate, and up to date, and the determination to have its indications respected, would have to pervade the whole community. To nourish and sustain that will must be the task not of any particular social or economic division of the community, but of the whole body of right-minded people in that community. The organization and preservation of that power of will is the primary undertaking, therefore, of a world revolution aiming at universal peace, welfare and happy activity. And through that will it will produce as the central organ the brain of the modern community, a great encyclopædic organization, kept constantly up to date and giving approximate estimates and directions for all the material activities of mankind.

The older and still prevalent conception of government is bullying, is the breaking-in and subjugation of the "subject," to the God, or king, or lords of the community. Will-bending, the overcoming of the recalcitrant junior and inferior, was an essential process in the establishment of primitive societies, and its tradition still rules our education and law. No doubt there must be a necessary accommodation of the normal human will to every form of society; no man is innately virtuous; but compulsion and restraint are the friction of the social machine and, other things being equal, the less compulsive social arrangements are, the more willingly, naturally, and easily they are accepted, the less wasteful of moral effort and the happier that community will be. The ideal state, other things being equal, is the state with the fewest possible number of will fights and will suppressions. This must be a primary consideration in arranging the economic, biological, and mental organization of the world community at which we aim.

We have advanced the opinion that the control of population pressure is practicable without any violent conflict with "human nature," that given a proper atmosphere of knowledge and intention, there need be far less suppression of will in relation to production than prevails to-day. In the same way, it is possible that the general economic life of mankind may be made universally satisfactory that there may be an abundance out of all comparison greater than the existing supply of things necessary for human well-being, freedom, and activity, with not merely not more, but infinitely less subjugation and enslavement than now occurs. Man is still but half born out of the blind struggle for existence, and his nature still partakes of the infinite wastefulness of his mother Nature. He has still to learn how to price the commodities he covets in terms of human life. He is indeed only beginning to realize that there is anything to be learnt in that matter. He wastes will and human possibility extravagantly in his current economic methods.

We know nowadays that the nineteenth century expended a great wealth of intelligence upon a barren controversy between Individualism and Socialism. They were treated as mutually exclusive alternatives, instead of being questions of degree. Human society has been is and always must be an intricate system of adjustments between unconditional liberty and the disciplines and subordinations of co-operative enterprise. Affairs do not move simply from a more individualist to a more socialist state or vice versa; there may be a release of individual initiative going on here and standardization or restraint increasing there. Personal property never can be socially guaranteed as the extremer individualists desired, nor can it be "abolished" as the extremer socialists proposed. Property is not robbery, as Proudhon asserted; it is the protection of things against promiscuous and mainly wasteful use. Property is not necessarily personal. In some cases property may restrict or forbid a use of things that could be generally advantageous, and it may be and is frequently unfair in its assignment of initiative, but the remedy for that is not an abolition but a revision of property. In the concrete it is a form necessary for liberty of action upon material, while abstracted as money, which is a liquidated generalized form of property; it is a ticket for individual liberty of movement and individual choice of reward.

The economic history of mankind is a history of the operation of the idea of property; it relates the conflict of the unlimited acquisitiveness of egoistic individuals against the resentment of the disinherited and unsuccessful and the far less effective consciousness of a general welfare. Money grew out of a system of abstracting conventions and has been subjected to a great variety of restrictions, monopolizations, and regulations. It has never been an altogether logical device, and it has permitted the most extensive and complex developments of credit, debt, and dispossession. All these developments have brought with them characteristic forms of misuse and corruption. The story is intricate, and the tangle of relationships, of dependence, of pressure, of interception, of misdirected services, crippling embarrassments, and crushing obligations in which we live today admits of no such simple and general solutions as many exponents of socialism, for example, seem to consider possible.

But the thought and investigations of the past century or so have made it clear that a classification of property, according to the nature of the rights exercisable and according to the range of ownership involved, must be the basis of any system of social justice in the future.

Certain things, the ocean, the air, rare wild animals, must be the collective property of all mankind and cannot be altogether safe until they are so regarded, and until some concrete body exists to exercise these proprietary rights. Whatever collective control exists must protect these universal properties, the sea from derelicts, the strange shy things of the wild from extermination by the hunter and the foolish collector. The extinction of many beautiful creatures is one of the penalties our world is paying for its sluggishness in developing a collective common rule. And there are many staple things and general needs that now also demand a unified control in the common interest. The raw material of the earth should be for all, not to be monopolized by any acquisitive individual or acquisitive sovereign state, and not to be withheld from exploitation for the general benefit of any chance claims to territorial priority of this or that backward or bargaining person or tribe.

In the past, most of these universal concerns have had to be left to the competitive enterprise of profit-seeking individuals because there were as yet no collectivities organized to the pitch of ability needed to develop and control these concerns, but surely nobody in his senses believes that the supply and distribution of staple commodities about the earth by irresponsible persons and companies working entirely for monetary gain is the best possible method from the point of view of the race as a whole. The land of the earth, all utilizable natural products, have fallen very largely under the rules and usages of personal property because in the past that was the only recognized and practicable form of administrative proprietorship. The development both of extensive proprietary companies and of government departments with economic functions has been a matter of the last few centuries, the development, that is to say, of communal, more or less impersonal ownership, and it is only through these developments that the idea of organized collectivity of proprietorship has become credible.

Even in quite modern state enterprises there is a tendency to recall the rôle of the vigilant, jealous, and primitive personal proprietor in the fiction of ownership by His Majesty the King. In Great Britain, for example, Georgius Rex is still dimly supposed to hover over the Postmaster General of his Post Office, approve, disapprove, and call him to account. But the Postal Union of the world which steers a registered letter from Chile to Norway or from Ireland to Pekin is almost completely divorced from the convention of an individual owner. It works; it is criticized without awe or malice. Except for the stealing and steaming of letters practised by the political police of various countries, it works fairly well. And the only force behind it to keep it working well is the conscious common sense of mankind.

But when we have stipulated for the replacement of individual private ownership by more highly organized forms of collective ownership, subject to free criticism and responsible to the whole republic of mankind, in the general control of sea and land, in the getting, preparation, and distribution of staple products and in transport, we have really named all the possible generalizations of concrete ownership that the most socialistic of contemporaries will be disposed to demand. And if we add to that the necessary maintenance of a money system by a central world authority upon a basis that will make money keep faith with the worker who earns it, and represent from first to last for him the value in staple commodities he was given to understand it was to have, and if we conceive credit adequately controlled in the general interest by a socialized world banking organization, we shall have defined the entire realm from which individual property and unrestricted individual enterprise have been excluded. Beyond that, the science of social psychology will probably assure us that the best work will be done for the world by individuals free to exploit their abilities as they wish. If the individual landowner or mineral-owner disappears altogether from the world, he will probably be replaced over large areas by tenants with considerable security of tenure, by householders and by licensees under collective proprietors. It will be the practice, the recognized best course, to allow the cultivator to profit as fully as possible by his own individual productivity and to leave the householder to fashion his house and garden after his own desire.

Such in the very broadest terms is the character of the world commonweal towards which the modern imagination is moving, so far as its direction and economic life are concerned. The organization of collective bodies capable of exercising these wider proprietorships, which cannot be properly used in the common interest by uncorrelated individual owners, is the positive practical problem before the intelligent portion of mankind to-day. The nature of such collective bodies is still a series of open questions, even upon such points as whether they will be elected bodies or groups deriving their authority from other sanctions. Their scope and methods of operation, their relations to one another and to the central bureau of intelligence, remain also to be defined. But before we conclude this essay we may be able to find precisions for at least the beginning of such definition.

Nineteenth-century socialism in its various forms, including the highly indurated formulae of communism, has been a series of projects for the establishment of such collective controls, for the most part very sketchy projects from which the necessary factor of a sound psychological analysis was almost completely wanting. Primarily movements of protest and revolt against the blazing injustices arising out of the selfishly individualistic exploitation of the new and more productive technical and financial methods of the eighteenth and nineteenth centuries, they have been apt to go beyond the limits of reasonable socialization in their demands and to minimize absurdly the difficulties and dangers of collective control. Indignation and impatience were their ruling moods, and if they constructed little they exposed much. We are better able to measure the magnitude of the task before us because of the clearances and lessons achieved by these pioneer movements.

11

IX. — NO STABLE UTOPIA IS NOW CONCEIVABLE

THIS unified world towards which the Open Conspiracy would direct its activities cannot be pictured for the reader as any static and stereotyped spectacle of happiness. Indeed, one may doubt if such a thing as happiness is possible without steadily changing conditions involving continually enlarging and exhilarating opportunities. Mankind, released from the pressure of population, the waste of warfare and the private monopolization of the sources of wealth, will face the universe with a great and increasing surplus of will and energy. Change and novelty will be the order of life; each day will differ from its predecessor in its great amplitude of interest. Life which was once routine, endurance, and mischance will become adventure and discovery. It will no longer be "the old, old story."

We have still barely emerged from among the animals in their struggle for existence. We live only in the early dawn of human self-consciousness and in the first awakening of the spirit of mastery. We believe that the persistent exploration of our outward and inward worlds by scientific and artistic endeavour will lead to developments of power and activity upon which at present we can set no limits nor give any certain form.

Our antagonists are confusion of mind, want of courage, want of curiosity and want of imagination, indolence, and spendthrift egotism. These are the enemies against which the Open Conspiracy arrays itself; these are the jailers of human freedom and achievement.

12

X. — THE OPEN CONSPIRACY IS NOT TO BE THOUGHT OF A

THIS open and declared intention of establishing a world order out of the present patchwork of particularist governments, of effacing the militarist conceptions that have hitherto given governments their typical form, and of removing credit and the broad fundamental processes of economic life out of reach of private profit-seeking and individual monopolization, which is the substance of this Open Conspiracy to which the modern religious mind must necessarily address its practical activities, cannot fail to arouse enormous opposition. It is not a creative effort in a clear field; it is a creative effort that can hardly stir without attacking established things. It is the repudiation of drift, of "leaving things alone." It criticizes everything in human life from the top to the bottom and finds everything not good enough. It strikes at the universal human desire to feel that things are "all right."

One might conclude, and it would be a hasty, unsound conclusion, that the only people to whom we could look for sympathy and any passionate energy in forwarding the revolutionary change would be the unhappy, the discontented, the dispossessed, and the defeated in life's struggle. This idea lies at the root of the class-war dogmas of the Marxists, and it rests on an entirely crude conception of human nature. The successful minority is supposed to have no effective motive but a desire to retain and intensify its advantages. A quite imaginary solidarity to that end is attributed to it, a preposterous, base class activity. On the other hand, the unsuccessful mass—"proletariat"—is supposed to be capable of a clear apprehension of its disadvantages, and the more it is impoverished and embittered, the clearer-minded it becomes, and the nearer draws its uprising, its constructive "dictatorship," and the Millennium.

No doubt a considerable amount of truth is to be found in this theory of the Marxist revolution. Human beings, like other animals, are disposed to remain where their circumstances are tolerable and to want change when they are uncomfortable, and so a great proportion of the people who are "well off" want little or no change in present conditions, particularly those who are too dull to be bored by an unprogressive life, while a great proportion of those who actually feel the inconveniences of straitened means and population pressure, do. But much vaster masses of the rank and file of humanity are accustomed to inferiority and dispossession, they do not feel these things to the extent even of desiring change, or even if they do feel their disadvantages, they still fear change more than they dislike their disadvantages. Moreover, those who are sufficiently distressed to realize that "something ought to be done about it" are much more disposed to childish and threatening demands upon heaven and the government for redress and vindictive and punitive action against the envied fortunate with whom they happen to be in immediate contact, than to any reaction towards such complex, tentative, disciplined constructive work as alone can better the lot of mankind. In practice Marxism is found to work out in a ready resort to malignantly destructive activities, and to be so uncreative as to be practically impotent in the face of material difficulties. In Russia, where—in and about the urban centres, at least—Marxism has been put to the test, the doctrine of the Workers' Republic remains as a unifying cant, a test of orthodoxy of as little practical significance there as the communism of Jesus and communion with Christ in Christendom, while beneath this creed a small oligarchy which has attained power by its profession does its obstinate best, much hampered by the suspicion and hostility of the Western financiers and politicians, to carry on a series of interesting and varyingly successful experiments in the socialization of economic life. Here we have no scope to discuss the N.E.P. and the Five Year Plan. They are dealt with in The Work, Wealth, and Happiness of Mankind. Neither was properly Communist. The Five Year Plan is carried out as an autocratic state capitalism. Each year shows more and more clearly that Marxism and Communism are divagations from the path of human progress and that the line of advance must follow a course more intricate and less flattering to the common impulses of our nature.

The one main strand of truth in the theory of social development woven by Marx and Engels is that successful, comfortable people are disposed to dislike, obstruct and even resist actively any substantial changes in the current patchwork of arrangements, however great the ultimate dangers of that patchwork may be or the privations and sufferings of other people involved in it. The one main strand of error in that theory is the facile assumption that the people at a disadvantage will be stirred to anything more than chaotic and destructive expressions of resentment. If now we reject the error and accept the truth, we lose the delusive comfort of belief in that magic giant, the Proletariat, who will dictate, arrange, restore, and create, but we clear the way for the recognition of an élite of intelligent, creative-minded people scattered through the whole community, and for a study of the method of making this creative element effective in human affairs against the massive oppositions of selfishness and unimaginative self-protective conservatism.

Now, certain classes of people such as thugs and burglars seem to be harmful to society without a redeeming point about them, and others, such as racecourse bookmakers, seem to provide the minimum of distraction and entertainment with a maximum of mischief. Wilful idlers are a mere burthen on the community. Other social classes again, professional soldiers, for example, have a certain traditional honourableness which disguises the essentially parasitic relationship of their services to the developing modern community. Armies and armaments are cancers produced by the malignant development of the patriotic virus under modern conditions of exaggeration and mass suggestion. But since there are armies prepared to act coercively in the world to-day, it is necessary that the Open Conspiracy should develop within itself the competence to resist military coercion and combat and destroy armies that stand in the way of its emergence. Possibly the first two types here instanced may be condemned as classes and excluded as classes from any participation in the organized effort to recast the world, but quite obviously the soldier cannot. The world commonweal will need its own scientific methods of protection so long as there are people running about the planet with flags and uniforms and weapons, offering violence to their fellow men and interfering with the free movements of commodities in the name of national sovereignty.

And when we come to the general functioning classes, landowners, industrial organizers, bankers, and so forth, who control the present system, such as it is, it should be still plainer that it is very largely from the ranks of these classes, and from their stores of experience and traditions of method, that the directive forces of the new order must emerge. The Open Conspiracy can have nothing to do with the heresy that the path of human progress lies through an extensive class war.

Let us consider, for example, how the Open Conspiracy stands to such a complex of activities, usages, accumulations, advantages as constitutes the banking world. There are no doubt many bankers and many practices in banking which make for personal or group advantage to the general detriment. They forestall, monopolize, constrain, and extort, and so increase their riches. And another large part of that banking world follows routine and established usage; it is carrying on and keeping things going, and it is neither inimical nor conducive to the development of a progressive world organization of finance. But there remains a residuum of original and intelligent people in banking or associated with banking or mentally interested in banking, who do realize that banking plays a very important, interesting part in the world's affairs, who are curious about their own intricate function and disposed towards a scientific investigation of its origins, conditions, and future possibilities. Such types move naturally towards the Open Conspiracy. Their enquiries carry them inevitably outside the bankers' habitual field to an examination of the nature, drift, and destiny of the entire economic process.

Now the theme of the preceding paragraph might be repeated with variations through a score of paragraphs in which appropriate modifications would adapt it to the industrial organizer, the merchant and organizer of transport, the advertiser, the retail distributor, the agriculturalist, the engineer, the builder, the economic chemist, and a number of other types functional in the contemporary community. In all we should distinguish firstly a base and harmful section, then a mediocre section following established usage, and lastly, an active, progressive section to whom we turn naturally for developments leading towards the progressive world commonweal of our desires. And our analysis might penetrate further than separation into types of individuals. In nearly every individual instance we should find a mixed composition, a human being of fluctuating moods and confused purposes, sometimes base, sometimes drifting with the tide and sometimes alert and intellectually and morally quickened. The Open Conspiracy must be content to take a fraction of a man, as it appeals to fractions of many classes, if it cannot get him altogether.

This idea of drawing together a proportion of all or nearly all the functional classes in contemporary communities in order to weave the beginnings of a world community out of their selection is a fairly obvious one—and yet it has still to win practical recognition. Man is a morbidly gregarious and partisan creature; he is deep in his immediate struggles and stands by his own kind because in so doing he defends himself; the industrialist is best equipped to criticize his fellow industrialist, but he finds the root of all evil in the banker; the wages worker shifts the blame for all social wrongs on the "employing class." There is an element of exasperation in most economic and social reactions, and there is hardly a reforming or revolutionary movement in history which is not essentially an indiscriminate attack of one functioning class or type upon another, on the assumption that the attacked class is entirely to blame for the clash and that the attacking class is self-sufficient in the commonweal and can dispense with its annoying collaborator. A considerable element of justice usually enters into such recriminations. But the Open Conspiracy cannot avail itself of these class animosities for its driving force. It can have, therefore, no uniform method of approach. For each class it has a conception of modification and development, and each class it approaches therefore at a distinctive angle. Some classes, no doubt, it would supersede altogether; others—the scientific investigator, for example—it must regard as almost wholly good and seek only to multiply and empower, but it can no more adopt the prejudices and extravagances of any particular class as its basis than it can adopt the claims of any existing state or empire.

When it is clearly understood that the binding links of the Open Conspiracy we have in mind are certain broad general ideas, and that—except perhaps in the case of scientific workers—we have no current set of attitudes of mind and habits of activity which we can turn over directly and unmodified to the service of the conspiracy, we are in a position to realize that the movement we contemplate must from the outset be diversified in its traditions and elements and various in its methods. It must fight upon several fronts and with many sorts of equipment. It will have a common spirit, but it is quite conceivable that between many of its contributory factors there may be very wide gaps in understanding and sympathy. It is no sort of simple organization.

13

XI. — FORCES AND RESISTANCES IN THE GREAT MODERN

We have now stated broadly but plainly the idea of the world commonweal which is the objective of the Open Conspiracy, and we have made a preliminary examination of the composition of that movement, showing that it must be necessarily not a class development, but a convergence of many different sorts of people upon a common idea. Its opening task must be the elaboration, exposition, and propaganda of this common idea, a steady campaign to revolutionize education and establish a modern ideology in men's minds and, arising out of this, the incomparably vaster task of the realization of its ideas.

These are tasks not to be done in vacuo; they have to be done in a dense world of crowding, incessant, passionate, unco-ordinated activities, the world of market and newspaper, seed-time and harvest, births, deaths, jails, hospitals, riots, barracks and army manoeuvres, false prophets and royal processions, games and shows, fire, storm, pestilence, earthquake, war. Every day and every hour things will be happening to help or thwart, stimulate or undermine, obstruct or defeat the creative effort to set up the world commonweal.

Before we go on to discuss the selection and organization of these heterogeneous and mainly religious impulses upon which we rest our hopes of a greater life for mankind, before we plan how these impulses may be got together into a system of co-ordinated activities, it will be well to review the main antagonistic forces with which, from its very inception, the Open Conspiracy will be—is now—in conflict.

To begin with, we will consider these forces as they present themselves in the highly developed Western European States of to-day and in their American derivatives, derivatives which, in spite of the fact that in most cases they have far outgrown their lands of origin, still owe a large part of their social habits and political conceptions to Europe. All these States touch upon the Atlantic or its contributory seas; they have all grown to their present form since the discovery of America; they have a common tradition rooting in the ideas of Christendom and a generic resemblance of method. Economically and socially they present what is known in current parlance as the Capitalist system, but it will relieve us of a considerable load of disputatious matter if we call them here simply the "Atlantic" civilizations and communities.

The consideration of these Atlantic civilizations in relation to the coming world civilization will suffice for the present chapter. Afterwards we will consider the modification of the forces antagonistic to the Open Conspiracy as they display themselves beyond the formal confines of these now dominant states in the world's affairs, in the social systems weakened and injured by their expansion, and among such less highly organized communities as still survive from man's savage and barbaric past.

The Open Conspiracy is not necessarily antagonistic to any existing government. The Open Conspiracy is a creative, organizing movement and not an anarchistic one. It does not want to destroy existing controls and forms of human association, but either to supersede or amalgamate them into a common world directorate. If constitutions, parliaments, and kings can be dealt with as provisional institutions, trustees for the coming of age of the world commonweal, and in so far as they are conducted in that spirit, the Open Conspiracy makes no attack upon them.

But most governments will not set about their business as in any way provisional they and their supporters insist upon a reverence and obedience which repudiate any possibility of supersession. What should be an instrument becomes a divinity. In nearly every country of the world there is, in deference to the pretended necessities of a possible war, a vast degrading and dangerous cultivation of loyalty and mechanical subservience to flags, uniforms, presidents, and kings. A president or king who does his appointed work well and righteously is entitled to as much subservience as a bricklayer who does his work well and righteously and to no more, but instead there is a sustained endeavour to give him the privileges of an idol above criticism or reproach, and the organized worship of flags has become—with changed conditions of intercourse and warfare—an entirely evil misdirection of the gregarious impulses of our race. Emotion and sentimentality are evoked in the cause of disciplines and co-operations that could quite easily be sustained and that are better sustained by rational conviction.

The Open Conspiracy is necessarily opposed to all such implacable loyalties, and still more so to the aggressive assertion and propaganda of such loyalties. When these things take the form of suppressing reasonable criticism and forbidding even the suggestion of other forms of government, they become plainly antagonists to any comprehensive project for human welfare. They become manifestly, from the wider point of view, seditious, and loyalty to "king and country" passes into plain treason to mankind. Almost everywhere, at present, educational institutions organize barriers in the path of progress, and there are only the feeblest attempts at any counter education that will break up these barriers. There is little or no effort to restrain the aggressive nationalist when he waves his flag against the welfare of our race, or to protect the children of the world from the infection of his enthusiasms. And this last is as true now of the American system as it is of any European State.

In the great mass of the modern community there is little more than a favourable acquiescence in patriotic ideas and in the worship of patriotic symbols, and that is based largely on such training. These things are not necessary things for the generality of to-day. A change of mental direction would be possible for the majority of people now without any violent disorganization of their intimate lives or any serious social or economic readjustments for them. Mental infection in such cases could be countered by mental sanitation. A majority of people in Europe, and a still larger majority in the United States and the other American Republics, could become citizens of the world without any serious hindrance to their present occupations, and with an incalculably vast increase of their present security.

But there remains a net of special classes in every community, from kings to custom-house officers, far more deeply involved in patriotism because it is their trade and their source of honour, and prepared in consequence with an instinctive resistance to any reorientation of ideas towards a broader outlook. In the case of such people no mental sanitation is possible without dangerous and alarming changes in their way of living. For the majority of these patriots by metier, the Open Conspiracy unlocks the gates leading from a fussy paradise of eminence, respect, and privilege,—and motions them towards an austere wilderness which does not present even the faintest promise of a congenial, distinguished life for them. Nearly everything in human nature will dispose them to turn away from these gates which open towards the world peace, to bang-to and lock them again if they can, and to grow thickets as speedily as possible to conceal them and get them forgotten. The suggestion of being trustees in a transition will seem to most of such people only the camouflage of an ultimate degradation.

From such classes of patriots by metier, it is manifest that the Open Conspiracy can expect only opposition. It may detach individuals from them, but only by depriving them of their essential class loyalties and characteristics. The class as a class will remain none the less antagonistic. About royal courts and presidential residences, in diplomatic, consular, military, and naval circles, and wherever people wear titles and uniforms and enjoy pride and precedences based on existing political institutions, there will be the completest general inability to grasp the need for the Open Conspiracy. These people and their womankind, their friends and connections, their servants and dependents, are fortified by time-honoured traditions of social usage, of sentiment and romantic prestige. They will insist that they are reality and Cosmopolis a dream. Only individuals of exceptional liveliness, rare intellectual power, and innate moral force can be expected to break away from the anti-progressive habits such class conditions impose upon them.

This tangle of traditions and loyalties, of interested trades and professions, of privileged classes and official patriots, this complex of human beings embodying very easy and natural and time-honoured ideas of eternal national separation and unending international and class conflict, is the main objective of the Open Conspiracy in its opening phase. This tangle must be disentangled as the Open Conspiracy advances, and until it is largely disentangled and cleared up that Open Conspiracy cannot become anything very much more than a desire and a project.

This tangle of "necessary patriots," as one may call them, is different in its nature, less intricate and extensive proportionally in the United States and the States of Latin America, than it is in the old European communities, but it is none the less virulent in its action on that account. It is only recently that military and naval services have become important factors in American social life, and the really vitalizing contact of the interested patriot and the State has hitherto centred mainly upon the custom house and the concession. Instead of a mellow and romantic loyalty to "king and country" the American thinks simply of America and his flag.

The American exaggeration of patriotism began as a resistance to exploitation from overseas. Even when political and fiscal freedom were won, there was a long phase of industrial and financial dependence. The American's habits of mind, in spite of his recent realization of the enormous power and relative prosperity of the United States and of the expanding possibilities of their Spanish and Portuguese-speaking neighbours, are still largely self- protective against a now imaginary European peril. For the first three quarters of the nineteenth century the people of the American continent, and particularly the people of the United States, felt the industrial and financial ascendancy of Great Britain and had a reasonable fear of European attacks upon their continent. A growing tide of immigrants of uncertain sympathy threatened their dearest habits. Flag worship was imposed primarily as a repudiation of Europe. Europe no longer looms over America with overpowering intimations, American industries no longer have any practical justification for protection, American finance would be happier without it, but the patriotic interests are so established now that they go on and will go on. No American statesman who ventures to be cosmopolitan in his utterance and outlook is likely to escape altogether from the raucous attentions of the patriotic journalist.

We have said that the complex of classes in any country interested in the current method of government is sustained by traditions and impelled by its nature and conditions to protect itself against exploratory criticism. It is therefore unable to escape from the forms of competitive and militant nationalism in which it was evolved. It cannot, without grave danger of enfeeblement, change any such innate form. So that while parallel complexes of patriotic classes are found in greater or less intricacy grouped about the flags and governments of most existing states, these complexes are by their nature obliged to remain separate, nationalist, and mutually antagonistic. You cannot expect a world union of soldiers or diplomatists. Their existence and nature depend upon the idea that national separation is real and incurable, and that war, in the long run, is unavoidable. Their conceptions of loyalty involve an antagonism to all foreigners, even to foreigners of exactly the same types as themselves, and make for a continual campaign of annoyances, suspicions, and precautions—together with a general propaganda, affecting all other classes, of the necessity of an international antagonism—that creeps persistently towards war.

But while the methods of provoking war employed by the patriotic classes are traditional, modern science has made a new and enormously more powerful thing of warfare and, as the Great War showed, even the most conservative generals on both sides are unable to prevent the gigantic interventions of the mechanician and the chemist. So that a situation is brought about in which the militarist element is unable to fight without the support of the modern industrial organization and the acquiescence of the great mass of people. We are confronted therefore at the present time with the paradoxical situation that a patriotic tradition sustains in power and authority warlike classes who are quite incapable of carrying on war. The other classes to which they must go for support when the disaster of war is actually achieved are classes developed under peace conditions, which not only have no positive advantage in war, but must, as a whole, suffer great dislocation, discomfort, destruction, and distress from war. It is of primary importance therefore, to the formally dominant classes that these new social masses and powers should remain under the sway of the old social, sentimental, and romantic traditions, and equally important is it to the Open Conspiracy that they should be released.

Here we bring into consideration another great complex of persons, interests, traditions—the world of education, the various religious organizations, and, beyond these, the ramifying, indeterminate world of newspapers and other periodicals, books, the drama, art, and all the instruments of presentation and suggestion that mould opinion and direct action. The sum of the operations of this complex will be either to sustain or to demolish the old nationalist militant ascendancy. Its easiest immediate course is to accept it. Educational organizations on that account are now largely a conservative force in the community; they are in most cases directly controlled by authority and bound officially as well as practically to respect current fears and prejudices. It evokes fewer difficulties for them if they limit and mould rather than release the young. The schoolmaster tends, therefore, to accept and standardize and stereotype, even in the living, progressive fields of science and philosophy. Even there he is a brake on the forward movement. It is clear that the Open Conspiracy must either continually disturb and revivify him or else frankly antagonize him. Universities also struggle between the honourable past on which their prestige rests, and the need of adaptation to a world of enquiry, experiment, and change. It is an open question whether these particular organizations of intellectual prestige are of any real value in the living world. A modern world planned de novo would probably produce nothing like a contemporary university. Modern research, one may argue, would be stimulated rather than injured by complete detachment from the lingering mediaevalism of such institutions, their entanglement with adolescent education, and their ancient and contagious conceptions of precedence and honour.

Ordinary religious organizations, again, exist for self-preservation and are prone to follow rather than direct the currents of popular thought. They are kept alive, indeed, by revivalism and new departures which at the outlet they are apt to resist, as the Catholic Church, for instance, resisted the Franciscan awakening, but their formal disposition is conservative. They say to religious development, thus far and no farther.

Here, in school, college, and church, are activities of thought and instruction which, generally speaking, drag upon the wheels of progress, but which need not necessarily do so. A schoolmaster may be original, stimulating, and creative, and if he is fortunate and a good fighter he may even achieve considerable worldly success; university teachers and investigators may strike out upon new lines and yet escape destruction by the older dons. Universities compete against other universities at home and abroad and cannot altogether yield to the forces of dullness and subservience. They must maintain a certain difference from vulgar opinion and a certain repute of intellectual virility.

As we pass from the more organized to the less organized intellectual activities, we find conservative influence declining in importance, and a freer play for the creative drive. Freshness is a primary condition of journalistic, literary, and artistic success, and orthodoxy has nothing new to say or do. But the desire for freshness may be satisfied all too readily by merely extravagant, superficial, and incoherent inventions.

The influence of this old traditional nationalist social and political hierarchy which blocks the way to the new world is not, however, exerted exclusively through its control over schools and universities. Nor is that indeed its more powerful activity. Would that it were There is also a direct, less defined contact of the old order with the nascent powers, that plays a far more effective part in delaying the development of the modern world commonweal. Necessarily the old order has determined the established way of life, which is, at its best, large, comfortable, amusing, respected. It possesses all the entrances and exits and all the controls of the established daily round. It is able to exact, and it does exact, almost without design, many conformities. There can be no very ample social life, therefore, for those who are conspicuously dissentient. Again the old order has a complete provision for the growth, welfare, and advancement of its children. It controls the founts of honour and self-respect; it provides a mapped-out world of behaviour. The new initiatives make their appearance here and there in the form of isolated individuals, here an inventor, there a bold organizer or a vigorous thinker. Apart from his specific work the innovating type finds that he must fall in with established things or his womenfolk will be ostracized, and he will be distressed by a sense of isolation even in the midst of successful activities. The more intensely he innovates in particular, the more likely is he to be too busy to seek out kindred souls and organize a new social life in general. The new things and ideas, even when they arise abundantly, arise scattered and unorganized, and the old order takes them in its net. America for example --both on its Latin and on its English-speaking side—is in many ways a triumph of the old order over the new.

Men like Winwood Reade thought that the New World would be indeed a new world. They idealized its apparent emancipations. But as the more successful of the toiling farmers and traders of republican America rose one by one to affluence, leisure, and freedom, it was far more easy for them to adopt the polished and prepared social patterns and usages of Europe than to work out a new civilization in accordance with their equalitarian professions. Yet there remains a gap in their adapted "Society." Henry James, that acute observer of subtle social flavours, has pointed out the peculiar headlessness of social life in America because of the absence of court functions to "go on" to and justify the assembling and dressing. The social life has imitated the preparation for the Court without any political justification. In Europe the assimilation of the wealthy European industrialist and financier by the old order has been parallel and naturally more logically complete. He really has found a court to "go on" to. His social scheme was still undecapitated until kingdoms began to change into republics after 1917.

In this way the complex of classes vitally involved in the old militant nationalist order is mightily reinforced by much larger masses of imitative and annexed and more or less assimilated rich and active people. The great industrialist has married the daughter of the marquis and has a couple of sons in the Guards and a daughter who is a princess. The money of the American Leeds, fleeing from the social futility of its land of origin, helped bolster up a mischievous monarchy in Greece. The functional and private lives of the new men are thus at war with one another. The real interests of the great industrialist or financier lie in cosmopolitan organization and the material development of the world commonweal, but his womenfolk pin flags all over him, and his sons are prepared to sacrifice themselves and all his business creations for the sake of trite splendours and Ruritanian romance.

But just so far as the great business organizer is capable and creative, so far is he likely to realize and resent the price in frustration that the old order obliges him to pay for amusement, social interest, and domestic peace and comfort. The Open Conspiracy threatens him with no effacement; it may even appear with an air of release. If he had women who were interested in his business affairs instead of women who had to be amused, and if he realized in time the practical, intellectual, and moral kidnap of sons and daughters by the old order that goes on, he might pass quite easily from acquiescence to antagonism. But in this respect he cannot a single-handed. This is a social and not an individual operation. The Open Conspiracy, it is clear, must include in its activities a great fight for the souls of economically-functional people. It must carve out a Society of its own from Society. Only by the creation of a new and better social life can it resist the many advantages and attractions of the old.

This constant gravitation back to traditional uses on the part of what might become new social types applies not merely to big people but to such small people as are really functional in the modern economic scheme. The have no social life adapted to their new economic relationships, and they forced back upon the methods of behaviour established for what were roughly their analogues in the old order of things. The various sorts of managers and foremen in big modern concerns, for example, carry on ways of living they have taken ready-made from the stewards, tradesmen, tenantry, and upper servants of an aristocratic territorial system. They release themselves and are released almost in spite of themselves, slowly, generation by generation, from habits of social subservience that are no longer necessary nor convenient in the social process, acquire an official pride in themselves and take on new conceptions of responsible loyalty to a scheme. And they find themselves under suggestions of class aloofness and superiority to the general mass of less cardinal workers, that are often unjustifiable under new conditions. Machinery and scientific organization have been and still are revolutionizing productive activity by the progressive elimination of the unskilled worker, the hack, the mere toiler. But the social organization of the modern community and the mutual deportment of the associated workers left over after this elimination are still haunted by the tradition of the lord, the middle-class tenant, and the servile hind. The development of self-respect and mutual respect among the mass of modern functional workers is clearly an intimate concern of the Open Conspiracy.

A vast amount of moral force has been wasted in the past hundred years by the antagonism of "Labour" to "Capital," as though this were the primary issue in human affairs. But this never was the primary issue, and it is steadily receding from its former importance. The ancient civilizations did actually rest upon a broad basis of slavery and serfdom. Human muscle was a main source of energy-ranking with sun, wind, and flood. But invention and discovery have so changed the conditions under which power is directed and utilized that muscle becomes economically secondary and inessential. We no longer want hewers of wood and drawers of water, carriers and pick and spade men. We no longer want that breeding swarm of hefty sweaty bodies without which the former civilizations could not have endured. We want watchful and understanding guardians and drivers of complex delicate machines, which can be mishandled and brutalized and spoilt all too easily. The less disposed these masters of our machines are to inordinate multiplication, the more room and food in the world for their ampler lives. Even to the lowest level of a fully-mechanicalized civilization it is required that the human element should be select. In the modern world, crowds are a survival, and they will presently be an anachronism, and crowd psychology therefore cannot supply the basis of a new order. It is just because labour is becoming more intelligent, responsible, and individually efficient that it is becoming more audible and impatient in social affairs.

It is just because it is no longer mere gang labour, and is becoming more and more intelligent co-operation in detail, that it now resents being treated as a serf, housed like a serf, fed like a serf, and herded like a serf, and its pride and thoughts and feelings disregarded. Labour is in revolt because as a matter of fact it is, in the ancient and exact sense of the word, ceasing to be labour at all.

The more progressive elements of the directive classes recognize this, but, as we have shown, there are formidable forces still tending to maintain the old social attitudes when arrogance became the ruler and the common man accepted his servile status. A continual resistance is offered by large sections of the prosperous and advantaged to the larger claims of the modernized worker, and in response the rising and differentiating workers develop an angry antagonism to these directive classes which allow themselves to be controlled by their conservative and reactionary elements. Moreover, the increasing relative intelligence of the labour masses, the unprecedented imaginative stimulation they experience, the continually more widespread realization of the available freedoms and comforts and indulgences that might be and are not shared by all in a modern state, develop a recalcitrance where once there was little but fatalistic acquiescence. An objection to direction and obligation, always mutely present in the toiling multitude since the economic life of man began, becomes articulate and active. It is the taste of freedom that makes labour desire to be free. This series of frictions is a quite inevitable aspect of social reorganization, but it does not constitute a primary antagonism in the process.

The class war was invented by the classes; it is a natural tradition of the upper strata of the old order. It was so universally understood that there was no need to state it. It is implicit in nearly all the literature of the world before the nineteenth century—except the Bible, the Koran, and other sequelae. The "class war" of the Marxist is merely a poor snobbish imitation, a tu quoque, a pathetic, stupid, indignant reversal of and retort to the old arrogance, a pathetic upward arrogance.

These conflicts cut across rather than oppose or help the progressive development to which the Open Conspiracy devotes itself. Labour, awakened, enquiring, and indignant, is not necessarily progressive; if the ordinary undistinguished worker is no longer to be driven as a beast of burthen, he has --which also goes against the grain—to be educated to as high a level of co-operative efficiency as possible. He has to work better, even if he works for much shorter hours and under better conditions, and his work must be subordinated work still; he cannot become en masse sole owner and master of a scheme of things he did not make and is incapable of directing. Yet this is the ambition implicit in an exclusively "Labour" movement. Either the Labour revolutionary hopes to cadge the services of exceptional people without acknowledgment or return on sentimental grounds, or he really believes that anyone is as capable as anyone else—if not more so. The worker at a low level may be flattered by dreams of "class-conscious" mass dominion from which all sense of inferiority is banished, but they will remain dreams. The deep instinctive jealousy of the commonplace individual for outstanding quality and novel initiative may be organized and turned to sabotage and destruction, masquerading as and aspiring to be a new social order, but that will be a blind alley and not the road of progress. Our hope for the human future does not lie in crowd psychology and the indiscriminating rule of universal democracy.

The Open Conspiracy can have little use for mere resentments as a driving force towards its ends; it starts with a proposal not to exalt the labour class but to abolish it, its sustaining purpose is to throw drudges out of employment and eliminate the inept—and it is far more likely to incur suspicion and distrust in the lower ranks of the developing industrial order of to-day than to win support there. There, just as everywhere else in the changing social complexes of our time, it can appeal only to the exceptionally understanding individual who can without personal humiliation consider his present activities and relationships as provisional and who can, without taking offence, endure a searching criticising of his present quality and mode of living.

14

XII. — THE RESISTANCES OF THE LESS INDUSTRIALIZED

So far, in our accounting of the powers, institutions, dispositions, types, and classes which will be naturally opposed to the Open Conspiracy, we have surveyed only such territory in the domain of the future world commonweal as is represented by the complex, progressive, highly-industrialized communities, based on a preceding landlord-soldier, tenant, town-merchant, and tradesman system, of the Atlantic type. These communities have developed farthest in the direction of mechanicalization, and they are so much more efficient and powerful that they now dominate the rest of the world. India, China, Russia, Africa present mélanges of social systems, thrown together, outpaced, overstrained, shattered, invaded, exploited, and more or less subjugated by the finance, machinery, and political aggressions of the Atlantic, Baltic, and Mediterranean civilization. In many ways they have an air of assimilating themselves to that civilization, evolving modern types and classes, and abandoning much of their distinctive traditions. But that they take from the West is mainly the new developments, the material achievements, rather than the social and political achievements, that, empowered by modern inventions, have won their to world predominance. They may imitate European nationalism to a certain extent; for them it becomes a convenient form of self-assertion against the pressure of a realized practical social and political inferiority; but the degree to which they will or can take over the social assumptions and habits of the long-established European-American hierarchy is probably very restricted. Their nationalism will remain largely indigenous; the social traditions in which they will try to make the new material forces subservient will be traditions of an Oriental life widely different from the original life of Europe. They will have their own resistances to the Open Conspiracy, therefore, but they will be different resistances from those we have hitherto considered. The automobile and the wireless set, the harvester and steel construction building, will come to the jungle rajah and the head hunter, the Brahmin and the Indian peasant, with a parallel and yet dissimilar message to the one they brought the British landowner or the corn and cattle farmers of the Argentine and the Middle West. Also they may be expected to evoke dissimilar reactions. To a number of the finer, more energetic minds of these overshadow communities which have lagged more or less ill the material advances t which this present ascendancy of western Europe and America is due, the Open Conspiracy may come with an effect of immense invitation. At one step they may go from the sinking vessel of their antiquated order, across their present conquerors, into a brotherhood of world rulers They may turn to the problem of saving and adapting all that is rich and distinctive of their inheritance to the common ends of the race. But to the less vigorous intelligences of this outer world, the new project of the Open Conspiracy will seem no better than a new form of Western envelopment and they will fight a mighty liberation as though it were a further enslavement to the European tradition. They will watch the Open Conspiracy for any signs of conscious superiority and racial disregard. Necessarily they will recognize it as a product of Western mentality and they may well be tempted to regard it as an elaboration and organization of current dispositions rather than the evolution of a new phase which will make no discrimination at last between the effete traditions of either East or West. Their suspicions will be sustained and developed by the clumsy and muddle-headed political and economic aggressions of the contemporary political and business systems, such as they are, of the West, now in progress. Behind that cloud of aggression Western thought has necessarily advanced upon them. It could have got to their attention in no other way.

Partly these resistances and criticisms of the decadent communities outside the Atlantic capitalist system will be aimed, not at the developing methods of the coming world community, but at the European traditions and restrictions that have imposed themselves upon these methods, and so far the clash of the East and West may be found to subserve the aims of the Open Conspiracy. In the conflict of old traditions and in the consequent deadlocks lies much hope for the direct acceptance of the groups of ideas centring upon the Open Conspiracy One of the most interesting areas of humanity in this respect is the great system of communities under the sway or influence of Soviet Russia. Russia has never been completely incorporated with the European system; she became a just passable imitation of a western European monarchy in the seventeenth and eighteenth centuries, and talked at last of constitutions and parliaments—but the reality of that vast empire remained an Asiatic despotism, and the European mask was altogether smashed by the successive revolutions of 1917. The ensuing system is a government presiding over an enormous extent of peasants and herdsmen, by a disciplined association professing the faith and dogmas of Marx, as interpreted and qualified by Lenin and Stalin.

In many ways this government is a novelty of extraordinary interest. It labours against enormous difficulties within itself and without. Flung amazingly into a position of tremendous power, its intellectual flexibility is greatly restricted by the urgent militant necessity for mental unanimity and a consequent repression of criticism. It finds itself separated, intellectually and morally, by an enormous gap from the illiterate millions over which it rules. More open perhaps to scientific and creative conceptions than any other government, and certainly more willing to experiment and innovate, its enterprise is starved by the economic depletion of the country in the Great War and by the technical and industrial backwardness of the population upon which it must draw for its personnel. Moreover, it struggles within itself between concepts of a modern scientific social organization and a vague anarchistic dream in which the "State" is to disappear, and an emancipated proletariat, breeding and expectorating freely, fills the vistas of time forevermore. The tradition of long years of hopeless opposition has tainted the world policy of the Marxist cult with a mischievous and irritating quality that focuses upon it the animosity of every government in the dominant Atlantic system. Marxism never had any but the vaguest fancies about the relation of one nation to another, and the new Russian government, for all its cosmopolitan phrases, is more and more plainly the heir to the obsessions of Tsarist Imperialism, using the Communist party, as other countries have used Christian missionaries, to maintain a propagandist government to forward its schemes. Nevertheless, the Soviet government has maintained itself for more than twelve years, and it seems far more likely to evolve than to persist. It is quite possible that it will evolve towards the conceptions of the Open Conspiracy, and in that case Russia may witness once again a conflict between new ideas and Old Believers. So far the Communist party in Moscow has maintained a considerable propaganda of ideas in the rest of the world and especially across its western frontier. Many of these ideas are now trite and stale. The time may be not far distant when the tide of propaganda will flow in the reverse direction. It has pleased the vanity of the Communist party to imagine itself conducting a propaganda of world revolution. Its fate may be to develop upon lines that will make its more intelligent elements easily assimilable to the Open Conspiracy for a world revolution. The Open Conspiracy as it spreads and grows may find a less encumbered field for trying out the economic developments implicit in its conceptions in Russia and Siberia than anywhere else in the world.

However severely the guiding themes and practical methods of the present Soviet government in Russia may be criticized, the fact remains that it has cleared out of its way many of the main obstructive elements that we find still vigorous in the more highly-organized communities in the West. It has liberated vast areas from the kindred superstitions of monarchy and the need for a private proprietary control of great economic interests. And it has presented both China and India with the exciting spectacle of a social and political system capable of throwing off many of the most characteristic features of triumphant Westernism, and yet holding its own. In the days when Japan faced up to modern necessities there were no models for imitation that were not communities of the Atlantic type pervaded by the methods of private capitalism, and in consequence the Japanese reconstituted their affairs on a distinctly European plan, adopting a Parliament and bringing their monarchy, social hierarchy, and business and financial methods into a general conformity with that model. It is extremely doubtful whether any other Asiatic community will now set itself to a parallel imitation, and it will be thanks largely to the Russian revolution that this breakaway from Europeanization has occurred.

But it does not follow that such a breakaway will necessarily lead more directly to the Open Conspiracy. If we have to face a less highly organized system of interests and prejudices in Russia and China, we have to deal with a vastly wider ignorance and a vastly more formidable animalism. Russia is a land of tens of millions of peasants ruled over by a little band of the intelligentsia who can be counted only by tens of thousands. It is only these few score thousands who are accessible to ideas of world construction, and the only hope of bringing the Russian system into active participation in the world conspiracy is through that small minority and through its educational repercussion on the myriads below. As we go eastward from European Russia the proportion of soundly prepared intelligence to which we can appeal for understanding and participation diminishes to an even more dismaying fraction. Eliminate that fraction, and one is left face to face with inchoate barbarism incapable of social and political organization above the level of the war boss and the brigand leader. Russia itself is still by no means secure against a degenerative process in that direction, and the hope of China struggling out of it without some forcible directive interventions is a hope to which constructive liberalism clings with very little assurance.

We turn back therefore from Russia, China and the communities of Central Asia to the Atlantic world. It is in that world alone that sufficient range and amplitude of thought and discussion are possible for the adequate development of the Open Conspiracy. In these communities it must begin and for a long time its main activities will need to be sustained from these necessary centres of diffusion. It will develop amidst incessant mental Strife, and through that strife it will remain alive. It is no small part of the practical weakness of present-day communism that it attempts to centre its intellectual life and its directive activities in Moscow and so cuts itself off from the free and open discussions of the Western world. Marxism lost the world when it went to Moscow and took over the traditions of Tsarism as Christianity lost the world when it went to Rome and took over the traditions of Caesar. Entrenched in Moscow from searching criticism, the Marxist ideology may become more and more dogmatic and unprogressive, repeating its sacred credo and issuing its disregarded orders to the proletariat of the world, and so stay ineffectively crystallized until the rising tide of the Open Conspiracy submerges, dissolves it afresh, and incorporates whatever it finds assimilable.

India, like Japan, is cut off from the main body of Asiatic affairs. But while Japan has become a formally Westernized nationality in the comity of such nations, India remains a world in itself. In that one peninsula nearly every type of community is to be found, from the tribe of jungle savages, through a great diversity of barbaric and mediaeval principalities, to the child and women—sweating factories and the vigorous modern commercialism of Bombay. Over it all the British imperialism prevails, a constraining and restraining influence, keeping the peace, checking epidemics, increasing the food supply by irrigation and the like, and making little or no effort to evoke responses to modern ideas. Britain in India is no propagandist of modern ferments: all those are left the other side of Suez. In India the Briton is a ruler as firm and self-assured and uncreative as the Roman. The old religious and social traditions, the complex customs, castes, tabus, and exclusions of a strangely-mixed but unamalgamated community, though a little discredited by this foreign predominance, still hold men's minds. They have been, so to speak, pickled in the preservative of the British raj.

The Open Conspiracy has to invade the Indian complex in conflict with the prejudices of both ruler and governed. It has to hope for individual breaches in the dull Romanism of the administration: here a genuine educationist, here a creative civil servant, here an official touched by the distant stir of the living homeland; and it has to try to bring these types into a co-operative relationship with a fine native scholar here or an active-minded prince or landowner or industrialist there. As the old methods of passenger transport are superseded by flying, it will be more and more difficult to keep the stir of the living homeland out of either the consciousness of the official hierarchy or the knowledge of the recalcitrant "native."

Very similar to Indian conditions is the state of affairs in the foreign possessions of France, the same administrative obstacles to the Open Conspiracy above, and below the same resentful subordination, cut off from the mental invigoration of responsibility. Within these areas of restraint, India and its lesser, simpler parallels in North Africa, Syria and the Far East, there goes on a rapid increase of low-grade population, undersized physically and mentally, and retarding the mechanical development of civilization by its standing offer of cheap labour to the unscrupulous entrepreneur, and possible feeble insurrectionary material to the unscrupulous political adventurer. It is impossible to estimate how slowly or how rapidly the knowledge and ideas that have checked the rate of increase of all the Atlantic populations may be diffused through these less alert communities.

We must complete our survey of the resistances against which the Open Conspiracy has to work by a few words about the Negro world and the regions of forest and jungle in which barbaric and even savage human life still escapes the infection of civilization. It seems inevitable that the development of modern means of communication and the conquest of tropical diseases should end in giving access everywhere to modern administration and to economic methods, and everywhere the incorporation of the former wilderness in the modern economic process means the destruction of the material basis, the free hunting, the free access to the soil, of such barbaric and savage communities as still precariously survive. The dusky peoples, who were formerly the lords of these still imperfectly assimilate areas, are becoming exploited workers, slaves, serfs, hut-tax payers, labourers to a caste of white immigrants. The spirit of the plantation broods over all these lands. The Negro in America differs only from his subjugated brother in South Africa or Kenya Colony in the fact that he also, like his white master, is an immigrant. The situation in Africa and America adjusts itself therefore towards parallel conditions, the chief variation being in the relative proportions of the two races and the details of the methods by which black labour is made to serve white ends.

In these black and white communities which are establishing themselves in all those parts of the earth where once the black was native, or in which a sub-tropical climate is favourable to his existence at a low level of social development, there is—and there is bound to be for many years to come—much racial tension. The steady advance of birth-control may mitigate the biological factors of this tension later on, and a general amelioration of manners and conduct may efface that disposition to persecute dissimilar types, which man shares with many other gregarious animals. But meanwhile this tension increases and a vast multitude of lives is strained to tragic issues.

To exaggerate the dangers and evils of miscegenation is a weakness of our time. Man interbreeds with all his varieties and yet deludes himself that there are races of outstanding purity, the "Nordic," the "Semitic," and so forth. These are phantoms of the imagination. The reality is more intricate, less dramatic, and grips less easily upon the mind; the phantoms grip only too well and incite to terrible suppressions. Changes in the number of half-breeds and in the proportion of white and coloured are changes of a temporary nature that may become controllable and rectifiable in a few generations. But until this level of civilization is reached, until the colour of a man's skin or the kinks in a woman's hair cease to have the value of shibboleths that involve educational, professional, and social extinction or survival, a black and white community is bound to be continually preoccupied by a standing feud too intimate and persuasive to permit of any long views of the world's destiny.

We come to the conclusion therefore that it is from the more vigorous, varied, and less severely obsessed centres of the Atlantic civilizations in the temperate zone, with their abundant facilities for publication and discussion, their traditions of mental liberty and their immense variety of interacting free types, that the main beginnings of the Open Conspiracy must develop. For the rest of the world, its propaganda, finding but poor nourishment in the local conditions, may retain a missionary quality for many years.

15

IN OUR

WE have dealt in the preceding two chapters with great classes and assemblages of human beings as, in the mass, likely to be more or less antagonistic to the Open Conspiracy, and it has been difficult in those chapters to avoid the implication that "we," some sort of circle round the writer, were aloof from these obstructive and hostile multitudes, and ourselves entirely identified with the Open Conspiracy. But neither are these multitudes so definitely against, nor those who are with us so entirely for, the Open Conspiracy to establish a world community as the writer, in his desire for clearness and contrast and with an all too human disposition perhaps towards plain ego-centred combative issues, has been led to represent. There is no "we," and there can be no "we," in possession of the Open Conspiracy.

The Open Conspiracy is in partial possession of us, and we attempt to serve it. But the Open Conspiracy is a natural and necessary development of contemporary thought arising here, there, and everywhere. There are doubts and sympathies that weigh on the side of the Open Conspiracy in nearly everyone, and not one of us but retains many impulses, habits, and ideas in conflict with our general devotion, checking and limiting our service.

Let us therefore in this chapter cease to discuss classes and types and consider general mental tendencies and reactions which move through all humanity.

In our opening chapters we pointed out that religion is not universally distributed throughout human society. And of no one does it seem to have complete possession. It seizes upon some of us and exalts us for one hour now and then, for a day now and then; it may leave its afterglow upon our conduct for some time; it may establish restraints and habitual dispositions; sometimes it dominates us with but brief intermissions through long spells, and then we can be saints and martyrs. In all our religious phases there appears a desire to hold the phase, to subdue the rest of our life to the standards and exigencies of that phase. Our quickened intelligence sets itself to a general analysis of our conduct and to the problem of establishing controls over our unilluminated intervals.

And when the religious elements in the mind set themselves to such self- analysis, and attempt to order and unify the whole being upon this basis of the service and advancement of the race, they discover first a great series of indifferent moods, wherein the resistance to thought and word for the Open Conspiracy is merely passive and in the nature of inertia. There is a whole class of states of mind which may be brought together under the head of "everydayism." The dinner bell and the playing fields, the cinema and the newspaper, the week-end visit and the factory siren, a host of such expectant things calls to a vast majority of people in our modern world to stop thinking and get busy with the interest in hand, and so on to the next, without a thought for the general frame and drama in which these momentary and personal incidents are set. We are driven along these marked and established routes and turned this way or that by the accidents of upbringing, of rivalries and loves, of chance encounters and vivid experiences, and it is rarely for many of us, and never for some, that the phases of broad reflection and self-questioning arise. For many people the religious life now, as in the past, has been a quite desperate effort to withdraw sufficient attention and energy from the flood of events to get some sort of grasp, and keep whatever grip is won, upon the relations of the self to the whole. Far more recoil in terror from such a possibility and would struggle strenuously against solitude in the desert, solitude under the stars, solitude in a silent room or indeed any occasion for comprehensive thought.

But the instinct and purpose of the religious type is to keep hold upon the comprehensive drama, and at the heart of all the great religions of the world we find a parallel disposition to escape in some manner from the aimless drive and compulsion of accident and everyday. Escape is attempted either by withdrawal from the presence of crowding circumstance into a mystical contemplation and austere retirement, or—what is more difficult and desperate and reasonable—by imposing the mighty standards of enduring issues upon the whole mass of transitory problems which constitute the actual business of life. We have already noted how the modern mind turns from retreat as a recognizable method of religion, and faces squarely up to the second alternative. The tumult of life has to be met and conquered. Aim must prevail over the aimless. Remaining in normal life we must yet keep our wills and thoughts aloof from normal life and fixed upon creative processes. However busied we may be, however challenged, we must yet save something of our best mental activity for self-examination and keep ourselves alert against the endless treacheries within that would trip us back into everydayism and disconnected responses to the stimuli of life.

Religions in the past, though they have been apt to give a preference to the renunciation of things mundane, have sought by a considerable variety of expedients to preserve the faith of those whom chance or duty still kept in normal contact with the world. It would provide material for an interesting study to enquire how its organizations to do this have worked in the past and how far they may be imitated and paralleled in the progressive life of the future. All the wide-reaching religions which came into existence in the five centuries before and the five centuries after Christ have made great use of periodic meetings for mutual reassurance, of sacred books, creeds, fundamental heart-searchings, of confession, prayer, sacraments, seasons of withdrawal, meditation, fasting, and prayer. Do these methods mark a phase in the world's development, or are they still to be considered available?

This points to a very difficult tangle of psychological problems. The writer in his earlier draft of this book wrote that the modern religious individual leads, spiritually speaking, a life of extreme wasteful and dangerous isolation. He still feels that is true, but he realizes that the invention of corrective devices is not within his range. He cannot picture a secular Mass nor congregations singing hymns about the Open Conspiracy. Perhaps the modern soul in trouble will resort to the psychoanalysts instead of the confessional; in which case we need to pray for better psychoanalysts.

Can the modern mind work in societies? May the daily paper be slowly usurping the functions of morning prayer, a daily mental reminder of large things, with more vividness and, at present, lower standards? One of the most distressful facts of the spread of education in the nineteenth century was the unscrupulous exploitation of the new reading public by a group of trash-dealers who grew rich and mighty in the process. Is the popular publisher and newspaper proprietor always to remain a trash-dealer? Or are we to see, in the future, publications taking at times some or all of the influence of revivalist movements, and particular newspapers rising to the task of sustaining a common faith in a gathering section of the public?

The modern temple in which we shall go to meditate may be a museum; the modern religious house and its religious life may be a research organization. The Open Conspirator must see to it that the museums show their meaning plain. There may be not only literature presently, but even plays, shows, and music, to subserve new ideas instead of trading upon tradition.

It is plain that to read and be moved by great ideas and to form good resolutions with no subsequent reminders and moral stocktaking is no enough to keep people in the way of the Open Conspiracy. The relapse to everydayism is too easy. The contemporary Open Conspirator may forget, and he has nothing to remind him; he may relapse, and he w hear no reproach to warn him of his relapse. Nowhere has he recorded vow. "Everyday" has endless ways of justifying the return of the believer to sceptical casualness. It is easy to persuade oneself that one is taking life or oneself "too seriously." The mind is very self-protective; has a disposition to abandon too great or too far-reaching an effort and return to things indisputably within its scope. We have an instinctive preference for thinking things are "all right"; we economize anxiety; defend the delusions that we can work with, even though we half realize they are no more that' delusions. We resent the warning voice, the critical question that robs our activities of assurance. Our everyday moods not only the antagonists of our religious moods, but they resent all outward appeals to our religious moods, and they welcome every help against religious appeals. We pass very readily from the merely defensive to the defensive aggressive, and from refusing to hear the word that might stir our consciences to a vigorous effort to suppress its utterance.

Churches, religious organizations, try to keep the revivifying phase and usage where it may strike upon the waning or slumbering faith of the convert, but modern religion as yet has no such organized rebinders. {sic-RW} They cannot be improvised. Crude attempts to supply the needed corrective of conduct may do less good than harm. Each one of us for himself must do what he can to keep his high resolve in mind and protect himself from the snare of his own moods of fatigue or inadvertency.

But these passive and active defences of current things which operate in and through ourselves, and find such ready sympathy and assistance in the world about us, these massive resistance systems, are only the beginning of our tale of the forces antagonistic to the Open Conspiracy that lurk in our complexities.

Men are creatures with other faults quite beyond and outside our common disposition to be stupid, indolent, habitual, and defensive. Not only have we active creative impulses, but also acutely destructive ones. Man is a jealous animal. In youth and adolescence egotism is extravagant. It is natural for it to be extravagant, then, and there is no help for it. A great number of us at that stage would rather not see a beautiful or wonderful thing come into existence then have it come into existence disregarding us. Something of that jealous malice, that self-assertive ruthlessness, remains in all of us throughout life. At his worst man can be an exceedingly combative, malignant, mischievous and cruel animal. None of us are altogether above the possibility of such phases. When we consider the oppositions to the Open Conspiracy that operate in the normal personality, we appreciate the soundness of the catechism which instructs us to renounce not only the trivial world and the heavy flesh, but the active and militant devil.

To make is a long and wearisome business, with many arrests and disappointments, but to break gives an instant thrill. We all know something of the delight of the Bang. It is well for the Open Conspirator to ask himself at times how far he is in love with the dream of a world in order, and how far he is driven by hatred of institutions that bore or humiliate him. He may be no more than a revengeful incendiary in the mask of a constructive worker. How safe is he, then, from the reaction to some fresh humiliation? The Open Conspiracy which is now his refuge and vindication may presently fail to give him the compensation he has sought, may offer him no better than a minor röle, may display Irritating and incomprehensible preferences. And for a great number of things in overt antagonism to the great aim of the Open Conspiracy, he will still find within himself not simply acquiescence but sympathy and a genuine if inconsistent admiration. There they are, waiting for his phase of disappointment. Back he may go to the old loves with a new animus against the greater scheme. He may be glad to be quit of prigs and humbugs, and back among the good fellowship of nothing in particular.

Man has pranced a soldier in reality and fancy for so many generations that few of us can altogether release our imaginations from the brilliant pretensions of flags, empire, patriotism, and aggression. Business men, especially in America, seem to feel a sort of glory in calling even the underselling and overadvertising of rival enterprises "fighting." Pill vendors and public departments can have their "wars," their heroisms, their desperate mischiefs, and so get that Napoleonic feeling. The world and our reveries are full of the sentimentalities, the false glories and loyalties of the old combative traditions, trailing after them, as they do, so much worth and virtue in a dulled and stupefied condition. It is difficult to resist the fine gravity, the high self-respect, the examples of honour and good style in small things, that the military and naval services can present to us, for all that they are now no more than noxious parasites upon the nascent world commonweal. In France not a word may be said against the army; in England, against the navy. There will be many Open Conspirators at first who will scarcely dare to say that word even to themselves.

But all these obsolete values and attitudes with which our minds are cumbered must be cleared out if the new faith is to have free play. We have to clear them out not only from our own minds but from the minds of others who are to become our associates. The finer and more picturesque these obsolescent loyalties, obsolescent standards of honour, obsolescent religious associations, may seem to us, the more thoroughly must we seek to release our minds and the minds of those about us from them and cut off all thought of a return.

We cannot compromise with these vestiges of the ancient order and be faithful servants of the new. Whatever we retain of them will come back to life and grow again. It is no good to operate for cancer unless the whole growth is removed. Leave a crown about and presently you will find it being worn by someone resolved to be a king. Keep the name and image of a god without a distinct museum label and sooner or later you will discover a worshipper on his knees to it and be lucky not to find a human sacrifice upon the altar. Wave a flag and it will wrap about you. Of yourself even more than of the community is this true; these can be no half measures. You have not yet completed your escape to the Open Conspiracy from the cities of the plain while it is still possible for you to take a single backward glance.

16

XIV. — THE OPEN CONSPIRACY BEGINS

A NEW and happier world, a world community, is awakening, within the body of the old order, to the possibility of its emergence. Our phrase, "the Open Conspiracy" is merely a name for that awakening. To begin with, the Open Conspiracy is necessarily a group of ideas.

It is a system of modern ideas which has been growing together in the last quarter of the century, and particularly since the war. It is the reaction of a rapidly progressing biological conception of life and of enlarged historical realizations upon the needs and urgencies of the times. In this book we are attempting to define this system and to give it this provisional name. Essentially at first it is a dissemination of this new ideology that must occur. The statement must be tried over and spread before a widening circle of people.

Since the idea of the Open Conspiracy rests upon and arises out of a synthesis of historical, biological, and sociological realizations, we may look for these realizations already in the case of people with sound knowledge in these fields; such people will be prepared for acquiescence without any explanatory work; there is nothing to set out to them beyond the suggestion that it is time they became actively conscious of where they stand. They constitute already the Open Conspiracy in an unorganized solution, and they will not so much adhere as admit to themselves and others their state of mind. They will say, "We knew all that." Directly we pass beyond that comparatively restricted world, however, we find that we have to deal with partial knowledge, with distorted views, or with blank ignorance, and that a revision and extension of historical and biological ideas and a Considerable elucidation of economic misconceptions have to be undertaken. Such people have to be brought up to date with their information.

I have told already how I have schemed out a group of writings to embody the necessary ideas of the new time in a form adapted to the current reading public; I have made a sort of provisional "Bible," so to speak, for some factors at least in the Open Conspiracy. It is an early sketch. As the current reading public changes, all this work will become obsolescent so far as its present form and method go. But not so far as its substantial method goes. That I believe will remain.

Ultimately this developing mass of biological, historical, and economic information and suggestion must be incorporated in general education if the Open Conspiracy is to come to its own.

At present this propaganda has to go on among adolescents and adults because of the backwardness and political conservatism of existing educational organizations. Most real modern education now is done in spite of the schools and to correct the misconceptions established by the schools. But what will begin as adult propaganda must pass into a kultur-kampf to win our educational machinery from reaction and the conservation of outworn ideas and attitudes to the cause of world reconstruction. The Open Conspiracy itself can never be imprisoned and fixed in the form of an organization, but everywhere Open Conspirators should be organizing themselves for educational reform.

And also within the influence of this comprehensive project there will be all sorts of groupings for study and progressive activity. One can presuppose the formation of groups of friends, of family groups, of students and employees or other sorts of people, meeting and conversing frequently in the course of their normal occupations, who will exchange views and find themselves in agreement upon this idea of a constructive change of the world as the guiding form of human activities.

Fundamentally important issues upon which unanimity must be achieved from the outset are:

Firstly, the entirely provisional nature of all existing governments, and the entirely provisional nature, therefore, of all loyalties associated therewith;

Secondly, the supreme importance of population control in human biology and the possibility it affords us of a release from the pressure of the struggle for existence on ourselves; and

Thirdly, the urgent necessity of protective resistance against the present traditional drift towards war.

People who do not grasp the vital significance of these test issues do not really begin to understand the Open Conspiracy. Groups coming into agreement upon these matters, and upon their general interpretation of history, will be in a position to seek adherents, enlarge themselves, and attempt to establish communication and co-operation with kindred groups for common ends. They can take up a variety of activities to develop a sense and habit of combined action and feel their way to greater enterprises.

We have seen already that the Open Conspiracy must be heterogeneous in origin. Its initial groupings and associations will be of no uniform pattern. They will be of a very different size, average age, social experience, and influence. Their particular activities will be determined by the things. Their diverse qualities and influences will express themselves by diverse attempts at organization, each effective in its own sphere. A group or movement of students may find itself capable of little more than self-education and personal propaganda; a handful of middle-class people in small town may find its small resources fully engaged at first in such things as, for example, seeing that desirable literature is available for sale or in local public library, protecting books and news vendors from suppression, or influencing local teachers. Most parents of school children can press for the teaching of universal history and sound biology and protest against the inculcation of aggressive patriotism. There is much scope for the single individual in this direction. On the other hand, a group of ampler experience and resources may undertake the printing, publication, and distribution of literature, and exercise considerable influence upon public opinion in turning education in the right direction. The League of Nations movement, the Birth Control movement, and most radical and socialist societies, are fields into which Open Conspirators may go to find adherents more than half prepared for their wider outlook. The Open Conspiracy is a fuller and ampler movement into which these incomplete activities must necessarily merge as its idea takes possession of men's imaginations.

From the outset, the Open Conspiracy will set its face against militarism. There is a plain present need for the organization now, before war comes again, of an open and explicit refusal to serve in any war—or at most to serve in war, directly or indirectly, only after the issue has been fully and fairly submitted to arbitration. The time for a conscientious objection to war service is manifestly before and not after the onset of war. People who have by their silence acquiesced in a belligerent foreign policy right up to the onset of war, have little to complain of if they are then compelled to serve. And a refusal to participate with one's country in warfare is a preposterously incomplete gesture unless it is rounded off by the deliberate advocacy of a world pax, a world economic control, and a restrained population, such as the idea of the Open Conspiracy embodies.

The putting upon record of its members' reservation of themselves from any or all of the military obligations that may be thrust upon the country by military and diplomatic effort, might very conceivably be the first considerable overt act of many Open Conspiracy groups. It would supply the practical incentive to bring many of them together in the first place. It would necessitate the creation of regional or national ad hoc committees for the establishment of a collective legal and political defensive for this dissent from current militant nationalism. It would bring the Open Conspiracy very early out of the province of discussion into the field of practical conflict. It would from the outset invest it with a very necessary quality of present applicability.

The anticipatory repudiation of military service, so far as this last may be imposed by existing governments in their factitious international rivalries, need not necessarily involve a denial of the need of military action on behalf of the world commonweal for the suppression of nationalist brigandage, nor need it prevent the military training of Open Conspirators. It is simply the practical form of assertion that the normal militant diplomacy and warfare of the present time are offences against civilization, processes in the nature of brigandage, sedition, and civil war, and that serious men cannot be expected to play anything but a röle of disapproval, non-participation, or active prevention towards them. Our loyalty to our current government, we would intimate, is subject to its sane and adult behaviour.

These educational and propagandist groups drawing together into an organized resistance to militarism and to the excessive control of individuals by the makeshift governments of to-day, constitute at most only the earliest and more elementary grade of the Open Conspiracy, and we will presently go on to consider the more specialized and constructive forms its effort must evoke. Before doing so, however, we may say a little more about the structure and method of these possible initiatory groupings.

Since they are bound to be different and miscellaneous in form, size, quality, and ability, any early attempts to organize them into common general action or even into regular common gatherings are to be deprecated. There should be many types of groups. Collective action had better for a time - perhaps for a long time—be undertaken not through the merging of groups but through the formation of ad hoc associations for definitely specialized ends, all making for the new world civilization. Open Conspirators will come into these associations to make a contribution very much as people come into limited liability companies, that is to say with a subscription and not with their whole capital. A comprehensive organization attempting from the first to cover all activities would necessarily rest upon and promote one prevalent pattern of activity and hamper or estrange the more original and interesting forms. It would develop a premature orthodoxy, it would cease almost at once to be creative, and it would begin to form a crust of tradition. It would become anchylosed. With the dreadful examples of Christianity and Communism before us, we must insist that the idea of the Open Conspiracy ever becoming a single organization must be dismissed from the mind. It is a movement, yes, a system of purposes, but its end is a free and living, if unified, world.

At the utmost seven broad principles may be stated as defining the Open Conspiracy and holding it together. And it is possible even of these, one, the seventh, may be, if not too restrictive, at least unnecessary. To the writer it seems unavoidable because it is so intimately associated with that continual dying out of tradition upon which our hopes for an unencumbered and expanding human future rest.

(1) The complete assertion, practical as well as theoretical, of the provisional nature of existing governments and of our acquiescence in them;

(2) The resolve to minimize by all available means the conflicts of these governments, their militant use of individuals and property, and their interferences with the establishment of a world economic system;

(3) The determination to replace private, local or national ownership of at least credit, transport, and staple production by a responsible world directorate serving the common ends of the race;

(4) The practical recognition of the necessity for world biological controls, for example, of population and disease;

(5) The support of a minimum standard of individual freedom and welfare in the world; and

(6) The supreme duty of subordinating the personal career to the creation of a world directorate capable of these tasks and to the general advancement of human knowledge, capacity, and power;

(7) The admission therewith that our immortality is conditional and lies in the race and not in our individual selves.

17

XV. — EARLY CONSTRUCTIVE WORK OF THE OPEN CON

IN such terms we may sketch the practicable and possible opening phase of the Open Conspiracy.

We do not present it as a movement initiated by any individual or radiating from any particular centre. In this book we are not starting something; we are describing and participating in something which has started. It arises naturally and necessarily from the present increase of knowledge and the broadening outlook of many minds throughout the world, and gradually it becomes conscious of itself. It is reasonable therefore to anticipate its appearance all over the world in sporadic mutually independent groupings and movements, and to recognize not only that they will be extremely various, but that many of them will trail with them racial and regional habits and characteristics which will only be shaken off as its cosmopolitan character becomes imperatively evident.

The passage from the partial anticipations of the Open Conspiracy that already abound everywhere to its complete and completely self-conscious statement may be made by almost imperceptible degrees. To-day it may seem no more than a visionary idea; to-morrow it may be realized as a world-wide force of opinion and will. People will pass with no great inconsistency from saying that the Open Conspiracy is impossible to saying that it has always been plain and clear to them, that to this fashion they have shaped their lives as long as they can remember.

In its opening phase, in the day of small things, quite minor accidents may help or delay the clear definition and popularization of its main ideas. The changing pattern of public events may disperse or concentrate attention upon it, or it may win the early adherence of men of exceptional resources, energy, or ability. It is impossible to foretell the speed of its advance. Its development may be slower or faster, direct or devious, but the logic of accumulating realizations thrusts it forward, will persist in thrusting it on, and sooner or later it will be discovered, conscious and potent, the working religion of most sane and energetic people.

Meanwhile our supreme virtues must be faith and persistence.

So far we have considered only two of the main activities of the Open Conspiracy, the one being its propaganda of confidence in the possible world commonweal, and the other its immediate practical attempt to systematize resistance to militant and competitive imperialism and nationalism. But such things are merely its groundwork undertakings; they do no more than clear the site and make the atmosphere possible for its organized constructive efforts.

Directly we turn to that, we turn to questions of special knowledge, special effort, and special organization.

Let us consider first the general advancement of science, the protection and support of scientific research, and the diffusion of scientific knowledge. These things fall within the normal scheme of duty for the members of the Open Conspiracy. The world of science and experiment is the region of origin of nearly all the great initiatives that characterize our times; the Open Conspiracy owes its inspiration, its existence, its form and direction entirely to the changes of condition these initiatives have brought about, and yet a large number of scientific workers live outside the sphere of sympathy in which we may expect the Open Conspiracy to materialize, and collectively their political and social influence upon the community is extraordinarily small. Having regard to the immensity of its contributions and the incalculable value of its promise to the modern community, science—research, that is, and the diffusion of scientific knowledge—is extraordinarily neglected, starved, and threatened by hostile interference. This is largely because scientific work has no strong unifying organization and cannot in itself develop such an organization.

Science is a hard mistress, and the first condition of successful scientific work is that the scientific man should stick to his research. The world of science is therefore in itself, at its core, a miscellany of specialists, often very ungracious specialists, and, rather than offer him help and co-operation, it calls for understanding, tolerance, and service from the man of general intelligence and wider purpose. The company of scientific men is less like a host of guiding angels than like a swarm of marvellous bees --endowed with stings—which must be hived and cherished and multiplied by the Open Conspiracy.

But so soon as we have the Open Conspiracy at work, putting its plainly and offering its developing ideas and activities to those most preciously preoccupied men, then reasonably, when it involves no special trouble for them, when it is the line of least resistance for them, they may be expected to fall in with its convenient and helpful aims and find in it what they have hitherto lacked, a common system of political and social concepts to hold them together.

When that stage is reached, we shall be saved such spectacles of intellectual prostitution as the last Great War offered, when men of science were herded blinking from their laboratories to curse one another upon nationalist lines, and when after the war stupid and wicked barriers were set up to the free communication of knowledge by the exclusion of scientific men of this or that nationality from international scientific gatherings. The Open Conspiracy must help the man of science to realize, what at present he fails most astonishingly to realize, that he belongs to a greater comity than any king or president represents to-day, and so prepare him for better behaviour in the next season of trial.

The formation of groups in, and not only in, but about and in relation to, the scientific world, which will add to those first main activities of the Open Conspiracy, propaganda and pacificism, a special attention to the needs of scientific work, may be enlarged upon with advantage here, because it will illustrate quite typically the idea of a special work carried on in relation to a general activity, which is the subject of this section.

The Open Conspiracy extends its invitation to all sorts and conditions of men, but the service of scientific progress is for those only who are specially equipped or who are sufficiently interested to equip themselves. For scientific work there is first of all a great need of endowment and the setting up of laboratories, observatories, experimental stations, and the like, in all parts of the world. Numbers of men and women capable of scientific work never achieve it for want of the stimulus of opportunity afforded by endowment. Few contrive to create their own opportunities. The essential man of science is very rarely an able collector or administrator of money, and anyhow, the detailed work of organization is a grave call upon his special mental energy. But many men capable of a broad and intelligent appreciation of scientific work, but not capable of the peculiar intensities of research, have the gift of extracting money from private and public sources, and it is for them to use that gift modestly and generously in providing the framework for those more especially endowed.

And there is already a steadily increasing need for the proper storage and indexing of scientific results, and every fresh worker enhances it. Quite a considerable amount of scientific work goes fruitless or is needlessly repeated because of the growing volume of publication, and men make discoveries in the field of reality only to lose them again in the lumber room of record. Here is a second line of activity to which the Open Conspirator with a scientific bias may direct his attention.

A third line is the liaison work between the man of science and the common intelligent man; the promotion of publications which will either state the substance, implications and consequences of new work in the vulgar tongue, or, if that is impossible, train the general run of people to the new idioms and technicalities which need to be incorporated with the vulgar tongue if it is still to serve its ends as a means of intellectual intercourse.

Through special ad hoc organizations, societies for the promotion of Research, for Research Defence, for World Indexing, for the translation of Scientific Papers, for the Diffusion of New Knowledge, the surplus energies of a great number of Open Conspirators can be directed to entirely creative ends and a new world system of scientific work built up, within which such dear old institutions as the Royal Society of London, the various European Academies of Science and the like, now overgrown and inadequate, can maintain their venerable pride in themselves, their mellowing prestige, and their distinguished exclusiveness, without their present privilege of inflicting cramping slights and restrictions upon the more abundant scientific activities of to-day.

So in relation to science—and here the word is being used in its narrower accepted meaning for what is often spoken of as pure science, the search for physical and biological realities, uncomplicated by moral, social, and "practical" considerations—we evoke a conception of the Open Conspiracy as producing groups of socially associated individuals, who engage primarily in the general basic activities of the Conspiracy and adhere to and promote the seven broad principles summarized at the end of Chapter Fourteen, but who work also with the larger part of their energies, through international and cosmopolitan societies and in a multitude of special ways, for the establishment of an enduring and progressive world organization of pure research. They will have come to this special work because their distinctive gifts, their inclinations, their positions and opportunities have indicated it as theirs.

Now a very parallel system of Open Conspiracy groups is conceivable, in relation to business and industrial life. It would necessarily be a vastly bulkier and more heterogeneous system of groups, but otherwise the analogy is complete. Here we imagine those people whose gifts, inclinations, positions and opportunities as directors, workers, or associates give them an exceptional insight into and influence in the processes of producing and distributing commodities, can also be drawn together into groups within the Open Conspiracy. But these groups will be concerned with the huge and more complicated problems of the processes by which even now the small isolated individual adventures in production and trading that constituted the economic life of former civilizations, are giving place to larger, better instructed, better planned industrial organizations, whose operations and combinations become at last world wide.

The amalgamations and combinations, the substitution of large-scale business for multitudes of small-scale businesses, which are going on now, go on with all the cruelty and disregards of a natural process. If a man is to profit and survive, these unconscious blunderings—which now stagger towards but which may never attain world organization—much be watched, controlled, mastered, and directed. As uncertainty diminishes, the quality of adventure and the amount of waste diminish also, and large speculative profits are no longer possible or justifiable. The transition from speculative adventure to organized foresight in the common interest, in the whole world of economic life, is the substantial task of the Open Conspiracy. And it is these specially interested and equipped groups, and not the movement as a whole, which may best begin the attack upon these fundamental readjustments.

The various Socialist movements of the nineteenth and earlier twentieth centuries had this in common, that they sought to replace the "private owner" in most or all economic interests by some vaguely apprehended "public owner." This, following the democratic disposition of the times, was commonly conceived of as an elected body, a municipality, the parliamentary state or what not. There were municipal socialists, "nationalizing" socialists, imperial socialists. In the mystic teachings of the Marxist, the collective owner was to be "the dictatorship of the proletariat." Production for profit was denounced. The contemporary mind realizes the evils of production for profit and of the indiscriminate scrambling of private ownership more fully than ever before, but it has a completer realization and a certain accumulation of experience in the difficulties of organizing that larger ownership we desire. Private ownership may not be altogether evil as a provisional stage, even if it has no more in its favour than the ability to transcend political boundaries.

Moreover—and here again the democratic prepossessions of the nineteenth century come in—the Socialist movements sought to make every single adherent a reformer and a propagandist of economic methods. In order to do so, it was necessary to simplify economic processes to the crudity of nursery toys, and the intricate interplay of will and desire in enterprise, normal employment, and direction, in questions of ownership, wages, credit, and money, was reduced to a childish fable of surplus value wickedly appropriated. The Open Conspiracy is not so much a socialism as a more comprehensive offspring which has eaten and assimilated whatever was digestible of its socialist forbears. It turns to biology for guidance towards the regulation of quantity and a controlled distribution of the human population of the world, and it judges all the subsidiary aspects of property and pay by the criterion of most efficient production and distribution in relation to the indications thus obtained.

These economic groups, then, of the Open Conspiracy, which may come indeed to be a large part of the Open Conspiracy, will be working in that vast task of economic reconstruction—which from the point of view of the older socialism was the sole task before mankind. They will be conducting experiments and observing processes according to their opportunities. Through ad hoc societies and journals they will be comparing and examining their methods and preparing reports and clear information for the movement at large. The whole question of money and monetary methods in our modern communities, so extraordinarily disregarded in socialist literature, will be examined under the assumption that money is the token of the community's obligation, direct or indirect, to an individual, and credit its permission to deal freely with material.

The whole psychology of industry and industrial relationship needs to be revised and restated in terms of the collective efficiency and welfare of mankind. And just as far as can be contrived, the counsel and the confidences of those who now direct great industrial and financial operations will be invoked. The first special task of a banker, or a bank clerk for that matter, who joins the Open Conspiracy, will be to answer the questions: "What is a bank?" "What are you going to do about it?" "What have we to do about it?" The first questions to a manufacturer will be: "What are you making and why?" and "What are you and we to do about it?" Instead of the crude proposals to "expropriate" and "take over by the State" of the primitive socialism, the Open Conspiracy will build up an encyclopædic conception of the modern economic complex as a labyrinthine pseudo-system progressively eliminating waste and working its way along multitudinous channels towards unity, towards clarity of purpose and method, towards abundant productivity and efficient social service.

Let us come back now for a paragraph or so to the ordinary adherent to the Open Conspiracy, the adherent considered not in relation to his special aptitudes and services, but in relation to the movement as a whole and to those special constructive organizations outside his own field. It will be his duty to keep his mind in touch with the progressing concepts of the scientific work so far as he is able and with the larger issues of the economic reconstruction that is afoot, to take his cues from the special groups and organizations engaged upon that work, and to help where he finds his opportunity and when there is a call upon him. But no adherent of the Open Conspiracy can remain merely and completely an ordinary adherent. There can be no pawns in the game of the Open Conspiracy, no "cannon fodder" in its war. A special activity, quite as much as a general understanding, is demanded from everyone who looks creatively towards the future of mankind.

We have instanced first the fine and distinctive world organization of pure science, and then the huge massive movement towards co-operating unity of aim in the economic life, until at last the production and distribution of staple necessities is apprehended as one world business, and we have suggested that this latter movement may gradually pervade and incorporate a very great bulk of human activities. But besides this fine current and this great torrent of evolving activities and relationships there are also a very considerable variety of other great functions in the community towards which Open Conspiracy groups must direct their organizing enquiries and suggestions in their common intention of ultimately assimilating all the confused processes of to-day into a world community.

For example, there must be a series of groups in close touch at one end with biological science and at the other with the complex of economic activity, who will be concerned specially with the practical administration of the biological interests of the race, from food plants and industrial products to pestilences and population. And another series of groups will gather together attention and energy to focus them upon the educational process. We have already pointed out that there is a strong disposition towards conservatism in normal educational institutions. They preserve traditions rather than develop them. They are likely to set up a considerable resistance to the reconstruction of the world outlook upon the threefold basis defined in Chapter Fourteen. This resistance must be attacked by special societies, by the establishment of competing schools, by help and promotion for enlightened teachers, and, wherever the attack is incompletely successful, it must be supplemented by the energetic diffusion of educational literature for adults, upon modern lines. The forces of the entire movement may be mobilized in a variety of ways to bring pressure upon reactionary schools and institutions.

A set of activities correlated with most of the directly creative ones will lie through existing political and administrative bodies. The political work of the Open Conspiracy must be conducted upon two levels and by entirely different methods. Its main political idea, its political strategy, is to weaken, efface, incorporate, or supersede existing governments. But there is also a tactical diversion of administrative powers and resources to economic and educational arrangements of a modern type. Because a country or a district is inconvenient as a division and destined to ultimate absorption in some more comprehensive and economical system of government, that is no reason why its administration should not be brought meanwhile into working co-operation with the development of the Open Conspiracy. Free Trade nationalism in power is better than high tariff nationalism, and pacificist party liberalism better than aggressive party patriotism.

This evokes the anticipation of another series of groups, a group in every possible political division, whose task it will be to organize the whole strength of the Open Conspiracy in that division as an effective voting or agitating force. In many divisions this might soon become a sufficiently considerable block to affect the attitudes and pledges of the national politicians. The organization of these political groups into provincial or national conferences and systems would follow hard upon their appearance. In their programmes they would be guided by meetings and discussions with the specifically economic, educational, biological, scientific and cultural groups, but they would also form their own special research bodies to work out the incessant problems of transition between the old type of locally centred administrations and a developing world system of political controls.

In the preceding chapter we sketched the first practicable first phase of the Open Conspiracy as the propaganda of a group of interlocking ideas, a propaganda associated with pacificist action. In the present chapter we have given a scheme of branching and amplifying development. In this scheme. this scheme of the second phase, we conceive of the Open Conspiracy as consisting of a great multitude and variety of overlapping groups, but now all organized for collective political, social, and educational as well as propagandist action. They will recognize each other much more clearly than they did at first, and they will have acquired a common name.

The groups, however, almost all of them, will still have specific work also. Some will be organizing a sounder setting for scientific progress, some exploring new social and educational possibilities, many concentrated upon this or that phase in the reorganization of the world's economic life, and so forth. The individual Open Conspirator may belong to one or more groups and in addition to the ad hoc societies and organizations which the movement will sustain, often in co-operation with partially sympathetic people still outside its ranks.

The character of the Open Conspiracy will now be plainly displayed. It will have become a great world movement as wide-spread and evident as socialism or communism. It will have taken the place of these movements very largely. It will be more than they were, it will be frankly a world religion. This large, loose assimilatory mass of movements, groups, and societies will be definitely and obviously attempting to swallow up the entire population of the world and become the new human community.

18

XVI. — EXISTING AND DEVELOPING MOVEMENTS

A SUGGESTION has already been made in an earlier chapter of this essay which may perhaps be expanded here a little more. It is that there already exist in the world a considerable number of movements in industry, in political life, in social matters, in education, which point in the same direction as the Open Conspiracy and are inspired by the same spirit. It will be interesting to discuss how far some of these movements may not become confluent with others and by a mere process of logical completion identify themselves consciously with the Open Conspiracy in its entirety.

Consider, for example, the movement for a scientific study and control of population pressure, known popularly as the Birth Control movement. By itself, assuming existing political and economic conditions, this movement lays itself open to the charge of being no better than a scheme of "race suicide." If a population in some area of high civilization attempts to restrict increase, organize its economic life upon methods of maximum individual productivity, and impose order and beauty upon its entire territory, that region will become irresistibly attractive to any adjacent festering mass of low-grade, highly reproductive population. The cheap humanity of the one community will make a constant attack upon the other, affording facile servility, prostitutes, toilers, hand labour. Tariffs against sweated products, restriction of immigration, tensions leading at last to a war of defensive massacre are inevitable. The conquest of an illiterate, hungry, and incontinent multitude may be almost as disastrous as defeat for the selecter race. Indeed, one finds that in discussion the propagandists of Birth Control admit that their project must be universal or dysgenic. But yet quite a number of them do not follow up these admissions to their logical consequences, produce the lines and continue the curves until the complete form of the Open Conspiracy appears. It will be the business of the early Open Conspiracy propagandists to make them do so, and to install groups and representatives at every possible point of vantage in this movement.

And similarly the now very numerous associations for world peace halt in alarm on the edge of their own implications. World Peace remains a vast aspiration until there is some substitute for the present competition of states for markets and raw material, and some restraint upon population pressure. League of Nations Societies and all forms of pacificist organization are either futile or insincere until they come into line with the complementary propositions of the Open Conspiracy.

The various Socialist movements again are partial projects professing at present to be self-sufficient schemes. Most of them involve a pretence that national and political forces are intangible phantoms, and that the primary issue of population pressure can be ignored. They produce one woolly scheme after another for transferring the property in this, that, or the other economic plant and interest from bodies of shareholders and company promoters to gangs of politicians or syndicates of workers—to be steered to efficiency, it would seem, by pillars of cloud by day and pillars of fire by night. The communist party has trained a whole generation of disciples to believe that the overthrow of a vaguely apprehended "Capitalism" is the simple solution of all human difficulties. No movement ever succeeded so completely in substituting phrases for thought. In Moscow communism has trampled "Capitalism" underfoot for ten eventful years, and still finds all the problems of social and political construction before it.

But as soon as the Socialist or Communist can be got to realize that his repudiation of private monopolization is not a complete programme but just a preliminary principle, he is ripe for the ampler concepts of the modern outlook. The Open Conspiracy is the natural inheritor of socialist and communist enthusiasms; it may be in control of Moscow before it is in control of New York.

The Open Conspiracy may achieve the more or less complete amalgamation of all the radical impulses in the Atlantic community of to-day. But its scope is not confined to the variety of sympathetic movements which are brought to mind by that loose word radical. In the past fifty years or so, while Socialists and Communists have been denouncing the current processes of economic life in the same invariable phrases and with the same undiscriminating animosity, these processes have been undergoing the profoundest and most interesting changes. While socialist thought has recited its phrases, with witty rather than substantial variations, a thousand times as many clever people have been busy upon industrial, mercantile and financial processes. The Socialist still reiterates that this greater body of intelligence has been merely seeking private gain, which has just as much truth in it as is necessary to make it an intoxicating lie. Everywhere competitive businesses have been giving way to amalgamated enterprises, marching towards monopoly, and personally owned businesses to organizations so large as to acquire more and more the character of publicly responsible bodies. In theory in Great Britain, banks are privately owned, and railway transport is privately owned, and they are run entirely for profit—in practice their profit making is austerely restrained and their proceedings are all the more sensitive to public welfare because they are outside the direct control of party politicians.

Now this transformation of business, trading, and finance has been so multitudinous and so rapid as to be still largely unconscious of itself. Intelligent men have gone from combination to combination and extended their range, year by year, without realizing how their activities were enlarging them to conspicuousness and responsibility. Economic organization is even now only discovering itself for what it is. It has accepted incompatible existing institutions to its own great injury. It has been patriotic and broken its shins against the tariff walls its patriotism has raised to hamper its own movements it has been imperial and found itself taxed to the limits of its endurance, "controlled" by antiquated military and naval experts, and crippled altogether. The younger, more vigorous intelligences in the great business directorates of to-day are beginning to realize the uncompleted implications of their enterprise. A day will come when the gentlemen who are trying to control the oil supplies of the world without reference to anything else except as a subsidiary factor in their game will be considered to be quaint characters. The ends of Big Business must carry Big Business into the Open Conspiracy just as surely as every other creative and broadly organizing movement is carried.

Now I know that to all this urging towards a unification of constructive effort, a great number of people will be disposed to a reply which will, I hope, be less popular in the future than it is at the present time. They will assume first an expression of great sagacity, an elderly air. Then, smiling gently, they will ask whether there is not something preposterously ambitious in looking at the problem of life as one whole. Is it not wiser to concentrate our forces on more practicable things, to attempt one thing at a time, not to antagonize the whole order of established things against our poor desires, to begin tentatively, to refrain from putting too great a strain upon people, to trust to the growing common sense of the world to adjust this or that line of progress to the general scheme of things. Far better accomplish something definite here and there than challenge a general failure. That is, they declare, how reformers and creative things have gone on in the past; that is how they are going on now; muddling forward in a mild and confused and partially successful way. Why not trust them to go on like that? Let each man do his bit with a complete disregard of the logical interlocking of progressive effort to which I have been drawing attention.

Now I must confess that, popular as this style of argument is, it gives me so tedious a feeling that rather than argue against it in general terms I will resort to a parable. I will relate the story of the pig on Provinder Island.

There was, you must understand, only one pig on Provinder Island, and Heaven knows how it got there, whether it escaped and swam ashore or was put ashore from some vessel suddenly converted to vegetarianism, I cannot imagine. At first it was the only mammal there. But later on three sailors and a very small but observant cabin boy were wrecked there, and after subsisting for a time on shell fish and roots they became aware of this pig. And simultaneously they became aware of a nearly intolerable craving for bacon. The eldest of the three sailors began to think of a ham he had met in his boyhood, a beautiful ham for which his father had had the caving knife specially sharpened; the second of the three sailors dreamed repeatedly of a roast loin of pork he had eaten at his sister's wedding, and the third's mind ran on chitterlings—I know not why. They sat about their meagre fire and conferred and expatiated upon these things until their mouths watered and the shell fish turned to water within them. What dreams came to the cabin boy are unknown, for it was their custom to discourage his confidences. But he sat apart brooding and was at last moved to speech. "Let us hunt that old pig," he said, "and kill it."

Now it may have been because it was the habit of these sailors to discourage the cabin boy and keep him in his place, but anyhow, for whatever reason it was, all three sailors set themselves with one accord to oppose that proposal.

"Who spoke of killing the pig?" said the eldest sailor loudly, looking round to see if by any chance the pig was within hearing. "Who spoke of killing the pig? You're the sort of silly young devil who jumps at ideas and hasn't no sense of difficulties. What I said was AM. All I want is just a Am to go with my roots and sea salt. One Am. The Left Am. I don't want the right one, and I don't propose to get it. I've got a sense of proportion and a proper share of humour, and I know my limitations. I'm a sound, clear-headed, practical man. Am is what I'm after, and if I can get that, I'm prepared to say Quits and let the rest of the pig alone. Who's for joining me in a Left Am Unt—a simple reasonable Left Am Unt—just to get One Left Am?

Nobody answered him directly, but when his voice died away, the next sailor in order of seniority took up the tale. "That Boy," he said, "will die of Swelled Ed, and I pity him. My idea is to follow up the pig and get hold of a loin chop. Just simply a loin chop. A loin chop is good enough for me. It's—feasible. Much more feasible than a great Am. Here we are, we've got no gun, we've got no wood of a sort to make bows and arrows, we've got nothing but our clasp knives, and that pig can run like Ell. It's ridiculous to think of killing that pig. But if one didn't trouble him, if one kind of got into his confidence and crept near him and just quietly and insidiously went for his loin—just sort of as if one was tickling him-one might get a loin chop almost before he knew of it."

The third sailor sat crumpled up and downcast with his lean fingers tangled in his shock of hair. "Chitterlings," he murmured, "chitterlings. I don't even want to think of the pig."

And the cabin boy pursued his own ideas in silence, for he deemed it unwise to provoke his elders further.

On these lines it was the three sailors set about the gratifying of their taste for pork, each in his own way, separately and sanely and modestly. And each had his reward. The first sailor, after weeks of patience, got within arm's length of the pig and smacked that coveted left ham loud and good, and felt success was near. The other two heard the smack and the grunt of dismay half a mile away. But the pig, in a state of astonishment, carried the ham off out of reach, there and then, and that was as close as the first sailor ever got to his objective. The roast loin hunter did no better. He came upon the pig asleep under a rock one day, and jumped upon the very loin he desired, but the pig bit him deeply and septically, and displayed so much resentment that the question of a chop was dropped forthwith and never again broached between them. And thereafter the arm of the second sailor was bandaged and swelled up and went from bad to worse. And as for the third sailor, it is doubtful whether he even got wind of a chitterling from the start to the finish of this parable. The cabin boy, pursuing notions of his own, made a pitfall for the whole pig, but as the others did not help him, and as he was an excessively small—though shrewd—cabin boy, it was a feeble and insufficient pitfall, and all it caught was the hunter of chitterlings, who was wandering distraught. After which the hunter of chitterlings, became a hunter of cabin boys, and the cabin boy's life, for all his shrewdness, was precarious and unpleasant. He slept only in snatches and learned the full bitterness of insight misunderstood.

When at last a ship came to Provinder Island and took off the three men and the cabin boy, the pig was still bacon intact and quite gay and cheerful, and all four castaways were in a very emaciated condition because at that season of the year shell fish were rare, and edible roots were hard to find, and the pig was very much cleverer than they were in finding them and digging them up—let alone digesting them.

From which parable it may be gathered that a partial enterprise is not always wiser or more hopeful than a comprehensive one.

And in the same manner, with myself in the röle of that minute but observant cabin boy, I would sustain the proposition that none of these movements of partial reconstruction has the sound common sense quality its supporters suppose. All these movements are worth while if they can be taken into the world-wide movement; all in isolation are futile. They will be overlaid and lost in the general drift. The policy of the whole hog is the best one, the sanest one, the easiest, and the most hopeful. If sufficient men and women of intelligence can realize that simple truth and give up their lives to it, mankind may yet achieve a civilization and power and fullness of life beyond our present dreams. If they do not, frustration will triumph, and war, violence, and a drivelling waste of time and strength and desire, more disgusting even than war, will be the lot of our race down through the ages to its emaciated and miserable end.

For this little planet of ours is quite off the course of any rescue ships, if the will in our species fails.

19

XVII. — THE CREATIVE HOME, SOCIAL GROUP AND SCHOOL

HUMAN society began with the family. The natural history of gregariousness is a history of the establishment of mutual toleration among human animals, so that a litter or a herd keeps together instead of breaking up. It is in the family group that the restraints, disciplines, and self-sacrifices which make human society possible were worked out and our fundamental prejudices established, and it is in the family group, enlarged perhaps in many respects, and more and more responsive to collective social influences, that our social life must be relearnt, generation after generation.

Now in each generation the Open Conspiracy, until it can develop its own reproductive methods, must remain a minority movement of intelligent converts. A unified progressive world community demands its own type of home and training. It needs to have its fundamental concepts firmly established in as many minds as possible and to guard its children from the infection of the old racial and national hatreds and jealousies, old superstitions and bad mental habits, and base interpretations of life. From its outset the Open Conspiracy will be setting itself to influence the existing educational machinery, but for a long time it will find itself confronted in school and college by powerful religious and political authorities determined to set back the children at the point or even behind the point from which their patents made their escape. At best, the liberalism of the state-controlled schools will be a compromise. Originally schools and colleges were transmitters of tradition and conservative forces. So they remain in essence to this day.

Organized teaching has always aimed, and will always tend to guide, train, and direct, the mind. The problem of reconstructing education so as to make it a releasing instead of a binding process has still to be solved. During the early phases of its struggle, therefore, the Open Conspiracy will be obliged to adopt a certain sectarianism of domestic and social life in the interests of its children, to experiment in novel educational methods and educational atmospheres, and it may even in many cases have to consider the grouping of its families and the establishment of its own schools. In many modern communities, the English-speaking states, for example, there is still liberty to establish educational companies, running schools of a special type. In every country where that right does not exist it has to be fought for.

There lies a great work for various groups of the Open Conspiracy. Successful schools would become laboratories of educational methods and patterns for new state schools. Necessarily for a time, but we may hope unconsciously, the Open Conspiracy children will become a social élite; from their first conscious moments they will begin to think and talk among clear-headed people speaking distinctly and behaving frankly, and it will be a waste and loss to put them back for the scholastic stage among their mentally indistinct and morally muddled contemporaries. A phase when there will be a special educational system for the Open Conspiracy seems, therefore, to be indicated. Its children will learn to speak, draw, think, compute lucidly and subtly, and into their vigorous minds they will take the broad concepts of history, biology, and mechanical progress, the basis of the new world, naturally and easily. Meanwhile, those who grow up outside the advancing educational frontier of the Open Conspiracy will never come under the full influence of its ideas, or they will get hold of them only after a severe struggle against a mass of misrepresentations and elaborately instilled prejudices. An adolescent and adult educational campaign, to undo the fixations and suggestions of the normal conservative and reactionary schools and colleges, is and will long remain an important part of the work of the Open Conspiracy.

Always, as long as I can remember, there have been a dispute and invidious comparisons between the old and the young. The young find the old prey upon and restrain them, and the old find the young shallow, disappointing, and aimless in vivid contrast to their revised memories of their own early days. The present time is one in which these perennial accusations flower with exceptional vigour. But there does seem to be some truth in the statement that the facilities to live frivolously are greater now than they have ever been for old and young alike. For example, in the great modern communities that emerge now from Christendom, there is a widespread disposition to regard Sunday as merely a holiday. But that was certainly not the original intention of Sunday. As we have noted already in an earlier chapter, it was a day dedicated to the greater issues of life. Now great multitudes of people do not even pretend to set aside any time at all to the greater issues of life. The greater issues are neglected altogether. The churches are neglected, and nothing of a unifying or exalting sort takes their place.

What the contemporary senior tells his junior to-day is perfectly correct. In his own youth, no serious impulse of his went to waste. He was not distracted by a thousand gay but petty temptations, and the local religious powers, whatever they happened to be, seemed to believe in themselves more and made a more comprehensive attack upon his conscience and imagination. Now the old faiths are damaged and discredited, and the new and greater one, which is the Open Conspiracy, takes shape only gradually. A decade or so ago, socialism preached its confident hopes, and patriotism and imperial pride shared its attraction for the ever grave and passionate will of emergent youth. Now socialism and democracy are "under revision" and the flags that once waved so bravely reek of poison gas, are stiff with blood and mud and shameful with exposed dishonesties. Youth is what youth has always been, eager for fine interpretations of life, capable of splendid resolves. It has no natural disposition towards the shallow and confused life. Its demand as ever is, "What am I to do with myself?" But it comes up out of its childhood to-day into a world of ruthless exposures and cynical pretensions. We are all a little ashamed of "earnestness." The past ten years have seen the shy and powerful idealism of youth at a loss and dismayed and ashamed as perhaps it has never been before. It is in the world still, but masked, hiding even from itself in a whirl of small excitements and futile, defiant depravities.

The old flags and faiths have lost their magic for the intelligence of the young; they can command it no more; it is in the mighty revolution to which the Open Conspiracy directs itself that the youth of mankind must find its soul, if ever it is to find its soul again.

20

XVIII. — PROGRESSIVE DEVELOPMENT OF THE ACTIVITIES

WE have now sketched out in these Blue Prints the methods by which the confused radicalism and constructive forces of the present time may, can, and probably will be drawn together about a core of modernized religious feeling into one great and multifarious creative effort. A way has been shown by which this effort may be developed from a mere propagandist campaign and a merely resistant protest against contemporary militarism into an organized foreshadowing in research, publicity, and experiment in educational, economic, and political reconstructions, of that Pax Mundi which has become already the tantalised desire of great multitudes throughout the world. These foreshadowings and reconstructions will ignore and transcend the political boundaries of to-day. They will continually become more substantial as project passes into attempt and performance. In phase after phase and at point after point, therefore, the Open Conspiracy will come to grips with the powers that sustain these boundaries.

And it will not be merely topographical boundaries that will be passed. The Open Conspiracy will also be dissolving and repudiating many existing restrictions upon conduct and many social prejudices. The Open Conspiracy proposes to end and shows how an end may be put to that huge substratum of underdeveloped, undereducated, subjugated, exploited, and frustrated lives upon which such civilization as the world has known hitherto has rested, and upon which most of our social systems still rest.

Whenever possible, the Open Conspiracy will advance by illumination and persuasion. But it has to advance, and even from the outset, where it is not allowed to illuminate and persuade, it must fight. Its first fights will probably be for the right to spread its system of ideas plainly and clearly throughout the world.

There is, I suppose, a flavour of treason about the assumption that any established government is provisional, and a quality of immorality in any criticism of accepted moral standards. Still more is the proposal, made even in times of peace, to resist war levies and conscription an offence against absolute conceptions of loyalty. But the ampler wisdom of the modern Atlantic communities, already touched by premonitions of change and futurity, has continually enlarged the common liberties of thought for some generations, and it is doubtful if there will be any serious resistance to the dissemination of these views and the early organization of the Open Conspiracy in any of the English-speaking communities or throughout the British Empire, in the Scandinavian countries, or in such liberal-minded countries as Holland, Switzerland, republican Germany or France. France, in the hasty years after the war, submitted to some repressive legislation against the discussion of birth control or hostile criticism of the militarist attitude; but such a check upon mental freedom is altogether contrary to the clear and open quality of the French mind; in practice it has already been effectively repudiated by such writers as Victor Margueritte, and it is unlikely that there will be any effective suppression of the opening phases of the Open Conspiracy in France.

This gives us a large portion of the existing civilized world in which men's minds may be readjusted to the idea that their existing governments are in the position of trustees for the greater government of the coming age. Throughout these communities it is conceivable that the structural lines of the world community may be materialized and established with only minor struggles, local boycotts, vigorous public controversies, normal legislative obstruction, social pressure, and overt political activities. Police, jail, expulsions, and so forth, let alone outlawry and warfare, may scarcely be brought into this struggle upon the high civilized level of the Atlantic communities. But where they are brought in, the Open Conspiracy, to the best of its ability and the full extent of its resources, must become a fighting force and organize itself upon resistant lines.

Non-resistance, the restriction of activities to moral suasion is no part of the programme of the Open Conspiracy. In the face of unscrupulous opposition creative ideas must become aggressive, must define their enemies and attack them. By its own organizations or through the police and military strength of governments amenable to its ideas, the movement is bound to find itself fighting for open roads, open frontiers, freedom of speech, and the realities of peace in regions of oppression. The Open Conspiracy rests upon a disrespect for nationality, and there is no reason why it should tolerate noxious or obstructive governments because they hold their own in this or that patch of human territory. It lies within the power of the Atlantic communities to impose peace upon the world and secure unimpeded movement and free speech from end to end of the earth. This is a fact on which the Open Conspiracy must insist. The English-speaking states, France, Germany, Holland, Switzerland, the Scandinavian countries, and Russia, given only a not very extravagant frankness of understanding between them, and a common disposition towards the ideas of the Open Conspiracy, could cease to arm against each other and still exert enough strength to impose disarmament and a respect for human freedom in every corner of the planet. It is fantastic pedantry to wait for all the world to accede before all the world is pacified and policed.

The most inconsistent factor in the liberal and radical thought of to-day is its prejudice against the interference of highly developed modern states in the affairs of less stable and less advanced regions. This is denounced as "imperialism," and regarded as criminal. It may have assumed grotesque and dangerous forms under the now decaying traditions of national competition, but as the merger of the Atlantic states proceeds, the possibility and necessity of bringing areas of misgovernment and disorder under world control increase. A great war like the war of 1914-1918 may never happen again. The common sense of mankind may suffice to avert that. But there is still much actual warfare before mankind, on the frontiers everywhere, against brigands, against ancient loyalties and traditions which will become at last no better than excuses for brigandage and obstructive exaction. All the weight of the Open Conspiracy will be on the side of the world order and against that sort of local independence which holds back its subject people from the citizenship of the world.

But in this broad prospect of far-reaching political amalgamations under the impulses of the Open Conspiracy lurk a thousand antagonisms and adverse chances, like the unsuspected gulleys and ravines and thickets in a wide and distant landscape. We know not what unexpected chasms may presently be discovered. The Open Conspirator may realize that he is one of an advancing and victorious force and still find himself outnumbered and outfought in his own particular corner of the battlefield. No one can yet estimate the possible strength of reaction against world unification; no one can foresee the extent of the divisions and confusions that may arise among ourselves. The ideas in this book may spread about without any serious resistance in most civilized countries, but there are still governments under which the persistent expression of such thoughts will be dealt with as crimes and bring men and women to prison, torment, and death. Nevertheless, they must be expressed.

While the Open Conspiracy is no more than a discussion it may spread unopposed because it is disregarded. As a mainly passive resistance to militarism it may still be tolerable. But as its knowledge and experience accumulate and its organization become more effective and aggressive, as it begins to lay hands upon education, upon social habits, upon business developments, as it proceeds to take over the organization of the community, it will marshal not only its own forces but its enemies. A complex of interests will find themselves restrained and threatened by it, and it may easily evoke that most dangerous of human mass feelings, fear. In ways quite unpredictable it may raise a storm against itself beyond all our present imaginings. Our conception of an almost bloodless domination of the Atlantic communities may be merely the confident dream of a thinker whose thoughts have yet to be squarely challenged.

We are not even sure of the common peace. Across the path of mankind the storm of another Great War may break, bringing with it for a time more brutal repressions and vaster injuries even than its predecessor. The scaffoldings and work sheds of the Open Conspiracy may fare violently in that tornado. The restoration of progress may seem an almost hopeless struggle.

It is no part of modern religion to incur needless hardship or go out of the way to seek martyrdom. If we can do our work easily and happily, so it should be done. But the work is not to be shirked because it cannot be done easily and happily. The vision of a world at peace and liberated for an unending growth of knowledge and power is worth every danger of the way. And since in this age of confusion we must live imperfectly and anyhow die, we may as well suffer, if need be, and die for a great end as for none. Never has the translation of vision into realities been easy since the beginning of human effort. The establishment of the world community will surely exact a price --and who can tell what that price may be?—in toil, suffering, and blood.

21

XIX. — HUMAN LIFE IN THE COMING WORLD COMMUNITY

THE new life that the Open Conspiracy struggles to achieve through us for our race is first a life of liberations.

The oppression of incessant toil can surely be lifted from everyone, and the miseries due to a great multitude of infections and disorders of nutrition and growth cease to be a part of human experience. Few people are perfectly healthy nowadays except for brief periods of happiness, but the elation of physical well-being will some day be the common lot of mankind.

And not only from natural evils will man be largely free. He will not be left with his soul tangled, haunted by monstrous and irrational fears and a prey to malicious impulse. From his birth he will breathe sweetness and generosity and use his mind and hands cleanly and exactly. He will feel better, will better, think better, see, taste, and hear better than men do now. His undersoul will no longer be a mutinous cavern of ill-treated suppressions and of impulses repressed without understanding. All these releases are plainly possible for him. They pass out of his tormented desire now, they elude and mock him, because chance, confusion, and squalor rule his life. All the gifts of destiny are overlaid and lost to him. He must still suspect and fear. Not one of us is yet as clear and free and happy within himself as most men will some day be. Before mankind lies the prospect not only of health but of magnanimity.

Within the peace and freedom that the Open Conspiracy is winning for us, all these good things that escape us now may be ensured. A graver humanity, stronger, more lovely, longer lived, will learn and develop the ever enlarging possibilities of its destiny. For the first time, the full beauty of this world will be revealed to its unhurried eyes. Its thoughts will be to our thoughts as the thoughts of a man to the troubled mental experimenting of a child. And all the best of us will be living on in that ampler life, as the child and the things it tried and learnt still live in the man. When we were children, we could not think or feel as we think and feel to-day, but to-day we can peer back and still recall something of the ignorances and guesses and wild hopes of these nigh forgotten years.

And so mankind, ourselves still living, but dispersed and reconstructed again in the future, will recall with affection and understanding the desperate wishes and troubled efforts of our present state.

How far can we anticipate the habitations and ways, the usages and adventures, the mighty employments, the ever increasing knowledge and power of the days to come? No more than a child with its scribbling paper and its box of bricks can picture or model the undertakings of its adult years. Our battle is with cruelties and frustrations, stupid, heavy and hateful things from which we shall escape at last, less like victors conquering a world than like sleepers awaking from a nightmare in the dawn. From any dream, however dismal and horrible, one can escape by realizing that it is a dream; by saying, "I will awake."

The Open Conspiracy is the awaking of mankind from a nightmare, an infantile nightmare, of the struggle for existence and the inevitability of war. The light of day thrusts between our eyelids, and the multitudinous sounds of morning clamour in our ears. A time will come when men will sit with history before them or with some old newspaper before them and ask incredulously, "Was there ever such a world?"

THE END

The New World Order

THE NEW WORLD ORDER

Published in 1940, The New World Order expands on many of the ideas Wells introduced in The Open Conspiracy. Written during the early stages of World War II, this book reflects Wells' urgent belief that only a unified world government could prevent future wars, economic instability, and social collapse.

Unlike some of his earlier works, which were more speculative or philosophical, The New World Order is a direct political argument advocating for global collectivism, centralized control, and the end of national sovereignty.

Key Themes & Proposals

A Single Global Government – Wells argues that nationalism and independent nation-states are outdated and destructive. To secure lasting peace, all countries must be subsumed into a World State governed by reason, science, and planning.

The End of National Sovereignty – Countries must relinquish control over their borders, economies, and military forces, integrating into a singular global system where laws and policies are determined by a central governing body.

Economic and Social Equality through Globalism – Wells envisions a world without poverty or class struggle, achieved through a planned, technocratic economy that redistributes resources efficiently across nations.

The Role of Education and Mass Media – For a global government to succeed, people must be educated (or conditioned) to reject nationalism and embrace global citizenship. Schools, universities, and media institutions would play a central role in shaping public perception.

Scientific and Rational Leadership – Traditional political systems are viewed as irrational and inefficient. Instead of democracy as we know it, Wells suggests that experts, scientists, and intellectuals should run the world based on logic and empirical data.

A Gradual Transition Rather Than a Violent Revolution – Similar to The Open Conspiracy, The New World Order does not advocate for an armed uprising but instead calls for strategic infiltration of governments, institutions, and key industries by those who believe in a unified global future.

Wells' Vision vs. Reality

At the time of writing, Wells saw World War II as evidence of the failure of nationalism. He believed that, once the war ended, the world would have no choice but to form a unified, international government to prevent another global conflict.

While the specific World State he envisioned never came to pass, many aspects of his ideas took root in institutions like:

The United Nations (UN) – 1945
The European Union (EU) – 1993
The World Economic Forum (WEF) – 1971
International Monetary Fund (IMF) & World Bank – 1944
Although Wells saw his vision as an idealistic and necessary evolution, many critics view The New World Order as a warning rather than a roadmap. Today, conversations about global governance, elite control, and centralized authority continue to spark controversy, with some seeing Wells as a prophet of the modern globalist movement.

Why The New World Order Matters Today
More than 80 years after its publication, The New World Order remains a foundational text in discussions on globalism, technocracy, and centralized control. Wells' arguments have influenced political thinkers, international organizations, and modern globalist agendas, making this book a must-read for anyone seeking to understand the origins of today's world order.

22

I. — THE END OF AN AGE

IN this small book I want to set down as compactly, clearly and usefully as possible the gist of what I have learnt about war and peace in the course of my life. I am not going to write peace propaganda here. I am going to strip down certain general ideas and realities of primary importance to their framework, and so prepare a nucleus of useful knowledge for those who have to go on with this business of making a world peace. I am not going to persuade people to say "Yes, yes" for a world peace; already we have had far too much abolition of war by making declarations and signing resolutions; everybody wants peace or pretends to want peace, and there is no need to add even a sentence more to the vast volume of such ineffective stuff. I am simply attempting to state the things we must do and the price we must pay for world peace if we really intend to achieve it.

Until the Great War, the First World War, I did not bother very much about war and peace. Since then I have almost specialised upon this problem. It is not very easy to recall former states of mind out of which, day by day and year by year, one has grown, but I think that in the decades before 1914 not only I but most of my generation--in the British Empire, America, France and indeed throughout most of the civilised world--thought that war was dying out.

So it seemed to us. It was an agreeable and therefore a readily acceptable idea. We imagined the Franco-German War of 1870-71 and the Russo-Turkish War of 1877-78 were the final conflicts between Great Powers, that now there was a Balance of Power sufficiently stable to make further major warfare impracticable. A Triple Alliance faced a Dual Alliance and neither had much reason for attacking the other. We believed war was shrinking to mere expeditionary affairs on the outskirts of our civilisation, a sort of frontier police business. Habits of tolerant intercourse, it seemed, were being strengthened every year that the peace of the Powers remained unbroken.

There was in deed a mild armament race going on; mild by our present standards of equipment; the armament industry was a growing and enterprising on; but we did not see the full implication of that; we preferred to believe that the increasing general good sense would be strong enough to prevent these multiplying guns from actually going off and hitting anything. And we smiled indulgently at uniforms and parades and army manoeuvres. They were the time-honoured toys and regalia of kings and emperors. They were part of the display side of life and would never get to actual destruction and killing. I do not think that exaggerates the easy complacency of, let us say, 1895, forty-five years ago. It was a complacency that lasted with most of us up to 1914. In

1914 hardly anyone in Europe or America below the age of fifty had seen anything of war in his own country.

The world before 1900 seemed to be drifting steadily towards a tacit but practical unification. One could travel without a passport over the larger part of Europe; the Postal Union delivered one's letters uncensored and safely from Chile to China; money, based essentially on gold, fluctuated only very slightly; and the sprawling British Empire still maintained a tradition of free trade, equal treatment and open-handedness to all comers round and about the planet. In the United States you could go for days and never see a military uniform. Compared with to-day that was, upon the surface at any rate, an age of easy-going safety and good humour. Particularly for the North Americans and the Europeans.

But apart from that steady, ominous growth of the armament industry there were other and deeper forces at work that were preparing trouble. The Foreign Offices of the various sovereign states had not forgotten the competitive traditions of the eighteenth century. The admirals and generals were contemplating with something between hostility and fascination, the hunger weapons the steel industry was gently pressing into their hands. Germany did not share the self-complacency of the English-speaking world; she wanted a place in the sun; there was increasing friction about the partition of the raw material regions of Africa; the British suffered from chronic Russophobia with regard to their vast apportions in the East, and set themselves to nurse Japan into a modernised imperialist power; and also they "remembered Majuba"; the United States were irritated by the disorder of Cuba and felt that the weak, extended Spanish possessions would be all the better for a change of management. So the game of Power Politics went on, but it went on upon the margins of the prevailing peace. There were several wars and changes of boundaries, but they involved no fundamental disturbance of the general civilised life; they did not seem to threaten its broadening tolerations and understandings in any fundamental fashion. Economic stresses and social trouble stirred and muttered beneath the orderly surfaces of political life, but threatened no convulsion. The idea of altogether eliminating war, of clearing what was left of it away, was in the air, but it was free from any sense of urgency. The Hague Tribunal was established and there was a steady dissemination of the conceptions of arbitration and international law. It really seemed to many that the peoples of the earth were settling down in their various territories to a litigious rather than a belligerent order. If there was much social injustice it was being mitigated more and more by a quickening sense of social decency. Acquisitiveness conducted itself with decorum and public-spiritedness was in fashion. Some of it was quite honest public-spiritedness.

In those days, and they are hardly more than half a lifetime behind us, no one thought of any sort of world administration. That patchwork of great Powers and small Powers seemed the most reasonable and practicable method of running the business of mankind. Communications were far too difficult for any sort of centralised world controls. Around the World in Eighty Days, when it was published seventy years ago, seemed an extravagant fantasy. It was a world without telephone or radio, with nothing swifter than a railway train or more destructive than the earlier types of H.E. shell. They were marvels. It was far more convenient to administer that world of the Balance of Power in separate national areas and, since there were such limited facilities for peoples to get at one another and do each other mischiefs, there seemed no harm in ardent patriotism and the complete independence of separate sovereign states.

Economic life was largely directed by irresponsible private businesses and private finance which, because of their private ownership, were able to spread out their unifying transactions in a network that paid little attention to frontiers and national, racial or religious sentimentality. "Business" was much more of a world commonwealth than the political organisations. There were many people, especially in America, who imagined that "Business" might ultimately unify the world and governments sink into subordination to its network.

Nowadays we can be wise after the event and we can see that below this fair surface of things, disruptive forces were steadily gathering strength. But these disruptive forces played a comparatively small role in the world spectacle of half a century ago, when the ideas of that older generation which still dominates our political life and the political education of its successors, were formed. It is from the conflict of those Balance of Power and private enterprise ideas, half a century old, that one of the main stresses of our time arises. These ideas worked fairly well in their period and it is still with extreme reluctance that our rulers, teachers, politicians, face the necessity for a profound mental adaptation of their views, methods and interpretations to these disruptive forces that once seemed so negligible and which are now shattering their old order completely.

It was because of this belief in a growing good-will among nations, because of the general satisfaction with things as they were, that the German declarations of war in 1914 aroused such a storm of indignation throughout the entire comfortable world. It was felt that the German Kaiser had broken the tranquillity of the world club, wantonly and needlessly. The war was fought "against the Hohenzollerns." They were to be expelled from the club, certain punitive fines were to be paid and all would be well. That was the British idea of 1914. This out-of-date war business was then to be cleared up once for all by a mutual guarantee by all the more respectable members of the club through a League of Nations. There was no apprehension of any deeper operating causes in that great convulsion on the part of the worthy elder statesmen who made the peace. And so Versailles and its codicils.

For twenty years the disruptive forces have gone on growing beneath the surface of that genteel and shallow settlement, and twenty years there has been no resolute attack upon the riddles with which their growth confronts us. For all that period of the League of Nations has been the opiate of liberal thought in the world.

To-day there is war to get rid of Adolf Hitler, who has now taken the part of the Hohenzollerns in the drama. He too has outraged the Club Rules and he too is to be expelled. The war, the Chamberlain-Hitler War, is being waged so far by the British Empire in quite the old spirit. It has learnt nothing and forgotten nothing. There is the same resolute disregard of any more fundamental problem.

Still the minds of our comfortable and influential ruling-class people refuse to accept the plain intimation that their time is over, that the Balance of Power and uncontrolled business methods cannot continue, and that Hitler, like the Hohenzollerns, is a mere offensive pustule on the face of a deeply ailing world. To get rid of him and his Nazis will be no more a cure for the world's ills than scraping will heal measles. The disease will manifest itself in some new eruption. It is the system of nationalist individualism and unco-ordinated enterprise that is the world's disease, and it is the whole system that has to go. It has to be reconditioned down to its foundations or replaced. It cannot hope to "muddle through" amiably, wastefully and dangerously, a second time.

World peace means all that much revolution. More and more of us begin to realise that it cannot mean less.

The first thing, therefore that has to be done in thinking out the primary problems of world peace is to realise this, that we are living in the end of a definite period of history, the period of the sovereign states. As we used to say in the eighties with ever-increasing truth: "We are in an age of transition". Now we get some measure of the acuteness of the transition. It is a phase of human life which may lead, as I am trying to show, either to a new way of living for our species or else to a longer or briefer degringolade of violence, misery, destruction, death and the extinction of mankind. These are not rhetorical phrases I am using here; I mean exactly what I say, the disastrous extinction of mankind.

That is the issue before us. It is no small affair of parlour politics we have to consider. As I write, in the moment, thousands of people are being killed, wounded, hunted, tormented, ill-treated, delivered up to the most intolerable and hopeless anxiety and destroyed morally and mentally, and there is nothing in sight at present to arrest this spreading process and prevent its reaching you and yours. It is coming for you and yours now at a great pace. Plainly in so far as we are rational foreseeing creatures there is nothing for any of us now but to make this world peace problem the ruling interest and direction of our lives. If we run away from it it will pursue and get us. We have to face it. We have to solve it or be destroyed by it. It is as urgent and comprehensive as that.

23

II. — OPEN CONFERENCE

BEFORE we examine what I have called so far the "disruptive forces" in the current social order, let me underline one primary necessity for the most outspoken free discussion of the battling organisations and the crumbling institutions amidst which we lead our present uncomfortable and precarious lives. There must be no protection for leaders and organisations from the most searching criticism, on the plea that out country is or may be at war. Or on any pretence. We must talk openly, widely and plainly. The war is incidental; the need for revolutionary reconstruction is fundamental. None of us are clear as yet upon some of the most vital questions before us, we are not lucid enough in our own minds to be ambiguous, and a mumbling tactfulness and indirect half-statements made with an eye upon some censor, will confuse our thoughts and the thoughts of those with whom we desire understanding, to the complete sterilisation and defeat of every reconstructive effort.

We want to talk and tell exactly what our ideas and feelings are, not only to our fellow citizens, but to our allies, to neutrals and, above all, to the people who are marshalled in arms against us. We want to get the same sincerity from them. Because until we have worked out a common basis of ideas with them, peace will be only an uncertain equilibrium while fresh antagonisms develop.

Concurrently with this war we need a great debate. We want every possible person in the world to take part in that debate. It is something much more important than the actual warfare. It is intolerable to think of this storm of universal distress leading up to nothing but some "conference" of diplomatists out of touch with the world, with secret sessions, ambiguous "understandings." ...Not twice surely can that occur. And yet what is going to prevent its recurring?

It is quite easy to define the reasonable limits of censorship in a belligerent country. It is manifest that the publication of any information likely to be of the slightest use to an enemy must be drastically anticipated and suppressed; not only direct information, for example, but intimations and careless betrayals about the position and movements of ships, troops, camps, depots of munitions, food supplies, and false reports of defeats and victories and coming shortages, anything that may lead to blind panic and hysteria, and so forth and so on. But the matter takes on a different aspect altogether when it comes to statements and suggestions that may affect public opinion in one's own country or abroad, and which may help us towards wholesome and corrective political action.

One of the more unpleasant aspects of a state of war under modern conditions is the appearance of a swarm of individuals, too clever by half, in positions of authority. Excited, conceited, prepared to lie, distort and generally humbug people into states of acquiescence, resistance, indignation, vindictiveness, doubt and mental confusion, states of mind supposed to be conductive to a final military victory. These people love to twist and censor facts. It gives them a feeling of power; if they cannot create they can at least prevent and conceal. Particularly they poke themselves in between us and the people with whom we are at war to distort any possible reconciliation. They sit, filled with the wine of their transitory powers, aloof from the fatigues and dangers of conflict, pulling imaginary strings in people's minds.

In Germany popular thought is supposed to be under the control of Herr Dr Goebbels; in Great Britain we writers have been invited to place ourselves at the disposal of some Ministry of Information, that is to say at the disposal of hitherto obscure and unrepresentative individuals, and write under its advice. Officials from the British Council and the Conservative Party Headquarters appear in key positions in this Ministry of Information. That curious and little advertised organisation I have just mentioned, the creation I am told of Lord Lloyd, that British Council, sends emissaries abroad, writers, well-dressed women and other cultural personages, to lecture, charm and win over foreign appreciation for British characteristics, for British scenery, British political virtues and so forth. Somehow this is supposed to help something or other. Quietly, unobtrusively, this has gone on. Maybe these sample British give unauthorised assurances but probably they do little positive harm. But they ought not to be employed at all. Any government propaganda is contrary to the essential spirit of democracy. The expression of opinion and collective thought should be outside the range of government activities altogether. It should be the work of free individuals whose prominence is dependent upon the response and support of the general mind.

But here I have to make amends to Lord Lloyd. I was led to believe that the British Council was responsible for Mr. Teeling, the author of Crisis for Christianity, and I said as much in The Fate of Homo Sapiens. I now unsay it. Mr. Teeling, I gather, was sent out upon his journeys by a Catholic newspaper. The British Council was entirely innocent of him.

It is not only that the Ministries of Information and Propaganda do their level best to divert the limited gifts and energies of such writers, lecturers and talkers as we possess, to the production of disingenuous muck that will muddle the public mind and mislead the enquiring foreigner, but that they show a marked disposition to stifle any free and independent utterances that my seem to traverse their own profound and secret plans for the salvation of mankind.

Everywhere now it is difficult to get adequate, far-reaching publicity for outspoken discussion of the way the world is going, and the political, economic and social forces that carry us along. This is not so much due to deliberate suppression as to the general disorder into which human affairs are dissolving. There is indeed in the Atlantic world hardly a sign as yet of that direct espionage upon opinion that obliterates the mental life of the intelligent Italian or German or Russian to-day almost completely; one may still think what one likes, say what one likes and write what one likes, but nevertheless there is already an increasing difficulty in getting bold, unorthodox views heard and read. Newspapers are afraid upon all sorts of minor counts, publishers, with such valiant exceptions as the publishers of this matter, are morbidly discreet; they get Notice D to avoid this or that particular topic; there are obscure boycotts and trade difficulties hindering the wide diffusion of general ideas in countless ways. I do not mean there is any sort of organised conspiracy to suppress discussion, but I do say that the Press, the publishing and bookselling organisations in our free countries, provide a very ill-organised and inadequate machinery for the ventilation and distribution of thought.

Publishers publish for nothing but safe profits; it would astound a bookseller to tell him he was part of the world's educational organisation or a publisher's traveller, that he existed for any other purpose than to book maximum orders for best sellers and earn a record commission--letting the other stuff, the highbrow stuff and all that, go hang. They do not understand that they ought to put public service before gain. They have no inducement to do so and no pride in their function. Theirs is the morale of a profiteering world. Newspapers like to insert brave-looking articles of conventional liberalism, speaking highly of peace and displaying a noble vagueness about its attainment; now we are at war they will publish the fiercest attacks upon the enemy--because such attacks are supposed to keep up the fighting spirit of the country; but any ideas that are really loudly and clearly revolutionary they dare not circulate at all. Under these baffling conditions there is no thorough discussion of the world outlook whatever, anywhere. The democracies are only a shade better than the dictatorships in this respect. It is ridiculous to represent them as realms of light at issue with darkness.

This great debate upon the reconstruction of the world is a thing more important and urgent than the war, and there exist no adequate media for the utterance and criticism and correction of any broad general convictions. There is a certain fruitless and unproductive spluttering of constructive ideas, but there is little sense of sustained enquiry, few real interchanges, inadequate progress, nothing is settled, nothing is dismissed as unsound and nothing is won permanently. No one seems to hear what anyone else is saying. That is because there is no sense of an audience for these ideologists. There is no effective audience saying rudely and obstinately: "What A. has said, seems important. Will B. and C, instead of bombinating in the void, tell us exactly where and why they differ from A.? And now we have got to the common truth of A., B., C, and D. Here is F. saying something. Will he be so good as to correlate what he has to say with A., B., C, and D.?"

But there is no such background of an intelligently observant and critical world audience in evidence. There are a few people here and there reading and thinking in disconnected fragments. This is all the thinking our world is doing in the face of planetary disaster. The universities, bless them! are in uniform or silent.

We need to air our own minds; we need frank exchanges, if we are to achieve any common understanding. We need to work out a clear conception of the world order we would prefer to this present chaos, we need to dissolve or compromise upon our differences so that we may set our faces with assurance towards an attainable world peace. The air is full of the panaceas of half-wits, none listening to the others and most of them trying to silence the others in their impatience. Thousands of fools are ready to write us a complete prescription for our world troubles. Will people never realise their own ignorance and incompleteness, from which arise this absolute necessity for the plainest statement of the realities of the problem, for the most exhaustive and unsparing examination of differences of opinion, and for the most ruthless canvassing of every possibility, however unpalatable it may seem at first, of the situation?

Before anything else, therefore, in this survey of the way to world peace, I put free speech and vigorous publication. It is the thing best worth fighting for. It is the essence of your personal honour. It is your duty as a world citizen to do what you can for that. You have not only to resist suppressions, you have to fight your way out of the fog. If you find your bookseller or newsagent failing to distribute any type of publication whatever--even if you are in entire disagreement with the views of that publication--you should turn the weapon of the boycott upon the offender and find another bookseller or newsagent for everything you read. The would-be world citizen should subscribe also to such organisation as the National Council for Civil Liberties; he should use any advantage his position may give him to check suppression of free speech; and he should accustom himself to challenge nonsense politely but firmly and say fearlessly and as clearly as possible what is in his mind and to listen as fearlessly to whatever is said to him. So that he may know better either through reassurance or correction. To get together with other people to argue and discuss, to think and organise and then implement thought is the first duty of every reasonable man.

This world of ours is going to pieces. It has to be reconstructed and it can only be effectively reconstructed in the light. Only the free, clear, open mind can save us, and these difficulties and obstructions on our line of thought are as evil as children putting obstacles on a railway line or scattering nails on an automobile speed track.

This great world debate must go on, and it must go on now. Now while the guns are still thudding, is the time for thought. It is incredibly foolish to talk as so many people do of ending the war and then having a World Conference to inaugurate a new age. So soon as the fighting stops the real world conference, the live discussion, will stop, too. The diplomats and politicians will assemble with an air of profound competence and close the doors upon the outer world and resume--Versailles. While the silenced world gapes and waits upon their mysteries.

24

III. — DISRUPTIVE FORCES

AND now let us come to the disruptive forces that have reduced that late- nineteenth-century dream of a powerful world patchwork of more and more civilised states linked by an ever-increasing financial and economic interdependence, to complete incredibility, and so forced upon every intelligent mind the need to work out a new conception of the World that ought to be. It is supremely important that the nature of these disruptive forces should be clearly understood and kept in mind. To grasp them is to hold the clues to the world's present troubles. To forget about them, even for a moment, is to lose touch with essential reality and drift away into minor issues.

The first group of these forces is what people are accustomed to speak of as "the abolition of distance" and "the change of scale" in human operations. This "abolition of distance" began rather more than a century ago, and its earlier effects were not disruptive at all. It knit together the spreading United States of America over distances that might otherwise have strained their solidarity to the breaking-point, and it enabled the sprawling British Empire to sustain contacts round the whole planet.

The disruptive influence of the abolition of distance appeared only later. Let us be clear upon its essential significance. For what seemed like endless centuries the swiftest means of locomotion had been the horse on the high-road, the running man, the galley and the uncertain, weather-ruled sailing ship. (There was the Dutchman on skates on skates on his canals, but that was an exceptional culmination of speed and not for general application.) The political, social and imaginative life of man for all those centuries was adapted to these limiting conditions. They determined the distances to which marketable goods could conveniently be sent, the limits to which the ruler could send his orders and his solders, the bounds set to getting news, and indeed the whole scale of living. There could be very little real community feeling beyond the range of frequent intercourse.

Human life fell naturally therefore into areas determined by the interplay between these limitations and such natural obstacles as seas and mountains. Such countries as France, England, Egypt, Japan, appeared and reappeared in history like natural, necessary things, and though there were such larger political efforts as the Roman Empire, they never attained an enduring unity. The Roman Empire held together like wet blotting-paper; it was always falling to pieces. The older

Empires, beyond their national nuclei, were mere precarious tribute-levying powers. What I have already called the world patchwork of the great and little Powers, was therefore, under the old horse- and-foot and sailing-ship conditions, almost as much a matter of natural necessity as the sizes of trees and animals.

Within a century all this has been changed and we have still to face up to what that change means for us.

First came steam, the steam-railway, the steamship, and then in a quickening crescendo came the internal combustion engine, electrical traction, the motor car, the motor boat, the aeroplane, the transmission of power from central power stations, the telephone, the radio. I feel apologetic in reciting this well-known story. I do so in order to enforce the statement that all the areas that were the most convenient and efficient for the old, time-honoured way of living, became more and more inconveniently close and narrow for the new needs. This applied to every sort of administrative area, from municipalities and urban districts and the range of distributing businesses, up to sovereign states. They were--and for the most part they still are--too small for the new requirements and far too close together. All over the social layout this tightening-up and squeezing together is an inconvenience, but when it comes to the areas of sovereign states it becomes impossibly dangerous. It becomes an intolerable thing; human life cannot go on, with the capitals of most of the civilised countries of the world within an hour's bombing range of their frontiers, behind which attacks can be prepared and secret preparations made without any form of control. And yet we are still tolerant and loyal to arrangements that seek to maintain this state of affairs and treat it as though nothing else were possible.

The present war for and against Hitler and Stalin and Mr. Chamberlain and so forth, does not even touch upon the essential problem of the abolition of distance. It may indeed destroy everything and still settle nothing. If one could wipe out all the issues of the present conflict, we should still be confronted with the essential riddle, which is the abolition of the boundaries of most existing sovereign states and their merger in some larger Pax. We have to do that if any supportable human life is to go on. Treaties and mutual guarantees are not enough. We have surely learnt enough about the value of treaties during the last half-century to realise that. We have, because of the abolition of distance alone, to gather human affairs together under one common war-preventing control.

But this abolition of distance is only one most vivid aspect of the change in the conditions of human life. Interwoven with that is a general change of scale in human operations. The past hundred years has been an age of invention and discovery beyond the achievements of the preceding three millennia. In a book I published eight years ago, The Work, Wealth and Happiness of Mankind, I tried to summarise the conquest of power and substances that is still going on. There is more power expended in a modern city like Birmingham in a day than we need to keep the whole of Elizabethan England going for a year; there is more destructive energy in a single tank than sufficed the army of William I for the conquest of England. Man is able now to produce or destroy on a scale beyond comparison greater than he could before this storm of invention began. And the consequence is the continual further dislocation of the orderly social life of our great-great-grandfathers. No trade, no profession, is exempt. The old social routines and classifications have been, as people say, "knocked silly". There is no sort of occupation, fisheries, farming, textile work, metal work, mining which is not suffering from constant readjustment to new methods and facilities. Our traditions of trade and distribution flounder after these changes. Skilled occupations disappear in the general liquefaction.

The new power organisations are destroying the forests of the world at headlong speed, ploughing great grazing areas into deserts, exhausting mineral resources, killing off whales, seals and a multitude of rare and beautiful species, destroying the morale of every social type and devastating the planet. The institutions of the private appropriation of land and natural resources generally, and of private enterprise for profit, which did produce a fairly tolerable, stable and "civilised" social life for all but the most impoverished, in Europe, America and East, for some centuries, have been expanded to a monstrous destructiveness by the new opportunities. The patient, nibbling, enterprising profit-seeker of the past, magnified and equipped now with the huge claws and teeth the change of scale has provided for him, has torn the old economic order to rags. Quite apart from war, our planet is being wasted and disorganised. Yet the process goes on, without any general control, more monstrously destructive even than the continually enhanced terrors of modern warfare.

Now it has to be made clear that these two things, the manifest necessity for some collective world control to eliminate warfare and the less generally admitted necessity for a collective control of the economic and biological life of mankind, are aspects of one and the same process. Of the two the disorganisation of the ordinary life which is going on, war or no war, is the graver and least reversible. Both arise out of the abolition of distance and the change of scale, they affect and modify each other, and unless their parallelism and interdependence are recognised, any projects for world federation or anything of the sort are doomed inevitably to frustration.

That is where the League of nations broke down completely. It was legal; it was political. It was devised by an ex-professor of the old-fashioned history assisted by a few politicians. It ignored the vast disorganisation of human life by technical revolutions, big business and modern finance that was going on, of which the Great War itself was scarcely more than a byproduct. It was constituted as though nothing of that sort was occurring.

This war storm which is breaking upon us now, due to the continued fragmentation of human government among a patchwork of sovereign states, is only one aspect of the general need for a rational consolidation of human affairs. The independent sovereign state with its perpetual war threat, armed with the resources of modern mechanical frightfulness, is only the most blatant and terrifying aspect of that same want of a coherent general control that makes overgrown, independent, sovereign, private business organisations and combinations, socially destructive. We should still be at the mercy of the "Napoleons" of commerce and the "Attilas" of finance, if there was not a gun or a battleship or a tank or a military uniform in the world. We should still be sold up and dispossessed.

Political federation, we have to realise, without a concurrent economic collectivisation, is bound to fail. The task of the peace-maker who really desires peace in a new world, involves not merely a political but a profound social revolution, profounder even than the revolution attempted by the Communists in Russia. The Russian Revolution failed not by its extremism but through the impatience, violence and intolerance of its onset, through lack of foresight and intellectual insufficiency. The cosmopolitan revolution to a world collectivism, which is the only alternative to chaos and degeneration before mankind, has to go much further than the Russian; it has to be more thorough and better conceived and its achievement demands a much more heroic and more steadfast thrust.

It serves no useful purpose to shut our eyes to the magnitude and intricacy of the task of making the world peace. These are the basic factors of the case.

25

IV. — CLASS-WAR

NOW here it is necessary to make a distinction which is far too frequently ignored. Collectivisation means the handling of the common affairs of mankind by a common control responsible to the whole community. It means the suppression of go-as-you-please in social and economic affairs just as much as in international affairs. It means the frank abolition of profit-seeking and of every devise by which human+beings contrive to be parasitic on their fellow man. It is the practical realisation of the brotherhood of man through a common control. It means all that and it means no more than that.

The necessary nature of that control, the way to attain it and to maintain it have still to be discussed.

The early forms of socialism were attempts to think out and try out collectivist systems. But with the advent of Marxism, the larger idea of collectivism became entangled with a smaller one, the perpetual conflict of people in any unregulated social system to get the better of one another. Throughout the ages this has been going on. The rich, the powerful generally, the more intelligent and acquisitive have got away with things, and sweated, oppressed, enslaved, bought and frustrated the less intelligent, the less acquisitive and the unwary. The Haves in every generation have always got the better of the Have-nots, and the Have-nots have always resented the privations of their disadvantage.

So it is and so in the uncollectivised world it has always been. The bitter cry of the expropriated man echoes down the ages from ancient Egypt and the Hebrew prophets, denouncing those who grind the faces of the poor. At times the Have-nots have been so uneducated, so helplessly distributed among their more successful fellows that they have been incapable of social disturbance, but whenever such developments as plantation of factory labour, the accumulation of men in seaport towns, the disbanding of armies, famine and so forth, brought together masses of men at the same disadvantage, their individual resentments flowed together and became a common resentment. The miseries underlying human society were revealed. The Haves found themselves assailed by resentful, vindictive revolt.

Let us note that these revolts of the Have-nots throughout the ages have sometimes been very destructive, but that invariably they have failed to make any fundamental change in this old, old story of getting and not getting the upper hand. Sometimes the Have-nots have frightened or otherwise moved the Haves to more decent behaviour. Often the Have-nots have found a Champion who has ridden to power on their wrongs. Then the ricks were burnt or the chateaux. The aristocrats were guillotined and their heads carried on exemplary pikes. Such storms passed and when they passed, there for all practical purposes was the old order returning again; new people but the old inequalities. Returning inevitably, with only slight variations in appearance and phraseology, under the condition of a non-collective social order.

The point to note is that in the unplanned scramble of human life through the centuries of the horse-and-foot period, these incessantly recurring outbreaks of the losers against the winners have never once produced any permanent amelioration of the common lot, or greatly changed the features of the human community. Not once.

The Have-nots have never produced the intelligence and the ability and the Haves have never produced the conscience, to make a permanent alteration of the rules of the game. Slave revolts, peasant revolts, revolts of the proletariat have always been fits of rage, acute social fevers which have passed. The fact remains that history produces no reason for supposing that the Have-nots, considered as a whole, have available any reserves of directive and administrative capacity and disinterested devotion, superior to that of the more successful classes. Morally, intellectually, there is no reason to suppose them better.

Many potentially able people may miss education and opportunity; they may not be inherently inferior but nevertheless they are crippled and incapacitated and kept down. They are spoilt. Many specially gifted people may fail to "make good" in a jostling, competitive, acquisitive world and so fall into poverty and into the baffled, limited ways of living of the commonalty, but they too are exceptions. The idea of a right-minded Proletariat ready to take things over is a dream.

As the collectivist idea has developed out of the original propositions of socialism, the more lucid thinkers have put this age-long bitterness of the Haves and the Have-nots into its proper place as part, as the most distressing part, but still only as part, of the vast wastage of human resources that their disorderly exploitation entailed. In the light of current events they have come to realise more and more clearly that the need and possibility of arresting this waste by a world-wide collectivisation is becoming continually more possible and at the same time imperative. They have had no delusions about the education and liberation that is necessary to gain that end. They have been moved less by moral impulses and sentimental pity and so forth, admirable but futile motives, as by the intense intellectual irritation of living in a foolish and destructive system. They are revolutionaries not because the present way of living is a hard and tyrannous way of living, but because it is from top to bottom exasperatingly stupid.

But thrusting athwart the socialist movement towards collectivisation and its research for some competent directive organisation of the world's affairs, came the clumsy initiative of Marxism with its class-war dogma, which has done more to misdirect and sterilise human good-will than any other misconception of reality that has ever stultified human effort.

Marx saw the world from a study and through the hazes of a vast ambition. He swam in the current ideologies of his time and so he shared the prevalent socialist drive towards collectivisation. But while his sounder-minded contemporaries were studying means and ends he jumped from a very imperfect understanding of the Trades Union movement in Britain to the wildest generalisations about the social process. He invented and antagonised two phantoms. One was the Capitalist System; the other the Worker.

There never has been anything on earth that could be properly called a Capitalist System. What was the matter with his world was manifestly its entire want of system. What the Socialists were feeling their way towards was the discovery and establishment of a world system.

The Haves of our period were and are a fantastic miscellany of people, inheriting or getting their power and influence by the most various of the interbreeding social solidarity even of a feudal aristocracy or an Indian caste. But Marx, looking rather into his inner consciousness than at any concrete reality, evolved that monster "System" on his Right. Then over against it, still gazing into that vacuum, he discovered on the Left the proletarians being steadily expropriated and becoming class-conscious. They were just as endlessly various in reality as the people at the top of the scramble; in reality but not in the mind of the Communist seer. There they consolidated rapidly.

So while other men toiled at this gigantic problem of collectivisation, Marx found his almost childlishy simple recipe. All you had to do was to tell the workers that they were being robbed and enslaved by this wicked "Capitalist System" devised by the "bourgeoisie". They need only "unite"; they had "nothing to lose but their chains". The wicked Capitalist System was to be overthrown, with a certain vindictive liquidation of "capitalists" in general and the "bourgeoisie" in particular, and a millennium would ensue under a purely workers' control, which Lenin later on was to crystallise into a phrase of supra-theological mystery, "the dictatorship of the proletariat". The proletarians need learn nothing, plan nothing; they were right and good by nature; they would just "take over". The infinitely various envies, hatreds and resentments of the Have-nots were to fuse into a mighty creative drive. All virtue resided in them; all evil in those who had bettered them. One good thing there was in this new doctrine of the class war, it inculcated a much needed brotherliness among the workers, but it was balanced by the organisation of class hate. So the great propaganda of the class war, with these monstrous falsifications of manifest fact, went forth. Collectivisation would not so much be organised as appear magically when the incubus of Capitalism and all those irritatingly well-to-do people, were lifted off the great Proletarian soul.

Marx was a man incapable in money matters and much bothered by tradesmen's bills. Moreover he cherished absurd pretensions to aristocracy. The consequence was that he romanced about the lovely life of the Middle Ages as if he were another Belloc and concentrated his animus about the "bourgeoisie", whom he made responsible for all those great disruptive forces in human society that we have considered.

Lord Bacon, the Marquis of Worcester, Charles the Second and the Royal Society, people like Cavendish and Joule and Watt for example, all became "bourgeoisie" in his inflamed imagination. "During its reign of scarce a century", he wrote in the Communist Manifesto, "the bourgeoisie has created more powerful, more stupendous forces of production than all preceding generations rolled into one .... What earlier generations had the remotest inkling that such productive forces slumbered within the wombs of associated labour?"

"The wombs of associated labour!" (Golly, what a phrase!) The industrial revolution which was a consequence of the mechanical revolution is treated as the cause of it. Could facts be muddled more completely?

And again: "...the bourgeois system is no longer able to cope with the abundance of wealth it creates. How does the bourgeoisie overcome these crises? On the one hand, by the compulsory annihilation of a quantity of the productive forces; on the other, by the conquest of new markets and the more thorough exploitation of old ones. With what results? The results are that the way is paved for more widespread and more disastrous crises and that the capacity for averting such crises is lessened.

"The weapons" (Weapons! How that sedentary gentleman in his vast beard adored military images!) "with which the bourgeoisie overthrew feudalism are now being turned against the bourgeoisie itself.

"But the bourgeoisie has not only forged the weapons that will slay it; it has also engendered the men who will use these weapons--the modern workers, the proletarians."

And so here they are, hammer and sickle in hand, chest stuck out, proud, magnificent, commanding, in the Manifesto. But go and look for them yourself in the streets. Go and look at them in Russia.

Even for 1848 this is not intelligent social analysis. It is the outpouring of a man with a B in his bonnet, the hated Bourgeoisie, a man with a certain vision, uncritical of his own sub-conscious prejudices, but shrewd enough to realise how great a driving force is hate and the inferiority complex. Shrewd enough to use hate and bitter enough to hate. Let anyone read over that Communist Manifesto and consider who might have shared the hate or even have got it all, if Marx had not been the son of a rabbi. Read Jews for Bourgeoisie and the Manifesto is pure Nazi teaching of the 1933-8 vintage.

Stripped down to its core in this fashion, the primary falsity of the Marxist assumption is evident. But it is one of the queer common weakness of the human mind to be uncritical of primary assumptions and to smother up any enquiry into their soundness in secondary elaboration, in technicalities and conventional formula?. Most of our systems of belief rest upon rotten foundations, and generally these foundations are made sacred to preserve them from attack. They become dogmas in a sort of holy of holies. It is shockingly uncivil to say "But that is nonsense". The defenders of all the dogmatic religions fly into rage and indignation when one touches on the absurdity of their foundations. Especially if one laughs. That is blasphemy.

This avoidance of fundamental criticism is one of the greatest dangers to any general human understanding. Marxism is no exception to the universal tendency. The Capitalist System has to be a real system, the Bourgeoisie an organised conspiracy against the Workers, and every human conflict everywhere has to be an aspect of the Class War, or they cannot talk to you. They will not listen to you. Never once has there been an attempt to answer the plain things I have been saying about them for a third of a century. Anything not in their language flows off their minds like water off a duck's back. Even Lenin--by far the subtlest mind in the Communist story--has not escaped this pitfall, and when I talked to him in Moscow in 1920 he seemed quite unable to realise that the violent conflict going on in Ireland between the Catholic nationalists and the Protestant garrison was not his sacred insurrection of the Proletariat in full blast.

To-day there is quite a number of writers, and among them there are men of science who ought to think better, solemnly elaborating a pseudo-philosophy of science and society upon the deeply buried but entirely nonsensical foundations laid by Marx. Month by month the industrious Left book Club pours a new volume over the minds of its devotees to sustain their mental habits and pickle them against the septic influence of unorthodox literature. A party Index of Forbidden Books will no doubt follow. Distinguished professors with solemn delight in their own remarkable ingenuity, lecture and discourse and even produce serious-looking volumes, upon the superiority of Marxist physics and Marxist research, to the unbranded activities of the human mind. One tries not to be rude to them, but it is hard to believe they are not deliberately playing the fool with their brains. Or have they a feeling that revolutionary communism is ahead, and are they doing their best to rationalise it with an eye to those red days to come? (See Hogben's Dangerous Thoughts.)

Here I cannot pursue in any detail the story of the Rise and Corruption of Marxism in Russia. It confirms in every particular my contention that the class-war idea is an entanglement and perversion of the world drive towards a world collectivism, a wasting disease of cosmopolitan socialism. It has followed in its general outline the common history of every revolt of the Have-nots since history began. Russia in the shadows displayed an immense inefficiency and sank slowly to Russia in the dark. Its galaxy of incompetent foremen, managers, organisers and so forth, developed the most complicated system of self-protection against criticism, they sabotaged one another, they intrigued against one another. You can read the quintessence of the thing in Littlepage's In Search of Soviet Gold. And like every other Have-not revolt since the dawn of history, hero worship took possession of the insurgent masses. The inevitable Champion appeared. They escape from the Czar and in twenty years they are worshipping Stalin, originally a fairly honest, unoriginal, ambitious revolutionary, driven to self-defensive cruelty and inflated by flattery to his present quasi-divine autocracy. The cycle completes itself and we see that like every other merely insurrectionary revolution, nothing has changed; a lot of people have been liquidated and a lot of other people have replaced them and Russia seems returning back to the point at which it started, to a patriotic absolutism of doubtful efficiency and vague, incalculable aims. Stalin, I believe, is honest and benevolent in intention, he believes in collectivism simply and plainly, he is still under the impression that he is making a good thing of Russia and of the countries within her sphere of influence, and he is self-righteously impatient of criticism or opposition. His successor may not have the same disinterestedness.

But I have written enough to make it clear why we have to dissociate collectivisation altogether from the class war in our minds. Let us waste no more time on the spectacle of the Marxist putting the cart in front of the horse and tying himself up with the harness. We have to put all this proletarian distortion of the case out of our minds and start afresh upon the problem of how to realise the new and unprecedented possibilities of world collectivisation that have opened out upon the world in the past hundred years. That is a new story. An entirely different story.

We human-beings are facing gigantic forces that will either destroy our species altogether or lift it to an altogether unprecedented level of power and well-being. These forces have to be controlled or we shall be annihilated. But completely controlled they can abolish slavery--by the one sure means of making these things unnecessary. Class-war communism has its opportunity to realise all this, and it has failed to make good. So far it has only replaced one autocratic Russia by another. Russia, like all the rest of the world, is still facing the problem of the competent government of a collective system. She has not solved it.

The dictatorship of the proletariat has failed us. We have to look for possibilities of control in other directions. Are they to be found?

NOTE

A friendly adviser reading the passage on p.47 protests against "the wombs of associated labour" as a mistranslation of the original German of the Manifesto. I took it from the translation of Professor Hirendranath Mukherjee in an Indian students' journal, Sriharsha, which happened to be at my desk. But my adviser produces Lily G. Aitken and Frank C. Budgen in a Glasgow Socialist Labour Press publication, who gave it as "the lap of social labour", which is more refined but pure nonsense. The German word is "Schoß", and in its widest sense it means the whole productive maternal outfit from bosom to knees and here quite definitely the womb. The French translation gives "sein", which at the first glance seems to carry gentility to an even higher level. But as you can say in French that an expectant mother carries her child in her "sein", I think Professor Mukherjee has it. Thousands of reverent young Communists must have read that "lap" without observing its absurdity. Marx is trying to make out that the increase of productive efficiency was due to "association" in factories. A better phrase to express his (wrong-headed) intention would have been "the co-ordinated operations of workers massed in factories".

26

V. — UNSALTED YOUTH

WE have now to examine these disruptive forces a little more closely, these disruptive forces which are manifestly overstraining and destroying the social and political system in which most of us have been reared. At what particular points in our political and social life are these disruptive forces discovering breaking-points?

Chief among these breaking-points, people are beginning to realise more and more clearly, is the common, half-educated young man.

One particular consequence of the onrush of power and invention in our time, is the release of a great flood of human energy in the form of unemployed young people. This is a primary factor of the general political instability.

We have to recognise that humanity is not suffering, as most animal species when they suffer to do, from hunger or want in any material form. It is threatened not by deficiency but by excess. It is plethoric. It is not lying down to die through physical exhaustion; it is knocking itself to pieces.

Measured by any standards except human contentment and ultimate security, mankind appears to be much wealthier now than in 1918. The qualities of power and material immediately available are much greater. What is called productivity in general is greater. But there is sound reason for supposing that a large part of this increased productivity is really a swifter and more thorough exploitation of irreplaceable capital. It is a process that cannot go on indefinitely. It rises to a maximum and then the feast is over. Natural resources are being exhausted at a great rate, and the increased output goes into war munitions whose purpose is destruction, and into sterile indulgences no better than waste. Man, "heir of the ages", is a demoralised spendthrift, in a state of galloping consumption, living on stimulants.

When we look into the statistics of population, there is irrefutable proof that everywhere we are passing a maximum (see for this Enid Charles' The Twilight of Parenthood, or R. R. Kuczynski's Measurement of Population Growth) and that a rapid decline is certain not only in Western Europe bur throughout the world. There is sound reason for doubting the alleged vast increase of the Russian people (see Souvarine's Stalin). Nevertheless, because of the continually increasing efficiency of productive methods, the relative pressure of this new unemployed class increases. The "mob" of the twentieth century is quite different from the almost animal "mob" of the eighteenth century. It is a restless sea of dissatisfied young people, of young men who can find no outlet for their natural urgencies and ambitions, young people quite ready to "make trouble" as soon as they are shown how.

In the technically crude past, the illiterate Have-nots were sweated and overworked. It was easy to find toil to keep them all busy. Such surplus multitudes are wanted no more. Toil is no longer marketable. Machines can toil better and with less resistance.

These frustrated multitudes have been made acutely aware of their own frustration. The gap of their always partly artificial disadvantage has been greatly diminished because now they all read. Even for incidental employment it has been necessary to teach them that, and the new reading public thus created has evoked a press and literature of excitement and suggestion. The cinema and the radio dazzle them with spectacles of luxury and unrestricted living. They are not the helpless Hodges and factory fodder of a hundred years ago. They are educated up to what must have been the middle-class level in 1889. They are indeed largely a squeezed-out middle class, restless, impatient and as we shall see extremely dangerous. They have assimilated almost all of the lower strata that were formerly illiterate drudges.

And this modernised excess population has no longer any social humility. It has no belief in the infallible wisdom of its rulers. It sees them too clearly; it knows about them, their waste, vices and weaknesses, with an even exaggerated vividness. It sees no reason for its exclusion from the good things of life by such people. It has lost enough of its inferiority to realise that most of that inferiority is arbitrary and artificial.

You may say that this is a temporary state of affairs, that the fall in population will presently relieve the situation, by getting rid of this surplus of the "not wanted". But it will do nothing of the sort. As population falls, consumption will fall. Industries will still be producing more and more efficiently for a shrinking market and they will be employing fewer and fewer hands. A state of five million people with half a million of useless hands, will be twice as unstable as forty million with two million standing off. So long as the present state of affairs continues, this stratum of perplexed young people "out of it" will increase relatively to the total community.

It is still not realised as clearly as it should be, how much the troubles of the present time are due to this new aspect of the social puzzle. But if you will scrutinise the events of the past half century in the light of this idea, you will see more and more convincingly that it is mainly through this growing mass of unfulfilled desire that the disruptive forces manifest themselves.

The eager and adventurous unemployed young are indeed the shock troops in the destruction of the old social order everywhere. They find guidance in some confident Party or some inspired Champion, who organises them for revolutionary or counter-revolutionary ends. It scarcely matters which. They become Communists or they become Fascists, Nazis, the Irish Republican Army, Ku Klux Klansmen and so forth and so on. The essence is the combination of energy, frustration and discontent. What all such movements have in common, is a genuine indignation at the social institutions that have begotten and then cold-shouldered them, a quasi-military organisation and the resolve to seize power for themselves embodied in their leaders. A wise and powerful government would at any cost anticipate and avert these destructive activities by providing various and interesting new employment and the necessary condition for a satisfying successful life for everyone. These young people are life. The rise of the successful leader only puts off the trouble for a time. He seizes power in the name of his movement. And then? When the seizure of power has been effected, he finds himself obliged to keep things going, to create justification for his leadership, exciting enterprises, urgencies.

A leader of vision with adequate technical assistance might conceivedly direct much of the human energy he has embodied into creative channels. For example he could rebuild the dirty, inadequate cities of our age, turn the still slovenly country-side into a garden and play-ground, re-clothe, liberate and stimulate imaginations, until the ideas of creative progress became a habit of mind. But in doing this he will find himself confronted by those who are sustained by the pre-emptions and appropriations of the old order. These relatively well-off people will bargain with him up to the last moment for their money and impede his seizure and utilisation of land and material resources, and will be further hampered by the fact that in organising his young people he has had to turn their minds and capacities from creative work to systematic violence and militant activities. It is easy to make an unemployed young man into a Fascist or gangster, but it is hard to turn him back to any decent social task. Moreover the Champion's own leadership was largely due to his conspiratorial and adventurous quality. He is himself unfit for a creative job. He finds himself a fighter at the head of a fighting pack.

And furthermore, unless his country is on the scale of Russia and the United States, whatever he attempts in order to make good his promises of an abundant life, has to be done in face of that mutual pressure of the sovereign states due to the abolition of distance and change of scale which we have already considered. He has no elbow-room in which to operate. The resultant of these convergent difficulties is to turn him and his fighting pack releasing flux of predatory war.

Everywhere in the world, under varying local circumstances, we see governments primarily concerned with this supreme problem of what to do with these young adults who are unemployable under present conditions. We have to realise that and bear it constantly in mind. It is there in every country. It is the most dangerous and wrong-headed view of the world situation, to treat the totalitarian countries as differing fundamentally from the rest of the world.

The problem of reabsorbing the unemployable adult is the essential problem in all states. It is the common shape to which all current political dramas reduce. How are we to use up or slake this surplus of human energy? The young are the live core of our species. The generation below sixteen or seventeen has not yet begun to give trouble, and after forty, the ebb of vitality disposes men to accept the lot that has fallen to them.

Franklin Roosevelt and Stalin find themselves in control of vast countries under-developed or so misdeveloped that their main energies go into internal organisation or reorganisation. They do not press against their frontiers therefore and they do not threaten war. The recent Russian annexations have been precautionary-defensive. But all the same both Russia and America have to cater for that troublesome social stratum quite as much as Europe. The New Deal is plainly an attempt to achieve a working socialism and avert a social collapse in America; it is extraordinarily parallel to the successive "policies" and "Plans" of the Russian experiment. Americans shirk the word "socialism", but what else can one call it?

The British oligarchy, demoralised and slack with the accumulated wealth of a century of advantage, bought off social upheaval for a time by the deliberate and socially demoralising appeasement of the dole. It has made no adequate effort to employ or educate these surplus people; it has just pushed the dole at them. It even tries to buy off the leader of the Labour Party with a salary of £2000 a year. Whatever we may think of the quality and deeds of the Nazi or Fascist regimes or the follies of their leaders, we must at any rate concede that they attempt, however clumsily, to reconstruct life in a collectivist direction. They are efforts to adjust and construct and so far they are in advance of the British ruling class. The British Empire has shown itself the least constructive of all governing networks. It produces no New Deals, no Five Year Plans; it keeps on trying to stave off its inevitable dissolution and carry on upon the old lines--and apparently it will do that until it has nothing more to give away.

"Peace in our time", that foolishly premature self-congratulation of Mr Chamberlain, is manifestly the guiding principle of the British elder statesman. It is that natural desire we all begin to feel after sixty to sit down comfortably somewhere. Unprogressive tranquillity they want at any price, even at the price of a preventive war. This astonishing bunch of rulers has never revealed any conception whatever of a common future before its sprawling Empire. There was a time when that Empire seemed likely to become the nexus of a world system, but now manifestly it has no future but disintegration. Apparently its rulers expected it to go on just as it was for ever. Bit by bit its component parts have dropped away and become quasi- independent powers, generally after an unedifying struggle; Southern Ireland for example is neutral in the present war, South Africa hesitated.

Now, and that is why this book is being written, these people, by a string of almost incredible blunders, have entangled what is left of their Empire in a great war to "end Hitler", and they have absolutely no suggestion to offer their antagonists and the world at large, of what is to come after Hitler. Apparently they hope to paralyse Germany in some as yet unspecified fashion and then to go back to their golf links or the fishing stream and doze by the fire after dinner. That is surely one of the most astounding things in history, the possibility of death and destruction beyond all reckoning and our combatant governments have no idea of what is to follow when the overthrow of Hitler is accomplished. They seem to be as void of any sense of the future, as completely empty-headed about the aftermath of their campaigns, as one of those American Tories who are "just out against F.D.R. Damn him!"

So the British Empire remains, paying its way down to ultimate bankruptcy, buying itself a respite from the perplexing problems of the future, with the accumulated wealth and power of its past. It is rapidly becoming the most backward political organisation in the world. But sooner or later it will have no more money for the dole and no more allies to abandon nor dominions to yield up to their local bosses, and then possibly its disintegration will be complete (R.I.P.), leaving intelligent English people to line up at last with America and the rest of the intelligent world and face the universal problem. Which is: how are we to adapt ourselves to these mighty disruptive forces that are shattering human society as it is at present constituted?

In the compressed countries which have little internal scope and lack the vast natural resources of the Russian and Atlantic communities, the internal tension makes more directly for aggressive warfare, but the fundamental driving-force behind their aggressiveness is still the universal trouble, that surplus of young men.

Seen in this broader vision, the present war falls into its true proportions as a stupid conflict upon secondary issues, which is delaying and preventing an overdue world adjustment. That is may kill hundreds of thousands of people does not alter that. An idiot with a revolver can murder a family. He remains an idiot.

From 1914 to 1939 has been a quarter of a century of folly, meanness, evasion and resentment, and only a very tedious and copious historian would attempt to distribute the blame among those who had played a part in the story. And when he had done it, what he had done would not matter in the least. An almost overwhelmingly difficult problem has confronted us all, and in some measure we have all of us lost our heads in the face of it, lost our dignity, been too clever by half, pinned ourselves to cheap solutions, quarrelled stupidly among ourselves. "We have erred and strayed.... We have lest undone those things that we ought to have done and we have done those things which we ought not to have done and there is no health in us."

I do not see any way to a solution of the problem of World Peace unless we begin with a confession of universal wrong-thinking and wrong-doing. Then we can sit down to the question of a solution with some reasonable prospect of finding an answer.

Now let us assume that "we" are a number of intelligent men, German, French, English, American, Italian, Chinese and so forth, who have decided in consequence of the war and in spite of the war, while the war is still going on, to wipe out all these squabbling bygones from our minds, and discuss plainly and simply the present situation of mankind. What is to be done with the world? Let us recapitulate the considerations that so far have been brought in, and what prospects they open, if any, of some hopeful concerted action, action that would so revolutionise the human outlook as to end war and that hectic recurrent waste of human life and happiness, for ever.

Firstly then it has been made apparent that humanity is at the end of an age, an age of fragmentation in the management of its affairs, fragmentation politically among separate sovereign states and economically among unrestricted business of organisations competing for profit. The abolition of distance, the enormous increase of available power, root causes of all our troubles, have suddenly made what was once a tolerable working system--a system that was perhaps with all its inequalities and injustices the only practicable working system in its time--enormously dangerous and wasteful, so that it threatens to exhaust and destroy our world altogether. Man is like a feckless heir who has suddenly been able to get at his capital and spend it as though it were income. We are living in a phase of violent and irreparable expenditure. There is an intensified scramble among nations and among individuals to

acquire, monopolise and spend. The dispossessed young find themselves hopeless unless they resort to violence. They implement the ever-increasing instability. Only a comprehensive collectivisation of human affairs can arrest this disorderly self-destruction of mankind. All this has been made plain in what has gone before.

This essential problem, the problem of collectivisation, can be viewed from two reciprocal points of view and stated in two different ways. We can ask, "What is to be done to end the world chaos?" and also "How can we offer the common young man a reasonable and stimulating prospect of a full life?"

These two questions are the obverse and reverse of one question. What answers one answers the other. The answer to both is that we have to collectivise the world as one system with practically everyone playing a reasonably satisfying part in it. For sound practical reasons, over and above any ethical or sentimental considerations, we have to devise a collectivisation that neither degrades nor enslaves.

Our imaginary world conference then has to turn itself to the question of how to collectivise the world, so that it will remain collectivised and yet enterprising, interesting and happy enough to content that common young man who will otherwise reappear, baffled and sullen, at the street corners and throw it into confusion again. To that problem the rest of this book will address itself.

As a matter of fact it is very obvious that at the present time a sort of collectivisation is being imposed very rapidly upon the world. Everyone is being enrolled, ordered about, put under control somewhere--even if it is only in an evacuation or concentration camp or what not. This process of collectivisation, collectivisation of some sort, seems now to be in the nature of things and there is no reason to suppose it is reversible. Some people imagine world peace as the end of that process. Collectivisation is going to be defeated and a vaguely conceived reign of law will restore and sustain property, Christianity, individualism and everything to which the respectable prosperous are accustomed. This is implicit even on the title of such a book as Edward Mousley's Man or Leviathan? It is much more reasonable to think that world peace has to be the necessary completion of that process, and that the alternative is a decadent anarchy. If so, the phrase for the aims of liberal thought should be no Man or Leviathan but Man masters Leviathan.

On this point, the inevitability of collectivisation as the sole alternative to universal brigandage and social collapse, our world conference must make itself perfectly clear.

Then it has to turn itself to the much more difficult and complicated question of how.

27

VI. — SOCIALISM UNAVOIDABLE

LET us, even at the cost of a certain repetition, look a little more closely now into the fashion in which the disruptive forces are manifesting themselves in the Western and Eastern hemispheres.

In the Old World the hypertrophy of armies is most conspicuous, in America it was the hypertrophy of big business. But in both the necessity for an increasing collective restraint upon uncoordinated over-powerful business or political enterprise is more and more clearly recognised.

There is a strong opposition on the part of great interests in America to the President, who has made himself the spear-head of the collectivising drive; they want to put the brake now on his progressive socialisation of the nation, and quite possibly, at the cost of increasing social friction, they may slow down the drift to socialism very considerably. But it is unbelievable that they dare provoke the social convulsion that would ensue upon a deliberate reversal of the engines or upon any attempt to return to the glorious days of big business, wild speculation and mounting unemployment before 1927. They will merely slow down the drive. For in the world now all roads lead to socialism or social dissolution.

The tempo of the process is different in the two continents; that is the main difference between them. It is not an opposition. They travel at different rates but they travel towards an identical goal. In the Old World at present the socialisation of the community is going on far more rapidly and thoroughly than it is in America because of the perpetual war threat.

In Western Europe now the dissolution and the drive towards socialisation progress by leaps and bounds. The British governing class and British politicians generally, overtaken by a war they had not the intelligence to avert, have tried to atone for their slovenly unimaginativeness during the past twenty years in a passion of witless improvisation. God knows what their actual war preparations amount to, but their domestic policy seems to be based on an imperfect study of Barcelona, Guernica, Madrid and Warsaw. They imagine similar catastrophes on a larger scale--although they are quite impossible, as every steady-headed person who can estimate the available supplies of petrol knows --and they have a terrible dread of being held responsible. They fear a day of reckoning with their long-bamboozled lower classes. In their panic they are rapidly breaking up the existing order altogether.

The changes that have occurred in Great Britain in less than a year are astounding. They recall in many particulars the social dislocation of Russia in the closing months of 1917. There has been a shifting and mixing-up of people that would have seemed impossible to anyone in 1937. The evacuation of centres of population under the mere exaggerated threat of air raids has been of frantic recklessness. Hundreds of thousands of families have been broken up, children separated from their parents and quartered in the homes of more or less reluctant hosts. Parasites and skin diseases, vicious habits and insanitary practices have been spread, as if in a passion of equalitarian propaganda, the slums of such centres as Glasgow, London and Liverpool, throughout the length and breadth of the land. Railways, road traffic, all the normal communications have been dislocated by a universal running about. For a couple of months Great Britain has been more like a disturbed ant-hill than an organised civilised country.

The contagion of funk has affected everyone. Public institutions and great business concerns have bolted to remote and inconvenient sites; the BBC organisation, for example, scuffled off headlong from London, needlessly and ridiculously, no man pursuing it. There has been a wild epidemic of dismissals, of servants employed in London, for example, and a still wilder shifting of unsuitable men to novel, unnecessary jobs. Everyone has been exhorted to serve the country, children of twelve, to the great delight of conservative-minded farmers, have been withdrawn from school and put to work on the land, and yet the number of those who have lost their jobs and cannot find anything else to do, has gone up by over 100,000.

There have been amateurish attempts to ration food, producing waste here and artificial scarcity there. A sort of massacre of small independent businesses is in progress mainly to the advantage of the big provision-dealing concerns, who changed in a night from open profiteers to become the "expert" advisers of food supply. All the expertise they have ever displayed has been the extraction of profits from food supply. But while profits mount, taxation with an air of great resolution sets itself to prune them.

The British public has always been phlegmatic in the face of danger, it is too stout-hearted and too stupid to give way to excesses of fear, but the authorities have thought it necessary to plaster the walls with cast, manifestly expensive, posters, headed with a Royal Crown, "Your courage, your resolution, your cheerfulness will bring us victory."

"Oh yus," said the London Cockney. "You'll get the victory all right. Trust you. On my courage, my resolution, my cheerfulness; you'll use up 'Tommy Atkins' all right. Larf at 'im in a kindly sort of way and use him. And then you think you'll out him back again on the dust-heap. Again? Twice?"

That is all too credible. But this time our rulers will emerge discredited and frustrated from the conflict to face a disorganised population in a state of mutinous enquiry. They have made preposterous promises to restore Poland and they will certainly have to eat their words about that. Or what is more probable the government will have to give place to another administration which will be able to eat those words for them with a slightly better grace. There is little prospect of Thanksgiving Services or any Armistice night orgy this time. People at home are tasting the hardships of war even more tediously and irritating than the men on active service. Cinemas, theatres, have been shut prematurely, black-outs have diminished the safety of the streets and doubled the tale of road casualties. The British crowd is already a sullen crowd. The world has not seen it in such a bad temper for a century and half, and, let there be no mistake about it, it is far less in a temper with the Germans than it is with its own rulers.

Through all this swirling intimidating propaganda of civil disorder and a systematic suppression of news and criticism of the most exasperating sort, war preparation has proceeded. The perplexed and baffled citizen can only hope that on the military side there has been a little more foresight and less hysteria.

The loss of confidence and particularly confidence in the government and social order is already enormous. No one feels secure, in his job, in his services, in his savings, any longer. People lose confidence even in the money in their pockets. And human society is built on confidence. It cannot carry on without it.

Things are like this already and it is only the opening stage of this strange war. The position of the ruling class and the financial people who have hitherto dominated British affairs is a peculiar one. The cast of the war is already enormous, and there is no sign that it will diminish. Income tax, super tax, death duties, taxes on war profits have been raised to a level that should practically extinguish the once prosperous middle strata of society altogether. The very wealthy will survive in a shorn and diminished state, they will hang on to the last, but the graded classes that have hitherto intervened between them and the impoverished masses of the population, who will be irritated by war sacrifices, extensively unemployed and asking more and more penetrating questions, will have diminished greatly. Only by the most ingenious monetary manipulation, by dangerous tax-dodging and expedients verging on sheer scoundrelism, will a clever young man have the ghost of a chance of climbing by the old traditional money-making ladder, above his fellows. On the other hand, the career of a public employee will become continually more attractive. There is more interest in it and more self-respect. The longer the war continues, the completer and more plainly irreparable will be the dissolution of the old order.

Now to many readers who have been incredulous of the statement of the first section of this book, that we are living in the End of an Age, to those who have been impervious to the account of the disruptive forces that are breaking up the social order and to the argument I have drawn from them, who may have got away from all that, so to speak, by saying they are "scientific" or "materialistic" or "sociological" or "highbrow", or that Providence that has hitherto displayed such a marked bias in favour of well-off, comfortable, sluggish-minded people is sure to do something nice for them at the eleventh hour, the real inconveniences, alarms, losses and growing disorder of the life about them may at last bring a realisation that the situation

in Western Europe is approaching revolutionary conditions. It will be a hard saying for many people in the advantage-holding classes, and particularly if they are middle-aged, that the older has already gone to pieces can never be put back. But how can they doubt it?

A revolution, that is to say a more or less convulsive effort at social and political readjustment, is bound to come in all these overstrained countries, in Germany, in Britain and universally. It is more likely than not to arise directly out of the exasperating diminuendos and crescendos of the present war, as a culminating phase of it. Revolution of some sort we must have. We cannot prevent its onset. But we can affect the course of its development. It may end in utter disaster or it may release a new world, far better than the old. Within these broad limits it is possible for us to make up our minds how it will come to us.

And since the only practical question before us is the question of how we will take this world revolution we cannot possibly evade, let me recall to your attention the reasons I have advanced in the second section of this book for the utmost public discussion of our situation at the present time. And also let me bring back to mind the examination of Marxism in the fourth section. There it is shown how easily a collectivist movement, especially when it is faced by the forcible-feeble resistances and suppressions of those who have hitherto enjoyed wealth and power, may degenerate into an old-fashioned class-war, become conspiratorial, dogmatic and inadaptable, and sink towards leader worship and autocracy. That apparently is what has happened in Russia in its present phase. We do not know how much of the original revolutionary spirit survives there, and a real fundamental issue in the world situation is whether we are to follow in the footsteps of Russia or whether we are going to pull ourselves together, face the stern logic of necessity and produce a Western Revolution, which will benefit by the Russian experience, react upon Russia and lead ultimately to a world understanding.

What is it that the Atlantic world finds most objectionable in the Soviet world of to-day? Is it any disapproval of collectivism as such? Only in the case of a dwindling minority of rich and successful men--and very rarely of the sons of such people. Very few capable men under fifty nowadays remain individualists in political and social matters. They are not even fundamentally anti-Communist. Only it happens that for various reasons the political life of the community is still in the hands of unteachable old-fashioned people. What are called "democracies" suffer greatly from the rule of old men who have not kept pace with the times. The real and effective disapproval, distrust and disbelief in the soundness of the Soviet system lies not in the out-of-date individualism of these elderly types, but in the conviction that it can never achieve efficiency or even maintain its honest ideal of each for all and all for each, unless it has free speech and an insistence upon legally-defined freedoms for the individual within the collectivist framework. We do not deplore the Russian Revolution as a Revolution. We complain that it is not a good enough Revolution and we want a better one.

The more highly things are collectivised the more necessary is a legal system embodying the Rights of Man. This has been forgotten under the Soviets, and so men go in fear there of arbitrary police action. But the more functions your government controls the more need there is for protective law. The objection to Soviet collectivism is that, lacking the antiseptic of legally assured personal freedom, it will not keep. It professes to be fundamentally a common economic system based on class-war ideas; the industrial director is under the heel of the Party commissar; the political police have got altogether out of hand; and the affairs gravitate inevitably towards an oligarchy or an autocracy protecting its incapacity by the repression of adverse comment.

But these valid criticisms merely indicate the sort of collectivisation that has to be avoided. It does not dispose of collectivism as such. If we in our turn do not wish to be submerged by the wave of Bolshevisation that is evidently advancing from the East, we must implement all these valid objections and create a collectivisation that will be more efficient, more prosperous, tolerant, free and rapidly progressive than the system we condemn. We, who do not like the Stalinised-Marxist state, have, as they used to say in British politics, to "dish" it by going one better. We have to confront Eastern-spirited collectivism with Western-spirited collectivism.

Perhaps this may be better put. We may be giving way to a subconscious conceit here and assuming that the West is always going to be thinking more freely and clearly and working more efficiently than the East. It is like that now, but it may not always be like that. Every country has had its phases of illumination and its phases of blindness. Stalin and Stalinism are neither the beginning nor the end of the collectivisation of Russia.

We are dealing with something still almost impossible to estimate, the extent to which the new Russian patriotism and the new Stalin-worship, have effaced and how far they have merely masked, the genuinely creative international communism of the revolutionary years. The Russian mind is not a docile mind, and most of the literature available for a young man to read in Russia, we must remember, is still revolutionary. There has been no burning of the books there. The Moscow radio talks for internal consumption since the Hitler-Stalin understanding betray a great solicitude on the part of the government to make it clear that there has been no sacrifice of revolutionary principle. That witnesses to the vitality of public opinion in Russia. The clash between the teachings of 1920 and 1940 may have a liberating effect on many people's minds. Russians love to talk about ideas. Under the Czar they talked. It is incredible that they do not talk under Stalin.

That question whether collectivisation is to be "Westernised" or "Easternised", using these words under the caveat of the previous paragraph, is really the first issue before the world today. We need a fully ventilated Revolution. Our Revolution has to go on in the light and air. We may have to accept sovietisation a la Russe quite soon unless we can produce a better collectivisation. But if we produce a better collectivisation it is more probable than not that the Russian system will incorporate our improvements, forget its reviving nationalism again, debunk Marx and Stalin, so far as they can be debunked, and merge into the one world state.

Between these primary antagonists, between Revolution with its eyes open and Revolution with a mask and a gag, there will certainly be complications of the issue due to patriotism and bigotry and the unteachable wilful blindness of those who do not want to see. Most people lie a lot to themselves before they lie to other people, and it is hopeless to expect that all the warring cults and traditions that confuse the mind of the race to-day are going to fuse under a realisation of the imperative nature of the human situation as I have stated it here. Multitudes will never realise it. Few human+beings are able to change their primary ideas after the middle thirties. They get fixed in them and drive before them no more intelligently than animals drive before their innate impulses. They will die rather than change their second selves.

One of the most entangling of these disconcerting secondary issues is that created by the stupid and persistent intrigues of the Roman Catholic Church.

Let me be clear here. I am speaking of the Vatican and of its sustained attempts to exercise a directive role in secular life. I number among my friends many Roman Catholics who have built the most charming personalities and behaviour systems on the framework provided them by their faith. One of the loveliest characters I have ever known was G.K. Chesterton. But I think he was just as fine before he became a Catholic as afterwards. Still he found something he needed in

Catholicism. There are saints of all creeds and of none, so good are better possibilities of human nature. Religious observances provide a frame that many find indispensable for the seemly ordering of their lives. And outside the ranks of "strict" observers many good people with hardly more theology than a Unitarian, love to speak of goodness and kindness as Christianity. So-and-so is a "good Christian". Voltaire, says Alfred Noyes, the Catholic writer, was a "good Christian". I do not use the word "Christianity" in that sense because I do not believe that Christians have any monopoly of goodness. When I write of Christianity, I mean Christianity with a definite creed and militant organisation and not these good kind people, good and kind but not very fastidious about the exact use of the words.

Such "good Christians" can be almost as bitterly critical as I am of the continual pressure upon the faithful by that inner group of Italians in Rome, subsidised by the Fascist government, who pull the strings of Church policy throughout the world, so as to do this or that tortuous or uncivilised thing, to cripple education, to persecute unorthodox ways of living.

It is to the influence of the Church that we must ascribe the foolish support by the British Foreign Office of Franco, that murderous little "Christian gentleman", in his overthrow of the staggering liberal renascence of Spain. It is the Roman Catholic influence the British and French have to thank, for the fantastic blundering that involved them in the defence of the impossible Polish state and its unrighteous acquisitions; it affected British policy in respect to Austria and Czechoslovakia profoundly, and now it is doing its utmost to maintain and develop a political estrangement between Russia and the Western world by its prejudiced exacerbation of the idea that Russia is "anti-God" while we Westerners are little children of the light, gallantly fighting on the side of the Cross, Omnipotence, Greater Poland, national sovereignty, the small uneconomic prolific farmer and shopkeeper and anything else you like to imagine constitutes "Christendom".

The Vatican strives perpetually to develop the present war into a religious war. It is trying to steal the war. By all the circumstances of its training it is unteachable. It knows no better. It will go on--until some economic revolution robs it of its funds. Then as a political influence it may evaporate very rapidly. The Anglican Church and many other Protestant sects, the wealthy Baptists, for example, follow suit.

It is not only in British affairs that this propaganda goes on. With the onset of war France becomes militant and Catholic. It has suppressed the Communist Party, as a gesture of resentment against Russia and a precaution against post-war collectivisation. The Belgian caricaturist Raemaekers is now presenting Hitler day after day as a pitiful weakling already disposed of and worthy of our sympathy, while Stalin is represented as a frightful giant with horns and a tail. Yet both France and Britain are at peace with Russia and have every reason to come to a working understanding with that country. The attitude of Russia to the war has on the whole been cold, contemptuous and reasonable.

It is not as if these devious schemes can take us somewhere; it is not that this restoration of the Holy Roman Empire is a possibility. You confront these Catholic politicians, just as you confront the politicians of Westminster, with these two cardinal facts, the abolition of distance and the change of scale. In vain. You cannot get any realisation of the significance of these things into those idea-proofed skulls. They are deaf to it, blind to it. They cannot see that it makes any difference at all to their long-established mental habits. If their minds waver for a moment they utter little magic prayers to exorcise the gleam.

What, they ask, has "mere size" to do with the soul of man, "mere speed, mere power"? What can the young do better than subdue their natural urgency to live and do? What has mere life to do with the religious outlook? The war, these Vatican propagandists insist, is a "crusade" against modernism, against socialism and free thought, the restoration of priestly authority is its end; our sons are fighting to enable the priest to thrust his pious uncleanliness once again between reader and book, child and knowledge, husband and wife, sons and lovers. While honest men are fighting now to put an end to military aggression, to resume indeed that "war to end war" that was aborted to give us the League of Nations, these bigots are sedulously perverting the issue, trying to represent it as a religious war against Russia in particular and the modern spirit in general.

The well-trained Moslem, the American fundamentalists, the orthodox Jew, all the fixed cultures, produce similar irrelevant and wasteful resistances, but the Catholic organisation reaches further and is more persistent. It is frankly opposed to human effort and the idea of progress. It makes no pretence about it.

Such cross-activities as these complicate, delay and may even sabotage effectively every effort to solve the problem of a lucid collectivisation of the world's affairs, but they do not alter the essential fact that it is only through a rationalisation and coalescence of constructive revolutionary movements everywhere and a liberal triumph over the dogmatism of the class war, that we can hope to emerge from the present wreckage of our world.

28

VII. — FEDERATION

LET us now take up certain vaguely constructive proposals which seem at present to be very much in people's minds. They find their cardinal expression in a book called Union Now by Mr Clarence K. Streit, which has launched the magic word "Federation" upon the world. The "democracies" of the world are to get together upon a sort of enlargement of the Federal constitution of the United States (which produced one of the bloodiest civil wars in all history) and then all will be well with us.

Let us consider whether this word "Federation" is of any value in organising the Western Revolution. I would suggest it is. I think it may be a means of mental release for many people who would otherwise have remained dully resistant to any sort of change.

This Federation project has an air of reasonableness. It is attractive to a number of influential people who wish with the minimum of adaptation to remain influential in a changing world, and particularly is it attractive to what I may call the liberal-conservative elements of the prosperous classes in America and Great Britain and the Oslo countries, because it puts the most difficult aspect of the problem, the need for collective socialisation, so completely in the background that it can be ignored. This enables them to take quite a bright and hopeful view of the future without any serious hindrance to their present preoccupations.

They think that Federation, reasonably defined, may suspend the possibility of war for a considerable period and so lighten the burden of taxation that the present crushing demands on them will relax and they will be able to resume, on a slightly more economical scale perhaps, their former way of living. Everything that gives them hope and self-respect and preserves their homes from the worst indignities of panic, appeasement, treason-hunting and the rest of it, is to be encouraged, and meanwhile their sons will have time to think and it may be possible so to search, ransack and rationalise the Streit project as to make a genuine and workable scheme for the socialisation of the world.

In The Fate of Homo sapiens I examined the word "democracy" with some care, since it already seemed likely that great quantities of our young men were to be asked to cripple and risk their lives for its sake. I showed that it was still a very incompletely realised aspiration, that its complete development involved socialism and a level of education and information attained as yet by no community in the world. Mr Streit gives a looser, more rhetorical statement --a more idealistic statement, shall we say?--of his conception of democracy, the sort of statement that would be considered wildly exaggerated even if it was war propaganda, and though unhappily it is remote from any achieved reality, he proceeds without further enquiry as if it were a description of existing realities in what he calls the "democracies" of the world. In them he imagines he finds "governments of the people, by the people, for the people".

In the book I have already cited I discuss What is Democracy? And Where is Democracy? I do my best there to bring Mr Streit down to the harsh and difficult facts of the case. I will go now a little more into particulars in my examination of his project.

His "founder democracies" are to be: "The American Union, the British Commonwealth (specifically the United Kingdom, the Federal Dominion of Canada, the Commonwealth of Australia, New Zealand, the Union of South Africa, Ireland), the French Republic, Belgium, the Netherlands, the Swiss Confederation, Denmark, Norway, Sweden and Finland."

Scarcely one of these, as I have shown in that former book, is really a fully working democracy. And the Union of South Africa is a particularly bad and dangerous case of race tyranny. Ireland is an incipient religious war and not one country but two. Poland, I note, does not come into Mr Streit's list of democracies at all. His book was written in 1938 when Poland was a totalitarian country holding, in defiance of the League of Nations, Vilna, which it had taken from Lithuania, large areas of non-Polish country it had conquered from Russia, and fragments gained by the dismemberment of Czechoslovakia. It only became a democracy, even technically and for a brief period, before its collapse in September 1939, when Mr Chamberlain was so foolish as to drag the British Empire into a costly and perilous war, on its behalf. But that is by the way. None of these fifteen (or ten) "founder democracies" are really democracies at all. So we start badly. But they might be made socialist democracies and their federation might be made something very real indeed--at a price. The U.S.S.R. is a federated socialist system, which has shown a fairly successful political solidarity during the past two decades, whatever else it has done or failed to do.

Now let us help Mr Streit to convert his "federation" from a noble but extremely rhetorical aspiration into a living reality. He is aware that this must be done at a price, but I want to suggest that that price is, from what I judge to be his point of view, far greater, and the change much simpler, more general and possibly even closer at hand, than he supposes. He is disposed to appeal to existing administrative organisations, and it is questionable whether they are the right people to execute his designs. One of the difficulties he glosses over is the possible reluctance of the India Office to hand over the control of India (Ceylon and Burma he does not mention) to the new Federation Government, which would also, I presume, take charge of the fairly well governed and happy fifty-odd million people of the Dutch East Indies, the French colonial empire, the West Indies and so on. This, unless he proposes merely to re-christen the India Office, etc., is asking for an immense outbreak of honesty and competence on the part of the new Federal officialdom. It is also treating the possible contribution of these five or six hundred million of dusky peoples to the new order with a levity inconsistent with democratic ideals.

Quite a lot of these people have brains which are as good or better than normal European brains. You could educate the whole world to the not very exalted level of a Cambridge graduate in a single lifetime, if you had schools, colleges, apparatus and teachers enough. The radio, the cinema, the gramophone, the improvements in both production and distribution, have made it possible to increase the range and effectiveness of a gifted teacher a thousandfold. We have seen intensive war preparations galore, but no one has dreamt yet of an intensive educational effort. None of us really like to see other people being educated. They may be getting an advantage over our privileged selves. Suppose we overcome that primitive jealousy. Suppose we speed up--as we are now physically able to do--the education and enfranchisement of these huge undeveloped reservoirs of human capacity. Suppose we tack that on the Union Now idea. Suppose we stipulate that Federation, wherever it extends, means a New and Powerful Education. In Bengal, in Java, in the Congo Free State, quite as much as in Tennessee or Georgia or Scotland or Ireland. Suppose we think a little less about "gradual enfranchisement" by votes and experiments in local autonomy and all these old ideas, and a little more about the enfranchisement of the mind. Suppose we drop that old cant about politically immature peoples.

There is one direction in which Mr Streit's proposals are open to improvement. Let us turn to another in which he does not seem to have realised all the implications of his proposal. This great Union is to have a union money and a union customs-free economy. What follows upon that? More I think than he realises.

There is one aspect of money to which the majority of those that discuss it seem to be incurably blind. You cannot have a theory of money or any plan about money by itself in the air. Money is not a thing in itself; it is a working part of an economic system. Money varies in its nature with the laws and ideas of property in a community. As a community moves towards collectivism and communism, for example, money simplifies out. Money is a necessary in a communism as it is in any other system, but its function therein is at its simplest. Payment in kind to the worker gives him no freedom of choice among the goods the community produces. Money does. Money becomes the incentive that "works the worker" and nothing more.

But directly you allow individuals not only to obtain goods for consumption, but also to obtain credit to produce material for types of production outside the staple productions of the state, the question of credit and debt arises and money becomes more complicated. With every liberation of this or that product or service from collective control to business or experimental exploitation, the play of the money system enlarges and the laws regulating what you may take for it, the company laws, bankruptcy laws and so forth increase. In any highly developed collective system the administration will certainly have to give credits for hopeful experimental enterprises. When the system is not collectivism, monetary operations for gain are bound to creep in and become more and more complicated. Where most of the substantial side of life is entrusted to uncoordinated private enterprise, the intricacy of the money apparatus increases enormously. Monetary manipulation becomes a greater and greater factor in the competitive struggle, not only between individuals and firms, but between states. As Mr Streit himself shows, in an excellent discussion of the abandonment of the gold standard, inflation and deflation become devices in international competition. Money becomes strategic, just as pipe lines and railways can become strategic.

This being so it is plain that for the Federal Union a common money means an identical economic life throughout the Union. And this too is implied also in Mr Streit's "customs-free" economy. It is impossible to have a common money when a dollar or a pound, or whatever it is, can buy this, that or the other advantage in one state and is debarred from anything but bare purchases for consumption in another. So that this Federal Union is bound to be a uniform economic system. There can be only very slight variations in the control of economic life.

In the preceding sections the implacable forces that make for the collectivisation of the world or disaster, have been exposed. It follows that "Federation" means practically uniform socialism within the Federal limits, leading, as state after state is incorporated, to world socialism. There manifestly we carry Mr Streit farther than he realises he goes--as yet. For it is fairly evident that he is under the impression that a large measure of independent private business is to go on throughout the Union. I doubt if he imagines it is necessary to go beyond the partial socialisation already achieved by the New Deal. But we have assembled evidence to show that the profit scramble, the wild days of uncorrelated "business" are over for ever.

And again though he realises and states very clearly that governments are made for man and not man for governments, though he applauds the great declarations of the Convention that created the American Constitution, wherein "we the people of the United States" overrode the haggling of the separate states and established the American Federal Constitution, nevertheless he is curiously chary of superseding any existing legal governments in the present world. He is chary of talking of "We the people of the world". But many of us are coming to realise that all existing governments have to go into the melting pot, we believe that it is a world revolution which is upon us, and that in the great struggle to evoke a Westernised World Socialism, contemporary governments may vanish like straw hats in the rapids of Niagara. Mr Streit, however, becomes extraordinarily legal-minded at this stage. I do not think that he realises the forces of destruction that are gathering and so I think he hesitates to plan a reconstruction upon anything like the scale that may become possible.

He evades even the obvious necessity that under a Federal Government the monarchies of Great Britain, Belgium, Norway, Sweden, Holland, if they survive at all, must becomes like the mediatised sovereigns of the component states of the former German Empire, mere ceremonial vestiges. Perhaps he thinks that, but he does not say it outright. I do not know if he has pondered the New York World Fair of 1939 nor the significance of the Royal Visit to America in that year, and thought how much there is in the British system that would have to be abandoned if his Federation is to become a reality. In most of the implications of the word, it must cease to be "British". His Illustrative Constitution is achieved with an altogether forensic disregard of the fundamental changes in human conditions to which we have to adapt ourselves or perish. He thinks of war by itself and not as an eruption due to deeper maladaptations. But if we push his earlier stipulations to their necessary completion, we need not trouble very much about that sample constitution of his, which is to adjust the balance so fairly among the constituent states. The abolition of distance must inevitably substitute functional associations and loyalties for local attributions, if human society does not break up altogether. The local divisions will melt into a world collectivity and the main conflicts in a progressively unifying Federation are much more likely to be these between different world-wide types and associations of workers.

So far with Union Now. One of Mr Streit's outstanding merits is that he has had the courage to make definite proposals on which we can bite. I doubt if a European could have produced any such book. Its naive political legalism, its idea of salvation by constitution, and its manifest faith in the magic beneficence of private enterprise, are distinctly in the vein of an American, almost a pre-New Deal American, who has become, if anything, more American, through his experiences of the deepening disorder of Europe. So many Americans still look on at world affairs like spectators at a ball game who are capable of vociferous participation but still have no real sense of participation; they do not realise that the ground is moving under their seats also, and that the social revolution is breaking surface to engulf them in their turn. To most of us--to most of us over forty at any rate--the idea of a fundamental change in our way of life is so unpalatable that we resist it to the last moment.

Mr Streit betrays at times as vivid a sense of advancing social collapse as I have, but it has still to occur to him that that collapse may be conclusive. There may be dark ages, a relapse into barbarism, but somewhen and somehow he thinks man must recover. George Bernard Shaw has recently been saying the same thing.

It may be worse that that.

I have given Mr Streit scarcely a word of praise, because that would be beside the mark here. He wrote his book sincerely as a genuine contribution to the unsystematic world conference that is now going on, admitting the possibility of error, demanding criticism, and I have dealt with it in that spirit.

Unfortunately his word has gone much further than his book. His book says definite things and even when one disagrees with it, it is good as a point of departure. But a number of people have caught up this word "Federation", and our minds are distracted by a multitude of appeals to support Federal projects with the most various content or with no content at all.

All the scores and hundreds of thousands of nice people who are signing peace pledges and so forth a few years ago, without the slightest attempt in the world to understand what they meant by peace, are now echoing this new magic word with as little conception of any content for it. They did not realise that peace means so complicated and difficult an ordering and balancing of human society that it has never been sustained since man became man, and that we have wars and preparatory interludes between wars because that is a much simpler and easier sequence for our wilful, muddle-headed, suspicious and aggressive species. These people still think we can get this new and wonderful state of affairs just by clamouring for it. And having failed to get peace by saying "Peace" over and over again, they are now with an immense sense of discovery saying "Federation". What must happen to men in conspicuous public positions I do not know, but even an irresponsible literary man like myself finds himself inundated with innumerable lengthy private letters, hysterical post-cards, pamphlets from budding organisations, "declarations" to sign, demands for subscriptions, all in the name of the new panacea, all as vain and unproductive as the bleating of lost sheep. And I cannot open a newspaper without finding some eminent contemporary writing a letter to it, saying gently, firmly and bravely, the same word, sometimes with bits of Union Now tacked on to it, and sometimes with minor improvements, but often with nothing more than the bare idea.

All sorts of idealistic movements for world peace which have been talking quietly to themselves for years and years have been stirred up to follow the new banner. Long before the Great War there was a book by Sir Max Waechter, a friend of King Edward the Seventh, advocating the United States of Europe, and that inexact but flattering parallelism to the United States of America has recurred frequently; as a phase thrown out by Monsieur Briand for example, and as a project put forward by an Austrian-Japanese writer, Count Coudenhove-Kalergi, who even devised a flag for the Union. The main objection to the idea is that there are hardly any states completely in Europe, except Switzerland, San Marino, Andorra and a few of the Versailles creations. Almost all the other European states extend far beyond the European limits both politically and in their sympathies and cultural relations. They trail with them more than half mankind. About a tenth of the British Empire is in Europe and still less of the Dutch Empire; Russia, Turkey, France, are less European than not; Spain and Portugal have their closest links with South America.

Few Europeans think of themselves as "Europeans". I, for example, am English, and a large part of my interests, intellectual and material, are Transatlantic. I dislike calling myself "British" and I like to think of myself as a member of a great English-speaking community, which spreads irrespective of race and colour round and about the world. I am annoyed when an American calls me a "foreigner"--war with America would seem to me just as insane as war with Cornwall--and I find the idea of cutting myself off from the English-speaking peoples of America and Asia to follow the flag of my Austrian-Japanese friend into a federally bunched-up European extremely unattractive.

It would, I suggest, be far easier to create the United States of the World, which is Mr Streit's ultimate objective, than to get together the so- called continent of Europe into any sort of unity.

I find most of these United States of Europe movements are now jumping on to the Federation band-wagon.

My old friend and antagonist, Lord David Davies, for instance, has recently succumbed to the infection. He was concerned about the problem of a World Pax in the days when the League of Nations Society and other associated bodies were amalgamated in the League of Nations Union. He was struck then by an idea, an analogy, and the experience was unique for him. He asked why individuals went about in modern communities in nearly perfect security from assault and robbery, without any need to bear arms. His answer was the policeman. And from that he went on to the question of what was needed for states and nations to go their ways with the same blissful immunity from violence and plunder, and it seemed to him a complete and reasonable answer to say "an international policeman". And there you were! He did not see, he is probably quite incapable of seeing, that a state is something quite different in its nature and behaviour from an individual human+being. When he was asked to explain how that international policeman was to be created and sustained, he just went on saying "international policeman". He has been saying it for years. Sometimes it seems it is to be the League of Nations, sometimes the British Empire, sometimes an international Air Force, which is to undertake this grave responsibility. The bench before which the policeman is to hale the offender and this position of the lock-up are not indicated. Finding our criticisms uncongenial, his lordship went off with his great idea, like a penguin which has found an egg, to incubate it alone. I hope he will be spared to say "international policeman" for many years to come, but I do not believe he has ever perceived or ever will perceive that, brilliant as his inspiration was, it still left vast areas of the problem in darkness. Being a man of considerable means, he has been able to sustain a "New Commonwealth" movement and publish books and a periodical in which his one great idea is elaborated rather than developed.

But I will not deal further with the very incoherent multitude that now echoes this word "Federation". Many among them will cease to cerebrate further and fall by the wayside, but many will go on thinking, and if they go on thinking they will come to perceive more and more clearly the realities of the case. Federation, they will feel, is not enough.

So much for the present "Federalist" front. As a fundamental basis of action, as a declared end, it seems hopelessly vague and confused and, if one may coin a phrase, hopelessly optimistic. But since the concept seems to be the way to release a number of minds from belief in the sufficiency of a League of Nations, associated or not associated with British Imperialism, it has been worth while to consider how it can be amplified and turned in the direction of that full and open-eyed world-wide collectivisation which a study of existing conditions obliges us to believe is the only alternative to the complete degeneration of our species.

29

VIII. — THE NEW TYPE OF REVOLUTION

LET us return to our main purpose, which is to examine the way in which we are to face up to this impending World Revolution.

To many minds this idea of Revolution is almost inseparable from visions of street barricades made of paving-stones and overturned vehicles, ragged mobs armed with impromptu weapons and inspired by defiant songs, prisons broken and a general jail delivery, palaces stormed, a great hunting of ladies and gentlemen, decapitated but still beautiful heads on pikes, regicides of the most sinister quality, the busy guillotine, a crescendo of disorder ending in a whiff of grapeshot....

That was one type of Revolution. It is what one might call the Catholic type of Revolution, that it is to say it is the ultimate phase of a long period of Catholic living and teaching. People do not realise this and some will be indignant at its being stated so barely. Yet the facts stare us in the face, common knowledge, not to be denied. That furious, hungry, desperate, brutal mob was the outcome of generations of Catholic rule, Catholic morality and Catholic education. The King of France was the "Most Christian King, the eldest son of the Church", he was master of the economic and financial life of the community, and the Catholic Church controlled the intellectual life of the community and the education of the people absolutely. That mob was the outcome. It is absurd to parrot that Christianity has never been tried. Christianity in its most highly developed form has been tried and tried again. It was tried for centuries fully and completely, in Spain, France, Italy. It was responsible for the filth and chronic pestilence and famine of medieval England. It inculcated purity but it never inculcated cleanliness. Catholic Christianity had practically unchallenged power in France for generations. It was free to teach as it chose and as much as it chose. It dominated the common life entirely. The Catholic system in France cannot have reaped anything it did not sow, for no other sowers were allowed. That hideous mob of murderous ragamuffins we are so familiar with in pictures of the period, was the final harvest of its regime.

The more Catholic reactionaries revile the insurgent common people of the first French Revolution, the more they condemn themselves. It is the most impudent perversion of reality for them to snivel about the guillotine and the tumbrils, as though these were not purely Catholic products, as though they came in suddenly from outside to wreck a genteel Paradise. They were the last stage of the systematic injustice and ignorance of a strictly Catholic regime. One phase succeeded another with relentless logic. The Maseillaise completed the life-cycle of Catholicism.

In Spain too and in Mexico we have seen undisputed educational and moral Catholic ascendancy, the Church with a free hand, producing a similar uprush of blind resentment. The crowds there also were cruel and blasphemous; but Catholicism cannot complain; for Catholicism hatched them. Priests and nuns who had been the sole teachers of the people were insulted and outraged and churches defiled. Surely if the Church is anything like what it claims to be, the people would have loved it. They would not have behaved as though sacrilege was a gratifying relief.

But these Catholic Revolutions are only specimens of one single type of Revolution. A Revolution need not be a spontaneous storm of indignation against intolerable indignities and deprivations. It can take quite other forms.

As a second variety of Revolution, which is in sharp contrast with the indignation-revolt in which so many periods of unchallenged Catholic ascendancy have ended, we may take what we may call the "revolution conspiracy", in which a number of people set about organising the forces of discomfort and resentment and loosening the grip of the government's forces, in order to bring about a fundamental change of system. The ideal of this type is the Bolshevik Revolution in Russia, provided it is a little simplified and misunderstood. This, reduced to a working theory by its advocates, is conceived of as a systematic cultivation of a public state of mind favourable to a Revolution together with an inner circle of preparation for a "seizure of power". Quite a number of Communist and other leftish writers, bright young men, without much political experience, have let their imaginations loose upon the "technique" of such an adventure. They have brought the Nazi and Fascist Revolutions into the material for their studies. Modern social structure with its concentration of directive, information and coercive power about radio stations, telephone exchangers, newspaper offices, police stations, arsenals and the like, lends itself to quasi-gangster exploitation of this type. There is a great rushing about and occupation of key centres, an organised capture, imprisonment or murder of possible opponents, and the country is confronted with fait accompli. The regimentation of the more or less reluctant population follows.

But a Revolution need be neither an explosion nor a coup d'etat. And the Revolution that lies before us now as the only hopeful alternative to chaos, either directly or after an interlude of world communism, is to be attained, if it is attained at all, by neither of these methods. The first is too rhetorical and chaotic and leads simply to a Champion and tyranny; the second is too conspiratorial and leads through an obscure struggle of masterful personalities to a similar end. Neither is lucid enough and deliberate enough to achieve a permanent change in the form and texture of human affairs.

An altogether different type of Revolution may or may not be possible. No one can say that it is possible unless it is tried, but one can say with some assurance that unless it can be achieved the outlook for mankind for many generations at least is hopeless. The new Revolution aims essentially at a change in directive ideas. In its completeness it is an untried method.

It depends for its success upon whether a sufficient number of minds can be brought to realise that the choice before us now is not a choice between further revolution or more or less reactionary conservatism, but a choice between so carrying on and so organising the process of change in our affairs as to produce a new world order, or suffering an entire and perhaps irreparable social collapse. Our argument throughout has been that things have gone too far ever to be put back again to any similitude of what they have been. We can no more dream of remaining where we are than think of going back in the middle of a dive. We must go trough with these present changes, adapt ourselves to them, adjust ourselves to the plunge, or be destroyed by them. We must go through these changes just as we must go through this ill-conceived war, because there is as yet no possible end for it.

There will be no possible way of ending it until the new Revolution defines itself. If it is patched up now without a clear-headed settlement understood and accepted throughout the world, we shall have only the simulacrum of a peace. A patched-up peace now will not even save us from the horrors of war, it will postpone them only to aggravate them in a few years time. You cannot end this war yet, you can at best adjourn it.

The reorganisation of the world has at first to be mainly the work of a "movement" or a Party or a religion or cult, whatever we choose to call it. We may call it New Liberalism or the New Radicalism or what not. It will not be a close-knit organisation, toeing the Party line and so forth. It may be a very loose-knit and many faceted, but if a sufficient number of minds throughout the world, irrespective of race, origin or economic and social habituations, can be brought to the free and candid recognition of the essentials of the human problem, then their effective collaboration in a conscious, explicit and open effort to reconstruct human society will ensue.

And to begin with they will do all they can to spread and perfect this conception of a new world order, which they will regard as the only working frame for their activities, while at the same time they will set themselves to discover and associate with themselves, everyone, everywhere, who is intellectually able to grasp the same broad ideas and morally disposed to realise them.

The distribution of this essential conception one may call propaganda, but in reality it is education. The opening phase of this new type of Revolution must involve therefore a campaign for re-invigorated and modernised education throughout the world, an education that will have the same ratio to the education of a couple of hundred years ago, as the electric lighting of a contemporary city has to the chandeliers and oil lamps of the same period. On its present mental levels humanity can do no better than what it is doing now.

Vitalising education is only possible when it is under the influence of people who are themselves learning. It is inseparable from the modern idea of education that it should be knit up to incessant research. We say research rather than science. It is the better word because it is free from any suggestion of that finality which means dogmatism and death.

All education tends to become stylistic and sterile unless it is kept in close touch with experimental verification and practical work, and consequently this new movement of revolutionary initiative, must at the same time be sustaining realistic political and social activities and working steadily for the collectivisation of governments and economic life. The intellectual movement will be only the initiatory and correlating part of the new revolutionary drive. These practical activities must be various. Everyone engaged in them must be thinking for himself and not waiting for orders. The only dictatorship he will recognise is the dictatorship of the plain understanding and the invincible fact.

And if this culminating Revolution is to be accomplished, then the participation of every conceivable sort of human+being who has the mental grasp to see these broad realities of the world situation and the moral quality to do something about it, must be welcomed.

Previous revolutionary thrusts have been vitiated by bad psychology. They have given great play to the gratification of the inferiority complexes that arise out of class disadvantages. It is no doubt very unjust that anyone should be better educated, healthier and less fearful of the world than anyone else, but that is no reason why the new Revolution should not make the fullest use of the health, education, vigour and courage of the fortunate. The Revolution we are contemplating will aim at abolishing the bitterness of frustration. But certainly it will do nothing to avenge it. Nothing whatever. Let the dead past punish its dead.

It is one of the most vicious streaks in the Marxist teaching to suggest that all people of wealth and capacity living in a community in which unco- ordinated private enterprise plays a large part are necessarily demoralised by the advantages they enjoy and that they must be dispossessed by the worker and peasant, who are presented as endowed with a collective virtue capable of running all the complex machinery of a modern community. But the staring truth of the matter is that an uncoordinated scramble between individuals and nations alike, demoralises all concerned. Everyone is corrupted, the filching tramp by the roadside, the servile hand-kissing peasant of Eastern Europe, the dole-bribed loafer, as much as the woman who marries for money, the company promoter, the industrial organiser, the rent-exacting landlord and the diplomatic agent. When the social atmosphere is tainted everybody is ill.

Wealth, personal freedom and education, may and do produce wasters and oppressive people, but they may also release creative and administrative minds to opportunity. The history of science and invention before the nineteenth century confirms this. On the whole if we are to assume there is anything good in humanity at all, it is more reasonable to expect it to appear when there is most opportunity.

And in further confutation of the Marxist caricature of human motives, we have the very considerable number of young people drawn from middle-class and upper-class homes, who figure in the extreme left movement everywhere. It is their moral reaction to the "stuffiness" and social ineffectiveness of their parents and their own sort of people. They seek an outlet for their abilities that is not gainful but serviceable. Many have sought an honourable life--and often found it, and death with it--in the struggle against the Catholics and their Moorish and Fascist helpers in Spain.

It is a misfortune of their generation, that so many of them have fallen into the mental traps of Marxism. It has been my absurd experience to encounter noisy meetings of expensive young men at Oxford, not one of them stunted physically as I was by twenty years of under-nourishment and devitalised upbringing, all pretending to be rough-hewn collarless proletarians in shocked revolt against my bourgeois tyranny and the modest comfort of my declining years, and reciting the ridiculous class-war phrases by which they protected their minds from any recognition of the realities of the case. But though that attitude demonstrates the unstimulating education of their preparatory and public schools, which had thrown them thus uncritical and emotional into the problems of the undergraduate life, it does not detract from the fact that they had found the idea of abandoning themselves to a revolutionary reconstruction of society, that promised to end its enormous waste of potential happiness and achievement, extremely attractive, notwithstanding that their own advantages seemed to be reasonably secure.

Faced with the immediate approach of discomfort, indignity, wasted years, mutilation--death is soon over but one wakes up again to mutilation every morning--because of this ill-conceived war; faced also by the reversion of Russia to autocracy and the fiscal extinction of most of the social advantages of their families; these young people with a leftish twist are likely not only to do some very profitable reexamination of their own possibilities but also to find themselves joined in that re-examination by a very considerable number of others who have hitherto been repelled by the obvious foolishness and insincerity of the hammer and sickle symbols (workers and peasants of Oxford!) and the exasperating dogmatism of the orthodox Marxist. And may not these young people, instead of waiting to be overtaken by an insurrectionary revolution from which they will emerge greasy, unshaven, class-conscious and in incessant danger of liquidation, decide that before the Revolution gets hold of them they will get hold of the Revolution and save it from the inefficiency, mental distortions, disappointments and frustrations that have over-taken it in Russia.

This new and complete Revolution we contemplate can be defined in a very few words. It is (a) outright world-socialism, scientifically planned and directed, plus (b) a sustained insistence upon law, law based on a fuller, more jealously conceived resentment of the personal Rights of Man, plus (c) the completest freedom of speech, criticism and publication, and sedulous expansion of the educational organisation to the ever-growing demands of the new order. What we may call the eastern or Bolshevik Collectivism, the Revolution of the Internationale, has failed to achieve even the first of these three items and it has never even attempted the other two.

Putting it at its compactest, it is the triangle of Socialism, Law and Knowledge, which frames the Revolution which may yet save the world.

Socialism! Become outright collectivists? Very few men of the more fortunate classes in our old collapsing society who are over fifty will be able to readjust their minds to that. It will seem an entirely repulsive suggestion to them. (The average age of the British Cabinet at the present time is well over sixty.) But it need not be repulsive at all to their sons. They will be impoverished anyhow. The stars in their courses are seeing to that. And that will help them greatly to realise that an administrative control to administrative participation and then to direct administration are easy steps. They are being taken now, first in one matter and then in another. On both sides of the Atlantic. Reluctantly and often very disingenuously and against energetic but diminishing resistances. Great Britain, like America, may become a Socialist system with a definitive Revolution, protesting all the time that it is doing nothing of the sort.

In Britain we have now no distinctively educated class, but all up and down the social scale there are well-read men and women who have thought intensely upon these great problems we have been discussing. To many of them and maybe to enough of them to start the avalanche of purpose that will certainly develop from a clear and determined beginning, this conception of

Revolution to evoke a liberal collectivised world may appeal. And so at last we narrow down our enquiry to an examination of what has to be done now to save the Revolution, what the movement or its Party--so far as it may use the semblance of a Party will do, what its Policy will be. Hitherto we have been demonstrating why a reasonable man, of any race or language anywhere, should become a "Western" Revolutionary. We have now to review the immediate activities to which he can give himself.

30

IX. — POLITICS FOR THE SANE MAN

LET us restate the general conclusions to which our preceding argument has brought us.

The establishment of a progressive world socialism in which the freedoms, health and happiness of every individual are protected by a universal law based on a re-declaration of the rights of man, and wherein there is the utmost liberty of thought, criticism and suggestion, is the plain, rational objective before us now. Only the effective realisation of this objective can establish peace on earth and arrest the present march of human affairs to misery and destruction. We cannot reiterate this objective too clearly and too frequently. The triangle of collectivisation, law and knowledge should embody the common purpose of all mankind.

But between us and that goal intervenes the vast and deepening disorders of our time. The new order cannot be brought into existence without a gigantic and more or less co-ordinated effort of the saner and abler elements in the human population. The thing cannot be done rapidly and melodramatically. That effort must supply the frame for all sane social and political activities and a practical criterion for all religious and educational associations. But since our world is multitudinously varied and confused, it is impossible to narrow down this new revolutionary movement to any single class, organisation or Party. It is too great a thing for that. It will in its expansion produce and perhaps discard a number of organisations and Parties, converging upon its ultimate objective. Consequently, in order to review the social and political activities of sane, clear-headed people to-day, we have to deal with them piecemeal from a number of points of view. We have to consider an advance upon a long and various front.

Let us begin then with the problem of sanity in face of the political methods of our time. What are we to do as voting citizens? There I think the history of the so-called democracies in the past half-century is fairly conclusive. Our present electoral methods which give no choice but a bilateral choice to the citizen and so force a two-party system upon him, is a mere caricature of representative government. It has produced upon both sides of the Atlantic, big, stupid, and corrupt party machines. That was bound to happen and yet to this day there is a sort of shyness in the minds of young men interested in politics when it comes to discussing Proportional Representation. They think it is a "bit faddy". At best it is a side issue. Party politicians strive to maintain that bashfulness, because they know quite clearly that what is called Proportional Representation with the single transferable vote in large constituencies, returning a dozen members or more, is extinction for the mere party hack and destruction for party organisations.

The machine system in the United States is more elaborate, more deeply entrenched legally in the Constitution and illegally in the spoils system, and it may prove more difficult to modernise than the British, which is based on an outworn caste tradition. But both Parliament and Congress are essentially similar in their fundamental quality. They trade in titles, concessions and the public welfare, and they are only amenable in the rough and at long last to the movements of public opinion. It is an open question whether they are much more responsive to popular feeling than the Dictators we denounce so unreservedly as the antithesis of democracy. They betray a great disregard of mass responses. They explain less. They disregard more. The Dictators have to go on talking and talking, not always truthfully but they have to talk. A dumb Dictator is inconceivable.

In such times of extensive stress and crisis as the present, the baffling slowness, inefficiency and wastefulness of the party system become so manifest that some of its worst pretences are put aside. The party game is suspended. His Majesty's Opposition abandons the pose of safeguarding the interests of the common citizens from those scoundrels upon the government benches; Republican and Democrats begin to cross the party line to discuss the new situation. Even the men who live professionally by the Parliamentary (Congressional) imposture, abandon it if they are sufficiently frightened by the posture of affairs. The appearance of an All-Party National Government in Great Britain before very long seems inevitable.

Great Britain has in effect gone socialist in a couple of months; she is also suspending party politics. Just as the United States did in the great slump. And in both cases this has happened because the rottenness and inefficiency of party politics stank to heaven in the face of danger. And since in both cases Party Government threw up its hands and bolted, is there any conceivable reason why we should let it come back at any appearance of victory or recovery, why we should not go ahead from where we are to a less impromptu socialist regime under a permanent non-party administration, to the reality if not to the form of a permanent socialist government?

Now here I have nothing to suggest about America. I have never, for example, tried to work out the consequences of the absence of executive ministers from the legislature. I am inclined to think that is one of the weak points in the Constitution and that the English usage which exposes the minister to question time in the House and makes him a prime mover in legislation affecting his department, is a less complicated and therefore more democratic arrangement than the American one. And the powers and functions of the President and the Senate are so different from the consolidated powers of Cabinet and Prime Minister, that even when an Englishman has industriously "mugged up" the constitutional points, he is still almost as much at a loss to get the living reality as he would be if he were shown the score of an opera before hearing it played or the blue prints of a machine he had never seen in action. Very few Europeans understand the history of Woodrow Wilson, the Senate and his League of Nations. They think that "America", which they imagine as a large single individual, planted the latter institution upon Europe and then deliberately shuffled out of her responsibility for it, and they will never think otherwise. And they think that "America" kept out of the war to the very limit of decency, overcharged us for munitions that contributed to the common victory, and made a grievance because the consequent debt was not discharged. They talk like that while Americans talk as if no English were killed between 1914 and 1918 (we had 800,000 dead) until the noble American conscripts came forward to die for them (to the tune of about 50,000). Savour for example even the title of Quincy Howe's England expects every American to do his Duty. It's the meanest of titles, but many Americans seem to like it.

On my desk as I write is a pamphlet by a Mr Robert Randall, nicely cyclostyled and got up. Which urges a common attack on the United States as a solution of the problem of Europe. No countries will ever feel united unless they have a common enemy, and the natural common enemy for Europe, it is declared, is the United States. So to bring about the United States of Europe we are to begin by denouncing the Monroe doctrine. I believe in the honesty and good intentions of Mr Robert Randall; he is, I am sure, no more in the pay of Germany, direct or indirect, than Mr Quincy Howe or Mr Harry Elmer Barnes; but could the most brilliant of Nazi war propagandists devise a more effective estranging suggestion?

But I wander from my topic. I do not know how sane men in America are going to set about relaxing the stranglehold of the Constitution, get control of their own country out of the hands of those lumpish, solemnly cunning politicians with their great strong jowls developed by chewing-gum and orotund speaking, whose photographs add a real element of frightfulness to the pages of Time, how they are going to abolish the spoils system, discover, and educate to expand a competent civil service able to redeem the hampered promises of the New Deal and pull America into line with the reconstruction of the rest of the world. But I perceive that in politics and indeed in most things, the underlying humour and sanity of Americans are apt to find a way round and do the impossible, and I have as little doubt they will manage it somehow as I have when I see a street performer on his little chair and carpet, all tied up with chains, waiting until there are sufficient pennies in the hat to justify exertion.

These differences in method, pace and tradition are a great misfortune to the whole English-speaking world. We English people do not respect Americans enough; we are too disposed to think they are all Quincy Howes and Harry Elmer Barneses and Borahs and suchlike, conceited and suspicious anti-British monomaniacs, who must be humoured at any cost; which is why we are never so frank and rude with them as they deserve. But the more we must contain ourselves the less we love them. Real brothers can curse each other and keep friends. Someday Britannia will give Columbia a piece of her mind, and that may clear the air. Said an exasperated Englishman to me a day or so ago: "I pray to God they keep out of the end of this war anyhow. We shall never hear the last of it if they don't...."

Yet at a different pace our two people are travelling towards identical ends, and it is lamentable that a difference of accent and idiom should do more mischief than a difference of language.

So far as Great Britain goes things are nearer and closer to me, and it seems to me that there is an excellent opportunity now to catch the country in a state of socialisation and suspend party politics, and keep it at that. It is a logical but often disregarded corollary of the virtual creation of All-Party National Governments and suspension of electoral contests, that since there is no Opposition, party criticism should give place to individual criticism of ministers, and instead of throwing out governments we should set ourselves to throw out individual administrative failures. We need no longer confine our choice of public servants to political careerists. We can insist upon men who have done things and can do things, and whenever an election occurs we can organise a block of non-party voters who will vote it possible for an outsider of proved ability, and will at any rate insist on a clear statement from every Parliamentary candidate of the concrete service, if any, he has done the country, of his past and present financial entanglements and his family relationships and of any title he possesses. We can get these necessary particulars published and note what newspapers decline to do so. And if there are still only politicians to vote for, we can at least vote and spoil our voting cards by way of protest.

At present we see one public service after another in a mess through the incompetent handling of some party hack and the unseen activities of interested parties. People are asking already why Sir Arthur Salter is not in control of Allied Shipping again, Sir John Orr directing our food supply with perhaps Sir Fredrick Keeble to help him, Sir Robert Vansittart in the Foreign Office. We want to know the individuals responsible for the incapacity of our Intelligence and Propaganda Ministries, so that we may induce them to quit public life. It would be quite easy now to excite a number of anxious people with a cry for "Competence not Party".

Most people in the British Isles are heartily sick of Mr Chamberlain and his government, but they cannot face up to a political split in wartime, and Mr Chamberlain sticks to office with all the pertinacity of a Barnacle. But if we do not attack the government as a whole, but individual ministers, and if we replace them one by one, we shall presently have a government so rejuvenated that even Mr Chamberlain will realise and accept his superannuation. Quite a small body of public-spirited people could organise an active Vigilance Society to keep these ideas before the mass of voters and begin the elimination of inferior elements from our public life. This would be a practical job of primary importance in our political regeneration. It would lead directly to a new and more efficient political structure to carry on after the present war has collapsed or otherwise ended.

Following upon this campaign for the conclusive interment of the played- out party system, there comes the necessity for a much more strenuous search for administrative and technical ability throughout the country. We do not want to miss a single youngster who can be of use in the great business of making over Great Britain, which has been so rudely, clumsily and wastefully socialised by our war perturbations, so that it may become a permanently efficient system.

And from the base of the educational pyramid up to its apex of higher education of teachers, heads of departments and research, there is need for such a quickening of minds and methods as only a more or less organised movement of sanely critical men can bring about. We want ministers now of the highest quality in every department, but in no department of public life is a man of creative understanding, bold initiative and administrative power so necessary as in the Education Ministry.

So tranquil and unobtrusive has been the flow of educational affairs in the British Empire that it seems almost scandalous, and it is certainly "vulgar", to suggest that we need an educational Ginger Group to discover and support such a minister. We want a Minister of Education who can shock teachers into self-examination, electrify and rejuvenate old dons or put them away in ivory towers, and stimulate the younger ones. Under the party system the Education Ministry has always been a restful corner for some deserving party politician with an abject respect for his

Alma Mater and the permanent officials. During war time, when other departments wake up, the Education Department sinks into deeper lethargy. One cannot recall a single British Education Minister, since there have been such things in our island story as Ministers for Education, who signified anything at all educationally or did anything of his own impulse that was in the least worth while.

Suppose we found a live one--soon--and let him rip!

There again is something to be done far more revolutionary than throwing bombs at innocent policemen or assassinating harmless potentates or ex- potentates. And yet it is only asking that an existing department be what it pretends to be.

A third direction in which any gathering accumulation of sanity should direct its attention is the clumsy unfairness and indirectness of our present methods of expropriating the former well-to-do classes. The only observable principle seems to be widows and children first. Socialisation is being effected in Britain and America alike not by frank expropriation (with or without compensation) but by increasing government control and increasing taxation. Both our great communities are going into socialism backward and without ever looking round. This is good in so far as that technical experience and directive ability is changed over step by step from entirely private employment to public service, and on that side sane and helpful citizens have little to do beyond making the process conscious of itself and the public aware of the real nature of the change, but it is bad in its indiscriminate destruction of savings, which are the most exposed and vulnerable side of the old system. They are expropriated by profit-control and taxation alike, and at the same time they suffer in purchasing power by the acceleration of that process of monetary inflation which is the unavoidable readjustment, the petition in bankruptcy, of a community that has overspent.

The shareholding class dwindles and dies; widows and orphans, the old who are past work and the infirm who are incapable of it, are exposed in their declining years to a painful shrinkage of their modes of living; there is no doubt a diminution of social waste, but also there is an indirect impoverishment of free opinion and free scientific and artistic initiative as the endless societies, institutions and services which have enriched life for us and been very largely supported by voluntary subscriptions, shrivel. At present a large proportion of our scientific, artistic, literary and social workers are educated out of the private savings fund. In a class-war revolution these economically very defenceless but socially very convenient people are subjected to vindictive humiliation -it is viewed as a great triumph for their meaner neighbours--but a revolution sanely conducted will probably devise a system of terminable annuities and compensation, and of assistance to once voluntary associations, which will ease off the social dislocations due to the disappearance of one stratum of relatively free and independent people, before its successors, that is to say the growing class of retired officials, public administrators and so forth, find their feet and develop their own methods of assertion and enterprise.

31

X. — DECLARATION OF THE RIGHTS OF MAN

LET us turn now to another system of problems in the collectivisation of the world, and that is the preservation of liberty in the socialist state and the restoration of that confidence without which good behaviour is generally impossible.

This destruction of confidence is one of the less clearly recognised evils of the present phase of world-disintegration. In the past there have been periods when whole communities or at least large classes within communities have gone about their business with a general honesty, directness and sense of personal honour. They have taken a keen pride in the quality of their output. They have lived through life on tolerable and tolerant terms with their neighbours. The laws they observed have varied in different countries and periods, but their general nature was to make an orderly law-abiding life possible and natural. They had been taught and they believed and they had every reason to believe: "This (that or the other thing) is right. Do right and nothing, except by some strange exceptional misfortune, can touch you. The Law guarantees you that. Do right and nothing will rob you or frustrate you."

Nowhere in the world now is there very much of that feeling left, and as it disappears, the behaviour of people degenerates towards a panic scramble, towards cheating, over-reaching, gang organisation, precautionary hoarding, concealment and all the meanness and anti-social feeling which is the natural outcome of insecurity.

Faced with what now amounts to something like a moral stampede, more and more sane men will realise the urgency for a restoration of confidence. The more socialisation proceeds and the more directive authority is concentrated, the more necessary is an efficient protection of individuals from the impatience of well-meaning or narrow-minded or ruthless officials and indeed from all the possible abuses of advantage that are inevitable under such circumstances to our still childishly wicked breed.

In the past the Atlantic world has been particularly successful in expedients for meeting this aspect of human nature. Our characteristic and traditional method may be called the method of the fundamental declaration. Our Western peoples, by a happy instinct, have produced statements of Right, from Magna Carta onwards, to provide a structural defence between the citizen and the necessary growth of central authority.

And plainly the successful organisation of the more universal and penetrating collectivism that is now being forced upon us all, will be frustrated in its most vital aspect unless its organisation is accompanied by the preservative of a new Declaration of the Rights of Man, that must, because of the increasing complexity of the social structure, be more generous, detailed and explicit than any of its predecessors. Such a Declaration must become the common fundamental law of all communities and collectivities assembled under the World Pax. It should be interwoven with the declared war aims of the combatant powers now; it should become the primary fact in any settlement; it should be put before the now combatant states for their approval, their embarrassed silence or their rejection.

In order to be as clear as possible about this, let me submit a draft for your consideration of this proposed Declaration of the Rights of Man--using "man" of course to cover every individual, male or female, of the species. I have endeavoured to bring in everything that is essential and to omit whatever secondary issues can be easily deduced from its general statements. It is a draft for your consideration. Points may have been overlooked and it may contain repetitions and superfluous statements.

"Since a man comes into this world through no fault of his own, since he is manifestly a joint inheritor of the accumulations of the past, and since those accumulations are more than sufficient to justify the claims that are here made for him, it follows:

"(1) That every man without distinction of race, of colour or of professed belief or opinions, is entitled to the nourishment, covering, medical care and attention needed to realise his full possibilities of physical and mental development and to keep him in a state of health from his birth to death.

"(2) That he is entitled to sufficient education to make him a useful and interested citizen, that special education should be so made available as to give him equality of opportunity for the development of his distinctive gifts in the service of mankind, that he should have easy access to information upon all matters of common knowledge throughout his life and enjoy the utmost freedom of discussion, association and worship.

"(3) That he may engage freely in any lawful occupation, earning such pay as the need for his work and the increment it makes to the common welfare may justify. That he is entitled to paid employment and to a free choice whenever there is any variety of employment open to him. He may suggest employment for himself and have his claim publicly considered, accepted or dismissed.

"(4) That he shall have the right to buy or sell without any discriminatory restrictions anything which may be lawfully bought or sold, in such quantities and with such reservations as are compatible with the common welfare."

(Here I will interpolate a comment. We have to bear in mind that in a collectivist state buying and selling to secure income and profit will be not simply needless but impossible. The Stock Exchange, after its career of four- hundred-odd-years, will necessarily vanish with the disappearance of any rational motive either for large accumulations or for hoarding against deprivation and destitution. Long before the age of complete collectivisation arrives, the savings of individuals for later consumption will probably be protected by some development of the Unit Trust System into a public service. They will probably be entitled to interest at such a rate as to compensate for that secular inflation which should go on in a steadily enriched world community. Inheritance and bequest in a community in which the means of production and of all possible monopolisation are collectivised, can concern little else than relatively small, beautiful and intimate objects, which will afford pleasure but no unfair social advantage to the receiver.)

"(5) That he and his personal property lawfully acquired are entitled to police and legal protection from private violence, deprivation, compulsion and intimidation.

"(6) That he may move freely about the world at his own expense. That his private house or apartment or reasonably limited garden enclosure is his castle, which may be entered only with consent, but that he shall have the right to come and go over any kind of country, moorland, mountain, farm, great garden or what not, or upon the seas, lakes and rivers of the world, where his presence will not be destructive of some special use, dangerous to himself nor seriously inconvenient to his fellow-citizens.

"(7) That a man unless he is declared by a competent authority to be a danger to himself and to others through mental abnormality, a declaration which must be annually confirmed, shall not be imprisoned for a longer period than six days without being charged with a definite offence against the law, nor for more than three months without public trial. At the end if the latter period, if he has not been tried and sentenced by due process of law, he shall be released. Nor shall he be conscripted for military, police or any other service to which he has a conscientious objection.

"(8) That although a man is subject to the free criticism of his fellows, he shall have adequate protection from any lying or misrepresentation that may distress or injure him. All administrative registration and records about a man shall be open to his personal and private inspection. There shall be no secret dossiers in any administrative department. All dossiers shall be accessible to the man concerned and subject to verification and correction at his challenge. A dossier is merely a memorandum; it cannot be used as evidence without proper confirmation in open court.

"(9) That no man shall be subjected to any sort of mutilation or sterilisation except with his own deliberate consent, freely given, nor to bodily assault, except in restraint of his own violence, nor to torture, beating or any other bodily punishment; he shall not be subjected to imprisonment with such an excess of silence, noise, light or darkness as to cause mental suffering, or to imprisonment in infected, verminous or otherwise insanitary quarters, or be put into the company of verminous or infectious people. He shall not be forcibly fed nor prevented from starving himself if he so desire. He shall not be forced to take drugs nor shall they be administered to him without his knowledge and consent. That the extreme punishments to which he may be subjected are rigorous imprisonment for a term of not longer than fifteen years or death."

(Here I would point out that there is nothing in this to prevent any country from abolishing the death penalty any country from abolishing the death penally. Nor do I assert a general right to commit suicide, because no one can punish a man for doing that. He has escaped. But threats and incompetent attempts to commit suicide belong to an entirely different category. They are indecent and distressing acts that can easily become a serious social nuisance, from which the normal citizen is entitled to protection.)

"(10) That the provisions and principles embodied in this Declaration shall be more fully defined in a code of fundamental human rights which shall be made easily accessible to everyone. This Declaration shall not be qualified nor departed from upon any pretext whatever. It incorporates all previous Declarations of Human Right. Henceforth for a new ear it is the fundamental law for mankind throughout the whole world.

"No treaty and no law affecting these primary rights shall be binding upon any man or province or administrative division of the community, that has not been made openly, by and with the active or tacit acquiescence of every adult citizen concerned, either given by a direct majority vote of his publicly elected representatives. In matters of collective behaviour it is by the majority decision men must abide. No administration, under a pretext of urgency, convenience or the like, shall be entrusted with powers to create or further define offences or set up bylaws, which will in any way infringe the rights and liberties here asserted. All legislation must be public and definite. No secret treaties shall be binding on individuals, organisations or communities. No orders in council or the like, which extend the application of a law, shall be permitted. There is no source of law but the people, and since life flows on constantly to new citizens, no generation of the people can in whole or in part surrender or delegate the legislative power inherent in mankind."

There, I think, is something that keener minds than mine may polish into a working Declaration which would in the most effective manner begin that restoration of confidence of which the world stands in need. Much of it might be better phrased, but I think it embodies the general good-will in mankind from pole to pole. It is certainly what we all want for ourselves. It could be a very potent instrument indeed in the present phase of human affairs. It is necessary and it is acceptable. Incorporate that in your peace treaties and articles of federation, I would say, and you will have a firm foundation, which will continually grow firmer, for the fearless cosmopolitan life of a new world order. You will never get that order without some such document. It is the missing key to endless contemporary difficulties.

And if we, the virtuous democracies, are not fighting for these common human rights, then what in the name of the nobility and gentry, the Crown and the Established Church, the City, The Times and the Army and Navy Club, are we common British peoples fighting for?

32

XI. — INTERNATIONAL POLITICS

AND now, having completed our picture of what the saner elements in human society may reasonably work for and hope for, having cleared away the horrible nightmares of the class war and the totalitarian slave-state from our imaginations, we are able to attack the immediate riddles of international conflict and relationship with some hope of a general solution. If we realise to the depths of our being that a world settlement based in the three ideas of socialism, law and knowledge, is not only possible and desirable, but the only way of escape from deepening disaster, then manifestly our attitude towards the resentments of Germany, the prejudices of America or Russia, the poverty and undernourishment of India or the ambitions of Japan, must be frankly opportunist. None of these are primary issues. We sane men must never lose sight of our ultimate objective, but our methods of getting there will have to vary with the fluctuating variations of national feeling and national policy.

There is this idea of federalism upon which I have already submitted a criticism in chapter seven. As I have shown there, the Streit proposals will either take you further or land you nowhere. Let us assume that we can strengthen his proposals to the extent of making a socialistic economic consortium and adhesion to that Declaration of Rights, primary conditions for any federal union; then it becomes a matter of mood and occasion with what communities the federal association may be begun. We can even encourage feeble federal experiments which do not venture even so far as that along the path to sanity, in the certainty that either they will fade out again or else that they will become liberal realities of the type to which the whole world must ultimately conform. Behind any such half-hearted tentatives an educational propaganda can be active and effective.

But when it comes to the rate and amount of participation in the construction of a rational world order we can expect from any country or group of countries, we are in a field where there is little more than guessing and haphazard generalisations about "national character" to work upon. We are dealing with masses of people which may be swayed enormously by a brilliant newspaper or an outstandingly persuasive or compelling personality or by almost accidental changes in the drift of events. I, for example, cannot tell how far the generality of educated and capable people in the British Empire now may fall in with our idea of accepting and serving a collectivism, or how strong their conservative resistance may be. It is my own country and I ought to know it best, and I do not know it detachedly enough or deeply enough to decide that. I do not see how anyone can foretell these swirls and eddies of response.

The advocacy of such movements of the mind and will as I am speaking of here is in itself among the operating causes in political adjustment, and those who are deepest in the struggle are least able to estimate how it is going. Every factor in political and international affairs is a fluctuating factor. The wise man therefore will not set his heart upon any particular drift or combination. He will favour everything that trends towards the end at which he aims.

The present writer cherishes the idea that the realisation of a common purpose and a common cultural inheritance may spread throughout all the English-speaking communities, and there can be no harm in efforts to give this concrete expression. He believes the dissociation of the British Empire may inaugurate this great synthesis. At the same time there are factors making for some closer association of the United States of America with what are called the Oslo powers. There is no reason why one of these associations should stand in the way of the other. Some countries such as Canada rest already under what is practically a double guarantee; she has the security of the Monroe Doctrine and the protection of the British fleet.

A Germany of eighty million people which has been brought to acquiesce in the Declaration of the Rights of Man and which is already highly collectivised, may come much earlier to a completely liberal socialist regime than Great Britain or France. If she participates in a consortium for the development of what are called the politically backward regions of the world, she may no longer be disposed for further military adventures and further stress and misery. She may enter upon a phase of social and economic recovery so rapid as to stimulate and react upon every other country in the world. It is not for other countries to dictate her internal politics, and if the German people want to remain united as one people, in federated states or in one centralised state, there is neither righteousness nor wisdom preventing them.

The Germans like the rest of the world have to get on with collectivisation, they have to produce their pattern, and they cannot give themselves to that if they are artificially divided up and disorganised by some old-fashioned Quai d'Orsay scheme. They must do the right thing in their own way.

That the belligerent tradition may linger on in Germany for a generation or so, is a risk the Atlantic powers have to take. The world has a right to insist that not simply some German government but the people generally, recognise unequivocably and repeatedly, the rights of man asserted in the Declaration, and it is disarmed and that any aggressive plant, any war plane, warship, gun or arsenal that is discovered in the country shall be destroyed forthwith, brutally and completely. But that is a thing that should not be confined to Germany. Germany should not be singled out for that. Armament should be an illegality everywhere, and some sort of international force should patrol a treaty-bound world. Partial armament is one of those absurdities dear to moderate-minded "reasonable" men. Armament itself is making war. Making a gun, pointing a gun and firing it, are all acts of the same order. It should be illegal to construct anywhere upon earth, any mechanism for the specific purpose of killing men. When you see a gun it is reasonable to ask: "Whom is that intended to kill?"

Germany's rearmament after 1918 was largely tolerated because she played off British Russophobia against the Russian fear of "Capitalist" attack, but that excuse can no longer serve any furtive war-mongers among her people after her pact with Moscow.

Released from the economic burdens and restrictions that crippled her recovery after 1918, Germany may find a full and satisfying outlet for the energy of her young men in her systematic collectivisation, raising the standard of her common life deliberately and steadily, giving Russia a lead in efficiency and obliging the maundering "politics" and discursive inattention of the Atlantic world to remain concentrated upon the realities of life. The idea of again splitting up Germany into discordant fragments so as to postpone her ultimate recovery indefinitely, is a pseudo-democratic slacker's dream. It is diametrically opposed to world reconstruction. We have need of the peculiar qualities of her people, and the sooner she recovers the better for the whole world. It is preposterous to resume the policy of holding back Germany simply that the old order may enjoy a few more years of self-indulgence in England, France and America.

A lingering fear of German military aggression may not be altogether bad for the minor states of South-Eastern Europe and Asia Minor, by breaking down their excessive nationalism and inducing them to work together. The policy of the sane man should be to welcome every possible experiment in international understandings duplicate and overlap one another, so much the better. He has to watch the activities of his own Foreign Office with incessant jealousy, for signs of that Machiavellian spirit which foments division among foreign governments and peoples and schemes perpetually to frustrate the progressive movement in human affairs by converting it into a swaying indecisive balance of power.

This book is a discussion of guiding principles and not of the endless specific problems of adjustment that arise on the way to a world realisation of collective unity. I will merely glance at that old idea of Napoleon the Third's, the Latin Union, at the possibility of a situation in Spanish and Portuguese South America parallel to that overlap of the Monroe Doctrine and the European motherlands which already exists in practice in the case of Canada, nor will I expatiate upon the manifold possibilities of sincere application of the Declaration of the Rights of Man to India and Africa--and particularly to those parts of the world in which more or less black peoples are awakening to the realities of racial discrimination and oppression.

I will utter a passing warning against any Machiavellian treatment of the problem of Northern and Eastern Asia, into which the British may be led by their constitutional Russophobia. The Soviet collectivism, especially if presently it becomes liberalised and more efficient through a recovery from its present obsession by Stalin, may spread very effectively across Central Asia and China. To anyone nourished mentally upon the ideas of an unending competition of Powers for ascendancy for ever and ever, an alliance with Japan, as truculent and militarised a Japan as possible, will seem the most natural response in the world. But to anyone who has grasped the reality of the present situation of mankind and the urgent desirableness of world collectivisation, this immense unification will be something to welcome, criticise and assist.

The old bugbear of Russia's "designs upon India" may also play its part in distorting the Asiatic situation for many people. Yet a hundred years of mingled neglect, exploitation and occasional outbreaks of genuine helpfulness should have taught the British that the ultimate fate of India's hundreds of millions rests now upon no conquering ruler but wholly and solely upon the ability of the Indian peoples to co-operate in world collectivisation. They may learn much by way of precept and example from Russia and from the English-speaking world, but the days for mere revolt or for relief by a change of masters have passed. India has to work out for itself, with its own manner of participation in the struggle for a world order, starting from the British raj as a datum line. No outside power can work that out for the Indian peoples, nor force them to do it if they have no will for it.

But I will not wander further among these ever-changing problems and possibilities. They are, so to speak, wayside eventualities and opportunities. Immense though some of them are they remain secondary. Every year or so now the shifting channels of politics need to be recharted. The activities and responses of the sane man in any particular country and at any particular time will be determined always by the overruling conception of a secular movement towards a single world order. That will be the underlying permanent objective of all his political life.

There is, however, another line of world consolidation to which attention must be drawn before we conclude this section, and is what we may call ad hoc internationalism is admirably set forth in Leonard Woolf s International Government, a classic which was published in 1916 and still makes profitable reading.

The typical ad hoc organisation is the Postal Union, which David Lubin, that brilliant neglected thinker, would have had extended until it controlled shipping and equalised freights throughout the world. He based his ideas upon his practical experience of the mail order business from which he derived his very considerable fortune. From that problem of freight adjustment he passed to the idea of a controlled survey of world, so that a shortage here or a glut there could be foreseen and remedied in time. He realised the idea in the form of the International Institute of Agriculture at Rome, which in its heyday made treaties like an independent sovereign power for the supply of returns from nearly every government upon earth. The war of 1914 and Lubin's death in 1919 checked the development of this admirable and most inspiring experiment in ad hoc internationalism. Its history is surely something that should be made part of the compulsory education of every statesmen and publicist. Yet never in my life have I met a professional politician who knew anything whatever or wanted to know anything about it. It didn't get votes; it seemed difficult to tax it; what was the good of it?

Another ad hoc organisation which might be capable of a considerable extension of its functions is the Elder Brethren of Trinity House, who control the lighthouses and charting of the seas throughout the world. But it would need a very considerable revision and extension of Mr Woolf s book and, in spite of the war stresses that have delayed and in some cases reversed their development, it would be quite beyond our present scope, to bring up to date the lengthening tale of ad hoc international networks, ranging from international business cartels, scientific and technical organisations, white-slave-trade suppression and international police co-operation, to health services and religious missions. Just as I have suggested that the United States and Great Britain may become complete socialisms unawares, so it is a not altogether impossible dream that the world may discover to its great surprise that it is already practically a cosmopolis, through the extension and interweaving of these ad hoc co-operations. At any rate we have this very powerful collateral process going on side by side with the more definite political schemes we have discussed.

Surveying the possibilities of these various attacks upon the complicated and intricate obstacles that stand between us and a new and more hopeful world order, one realises both the reasons for hope in that great possibility and the absurdity over over-confidence. We are all like soldiers upon a vast battlefield; we cannot be sure of the trend of things; we may be elated when disillusionment is rushing headlong upon us; we may be on the verge of despair, not knowing that our antagonists are already in collapse. My own reactions vary between an almost mystical faith in the ultimate triumph of human reason and good-will, and moods of stoical determination to carry on to the end in the face of what looks like inevitable disaster. There are quantitative factors in the outlook for which there are no data; there are elements of time and opportunity beyond any estimating. Every one of these activities we have been canvassing tends to delay the drift to destruction and provides a foothold for a further counter-offensive against the adversary.

In the companion predecessor to this book, The Fate of Homo sapiens, I tried to drive home the fact that our species has no more reason to believe it can escape defeat and extinction, than any other organism that plays or has played its part in the drama of life. I tried to make clear how precarious is our present situation, and how urgent it is that we should make a strenuous effort at adjustment now. Only a little while ago it seemed as though that was an appeal to a deaf and blind world, invincibly set in its habitual ways into the question whether this inclination towards pessimism reflected a mood or phase in myself, and I threw out a qualifying suggestion or so; but for my own part I could not find any serious reason to believe that the mental effort that was clearly necessary if man was to escape that fate that marched upon him would ever be made. His conservative resistances, his apathy, seemed incurable.

Now suddenly everywhere one meets with alarmed and open and enquiring minds. So far the tremendous dislocations of the present war have been immensely beneficial in stripping off what seemed to be quite invincible illusions of security only a year ago. I never expected to live to see the world with its eyes as widely open as they are to-day. The world has never been so awake. Little may come of it, much may come of it. We do not know. Life would amount to nothing at all if we did.

33

XII. — WORLD ORDER IN BEING

THERE will be no day of days then when a new world order comes into being. Step by step and here and there it will arrive, and even as it comes into being it will develop fresh perspectives, discover unsuspected problems and go on to new adventures. No man, no group of men, will ever be singled out as its father or founder. For its maker will be not this man nor that man nor any man but Man, that being who is in some measure in every one of us. World order will be, like science, like most inventions, a social product, an innumerable number of personalities will have lived fine lives, pouring their best into the collective achievement.

We can find a small-scale parallel to the probable development of a new world order in the history of flying. Less than a third of a century ago, ninety-nine people out of a hundred would have told you that flying was impossible; kites and balloons and possibly even a navigable balloon, they could imagine; they had known of such things for a hundred years; but a heavier then air machine, flying in defiance of wind and gravity! That they knew was nonsense. The would-be aviator was the typical comic inventor. Any fool could laugh at him. Now consider how completely the air is conquered.

And who did it? Nobody and everybody. Twenty thousand brains or so, each contributing a notion, a device, an amplification. They stimulated one another; they took off from one another. They were like excited ganglia in a larger brain sending their impulses to and fro. They were people of the most diverse race and colour. You can write down perhaps a hundred people or so who have figured conspicuously in the air, and when you examine the role they have played, you will find for the most part that they are mere notorieties of the Lindbergh type who have put themselves modestly but firmly in the limelight and can lay no valid claim to any effective contribution whatever. You will find many disputes about records and priority in making this or that particular step, but the lines of suggestion, the growth and elaboration of the idea, have been an altogether untraceable process. It has been going on for not more than a third of a century, under our very eyes, and no one can say precisely how it came about. One man said "Why not this?" and tried it, and another said "Why not that?" A vast miscellany of people had one idea in common, an idea as old as Daedalus, the idea that "Man can fly". Suddenly, swiftly, it got about--that is the only phrase you can use --that flying was attainable. And man, man as a social being, turned his mind to it seriously, and flew.

So it will certainly be with the new world order, if ever it is attained. A growing miscellany of people are saying--it is getting about--that "World Pax is possible", a World Pax in which men will be both united and free and creative. It is of no importance at all that nearly every man of fifty and over receives the idea with a pitying smile. Its chief dangers are the dogmatist and the would-be "leader" who will try to suppress every collateral line of work which does not minister to his supremacy. This movement must be, and it must remain, many-headed. Suppose the world had decided that Santos Dumont or Hiram Maxim was the heaven-sent Master of the Air, had given him the right to appoint a successor and subjected all experiments to his inspired control. We should probably have the Air Master now, with an applauding retinue of yes-men, following the hops of some clumsy, useless and extremely dangerous apparatus across country with the utmost dignity and self-satisfaction ....

Yet that is precisely how we still set about our political and social problems.

Bearing this essential fact in mind that the Peace of Man can only be attained, if it is attained at all, by an advance upon a long and various front, at varying speed and with diverse equipment, keeping direction only by a common faith in the triple need for collectivism, law and research, we realise the impossibility of drawing any picture of the new order as though it was as settled and stable as the old order imagined itself to be. The new order will be incessant; things will never stop happening, and so it defies any Utopian description. But we may nevertheless assemble a number of possibilities that will be increasingly realisable as the tide of disintegration ebbs and the new order is revealed.

To begin with we have to realise certain peculiarities of human behaviour that are all too disregarded in general political speculation. We have considered the very important role that may be played in our contemporary difficulties by a clear statement of the Rights of Man, and we have sketched such a Declaration. There is not an item in that Declaration, I believe, which a man will not consider to be a reasonable demand--so far as he himself is concerned. He will subscribe to it in that spirit very readily. But when he is asked not only to concede by the same gesture to everybody else in the world, but as something for which he has to make all the sacrifices necessary for its practical realisation, he will discover a reluctance to "go so far as that". He will find a serious resistance welling up from his sub-conscious and trying to justify itself in his thoughts.

The things he will tell you will be very variable; but the word "premature" will play a large part in it. He will display a tremendous tenderness and consideration with which you have never credited him before, for servants, for workers, for aliens and particularly for aliens of a different colour from himself. They will hurt themselves with all this dangerous liberty. Are they fit, he will ask you, for all this freedom? "Candidly, are they fit for it?" He will be slightly offended if you will say, "As fit as you are". He will say in a slightly amused tone, "But how can you say that?" and then going off rather at a tangent, "I am afraid you idealise your fellow-creatures."

As you press him, you will find this kindliness evaporating from his resistance altogether. He is now concerned about the general beauty and loveliness of the world. He will protest that this new Magna Carta will reduce all the world to "a dead level of uniformity". You will ask him why must a world of free-men be uniform and at a dead level? You will get no adequate reply. It is an assumption of vital importance to him and he must cling to it. He has been accustomed to associate "free" and "equal", and has never been bright-minded enough to take these two words apart and have a good look at them separately. He is likely to fall back at this stage upon that Bible of the impotent genteel, Huxley's Brave New World, and implore you to read it. You brush that disagreeable fantasy aside and continue to press him. He says that nature has made men unequal, and you reply that that is no reason for exaggerating the fact. The more unequal and various their gifts, the greater is the necessity for a Magna Carta to protect them from one another. Then he will talk of robbing life of the picturesque and the romantic and you will have some difficulty in getting these words defined. Sooner or later it will grow clear that he finds the prospect of a world in which "Jack's as good as his Master" unpleasant to the last degree.

If you still probe him with questions and leading suggestions, you will begin to realise how large a part the need for glory over his fellows plays in his composition (and incidentally you will note, please, you own secret satisfaction in carrying the argument against him). It will become clear to you, if you collate the specimen under examination with the behaviour of children, yourself and the people about you, under what urgent necessity they are for the sense of triumph, of being better and doing better than their fellows, and having it felt and recognised by someone. It is a deeper, steadier impulse than sexual lust; it is a hunger. It is the clue to the unlovingness of so much sexual life, to sadistic impulses, to avarice, hoarding and endless ungainful cheating and treachery which gives men the sense of getting the better of someone even if they do not get the upper hand.

In the last resort this is why we must have law, and why Magna Carta and all its kindred documents set out to defeat human nature in defence of the general happiness. Law is essentially an adjustment of that craving to glory over other living things, to the needs of social life, and it is more necessary in a collectivist society than in any other. It is a bargain, it is a social contract, to do as we would be done by and to repress our extravagant egotisms in return for reciprocal concessions. And in the face of these considerations we have advanced about the true nature of the beast we have to deal with, it is plain that the politics of the sane man as we have reasoned them out, must anticipate a strenuous opposition to this primary vital implement for bringing about the new world order.

I have suggested that the current discussion of "War Aims" may very effectively be transformed into the propaganda of this new Declaration of the Rights of Man. The opposition to it and the attempts that will be made to postpone, mitigate, stifle and evade it, need to be watched, denounced and combatted persistently throughout the world. I do not know how far this Declaration I have sketched can be accepted by a good Catholic, but the Totalitarian pseudo-philosophy insists upon inequality of treatment for "non- Aryans" as a glorious duty.

How Communists would respond to its clauses would, I suppose, depend upon their orders from Moscow. But what are called the "democracies" are supposed to be different, and it would be possible now to make that Declaration a searching test of the honesty and spirit of the leaders and rulers in whom they trust. These rulers can be brought to the point by it, with a precision unattainable in any other fashion.

But the types and characters and authorities and officials and arrogant and aggressive individuals who will boggle at this Declaration and dispute and defy it, do not exhaust the resistances of our unregenerate natures to this implement for the establishment of elementary justice in the world. For a far larger proportion of people among the "democracies" will be found, who will pay it lip service and then set about discovering how, in their innate craving for that sense of superiority and advantage which lies so near the core of our individuals wills, they may unobtrusively sabotage it and cheat it. Even if they only cheat it just a little. I am inclined to think this disingenuousness is a universal weakness. I have a real passion for serving the world, but I have a pretty keen disposition to get more pay for my service, more recognition and so on than I deserve. I do not trust myself. I want to be under just laws. We want law because we are all potential lawbreakers.

This is a considerable digression into psychology, and I will do no more than glance at how large a part this craving for superiority and mastery has played in the sexual practices of mankind. There we have the ready means for a considerable relief of this egotistical tension in mutual boasting and reassurance. But the motive for his digression here is to emphasise the fact that the generalisation of our "War Aims" into a Declaration of Rights, though it will enormously simplify the issue of the war, will eliminate neither open and heartfelt opposition nor endless possibilities of betrayal and sabotage.

Nor does it alter the fact that even when the struggle seems to be drifting definitely towards a world social democracy, there may still be very great delays and disappointments before it becomes an efficient and beneficent world system. Countless people, from maharajas to millionaires and from pukkha sahibs to pretty ladies, will hate the new world order, be rendered unhappy by frustration of their passions and ambitions through its advent and will die protesting against it. When we attempt to estimate its promise we have to bear in mind the distress of a generation or so of malcontents, many of them quite gallant and graceful-looking people.

Ant it will be no light matter to minimise the loss of efficiency in the process of changing the spirit and pride of administration work from that of an investing, high-salaried man with a handsome display of expenditure and a socially ambitious wife, into a relatively less highly-salaried man with a higher standard of self-criticism, aware that he will be esteemed rather by what he puts into his work than by what he gets out of it. There will be a lot of social spill, tragi-comedy and loss of efficiency during the period of the change over, and it is better to be prepared for that.

Yet after making allowances for these transitional stresses we may still look forward with some confidence to certain phases in the onset of World Order. War or war fear will have led everywhere to the concentration of vast numbers of workers upon munition work and the construction of offensive and defensive structures of all sorts, upon shipping, internal communications, replacement structures, fortification. There will be both a great accumulation and control of material and constructive machinery and also of hands already growing accustomed to handling it. As the possibility of conclusive victory fades and this war muddle passes out of its distinctively military phase towards revolution, and as some sort of Peace Congress assembles, it will be not only desirable but necessary for governments to turn over these resources and activities to social reconstruction. It will be too obviously dangerous and wasteful to put them out of employment. They must surely have learnt now what unemployment means in terms of social disorganisation. Governments will have to lay out the world, plan and build for peace whether they like it or not.

But it will be asked, "Where will you find the credit to do that?" and to answer this question we must reiterate that fact that money is an expedient and not an end. The world will have the material and the hands needed for a reconditioning of its life everywhere. They are all about you now crying out to be used. It is, or at any rate it has been, the function of the contemporary money-credit system to bring worker and material together and stimulate their union. That system always justified its activities on that ground, that is its claim to exist, and if it does not exist for that purpose then for what purpose does it exist and what further need is there for it? If now the financial mechanism will not work, if it confronts us with a non possumus, then clearly it resigns its function.

Then it has to get out of the way. It will declare the world has stopped when the truth will be that the City has stopped. It is the counting-house that has gone bankrupt. For a long time now an increasing number of people have been asking questions about the world counting-house, getting down at last to such fundamental questions as "What is money?" and "Why are Banks?" It is disconcerting but stimulating to find that no lucid answer is forthcoming.

One might have imagined that long before this one of the many great bankers and financial experts in our world would have come forward with a clear and simple justification for the monetary practices of to-day. He would have shown how completely reasonable and trustworthy this money-credit system was. He would have shown what was temporarily wrong with it and how to set it working again, as the electrician does when the lights go out. He would have released us from our deepening distress about our money in the Bank, our little squirrel hoard of securities, the deflating lifebelt of property that was to assure our independence to the end. No one of that quality comes forward. There is not so much as a latter-day Bagehot. It dawns upon more and more of us that it is not a system at all and never has been a system, that it is an accumulation of conventions, usages, collateral developments and compensatory expedients, which creaks now and sways more and more and gives every sign of a complete and horrifying social collapse.

Most of us have believed up to the last moment that somewhere distributed among the banks and city offices in a sort of world counting-house, there were books of accounts, multitudinous perhaps and intricate, but ultimately proper accounts. Only now is it dawning upon comfortable decent people that the counting-house is in a desperate mess, that codes seem to have been lost, entries made wrong, additions gone astray down the column, records kept in vanishing ink....

For years there has been a great and growing literature about money. It is very various but it has one general characteristic. First there is a swift exposure of the existing system as wrong. Then there is a glib demonstration of a new system which is right. Let this be done or that be done, "let the nation own its own money", says one radio prophet earnestly, repeatedly, simply, and all will be well. These various systems of doctrine run periodicals, organise movements (with coloured shirt complete), meet, demonstrate. They disregard each other flatly.

And without exception all these monetary reformers betray signs of extreme mental strain.

The secret trouble in their minds is gnawing doubt that their own proper "plan", the panacea, is in some subtle and treacherous way likely to fail them if it is put to the test. The internal fight against this intolerable shadow betrays itself in their outer behaviour. Their letters and pamphlets, with scarcely an exception, have this much in common with the letters one gets from lunatics, that there is a continual resort to capital letters and abusive terms. They shout out at the slightest provocation or none. They are not so much shouting at the exasperating reader who remains so obstinate when they have been so clear, so clear, as at the sceptical whisper within. Because there is no perfect money system by itself and there never can be. It is a dream like the elixir vitas or perpetual motion. It is in the same order of thought.

Attention has already been drawn, in our examination of Mr Streit's proposals for Union Now, to the fact that money varies in its nature and operations with the theory of property and distribution on which society is based, that in a complete collectivism for example it becomes little more than the check handed to the worker to enable him to purchase whatever he likes from the resources of the community. Every detachment of production or enterprise from collective control (national or cosmopolitan) increases the possible functions of money and so makes a different thing of it. Thus there can be endless species of money--as many types of money as there are types and varieties of social order. Money in Soviet Russia is a different organ from money French or American money. The difference can be as wide as that between lungs and swimming bladders and gills. It is not simply a quantitative difference, as so many people seem to imagine, which can be adjusted by varying the rate of exchange or any such contrivance, it goes deeper, it is a difference in quality and kind. The bare thought of that makes our business and financial people feel uncomfortable and confused and menaced, and they go on moving their bars of gold about from this vault to that, hoping almost beyond hope that no one will say anything more about it. It worked very well for a time, to go on as though money was the same thing all the world over. They will not admit how that assumption is failing to work now.

Clever people reaped a certain advantage from a more or less definite apprehension of the variable nature of money, but since one could not be a financier or business director without an underlying faith in one's right to profit by one's superior cleverness, there did not seem to be any reason for them to make a public fuss about it. They got their profits and the flats got left.

Directly we grasp this not very obscure truth that there can be, and are, different sorts of money dependent on the economic usages or system in operation, which are not really interchangeable, then it becomes plain that a collectivist world order, whose fundamental law is such a Declaration of Rights as we have sketched, will have to carry on its main, its primary operations at least with a new world money, a specially contrived money, differing in its nature from any sort of money conventions that have hitherto served human needs. It will be issued against the total purchasable output of the community in return for the workers' services to the community. There will be no more reason for going to the City for a loan than for going to the oracle at Delphi for advice about it.

In the phase of social stress and emergency socialisation into which we are certainly passing, such a new money may begin to appear quite soon. Governments finding it impossible to resort to the tangled expedients of the financial counting-house, may take a short cut to recuperation, requisition the national resources within their reach and set their unemployment hands to work by means of these new checks. They may carry out international barter arrangements upon an increasing scale. The fact that the counting-house is in a hopeless mess because of its desperate attempts to ignore the protean nature of money, will become more manifest as it becomes less important.

The Stock Exchange and Bank credit and all arts of loaning and usury and forestalling will certainly dwindle away together as the World Order establishes itself. If and when World Order establishes itself. They will be superseded, like egg-shells and foetal membranes. There is no reason for denouncing those who devised and worked those methods and institutions as scoundrels and villains. They did honestly according to their lights. They were a necessary part of the process of getting Homo sapiens out of his cave and down from his tree. And gold, that lovely heavy stuff, will be released from its vaults and hiding-places for the use of the artist and technician -probably at a price considerably below the present quotations.

Our attempt to forecast the coming World Order is framed then in an immense and increasing spectacle of constructive activity. We can anticipate a rapid transfiguration of the face of the earth as its population is distributed and re-distributed in accordance with the shifting requirements of economic production.

It is not only that there is what is called a housing shortage in nearly every region of the earth, but most of the existing accommodation, by modern standards, is unfit for human occupation. There is scarcely a city in the world, the new world as well as the old, which does not need to have half its dwelling-places destroyed. Perhaps Stockholm, reconditioned under a Socialist regime, may claim to be an exception; Vienna was doing hopefully until its spirit was broken by Dollfuss and the Catholic reaction. For the rest, behind a few hundred main avenues and prospects, sea and river fronts, capitols, castles and the like, filthy slums and rookeries cripple childhood and degrade and devitalise its dulled elders. You can hardly say people are born into such surroundings; they are only half born.

With the co-operation of the press and the cinema it would be easy to engender a world-wide public interest and enthusiasm for the new types of home and fitment that are now attainable by everyone. Here would be an outlet for urban and regional patriotism, for local shame and pride and effort. Here would be stuff to argue about. Wherever men and women have been rich enough, powerful enough and free enough, their thoughts have turned to architecture and gardening. Here would be a new incentive to travel, to see what other towns and country-sides were doing. The common man on his holidays would do what the English milord of the seventeenth century did; he would make his Grand Tour and come back from his journeys with architectural drawings and notions for home application. And this building and rebuilding would be a continuing process, a sustained employment, going on from good to better, as the economic forces shifted and changed with new discoveries and men's ideas expanded.

It is doubtful in a world of rising needs and standards if many people would want to live in manifestly old houses, any more than they would want to live in old clothes. Except in a few country places where ancient buildings have wedded themselves happily to some local loveliness and become quasi- natural things, or where some great city has shown a brave facade to the world, I doubt if there will be much to preserve. In such large open countries as the United States there has been a considerable development of the mobile home in recent years. People haul a trailer-home behind their cars and become seasonal nomads.... But there is no need to expatiate further on a limitless wealth of possibilities. Thousands of those who have been assisting in the monstrous clumsy evacuations and shiftings of population that have been going on recently, must have had their imaginations stirred by dim realisation of how much better all this might be done, if it were done in a new spirit and with a different intention. There must be a multitude of young and youngish people quite ripe for infection by this idea of cleaning up and resettling the world. Young men who are now poring over war maps and planning annexations and strategic boundaries, fresh Maginot lines, new Gibraltars and Dardanelles, may presently be scheming the happy and healthy distribution of routes and residential districts in relation to this or that important region of world supply for oil or wheat or water-power. It is essentially the same type of cerebration, better employed.

Considerations of this sort are sufficient to supply a background of hopeful activities to our prospective world order. But we are not all architects and gardeners there are many types of minds and many of those who are training or being trained for the skilled co-operations of warfare and the development of a combatant morale, may be more disposed to go on with definitely educational work. In that way they can most easily gratify the craving for power and honourable service. They will face a world in extreme need of more teachers and fresh-minded and inspiring teachers at that. At every level of educational work from the kindergarten to the research laboratory, and in every part of the world from Capricornia to Alaska and from the Gold Coast to Japan, there will be need of active workers to bring minds into harmony with new order and to work out, with all the labour saving and multiplying apparatus available, cinema, radio, cheap books and pictures and all the rest of it, the endless new problems of human liaison that will arise. There we have a second line of work along which millions of young people may escape the stagnation and frustration which closed in upon their predecessors as the old order drew to its end.

A sturdy and assertive variety of the new young will be needed for the police work of the world. They will be more disposed for authority and less teaching or creative activities than their fellows. The old proverb will still hold for the new order that it takes all sorts to make a world, and the alternative to driving this type of temperament into conspiracy and fighting it and, if you can, suppressing it, is to employ it, win it over, trust it, and give it law behind it to respect and enforce. They want a loyalty and this loyalty will find its best use and satisfaction in the service of world order. I have remarked in the course of such air travel as I have done, that the airmen of all nations have a common resemblance to each other and that the patriotic virus in their blood is largely corrected by a wider professionalism. At present the outlook before a young airmen is to perish in a spectacular dog-fight before he is five and twenty. I wonder how many of them really rejoice in that prospect.

It is not unreasonable to anticipate the development of an ad hoc disarmament police which will have its greatest strength in the air. How easily the spirit of an air police can be denationalised is shown by the instance of the air patrols on the United States-Canadian border, to which President Roosevelt drew my attention. There is a lot of smuggling along that border and the planes now play an important part in its suppression. At first the United States and Canada had each their own planes. Then in a wave of common sense, the two services were pooled. Each plane now carries a United States and Canadian customs officer. When contraband is spotted the plane comes down on it and which officer acts is determined by the destination of the smuggled goods. There we have a pattern for a world struggling through federation to collective unity. An ad hoc disarmament police with its main strength in the air would necessarily fall into close co-operation with the various other world police activities. In a world where criminals can fly anywhere, the police must be able to fly anywhere too. Already we have a world-wide network of competent men fighting the white-slave traffic, the drug traffic and so forth. The thing begins already.

All this I write to provide imaginative material for those who see the coming order as a mere blank interrogation. People talk much nonsense about the disappearance of incentive under socialism. The exact opposite is the truth. It is the obstructive appropriation of natural resources by private ownership that robs the prosperous of incentive and the poor of hope. Our Declaration of Human rights assures a man the proper satisfaction of all his elementary needs in kind, and nothing more. If he wants more than that he will have to work for it, and the healthier he is and the better he is fed and housed, the more bored he will be by inactivity and the more he will want something to do. I am suggesting what he is likely to do in general terms, and that is as much as one can do now. We can talk about the broad principles upon which these matters will be handled in a consolidating world socialism, but we can scarcely venture to anticipate the detailed forms, the immense richness and variety of expression, an ever-increasing number of intelligent people will impose upon these primary ideas.

But there is one more structural suggestion that it may be necessary to bring into our picture. So far as I know it was first broached by that very bold and subtle thinker, Professor William James, in a small book entitled The Moral Equivalent of War. He pointed out the need there might be for a conception of duty, side by side with the idea of rights, that there should be something in the life of every citizen, man or woman alike, that should give him at once a sense of personal obligation to the World State. He brought that into relation with the fact that there will remain in any social order we can conceive, a multitude of necessary services which by no sort of device can be made attractive as normal life-long occupations. He was not thinking so much of the fast-vanishing problem of mechanical toil as the such irksome tasks as the prison warder's, the asylum attendant's; the care of the aged and infirm, nursing generally, health and sanitary services, a certain residuum of clerical routine, dangerous exploration and experiment. No doubt human goodness is sufficient to supply volunteers for many of these things, but are the rest of us entitled to profit by their devotion? His solution is universal conscription for a certain period of the adult life. The young will have to do so much service and take so much risk for the general welfare as the world commonwealth requires. They will be able to do these jobs with the freshness and vigour of those who know they will presently be released, and who find their honour through performance; they will not be subjected to that deadening temptation to self-protective slacking and mechanical insensitiveness, which assails all who are thrust by economic necessity into these callings for good and all.

It is quite possible that a certain percentage of these conscripts may be caught by the interest of what they are doing; the asylum attendant may decide to specialise in psychotherapeutic work;

the hospital nurse succumb to that curiosity which underlies the great physiologist; the Arctic worker may fall in love with his snowy wilderness....

One other leading probability of a collectivist world order has to be noted here, and that is an enormous increase in the pace and amount of research and discovery. I write research, but by that I mean that double-barrelled attack upon ignorance, the biological attack and the physical attack, that is generally known as "Science". "Science" comes to us from those academic Dark Ages when men had to console themselves for their ignorance by pretending that there was a limited amount of knowledge in the world, and little chaps in caps and gowns strutted about, bachelors who knew all that there was to be known. Now it is manifest that none of us know very much, and the more we look into what we think we know, the more hitherto undetected things we shall find lurking in our assumptions.

Hitherto this business of research, which we call the "scientific world", has been in the hands of very few workers indeed. I throw out the suggestion that in our present-day world, of all the brains capable of great and masterful contributions to "scientific" thought and achievement, brains of the quality of Lord Rutherford's, or Darwin's or Mendel's or Freud's or Leonardo's or Galileo's, not one in a thousand, not one in a score of thousands, ever gets born into such conditions as to realise its opportunities. The rest never learn a civilised language, never get near a library, never have the faintest chance of self-realisation, never hear the call. They are undernourished, they die young, they are misused. And of the millions who would make good, useful, eager secondary research workers and explorers, not one in a million is utilised.

But now consider how things will be if we had a stirring education ventilating the whole world, and if we had a systematic and continually more competent search for exceptional mental quality and a continually more extensive net of opportunity for it. Suppose a quickening public mind implies an atmosphere of increasing respect for intellectual achievement and livelier criticism of imposture. What we call scientific progress to-day would seem a poor, hesitating, uncertain advance in comparison with what would be happening under these happier conditions.

The progress of research and discovery has produced such brilliant and startling results in the past century and a half that few of us are aware of the small number of outstanding men who have been concerned in it, and how the minor figures behind these leaders trail off into a following of timid and ill-provided specialists who dare scarcely stand up to a public official on their own ground. This little army, this "scientific world" of to-day, numbering I suppose from head to tail, down to the last bottle-washer, not a couple of hundred thousand men, will certainly be represented in the new world order by a force of millions, better equipped, amply co-ordinated, free to question, able to demand opportunity. Its best will be no better than our best, who could not be better, but they will be far more numerous, and its rank and file, explorers, prospectors, experimental team workers and an encyclopaedic host of classifiers and co-ordinators and interpreters, will have a vigour, a pride and confidence that will make the laboratories of to-day seem half-way back to the alchemist's den.

Can one doubt that the "scientific world" will break out in this way when the revolution is achieved, and that the development of man's power over nature and over his own nature and over this still unexplored planet, will undergo a continual acceleration as the years pass? No man can guess beforehand what doors will open then nor upon what wonderlands.

These are some fragmentary intimations of the quality of that wider life a new world order can open to mankind. I will not speculate further about them because I would not have it said that this book is Utopian or "Imaginative" or anything of that sort. I have set down nothing that is not strictly reasonable and practicable. It is the soberest of books and the least original of books. I think I have written enough to show that it is impossible for world affairs to remain at their present level. Either mankind collapses or our species struggles up by the hard yet fairly obvious routes I have collated in this book, to reach a new level of social organisation. There can be little question of the abundance, excitement and vigour of living that awaits our children upon that upland. If it is attained. There is no doubting their degradation and misery if it is not.

There is nothing really novel about this book. But there has been a certain temerity in bringing together facts that many people have avoided bringing together for fear they might form an explosive mixture. Maybe they will. They may blast through some obstinate mental barriers. In spite of that explosive possibility, that explosive necessity, it may be this remains essentially an assemblage, digest and encouragement of now prevalent but still hesitating ideas. It is a plain statement of the revolution to which reason points an increasing number of minds, but which they still lack resolution to undertake. In The Fate of Homo sapiens I have stressed the urgency of the case. Here I have assembled the things they can and need to do. They had better summon up their resolution.

THE END

The Fate of Man

The Fate of Man

Published in 1939, on the eve of World War II, The Fate of Man is one of H.G. Wells' most urgent and philosophical works. In it, Wells explores the existential crisis facing humanity, emphasizing the need for a radical restructuring of civilization to prevent self-destruction. He argues that war, nationalism, economic instability, and ignorance are pushing humanity toward collapse, and only a scientifically managed world system can save it.

Key Themes & Arguments

Humanity Stands at a Crossroads – Wells views the world of 1939 as a moment of reckoning. Nations are preparing for another devastating war, totalitarian regimes are rising, and economic struggles are fueling instability. He warns that without drastic changes, humanity is doomed to repeat its failures.

War Is an Outdated and Preventable Tragedy – Wells sees war as a result of ignorance and tribalism. He believes that modern technology and communication make global conflict unnecessary—if only a rational governing system were in place to prevent it.

The Need for a World State – Like in The Open Conspiracy and The New World Order, Wells proposes that only a unified global authority can prevent war and ensure stability. He sees sovereign nation-states as a dangerous relic of the past, responsible for endless cycles of conflict.

Scientific and Intellectual Leadership – The book argues that governance should be in the hands of experts, scientists, and intellectuals, rather than politicians driven by nationalistic or self-serving agendas. The future should be planned, logical, and based on scientific principles.

Education as a Tool for Global Transformation – To achieve his vision, Wells believes that people must be re-educated to accept a global perspective rather than a national identity. Schools and media must reshape public thought to prepare future generations for a united world.

The Individual vs. The Collective – While Wells acknowledges individual freedoms, he suggests that personal liberties must sometimes be sacrificed for the greater good of humanity's survival. He argues that a rational, centrally planned society is preferable to the chaos of democracy and free-market competition.

Historical Context & Influence

Written just before the outbreak of World War II, The Fate of Man reflects Wells' deep anxiety over the self-destructive nature of human civilization. His solution—a global scientific dictatorship—was controversial at the time and remains so today.

Some see Wells as a visionary, predicting the need for international cooperation, leading to institutions like the United Nations, the European Union, and the World Bank.

Others view him as an advocate of technocratic authoritarianism, promoting a system that would strip nations and individuals of their autonomy in the name of global stability.

Wells believed the survival of humanity required radical change—a theme that remains relevant in modern discussions about global governance, artificial intelligence, and the control of world resources.

Why The Fate of Man Matters Today

As modern society faces geopolitical tensions, economic crises, and technological upheaval, The Fate of Man serves as a compelling study in both the utopian dreams and authoritarian dangers of globalist thought. Wells saw scientific governance as the only way forward, but whether his ideas represent salvation or tyranny is left for the reader to decide.

34

INTRODUCTION

I HAVE been asked to set down as simply and clearly as I can, in one compact book, the reality of the human situation; that is to say I have been asked to state the world as I see it and what is happening to it. This is the result.

A very large part of my conscious life has been a struggle for effective knowledge. I have attempted to collect and summarise existing knowledge so that it could be made available in human living, and to induce other and abler people to take up the same work, I have worked also to bring together incompatible systems of thinking about reality, systems which ignore each other stupidly and wastefully, and are manifestly answerable for much fundamental confusion in human thought. These unresolved, contradictory philosophies and theologies encumber the human mind, and their irresolution is largely due to an elaborate mutual disregard. I am exceptionally intolerant of such inconsistencies, because if I attempt to deal with them they worry and entangle me. I cannot make the necessary reservations and adjustments.

The peculiar strength and the peculiar weakness of my mind are one and the same quality. Put favorably, mine is a very direct mind; put unfavorably, it is unsubtle. I am impatient of complicating details and conventional mis-statements because I am afraid of them. The reader will find this book ego-centered, for so we all began, and also insistent. I hammer at my main ideas, and this is an offense to delicate-minded people. If a door is not open I say it is shut, and I am impatient with the suggestion of worldly wisdom that it may be possible to wangle a way round. Yet there may be a way round if you do not lose yourself getting there. You have been warned that I shall not be with you in any such uncertain enterprise. I work not simply for knowledge but for a stark clarity of thought about it. It seems to me a fair challenge to demand a lucid statement of the vision of the universe to which this directness of inquiry and assemblage have brought me.

That vision may affect many readers as unflattering to human self-esteem. I cannot help that; it is the way in which reality has unfolded itself before me.

By way of Introduction I will tell how I came to see the world as I do. Then in the subsequent sections I will give the conclusions at which I have arrived today. I will tell what I first saw of life. How I saw it. How I was allowed to see it. How my range of vision extended. How knowledge, experience and imagination accumulated and horizon opened beyond horizon.

I was born in a rather unprosperous home; there was no nursery and most of my waking day was spent in an underground kitchen. Very little remains in my memory now of that first world, my infantile world. As I saw it then, it seemed to be the only world. When I put together the notes for this Introduction, I sat for a time, doing my utmost to recall what picture of the world I had in early childhood. I get scarcely anything at all.

It must have been a very limited picture. I had few general ideas. Or none. For instance, my mind was not living in a that world or a round world or anything of that sort, I was not bothering about any shape or size of the world. I was entirely incurious about all that. I was just living in "the world." I was informed that there was a home for little children above the bright blue sky, but I do not remember that that interested me in the slightest degree. I was rather more concerned about Old Bogey who would come and fetch me if I told fibs and so on, and I rather disliked (but I did not think very much about) a certain divine eye that was always watching me—generally with disapproval But as far as my recollections go, I was much more afraid of bears, tigers, black men, red Indians and other dangers, lurking in the shadows upstairs and round the corner. That infantile world was a world of vivid, immediate, inconsecutive realities against a background of nothingness that evoked no curiosity. There was the house next door, there was the moon, there was night, there was day and so forth. Why not? With the utmost effort, that is all I can reconstruct of the world I saw before I began to read books and see pictures, go for walks, go to school, and inspect and inquire with the freedom of seven or eight years old.

I have a fuller conception of what I was seeing after that stage. My imagination was being used to amplify and extend what I saw and heard and felt directly. A rather foggy time-background was taking shape. I heard about "Once upon a time" before I existed. I had a jumbled idea of old England, mostly forests with turrets peeping out of them, old Paris, Rome, where it was always -- Nero and Christians fighting beasts in the Coliseum. My historical ideas centered upon Windsor Castle. I had seen Windsor Castle, and I firmly believed that that grandiose round tower, which George the Fourth clapped upon it, was built by William the Conqueror. Rome, Greece, Babylon, Jerusalem and Egypt, arranged anyhow, crowded the background, and the Creation, seen across the shining waters of the Flood and a curious procession of very, very, very old gentlemen—Methuselah beat the record—sealed up the vista of the past.

I was interested in geography chiefly because it provided varied scenery for imaginary adventures. I thought China and Japan were made to be laughed at, though their porcelain and silks and fans were clever. I knew that there were also savages for whom Britain provided missionaries and machine-guns. Savages were generally cannibals and wore few or no garments, which seemed to me very rude of them indeed. I knew the world was round because everybody told me so. If they had told me the world was cone-shaped or flat, I should have known that with equal conviction—and it was only years afterwards that I realized how difficult it is to prove that the world is a globe. There were upper classes one respected and lower classes that one didn't, and poor people had to work, and that was how things were. The nearer I could edge up to the upper classes the better it would be for me.

I forget when it was I began to realize that the world as it had been presented to me was not a trustworthy picture of reality, that in effect I was being lied to about life. I began doubting quite early in life. The religion they put before me was queer, muddled stuff, metaphors about unfatherly fathers and sacrificial sons, blood offerings and blood-dripping sacrificial lambs (in suburban London!), an irrational fall and a vindictive judgment, stuff that took refuge from any intelligent questions behind a screen of awe, mystery and menace, so that my reason did not so much reject it as fail altogether to accept it. What they called morality seemed planned to thrust me into some nasty secret corners and leave me there. I had some bad times, fearing a God whom I felt but did not dare to think a spy, a bully, a tyrant and fundamentally insane, and it was only after terrific distresses and terrors that I achieved disbelief. Fear lingered in my mind long after definite faith had dissolved.

The sublunary world they imposed upon me was equally difficult to accept. The history they taught me wound up at 1700, which was queer when one came to think about it. But even then I must have read books about the French Revolution and George Washington and the Roman Republic, and they had upset my simple faith in the inevitability of our political order, the dear Queen and all the rest of it. A sixpenny book by the late Henry George came into my hands and set me thinking crudely, destructively, but profitably about rent, wages and suchlike matters. Some rumors about a science called geology reached me. I had already observed for myself in the pictures in Wood's Natural History that different species of animals had quite needless resemblances to one another, if it was indeed true that they had all been made separately. Then about that time my schoolmaster set me reading science textbooks to earn Education Department grants for him, and suddenly I woke up to the existence of a vast and growing world of thought and knowledge outside my ordinary circle of ideas altogether. My heavens opened, and the world as I had seen it hitherto became a flimsy veil upon the face of reality.

I have heard other people who have had similar experiences to mine tell of the thirst for knowledge they experienced. I suppose I had that thirst in good measure, but far stronger was my anger at the paltry sham of an education that had been fobbed off upon me; angry resentment also at the dismal negligence of the social and religious organizations responsible for me, that had allowed me to be thrust into the hopeless drudgery of a shop, ignorant, misinformed, undernourished and physically under-developed, without warning and without guidance, at the age of thirteen. To sink or swim. I was too young to make allowances for the people who were exploiting and stifling me. I did not realize that they were quite charming people really, if a little too self-satisfied and indolent. I thought they had conspired to keep me down. It wasn't true that they had conspired to keep me down. But I was down and they didn't bother. They took my inferiority as part of the accepted order. They just trod on me. But I did not discriminate about their responsibility. I hated them as only the young can hate, and it gave me the energy to struggle, and I set about struggling, for knowledge. I was bitterly determined to see my world clearer and truer, before it was too late.

To this day I will confess I dislike the restriction and distortion of knowledge as I dislike nothing else on earth. In this modern world it is, I hold, second only to murder to starve and cripple the mind of a child. Emasculation of the mind is surely more horrible than any degrading bodily mutilation. In our modern world we recoil from the deliberate manufacture of human dwarfs, harem attendants and choristers, but the world still swarms with mental cripples, who follow the laws of their own distortion and scarcely suspect they are distorted.

I have indicated the limits of my world outlook in 1880. By extraordinary good luck I caught up to something like contemporary knowledge in the course of a few years. In seven years, before I was twenty-one, I contrived—never mind how—to secure four years of almost continuous study, and three of these were at the Royal College of Science, and one under the professorship of the great Huxley, Darwin's friend; and by 1887 the world as I saw it had become something altogether greater, deeper and finer than the confused picture I had of it in 1880. Mentally, we all travel at our fastest, I suppose, between fourteen and twenty-one. Many of my readers will know from their own experience what I mean when I say that for me these years remain in my memory as if all the time I was putting together an immense jig-saw puzzle in a mood of inspiration. These were the most exciting years in my life. I had been blind and I was learning to see. The world opened out before me. By '88 I saw the world, not precisely as I see it today, but much more as I see it today than as I saw it in 1880. There has been a lot of expansion and supplementing since, but nothing like a fundamental reconstruction.

Now how did we—because I was one of a generation of science students—how did we see the world in '88? Time had opened out for us, and the Creation, the Fall of Man and the Flood, those simple fundamentals of the Judaeo-Christian mythology, had vanished. Forever. Instead I saw a limitless universe throughout which the stars and nebulae were scattering like dust, and I saw life ascending, as it seemed, from nothingness towards the stars.

In the eighties the prevailing ideas about space and time, matter and energy, were simpler than they are now. Space and time just went on forever, we thought. We students used to talk about the fourth and other dimensions, but when I wrote a story for the students' magazine and identified time with the fourth dimension, I thought I was being very original and paradoxical indeed. We also had very definitely limited ideas about the amount of energy latent in the universe, and it seemed to us that our world would probably "freeze up" in a few million years. Still even that gave us a long time ahead, and we thought humanity might see and do tremendous things. We knew the broad outline of the history of life in time; we knew that our ancestors were apes, and it seemed possible that man would go on to a power and wisdom beyond all precedent.

But our ideas of that progress we anticipated were remarkably restricted. Our imaginations were relatively unstimulated. For example, our world, as we saw it then, knew nothing of radio—or to be exact it knew of radio transmission as a curious laboratory experiment, the Hertzian waves—and its ideas about atoms and the statement of physical processes, were naive in the extreme. We doubted if aviation was possible, we doubted if electric fraction was possible, we associated submarines with the fantasies of Jules Verne, and we considered his Around The World In Eighty Days an extravagant dream. Our interpretation of mental actions was trivial and shallow almost beyond comparison with what we have now.

As I compare the world as I see it now, with that world I contemplated fifty years ago, I realize how greatly the picture has unfolded and how much understanding has intensified. So far as its scale and texture go, so far as space and time, the atoms and the threads and substance of the picture go, the world as I see it today is altogether more marvelous, mysterious and profound.

It is not only that our analysis of the rhythms and interplay of the physical elements of the universe has been elaborated and rephrased in far more effective modes. In the foreground and middle distance also, concerning affairs upon this planet and the more obvious and immediate activities of life, our enlightenment has been immense. Thanks largely to Freud and his disciples and successors, there has been an immense advance in our self-knowledge. I would put Freud side by side with Darwin as a significant figure in human enlightenment. These two men are cardinal not so much on account of the actual elucidations they produced but 'because of the questions they asked and the method of their questioning. Our knowledge first of our own motives and impulses and then of mass-thought and mass-action, has become beyond comparison more lucid and practical, thanks primarily to the initiatives of Freud.

One immediate result of this rapid progressive enlargement and confirmation of our former outlook has been a tremendous wave of optimistic assurance in the minds of liberal-minded, freely thinking people. They have taken progress in discovery, in intelligent social organization, in the conquest of want, disease, ignorance, as something almost as inevitable as the precession of the Equinoxes. That progress has had the air of something quite independent of the daily lives and mass responses of everyday people. There was nothing anyone need do about it. It came; it unfolded; it increased. Progress! The men of science, the inventors, clever people somewhere were doing it all for us and all we had to do was to sit back and marvel and accept the cornucopia. There are the facts before us, the novelties, the triumphs, perpetually reinforced. In the world as I see it today, the powers and possibilities of human effort appear enormously greater than they did in 1888. And still they increase. Still the prospect and the promise expand.

The case for optimism about physical wants is stronger now than ever. So far as economic circumstances go, the world could be organized to provide every living soul upon it with abundant food, housing and leisure, and that without either direct compulsion to toil or any irksome monotony of employment. We have passed in a single lifetime from a general neediness to a practicable plenty for all The story is too familiar to need exhaustive recapitulation here. Aviation and radio communication have abolished distance. In 1888 the unity of the world as one community was a remote aspiration; now it has become an imperative necessity. Fifty years ago none of us dreamt of the freedom and fullness of life that is now a plain possibility for everyone. To many hopeful people in die past few decades, an age of power, freedom and abundance has seemed close at hand. Eye has not seen nor ear heard, it is only now entering into the human imagination to conceive, the wonder of the years to come.

And now suddenly we are confronted by a series of distresses and disasters, of a nature to convince the most hopeful of us that all this happy assurance was premature. We anticipated too easily, too greedily and too uncritically. These new powers, inventions, contrivances and methods, are not the unqualified enrichment of normal life that we had expected. They are hurting, injuring and frustrating us increasingly--They are proving dangerous and devastating in our eager but unprepared hands. We are only beginning to realize that the cornucopia of innovation may perhaps prove far more dangerous than benevolent.

What we may call the scientific world has recognized this quite recently. There have been great stirrings of conscience in various scientific organizations upon the question of the misuse of science and invention, and how far the man of science may be held responsible for that misuse. The Associations for the Advancement of Science in Britain, America and Australia have been moving under the initiatives of such men as Sir Frederick Gowland Hopkins, Lord Rutherford and Sir Richard Gregory. The British Association has created a special Division, not merely a new section but a sort of collateral to itself, for the study of the 1 social relations of science. The fate of this Division will be of considerable interest from our point of view. I have been privileged to attend some of its deliberations and two divergent lines of tendency have been very evident. One is plainly to organize and implement the common creative impulse in the scientific mind so as to make it a vital factor in public opinion; that was the original impulse which evoked the Division; the other is to restrain any such development of an authoritative and perhaps embarrassing criticism of the conduct of public affairs and to keep the man of science modestly to his present subordination.

It would carry us too far afield to discuss here how far the consciences of men of science may be able to get the upper hand of a trained and experienced governing class, so as to insist upon such collective ideals as they are able to formulate, and how far a trained and experienced governing class may maneuver this medley of distressed and protesting intelligences into the position of a roster of mere "experts" available if called upon by the authorities, and otherwise out of consideration.

It is conceivable that the scientific worker is even now walking into a net; that increasing areas of his inquiries and experiments are falling under the restrictions of "official secrets"; and that far beyond the more obvious realms of physics and chemistry, fields of investigation that have no direct bearing upon warfare are likely to come under control, as favoring subversive ideas undermining the military morale of the community. In Nazi Germany this has happened already to psychological science, to mathematical physics and ethnology—matters quite outside armament and strategy. An almost complete strangulation of the unhampered publication and exchanges of the free scientific period is visibly within the range of contemporary possibility, and the world of scientific workers, as we know them, even with that "Division" to rally them, appears a feeble folk to resist the influences making for that extinction.

No one has ever explored the bases of intellectual freedom in the modern community, and they may prove to be far more flimsy than the intellectual worker, flinging his mind about in the apparent security of his study, imagines.

It is not simply the forcible misuse of purely mechanical inventions that is producing such frightening retrogressions of those brave, free hopes that culminated in the later twenties. Every fresh development of radio, of the film and mass information generally, and all the new educational devices to which we had looked for the rapid spread of enlightenment and a common world understanding, are being subordinated more and more to government restriction and the service of propaganda. They were to have been the artillery of progress. They are rapidly being turned against our mental freedoms with increasing effectiveness.

Plainly, it is high time we looked more closely into the causes of these disconcerting frustrations of our recent large, bright anticipations of a world of plenty and expansion. What is the real position of Homo sapiens in relation to his environment? Has he the mastery we assumed he had, or did we make a profound miscalculation of his outlook? Have we been indulging in hopeful assumptions rather than facing the realities of his case? Upon that question the subsequent summary concentrates.

35

§ 1. — PRELIMINARY STATEMENT

SINCE the day when Herbert Spencer launched the word "Sociology" upon the world, the study of the general question of what is happening to mankind has made great advances. Sociology—or, to give it a more recent and better name, human ecology—has become a real science, analyzing operating causes and forecasting events. Our awareness of our circumstances is altogether more lucid than the world outlook even of our fathers. We have, flowing into the problem of human society, a continually more acute analysis of its population movements, of its economic processes, of the relation of its activities to the actual resources available. We no longer talk with quite the same pompous ignorance as the history teachers of our youth, of the rise and decay of Empires and of the march of civilization from East to West—or from West to East, it is much the same—and suchlike plausible caricatures of the current of events. With the increase in our knowledge and understanding quite new conceptions of the prospects and problems of humanity unfold before us.

The infiltration of biological ideas into sociology and human history, it has to be recognized, is a process still only beginning. The enlightenment of the middle nineteenth century through the destructive analysis of the Creation myth, went on in the face of vast resistances, and not the least of these were in the schools. The new conceptions threatened the very bases of belief oh which right conduct seemed to rest. Men shrank from following out the plain implications of the new discoveries. And so either they were denied, irrationally and frantically, or they were minimized, they were admitted, yes, but as obscure, remote matters, that had little or no significance in the "broader issues" of life. So that they could be taught in a sterilized form or ignored altogether. There was a period of controversy, very disastrous to the old dogmas, and then a phase of defensive silences. Open fighting was abandoned and the established beliefs dug themselves in.

It is still possible for bright youngsters at the universities to enter upon the "advanced" study of history, philosophy and economics, in the blackest ignorance of general biology. A majority of them remain in that ignorance, with a deepening scholastic hostility to this science, which sits like a neglected creditor at their doors. They have established a social prejudice against this dreaded line of thought and body of knowledge in which they have no share. They succeed in putting it upon the all too snobbish and sensitive young that somehow the biological reference is not quite the thing. It isn't done. It isn't to be thought about. There is an indecency in it. The young university philosopher, historian or economist is in many cases not so much biologically ignorant as biology-proofed.

It is because of such mental gaps and barriers that it is necessary to recapitulate here certain facts about life, which, although they are matters of general knowledge today beyond question and almost beyond cavil, might nevertheless, so far as any effective realization of their bearing upon our general social, political and religious behavior goes, be totally unknown. Yet they bear upon the problems of the present urgently. Contemporary political discussion remains indeed mere maundering empiricism, a tissue of guesses, ill-founded assertions and gossip, until they are brought into court.

This contrast of established knowledge and its effective application is a very remarkable one. Men can know a thing and yet know it quite ineffectively if it contradicts the general traditions and habits in which they live. It is well to understand that at this stage in our analysis, because it bears very directly upon the review of human possibilities to which this summary is directed.

36

2. — BIOLOGY INVADES HISTORY

ONE of the most striking differences between the outlook of our grandparents and that of a modern intelligence today is the modification of time values that has occurred.

By the measure of our knowledge their time-scale was extremely shallow. They had scarcely any historical perspective at all. They looked back to a past of a few thousand years and at the very beginning of time as they conceived it, they saw human life very much as it is now: it was a more or less balanced system of certain social types: rulers and ruled, hunter and cultivator, priest and soldier. This they regarded as the immemorial life of man. They saw the life of city and cultivated land, desert and sea, throughout all the interval, spreading perhaps, changing in a few particulars, enriched rather than altered by inventions and discoveries, but essentially the same. Their range of observation and comparison was too limited for them to realize that by clearing forests, over-stocking grasslands, destroying soil, they were slowly impoverishing and devastating many of the regions into which they spread. They did not connect the rise and fall of empires with a factor of unforeseeing waste in that normal life of theirs. They ascribed such drifting of population and energy as they observed to other causes. These processes of primitive waste were too relatively slow to be perceptible from lifetime to lifetime. So these thinkers of yesterday talked of unchanging human nature. You cannot change human nature, they said. They relied upon the fabled promise of the rainbow, they had it straight from the Creator's mouth, that while the earth still remained, seedtime and harvest should endure.

The order of events seemed a sure, unfailing routine. And in much the same way, our ancestors, until a couple of dozen centuries ago, thought the world was flat. They thought the sea they sailed upon flat without qualification, and it required a considerable amount of mental exercise for them to realize that the apparent plane of the ocean surface was really curved and that the faster and farther they sailed the more effectively they would realize how the round earth was falling away from their first assumptions. All their old landmarks would then vanish one after another. Astounded navigators found unfamiliar constellations in the heavens. Within two dozen centuries man has been discovering that he lives not on a flat earth but upon a globe, and within the last ten, that he is not the center of the universe but a denizen of a very second-rate planet. He has had to readjust his general ideas about life to that, and to a certain extent he has adjusted them. To a certain extent only.

And similarly our historical imaginations, quite as much as our geographical imaginations, live today in a vastly enlarged system of perspectives. We know that the everlasting hills are not everlasting, that all our working conceptions of behavior and destiny are provisional and that human nature and everything about it is being carried along upon an irreversible process of change. Our historical ideas reach back now through vistas of millions of years, we see humanity emerging from sub-human conditions, from the life of relatively solitary apes, at distances in the nature of a quarter of a million years, we know with increasing precision of the onset of a social hunting life in those distant ages, we are able to trace the beginnings of agriculture in a period of two or three hundred centuries, and by the new scale, the development of cities, language, law, religious organization, and all the various adaptations of humanity to the new conditions of a regular food supply, all that social system which seemed as eternal as the heavens, appear now events of yesterday, devoid of any finality whatsoever. That fixity of the normal human life which our great-great-grandfathers assumed as a matter of plain common sense, we discover was a transient dream. As our perspectives open, it vanishes.

The rapid progress of social psychology, human ecology and all the ill- defined activities of human and general biology is opening our eyes, it is opening even the eyes of our trained historians and our social teachers, to the real nature of our everyday social life. It is brought home to us that the human species for the last twenty or twenty-five thousand years has been living in such a continuously accelerating process of change as no other animal species has ever been called upon to face. And it is also being forced upon our reluctant attention that the species Homo sapiens is no privileged exception to the general conditions that determine the destinies of other living species. It prospers or suffers under the same laws. These laws can be stated compactly, and there is nowadays very little dispute about them, even in matters of detail.

37

3. — HOW SPECIES SURVIVE

WHAT in general terms are the relations of a species to the world about it?

A species may be living in practical harmony with its environment or it may be more or less out of balance with its surroundings.

In the former case it may continue recognizably the same species, living the same life, age after age. Any tendency to excessive numbers may be corrected by a correlated increase in the types that prey upon it, and there will be no definite biological encouragement for such variations and mutations as occur. Harmless mutations may indeed produce varieties and sub-species, and, as Henry Fairfield Osborn long ago pointed out, there may be purely mutational. efflorescences; the correlation of a species to its environment is never hard and exact; but only a minority of mutations seem to be without some quality of advantage or disadvantage. Abnormal individuals in a species in practical equilibrium will generally be eliminated, and the species as a whole will pursue the even tenor of its way indefinitely.

There are species that have been under no necessity to adjust themselves to circumstances over vast periods of geological time. But they are exceptions to the general ecological spectacle of species balancing themselves in a changing world. Most existing species, when their affairs are scrutinized as a whole, are discovered to be in a state of imperfect adjustment to their circumstances, and to be either undergoing adaptation to meet new requirements or to be losing ground in the struggle—if one may call anything so essentially passive a struggle-to survive. Over a large part of the animal and vegetable kingdoms, adaptation, the working adjustment of the species under stress, is made, if it is made at all, by the selective frustration and killing off of less well-adjusted individuals. Variations and mutations—it is not necessary to enter here into the controversial question of their causes; suffice it that they occur—variations and mutations, indifferent, favorable and unfavorable, play a considerable part in this selective adjustment. The adjustment is either sufficient or insufficient. In the latter case, the species dwindles and disappears. In the former, the species undergoes modification; it survives, changed, as a new species or as several new species according to the imperatives of its altered conditions.

All this again is practically common knowledge today. Most educated people know about it even if they do not think very much about it, or link it up with other systems of ideas in their minds. It needs to be repeated plainly here in view of that possibility of disregard.

The general history of life in the past is, as everybody knows, one of failure and defeat rather than adaptation. Great groups of living things have arisen, had their heyday, and then passed altogether from the scene, giving place to more plastic and adaptable forms of life. Comparatively insignificant forms with novel accommodations arise to take their place.

When we contemplate that greater past that science has unfolded for us, we see great groups and orders of mighty creatures dominating the earth, enormous reptiles, huge mammals flourishing and then waning and passing away. They have not kept pace with change; their exuberance has been almost a defiance of change; and change has overcome and obliterated them. The geological record can be presented, certain assumptions being granted, as on the whole a great progression, but that does not alter the fact that it is also a history of the ruthless extinction of whole species, genera and orders of living things. There are tremendous massacres in the geological record.

One of the greatest of these occurred at the close of the Mesozoic period, when in the course of perhaps only a few hundred thousand years, a vast reptilian fauna, ichthyosaurus, plesiosaurus, tyrannosaurus and so forth, an equally wonderful flora, scores of genera of ammonites and so on and so forth, were thrust out of existence. We know little or nothing of the changes that made so many hitherto successful forms of life impossible. We know surely only that they occurred. A change from conditions of all-the-year-round equable temperature to wide seasonal alternations of heat and cold may have resulted from some planetary disturbance. More recently there have been parallel massacres of groups of the early mammals, and there can be no question that today we are, from the geological point of view, living in a phase of exceptional climatic instability,-in a series of glacial and interglacial ages, and witnessing another destruction of animal and plant species on an almost unparalleled scale. The list of species extinguished in the past hundred years is a long one; the list of species threatened with extinction today is still longer. No new species arise to replace those exterminated. It is a swift, distressful impoverishment of life that is now going on. And this time the biologist notes a swifter and stranger agent of change than any phase of the fossil past can show—man, who will leave nothing undisturbed from the ocean bottom to the stratosphere, and who bids f air to extinguish himself in the process.

This species man is, as we all know, one of a great series of species which we can speak of roughly as cerebral animals. These are the mammals who have dominated the earth since the beginning of the Tertiary period and which display throughout a rapid development of the cerebral cortex. This cerebral cortex was a novelty in the history of life, and it brought with it a fresh, distinctive method of individual adaptation to special circumstances. It quickened the response of a species to changing conditions very greatly. Learning from experience appears indeed but very rudimentarily in cold-blooded vertebrata; it is only in the birds and mammals, and particularly in the latter, that it becomes of real importance in adaptation. Essentially the cerebrum is an organ for the storage and application of memories. It enables individuals to learn by experience. The history of the mammals in particular is a history of memory development. All through the Tertiary period, it is to be noted, brains in every group of mammals increase in relative size and complexity. With every increase, the power of learning from experience and of supplementing direct impulse by conditioned reflexes increases. A young fish or reptile comes into the world with a practically complete, almost unalterable set of instinctive responses. It survives or fails by its inherited outfit. Apparently it can learn to a certain extent, but it learns very little. A young mammal comes into life far less conclusively equipped, a tabula rasa, prepared to learn. It learns. And the ampler its cerebral equipment, the more it learns to take care of itself. To begin with, it is sillier and less certain than the cold-blooded type; it stands in need of protection; in the end it is far better adapted to meet the special conditions it faces.

Moreover, the young mammal and, to a rather different extent and in a rather different fashion, the young bird do not simply learn from individual experience. Generally speaking there is also a protective relationship between the parent and the new individual. By example and often by direct intervention the young individual is taught. It heeds and imitates.

As we ascend the scale of cerebral development the possibility of teaching increases. It becomes possible to domesticate and train these higher-brain animals in just the measure that their brains are developed. You can teach very little to a fish or a reptile, but directly you come to the higher cerebral mammals you are confronted by the new possibility of establishing an artificial, taught, motive system to control, supplement or altogether replace natural instinct. You must catch them young. Then you can socialize them and get to quite remarkable working understandings with them. The shepherd's dog, the blind man's dog, the polo pony, the polite, house-trained cat, are examples of the immense individual adaptability which is achieved through the establishment of a taught, secondary self in the cerebral cortex. None of these creatures are behaving in accordance with the primary tendencies they have inherited. They are behaving in accordance with an adaptive mental superstructure imposed upon their natural dispositions. It enables them to survive not simply as tolerated but as contributing individuals in a complex social organization which otherwise would have had no alternative but their extermination. They would have suffered the fate that is overtaking the unteachable Tasmanian Devil or the unteachable Tasmanian Wolf.

38

4. — HISTORY BECOMES ECOLOGY

AT this point again it may be well to take stock of the discussion we are unfolding. We have been restating, very plainly and directly, established facts in general ecology, and we are going on now to develop this restatement in relation to the particular position and outlook of the human species. There is no need to apologize for this biological resume, elementary though it is. It is vitally necessary to our statement. It is absolutely impossible to approach the urgent and distressful problems of the present time with any hope of lucid solution until this general background of knowledge is definitely present in the mind.

From now on we shall encounter an increasing amount and variety of resistance to our application of these almost universally admitted facts. From this' point on, many readers will be quite unaccustomed to seeing human social life in the light of ecological science. There is a sort of barrier in their minds. It is not because they do not know, but because they see the two sets of facts apart. They will experience a strong resistance to this invasion of this reserved region of human affairs by these really quite incontrovertible ideas, because in this reserved region their minds are already strongly occupied by idea systems that are incompatible with it....

It has been pointed out how the species of brain-animals cooperate with circumstances in teaching their offspring to adapt themselves to the exactions of their environment. But in th£» case of man, and to a quite exceptional extent, because of an immense development of speech and gesture, the taught stuff in the cerebrum becomes of overpoweringly greater importance than mere hard experience, and we find the behavior system of the individual' molded to social cooperation and collective needs, not only by tradition and other forms of education but by institutions and law. Man, above everything else, is an educated animal, socially controlled. He is no longer primarily or even mainly a creature of instinct and brief individual experience. That phase in evolution lies a million years behind him. His instincts alone and without correction would fail him utterly as a behavior control in his present circumstances.

There is a relatively enormous artificial supplement to the natural man in all of us. We talk of our "selves" and of being freemen, but much the greater part of our activities today we perform as parts not of one simple, greater organism, human society, but, what is more complex, as parts of a number of greater organisms—profession, township, nation, religion, club, class, and so forth, which are all woven together into what we call human society and our social reactions. What we do as purely spontaneous individuals is -hardly more than a narrow choice between prescribed things. The home we live in, the clothes we wear, the food we eat, the way we go about the world, are all substantially imposed upon us by forces exterior to our personalities.

They are social products and more and more do they become social products.

The socialization of human life, the relative increase of the factor supplied by society, is still going on quite rapidly. There was a time, for instance, not so many generations ago, when most people built their own homes, made their own clothes, got their own food, taught their own children. Now the building trade, clothing trade, the provision shop, and the public school see to all that.

This applies with even greater truth to our minds. A mere fraction of our knowledge is self-taught. What we know again is nine-tenths hearsay. We have heard, we have read. The stuff in our heads was mainly put there by society. To the biologist an ordinary ape is just a natural ape, but a man is a natural man plus a great cerebral accumulation of directive ideas, prejudices, antagonisms, tolerances and conceptions of what he ought and ought not to do, which wrap about him and fit him into the social body to which he belongs. From the biological point of view all this cerebro-social accumulation of knowledge, beliefs and ideas, responsibilities and dependency, is as much a natural adjustment to needs and environment as a claw or a skull or a swimming bladder; it is a thing of the same kind, though it differs enormously in the relative swiftness and breadth of its adaptability to changing conditions. It is subject to the same ecological laws.

The growth of this mental superstructure upon the primitive ape-man of the later Tertiary period can now be traced in its broad lines without very much difficulty. Any attempt to make a general outline of human history falls almost uncontrollably into the form of a story of developing communication, learning and co-operation between the primordial ape-man family groups. The outline of history as one whole is, and must be, a history of communication and socialization. It is compelled to apprehend primary processes that the older type of history, with its preoccupation with separate communities, was equally compelled to ignore. It begins necessarily with the origins of speech, gesture, drawing, observances, and taboos.

With every such development, the association of human animals in groups collectively more efficient in the appropriation of food supplies became easier. The family group grew into the tribe and tribes grew larger. Their growing awareness of the seasons is apparent in the archaeological record; their growing ability to co-operate in the semi-domestication of animals and the first agricultural tentatives is now quite clearly traceable. These are no longer matters to dispute about. With the development of agriculture and the beginnings of settlement, man, the new sort of socialized man, appears as a rapid and immense biological success. His growing communities spread swiftly, growing as well as multiplying and spreading, and displaying every symptom of an unprecedented surplus of biological energy.

A few millenia ago the life which our great-grandfathers considered to be the normal and immemorial life of mankind was well under way. It had grown up, biologically speaking, speaking by the standards of geological time, with the rapidity of a puff-ball, and those who lived it were unaware that there had ever been any other way of human living. Such was life. And it was still, although they did not perceive it in the least, under a stress of accelerating change.

The changes in the conditions of human life during the last twenty or thirty thousand years have been mainly brought about by the acceleration of invention through increasing co-operation and the release of material and social power. There have been no doubt climatic and geographical changes, but their share has been relatively less important. The essential story of history and pre-history is the story of the adaptation of the social- educated superstructure of the animal man to the novel problems with which his own enterprise and inventiveness have been continually confronting him. Law, religion, education, are from the ecological point of view, names we give to the cardinal aspects of this process of adaptation. Each generation in these growing and spreading societies was told a story of its relation to the community into which it had to fit itself and given an account of the acquiescences and co-operations expected from it. The imperatives of law, education, religion, all flowing into one another and sustaining one another, were expressed, and in these early stages of mental development could only be expressed, by anthropomorphic myths. Natural selection has no care for scientific precision. There is no immediate survival value in truth. To this day the survival value of the critical habit of mind is questionable. It sufficed for the purposes of nature if the myths and the system of observance, the things that were too awful to do and the things that it was fatal to leave undone, made for the survival of the community as a whole. The adaptive superstructures, the laws, rules and beliefs, that were favoring human survival, varied in different regions, but they varied within the limits set by the conditions of specific survival. A certain primary resemblance of the tribal gods and of the tribal stories and of the behavior systems of the differentiating social classes, waited upon the spread of the "normal" way of life about the earth. Parallel circumstances evoked parallel adjustments. Generally the pattern included a tribal ancestor god, a priesthood taking care of the calendar and medicine, a morality of propitiation and self-restraint.

Step by step, as human inter-communication increased, communities grew larger. And as they grew larger they developed something, of which curiously enough we are only beginning to grasp the profound importance today; they developed a superfluity of young men.

From the point of view of the biologist Homo sapiens was making an almost excessive success. He was repeating the exuberance of the great Mesozoic reptiles or the early Tertiary deinotheria. The species was not only holding its own, it was spreading and multiplying by leaps and bounds. And the front of its biological advance was this surplus of young men. Young men, full of beans as people say, and looking for trouble.

Hitherto historians have failed to recognize the great importance of this trouble-making stratum. It is well to underline it here. It is a primary social fact. I have been reading recently the works of Mark Benney, Low Company and The Truth About English Prisons (Fact, March 1938), who is rapidly becoming a leading authority on criminology, and he reminds me very strikingly of how nonsensical it is to talk of a criminal class as a different sort of human being. It is in its origins more and more of an age class. Every sort of energetic male human being is a potential criminal, if nothing else is found to occupy and interest him. These expanding human societies in the past were needing less and less energy per head to be sure of their food supply and security. Something had to be done to and for these young men, and the easiest way of keeping them out of mischief, keeping them disciplined in fact and the numbers of them down, was war.

Primitive war was a necessity forced upon the human community by biological success through the production of a surplus of young males. It appeared with herding and agriculture and it was naturally associated with them. In Papua and the Mandated Territory of New Guinea, one can still see humanity in a sort of equilibrium at that stage of development. There you have a population of over half a million, still living in small independent communities, each with its own conceit of itself, its peculiar petty customs and prejudices. These New Guinea peoples are by no means a monotony of barbarism. They present indeed a great variety of physical and mental types, and their social and artistic possibilities are very considerable. Up to the present they have solved their population pressure by spells of not too destructive warfare. There is a little killing-off and then things settle down again. Now, under the parental care of the Canberra government, their warfare is to cease, and what will happen to these peoples is very uncertain. They may be subjected to economic exploitation far more tragic than warfare.

You can write human history in a variety of ways, but one way of writing it would be to consider how, age after age, humanity has met the problem of What to do with out sons. There was war and what was generally associate i with war, conquest and colonization. Roman Britain, for instance, was conquered by the surplus offspring of the Saxon shore. In my native county, Kent, traces survived until a very recent period of the custom of gavelkind. The elder sons were sent off marauding and the youngest kept the home. You can re-write the history of all the great population movements in terms of the pressure of the young male surplus.

It should be particularly evident as an operating cause in the history of the last two centuries, and it would be if history were properly told. Every community can be shown to be either sending out the plethora of its population as emigrants and settlers, or reducing it by warfare, or else suffering from acute social trouble, such social trouble as the words Russian Hooligans, Chinese Boxers, Moonlighters, Nazis, Fascists, revolutionary terrorists, gangsters, will call to mind. The young man surplus, if it is not consumed, is the main source of rebels, revolutionaries and disturbances of all kinds. Somehow that tension must find relief. The comparative social stability of the nineteenth century was largely due to emigration and the settlement of new lands. Now there are no more new lands open to immigration.

Moreover this tension has been greatly intensified by the huge increase of productive efficiency through invention and the use of mechanical power, which has diminished the number of young men who could look forward to a fairly secure, properly rewarded, sufficiently interesting married life.

Invention and discovery in production have intensified this age-long human problem and contributed to the present exceptional drift towards warfare and social convulsions. People stand in the young man's way and he is ready to get rid of them in any fashion suggested to him. That drift towards a social killing-off, and the necessity of justifying it, explain the eagerness with which race difference, class difference, any sort of difference of complexion, language or usage, nationalism and imperialism, are exalted into combatant provocations today. You can waste a lot of time arguing about this or that ism. The essential fact is the accumulating tension of unsatisfied youth, and these isms are mere formulae of relief.*

* See Note 4A. A falling birth-rate does not affect this.

Warfare and social conflict have for long ages released the plethoric human species towards the relief of a bloodletting. So it has been through all the ages of recorded history. With the relatively puny means of destruction available before the age of invention and innovation, it was no more than an excretion of inconvenient energy. For some hundreds of centuries humanity got along in this way. War became part of the accepted human rhythm, just as the massacre of the drones is part of the natural rhythm of the honey bee. Laws, customs, morals, sentiments and thoughts were adapted to it so as to make it natural and easy. If it were not for the outbreak of invention and discovery during the past century, man might have gone on drumming and trumpeting his way through long ages yet to come, going to his priest to bless his flags, facing the day of battle bravely, and either dying on the field of honor, or surviving to raise another generation for the same experience.

But that inventive urge in the species has suddenly, in—what is by the geological and biological scales—a mere flash of time, altered all that. It has made war something entirely different and it has put quite a new face on the political ideas, the working conceptions of right and wrong, of duty and service that have hitherto kept the varied and fluctuating patchwork of human communities going. It has strained and distorted the problem of adaptive survival almost beyond recognition. That, concisely, is the clue to the human situation today.

Let me try to give the gist of this vast change. It is a change in human power and scope.

First as to the increase in socially available power. Before the change, except for a little wind power or water power, the only power available for human purposes was a little animal power, horse, ox, elephant, camel, llama, or what not, and man power. The gross total of power units that sufficed to run everything that was going on in Great Britain in a day in the reign of Queen Elizabeth, everything, was probably much less than the total of units that is consumed today in running the lighting and transport alone of such a city as Manchester or Kansas City. And again all the energy of marching, shooting, stabbing, hacking, running to and fro at the battle of Agincourt was probably less than the energy released by one single high explosive shell in a modern bombardment.

Until this change in the total of available power occurred, the great majority of mankind toiled habitually to get food, clothing and shelter. They were under an obligation to do so or want. A small minority contrived in various ways to live by the toil of others and spend, and except for such parasitism there was no way to leisure. Now a steadily dwindling number of people, using power machinery and modern contrivances, can produce the essentials of life in excess of all our requirements. Never before in the history of life has any animal had such a fantastic increase in its ability to make or destroy.

That is the first aspect of the contemporary change. A second is what is called the abolition of distance. Even more fantastic in relation to past tradition is the increase of speed from point to point. The maximum of speed at which an Elizabethan man could travel was limited by a horse. He could send an uncertain and difficult message a hundred miles a day. He had beacon fires of course, but they do not carry any explicit messages.*

* See Note 4B.

He could see for a few miles. Now abruptly this creature can travel in comfort three hundred miles an hour, he can see and talk to his fellow-man on die other side of the earth, he can murder him at vast, increasing distances, he knows what is happening all over the world almost instantaneously. And his health improves and his vitality is greater. On the average he lives almost twice as long and twenty times as actively and variously as his great-great-grandfather. Now that distance has been abolished, he lives with increasing restlessness cheek by jowl with all the rest of mankind. So far a biologist might count him an unqualified success in the struggle for life—except for one disconcerting thing. He is ceasing to breed. His numbers are now passing a maximum and seem fated to decline, at least for some decades ahead. Woman for a variety of reasons is betraying an increasing disinclination to bear children. Man's conquest of nature may prove a sterile conquest.

His reproduction is falling off and his behavior traditions and controls, and more particularly the war tradition, are producing the most devastating tragedies among his communities. The effect of the increase of power has been to exaggerate the impact of the war drive monstrously. One may compare the human species today to a steamship that has long sailed the seas with engines roughly adequate to its needs, until some malign influence has suddenly gone down into the engine-room and, without any consultation with the ship's officers, amplified the power of the engines a thousandfold. Now they are flying loose out of control, lashing the ship to pieces, and threatening to sink it altogether. The captain upon the bridge gives impotent orders; the engineers dodge the pounding shafts and the escaping, searching, scalding steam.

Because of the way in which science and invention have brought us all into intimate contact and put high explosives into our hands, war has become a process of destruction that spares neither age nor sex, it is no longer a selective elimination of the surplus young men, it is a colossal wastage of material resources, a rapid disintegration of the social organization, robbed of all the glories and gallantries that once adorned it. In the past it was a corrective and almost tonic process. Now it has become a rapid wasting disease, a galloping consumption of the human species.

39

5. — UNION NOW?

IS it possible for man to recover control, or is this shattering return to destructive violence the beginning of the end of the career of Homo sapiens? Let us hold firmly to the broad conceptions of ecological science that have brought us thus far. The human species is, as a whole, dangerously out of harmony with these new conditions. Either its powers of adaptation will be sufficient to readjust it to the new demands, and it will go on to a new phase of survival, or, like any other living species, it will be defeated, shattered and ultimately wiped out. There are no other possibilities.

There is no time for any of the slower and more ancient methods of adaptation. The readjustment needed must be a mental readjustment. In that alone is there any hope for mankind.

In view of what has gone before it is plain that that mental readjustment must involve three main essentials. In varying measure these essentials are already widely recognized.

First and most obviously the idea and tradition of war must be eliminated. For that, quite a large number of people seem to be more or less prepared. They desire it, even if they have yet to discover the price that must be paid for it. Secondly, and what is not nearly so widely conceded, the vast and violent wastage of natural resources in the hunt for private profit that went on during the nineteenth century, must be arrested and reversed by the establishment of a collective economy for the whole world. And thirdly, in view of the stress of those young people, the resultant world organization must be of an active, progressive, imaginatively exciting nature. That surplus energy of youth, male and female, must be used up. It is the drive and essence of life; it is life itself. It must in each generation be "getting on." It must be doing things, making or remaking with an effect of conquest and general participation. The earlier years were preparation; the later, relieved of the high fever and impatience of that full onset of vitality, are appreciation, deliberation and the continual broadening-out of the human agenda.

These three propositions, peace, collectivism and incessant new enterprise, are interdependent and practically inseparable. One cannot be realized without the other two. In stating these propositions we are not in any way "laying down the law." The law is in the nature of things. We are merely stating as precisely as possible the unconditional terms that our race manifestly has to expect.

To what extent is contemporary thought and education moving towards the abolition of war?

An increasing number of us are realizing that the age of independent sovereign states and empires throughout the world, free to make war and prepared to make war, each separated from the other by barriers of language, religion, historical delusions and those differences in habits of life which are called national cultures, is coming to an end, obviously, rapidly; and at present not one of us can say with any confidence what sort of world order can replace it. A world order we feel there must be, but as to how it is to be attained, we are all at sixes and sevens.

The world of man has to become, has—in a chaotic disorder of conflict—already become, one community—one disorderly community. In the days of Oliver Goldsmith, what happened in China, happened in China, and did not matter a rap to anyone in England, If every time one fired a gun in England, he remarked, a man died in China, nobody would mind in the least. The shooting would go on. Now what happens in China, happens everywhere in the world; that is to say it is known and affects life everywhere. The crude fact of the world-wide community is here now. The open questions arise when we consider how this inevitable coming together of our communities can and will be recognized and established as a world order.

We have indeed already seen one attempt to reconstitute human affairs so as to eliminate this destructive process of modern war, in the League of Nations experiment. That, we realize now, was an extremely naive attempt to stop the current of history and to preserve forever just those national separatisms and strangulating boundaries against which the stars in their courses are fighting. Certain minimum changes were to be made to "end war" while everything else was to go on just as it had been going on before. Sovereign states, organized essentially for defense and aggression, were to form a League to end combat. Simply that. The conception of an organized World Pax, after it had played its part in the warfare of propaganda, after it had been used to build up false expectations of a new start in life for the German people, was taken over at Versailles and translated into the ideology of Foreign Offices and the diplomatic services. These essential organs of the old regime were instructed to supersede themselves and they were left to work out the task, and quite naturally they did nothing of the sort. The League Covenant completely disregarded that perennial problem of the restless young men, and it gave no attention to the absolute necessity of reconstructing economic life upon a collective basis throughout the world. These are matters about which diplomacy has never concerned itself. They do not enter into diplomatic or political education, which is at least the better part of a century out of date.

At the end of less than a score of years the failure of the League of Nations experiment is complete, and we will spend no time on enlarging upon that fruitless interlude of half-hearted idealism. Suffice it to say that for many excellent minds it has blocked the way to a realistic treatment of the human problem for two decades. We find now in 1939, a rough reproduction of the world situation of 1914-18. We find three aggressive military states threatening the whole world, and we find a number of threatened states contemplating some sort of loosely organized resistance to that aggression.

How loosely—with what dangerous looseness—that organization is still contemplated is illustrated by a book that has recently been given quite serious attention in Britain and America. This is Union Now by Clarence K. Streit He proposes that right now there shall be a "federal" union of fifteen now independent states which he describes as democracies. They are the United States of

America, the British group, Finland, France, Holland, Belgium, Switzerland, Denmark, Norway, Sweden. It is not a League or a war alliance he proposes but a permanent federation on the American model, with a common foreign policy, common money, common armed forces, common control of interstate and foreign trade and a common citizenship. He sweeps aside such questions as the status of India, colonial possessions, the various monarchist traditions involved, as secondary questions. Soviet Russia he balances on the brim of his project with a query—on the whole an encouraging query. Apparently the federated democracies are to have great local economic autonomy within the limits of the federal constitution.

Before we look into Mr. Streit's proposals more closely, it will be worth while to get this loose word "democracy" defined. The special interest of his book here lies in the fact that it has been well received by a considerable number of considerable people. It is an intimation of how rapidly opinion is moving towards the conception of a new world order transcending existing boundaries. So far it is a book to be welcomed. But it is also an indication of the extreme vagueness still prevalent about the necessary material and mental conditions of such a world order. Its pseudo-practical short-sightedness is almost as manifest as the boldness of its intention.

I do not believe that a world order can come into existence without a preliminary mental cosmopolis. I may be mistaken in that. Political federation, loose and confused at first, may precede and impose the necessary mental adaptations. That is too round-about and slow a process for the limitations of my imagination. World democracy, I believe, would get lost on the way.

40

6. — WHAT IS DEMOCRACY?

SINCE at any time now we may find ourselves fighting, enduring and dying for "democracy," it seems worth while to ask for some clear definition of what democracy means, so that we shall not only fight for it, but be prepared to see that in the end we get it. When you question people closely in the matter, you will encounter a considerable variety of answers, but you will find as you sort them out and arrange them that they do tend to converge and point in a common direction. There is a vital intention beneath the endless misuses and perversions of the word.

Towards what do these diverse statements converge? What is the reality, implicit and potential, that gives its living, present appeal to the word democracy?

Two words that will come out very frequently in the definitions that are given you are "freedom" and "liberty." Frequent, but not quite so frequent, are such phrases as the "right" of individuals and communities to "self-government." A few people will make a vote the symbol of democracy. But all of them can be brought into agreement that democracy means the subordination of the state to the ends and welfare of the common individual Very prevalent is an attitude of negation. Democracy, it is declared, is an anti-movement. It demands the protection of the individual life from the state. It is anti-Fascist, anti-Nazi, anti-Communist, anti-war—since there is no liberty in a state of siege—it is the denial of the right of the state organization to interfere in the life of the common individual except for the common convenience and with the common consent.

All this is matter of general agreement, but in all these phrases, there is an element of idealistic overstatement, and as soon as we attempt to bring them into effective contact with the realities of life, we find ourselves involved in some of the standing controversies that have exercised humanity since human thought and discussion began. We are reminded that there is no such thing as absolute freedom or absolute servitude. Limitless freedom, anarchy, would be a world of chaotic conduct, ruled only by impulse, a jungle life. All freedom in any society is conditional; it is a compromise; it implies "rules of the game," that is to say, law. Behind all actual social behavior there is the suggestion of a defined give-and-take, a "social contract." The social contract may vary between the extremes of a contract of blind obedience on the one hand and a contract to undertake no collective action whatever without a plebiscite, an entirely impracticable subordination of the law to mass impulse, on the other. Between these extremes and with a declared bias for conscious, free, individual action whenever it is practicable, this democracy falls.

Now the desire for conscious, free, individual action is innate in the normal human being. But it can be inhibited by fear of known or unknown consequences, by indolence and following the drift, and by a complex of infantile dispositions to imitate and obey. The herd instinct is very strong in the immature human animal. It will follow a leader or stampede like a cow, and find great relief from perplexity in doing so. The preference of democracy for the practical maximum of conscious, free, individual action requires a justification beyond the mere faltering desire in our hearts to "stand up, look heaven in the face and be a man."

For the normal man, unrestrained democracy is a very exacting way of living indeed. It asks too much of his natural resources. In a thousand situations even a wise or able man may find himself unable to decide upon the line of action that is fairly the best for himself and also the best for the general good, and in ten thousand he will find a fatal delay in his decisions. For that reason, a detailed, comprehensive, agreed-upon, accessible and understandable system of laws, which are really rules for behavior in predigested situations, is a necessary preliminary condition for a modern democracy. A taxi-cab tariff or the rule of the road or a minimum wage is a convenient elementary instance of the way in which conscious, free, individual action is set aside to the general benefit in a modern, democratic community. We extend that principle nowadays to rates of interest and inordinate profits, to the acquisition of land and many forms of property and to an increasing number of ordinary transactions. Our modern democratic community would frustrate its own declared aims without a complete, detailed, legal framework enforced by a judiciary and a police acting strictly under the law. The man who in a breath will say "I am a democrat" and also "I am a rebel" is simply a fool.

The contrast between democracy and the forms of community with which it is generally contrasted lies essentially in this reliance upon law. In a democracy a man does or should know, or should be easily able to ascertain, exactly "where he stands," what he must do, what he may do, what cannot be done, and he should be able to say with the utmost confidence, "You be damned" to any illegal order or request. The laws that restrain and protect him have received his implicit or expressed consent, and he has a reasonable right to attempt to alter them if he finds them uncongenial, but until they are altered they must be respected by all, small or great, in the community. The President or ruling assembly is as much bound by the law as the meanest citizen.

On the other hand the dictatorships and undemocratic social organizations generally, subject a large part of the common man's activities to uncovenanted restrictions, interference and compulsion. It is plainly contrary to the spirit of democracy that a man should sell himself into slavery or bind himself indefinitely to unquestioning obedience. The care of democracy for freedom extends to the protection of a man from his own desperate necessity. No democracy would tolerate Esau's bargain. Most existing dictatorships, indeed, claim a sort of legality based upon some forced plebiscite, some snatched election. But your inquiries will make it plain that the consent of the governed in a democracy can never be a finally silenced and irrevocable consent. It must be a continuing consent. It must be subject to sustained revision and renewal. From the point of view of democracy all absolutisms are illegal, and resistance to their commands is as justifiable as resistance to any less general hold-up or act of violence.

This fundamental legalism of democracy has been and is a deterrent to swift collective action, and the history of human government is very largely a history of attempts to reconcile the bickering gradualism of legal and deliberative government under democratic conditions with the needs of special emergencies. Before flood, fire, pestilence, earthquake, war, and especially in war, men have had to relinquish their liberty of individual action more or less completely to a higher command of some sort with unqualified immediate powers. The original "dictators" of the Roman system were essentially legal officials, and one of the primary riddles of human society has been the resumption of power by the community at the end of a period of crisis. A democracy needs to be in a state of perpetual vigilance against the specialist. From Caesar to Stalin, democracy has been trapped into one-man tyrannies by crises.

But historical analogies are always misleading, and modern crises become more and more elaborate affairs and less and less controllable by single individuals. None of these modern dictatorships has yet been tried out in a sustained war. It is at least highly doubtful whether the vast communities of today, if they are able to develop a class of competent public servants, with a co-operative morale and a sense of public criticism, may not attain an efficiency and a toughness far beyond that of a system subjected to the freaks and inspirations of a single individual. But they must work in the light. They must work with the distinctive freedom and the conscious individual co-operation of a team of football players, and they must be subjected to the continual criticism of an understanding public opinion with unlimited freedom of expression and with an ultimate, if deferred, right of intervention.

This conception of the superior flexibility and efficiency of free teamwork, as against dictatorially planned work, is very attractive to the democratically-minded, but it may easily be exaggerated. For example, Tom Wintringham in his English Captain lays great stress on the technical superiority of free men, inspired by a common idea, over the conscript soldiers of a dictatorship. He was in the fortunate position of leading a battalion of English volunteers, exceptionally intelligent and enthusiastic, picked men who wanted to fight, who were keen to fight, and unanimous at least in their hostility to the Franco pronunciamento. Of such individuals, unanimous for the services that engage them, an enlightened democracy should no doubt consist. But when one turns to the story Major Jose Martin Blasquez tells in I Helped To Build An Army, of the internal struggles and indiscipline of the defenders of the Republic, one realizes that practical freedom of initiative may achieve the most disastrous confusion.

There is indeed no guarantee of either immediate or ultimate victory in democracy. On that we must insist. There is no inherent magic successfulness in democratic freedom. Democratic freedom may be much more vulnerable than slavery, less easy both to attain and maintain. It may be that few or none of us realize yet the full price that may have to be paid for it.

None the less it is only through the attainment of a real world democracy that there is any hope for the ultimate survival of our species.

In many of the replies one will receive to the demand for a clear definition of democracy, one will get some reference to that magnificent outbreak of the common sense of mankind, the first French Revolution, That remains still a cardinal event in the history of human liberation. It was not the beginning of liberation but it was its most outstanding assertion. The democracy of America, the radicalism of Britain in its most vigorous phase, derived plainly from that French initiative. And since in those days titles and privileges were the most conspicuous infringements of men's liberties, democracy from the outset would have none of them; it was equalitarian without qualification. It was republican, it denied and repudiated any form of class rule whatever—and whenever it is still in health it remains republican and equalitarian.

But conditions in eighteenth-century France were peculiar in the fact that then the conspicuous offense against human liberty was class privilege. For many people in those days the possession of private property was a means of independence, freedom of ownership seemed a reasonable provision for democratic liberty, and only a few realized that, released from class tyranny, the free play of proprietorship might create advantages and disadvantages as wide and socially wasteful, as subject to "abuses," as the class privileges of the older regime. Throughout the first revolutionary period the spirit of democracy found itself puzzled, mocked and frustrated by economic inequality. Men freed from the tyranny of privileges found themselves oppressed by a tyranny of advantages. The common man, theoretically free and independent, discovered himself in the grip of an expanding economic system that made free competitive employment only another form—and to many it seems a scarcely preferable form—of serfdom. Political equality by itself proved in practice to be no equality at all.

Accordingly when we pursue our inquiries into the meaning of democracy today, we find a definite cleavage from this point onward in the replies to the question of "What is democracy?" An increasing number will be forced to agree that collective economic controls, "Industrial Democracy," as Beatrice Webb first phrased it very happily, in her study of co-operation (1891), constitute a necessary completion of the democratic proposition. A dwindling minority clings to the private profit system as the logical method of the sturdy individualism of the revolution. But the general implication of modern democracy is that unrestrained economic advantage can be an even graver infringement of human liberty than privilege. Modern democracy is not only legalism and equalitarianism; it is socialism. It sets its face against all abuse of the advantages of ownership.

Democracy is socialism, and also, by a natural extension of its equalitarianism as the problem of world law becomes urgent, it is cosmopolitan. Almost tacitly democracy has accepted and assimilated the necessity that law must be world law and equally protective of every individual human being.

So far as cosmopolitanism goes, modern democracy reverts to far older revolts of human common sense against racial, national and class distinctions. Since the rise of Buddhism there has been hardly any broad religious initiative that has not at least paid lip service to this idea which, in Christianity for example, is incorporated in the formula of an impartial divine fatherhood and an equal brotherhood of man. In The Outline Of History the association of cosmopolitanism with theocrasia and the appearance of the syncretic universal religions is traced. There was a double impulse from below and from above; the desire of the expanding empires to fuse local particularisms into a larger order under the God-Emperor was in accordance with the craving of normal common sense to escape from the irksomeness of obviously artificial estrangements. Dr. T.J. Haarhoff, quoting W.W. Tarn's Alexander And The Unity of Mankind, declares that Alexander "was the pioneer of one of the supreme revolutions in the world outlook, the first man known to us who contemplated the brotherhood of man or the unity of mankind." This is an exaggeration of a significant fact. Cosmopolitanism, universal brotherhood, has indeed been appearing and reappearing in human thought for at least the past four and twenty centuries, like sunshine trying to break through a cloudy sky.

Now the "democracy" that found its expression in the first French Revolution, the American Revolution and the liberal movement throughout the world, was not only incomplete upon the economic side and had, later and with difficulty, to become socialist in order to preserve its liberating intention, but also it was very sketchy and indefinite in the matter of education.

This was due to the fact that the ideology of the Great Revolution was essentially middle-class in its origins. It sprang from a social stratum already educated and so satisfied with the sufficiency of its general education and so accustomed to a supply of books and pamphlets, that it did not realize that there was anything exceptional in the knowledge and freedom of thought it enjoyed. It did not even apprehend its immense and immediate obligations to the Encyclopaedists in organizing its ideas. It took their contribution for granted. It launched its generous proposition of universal equality indeed, but not only did it fail to realize the need to insure freedom from economic pressure, but also it neglected to organize the education of the community as one whole. The American Revolution, in this respect, with, for example, its provision of State universities, seems to have been ahead of the French. Nevertheless it took the better part of a century for democracy to realize, even to a limited extent, the third vital implication of its demand for liberty, equality, and fraternity, which was the free and necessary universal education of the democratic community to a common level of understanding and co-operation. Communities in which every mentally normal citizen can at least read and write, have existed for less than a century. Communities in which the common education rises much above that level do not yet exist.

That freedom and equality are incomplete without freely accessible knowledge and free and open discussion is a necessary completion of the democratic idea, but it is one upon which the inquirer into the meaning of democracy will get the least assurance. If he asks leading questions, he will get a general admission that universal education and sound, ample information upon every matter of collective concern are necessary elements in the democratic proposition, but unless he himself introduces the matter he will hear very little insistence upon this vital completion of the democratic ideal.

He will indeed encounter a certain amount of impatience if he stresses this matter. Ordinary people resent being told that they are undereducated or wrongly educated. To the common man and woman today, prepared though their minds seem to be now for a socialist cosmopolis of a quite , and news is what a press run entirely for profit and political and social ends, and (in the British system) a government-controlled radio, choose to tell them. It is the education they have grown up to, and so far they have not been awakened to its insufficiency. They want to carry out these new conceptions of life at that level To raise that level seems to them irksome and uncalled for.*

* See Note 6A.

It is still possible therefore for the equalitarian impulse to be effectively frustrated in practice by deliberate and systematic miseducation and misinformation. The common man and woman know now in general terms and pretty definitely what they want, but they still do not know how to state and demand what they want. Private enterprise is able to defend its appropriations quite effectively, because it owns the press almost entirely, the news agencies and the distributing trades, and so it can distort values and distract the public from crucial issues in the boldest fashion. There is no countervailing equipment of the public mind in the common schools. These are essentially conservative institutions, adapting the common man to the social order in which he finds himself, preparing him for that state of life to which he has been called, and giving him no reasonable intimations of the great drama of change in which he has to play his part. As we have shown, the whole mechanism of modern life demands organized collective control. The stars in their courses will not suffer the world scramble of exploitation that wasted so much human possibility in the nineteenth century to go on. Our species cannot afford it under any conditions. But in face of the essential ignorance of the modern "democratic" community, the enterprising owner, the profiteer that is to say, can keep his grip upon his advantages far more effectively than he can in the face of a dictator with unqualified powers. He can resist socialization far more effectively.

Against the capitalist's obstructive power the willfulness of the dictator is able to operate far more vigorously than the will of the under-educated, ill-informed and suggestible "democracies." So that in certain ways the dictatorships have undoubtedly been able to get ahead of the "democratic" states. They have gone further on the way to socialization. While the industrial exploiter or the rich man struggles to keep his grip on the recalcitrant worker below, the dictator of the totalitarian state takes him firmly by the collar. Wealth finds itself handled with an extraordinary disrespect. Dictatorships imply collectivism. They are forced to collectivism in the face of bargaining wealth and the uneasy claims of their own supporters. They are forced towards a comprehensive efficiency. The only effective response to totalitarian collectivism on the part of a freedom-seeking community is a scientifically planned and directed socialism.

From the economic point of view, the whole difference now between the reality of dictatorship and the ideal of democracy, when it is worked out to its practical completion, is the difference between socialization in the dark, with all the progressive corruption, appropriation and inefficiency that spring up in the dark, and socialization in the light of an alert and implemented public opinion; between socialization by compulsion or socialization by enlightened consent.

From the point of view of the individual the difference is one between a deadening servitude and a continual participating enlargement of responsible life. No existing institutions coming to us from the past can represent democracy as it is thus conceived; it is a far bolder thrust towards a new order than any of these adventurer systems that stand in its path.

If now we fill in the gaps in the current conception of democracy by insisting upon complete educational equalitarianism, if we dot the i's and cross the /s that are still undotted and uncrossed, if we transcend any accepted contemporary rendering of the idea, then "democracy" does indeed become a very magnificent conception of a new life for man.

If democracy means economic justice and the attainment of that universal sufficiency that science assures us is possible today; if democracy means the intensest possible fullness of knowledge for everyone who desires to know and the greatest possible freedom of criticism and individual self-expression for anyone who desires to object; if democracy means a community saturated with the conception of a common social objective and with an educated will like the will of a team of football players to co-operate willingly and understandingly upon that objective; if democracy means a complete and unified police control throughout the world, to repress the financial scramble and gangster violence which constitute the closing phase of the sovereign state and private ownership system; then we have in democracy a conception of life for which every intelligent man and woman on earth may well be prepared to live, fight or die, as circumstances may require.

But that rounded-off and completed realization of democracy is still only establishing itself against great resistances in the human mind. It is not as yet established there. And still less is it established as the guiding faith of any political or social organization whatever.

41

7. — WHERE IS DEMOCRACY?

WHERE in all this collection of governments Mr. Streit would have us federate, is there one that satisfies this plain bare statement of the growing and deepening significance of the democratic idea?

France depends for its mental expression upon an alliance of reactionary papers and for its foreign policy upon an association of diplomatists and army chiefs, which has held together throughout its dynastic and political fluctuations in one consistent policy for the security and advancement of La France. America tempers a wide tolerance of free speech and personal criticism with a press-sustained persecution of labor leaders, radicals, "reds" and "agitators" generally. Its press, if less centralized than the French and so less concerted, is equally commercial. The freedom of expression of its university professors is pinched between the possibility of dismissal for excessive outspokenness from above and the attacks of the press-man from below. The American record of successfully framed-up cases against troublesome workers' leaders is a long and discreditable one, and one need only glance reproachfully at the distressful history of color prejudice, unincorporated townships and the exploitation of penal labor in the more backward states. And yet these two are the "democracies" par excellence.

Most of the European states invited to Mr. Streit's federation are not even democratic in profession. Sweden, Norway, Denmark, Holland and the British Empire are monarchies; the monarch professes to act only on the advice of his or her ministers, but as a matter of fact the court is a center of social and administrative influence of an entirely undemocratic sort. A crown is the symbol of graded privilege. In the place of Heil Hitler or the Fascist salute, these royalist peoples, at the sound of their particular Royal Anthem, stand stiffly to attention with an air of ineffable reverence. It is a quite parallel act of worship, and as complete a repudiation of the personal responsibility of democracy.

The disintegrating British Empire is now, one has to recognize, a system of government almost completely out of popular control. Practically it has undergone a reactionary revolution in the last decade, and a loose-knit combination of court, church, army and wealth, intensely class-conscious, intensely self-protective, has resumed control of affairs. It is an oligarchy skillful in the assimilation of useful or formidable individuals but without the slightest disposition to amalgamate with anything else on earth. Its ruling motive is the fear of dispossession. Decisions involving peace or war are made without any pretense of consulting any surviving popular will, and the whole capitalist press, the cinema, the radio and indeed all possible means of influencing opinion, concentrate upon the assertion of the rightness and inevitableness of these decisions. Dissent is a muffled and ineffective squeaking, and any inconvenient facts are kept from the public by requests for suppression that are in effect commands. There is a special Form D sent round to the press which it is extremely unwise to defy. Most of the acts of Mr. Chamberlain since September 1938 have been as irresponsible as those of any Dictator, equally unscrupulous and far more shameful. He has indeed made himself a Dictator by tact and betrayal instead of by violent seizure. There is in the long run very little to choose between a bully dictatorship and a "tact" dictatorship. The latter may be less crushing but more insidious in its attack upon human dignity.

These are the practical realities Mr. Streit has to face. The will for federation in any of these governments is more than doubtful—even if presently they have their backs to the wall. They will all fight for their separate sovereignty to the last.

No doubt it is true that, in spite of much human inconsistency, much confused thinking and many local abuses, there is still a powerful disposition throughout all the Atlantic and Scandinavian communities towards liberty, equality and world brotherhood. It breaks out in literature, discussion and conduct. It expresses itself plainly in books, spontaneous press writing, plays and films. This is most manifest in America and there is in consequence a growing disposition of the British authorities to intercept and censor the too outspoken American weekly press. An increasing number of English readers subscribe to American periodicals to learn what is being hushed up in their own country.

With every acceleration of communications this American influence will increase. Moreover, there are plenty of American professors manifestly disposed to take the risk of outspokenness and say what they like. If at times they veil their meaning a little from the possible hostility of the unintelligent in a deliberate obscurity of technicality that sometimes borders on jargon, that does not prevent their speculating very boldly about economic, social and international processes, muck more boldly and freshly than their English equivalents.

Again the bitter jests of such a French periodical as Le Canard Enchaîné are saturated with the soundest democratic scorn and derision. The desire of a considerable section of enlightened Frenchmen to sustain and complete the mighty impetus of the Declaration of the Rights of Man is genuine and obstinate. They will not willingly suffer France to desist from her traditional task of world enlightenment. For some years, in the face of overwhelming financial and political difficulties, there has been a gallant attempt to produce a modern encyclopaedia, which might repeat the preparatory role of the original Encyclopaedists for the vaster needs of today.*

* See Note 7A, the Italian Encyclopedia.

Neither Americans nor British, with their vastly greater resources, have attempted anything so comprehensive and illuminating. It would be possible to quote hundreds of instances, names, books, speeches, utterances and acts, to show that all round and about the world in a great multitude of still all-too-dispersed intelligences, democracy lives and advances.

But these evidences of a considerable and growing will for a reasonably complete democracy do not alter the fact that the directive forces in control of this miscellany of states Mr. Streit and his disciples would have us federate, are scarcely more democratic in structure and method than those running the frankly anti-democratic states.

Indeed, to call the present world convulsion a war between the "allied democracies" of the world and "totalitarian states," is putting all too fine a name upon it. The reality will be a war of established governments and governing systems claiming to represent "democracy" but quite unwilling and unprepared to set themselves to realize the modern democratic idea, against expansive desperado governments that have shown themselves -contemptuous of democratic pretensions and dangerous to the general peace. It will be another war for the alteration or preservation of frontiers.

It is almost impossible to hope that this complex of warfare towards which the world is drifting can assume any other form than a confused alliance against these more lawless military powers, whatever formal victories or defeats ensue. It is incredible that there will not be a steady deterioration in human morale through the stresses of the struggle. If the so-called aggressor states are defeated, their unfortunate common people will be saddled with the war guilt of the governments that have enslaved and ruined them. They will be made to "pay" again. Another insincere attempt to organize "collective security" on the lines of the League of Nations, another unstable League of victors, will simply accumulate the necessary resentments for another collapse into still more violent conflict. Fresh brigand adventurers will appear, trading on the shame and despair of the vanquished.

It is this that makes the approach of this second world-war storm so black. Whichever side emerges at any particular phase as victorious, is really a secondary issue. The practical loss of freedom, the usurpation of controls, seems inevitable.

The possibility of an emergence of any sort of enhancement of democracy from the threatened mêlée seems very slight indeed. Democracy is still too incomplete, unorganized and unprepared to bring about any such happy ending. Catastrophe is still steadily outrunning education. We are at present rapidly experiencing a repetition of 1914-1919 on a vastly more disastrous scale.

42

8. — WHAT MAN HAS TO LEARN

IF we hold firmly to that same systematic assembling of universally acceptable statements which has brought us thus far, it is not overwhelmingly difficult to state the nature of the mental adaptation that is needed to arrest this present drive towards biological disaster for Homo sapiens. If it has become necessary for him to be re-educated as a conscious world citizen, to be prepared to take his place in a collective world fellowship, then plainly the realization of this necessity is the framework upon which his social being must be rebuilt. The scientific vision of life in the universe and no other has to be his vision of the universe. Any other leads ultimately to disaster. And since the existing educational organization of the world does not provide anything like that vision nor establish the necessary conceptions of right conduct that arise out of it, it needs to be recast quite as much and even more than the political framework needs to be recast. This may involve, it will almost certainly involve, such a Kulturfkampf as the world has never seen before. But since it is the only possible line of survival, that effort has to be faced. Unless there is sufficient mental and moral vigor in our race to achieve the educational readjustment, then there seems to be nothing that can possibly arrest the present dégringolade of Homo sapiens.

43

9. — SAMPLE OF A GENERATION

LET us be as full and explicit as possible about this reorganization of man's mental superstructure, this reconditioning of his apparatus for adaptation, that we are stressing.

And here again there is nothing original and hardly anything that is fairly controversial in what will be stated here. The only originality lies in an adherence to one consistent line of thought, to carrying the broad and practically indisputable statements of modern ecological science, unimpaired, into the field of current human affairs and refusing to be deflected or complicated by secondary and irrelevant considerations.

It happens to have been my role throughout life to assemble facts and interpretations of fact, bearing upon man's power of controlling his future. From the days of that paradoxical fantasy, The Time Machine (1894) onward, my mind, partly no doubt by the accidents of life, but partly also, I think, by a natural predisposition, has been directed more and more definitely to the question of what is likely to happen in the future. And looking back upon this half-century of discussion and suggestion and tracing its development phase by phase, a very remarkable change in the whole tenor of human thought becomes manifest.

It is only now, indeed, as I bring all these things together to review, that I realize how our attitude to past and future has changed since the later-Victorian period. There has been an almost complete reorientation, at once profound and subtle, of our minds with regard to time.

Briefly: the intelligence of the nineties attached much more importance to the past and much less to the probabilities of the days to come, than do any contemporary minds now. It was living in what appears now as an almost static present. The past supplied a picturesque system of justifications for the established state of affairs, but it was the established state of affairs alone which had any quality of reality. There was a widespread feeling that nothing more of primary importance was ever likely to happen. Life as we knew it was a leisurely game of consequences. It is difficult now, even for those of us who were already living in those days, to recall the entire absence of urgency that prevailed. We were carried along by habit and that false sense of security which the absence of fundamental crises engenders. To most of my generation in the eighties and nineties, all the cardinal discoveries of science seemed to have been made, all the great political systems established for good, the world permanently apportioned among the Powers. We had a sort of feeling that Queen Victoria, under whose rule everybody up to high middle age had been born, would go on living forever. The future was something in another universe, in another dimension. One could say or think anything one liked about it because it did not seem to matter in the least.

This habit of mind lingered long after the beliefs on which it had been established had decayed. It lingers still.

One factor in the steadily accelerated swing from traditionalism and legalism to futurism, that presently began, was certainly the enlargement of our horizons by the realization of evolution and geological time and the breaking of the barriers set to our imaginations by the myth of the Creation and the Fall. But at first there was—how can one put it?—an intellectual but not a practical release. It was still possible in The Time Machine to imagine humanity on the verge of extinction and differentiated into two decadent species, the Eloi and the Morlocks, without the slightest reflection upon everyday life. Quite a lot of people thought that idea was very clever in its sphere, very clever indeed, and no one minded in the least. It seemed to have no sort of relation whatever to normal existence.

To a large extent, I shared that detachment. If I was imaginatively futurist, I was for all practical purposes contemporaneous. The possible extinction of humanity appeared to be something so remote that it never gave me a moment's real uneasiness in those days. The future was still no more real than dreamland.

But all that has changed, and I have come through the phases of that change. Now the questions: "What is going to happen?" and "And then what will happen?" dominate an increasing number of awakening minds among which I am moving. We live in a planning world. Everything we do is becoming preparatory and anticipatory. Today has vanished almost completely in our enormous preoccupation with tomorrow.

I suppose I have responded as much as anyone in my generation to this mental rotation. There is no need therefore for me to apologize for using myself as the trace of the flow of thought during the past half century. I happen to be the most convenient trace. If I were not so, then somebody else should be writing this book instead of me.

To begin with I used the future as a field for purely imaginative play. After The Time Machine I wrote some more futuristic stories. But as one followed another I found I was less and less interested in the artistic business of making the tale plausible and more and more in the scientific interest of making it probable. The turn of the century set many of us forecasting in earnest. My natural bias or my journalistic instinct, or maybe both in unison, moved me to write Anticipations (1900), in which I threw the teller of fantastic tales aside altogether and set myself speculating about the coming years. I was moving with the times. The book caught on; it was more successful than most novels; it was one of the first of such books to sell well. I will not say anything of its guesses, some happy, some wildly out. But it left me with the persuasion that here was something needing to be done and which could be done much more thoroughly than I had done it. My sense of the importance and reality of the future increased.

In 1902 I was reading a paper to the Royal Institution, The Discovery Of The Future, in which I was boldly asserting the need to realize and accept a forward-looking system of values. I presently found myself in correspondence with various parallel groups abroad which, half in defiance and half in burlesque, were proclaiming the Futurist doctrine. Among them was Signer Marinetti, who came to London reciting, in a tremendous voice, the most astounding Futurist poetry. He resented with extreme bitterness the English and American tourists in Italy with their red guide-books like catalogues at a sale. He was, he said, prepared to destroy all the historical monuments in the peninsula. He demanded, loudly and violently, a living country and not a museum of antiques.

The impulse spread, but still for a great number even of progressive-minded people it retained a quality of unreality. It was an exuberance for them, a lark, a fashion. This Futurist stuff, they felt, could not last. In practice they still clung to the established order for their permanent values. It was the shock and stresses of the Great War that wrenched them away finally from this assumption of permanent stability towards a reluctant, imperfect recognition of the greater importance of the anticipatory aspect of life. It was like the internal change-over that must happen in a bar of iron when it is magnetized. And many quite intelligent people were not wrenched away. They kept up their resistances, and a large body of the educated still resist—as we shall see. But the forward-looking section accumulated conviction; their sense of reality continued to shift away more and more decisively from the thing that is to the thing that is to be. The Discovery Of The Future became by degrees a matter-of-fact statement for me instead of a daring thesis. I believed in it as time went on much more than I had done when first I launched it.

As the war unfolded before me, my mind was increasingly obsessed by the problem of how the war would end and what would come after the war. Imaginative people were guessing and inferring and making plans. The word "plan" became more and more frequent; at length no newspaper was complete without it. A Ministry of Foresight was suggested. We busied ourselves in making the New Map of Europe, the New Map of the World. The idea of a "League of Nations" emerged amidst this ferment of anticipatory projects. An interesting phase in all this forward-looking peering was the War Aims controversy, I happened to be working in Northcliffe's Ministry of Propaganda in Enemy Countries.*

[* See Secrets Of Crewe House by Sir Campbell Stuart.]

I was in particular directing the propaganda in Germany, and, in co-operation with Dr. J W. Headlam-Morley, I induced our Crewe House colleagues to draw up a memorandum upon the allied war aims and submit it to the Foreign Office for endorsement. "This," we said, "is what we suppose we are fighting for, and if we can get this we shall be satisfied and the war will be at an end. Is that so? We cannot go on with our work properly unless we know its objective." The War Office was profoundly shocked. Whatever else in the world had been affected by the rotation of the human mind towards the future, the Foreign Office has remained immune. There, at any rate, war was what it always had been. You fought your way to your enemy's capital and you then "dictated terms." The objective of a war was victory. To reveal your terms beforehand was not done. So the Foreign Office never committed itself to a binding endorsement of our War Aims Memorandum, and it never warned us of various secret understandings that affected it. It remained in the self-satisfying pose of a superior body tolerating us and using us according to the best diplomatic traditions. And at length at Versailles the terms were dictated.

Until the German capitulation we went on with our development of the League of Nations movement, committing ourselves to very definite promises to the German people, in the hope that our engagements would be honored at the Peace. They were not honored. We had taken the utmost pains in our propaganda to distinguish between the German people and the Hohenzollern government, and to hold out hopes of a speedy return to the fellowship of nations and a reasonable prospect of recuperation to a chastened and republican Germany. The victorious Foreign Offices treated all that as new-fangled rubbish. The Quai d'Orsay in particular seemed obsessed with a dream of obliterating Germany, of dividing it up so that it would never reassemble itself. They continued to kick Germany about until Germany became frantic with shame and hate, until Germany passed from reason to screaming fury. Its screaming fury found its incarnation at last in Hitler. He did not hesitate at the thought of war. He demanded war. He did not hesitate at the possibility of a subsequent social revolution. The victors of Versailles found Red Revolution even more terrifying than flaming war, and he played upon that terror. They passed from arrogance to propitiatory terror. This madman, they felt, might do anything. History became an attempt to humor and appease a lunatic who after all—and that was the worst of it for them—was not always quite so mad as he seemed.

All that is now quite familiar to everyone. What concerns us more directly here are those meetings and movements and discussions that occurred when the idea of the League of Nations was being shaped. These deliberations brought home to me the confused divergence of historical preoccupations among those taking part in them. Their minds were full of broken scraps of history, irrational political prejudices, impossible analogies. Everyone saw the idea from a different angle and seemed prepared to realize it by the hastiest of compromises. The Outline of History was the direct outcome of the experience I gathered in these discussions. At first, in conjunction with L.S. Woolf* and one or two others, I tried to organize a Research Committee, which would set itself to think out the full significance and possibilities of this great idea. We made William Archer, who was badly out of a job just then, the salaried secretary of this body.

* Author of an excellent book, International Government (1916).

With much internal friction we compiled The Idea Of A League Of Nations, Prolegomena To The Study Of World Organization, and The Way To The League Of Nations: A Brief Sketch Of The Practical Steps Needed For The Formation Of A League. These booklets are still available for the collector. Then President Wilson came to Europe and we were swept aside, because he had his own ideas, and very crude ideas they were, of a League that would make the world safe for democracy. But the difficulty of producing these two reports opened my eyes to the enormous obstacles in the way of all volunteered co-operation. It seemed impossible to hold a team together. They differed upon endless points and they would not come together to hammer diem out. They were all too intent upon what they considered more immediately important things. Our chief financial supporter deserted us to go off wool-gathering upon his own lines.* He could not see what need there was for all this highbrow research. But we were all going off upon our own lines. We had already disintegrated before we were disregarded.

* See Note 9A, expanding this.

At a conference with some representative Americans at the Reform Club during the war, I pointed out the urgent need for a general history of mankind which would consolidate people's ideas about the establishment of some sort of World Pax. Everyone thought it was a good idea. But here again was something which was nobody's business in particular. There was no time to go about collecting, persuading and editing the academically right people. One might as well have asked Lord Acton to write something. An Outline of History had to be done soon, even if it had to be flung together—and, getting help wherever I could find it, I flung one together.

I did it as well as I could, I worked enormously, and the strenuous hostile criticism to which it has since been subjected has revealed hardly any serious errors of statement. But a lot of it was headlong writing. It seemed to me at the time that if I and a few people could show that there was a shape to history, then it would be easy, since there is no copyright in the past, for the professional historians to rectify any serious flaws and do it better. They did nothing of the sort, and, failing that better performance, The Outline of History was launched upon a world conspicuously in need of just that assemblage of information. It had a fantastic success. Millions of copies have been sold and it has been translated into practically every important language in the world—except Italian. Fascist Italy could not tolerate the candid criticism of the Roman Empire.

I was probably rather excited by this astonishing boom. I do not know about that because I was not watching myself very closely. But I think that even at the time I did realize that this immense sale was no tribute to my authorship. It was something much more significant. It was the revelation of a world-wide hunger for adequately summarized knowledge on the part of multitudes whom the schools had sent empty away.

It seemed to me that this aching void probably extended far beyond the field of history. I knew that the general public throughout the world was being kept in the blackest ignorance of modern biological knowledge, evolutionary thought, modern ideas about individuality and modern psychology. I have already told in the Introduction how I realized that in my own case. With the assistance of Dr. Julian Huxley and my son, G.P. Wells, I produced a far more competent companion volume to The Outline Of History, The Science Of Life. It is fuller and more searching and better done than its predecessor, but its success was by no means astronomical.

Then I turned to the most difficult and original of all these encyclopaedic essays, The Work, Wealth And Happiness Of Mankind. This was an attempt to rescue social, economic and monetary "science" from the medieval scholasticism, the theorizing unworldliness, in which it still wanders. It was also an attempt to get behind the arbitrary assumptions upon which the Marxist doctrine of a necessary class war is based. Instead of jumping into the matter in the accepted academic style from some crudely plausible assumption, I approached these questions as a special branch of human ecology, and opened the matter out from a realistic survey of human life as a going concern. I began with a survey of the substances and power in the service of man, and thence I pursued a series of interrogations, How? and Why? up to government and education.

It was a laborious task; I chose some unsuitable collaborators from whom I had to disentangle the enterprise with considerable expense and difficulty; but in the end I managed to get every section of it "vetted" by authorities of the first rank. It is sound and tested matter.

In the end the book failed to earn the attention I think it deserved. The title may have been unpromising to the ordinary reader, the manner of its marketing unsuitable. It might have had better fortune as An Outline Of Social And Economic Knowledge. I am convinced there is as great a public ready for a summary of facts and ideas upon social, political and monetary matters as there is for historical and biological digests. The book did not get to them. The world of economists and so forth ignored it completely—but then it is their practice also to ignore one another completely, to ignore almost everything completely. I find a sort of recognition of it in Barbara Wootton's brilliant Lament For Economics (1938), for which I am discouraged enough to be grateful. She is not biologically trained, she is probably quite ignorant of general ecology, but her realization that economics has still to become a science and can only become a science by admitting the descriptive treatment and examination of actual things and processes, is perfectly clear.

One other book I must mention here. The Salvaging of Civilization was written originally to be delivered as lectures in America, a project frustrated by a bout of influenza. Therein, borrowing a phrase from Dr. John Beattie Crozier,* I launched the idea of a "Bible" for civilization. In this idea of a "Bible" for the new social and political order, it is plain that Dr. Crozier and myself are groping our way and getting very near to a full realization of the scale and nature of the mental readjustment incumbent upon the world.

* See Note 9B

This new "Bible" of ours is the World Encyclopaedia, to which I am coming, in embryo. I will not recapitulate the various other papers, pamphlets, books, with which I documented my successive mental readjustments, because they are ceasing to have anything more than a minor, personal significance. I was traveling along a road that a number of my contemporaries were following.

Step by step the more responsive elements in my generation were being forced towards a complete recognition of the need for a realistic preparation for the future, if our existence henceforth was to be anything better than a mechanical response to the blows of adverse fate that were beating upon us now, faster and faster. We were asking "What shall we do?" and more realistically "What have we to do?" and it was plain that the answers to these questions needed setting down as the necessary articles of association for a world-wide revolutionary effort. There may have been a slight slackening of this mental fermentation during the phase of the Fatuous Twenties, but it was revived with the mounting sense of urgency that came with the Frightened Thirties. Crisis appeared following crisis, each more menacing than the last—it was like the Pacific surf coming in before a rising gale—and what had we prepared for these crises?

By the early thirties I was one of those who were becoming fully aware that the systematic reconditioning of our mental life was not a secondary but a primary need for all mankind. It has beyond all question become now the most urgent and important thing in the world.

And also I was realizing the unsatisfactoriness of such detached, uncoordinated work as writers of my type were doing. A number of us were all saying very much the same sort of thing, but without much co-ordination or anything mutual in the way of consequences. We could plead that we were pioneering and exploring, but that is merely a provisional plea. There comes a time to have done with sketches and samples. There is a quantitative element in real affairs. Doing something does not amount to very much unless you do enough.

The achievement of the French Encyclopaedists has always appealed very strongly to my imagination. Diderot and his associates had scented the onset of change; they had set themselves, in the measure of their times, to prepare and equip the ideology of the new world they anticipated. They worked against great difficulties and within hampering limitations, but they did produce a new, inspiring conception of a world renewed. They gave a definite form and direction to the confused and powerful liberal impulses of their time. Their assembled thought materialized in the American and French revolutions and in a great heartening of the creative spirit of man throughout the whole world. They lived in an age of comparatively small things. The public capable of understanding and transmitting their ideas was a limited one. But it became very clear to me that what was needed in the face of the oncoming challenges of our time was essentially a new Encyclopaedism commensurate with the relative vastness of our new occasions.

I set myself to the development of this idea of a modern Encyclopaedism which should assemble facts and suggestions with the same insistence upon scientific reality and the same exclusion of irrelevances that has controlled the establishment of the world outlook I have put before the reader.

In a small book, World Brain (1938), the reader will find the substance of my proposals stated more fully and explicitly than is convenient here. I would be glad if the reader could find time to get and read it. I have made a sort of campaign for this new Encyclopaedism and I continue to work for it to the best of my ability. World Brain is a book, quite bold and uncompromising in substance, but still with a distinctly propitiatory manner. It makes clear and definite proposals for a world-wide reconstruction of what we call higher education. What I call the permanent World Encyclopaedia is projected as a permanent institution, a mighty super-university, holding together, utilizing and dominating all the teaching and research organizations at present in existence. This is shown to be not only a plausible and practicable idea, but an idea already finding a material embodiment in part and detail, through the common-sense needs of the scientific and technical world. A permanent World Encyclopaedia, as I show in that book, is indeed crystallizing into existence, but at a pace altogether too slow for the urgency of the human situation. Bound up with this in the same book is a frank survey of what the citizen of a modern democratic world should know—that is to say, a scheme for an adequate modern education. This survey constituted my address as President of the Education Section of the British Association at Nottingham in 1937. It is much more provocative in its manner than the Royal Institution lecture of which it forms the complement. It completely excluded both the Bible mythology and national and imperial history from the educational scheme.

Throughout 1937 I was doing what I could to promote this new Encyclopaedism I had in mind, but with very little effect, and in the autumn I went to America and lectured, as World Brain relates. There is no need to recapitulate that American discourse here, but what is very apparent to me as I re-read the book, is the sacrifice of intensity in the effort to make it interesting and attractive. I am trying out ways and means in a very discursive spirit. I attempt some disarming jests. I write as though there was still quite sufficient time in hand to bring about the new mental orientation. I still had that feeling. Taking myself as a fair sample of the more progressive thought of my time, it is plain that up to the publication of World Brain in the spring of 1938 we were still not fully aware of the nearness of a culminating crisis in human affairs.

That forced itself upon our attention in spite of ourselves. We were compelled by the rush of circumstances to realize not only the unqualified soundness, but also, what is by no means the same thing, the urgent and fundamental importance of our intellectual convictions.

In the summer I was invited to be the guest of the Australian and New Zealand Association for the Advancement of Science at Canberra, and this involved giving an hour's discourse. I was becoming more and more impatient with the failure of the new encyclopaedia idea to secure any energetic support, and also I was growing more and more impatient with my own personal ineffectiveness in the matter. I determined to use this invitation to assert still more plainly and clearly—to myself among other hearers—the case for a new encyclopaedia and a radical revision of the world's educational organization. In Canberra I gave this address the tide of The Role of English In The Development Of The World Mind, for reasons I have set out in a note at the end of this book.*

* For the advantages of English see Note 9C

I repeated this lecture with some slight modifications as a public lecture in Sydney Town Hall, under the title of The Human Outlook. Substantially this book is an expansion of that address. Its line of thought is the same; its conclusions are the same. It is fuller, much more explicit and more closely reasoned, and its application to current affairs is closer and, to my mind, inescapable.

In addition I volunteered to read another paper to the Education Section at Canberra. I called it A Provocative Paper On The Poison Called History. This also was made into a very largely attended public lecture, at which debate would have been impossible. It was an hour's show. As I wanted to bring whatever opposition there might be to my thesis into the light of clear statement, I suggested that the Education Section should provide time for its discussion.

The reception of these lectures and addresses was very typical of the transitional state of mind in which we are all living, even the most enlightened of us. They were, you must take my word for it, vividly successful. They were delivered in a setting of compliments and applause. I had been stimulating, amazingly stimulating. I had said things that had long needed saying. I had given them all food for thought of the most invigorating kind. Distinguished men of science came to thank me earnestly for the plainness of my statements. And so on.

And then everything went on just as it had been going on before. The stimulant seemed to evaporate at once and the food was certainly not assimilated.

The Right Honorable William Hughes, that distinguished Australian statesman, had very kindly consented to preside over my Town Hall lecture and at the end of it he expressed his appreciation. "God save us all," he said, and then, advancing to the front of the platform, he led the audience with the singing of "God Save the King." Everybody stiffened up to attention. I had been stating as lucidly as I could the reasons for believing that the human species was already staggering past the zenith of its ascendancy and on its way through a succession of disasters to extinction. And then we shook off the disagreeable vision, and lifted up our voices in simple loyalty to things as they are.

The discussion of that "provocative paper" by the Education Section was still more remarkable. I had denounced the teaching of the Judaeo-Christian mythology as historical fact, in the most emphatic terms. Not a single Christian teacher appeared to reply to that challenge. Most of them, including the masters in one or two progressive schools who had been most anxious to turn my publicity value to account, contrived to have a parallel conference with another Section. In place of a discussion upon the crucial points I had sharpened, we had a series of brief, disconnected addresses by various educational officials, public characters and thoughtful people, about education in general, speaking in an elevated and discursive spirit, making many admirable but irrelevant philosophical remarks and including much autobiographical material. The avoidance of the essential issue was complete. And it was quite deliberate. The discussion was over and nothing had come of it and things were still very agreeably as they always had been. Tea was ready.

Now these were not consciously backward people. They knew indeed that they were the elite of Australasian progress. These Associations for the Advancement of Science throughout the world, the British, the American and the Australasian, are essentially assemblies of well-informed and liberal and progressive minds. But the real world of our Conference was still this wholly present world in which there are parents to consider, promotion to consider, dismissals, retirements, a world of knighthoods and honors. I went away pondering these things. Presently—let me confess it, lest I seem to claim to be anything better than a sample of a generation—I found myself discussing rather keenly the terms upon which I would lecture in Sydney.

Plainly we are not moving fast enough. We are still balancing in this strange phase of indecision between the actual present and the inevitable future. Even what we may call the more advanced intelligences vacillate and fail to sustain their constructive faith. The established, habitual present remains their real world. They may be profoundly disturbed—intellectually. They may be greatly unsettled and alarmed by the ever-increasing uncertainty of life, but still, in the exact sense of the word "realize," they fail to realize the urgent, implacable future. As the legendary gentleman who sat over his drink in the bar of the sinking Titanic remarked: "Well, anyhow, the damn thing hasn't gone down yet."

They are all continually relapsing towards acceptance of the prevalent contemporaneous outlook because that is what is most natural in the normal human make-up. At any sign of respite they yield to it. Alertness to the future, we have to realize, is a novel and artificial thing in life. It has to be constantly refreshed and sustained. Minds must be trained and accustomed to it; it is a matter of social atmosphere much more than individual intelligence. They have to be held up to it by something stronger and more permanent than themselves.

It is only in such an educational organization as I have been deducing from our present needs and, I hope, forecasting here, in such a permanent organization of knowledge, systematically assembled, continually extended and renewed and made freely and easily accessible to everyone, that there is the slightest hope of our species meeting the serried challenges of destiny that advance upon it. It is impossible to be steadily futuristic, solo, without a sustaining social organization which will give as assured and habitual a quality to the forward orientation of the everyday life as is now possessed by the unprogressive world of today.

And that organization fails to materialize.

I am impatient and at the same time I do not know how to accelerate matters. I do not think this is simply a case of the distress of an old man in a hurry. There is every justification for hurry in the world about us. I think that however young and hopeful I might be, I should still be intensely impatient to see this movement for human re-education quickened and implemented.

This reconditioning and reorientation of the human mind has to be undertaken not merely against the innate resistances to changing conditions in everyone's make-up. These innate resistances are organized very powerfully and effectively, and the nature of their organization is one we have now to examine. And also we are working against time. It is this time factor that casts the darkest shadow upon the possibility of a single, clear-headed, creative, happily interested, war-free human community emerging from the returning chaos of the present to dominate our planet through long ages still to come.

Years ago I threw out a sentence that caught the attention of that very great and lucid historian, James Harvey Robinson. He picked it up and repeated and commended it and gave it a wide publicity. The outlook for mankind, I had written—I think in The Salvaging Of Civilization—"a race between education and catastrophe."

Today catastrophe is well on its way, it is losing no time at all, but education seems still unable to get started, has indeed not even readjusted itself to start. The race may, after all, prove a walk-over for disaster.

44

10. — ESTIMATING HOPE

HERE a personal factor comes in, which, I think, should be explained to the reader.

We are now in a field of thought from which it is impossible to banish a temperamental estimate of values. I find a certain defeatism has invaded my mind in the course of the past year. I anticipate very little happiness in the residue of my life. I feel that the odds are very heavily against any such educational revolution being even attempted in my lifetime—there will be no Pisgah glimpse of the promised world for me—and that in all probability my last years will be passed in a very ugly and distressful phase of human history. In many quarters I am unlikely to be a persona grata, A spell of ill-health involving bodily discomfort and a considerable ebb of mental resilience is contributing to this depression. These are my circumstances. That matter of health is comparatively a minor issue. But quite apart from any bodily depression, the spectacle of evil in the world during the past half-dozen years—the wanton destruction of homes, the ruthless hounding of decent folk into exile, the bombings of open cities, the cold-blooded massacres and mutilations of children and defenseless gentle people, the rapes and filthy humiliations and, above all, the return of deliberate and organized torture, mental torment and fear to a world from which such things had seemed wellnigh banished—has come near to breaking my spirit altogether.

Said an old friend of mine the other day: "If only we could get away from events for a spell! If only we could get together as we used to get together and laugh!"

Children still laugh. Laughter is born again in each generation. What is past is over and done with for those who did not share in it. Life begins again incessantly. The sequence of birth and death is a continuing amnesty, but for my generation there have been things so unforgettable and disappointments so bitter that for us laughter has become almost a brutality. The dead past is dead—but not for us. We have been too near it and we are splashed with blood.*

* See Note 10A for a schoolgirl's reaction to A.R.P.

It is well to remind the reader that though all that follows is written as. objectively and truly as I can, it is overshadowed by these misadventures of my generation and mental type. The younger the reader is the more he or she should be able to discount the discouragement of our shadows.

And a consideration he must bear in mind in weighing what I am putting before him is the probability that there is a kind of egotistical intolerance in every definitely elderly mind. That is almost inevitable. Through a long life a complex system of ideas is built up upon a framework of concepts and associations determined by early circumstances. One qualifies, modifies, extends, superimposes significance upon this primary structure, but after a time it becomes irreplaceable. It may not be the best possible foundation, but the more it has to carry, the less it can be changed. It is like a business that has grown up in reasonably convenient premises, they might be better laid out perhaps, but there is no possibility now of completely revising the lay-out. The going concern must carry on. But it becomes more and more difficult to rephrase one's ideas or to recognize them when they are rephrased. So that I may be much less alone and outstanding than I am disposed to think.

The nearer my beliefs are to reality the more probable it is that similar minds may be traveling along parallel, if not identical, lines of thought to practically the same conclusions, approached perhaps from a different starting-point and so differently phrased. I suspect and indeed I hope that I do not allow fully for that.

For example, there is the peculiar dialect of so many minds in the war generation who resorted to communism and the Communist Party to express their recoil from the existing state of affairs. It was the handiest formula for any sort of organized dissent. Many of them—not all, alas!—are emerging to a broader conception of what can be done with life, but they still speak with a strong Marxist accent. Some few, and my friend J.B.S. Haldane is among their number, seem to be resolved like Lenin (but without the justification of his circumstances) to read a wisdom and profundity into the sage of Highgate which was certainly not there. His Haldane Memorial Lecture (Birkbeck College, May 24th, 1938), was, to my mind, a brilliant yet obstinately perverse overvaluation of the role of Marx (and Engels) in human thought, which may well have made the worthy uncle whom he was commemorating turn in his grave. Lord Haldane also professed the Hegelian faith and that was his nephew's justification. This lecture made the most of Marx, I insist, and more also. And then more.

Now I have always had a peculiar contempt and dislike for the mind and character of Karl Marx, a contempt and dislike that have deepened with the years. I have given it the liveliest expression I could contrive in "The Shaving of Karl Marx" in Russia In The Shadows and in the "Psychoanalysis of Karl Marx" in The World Of William Clissold. My only regret for these brief essays is that I could not infuse more sting and challenge into them. I have watched the tradition of Marxian bad manners and Marxian dogmatism wrapping like a blanket of fog round the minds of two crucial generations. They seemed to me to be lost in the fog. It was difficult for me to think they could be advancing under that fog.

Yet when, for example, I turn over such a book as The Social Function Of Science by that very considerable writer, Professor J.D. Bernal, F.R.S., I get at times, in spite of his very distinct Marxist twang, a curious sense of parallelism and co-operation. And much that J.B.S. Haldane said in his lecture, I find as I read it over again, I could subscribe to, except that I reject the Marxist attribution.

I am reminded of the story of an Englishman who had a more or less rudimentary cultural conversation with a Japanese gentleman. The latter broke into an oration, a gabble, a flow of unfamiliar sounds which sounded like no known human speech. Then something clicked over in the hearer's mind. He made some rapid transpositions and light broke upon him. He was hearing one of the most familiar of Shakespeare's speeches in English! English of a different tint.

I have been asserting, in a phraseology that no doubt owes much more than I realize to the phrases and assumptions of the liberal, protestant, progressive world of half a century ago, a view of the human outlook, that seems to me to be irresistibly convincing if one accepts a known series of facts. The truer and more inevitable that view is, the more probable it is that intelligent men, starting from all sorts of different standpoints, will converge upon the same conclusions. In English of a different tint. Indeed, it will be the completest disproof of my contentions, if there is not that convergence, if my conclusions do not reappear independently, crop up from a variety of starting-points and yet work out towards practically the same pattern. If the compelling facts do, as I assert, lie plainly on the face of things, that must be so. But probably, because I have a phraseology of my own, I shall be among those least able to recognize it.

And another thing that anyone who has spent most of his mental energy in trying to give the fullest and most emphatic expression to the truth as he perceives it, may easily underrate, is the tacit insubordination of many of the suppressed and formally silenced minds who are apparently disciplined against us. It is well to recall that all that outbreak of liberal questioning, the Protestant Reformation, which did so much to prepare the way for the French Revolution, was due almost entirely to the mental insurrection of friars or priests. They had had to take their creeds seriously, and they had brooded over their dogmas until they found them unbearable. There was no effective attack from without upon Church teaching throughout the whole Reformation period. There were close at hand in the alien disbeliefs of Jew and Moslem, a tacit denial of the Catholic faith, but these provoked no reforming zeal. All that came from within. And conversely the Jesuit Counter Reformation was the work of a group of romantic-minded laymen led by a court-bred gallant who had been wounded and crossed in love. The seven founders of the Society of Jesus were with one exception laymen. They were excited outsiders. They believed crudely and without qualification. They had had none of that intimate instruction of the mind from which questionings arise. They were, so to speak, the Nazis of Roman Catholicism.

But that is a passing comment. The more relevant point is the indisputable, obstinate tendency of common sense to assert itself in minds deliberately trained in any elaborate system of intolerance and error. Fanatics are madmen who find a masochist pleasure in strangling their own doubts, there is no dealing with them; but wherever there is discussion and mental training there lurks in every organized dogmatism a class of potential rebels. Hidden allies and half-hearted antagonists may be waiting to come over to a movement for the radical reconstruction of human ideology as it gathers strength. They are, so to speak, among the undisclosed reserves of progress.

Moreover, in further mitigation of my defeatist mood, it has to be borne in mind that while there is still life in a species no biological defeat is complete. Men and women of my type of mind and my generation, however the odds work against us, have no alternative to a stoical persistence in our convictions until our courses are run. We may have to admit regretfully a loss of buoyancy and of the ability for flexible mental co-operations. That is our private affair. In that we are just as much war casualties as those who may have suffered physical disablement in battle but are not yet completely incapacitated. Our injuries narrow down the scope of our service, but they furnish no justification for abandoning a loyal participation in the struggle. Our cause may still be winning.

Finally, as to the urgency of all this, let it be remembered that nothing is more difficult than estimating possibilities in time, and that timing here is a factor of primary importance. Disaster seems to me to be advancing upon us, but it may be that I am overlooking or underestimating the possibility of some intercalary slowing-down in the pace of change. I may be failing to perceive possible delaying forces. Some unexpected development of anti-aircraft technique might, for example, greatly minimize the destructiveness of air raids and the possibility of surprise wars.* The world may be held back from disaster for a time by the very weight and strain of its own armaments. It may be false to assume that sooner or later guns will go off of their own accord. Guns can rust and explosives disintegrate. A balance of power may be possible for longer years than I suppose, heavy and burthensome years perhaps, but still not years of complete catastrophic collapse.

* See Note 10B for such a possibility.

In that pause, many people will be thinking hard, and the human intelligence may find methods of discussion and organization unknown to us. I find myself unable to imagine any such respite, and so I cannot bring it honestly into my account-rendered of the world, but there may be such a possibility. That gives no excuse for slackening, but it does justify a certain hopefulness.

With that I think I can finish with myself as a typical sample in evidence in this survey of the reaction of Homo sapiens to his present dangers. These ego-centered passages are not really so egotistical as they will seem to be to the antagonistic reader. It is auto-vivisection. I was by far the best and handiest rabbit for this demonstration.

Allowing for my own loss of individual hopefulness and that probable narrowing down of co-operative tolerance in my mind, the conclusions I am presenting to you remain nevertheless sound, grimly sound. The prospect for our species is just as stern and implacable, charged just as much with bracing uncertainty. The issue upon which I am in doubt is not whether I am right or wrong about the facts I have assembled; it is simply whether you of the new generation can be sufficiently braced in time. There, maybe, I do you an injustice. That is what I am saying.

What I have admitted in qualification of my own ebb of confidence, is no justification whatever for mere optimistic trumpetings—"I believe in the ultimate triumph of civilization"—and so forth. We have heard so much of that kind of hysteria. Without personal and organized devotion it means less than nothing. It is desertion under cover of a declaration of faith.

There are always plenty of well-meaning people in the world ready to relax at the slightest encouragement, and the surest preparation for disaster is the enervation of sentimental overconfidence. Face your adversary at his worst and most menacing, and then you will know best how to set about him. Rational adaptation, I admit, may be achieved ultimately, but only heroically, at a great cost. The odds are against it, rest assured, if not perhaps so heavily against it a$ nowadays they seem to be, to me.

45

11. — SURVEY OF EXISTING FORCES

WE are now in a position to reconsider the nature of the various established systems that block the way to the readjustment of the human species as one single, continually progressive and creative world community, and to make a rough estimate of the way in which they are operating at the present time. We arrive with minds cleansed and refreshed by our survey of the biological situation, at the political, social and religious realities of today.

Legally the world's affairs are in the control of a miscellany of sovereign states, and each embodies itself in a government of politicians and officials, deeply concerned in maintaining the bargaining autonomy of the particular regime which gives them their importance, and prepared to offer a spirited resistance to any invasion, conquest or amalgamation of brave little (or big or old) Ruritania, or whatever state it is. That is how the political map of the world presents things to us. But very few of these legal governments are real cultural entities. It is only one or two sovereignties that embody a complete cultural system of their own. For all practical purposes the British Empire is such a system, with a curiously loose yet persistent will and tradition, sustained by a very distinctive literature of biographies, memoirs, collected letters and speeches and the like, and a quite definite religion—or religious substitutes—the Anglican compromise between Protestant and Catholic Christianity. Still more complete is the Nazi Germany of today, which indeed is now strenuously self-sufficient even to the extent of a distinctive science, art, literature, history, clothing, dietary of its own. But most of the other states play their game of international competition over a sort of map which does not necessarily correspond to their spheres of sovereignty. They are like estates, farms and fields spreading over a substratum of soils and geological formations.

It is to these underlying foundation realities of the world situation that we must first direct our attention.

As the facts assembled in The Outline Of History showed very clearly, the expansion in size of the early empires (saving only Egypt with its Nile) was dependent upon two advances in communication, writing and road-making. These expanding empires of the second and first millennia B.C. put a great strain upon the tribal and petty national religions (which in those days included the science and morality) of the smaller states they incorporated. A working compromise was found in a sort of fusion of the absorbing and absorbed cultures. A rejuvenated religion was produced by a mutual modification of ceremony and myth. The corresponding gods of these syncretic religions adopted each other's names as aliases, or they became different "aspects" of a consolidated deity (theocrasia). A general similarity in these more primordial tribal cults greatly facilitated this syncretic process.

About these primordial religions we now have a considerable body of assured knowledge. And this is not—we must underline here—knowledge in dispute. It is not a collection of theories we are bringing into court; it is an assemblage of facts. What we have to cite here is no more questionable than the facts of evolution and ecology that have been assembled in the earlier sections of this book. It is indeed knowledge that is not made accessible to everyone; that is the default of our educational systems; it is steadfastly ignored by many people who find it inconvenient and distasteful; but that does not affect its truth.

We know that these early religions were systems of fear and propitiation, that they centered upon the primary importance of a seasonal blood sacrifice, and that that sacrifice was the function of a priesthood, which was also in charge of the calendar and of whatever medical knowledge existed. From The Golden Bough of Sir James George Frazer, O.M., and from Forerunners And Rivals Of Christianity, by F. Legge (published by the Cambridge University Press), the unbiased reader can realize for himself how this cannibal blood sacrifice has been refined at last into the Mystery of the Mass, which will indeed have very little mystery left for him if he faces the facts these writers, with no unnecessary emphasis nor any partisan purpose, put plainly before him.*

* See Note 11A

These investigations into the beginnings of religion have accumulated steadily throughout the past half-century. It is only by great efforts of censorship, by sectarian education of an elaborately protected sort and the like, that ignorance about them is maintained.

These seasonal blood-sacrifice religions had a wide range of local variation, their theogonies differed widely—in some of them, mystical, secret mother-nature goddesses lurked behind the great father god; in others, the totem animal prevailed—but in all their forms they sustained the fear-begotten idea of blood salvation. Two dozen centuries ago they were already suffering through the pressure not only of syncretic necessity but from the increasing skepticism of the awakening human intelligence. They still cumbered the earth with a multitude of temples and priesthoods, for where there is an endowment you can always find someone to be a priest, but they were producing complex developments of their theological explanations.

Ptolemaic Alexandria was a hot-bed of religious elaboration. At the Serapeum, before the middle of the third century B.C., it had produced a trinity with a sacrificial son, who is slain and ascends to the Father and becomes the Father. There were a regular and secular clergy, monks with tonsures, a choral Easter ceremony; and the worship of the goddess Isis bearing the infant Horus in her arms anticipated the Catholic adoration of the Virgin Mary down even to minor details. The hymn "Sun of my Soul, thou Saviour dear," addressed originally to the hawk-sun-god Horus, has become a Christian hymn. In the temples one saw collections of ex-votos hung up in gratitude for miraculous cures and escapes, and the ceremonial purchase and burning of votive candles was encouraged. The hope of a glorious immortality—which was little stressed in the earlier religions outside Egypt—was a central fact in this religious scheme, and so, too, was an insistence upon the material resurrection of the (in Egypt usually pickled) body. All this was going on nearly three centuries before there was a Christian in the world.

But very few Christians know these facts. They are all to be found fully documented in Legge (op. cit.).

We must turn now to a second factor in the basis of 'the cultural life of Europe and the Europeanized world, the Sacred Book.

While religious cults were limited in their range and appealed at most to a few thousand votaries, it was possible to sustain 'them by direct teaching and initiation, but as greater empires grew with the development of writing and land and sea communications, there appeared a new demand and also a new facility for mental organization. This was the written word. Spreading over the old sacrificial paganism, there presently appeared what one may distinguish as Book religions. Every great religion in the world today, whether it does or does not preserve the tradition of the cannibalistic blood sacrifice, is a Book religion.

The first of the Sacred Books to affect the Western world was the collection of Hebrew writings constituting the core of what is now called the Old Testament. It came into existence as a natural result of the series of misfortunes that happened to the various communities speaking the closely related Semitic languages which had dominated the Western world a thousand years before the Christian era. These were the Babylonian, Phoenician and Carthaginian states, the Jews who had been deported to Babylon and then returned to Palestine, and a variety of trading colonies and settlements in association with these Semitic-speaking centers. In the course of a few centuries these highly civilized and intelligent trading empires and cities, in common with various other old-world communities, collapsed under a series of barbarian raids and conquests coming from the North. Most of these Northern barbarians spoke languages of the Aryan group. Between the Homeric Age and the third century B.C. they had, as the Persians, the Greeks and Macedonians, the Romans and Gauls, become masters of the larger part of the Mediterranean world, leaving the less warlike, Semitic-speaking peoples, inter alia, subdued and scattered and defeated but still trading, sustaining a financial network, navigating the seas and going to and fro in the world. They remained in possession of these roles because they knew more about them. The conquerors, as they became civilized, availed themselves, with a certain suspicion and resentment, of these superior gifts and facilities of the defeated. The Semitic business methods were ready-made for the new kings and aristocrats and warriors. They learnt to use them slowly and left them largely in Semitic hands.

During the course of these conquests there was naturally a great intermingling of blood. The subjugated Semitic and pre-Semitic peoples were certainly in the majority in the Latin, Greek, Persian 'and Macedonian empires; history records no general ban upon intermarriage, and we can hardly doubt that the actual blood of the ruling Aryan-speaker was the smaller factor in that continually stirred-up mixture which is now the European and Europeanized world of today.*

* See Note 11B on the racial unity of mankind.

But traditions were less easily assimilated. Throughout that millennium which culminated in the Roman Empire, in all the ports and cities there must have been groups of households and business organizations struggling to maintain a level of refinement and behavior higher than that of their rulers, and eager also to preserve their business correspondence and a sympathetic understanding with their kindred throughout this new world that had annihilated and discredited their separate religious systems. They needed a Book to unify them, they were ripe for a Book, and the Book was ready for them.

It was in Babylon and Judaea and in the towns of these regions that those Jewish sacred writings first appeared. They contained two overlapping versions of the old Babylonian cosmogony, together with the myths of the Creation, the Serpent-Enemy, the Fall, the Flood and the Tower of Babel. They also contained the story of a Promise and of a Chosen People who were destined to recover all and more than their ancient ascendancy. But at a price. These Chosen People had to keep themselves aloof from the Gentile world. They must preserve their precious distinctive habits and usages intact. They must remain aloof and enduring, until a promised Messiah came to lead Israel to its final triumph over the rest of mankind.

The appeal of these Scriptures to. the needs and imaginations of these scattered peoples on the defensive must have been irresistible. In a century or so Carthaginians, Phoenicians, Babylonians disappear from history, and all over the world of their former activities the Jewish communities appear, centering upon the schools of Babylon and Jerusalem with a consolidating literature and a religion. In this stage they proselytized freely. Probably the proselytizing was chiefly among kindred and sympathetic Semitic-speakers, but there were also Tartar and other tribes which were won over. The blood-sacrifice tradition was sustained by the priests in the Temple until the fall of Jerusalem to Vespasian in 70 A.D. Then the sacrifices ceased and the Sacred Book with its semi-authoritative accretions became the link of Jewry throughout the world....

So the first of the great Book religions on which our civilization rests arose. Hard upon its diffusion followed Christianity, its unidentical twin.

Christianity began as a Jewish sect, as the Books of the New Testament tell very simply and clearly; it was still entirely Jewish after the Crucifixion; and it was only through the initiative of Saint Paul that the ranks of the elect were opened to the uncircumcised. After the Four Gospels, the New Testament is largely occupied with Paul's reconstruction of the Nazarene cult. It is all very plain to anyone who reads these books without theological prepossessions. His brilliant intelligence seized upon the idea of presenting Jesus as the sacrificial king of the blood-sacrifice tradition. Jesus, he declared, was the Lamb by whose blood we were saved—though as a matter of fact crucifixion is hardly a more bloody death than hanging. He had died, said Saint Paul, not only for the Jews but for all men who would accept his sacrifice. This, for the stricter Jews, was an intolerable relaxation of their divine bargain. But some, less profoundly convinced of the Messianic hope, realized the attractive quality of the Pauline teaching.

The medium of diffusion for Christianity remained for a time the scattered Jewish communities. Throughout the first and second centuries Judaism and its offshoot, Christianity, the latter becoming more and more Gentile and anti- Jewish, spread and bickered side by side throughout the whole extent of the Roman Empire. The pagan world, although it was also in a state of great social and religious unrest—the two things seem to be inseparable—had no comparable nexus for the production of alternative sacred writings that could stand up against the dissemination of these Judaeo-Christian legends and mythology. So that these latter provided the written factor in the foundations of civilization throughout the entire Western world.

Later, another Book religion, Islam, swept for a time across the Mediterranean scene, with very considerable reactions upon medieval science and thought. But that influence, and the effects of a vast multitude, myriads indeed, of less distinguished "Sacred Book" cults, are outside our present discussion.

It is necessary to recall these well-known—though persistently neglected—facts--here because they establish a general statement that what we may call roughly Western culture—the mental adaptation of mankind to social and political life, from -the Pacific coast westward across the Atlantic to farthest eastern Russia, up to as late as the second Russian Revolution in 1917—was based upon an interrelated system of Bible-centered Book religions which had either obliterated or assimilated the more ancient blood-sacrifice cults.

Let us now review the chief forms these foundation religions take in our world today.

46

12 — THE JEWISH INFLUENCE

FIRSTLY, because of its illuminating quality, we must consider the progressive segregation of the Jewish community. It has diverted, wasted and sterilized an amount of ability and moral energy that mankind at large can ill spare. In the previous section we have shown how naturally it arose out of the state of world affairs of the centuries before and after the Christian era, and how the realistic genius of Saint Paul sought an escape from its perilous limitations. From the very beginning, there must have been men of vision among the Jews who realized and rebelled against the moral isolation to which they were being condemned, there must have been a continual seeping-away of individuals to the larger opportunities of the outer world, but the uncompromising tradition carried by the old Bible and the associated writings which grew into the Talmud has been sufficient to hold together a core of inassimilable and aggressive orthodoxy to this day clinging obstinately to every detail of ritual, behavior and avoidance that emphasized the central legend of a Chosen People. It is this orthodox remnant and its behavior and influence, the repercussions it evokes and the dangers to which it has exposed the whole Jewish community, which constitute the Jewish problem. There would be no distinctive Jewish question at all were it not for this remnant and its activities.

The whole question turns upon the Chosen People idea, which this remnant cherishes and sustains, which it is the "mission" of this remnant to cherish and sustain. It is essentially a bad tradition, and the fact that for two thousand years the Jews on the whole have been very roughly treated by the rest of mankind does not make it any the less bad. Almost every community with which the orthodox Jews have come into contact has sooner or later developed and acted upon that conspiracy idea. A careful reading of the Bible does nothing to correct it.

Every sort of man is disposed to get together with his own sort of people and prefer them to strangers. That is the natural disposition of our species, fair play to the outsider is one of the last and least assured triumphs of civilization, but the indictment against the Jewish community is 'that their religion of a Chosen People takes this universal human vice, justifies it and stimulates it to the form of a persistent organized attitude of self-exclusion from the common fellowship of the world.

Everywhere the same reaction occurs and everywhere the Jew expresses his astonishment. Not only Christians but Turks have resorted to pogroms. In contact with the Arab, the Koran-taught

Arab from the desert, who shares the Jew's cosmogony, who practices similar dietetic taboos, who is equally free from Trinitarian theology and sacrificial bloodshed, and has indeed a much stronger claim to be called Semitic, the angry reaction to the theory and practice of a Chosen People, to the practice much more than the theory, is just as violent as it is in any other part of the world.

It is this Chosen People tradition and still more the habit of mind which betrays itself in those who have come under its influence, which is the ever- recurrent cause of the trouble. It seems to me beside the mark to look for any other.*

* See Note 12A for a further discussion of this point.

Estimates of the number of Jews in the world vary between fourteen and sixteen million. The latter figure is given by Louis Golding in The Jewish Problem and by Lewis Browne in the careful and scholarly work he has entitled so flippantly, How Odd Of God. ("How odd of God to choose the Jews!"—W.N. Ewer.) This is not a very great total. They have and always have had abundant and well-cared-for families. Probably outside the range of definitely associated Jews, there has always been a much larger world of sympathetic kin, sharing and affected by the feelings of the stricter core, capable of co-operating with it and responding to modifications of the central idea, but gradually slipping away beyond recall.

As we have noted in § 11 (and see also Note 11B) most of us probably have a more or less considerable proportion of "Jewish" blood in our veins, using "Jewish" in the larger sense. But orthodox Judaism has always been a narrower and intenser strain. It has passed through phases of leakage and recovery. The Protestant Reformation was a phase of leakage. Browne doubts whether there were half a million Jews in Europe in 1600, "fewer than were to be found in Castile alone four hundred years earlier."

Of the sixteen million Jews today, Browne estimates that there cannot be more than four million who are strict adherents to and observers of the Law and that perhaps another six million are what he calls semi-observant; they are lax about food and drink and the Sabbath, but when it comes to celebrating marriages, funerals, taking an oath and so forth they follow the ancient formulae, they attend the main annual feasts, they pay their pew rents and do their full duty by the Jewish charities. They are very much like the Anglicans who don't go to Church very much but would never dream of being married in a registry office. Then comes another three million who have become entirely indifferent to the Law. They do not attack it, but they put it aside. Yet they cling as nationalists to the solidarity it has preserved through the ages. They are Reform Jews or Radical Nationalists, like the law-disregarding young Jews of Palestine. Mr. Browne is himself a Reform Rabbi and he can write incidentally:

"There are certain writers who become tremulously nostalgic and tender when describing the life of those pietist Jews. Ensconced in laurel-embowered English cottages, or seated in cafes on Montparnasse, such writers will wax ecstatic as they discourse on the effulgent 'mysticism' enhaloing the ghetto hovels. But that, I fear, is because they have never entered those hovels. Had they done so they would in all likelihood realize—unless sentimentality had too thickly blurred their sight—that life in them is not bathed in the lambent light of unearthly wisdom: that instead it is dark and scabrous with superstition."

The remaining three of these sixteen million Jews are rapidly ceasing to be Jews at all, and he notes with a sort of calm amazement that "a cult which has lasted for centuries could be shattered in a decade." The younger generation has been given equality in the U.S.S.R,, excellent schools and a new and exciting creed. Nominally they remain Jews, and their language, Yiddish, is one of the national languages recognized by the Union. But Hebrew has vanished—the Law, the Promise and Jehovah!

And at this point Browne and I part company. Judaism may vanish in Russia under communism, he has to admit, but it will live on elsewhere not by virtue of its own quality but because of Gentile intolerance. He argues that Gentile intolerance makes the Jews and keeps them together. I argue that the Jews make themselves and that Gentile intolerance is a response to the cult of the Chosen People. To get down to ultimate things, we are in substantial agreement, I find, in that we desire a world, enlightened, scientifically administered, free, a world-wide new civilization open to everyone, where there will be neither Jew nor Gentile, bond nor free. Nevertheless we differ diametrically in our interpretation of the root cause of the Jewish problem, and as a consequence upon the question where the tentative for denationalization should begin. Thirteen million Jews—at least—still make the implacable Gentile the justification for their own persistence. They still hold to that hard core of national separatism in spite of the steady evaporation of every traditional religious justification. Yet they have a world-wide organization for calling off that attitude and the Gentiles have no corresponding representative network to speak for them to the same extent. The Holy See has recently condemned racialism very clearly and definitely. So has the White House....

But let me go on with what I believe is the truer version of the Jewish story, and the reader, with a glance at the notes at the end whenever he needs confirmation, must judge between me and the defenders of persistent Jewish nationalism.*

* See Note 12B for that fuller discussion.

The hostile reaction to the cult of the Chosen People is spreading about the entire world today. In the past the Jews have been subjected to much resentful treatment and much atrocious cruelty and injustice, now here, now there, but there has never been such a world-wide—I will not use the word anti-Semitism because of the Arab—I will say anti-Judaism. Now, because of the physical unification of the world, the resentment against the theory and practice of a Chosen People is much quicker and more contagious than it used to be; it is becoming world-wide and simultaneous. The idea is becoming everywhere more and more intolerable than it has ever been before.

The cultivated, exaggerated, national egotism of the Chosen People has never been so conspicuous as it has been in the present century and particularly since the War. As their ritualism has weakened their nationalism has increased. I recall a conference that took place in '19 or '20 in a room in the House of Commons. A number of French writers had deputed Madame Madeleine Marx to discuss with various English men and women of letters the possibilities of concerted action and possibly organization in the cause of world peace and world understanding. In those days Israel Zangwill had adopted the role of Champion of the downtrodden and suffering Jewish race, and more particularly of that section of it which was to be found in the wealthier mansions of West Kensington and Tyburnia, en route from the East End to the House of Lords. He sustained its racial pride, if indeed that needed sustaining. He insisted upon Israel's distinction and its inappeasable hunger for restoration to the land of the protracted Promise. He told them of the Dreamers of the Ghetto. He reminded them of their origins with humor and emotion. He helped them to feel "different," as the American car salesmen say, and mystically better. They were, he persuaded them, not really having the good time they seemed to be having; behind the brave face they put upon things they were weeping by the waters of Babylon. The true voice of Israel was to be heard not in the West End of London -but when it went off for a trip to Palestine and, following the customary routine, wailed at the Wailing Wall. Always he spoke of "My people."

He brought his championship to our deliberations. We various British authors had had our trivial shares in the "war to end war," and we were very willing to fall in with any proposals that would help to rationalize the heated and punitive atmosphere of the Versailles peace. We felt that a peace that would indeed end war was slipping away from us. But we found this conference dominated by the communist dogmatism of Madame Marx, against which Bernard Shaw protested, and Zangwill's preoccupation with his "people." He laid down the conditions that would satisfy their needs; he insisted on what would satisfy them, what would make them willing to help us, and the difficulties an offended Jewry could create for us. So far as I could grasp his drift he was dealing with us as the British Empire. We were not the British Empire, but it was vain to protest. Zangwill was a very resolute character and that was the drama he had in mind. Just as in our private disputes he would insist on treating me as a devout Christian. Then he could say: "But your Saviour was a Jew!" Useless to plead that I was not a Christian, and that there might be considerable prepotency in the Holy Ghost. Zangwill was being the captive nation making his terms with the oppressor. It is the drama so many people still have in mind when discussing this question.

In those days we in the victorious allied countries were all ready to believe that the world was really recovering from the War and entering upon a phase of comparative freedom and hope. We did our best not to think too much about the state of affairs in Germany. Everybody was talking of reconstruction and rationalization, and it was possible to deal jestingly with things that have now become intolerably grim.

The Zionist movement was the crowning expression of what I, in flat contradiction to Mr. Browne, hold to be the obdurate insistence of orthodox and semi-orthodox Jewry upon their peculiarity. In the years immediately following the war, there was a lull even in the normal persecutions in Eastern Europe to which the orthodox were subjected. They suffered indeed during the civil disorders that preceded the consolidation of the Bolshevik government; Whites, Reds and Greens were alike guilty of pogroms of varying degrees of virulence, and there was in consequence a certain exodus westward, but as the new law and order were established in Russia these outrages ceased and the process of rapid assimilation, to which reference has already been made, began. But already the champions of Judaism were advertising to the whole world how implacably they insisted upon their eternal essential foreignness. They had demanded a national home, so that elsewhere they could be forever foreigners. They might within limits accept the advantages of citizenship of the country they lived in, but essentially they would not belong. They would vote, hold office, rule, but always with Zion in their hearts. They ignored the manifest fact that the day of small sovereign states is drawing to an end, and that in a world of ever-growing violence, to plant themselves massively in any particular area was to invite a wholesale disaster.

Today when the whole world is being subtly pervaded with anti-Jewish feeling, and when the restraints upon the predatory and persecuting impulses in the human animal are being rapidly weakened, these implacable nationalists are still conspicuously seeking suitable regions where they can go on being a people by themselves, where, pursuing an ancient and irrational ritual so far as it suits them, they can sustain a solidarity foreign and uncongenial to all the people about them.

No country wants them on such conditions. Why should any country want these inassimilable aliens bent on preserving their distinctness? Palestine is an object lesson. Until they are prepared to assimilate and abandon the Chosen People idea altogether, their troubles are bound to intensify. No one can help them while even a die-hard minority—a minority that the general body of them does not disavow, a nucleus about which habit and association and sentiment gather very readily and to which it is easy for lost sheep to return—prefers these exasperating pretensions of a special right and claim to becoming frankly and of their own accord common citizens of the world.

These are the elementary facts of the quandary to which the Chosen People have come, the more relentless dragging the doubters and half-hearted with them. They are facts that have to be stated, even though matters are now coming to a complexion which gives a flavor of ruthlessness to their bare statement.

Because this obdurate separatism which, after all, except for the growing trouble in Palestine, has been hitherto more of an irritant than a downright evil, is now conspicuous and challenging just at a phase in human affairs when it is becoming extremely dangerous to be in any manner alien and provocative.

In the last two paragraphs of § 4, the essential facts of the present rapid dislocation of social order have been stated. Social disintegration is now a world-wide reality, it is a convulsive breaking-down everywhere of long-established systems of law and order, an almost cataclysmal dissolution. It is a process far vaster than this Jewish question we are discussing and it arises from causes that have no special connection with that trouble. But it catches up the Jewish question in its swirling eddies and spins it about so that its fluctuations become indicative of the character of the entire process.

The Jewish question is already something very different from what it was a score of years ago when Zangwill championed and threw that glamor of racial romance and Maccabean heroism about the ancient ways. Those were tolerant days. At that time it was easy for people to fall away from the old observances if they chose and become Christians or unconforming skeptics. Now, and it is the most ominous aspect of the new phase, in many parts of the world the doors of escape from orthodox Jewry are being closed. These doors are not being closed from the inside; there i£ no way of closing them from the inside. They are being closed from the outside. Those who are disposed to apostasy are being turned back by the outer world. Nothing of this sort was happening twenty years ago. A number of people, and some of them are very sinister people indeed, are beginning to say, "You insisted upon being Jews. Jews you shall be."

The operating causes in those wide alternations between social confidence, a sense of stability and a prevailing lawfulness and intolerance, and phases of insecurity, fear, dishonesty and general unrighteousness, which have manifestly occurred in the human story, have still to receive anything but the most casual attention from the historian. Those happier periods, when the social machine was running smoothly, when men were able to move about freely and almost fearlessly, work with a sense of fair reward, when there was something definite and reasonably satisfactory and hopeful for most of the young men to do, have been by far the less frequent and the least secure. Order and peace have been precarious always in the growing human societies of the last four or five thousand years. There have been constantly recurrent phases of mutual pressure, expansion and that dislocation without which readjustment is impossible. Then doubt and suspicion invade men's minds. They lose that feeling that they are being properly taken care of; there is no confidence that services will be rewarded or debts paid; mutual trust gives way to suspicion. Social behavior deteriorates. The strong and cunning no longer feel that the weak will be protected. The suspicious look for scapegoats to blame, for evil doers who have offended the gods, for conspirators. Particularly for conspirators.*

* See Note 12C for The Protocols Of The Elders Of Zion, etc.

We do know and we have already stated in general terms the forces that have produced the particular phase of violent social disintegration that is going on today. They are world-wide and unprecedented. Socially they are more destructive than anything our species has ever faced before. The disintegrating changes in the social order of the past were probably due to much more localized and quite different influences: to unrecorded fluctuations in the relative welfare of classes, to the social shifting due to new economic processes, to the infiltration of foreign ideas and practices, to foreign pressure, to epidemics—no history can be complete without a proper study of the social sequelae of plague, the Black Death and the like—to sustained bad weather, drought for example, over a number of years, to a stimulating and disorganizing influx of gold such as happened after the discovery of America. These and a thousand other disturbing forces have been enough to tilt the always unstable and insecure social balance back to general distrust and convulsive, self-protective dishonesty. The adaptive culture fails. Things go to pieces, Man reverts to his more natural state of a fear-and-desire-driven beast.

In the history of any social system such periods of disorganization display almost parallel phenomena of demoralized mass action. The strong are looking for the weak not only individually but collectively in order to gratify their craving for power, the crowd is seeking the furtive enemies of the state, the fearful are looking for the strange wickedness and secret mischiefs that have brought about the discomforts of the time. In such an atmosphere any marked kind of people are liable to set upon, are liable to be ringed about for victimization and punitive plunder.

Such a convergence of hostility has by no means been confined to the Jews. The Albigenses, for example, in the south of France, had no very special relationship to the Jewish community. They were a Christian sect with certain heretical ideas derived by way of Bulgaria from the Gnostics and Manichaeans. They were charged, by their exterminators, to whom we owe most of the knowledge we have of their beliefs, with abnormal sexual practices. What is more certain is that they protested vigorously against the corruptions of the Church and were markedly anti-sacerdotal. They spread throughout Provence and prospered throughout the twelfth century. Their movement was in several respects an anticipation of the Protestant Reformation. Whereupon the Church invoked the harder, ruthless and more Catholic north, and preached a Crusade against them. Moral and religious indignation and the prospect of loot implemented their destruction. Here we cannot tell the tale of massacres, burnings alive—two hundred in one auto-da-fé—the sadistic terrorism and blackmail of the Holy Inquisition....

The Armenians again are another much massacred, non-Jewish but distinctive people.

But it is the Jews who have generally been the marked people throughout the realms of Christendom and Islam. They have generally "got it first." And repeatedly the door has been slammed upon Jews who have been seeking to get away or were actually getting away from the threats that darkened over them.

Lewis Browne gives a compact and effective account of the fate of the Marranos in Spain and Portugal. He tells of the forcible baptism and conversion of the Jews in 1391 in the face of a storm of popular hostility. The government, because of their financial and administrative usefulness, opened a door of escape for them. They were given the choice between exile and massacre or Christianization. A great majority chose the latter, and since all the synagogues were closed and the practice of the Jewish law sedulously suppressed, within three or four generations most of these baptized Jews became just as good or better Catholics than their neighbors. This from the outset was a huge disappointment for those neighbors who had been whetting the knife, so to speak, for an orgy of murder and plunder. It seemed to them the meanest trick conceivable. They called these desperate converts the New Christians or more familiarly swine (=Marranos), and set as rigid a bar as possible on any intercourse with them. As Jews they had been "dogs" but now they were "swine." "Conversion indeed!" they said. "You don't get away with that."

In complete good faith the majority of the Marranos in the next generation or so were Catholics, "These hapless creatures," says Browne, "took no pride in their past. On the contrary they were through and through ashamed of it and groaned that it be forgotten." That did not help them in the least. Massacre and detailed persecution closed in on them. The tale is fully told in Mr. Cecil Roth's History Of The Marranos. It is a frightful story, but from the point of view of the present discussion it is almost the same story, Inquisition and all, as that of the Albigenses who were not Jews at all.

An entirely parallel treatment has been meted out in the last decade to the Christian Jews in Germany. They have been herded back upon their orthodox brethren, in the same spirit and for the same reason that the Marranos were kept apart for destruction. We are witnessing now a swifter and vaster repetition of that Marrano tragedy.

A time has come when a multitude of men and women of more than average intelligence, men and women who in reality have no essential racial difference from the average European, are finding themselves with no foothold whatever upon the earth, dispossessed and hunted from country to country, marooned in impossible regions, deprived of the normal protection of the law, beaten up by anyone who chooses to beat them up, outraged, tortured, sterilized, stripped of everything, ill-treated in every possible way. They seek escape from one country to another, and the countries where they would take refuge, suffering now from the fast-spreading economic and social malaise of this current phase in human history, are more and more chary of receiving them even as assimilable individuals. Everywhere employment is dislocated. Everywhere they encounter the protest: "We have our own unemployed!"*

* See Note 12D upon the refugee question.

A great book, a book of victims with thousands of authenticated cases, could be filled already with the tale of forced suicides, murders and abominations done upon these refugees, and there is no reasonable prospect of surcease. From the narrower point of view the compilation might be called The Jewish Book Of Martyrs, but from another it could be entitled The Natural Man, because its broader interest lies in the clear demonstration of what the inherent brute in man can do when the grip of law and order relaxes. It is a horrible recrudescence of primordial human reactions, but that is no reason why we should shut our eyes to the role of the alien nationalism of the Chosen People in exposing them first and foremost before any other people to this accumulating outbreak of hatred, cruelty, bestiality and every sort of human ugliness. They are the first to suffer in the social dissolution of our epoch, because they have stood 1 out most conspicuously. They are the most obvious "murderees" and "plunderees." They come first. But they are only the first....

I have enlarged upon their case because it is not only conspicuously challenging at the present time but because it brings into the picture most of the elements of the present human situation, the general disposition of any established community to adhere to forms and traditions of living long after their survival value has disappeared, the normal blindness of human beings to the onset of novel and more exacting conditions until disaster actually supervenes, the swiftness with which social balance can now be overturned.

I can see no other destiny for orthodox Judaism and those who are involved in its obloquy, unless that enormous effort to reconstruct human mentality for which I have been pleading arrives in time to arrest their march to destruction. That, if it is to save our species, must be a reconstruction so bold and wide, an amnesty so fundamental, that it will sweep the religion of the Chosen People and this age-long feud of Juif and anti-Juif out of the living interests of mankind altogether.*

* For a practically identical view vividly expressed, read Wyndham Lewis's The Jews, Are They Human?

47

13. — CHRISTENDOM

FROM the tragedy of Judaism we must turn now to Christianity, that second and greater branch of the Bible tradition, which is the basis of contemporary Western civilization. The word Christianity has covered and still covers an immense variety of idea systems, but today it finds its most highly organized and active expression in the Roman Catholic Church. That too is a power transcending national and state boundaries and playing a distinctive part in molding human thought and destiny today.

In certain respects Catholic Christianity is in diametric contrast to Judaism; in certain others the two cults run side by side. They have this in common that nearly everywhere they produce the feeling that they are alien cultures. They are apt to be suppressed by governments together, as in Hanoverian England and Hitlerian Germany, and to be emancipated together. But they differ fundamentally in the fact that while participation in Judaism after the early phase of eager proselytism became for many reasons difficult, Christianity from its beginning with Saint Paul (Acts xi, 26) onward has been a missionary religion, seeking and incorporating converts throughout the whole world.

It not only incorporated converts but it incorporated ideas. It sprang from the Jewish sect of the Nazarenes, but in the course of the three centuries before its forcible stabilization by Constantine the Great in 325 at the Council of Nicaea and the definitive formulation of its three creeds, the third-century Apostles Creed, the fourth-century Nicene Creed, so much more explicit about the Trinity, and the Athanasian (of uncertain date and authorship) which finally cleared up the Trinity business for good and all in a drumming storm of intolerant nonsense, it had practically become a synthesis of all the chief religious cults of that mentally festering age.

The Catholic Church emerged from these formative centuries as an organization of very considerable tenacity, but intellectually it was already the most extraordinary jumble of absurdities and incompatibilities that has ever exercised and perplexed the human intelligence. It accumulated accretions like a caddis worm. Still—though now with more deliberation—it assimilates. At a very early stage it developed sexual obsessions unknown to its cognate Judaism. The Virgin Birth began to worry its usually celibate theologians. Jesus on one occasion (Matthew xx, 47-50) had very definitely denied any religious importance to his mother, but with the taking-over of Isis and the Infant Horus, as the Virgin and Child, this was disregarded. The Virgin became a divine queen, very beautiful and adorable. St. Ignatius Loyola, contemptuous of the earthly attractions he had found unsatisfactory, vowed himself her Knight, and believed there was a mutual devotion. That the intenser religious succumb very readily to the suggestions of such phrases as "The Bride of Christ," one can find ample evidence for in the vast literature of the Christian mystics. It became necessary to sublimate the Virgin, the attractive Queen of Heaven. She had to be made "sinless" and born without "sin." So the theologians excogitated a "sinless" begetting for her. It is difficult to tell these things without a touch of derision. The doctrine of the Immaculate Conception emerged from their meditations. It was mainly a Spanish product, and there is a monument to the Immaculate Conception outside the Alcazar in Seville. It is perfectly decent; it is a grouping of the divines, thinkers and spiritual heroes, grave and dignified figures, who contributed to the perfection of this profound discovery. For centuries, however, this Immaculate Conception was not a matter of faith. It was made so by a bull of Pope Pius IX as recently as 1854. There was a great assembly of bishops and dignitaries in Rome from all parts of the world, a great gathering of adult men robed very beautifully and carrying themselves very seriously. A happy sense of a great consummation pervaded them. And now all good Catholics must believe in the Immaculate Conception of the Virgin Mary, though what it is they think they are believing in I cannot imagine.

And so, century by century, the great fabric of the faith goes on accumulating. It has become a sort of Cumberland Market of religious notions.*

* For a frank Catholic admission of this, see Note 13A

There is something from everywhere in it and, wherein lies its chief attractiveness, something for everybody. No single mind can cover that mighty mental jumble sale in its entirety, so that anyone willing to be converted has no difficulty in ignoring the less congenial articles of the collection. You will, for example, find the sternest condemnation of socialism, no Catholic can be a Socialist, and then you will find that the author of the completest forecast of communism, commissars and all that, Sir Thomas More, has been canonized as a saint.

The organization of the Church, with its confessional and its spiritual direction, facilitates this fragmentary approach to faith in every possible way. The convert is invited and trained to help in his own subjugation. He is implored to pray for light. He must bury his sense of humor. These, he is told, are serious matters. A hearty laugh at the metaphors of relationship in the triplex composition of the divinity would -shatter the whole process. Derision is the deadly enemy of Catholicism; it drives it to indignant persecution, indignant silence or indignant flight, according to the exigencies of the situation.

Christianity picked up the Holy Trinity, it would seem, in the second century, and very manifestly from Alexandria. By that time Alexandria far more than Jerusalem had become the spiritual home of Christianity. Neither St. Paul nor Jesus insisted upon the fundamental importance of right views about the Mystery of the Trinity to their followers. To say the least of it, it was inconsiderate of them to leave it to the author of the Athanasian creed, centuries later, to formulate in terms of the now long-abandoned metaphysics of Alexandria, "The Catholic faith, which except a man believe faithfully he cannot be saved." Did Matthew know? Did Peter understand? It leaves one anxious about the ultimate fate even of St. Paul himself.

Why do intelligent people accept this strange heap of mental corruption as a religion and a rule of life? That question will bring us back to that reorientation of the human mind, and that conflict between the actuality of the present and the accumulating reality of the future, to which I have devoted § 9. They accept it because it is there before them and because it existed long before they did. They grew up to it and even if they were not actually born and bred Catholics, they saw it everywhere taken for granted and treated with respect, cathedrals and shrines, saints and martyrs, in art, in literature, in history, in the world about them. There is no reasoning in a stained-glass window, but there is an immense amount of conviction. To turn from the menaces of stark reality to established religion is to be immediately reassured. To turn from active, questioning minds to the company of the faithful is inexpressibly comforting. And with that you get prescription and direction for all the main issues of life. The Church, the faithful about one, a vast volume of literature and history, agree in saying: "Don't trouble. You are all right. Do as we do and all will be well." At times I have tried to imagine what such a natural born scoffer and rebel as Mr. Hilaire Belloc, whose mental processes have always interested and distressed me, thinks at Mass. But that is just when he suspends all thinking. Credo quia absurdum, I suspect is the note of it, a triumphant revolt against his own intelligence. He became a scoffer and rebel against liberalism and scientific revelation because he resented their compelling convincingness. Any fool, he felt, could believe that.

And it is equally easy to understand the attraction of the Catholic Church to those outside but within the influence of the fold. They are already half converts. They "go over" without the slightest examination of the fundamental absurdities of the faith. Conviction comes after a discussion of the Apostolic Succession and the validity of the Protestant Orders. Such things are deliberated very gravely. With a sense of enhanced importance, the convert takes to fish on Fridays, is received, attends Mass, feels unutterable things. Unutterable even to himself. It is all so tremendously established. Quiescence, spiritual peace ensues. Until the anxiety of the times takes hold of these refugess from fact, they will not recognize the element or malignity in the activities of this great organization to which they, are clinging. Even then they will feel the utmost reluctance in leaving go. It is their last protection against that terrifying readjustment to creative reality, which would make them responsible adults in this world of limitless danger, limitless difficulty and limitless possibility.

Fantastic, defiantly absurd as this vast pile of the Faith becomes to anyone who dares to go into it and question it fearlessly, it is far less fantastic than the actual organization of the Church. Its central control rests with a close corporation of priests, mainly Italians, the cardinals, who with scarcely a break have elected a continuity of Italian Popes for the last three centuries. Spiritually Italians must be a very superior people.

In the Vatican, in entirely unveracious succession to St. Peter, sustained by a handsome subsidy from the Fascist government and the less reliable contributions of the faithful at large, the Holy Father, in the measure of his intelligence and the quality of his advisers, keeps his court and steers the Church through the pitfalls of this world. He has had the medieval education of a priest; his advisers have worn the mental blinkers of the devout, and just as far as they dare, they influence the political life of the world, according to their limitations and prejudices. In all the democracies the "Catholic vote" obeys the tortuous wisdom of these scheming old anachronisms. Here tyrannies are blessed and here revolts are fomented. The devout in France or Britain, for example, must support the Franco pronunciamento to the infinite injury of their own countries.

Joseph McCabe in his History Of The Popes tells the story of the Papacy with a certain bitter accuracy and an ample citation of authorities. The Catholic reader will, I know, feel that my recommendation of that outspoken book is in the worst possible taste. But let me nevertheless urge it upon his attention. It will trouble his mind, but it will purge it. But if he asks his co-religionists questions about it, they will make him feel as if he were making rude noises.

When we try to estimate the role the Church is now playing in mundane affairs we have to realize that on earth it has no definite objective at all. It is a vast, self-protective organization which seeks merely to exist and if possible spread. Its friends are those who support and serve it; its enemies—and its enmity has the unrelenting quality of an instinct—are those who have thwarted, controlled and suppressed it. It is against Soviet Russia, against every Protestant system, against every country which insists upon secular education; it is on the side of every government, however corrupt and evil, which attends Mass and makes the sign of the cross. Its real objectives, it alleges, lie in another world. In some strange existence outside time and space the reckoning will be made, and those who have swallowed the Athanasian metaphysics, taken the advice of their priests, and performed all their religious duties, will enjoy heaven, and those who have fallen short will pass to heaven through a state called purgatory or descend into hell forever, according to the enormity of their disrespect. Bolsheviks, I assume, will all go to hell.

In the past it was the custom of the Church to suggest that the sufferings in hell and purgatory were essentially physical tortures, and simple folk were given pictures of the damned being burnt in flaming bowls, tormented by red-hot pincers, racked and maltreated very richly and variously. The state of bliss was less fully particularized. Nowadays one hears remarkably little of either the upper or lower aspect of the future state. Yet why is there no copious and attractive literature upon the subject? Why are there no speculative anticipations? Why have Catholic poets recoiled? It should be a most fascinating preoccupation to imagine that unearthly loveliness ahead. There are not even impostors to offer us dreams and visions. No one has ever produced a plausible page from a celestial Baedeker. Even Bunyan's Pilgrim's Progress stops short at the gates of the Celestial City. We are left to imagine "these endless Sabbaths the blessed ones see." There is the Book of Revelation indeed, but who except cranks and lunatics reads the Book of Revelation? And that, after all, is symbolic prophecy and not to be mistaken for a picture of reality. The fact of it is that the majority of Christians are not even reasonably curious about the future life, and they are not curious because they have no more positive belief in it than I have. They are Christians because it is the most convenient and agreeable pattern of life for them, and for no other reason whatever.

And yet the Church is something more than a picturesque and reassuring frame for an everyday mode of living. It provides that, just as it provides dispensations, annulments of marriages for the wealthy, titles, blessings, missions, festivals and displays, but such things are by the way. It exists primarily for itself. It is always anticipating and warding off dangers and occasionally it counter-attacks. There is an incessancy in its self-preserving activities, and in this present phase of world crisis it is encouraging much partisan activity.

There comes to hand as I write a book, Crisis For Christianity by William Teeling, which summarizes very clearly the ideas of a Catholic reaction and recovery that are stirring the imaginations of the more active faithful I do not know who William Teeling is. His title page supplies no information beyond his bare name; he has written at least one other book, The Pope In Politics; but he seems to have met and discussed affairs with most of the leading Catholics in Europe; and I understand that that very peculiar body, the British Council, which spends £100,000 a year in endearing England to foreigners by sending them carefully chosen, if occasionally highly unrepresentative, samples of British thought and behavior to lecture and talk to them, has availed itself of his services. So that his book gives us not only the present Catholic outlook, but one at least of the many faces the now highly diplomatic and incalculable British Empire turns to the world.

The first thing to remark about this book is that it completely ignores the existence of any modern, scientific picture of the world. So far as I am able to judge, this is a real and not a deliberate ignorance. Mr. Teeling was probably educated in a Catholic atmosphere from which such knowledge is excluded. He seems to have no idea of the Good Life except in what survives today of Christendom, White Christianity that is to say, finding its completest embodiment in the Roman Catholic Church. Regardless of the foreign missions, he fears that Christ may "desert Europe" and leave it "to be completely overrun by the Yellow Races or the Black or the Communists and to pass through horrors undreamt of even today." The most Christian countries of Europe now, he says, are "Franco's Spain, Catholic Belgium and God-fearing Britain." Mrs. Nesta Webster, to whose mentality I have devoted a Note at the end of this book (Note 12c), could not have a livelier horror of Jews and Russia. Outside the Christian pale there is one single movement to which he turns with a certain hope and kindliness, and there I think he is probably giving us a fair reflection of the Vatican-centered mentality. He has met and discussed matters, it is to be noted, with the present Pope. He seems to be a fair sample of how Catholics think.

He writes: "No matter what we may think of the Nazi leaders, or the methods they employ, they are at least instilling into the nation as a whole, and not only into those who might be their willing converts in a free country, a desire to help the maimed, to support one's neighbors, to work and live clearly, such as no democratic country is able to show. The democratic governments pay only lip service to much that is Christian, and they scarcely ever try to enforce it, while the Trade Unions and other socialist groups in this country" (i.e., Britain) "encourage, as indeed do some of the less-thoughtful Conservative die-hards, a form of class warfare which Christianity can never tolerate.

"My own feelings are all in favor of a free democracy giving the opportunity to lead a Christian life, seeing that a willing Christian is worth more to God than an unwilling one. But if the democrats do not respond, and under the cloak of freedom carry on a most un-Christian life, can we expect that God should favor them, rather than a disciplined body that at least is practicing some of the teachings of the Sermon on the Mount?"

That is how the Church wishes to see the Nazis today. Our exponent ignores the implacable resolution with which the education of the young is being wrested from the Catholic teachers in favor of Wotan, and the bulk of this edifying book is a discussion of the possibilities of a sympathetic swamping of this Nazi movement by the incorporation of more and more Catholics into the Reich so that at last it will be possible to chip off the flapping ends of the swastika and restore the cross. It is all set out very attractively. The curious reader can learn how Dollfuss on "Great Catholic Day" (Sept. 11th, 1933) inaugurated the first German Corporative Christian State, and less explicitly how he stamped down socialism and labor. It was Dollfuss who betrayed and destroyed the radical republic that had ruled in Austria from the end of the War. It was he who stood behind Major Fey's smashing-up of the workmen's dwellings that had been the pride of the socialist regime in Vienna (Feb. 1934). This was not only a frankly uncivilized act but a piece of political folly.*

* John Gunther's Inside Europe is particularly good on this.

It left him face to face with the Nazis. They assassinated him in July 1934, but the Catholic Corporative movement went on less confidently under Schuschnigg, until the forcible realization of the Anschluss in 1938 by the Nazi army made Austria an integral part of the Reich.

Ultimately Mr. Teeling thinks Nazi Germany will have an indigestion of Catholics. That is his hope. Large parts of Bavaria, Baden and possibly Wurttemberg and the Rhine-land, are to break away and join up with Austria. Communism may gain control in Italy—Mr. Teeling throws that out quite abruptly and gives no reason for his assumption—and then the Vatican will have to make Vienna its headquarters, Nazism and Fascism will be at a discount, and the Authoritarian State, founded on the suggestions of the Papal Encyclical Quadragesima Anno (Pius XI, 1931) for a corporative society will be installed in Vienna, with the Emperor Otto at its head and the Pope near by.

There you have the sort of thing the energetic young Catholics of today can imagine; the sort of thing the present "God-fearing" British government is unobtrusively subsidizing and spreading about, to the ultimate confusion of all Jews, atheists, men of science, Bolsheviks, Russians (but see the Note 12c on Mrs. Nesta Webster.)...

So much for the Catholic contribution to human adjustment today.

We are too apt to forget the narrow educational limitations of those who figure as wise, unquestionable leaders of men. Everywhere that applies, we live in a medley of ignorant systems, but it is the Catholic culture I am now discussing. It is a common tendency in our minds to believe that what we know clearly is also known clearly to other people. We are all too apt to believe that these dignified directors of human consciences know and understand the body of modern knowledge, that they have studied, judged it and rejected it.

But these Catholic prelates, so imposing in their triple crowns and miters and epicene garments, are in fact extremely ignorant men, not only by virtue of the narrow specialization of their initial education, but also by the incessant activities of service and ceremony that have occupied them since. They can have read few books, they can have had no opportunities of thinking freely. They are not nearly the cynical rogues so many non-Catholics think them; most of them are trying most earnestly to do right by the dim and dwindling oil-lamps inside their brains. They are quite ready to believe Mr. Belloc when he tells them, with that buoyant assurance of his, that Darwin was inspired by the ambition to abolish God in the universe. That fits in completely with their prepossessions. Why should they seek further? Mentally they live in another universe from ours, and the pity is that materially our universes intersect.

The slovenly, unorganized, intellectual world in which we and they live together, gives them no opportunity of grasping modern ideas without an impossible expenditure of perplexing inquiry. And to set against that we must remember that their world of theological elaborations remains an unmapped jungle to the unbeliever. They may have something to say to us but we are quite unable to get it, and conversely. The mind of mankind is still like a scattered jigsaw puzzle, bits of knowledge here and bits of knowledge there and no common pattern visible. And until we have something in the nature of that permanent world encyclopaedia I have tried to foreshadow, so matters must remain. That revival of the Holy Roman Empire under the Emperor Otto, which strikes a realistic modern intelligence as fantastically absurd, presents itself to the Vatican intelligence in the guise of sober and subtle statecraft.

It is not necessary for us to wait for the return of the Holy Roman Empire to appreciate the nature of the Roman Catholic Christian State. In Eire (formerly Southern Ireland) and in Spain, the Church rules and we can watch it in operation. Franco's Spain is still too busy cleaning up the Republican Opposition, by shootings, expulsions and proscriptions, to develop the Christian life in its complete beauty, but in Ireland, Catholicism has been in control for some years.

A stringent censorship of books and publications and a fairly complete control of education have produced a first crop of young men, as blankly ignorant of the modern world as though they had been born in the thirteenth century, mentally concentrated upon the idea of bringing the Protestant North under Catholic control in the sacred name of national unity. That tension of the young men to which so much social disturbance is due seems to be increasing. There has been a steady flow of emigrants to Great Britain, and recently there have been a number of bomb outrages designed to terrorize the British government into an abandonment of Northern Ireland. These patriotic zealots set about their business in a vein of pious devotion. They take Mass and purify their souls by confession—of everything but -the particular enterprise they have in hand. And if the British police deal sternly with these foolish, misguided youngsters, all Catholic Ireland will set up a.great outcry, possibly with more and better bombing, to avenge or release this new crop of national martyrs.

The future of Ireland is incalculable. Hopeful Irishmen abroad have indulged in dreams of a restless and independent-minded people tiring of priests, piety and patriotism and returning presently as an animating influence to world civilization. But how can these young men get the idea of that? We may perhaps find sounder intimations of Ireland's future in the experiences of the Catholic South American States. A people which learns little forgets nothing, and the Church in Eire may be trusted to see to it that the young men of Ireland learn little and so sustain their tradition that inveterate animosities are dignified and desirable. The probabilities seem to point to murderous faction fighting, with Northern Ireland and England always to fall back upon in phases of comparative unity. There is a close temperamental kinship between the Irish and the Spanish, and the history of South America has already produced a series of bosses and pronunciamentos, vindictive massacres and pitiless wars.

Never has there been such heroic, cruel, senseless warfare as those little Christian hells in South America have known. Paraguay under Solano Lopez fought on until its population was reduced from 1,300,000 to under a quarter of a million. Regiments were made up of boys between twelve and fifteen, and women were enrolled to carry ammunition and stores. When these women could keep up no longer, they were either left to die by the roadside or, i£ there was any chance of their falling into the enemy's hands and yielding information, butchered out of hand. No doubt many a wretched young conscript rebelled against his lot, but what could he do? He might hope for a change of leaders. He had no other ideas. It was impossible for him to have other ideas.

The Roman Catholic Church, that clumsy system of frustrations, that strange compendium of ancient traditions and habit systems, since it lies in the closest entanglement with the intellectual life of the Western world and still holds many millions in its grip, is certainly the most formidable single antagonist in the way of human readjustment to the dangers and frustration that now close in upon us all.

48

14. — WHAT IS PROTESTANTISM?

THE conflict of Judaism and anti-Judaism is a tragedy involving the misery and destruction of at most a few million people, and were it not that the abolition of distance has made every one of us his brother's keeper, it would be an incident of secondary importance in the general collapse 'of civilization that is now going on. But the struggle of Christianity to maintain its present ascendancy affects the larger part of the human race. The Roman Catholic Church is the most highly organized and efficient embodiment of Christian teaching, the Orthodox Churches of Greece, Serbia, Russia and the like are relatively negligible systems of ceremony and superstition, the British Imperial culture it will be more convenient to consider later, and the next group of world forces to which we must direct our attention is the Protestantisms, that series of movements and organizations which has arisen through the incapacity or unwillingness of people to accept this or that outstanding incredibility of the Catholic faith.

They protested. But for the most part they did not protest outright against the ensemble of Church beliefs. That would have been too awful for them. The earlier reaction was to discover some incompatibility between the Bible and the practice and teaching of the Church. The courage of the Protestant has grown by degrees. None of these earlier doubters were capable of facing, even in their secret hearts, the terrific isolation of denying Christianity. Such a denial was almost unthinkable in Christendom for those born within the pale, and they did not think it. For reasons we made plain in the preceding section, when we asked why it is that fairly well-educated people cannot merely remain but become Roman Catholics, these early dissentients clung quite desperately to the assertion of their essential orthodoxy.

A convergence of mechanical inventions occurred in the sixteenth century to strengthen the Book against the priest; paper in sheets of a uniform size replaced parchment, and the rapid multiplication of books by printing from movable type became possible. Suddenly Europe was sprayed with Bibles and vernacular translations of the Bible, and the Church found itself assailed by a variety of new Protestantisms that steadily gathered strength and enterprise. Men brooded dubiously over the inspired word. All the Protestants began as "reformers," and their original protests were the distressful cries of honest men, who were—as I have noted in an earlier section—usually priests.

But though the Church monopolized education, ruled men's minds, sanctioned and condemned conduct, adjudicated on political claims, preached crusades, excommunicated, put states under interdicts, and held an ever increasing accumulation of land and wealth, it had never secured a physical grip upon the secular arm. It trusted for obedience to the spiritual fears it could arouse and the civil inconveniences it could cause. It could turn state against state and subjects against their rulers. It could dissolve allegiances. In an illiterate world this gave it an effective security. Many monarchs and princes lived in a 'state of uneasy resentment against the restrictions imposed upon their conduct. There was a continual struggle going on over such things as the appointment of bishops, the restriction of gifts and bequests to the Church, the taxation of its accumulating property. These lords and princes struggled and lived and died, but the Church had a massive continuity. Sooner or later it recovered its concessions and advanced to further aggrandizements. So long, that is, as its moral power, its grip upon the minds and consciences of the people, remained.

It could bluff its way through many scandals and abuses so long as faith was unimpaired. But these honest doubters and critics, with their arguments and proofs, gave a novel strength to the recalcitrance of the princes. Before, they had been recalcitrant like naughty boys, there had been fear and the possibility of repentance behind their outrages, but now they began to behave like youths growing up and discovering flaws and weaknesses in the character of the governess that hitherto even in their disobedience they had respected. They seized very gladly upon this new destructive criticism of the doctrines of the Church. They gave the reformers their protection and ample opportunity to spread their doctrines. So that a thinly concealed desire for autonomy and the confiscation of the vast estates of the Church, mingled very remarkably with honest protestations in the Protestant Reformation.

All this is a matter of history. We need not recapitulate the process by which the new Protestant States that detached themselves from Rome sought first to utilize and then to limit this process of protesting and questioning, of which they had made such good use, by setting up government-controlled Established Churches. Nor need we do more than glance at the way in which Peter the Great took a leaf from the English Establishment and applied the same process of nationalization to the Orthodox Church in Russia. These Protestant State Churches play a diminishing role in the present drama of human affairs. What is of greater interest for the purposes of our present inquiry is the inability of any of these would-be-religious settlements, as reading, writing and controversy spread, to arrest the progressive release of the human intelligence.

The implementing of the Bible by printing had two divergent results. The most conspicuous at first was a definite return towards the spirit of Old Testament Judaism. The Old Testament is the larger, more various and intriguing part of the Word. One theme in it, which appealed more to the reformers and thoughtful subjects generally than to the princes, was the Calvinistic theme, the assertion of a stern Theocracy, the rebuking and warning of kings by prophets, a republicanism under God. The other, politically more agreeable to the established rulers, attached less importance to predestination and more to the good works that came naturally from the Christian monarch. According to the former doctrine he might fail to be one of the elect and be denounced and disobeyed in this life and damned forever in the next, however amiable his behavior. According to the Lutheran alternative he justified himself by the inevitable rightness of his works.

Here we cannot enlarge on these attempts to adjust the new Bible Christianity to the needs of that period. But one very natural mental twist may be noted, and that was the widespread disposition of the Protestant Christians to identify themselves with the Chosen People, either mystically or physically. It would need a small encyclopaedia to recapitulate the writers, movements and societies that have sought to prove some magical migration of the "Lost Ten Tribes" to Western Europe. There are British Israelites of that persuasion today. Such a jungle of absurdities it is, as could only flourish in an ill-instructed world. But one curious variant upon this craving to be an elite with specific divine favor we shall have to consider when we come to estimate the value of the Nazi movement in the complication of human destiny....

The reversion of large parts of Christendom to Bibliolatry and the Chosen People idea was however only the first and most immediate result of the invention of printed books. Many accepted the authority and read and believed. But some read and thought and compared as they read. Gathering momentum more slowly was a new skepticism, which began to question the divinity of the Bible itself.

The doctrine of the Trinity was on the whole one of the less fortunate acquisitions of the Catholic Church. It has always given trouble from the days of the Arian heresy onward. It gave Charlemagne an excuse for breaking with Greek orthodoxy on the profoundly important point whether the Holy Ghost proceeds from the Father only or from the Father and the Son. Arian and Trinitarian, Latin and Greek—the history of their wars was written in the blood of millions. With the increase of questioning in Christendom, that triplex divinity began presently not merely to untwist but to lose its second and third strands altogether.

Men dared presently to call themselves Unitarian, bowing politely but distantly to the Biblical record.

Then came another step. A fashion of skepticism spread among the European nobility and gentry in the seventeenth and eighteenth centuries; bold spirits encouraged each other to the pitch of doubting and ridiculing the Bible altogether. They became naughtily wicked about it. They were deists. There were soon enough of them to live in easy understanding with each other. Voltaire and Gibbon typify their quality. But atheism still remained a rather shocking extravagance. Only temerarious individuals professed so extreme a lack of belief, and usually it was associated with defiant blasphemies and a general pretension to extreme depravity. By this note of defiance in their excesses, these eighteenth-century atheists betrayed a lingering belief in the God they had denied. It was the ideas of God and good not only in the world about them but in themselves that they fought down.

The bright young people who gathered about Sir Francis Dashwood at Medmenham Priory set out to be terrible fellows with their Hell Fire Club and their Black Masses, but how could one get the slightest thrill out of a Black Mass unless one had a lingering awe of the Mass itself? Without that much belief a Black Mass is an inane burlesque of nothing in particular.

It is only in our own time that Protestantism, the progressive etching away of belief by inquiry, has reached its natural finality in complete, untroubled disbelief in superhuman authority. Even now many atheists prevaricate. If the word "God" means anything at all, it means a powerful being sufficiently anthropomorphic to have reciprocal relations with the individual man. A God who is not a personality is a contradiction in terms. But because of the ribald and ungenteel associations of the word "atheist," a great number of atheistic thinkers and teachers and writers have clung ambiguously to the entirely deflated name of "God." God, they say, is -the Absolute, he is a force not ourselves making for righteousness, he is the whisper of conscience, he is the brainless Thinker responsible for the mathematical order of the world, he is immanence. These are mere subterfuges, God-shaped vacuums.

A sort of theism in effect, a theistic feeling at the beginning of life, may be as innate as suckling. The natural and necessary disposition of all immature creatures to believe they are being taken care of, survives and will no doubt survive always. Even if they do not think in theistic terms they will still believe in protection. And throughout the Western world, in Christendom and Islam and Israel, children will be constantly hearing talk of God, so that a father-like divinity becomes the form of this basic feeling. Until a mind is fully adult, it finds great comfort in that ancient personification of a natural but transitory need. And there is still a disposition on the part of unbelieving parents and of teachers who should know better to utilize this craving for dependence in the moral training of their children. Most educational psychologists are convinced that it gives a better result in behavior to teach children that the right thing should be done, not because of an all-seeing eye or a loving Father in Heaven, but because it is simply just that—the right thing to do. Innumerable Confucians and Buddhists have lived noble and beautiful lives without the assistance of an unseen Inspector.

Protestantism carried on to its end is a complete acceptance of the limitless, impartial and continually more wonderful universe that scientific inquiry is illuminating for us; that is to say, it culminates in atheism without qualification. Its final stage is a world of grown men, free from superstitious fear and free equally from belief in any guidance of the world that can relieve them from responsibility for the shortcomings and failures of our race.

49

15. — THE NAZI RELIGION

WE come now to the Nazi movement, which is, in its possibilities of destruction, the most urgent challenge the human mind and will have ever had to face. Nazi Germany may well bring down conclusive disaster on our species. Yet its intellectual content is naive, and its sudden extreme importance the result of a convergence of accidents. A people almost stupidly warlike, led by a maniac, threatens the world and holds in its hands all the exaggerated powers of destruction modern science and invention have created.

It is plain that the Fuehrer is insane; he shows all the symptoms of a recognized form of sex mania, the jealous fear and hate of the great raping black man—who in his case becomes the Jew. Since in his case his obsession endangers the lives of people about him, he should be certified and put under restraint. But insanity has its advantages as well as its handicaps. It involves an abnormal concentration of purpose and nervous energy. In its phase of mania it abolishes or at least defers fatigue and sustains long spells of sleepless vigilance and penetrating distrust far beyond the compass of the normal man. These qualities alone never made any man the leader of a mighty nation. Hitler's insanity would have had little effect upon the world if it had not slotted very easily into certain essential needs of the German situation. But for that he might be shouting, frothing and orating in a madhouse at the present time. But it happened that he supplied just the inflexible spearhead, the inhuman pertinacity, required to give extreme expression to the feelings of a humiliated and outrageously treated people.

The Nazi movement, or something essentially like it, was inevitable. Had there been no Hitler, or were Hitler to vanish tomorrow, Germany would still be the problem sister among the European states, the embittered and crazy sister clutching the high explosive bomb.

The Nazi movement was inevitable because she had a greater surplus of young people without reasonable hope of life than any other country in the world. They had no colonies to go to, no great business enterprises to develop; no employment of any sort. There you have the primary condition for a desperate outbreak. If you want the state of mind of pre-Nazi Germany compactly rendered, read Hans Fallada's Little Man, What Now? That post-war generation grew up to explode and it has exploded. What else could have happened?

In § 12 the conditions under which social order may degenerate into phases of suspicion, persecution, and plunder have been discussed. Post-war Germany displayed these conditions to an exaggerated degree. A new regime should have its own new education to explain itself to the community, but the staggering liberal Republican Germany of the twenties carried on without any revolution in its schools and colleges. They had become a great means of patriotic consolidation under the Hohenzollern regime, they had been purged and vetted for a third of a century to that end, and now they were hard at work establishing in the minds of a new generation the innocence of Germany for the war and the conviction that she had never been defeated; she had been cheated and betrayed. She was suffering bitterly through no fault of her own. The teachers mined the democratic republic. Everything was ripe for an outbreak of hysterical patriotism and a great pogrom before Hitler became of the slightest importance.

And here another factor in the mentality of that dominating section of the German peoples which we may call Nordic-conscious came into play. Much of it was only less anti-Catholic than it was anti-Jewish. Its mentality had been framed upon the Lutheran interpretation of the Bible, and with a certain acceptable reversal it was possible to apply the conception of a Chosen People to the Germanic world. The Nazis took that over in one magnificent plagiarism. The Slav Prussians, the Alpine Bavarians, the melange of Gothic and Celtic peoples in the Rhineland, discovered that they were one single, pure race of beautiful blonds. They saw through their mirrors to the inner truth of themselves. They knew that in spite of appearances they had lovely, pure, blond souls. They turned upon the Jews and all foreigners with the completest paraphrase of the old Bible nationalism. And, wiser in their generation than the post-war liberal Republic, they have seized upon the schools and universities, and are doing their best to mold the mentality of the entire Reich to this fundamentally Biblical idea of a militant Chosen People—Germanized.

Explicitly the new teaching retranslates Jehovah as Wotan, the old Kaiser's unser alter Gott and flouts the most elementary concepts of Christianity. But it is impossible to estimate with what consistency this new religion of heroic combat is being imposed upon the youth of the Reich. Variations in statement may set the brighter ones thinking. All the books have not been burnt. We do not know how much of social democracy remains beneath the Nazified surface. We do not know how much counter-propaganda is going on in the outwardly submissive and still tolerated Protestant and Roman Catholic congregations.

I have cited Mr. William Teeling to show the Roman Catholic expectation of a German return to the faith, but I doubt whether he fully realizes the relentless vigor of the educational drive of the new religion. In Austria just as much as in Germany they are turning the children against parent and priest. Mr. Teeling, I think, counts his Catholics before they are hatched. He would be wiser to count them after they are educated. The complete de-Christianization of the entire Reich, of southern as of northern Germany, is, I think, the greater probability.*

* See School For Barbarians by Erika Mann (1939).

But that involves no release of German thought; it is only a relapse into organized, relentless barbarism. Science in Germany has been silenced completely. There is no free scientific opinion any more. What remains of German science is enslaved to produce either secret discoveries of military importance or sustain the crazy ethnology of race superiority. But if research in non-German countries is forced, barbarism for barbarism, to adopt a reciprocal protective secrecy, it may not be long before Germany realizes a decline in her technical efficiency. She may cease to make discoveries herself and she may be able no longer to borrow them from abroad and develop them for her own purposes. This may move her to some loosening of the gag on her laboratories and an attempt to re-open communications with the alien world outside. And that again may undermine that still very unstable Wotan.

The problem of what will happen in Germany is the major problem of our immediate future. If the Nazi process continues upon its present lines, then all die world must be given over to the .servitude of war preparation, at least until Nazi Germany ceases to exist. So far, Germany has conquered the earth already. The demonstration of the impossibility of independent sovereign states under modern conditions is complete. This finishes it. The declared Nazi objective is to create a unanimous, belligerent Germany, a bloodthirsty nation, entirely tough and ruthless, resolved to use any weapons and any methods, however monstrous and destructive, in its march to world dominion. It will fight and conquer, or blow the world to pieces.

How will that drive to destruction end? It is possible but highly improbable that this desperate adventure may succeed, and the whole world, or what is left of it, may cower at last at the feet of Wotan's Chosen People, its masters. Or that after a world storm of war, more horrible than any war has ever been, Germany may be defeated and stamped out by victors become at last as ruthless as their enemies. Or as a third possibility; something may occur within Germany to shake the Nazi solidarity. Many accidents are possible. Mental forces at present unrevealed may appear. All German thought is not in concentration camps. Individuals may die, new groupings may occur, resolution may falter at the eleventh hour. Every month that this tension endures without an actual explosion, the search for escape from

Armageddon will become more intelligent both within and without Germany. The magnitude of the still impending danger will help more and more people to realize the magnitude of the reconstruction needed to restore safety and hope to mankind. Which means, inter alia, restoring security, hope and ample scope for energetic activities, to the stifled youth of Germany—from whose exploited frustrations all this trouble has arisen.

Before we leave this vital question of the German outlook, it may be well to note one sinister possibility in contemporary thought. Because of the peculiar filthiness and malignity of the Nazi concentration camps, because of the sheer horror of the stories told by the more or less broken creatures who have escaped from them, there is a widespread disposition to assert that Germans are particularly cruel; that they are indeed a specially evil-spirited variety of human being. Old stories of atrocities are being revived. Now this is to concede the Nazi claims to be a unique people. We cannot have it both ways, and, if we argue, as we have done in the preceding sections, that the Germans are not the pure blond Chosen People they imagine themselves to be, but a melange of Slav, Celtic, Gothic and Alpine elements with only a language to bind .them together, then we cannot also entertain this idea of a specific sadistic streak in Germans.

Yet when we compare the evidence of those who have been interned in various countries, we find a general agreement in one respect, in regard to the attitude of the minor officials towards the prisoners, which at the first glance does seem to justify this particular charge against the Germans. There is a consensus of evidence by those who have been there, that in British and Russian prisons the attitude of the guard, the warder, the turnkey and so forth is generally sympathetic to his charges. Fellow feeling is his quality. He regrets his instructions and does his best to mitigate them. At times he may lose his temper or dislike and bully someone, but that is an individual lapse. But his German equivalent, there is no doubt of it, does his tortures with zest, hates his charges as though they were loathsome animals, and is ingenious in devising new pains and abasements and suffering for them. It is important that we should make up our minds about the real nature of this difference. If it is innate, then biologically it would be an excellent thing to kill all Germans.

But most of us who have known and seen Germans intimately have found them as humane and helpful as most people. They are generally more law-abiding than the Irish or the English. They like to be relieved of the dangers and troubles of responsibility by explicit directions. That may be a habit of mind due to a persuasion that this is a dangerous world with which it is unwise to take liberties, and it is quite compatible with these cruelties. The position of the Germans in Central Europe has always exposed them to an exceptional imminence of warfare. The country has been overrun time after time by alien armies. Plunder and rapine have flowed over the land. The German-speakers lived for the most part in a great plain, they had no mountains in which they could hide. It was only by screwing themselves up to fighting pitch and facing all comers, that the divided German states were able to maintain themselves at all. They were called upon by their circumstances to be tougher fighters than any other Europeans.

Toughness therefore is as much in the German tradition as it was, for other reasons, in the Spartan. They had to despise fear and pain in themselves, and that for most human beings means despising fear and pain in others. The Nazi is not a born tough. If he were changed at birth and put among gentle, fearless people, he would not be a tough at all He is a being innately as gentle as you and I, only he is inspired by an hysterical desire to be utterly tough. He refuses to give way to the horror of other people's torments, because from doing that it is only a step to giving way to pain and fear himself. And, attacking his own shrinking and disgust, he goes out of his way in a sort of desperation, to devise and inflict ruthless, disgusting and intolerable things on the recalcitrants, the evil-doers, the detected conspirators—and we must remember that he has been made to believe them that—committed to him for reformation. Deliberate cruelty is not a characteristic of limitless strength. Great strength may be heedless and unconsciously cruel, but not ingeniously and appreciatively cruel. It would get no thrill out of it. That is reserved for men and women who are inwardly afraid. It is sensitive people who seek to sustain and fix themselves by outrages.

Here it would take us too far from our main argument to examine other cases of torture and cruelty, the abominations done by Red Indian and Arab women for example, after battles. There is indeed no people on earth against whom some phase of cruelty cannot be brought. The English assume themselves to be a particularly gentle people, and with some truth now. Yet consider the cockshies and bear- and bull-baiting that delighted their ancestors in the past and the extreme savagery of the penal laws at the end of the eighteenth century. There is a strain of cruelty, suppressed or overt, in every human being. It is inseparable from self-assertion and the craving to exercise power....

But enough has been said to qualify this charge of a special German cruelty. Those concentration camps must be forgotten if ever Germany comes to judgment. Vindictive reprisals may be part of the behavior pattern of a patriotic Irish Catholic who knows no better, but not of a civilized man. Let the dead past bury its grievances. They can have no part in the rational reconstruction of human life....

And here, apt to my argument, comes confirmation. Since I wrote the above I have had a talk with a man who has been in a German concentration camp, and he told me of how an official, instructed to give him, for no particular reason, thirty lashes, fell into conversation with him after the second stroke, found out that he had been the editor of an illustrated paper he liked, sat talking journalism, omitted the rest of the prescribed beating, saying only, "I suppose your friend here won't give us away," quite after the Russian or English pattern. The friend was trustworthy. All fellow-prisoners are not trustworthy. One of the minor vilenesses of Dachau is that prisoners are bribed by petty indulgences and payments to report small relaxations of discipline. And many are in such physical misery, craving to smoke, craving for taste of sweetness, that they do.*

* See Stefan Lorant's I Was Hitler's Prisoner.

50

16. — TOTALITARIANISM

TOTALITARIANISM is no new thing in the Western world. It is stated very completely in Hobbes' Leviathan. Leviathan is the State into which the individual life is almost completely incorporated. Its will is concentrated on the sovereign who heads the collective monster by right divine. He makes war and peace, he raises up and casts down, he levies taxes as he will. Even while Hobbes was preparing his book for press, England decapitated Leviathan in the person of Charles the First. The practical difficulty of the Corporative State has always been the question who should be the head and how a new head should succeed its predecessor. The High Anglican Church upheld the monarchy and maintained the hereditary principle, but the liberal gentry, the merchants and the tax-paying classes generally, were too much for the state monster.

Except in the case of Franco's Spain and the extinguished Catholic Corporative State of Dollfuss, the heads of the totalitarian states of today are usually sustained by "parties" of a distinctly gangsterish quality. At the cost of mental flexibility and adaptability, the corporate state gains a certain immediate concentration of will. Our problem is to estimate what amount of mischief these obstinately knotted will systems may do with the monstrous weapons of the present time, before they themselves can be undone. It may be irreparable mischief.

The Nazi culture has been weighed in the previous section. Now we turn to its weaker associate, fascism. This is immediately interwoven with the career of one single man, Benito Mussolini. Compared with Hitler he is sane, intelligent and human. He is vain, rhetorical and immensely energetic, with the energy not of morbid concentration but physical abundance. He is what many men would like to be. His career from his early days as a socialist conspirator, when oddly enough he was already nicknamed il Duce, to his present supremacy on the crest of middle age, is a fairly open book. It is laced throughout with a thread of the ridiculous. Where Hitler is an unqualified horror, Mussolini often is, as schoolboys say, a bit of an ass, which is much more endearing. Until we remember the castor oil campaign and the poison bombs in Abyssinia and the Lipari Islands, and Amendola and Mateotti and Roselli and the like, he is a lark. But then the lark stops singing. We know absurdities about him from which he cannot escape, we have the researches of the curious and the revelations of intimates. Madame Balabanoff* tells a fairly convincing story of his life at Geneva, Mr. G. Megaro† gives the particulars of his upbringing among the rebel spirits of the Romagna, quotes relentlessly from his early speeches, and shows with chapter and verse how strenuous have been his efforts to conceal the truth about his early career. That anxious eye on posterity, these absurd and belated efforts to escape the unrelenting pens that pursue him, are naturally pleasing to a writer with a weakness for derision.

* My Life as a Rebel (1938).

† Mussolini in the Making (1938).

But do not let us judge Mussolini only by the writings of his enemies. A more flattering study, written indeed in terms of unrestrained admiration, is My Autobiography. It was dictated by the Duce himself at the request of Mr. Richard Washburn Child, if possible a more fulsome hero-worshiper than the autobiographer himself, and it is amusing to compare its evasive flourishes with the relentless documentation of Megaro. If one learns little about the blacksmith father one gets hitherto disregarded particulars about the aristocratic Mussolinis of former days and their armorial bearings and castles and so forth. Anybody on record who was ever called Mussolini seems to have been his ancestor and to have anticipated some or all of his distinctive qualities.*

* See also Professor Salvemini's The Fascist Dictatorship In Italy (1928).

Here we are not concerned either with biography or history except in so far as they throw light on the present world situation, but it is of very great importance in our estimate of the future of fascism to realize that the personal vitality of its creator must now be passing its maximum. He was born in 1883. For some years there has been an increasing appearance of effort and uncertainty in his grandiose gestures. It is as if he felt Italy was slipping away from beneath him. He has manifestly become dependent on the tougher initiatives of Nazi Germany. He is less sure of the Church. Six years ago he was holding up Dollfuss in Austria as a barrier against Hitler. And where is that barrier now? The Nazis look down on him from the Brenner Pass. He is losing face with his own people and his Nazi friends do little to help him in that matter. A few years ago it was dangerous to talk about him in Italy. Now they are talking.

Can there be a second Duce to follow the first? His high-spirited daughter and his son-in-law, Count Ciano, seem impatient to outdo his Fascist intemperance, but they will scarcely dare to attack and oust him, and it is not in his character to resign. Unless some unanticipated accident removes him from the scene, we shall have, not Giovinezza, but a middle-aged fascism to reckon with from now on.

The Italian situation has several incongruous elements and their relative importance varies continually. The Vatican (pace Mr. Teeling and his friends) seems now firmly dug in at Rome. Its relations to fascism have always lacked enthusiasm; it has ideas of its own. In the case of Fascist collapse or national defeat, the monarchy also stands ready to return and save the country. If the monarchy returned, would it be liberal or Catholic totalitarian? And the foreigner knows nothing of the possibilities of social discontent in Italy. Italy is a land peculiarly unfitted to stand the stresses of modern war. She is mostly coast line. She has no coal, and the Apennines are a thousand feet too low for her to have snowfields that would give her irrigation or water power. She can better defend herself against Germany in the Alps than against the sea power of France and Britain.

All these considerations lead towards the same conclusion, that in the probable war tornado of the near future, Italy, if she is not clever enough to keep out of it, will play a secondary and gesticulating role. She may suffer many things. She has not the fixed will, and she cannot afford to have the fixed will, for war, at which the Nazi culture aims. It is Nazi Germany which remains the danger center of mankind.

51

17. — THE BRITISH OLIGARCHY

THE next network of thought and behavior we must bring into this reckoning of world forces is the British Empire. British Imperialism, like Roman Catholicism, is a natural aggregation. No man planned it; it discovered itself in being. It is a crowned oligarchy, claiming to be democratic because it uses universal suffrage for election to one of its two Houses of Parliament, and to correct that it has an easily manipulated voting system and a proprietary press dependent on advertisement revenue for the information of its citizens. At no phase in history have the common people played a dominant part in the government of Great Britain, and in every phase the baronial oligarchy has prevailed. It is the tradition and education of this oligarchy which determines the behavior of the Imperial Government and its role in contemporary world affairs.

Runnymede is the typical scene in the pageant of English liberties; Magna Carta documents the fundamental British situation. Magna Carta secures the liberties of the baron and free yeomen of the realm from all the main abuses of unqualified monarchy. It concedes no more rights to the churls and common folk of the land than it does to cats and dogs. About this central picture of the monarch amidst his barons English history groups itself. The king is restive, but his peers are stern. They war with the Scots and the French and they conquer and parcel out Ireland. The Church carries on its habitual struggle for existence, asserts itself, is restrained; it becomes rich and is reformed and plundered. The Crown, with a Tory following and a sympathetic Church, tries to go back upon Magna Carta, asserting its divine right to absolutism, and one king is beheaded and another goes into exile with his family, leaving the oligarchy, with a manageable new dynasty of Hanoverians, in possession. It over-exploits its American colonies and loses them, and it happens upon a greater Empire in the East.

Never once in the proud island story does the will of the common people matter a rap. Occasionally they give trouble; they get rather out of control after the Black Death; and a little later we find them asking quite inconclusively:

"When Adam delved and Eve span
Who was then the gentleman?"

They subside into deepening misery with the industrial revolution, and they reappear in the nineteenth century struggling for nothing more than better wages and rather more tolerable living conditions. There was nothing very democratic about British trade unionism—as we have defined democracy in § 6—and hardly more in the Labor Party that derived from it. The British Labor Party has never displayed any ambition to direct the affairs of the Empire. It aspires to nothing of the sort. It acknowledges the class inferiority of the workers and haggles by means of strikes and votes for a more tolerable but admittedly inferior way of living. By diminishing the discomfort of the masses and mitigating and soothing the exasperations caused by excessive business enterprise, it plays a stabilizing role in the existing system. Not only is it utterly absurd to call the British government now or at any time in the past a democratic government, but it flies in the face of manifest facts to deny that it is farther off now from anything that can be recognized as a democracy than it was thirty years ago. The old Liberal Party was liberal in its professions at any rate; the Labor Party is densely conservative. The British masses neither rule nor want to rule. They are politically apathetic. They do not produce outstanding individuals to express their distinctive thoughts or feelings, because they have no distinctive thoughts or feelings to express. Outstanding individuals of humble origin are obliged to fall into more or less easy acquiescence with the ruling system. There is nothing else for them to do. The oligarchy is privileged, it has to be served first at table with everything, office, honors, opportunity, but it is not exclusive, and that is one of the factors in its continued existence.

I do not know of any comprehensive study of the education and training of the British ruling class throughout the ages. The feudal world was limited enough for a lord to get away with very little reading and writing. He had his clerk, his cleric, at his elbow, and he felt he could keep his eye on him. His world was all in sight. Leech, lawyer and priest knew their places and stuck to them. The renascence and the coming of the printed book altered all that. The medieval universities were swarms of poor scholars. The gentleman of the renascence had his tutor at home and went to grammar school and university. The grammar school became the narrowing portals through which the poor scholar had now to pass on his way to the learned professions. The Latin and Greek classics came into the Western world first as a stimulant and then, as the pedagogues watered learning down to scholarship, as a distinctive culture. The British oligarchy of the sixteenth and seventeenth centuries conceived of itself as Roman patricians and was rather ashamed of its illiterate members. It made the grand tour with its tutor, achieved a sort of French and Italian and became artistic and architectural. The apt classical quotation adorned the Parliamentary debates into the middle of the nineteenth century. After -that it became infrequent. It was not that the classics were going out of fashion but that the standard of learning was sinking.

Culturally the British oligarchy was at its best in the seventeenth century. It knew what it wanted and how to get it. It managed its estates ably. It built fine houses, it made great progress in agriculture; its younger sons went into trade and spread adventurously into America, India, China. A prolific Protestant clergy supplemented the supply of enterprising young men. Yet a shadow fell upon the outlook with the Hanoverian importation, and Pope's Dunciad marked the change. The Goddess Dullness is enthroned:

"And at her fell approach and secret might
Art after art goes out and all is night."

The oligarchy still ruled and flourished materially under that unstimulating dynasty, but it made no further progress mentally; it ceased to be alert and adaptable, it became acquisitive, tenacious and conservative. Because of these qualities it presently irritated the thirteen American colonies into separation. The French Revolution took it by surprise. When the French in their turn decapitated their king it was not flattered by the imitation. It was scared. The revolutionary mob, it realized, was something different from the Ironsides. The Ironsides sang hymns and were sternly respectable. These people from Marseilles sang a much more alarming song.

The deterioration of an education is usually a complicated process. The mere fact that it is materially successful makes for uncritical contentment, and discredits change. Teaching falls into the hands of sound, orthodox, unenterprising men. It becomes humdrum. Interest shifts to the greater reality of the playing fields. The history of British education—of the education of the oligarchy, that is to say, for popular education had hardly begun—from 1760 to 1860 is a history of resistance to change and steady deterioration.

The nineteenth-century British gentry had nothing like the full-bodied classical education of the preceding centuries; they had only the pedagogic vestiges of that education. Mathematical studies had been introduced, but they were as stylistic and useless as the pedants could make them. By the middle of the nineteenth century the self-complacency of the British governing classes was being protected educationally not only from the subversive ideas of the French Encyclopaedists and the French Revolution, but also from that more fundamental upheaval which was making biological science the key to a modernized mentality. A dwindling section of the upper classes could read French still; there was an attractive breadth in the French novel that the domestic fiction of the period did not display; but Voltaire and Gibbon were passing out of fashion. When gentlemen scoffed, Queen Victoria was "not amused."

Within the narrowing field of their cultivated ignorance, the young gentlemen prepared themselves vigorously for Parliamentary and administrative careers, and they developed an -enthusiasm for open-air sport and that primitive form of bath called the Englishman's tub, which was quite outside the ideology of their Tudor and Stuart ancestors. Many of them still shoot with distinction; others devote much time and attention to fly-fishing; others again cultivate gardens and watch birds. They have developed a peculiar literature of their own; memoirs, biographies and autobiographies, collections of letters and speeches, which establish their social values and supply them with patterns for the careers they follow. This constitutes the bulk of their reading. So equipped, the British oligarchy, at the head of a vast and scattered medley of dominions, crown colonies, mandated territories, India, faces the vast occasions of our time.

It is questionable whether it faces them with any ideas about their future at all. Or its own future or any future. Like the Catholic Church, its main purpose seems to be to hold on, aimless except for self-preservation. It means to go on with the sort of life its fathers have left it, forever if possible, and that apparently is all it means. Crown, Church, lords and gentry will just stick at what they are where they are, until something shatters and replaces them. And they will do this not out of any essential wickedness but because in fact they know of nothing better to do.

The English-speaking world produces an abundance of thought and new ideas, and it has a reading public sufficiently large to secure the translation of any really original book written in any language under the sun. But that reading public is widely dispersed and the major part of it is probably outside the boundaries of the Empire. The British ruling class is shy of ideas and imaginative creation, it dreads and hates what it calls highbrow conversation, and it can have very little time to explore beyond its distinctive literature of personalities. A number of concepts and understandings, a vast multitude of facts, that are known and clear to all well-informed people, seem never to have entered the British ruling-class mind or to have entered it only in a crippled or belittled state.

Here again, just as in our examination of the mutual unawareness of Catholicism and skepticism, we may fall into the error of imagining that what is known to us must necessarily be known to other people. But in reality these people who rule the British Empire do not willfully ignore a great number of things, they are simply ignorant of them or ignorant about them—which is quite a different matter. Ever since the first French Revolution, for example, the mind of the British ruling class has remained barred against any understanding of revolutionary democratic ideas. The French Revolution frightened them and they pulled down the blinds upon it. They chose to think that liberty means nobody doing any work, that equality means bringing the under-housemaid up into the drawing-room and sitting her down to play the grand piano, to her and the general embarrassment, and that fraternity means embracing extremely unwashed—untubbed—people. Socialism again they regard as a dividing-up of all the property in the world into exactly equal shares for everyone. ("Inequality would come again tomorrow.")

Since the advent of a real social democracy would certainly mean very profound readjustments in life for them, these quick shorthand interpretations so to speak, are far more satisfying and sufficient than a sustained argument. They insist upon thinking like that, and if their sons and daughters get other ideas they discourage them and "laugh them out of it" if they can. Everything indeed outside that little anecdotal world of theirs with its importances and routines, that world they would like to go on forever, they know as little about as possible; and since they have never looked at such projects and interpretations directly and intelligently, they cease to be projects and interpretations and are apprehended vaguely as prowling monsters, threats and perils—the Red Peril, the Yellow Peril, the Black Peril—outside rational existence altogether.

I have had plentiful opportunity of sounding the minds of socially well- placed people, and in common with all the world I have watched the political conduct of the Empire during the past few searching years. Manifestly the mentality now ruling is one in which "Bolshies" are the enemies of God and man, men who go east are "pukka sahibs," royalties, beloved mascots whose very pet dogs are adorable, and workers honest drudges so long as they are not "spoilt," with only one weakness, susceptibility to foreign agitators. Americans it is understood are snobs in grain, but rich, and they should be kindly entreated. They will just simply fall down before the dear king and queen, whenever they get a chance. And also remember, "they cannot afford to see the British Empire overthrown,"

If the men get a little away from that sort of thing, the chatter of their women brings them back to it. Their women interfere a lot; the Colonel's lady is the typical figure of feminine influence throughout the social scale. In the army, in the Church, in politics, her good word raises up or casts down. All this is recognized openly in novels, in plays and social intercourse, but when it comes to political discussion and Times leading articles, then reality has to be wrapped up in a lofty pretentiousness....

This is undignified writing. This is in the worst possible taste. Yet I cannot explain the twists and turns of Mr. Neville Chamberlain unless I use the terms I do. How can I adorn him with splendid prose? I cannot see him as anything but essentially ignorant, narrow-minded, subconsciously timid, cunning and inordinately vain. He and his father, Joseph, before him appear to me as the appointed scavengers of the fading Imperial dream. Joseph Chamberlain, with his mean yet extravagant idea of monopolizing the vast resources under the flag by means of an Empire Zollverein, aroused that convergent hostility of the Have-Not States, to which his son, with a sort of poetic justice, now makes his propitiatory surrenders.

I do not think Mr. Chamberlain wants to "save the Empire." The Empire came and the Empire may have to go. He adheres to something less transitory. His more immediate purpose, unless all his acts belie him, is to save the oligarchy and its way of life from its predestined end. He cannot understand that that way of life is over forever.

His family have been at such pains to achieve it, have been so eager, so clumsily eager, to serve it. Still he and his kind dream of friendly hospitable chateaux in a restored Holy Roman Empire or under a Spanish monarchy, and of a France, an Italy, a Greece made safe for the gentry again by the crushing out of all subversive forces. That I am convinced gives the ultimate range of the political vision of Mr. Chamberlain and his class.

When New York made an Exhibition to stimulate imaginations about The World Of Tomorrow, the British pavilion stressed the sentimental past, exhibited Magna Carta, crown jewels, pedigrees and an old English village. There was a genealogical diagram to demonstrate that George Washington was "one of us." There was not the faintest anticipation of that great fusion of English-speaking thought and activity throughout the world, of which all modern-minded men are dreaming. World Federation? Instead there was the most definite reminder that the British Crown and Church stood gently but inexorably in the way of anything of the sort.

In the days before "Tariff Reform," it was possible for young Englishmen to dream of the Empire as a great propaganda and medium for liberal and broadening democratic methods, free migration, free trade and open speech, steadily weaving all the world together. It was a dream that captured many an alien imagination, as for example, Joseph Conrad's, but now it is an altogether abandoned dream. The idea of the Empire as a step towards world unification has lost all plausibility, and while the Chamberlain school of statecraft engages in its propitiatory dispersal, the creative imagination turns to the still living possibilities of one common culture of the English-speaking peoples.

An increasing number of British people look now to the present President of the United States for some sort of world leadership. He is a good, liberal-minded fellow anyhow, but in a sort of despair of anything better they do their best to exaggerate him. Britain herself produces no one to speak whatever liberal thoughts she has to the world. She has nobody of that quality, and even were there such a man it is difficult to imagine how under existing conditions he could emerge to popular attention. Without an objective, dumb, the Empire is becoming an anachronism, an Empire of passive and inadequate resistance. Its progressive disarticulation seems inevitable, and if after all the dream of a federal reassembling of the English-speaking and English-reading communities struggles towards realization, it will owe very little to the Imperial tradition and organization. North America, with its looser, freer and more abundant mental activities, is far more likely to become the backbone of such a reconstruction, and to carry it out on a democratic rather than oligarchic ideology. Monarchy, Church, influential families, experienced administrators and old Parliamentary hands, would merely clog and encumber the development of the social machinery necessary for a modernized world state.

So far from exercising any further leadership in world affairs, Great Britain is much more likely to withdraw into itself. With a dwindling population, an inadequately progressive educational system falling more and more behind the headlong needs of our time, and a shriveled prestige, the island may become unimportant enough to stand out altogether from the effort to effect a world synthesis. It may remain a crowned oligarchy yet for many years, fatuously content with itself and still as unaware as it is today of its continual decadence. Today in the Eastern world one can find a dozen anticipatory parallels, the self-satisfied and self-contained vestiges of what were once proud and important ruling powers.

Possibly this residual Old England, in addition to its hunting and shooting and fishing and race meetings and so forth, will carry on, will be almost forced to carry on, a small but bickering warfare with the equally decadent dictatorship of Catholic Ireland. In that manner, if the world fails to reconstruct itself, the British Islands seem likely to pass into the gathering darkness of the future. And if after all, mankind as a whole does meet the challenge of facts and the scientifically organized world state emerges, it will be into enlightenment rather than darkness that these island residues will dissolve. Macaulay's New Zealander may arrive after all, and when, according to the prophecy, he has visited the ruins of St. Paul's, he will be shown over the Houses of Parliament ("curious and rewarding," as Baedeker would put it) and do his puzzled best to imagine what that strange narrow life was like, assisted by extracts from Hansard, carefully preserved gramophone records of important speeches, enlarged photographs of Mr. Gladstone, movie glimpses of Mr. Neville Chamberlain in a state of indignation, and the still surviving political novels of Mrs. Humphry Ward.

52

18. — SHINTOISM

AND now we may consider another great mental system ruling the minds and behavior of millions of men and women, which has recently become a leading factor in world destiny. This is Shinto, the official and compulsory religion of the Japanese. Formally, other religions are still tolerated, the Roman Catholic for example, but only on condition of ceremonial and practical acquiescence in the main doctrine of the creed, the recognition of the supreme divinity of the Mikado. Mr. A. Morgan Young has recently published an admirable summary of this culture,* and to this mainly I am indebted for the material of this section. He in turn gives his sources for whatever statements he makes, so that the interested reader can easily verify and expand what is given here.

* The Rise Of A Pagan State (1939).

The basis of Shinto is the Kojiki, a compilation of the eighth century A.D. It is readable in its entirety only by scholars, its language being far more remote from the Japanese of today than eighth-century Anglo-Saxon would be from current English. For various reasons only portions of it have been modernized for general use. It begins with a sort of storm of Gods neither made nor begotten but passing away. From this tumult emerge two highly sexual figures, Izanagi and Izanami, who might be described in Hollywood language as male and female "sex appeal." They respond to each other with tremendous vigor, begetting gods and islands and at last a Fire God who burns up his mother Izanami. But by this time Izanagi is so set on procreation that everything about him procreates; he throws off his clothes and they become sea gods and land gods. Finally he produces the Sun Goddess from his left eye, the Moon God from his right eye and the headlong Susa-no-o by blowing his nose. After which he seems to have retired and the Sun Goddess and Susa-no-o occupy the stage.

After various remarkable adventures, no doubt of the greatest spiritual significance and full of lessons for the true believer, Susa-no-o meets a formidable damsel-devouring dragon with eight heads and other alarming accessories, makes the beast drunk with saki, and then kills it and cuts it up. But one of the tails resists and breaks his sword, because in it there is hidden a better sword. This he extracts and presents to his sister the Sun Goddess. It lies today, thickly swathed in brocade, in the Family Shrine of the Imperial House in Tokio. It is one of the Three Sacred Treasures, the sword, the mirror and the jewel, which the Sun Goddess transmitted to her heirs, the divine Emperors, the living Gods of Japan.

To the Western mind accustomed to a widely different system of myths and absurdities, this reads like monstrous nonsense. But it is wiser not to say that in Japan. For example, Mr. Morgan Young tells of what befell Dr. Inoue Tetsujiro, a loyal but liberal-minded Shintoist who ventured to doubt the authenticity of the Three Sacred Treasures. He was denounced, his publisher was penalized, and he was expelled from the Imperial University. Later on, while attending the memorial service of a friend, he was set upon by a gang of pious ruffians and beaten so that one eye was destroyed. So much for a man who had attempted to spiritualize and rationalize the Japanese faith. No one was punished for the outrage upon him, which indeed is only one sample among many of the spirit of renascent Shintoism. It is quite good form to jump at a man who uses a phrase or makes a gesture that seems lacking in piety, and stab him. It is like those fierce old colonels in England who assault people for not standing stiff to "God Save the King."

Mr. Morgan Young makes some interesting suggestions about the temperamental make-up of the Japanese. There are important Mongolian strains in them, but he quotes Putnam Weale (The Truth About China And Japan) to support the thesis that the virile and dominating factor is Malay. Their clothing beneath the kimono, the construction of their houses, their lapses into moody murderousness are all Malay. He insists upon the constant recurrence of head hunting proclivities in their history. An unintelligent blood-thirstiness is in their nature and tradition. They have an inferiority complex with regard to Chinese and Western civilization, which takes the form of an extravagantly aggressive and assertive patriotism. I have followed my authorities in these generalizations. So far as official Japan is concerned they seem to be thoroughly justified. They account for the fact that the head of the state is not so much a leader as a mystically sacred symbol. The rulers of Japan today are Nazis without a Hitler, Fascists without a Mussolini. In the animal world an acephalous monster is sometimes, tougher to tame or destroy than one with a head.

From the deliberate isolation of Japan in the seventeenth century—when all the bickering Christian sects and in particular Xavier's Jesuits were expelled, and the entry of foreigners and foreign travel prohibited absolutely—until the barrier was broken down by Commodore Perry in 1853, there was an age of internecine feuds and exciting strife of every sort. Vendettas were honored. The play of the Forty-Seven Ronin, the most popular of Japanese plays, is the heroic consummation of a vendetta, ending, after the decapitation of the initiator of the feud, with the hara-kiri of these forty-seven heroes. Japan was indeed a romantic head-hunting preserve for the tough. And among the tough everywhere loyalty to the gang is the supreme virtue, loyalty to the gang and no mercy for the flats, the serfs, the common cattle, outside the gang.

This is as true of the "wise guys" of Soho as it is of the gangsters of San Francisco. Wherever there are young men without proper employment the tough guy reappears. The ultimate sin is "squealing"; the crowning heroism is silence under the severest questioning; the master triumph is brilliant outrage. These gallant fellows in Japan would rape or try their swords on peasants without compunction. In such an atmosphere of swagger and loyalty lived the Daimios, the feudal noblemen, and their henchmen the Samurai, until the barriers were forced and the outer world broke in.

About the beginning of this century, the code of honor of these bickering toughs, the noble warrior's way of life, was idealized by a certain Dr. Nitobe, who wrote a book in English called Bushido, "through which the word was for many years far better known abroad than in Japan." He incorporated all the finest pretensions of European chivalry. His Samurai became the disciplined and fearless knights-errant of the world. It took in a lot of people—including myself. In A Modern Utopia (1905), the world was taken care of by an order of "Samurai." They assumed the role of the Syphograuntes in the original Utopia, and in that they anticipated the Communist Party commissars very strikingly. Since 1900 we have had, inter alia, the Nazis, the Fascists, the Phalangists. I was thinking with my generation.

In a lecture at the Sorbonne, in 1927, Democracy Under Revision, I returned to that idea of a disciplined liberal "party." It arises naturally and inevitably out of the problem of contemporary indefiniteness and the relative ineffectiveness of intelligent people.

Perry's guns in 1853 aroused that ringed-in Japan of blood feuds, hara-kiri and heroic decapitations to the existence of a dangerous and aggressive outer world. The Japanese nobles and their Samurai, given over altogether to pride, realized their enormous practical inferiority. While they had been enjoying life after their fashion, the outer world had stolen a march on them. It was plain they had to modernize or succumb—like India, like Java. They had to learn the tricks of these foreigners and learn them quickly, their machinery, their weapons and generally how they did it. At first it seemed that Christianity might be part of the coveted advantages, and Japan thought seriously of making Christianity a state religion. After much recalcitrance and rebellion, the Shinto religion was revived and the country was unified under the divinity of the Mikado.

Happily for the renascent Japanese, the British Empire suffers from practically incurable Russophobia. It is a constitutional disease of the British ruling class. Every assistance was given, material and mental, to the new forces of consolidation, and in the Russo-Japanese War (1904-1905) an Eastern Asiatic power shattered the prestige of Europe on land and sea alike. The Great War completed the job. After that there were no more inquiries for an adaptation of Christianity to the headship of a divine monarch—a slight improvement upon the Royal Headship of the Established Church of England. Instead of Christianity, Shinto, a genuine home product, came into its own.

And gradually, in association with the concentration of power in the warrior class, it has consolidated itself and all its absurdities as the sole religion of Japan, driving every alternative faith and conception underground. For the better part of the period of modernization since 1868, there has been a steady influx of Western science, Western ideas, Western radicalism into Japan. There were endless circles in which "advanced" ideas were discussed freely. With an astonishing swiftness that liberal Japan has disappeared. A few murders, a clean-up of schools and colleges, and the thing has been done. In the place of an intelligent people we face a national monomaniac. This, from our present point of view, is the most important aspect of the whole business.

With an apparent singleness of purpose Japan has flung itself into the attempted conquest of China and the most reckless defiance of the chief naval powers of the world. Here, as in the case of Nazi Germany, we are left asking, "Where have all these reasonable mitigating people gone?"

"Where"—and this is perhaps even more to the point—"has the rational element gone in those who have succumbed?" So many who once talked liberalism, seem now to be wholehearted belligerent patriots.

Our essential theme in this book is the possibility of changing the mental superstructure, the knowledge, idea and habit system of mankind. In that we hope. The tremendous rapidity of this last Japanese change-over is almost incredible. Is it an irreversible process? And if so, what will it go on to next? Can it stand military defeat in China?

Many things seem possible in this catastrophic world of today, but one of the higher probabilities of the present world situation seems to be the failure of the Japanese attack on her greater neighbor. China has astonished the world by her tenacity, by the steady unification of her resistance, by the emergence of a sort of pervading militant wisdom. The Japanese have been stupendously energetic and stupendously unoriginal. There has been much detailed cunning in their operations but no essential wisdom. Desperadoes may murder many people but they cannot divide and rule a hostile country. What will happen in their heads as they realize defeat with nothing but that childish Shintoism of theirs and a tradition and cant of swaggering victory to sustain them?

Will it be wrath and social revenge? Many of these young warriors who landed in China full of the toughest dreams of heroism, victory, rape and authority, must now be in a state of profound disillusionment. They will have a sense of having been fooled. And in China—unless I underestimate the quality of Chinese and Communist propaganda—they will have met not only hardship but ideas. Sooner or later they must go back to a country where the endurance of the peasantry and the people has been tried to the breaking point.

Here are the same factors that existed in Russia in 1918, the factors for a crude and violent social revolt. There is no greater threat to a government than the return of a defeated army. It will go ill in such an event with nobles and dignitaries and priests, and it is quite among the possibilities of the next few years that the last divine heir of the Sun Goddess, shorn of all divinity, may share a parallel fate to that of the last Little Father of Russia. Then, starting from an even lower level than Russia in 1918, Japan will have to reconstruct its social and economic life.

That may be one possibility, but history never repeats itself exactly, and revolutionary methods have changed very greatly in the last twenty years. As one turns these matters over in the mind, China looms not merely as a military but as a mental reality of the first importance. What systems of thought are operative there, what new systems of thought are worming their way into the brains—and many authorities declare that they are rather above the human average—of that immense multitude? That is a question of more importance in a forecast of the human outlook than any we have hitherto discussed.

53

19. — THE CHINESE OUTLOOK

THE primary importance of China in the current interplay of human forces is due not only to the fact that it is the greatest mass of human beings with any sort of solidarity in the world, but also to its manifest educability. It is not only the largest but now it is probably the most plastic mass on earth. Hitherto we have been weighing the influence and destinies of set and blinkered cultures. But in China, tradition, cultural ideas, cultural methods are passing through a phase of extreme dissolution, the mind of every intelligent man is in a state of stimulated inquiry, and creative propositions, if they could be presented there, would surely have a freedom and effectiveness such as no other part of the world can display.

The immemorial basis of Chinese life is an industrious peasantry, the primary source of wealth, on whom the landlord, the loan manager, the merchant, the tax collector have lived in a state of inconsiderate refinement for a long period. When the pressure of taxation or population becomes intolerable, the peasant becomes a bandit and the tension is relieved. Bandits, says J.D.M. Pringle, are the Chinese equivalent of the "unemployed," they levy an unsystematic dole. There have never been any fixed impediments to peasants acquiring wealth or gentlefolk becoming poor, and so, though there has always been much poverty, it has produced little class antagonism. No race difference exists between rich and poor; there is no superimposed nobility, no chivalry with a strong military and hunting tradition. The absence of great natural barriers led to a precocious expansion of governments to a size that, almost from the outset, made a class of literate administrators more necessary and more important than soldiers.

The early need for writing in China arrested its development beyond a quasi-pictorial and clumsily elaborate stage. It was wanted too soon, before it could undergo simplification into a syllabic or alphabetical system. This also contributed to the distinctive quality of China, to the Chinese—if we may coin a word—para-democracy. The extreme difficulty of the written language did indeed put popular education out of the question and set a practical barrier between literate and illiterate more effective as between man and man than any Western class distinction, but at the same time the very difficulty of scholarship obliged the mandarinate to draw continually upon the clever sons of poorish homes. These special conditions converged to give China its distinctive social and political structure, a structure so difficult to alter without complete destruction, that so far neither invasion nor civil commotion has ever changed it in any essential particular. When for example the Manchus conquered the land, they merely founded a new dynasty and imposed the now vanished pigtail—rather by way of assimilation than sublimation. So far. But now this refractory system has to face something more powerful than Hun or Manchu or Japanese; it has to face the change of scale, the change of pace, that is shattering all other human societies.

The religious basis of the Chinese system is equally in contrast with the God-centered beliefs of the West. Confucianism, Taoism and Buddhism are all alike atheisms. There is no one God standing in any personal relationship to man. Confucianism is concerned entirely with the present life, it discourages speculation and inculcates an excessive ancestor worship and respect for the state. It insists upon public service and dignified self-control, not to please a god but simply because that is the right way of living. Taoism is in contrast a religion of abandonment to nature. Politically it is anarchistic and around it cluster a great accumulation of superstitions, spiritualisms, spookisms and quasi-magic beliefs, incantations and astrology. Every folly of the wonder-lovers of today has been anticipated by Taoism. Buddhism teaches a transmigration of souls, souls that may be entirely unaware that the good and evil they experience is due to their behavior in a previous embodiment.

Essentially these religions are behavior systems—or misbehavior systems. Taoism is frankly anti-social, an imaginative dissipation of the mind and will, and Buddhism is at least a withdrawal from life. They are both what it is now fashionable to call escape systems. Their teaching finds its Western equivalent in the "detachment" of Mr. Aldous Huxley. Both foster religious orders and inflict a great multitude of monks and nuns upon the community, and neither has anything of importance to contribute to that intelligent reconditioning 3f the human mind which the present world situation demands. Politically and educationally, the yellow- (or gray) clad Buddhist monk with his begging bowl and his pimping possibilities is a social nuisance; the convent passes by insensible degrees into a common brothel.* But Confucianism is almost pedantically upright. It is the religion of a respectable totalitarianism. Whatever political backbone is found among the older generation of Chinese is in the tradition of Mencius, the disciple and exponent of the master.

* See Lin Yutang's My Country And My People (1936).

In the crucial period of the nineteenth century, China was more self- satisfied with itself than Japan, and altogether indisposed for fundamental change. It had no such sudden shock as Commander Perry gave the Japanese, and it had no consciously ruling caste to react effectively to a warning. It knew the European better than the isolated Japanese, and it had long since formed a poor opinion of the physical and moral bustle and inelegance of Western living. It found the Westerners ugly, truculent and requiring cautious management; but although they had a variety of curious mechanical advantages it deemed them despicable. Since it took on an appearance of Westernization, China held out against modernization for half a century after the Japanese awakening. It endured much. We cannot even sketch that story here from the British Opium War onward. China's first reaction to these aggressions was violent xenophobia. This culminated in the Boxer outbreak (1900) and the punitive looting of the Summer Palace at Peking by the allied European powers. Still China would not pull itself together to fight Outlying parts of its Empire fell away; ports and provinces were seized; this did not affect the routine in the regions still intact.

Even under direct foreign rule much of the old life still carried on. The ancient order seemed as incurably contented with itself as the British.,

Here is how that keen and witty writer Mr. Lin Yutang characterized the Chinese way of living—so recently as 1936. "...Face, Fate and Favor. These three sisters have always ruled China, and are ruling China still. The only revolution that is real and that is worth while is a revolution against this female triad. The trouble is that these three women are so human and so charming. They corrupt our priests, flatter our rulers, protect the powerful, seduce the rich, hypnotize the poor, bribe the ambitious and demoralize the revolutionary camp. They paralyze justice, render ineffective all paper constitutions, scorn at democracy, contemn the law, make a laughing stock of the people's rights, violate all traffic rules and club regulations, and ride roughshod over the people's home gardens. If they were tyrants, or if they were ugly, like the Furies, their reign might not endure so long; but their voices are soft, their ways are gentle, their feet tread noiselessly over the law courts, and their fingers move silently, expertly, putting the machinery of justice out of order while they caress the judge's cheeks. Yes, it is immeasurably comfortable to worship in the shrine of these pagan women."

So Mr. Lin Yutang in 1936, and in 1936 he still despaired of any purposeful consolidation of his country for many years to come. But in three years Japanese military savagery has brought about a desperate unification beyond any foresight.

Mr. Lin Yutang is by nature and disposition a Taoist of the finer sort. He betrays at times a certain patriotic uneasiness and impatience, but these are lapses from his usual artistic self. For the most part he sustains a genteel detachment from the revolution of 1911 which ended the Manchu regime and the pigtail forever. He deplores the novel energy of Sun Yat Sen who "kept up his reading." He notes that Chiang Kai Shek and his financial ally T.V. Soong work "like horses." His heart turns back to "Merry old China" in all the infinite strength of laziness. "The racial tradition," he concludes, "is so strong that its fundamental pattern of life will always remain."

Nothing in the world is so perennial as that. The history of China since the fall of the Manchus displays altogether new forces at work. It is not the old, old story. However reluctantly, she now faces towards Cosmopolis, The republic was the creation of Chinese students who had been educated abroad or by foreign missions, and mostly they had been trained in America. Never before had there been a Chinese revolution fostered in exile. But this last one, like the kindred Russian one, was made by expatriates. Its revolutionary technique followed Western patterns. The Chinese Republicans borrowed ideas from the Communist Party, and the organization of the Kuomintang provided a nexus for the restless and intelligent throughout the Empire. Numerically the Kuomintang, like the Communist Party in Russia in 1917, was a relatively small organization, but it was the only thing that had continuity and a definite will of its own in an otherwise planless chaos.

This is not the place to review the stormy confusion of Chinese affairs since the establishment of the Republic;* the experimental policies of Sun Yat Sen and the significance of his will, the treason of Yuan Shih Kai and his transitory usurpation of the Imperial throne, the clumsy attempts of the Russian Borodin to introduce an uncongenial class war and to revive xenophobia in the form of anti-British Imperialism as a fundamental motive. He failed, and returned to obscurity in Russia, but the Party, under Chou En-lai, organized a successful peasant communist state in Kiangsi—I say peasant communist because there was no attempt at collective farming—and a very efficient Red Army.

* A compact summary is to be found in China Struggles For Unity, by J.D.M. Pringle and Marthe Rajchman.

Driven out of Kiangsi, this Red Army retreated fighting for six thousand miles in one of the greatest retreats in history, and stood at last with its back to Soviet Russia in Shensi and the northwest. The intricate struggles between the Nanking government, the private armies of various warlords and the Red Army, need not concern us, nor the romantic and mysterious cessation of the war against the "Reds." The fact became apparent to the Japanese that slowly and steadily China was being unified under one government. There was no time to lose. Like a fiery new birth came the tragic consolidation of the Chinese national spirit in the face of intolerable Japanese outrages. Today under the military and administrative ability of the energetic Chiang Kai Shek we have a China more united and purposeful than it has ever been before, and apart from its resolve for complete national emancipation, more incalculable than any other human aggregation.

So faded and nerveless are the old conceptions of life, so Taoist, that the entire collective mentality of China is now in effect a tabula rasa upon which it is possible to write almost any constructive idea. And what is written will be evidently determined very largely by movements in the general world mind outside the boundaries of China. The native contribution is in the nature not of initiatives but adaptive qualifications. Lin Yutang, in one of those involuntary lapses of his from "detachment" into patriotic distress and irritation, notes that a dozen years after the death of Sun Yat Sen, who is by universal consent the father of the new China, no Chinese writer has yet displayed the energy and intellectual power .needed to write a full and competent account of the Founder's life and teaching. It would certainly be an immense commercial success; it would be of the greatest political importance; and in that land of lassitude, evasion and passive resistance to change, nobody produces it.

It would seem as though a Chinese mind must needs go abroad and lead a foreign life, before it can even begin to see China. And when it sees China it still depends upon a push from the exterior, for action.

The most vital new thing so far that has been written upon this blank Chinese intelligence is a sort of communism. In a later section we must examine communism as a world force, but here it is to be observed that just as Chinese democracy is not the same thing as Western democracy but a para-democracy, so Chinese communism is not by any means the Russian article, but a para-communism. It has rejected Borodin's crude ideas of liquidating the "rich," the class war and collectivized farming. It is essentially a peasant communism, a revolt against rent, taxes, debt, forestalling, speculative marketing and all the handicaps that enslave the little man. Its leaders are often the fanatical enthusiastic sons of wealthy men, sons who have read Marx and Lenin, but the responding rank and file are the commonalty. It educates earnestly and well, it carries on a propaganda by means of plays, concerts, meetings. It promotes a modernized script. It is making its people into newspaper readers. It is in fact producing a new sort of Chinese common man, with a genuine workers' and soldiers' solidarity. Everywhere the peasants, even those who do not belong to the Party formally, believe in it. Its "Red" Army is as sturdy as any China has ever seen, with partisan tactics peculiarly adapted to the country.

A second set of ideas which is being scrawled across the Chinese tabula rasa is the New Life movement. This was deliberately created by Chiang Kai Shek as a rival and substitute for communism. Chiang Kai Shek is at present the central figure on the Chinese stage; he has been fairly explicit about his ideas and motives, and there is considerable artlessness in what he says. He has an interestingly responsive and representative mind. He speaks with profound reverence of the influence of his mother in forming his character. She remained an earnest Buddhist to the end. She watched over his tender years. She trained him for an energetic life of public service and self-subordination. He took his early political leadership from Sun Yat Sen and the Kuomintang. Sun Yat Sen was a Methodist with a passionate desire to free his country from 'Western Imperialism." This brought him at last into close association with the anti-Imperialist Borodin. It was Borodin's aggressiveness and the killing of rich people and foreigners that estranged Chiang Kai Shek from Sun Yat Sen.

Chiang Kai Shek became for a period militantly anti-Communist. His marriage with Miss Mayling Soong, a member of one of the richest families in China, may have had its subconscious influence upon him. His close association with the Soong family, and particularly with T.V. Soong, has relieved him of many temptations that have overcome other leaders less financially secure. Madame Chiang Kai Shek is a woman of manifest beauty and force of character, and for some time she seems to have done the religious thinking for her husband. He was baptized as a Christian in 1930. Their type of Christianity is a simple evangelical bibliolatry, inclining to fundamentalism rather than to either modernism or Catholicism; it is fundamentalism with a dash of Buchmanism. Every day the Generalissimo reads his Bible and prays for guidance. He prays regularly and abundantly and says grace before he eats. In moments of doubt the sacred book is opened and consulted for an omen.

The New Life Movement is not however professedly Christian, though it speaks in the name of the Christian Sun Yat Sen. It is essentially a patriotic behavior system, attacking opium, polygamy and "immorality" generally, tobacco, alcohol, tea, coffee, meat. It is in violent reaction from the enervation of Taoist self-indulgence. It expresses the realization of the middle and upper classes that things are getting serious for them. Its ambition is to be stern and powerful, to promote a "clean" and strenuous life.

Chiang Kai Shek has been immensely impressed by Fascist and Nazi propaganda, he speaks in profound admiration of "the strength of present-day Italy and Germany," he swallows, as I did, the legend of Bushido (§ 18) and like Mr. Teeling (§ 13) he believes that the Nazi disciplines make for brotherhood, obedience and particularly for that "cleaner" life of sexual and imaginative suppression which leaves the mind free for militant authority. (Both he and Mr. Teeling would be all the wiser and better for a cleansing month in the latrines at Dachau.) But since the aim of the New Life is power even more than purity, it is flatly opposed to any infringement of the rights of private property. It was indeed primarily organized for that end, as a counterblast to communism, and by its emphatic denunciation of Communists and "traitors" and its rigid insistence upon the payments of debts, it makes a special appeal to foreign finance. Its Methodist virtues are a means to an end. The end is self-righteous power. No doubt the New Life stimulates the open campaign against opium, vice and insanitary living, and no doubt it releases a genuine streak of solemn masochism in the composition of the Generalissimo, but how far the natural Chinaman will give himself wholeheartedly to the New Life remains to be shown. The failure of Prohibition in America and the social demoralization caused by it, seem to have had no lesson for Chiang Kai Shek.

For my own part I believe in the complete honesty of Mr. and Mrs. Chiang Kai Shek, but it is plain that they have not the faintest conception of the demands that fate is making upon mankind. They sound indeed in all their published utterances, terribly limited and self-satisfied, and however much we may be pleased to see China led to victory against the Japanese, that is no reason why we should exaggerate the intelligence and vision of these two leaders, because they are instrumental in that hoped-for debâcle.

Such are the chief forces that are operating to produce the China of tomorrow—Chinese communism, or, to define it more clearly, para- communism, and this New Life which is plainly para-fascism. Neither is yet what one can call a commanding force. They combine against the common enemy, but they have no real convergence. The end of the war with Japan will release rather than conciliate their oppositions. China liberated will become more and more definitely a battleground of world ideologies. She will waver between Soviet Russia and fascism, between Christianity of the J.D. Rockefeller type on the one hand and a tentative socialism after the fashion of the New Deal, rather to the left of the New Deal, on the other. One may well doubt if she has any initiative of her own to give the world.

In most Chinamen there struggle a Confucian, a Taoist and a Bandit. To judge by the present state of things that completes the inventory. And yet there is an accumulation of artistic work, a record of invention and ingenuity to the credit of China, witnessing to something not covered by any of these three factors, to some constructive element that existing circumstances have failed to release, some higher intellectual development which may still be waiting there—for the proper evocation.

This raises what is from our present point of view a very important issue. Is there a real scientific modernism, a constructive originality, latent in that very respectable Chinese brain? Has it unexploited mental reserves? That is a question that might be extended far beyond the Chinese horizon. At present China is almost completely unaware of the ecological view of life. She has never heard about it. Science subsidizes no missions; it has failed even to organize its friends in defense of its own freedoms. Almost all this "new education" in China, that has been replacing the classics since the revolution, has been ear-marked for the service of some narrow dogmatism or other. Her brightest intelligences have had but a poor chance of any broader vision. So in China even more than in our Western world, political and social life is still a disastrous clashing-together of blinkered minds. What she thinks new is already old. She is no more prepared to attack the gigantic problems of adjustment that close in upon her, in common with the rest of the world, than she was thirty years ago.

In these thirty years she has done great things. The greatest has been to discover and assert her national independence and solidarity. And still she has everything to do. It is either a prelude to renascence or failure, to have installed a Methodist-Generalissimo in the place of the Son of Heaven, got rid of pigtails, given up smoking, drinking, swearing, necking and suchlike scandalous behavior, and driven the opium traffic underground. Things will not stay at that.

So China, because of its nascent state, because at present there is no deep-rooted system of ideas imposed upon her character and habits, presents, in the barest form, the universal human problem. What prospect is there of an effective drive towards a scientific understanding of history and present realities, and of a reconstruction upon the lines of that knowledge?

Here again we must repeat the refrain of this book.

There exist already scattered about the world, all the knowledge and imaginative material required to turn not merely these seething four hundred million people but the whole world into one incessantly progressive and happily interested world community. All that is needed is to assemble that scattered knowledge and these constructive ideas in an effective form. The world cannot go on, a hydra-headed confusion of sovereignties; it has to concentrate its direction in a World Brain. The organization of a few thousand workers and the expenditure of a few score million pounds could bring that indispensable organization into being. And I doubt if it will ever be done.

It would give this rudderless world, as it drifts towards the rocks, a chart-room, a compass, a bridge and steering-gear

It would change the face of human politics from the aimless stare of dementia to understanding purpose....

To vary the image once more, in China, the greatest, most central and representative human accumulation in the world, the fields are manifestly "white unto harvest" for a comprehensive renewal of civilization, the whole land aches for it, and there are no reapers; there are only spreading fires, trampling beasts in the corn, and a few weaklings gathering a handful of ears.*

* A very convincing and readable picture of China in dissolution is to be found in Miss Nora Wain's The House Of Exile, and there are also the various effective and well-informed novels of Mrs. Pearl Buck, The Patriot for example, and The Good Earth. Edgar Mowrer's Mowrer In China is a convenient little book, compact, full, and understanding.

54

20. — SUBJECT PEOPLES

ONLY very briefly and, as it were, in parenthesis, is it possible to glance at the future of the black peoples massed in Africa and their kindred in America.

The argument of this book is framed on such a scale that the lives and deaths of scores of millions appear as details of microscopic size in relation to the general ant-hill Moreover, it has a perspective of its own. It looks from the directive centers of human thought, outwardly. Estimates of the population of tropical and southern Africa vary round and about one hundred and fifty million. Probably it is subject to considerable fluctuations. These millions live, hope, desire and suffer. But this great population is so remote from the central intellectual processes of mankind, it contributes so little to these processes, that it counts for far less than the sixteen million Jews, from whom, in spite of great handicaps, come men of science, original thinkers, mental workers of all sorts by the thousand. Later, but many decades later, the Negro mind may make a steadily increasing contribution to the World Brain. But at present it is held off by such a tangle of difficulties, obstructions and mind-traps as only the rarest and luckiest of natural geniuses may hope to overcome.

In Lord Hailey's An African Survey (1938) and in Julian Huxley's Africa View (1931), the reader may learn something of that tangle. There, for example, he will find a discussion of the language problem. Is the young Negro of genius to begin his learning in some narrow dialect or in such a wider medium as Swahili, which still provides only a very limited literature for his study, or shall he be given as soon as possible the key to contemporary knowledge and thought, in English or some other European tongue? And where are the teachers and schools to be found for that? Even if he gets English, will it be good, fresh English? Will he encounter anything better than the faded methods, half a century stale, of a lower type of English school? Will it let him get to anything better than Bible Christianity, the history of England and a nice Christmas story or so about holly and robins? Where the Negro is apt to become a little ridiculous is in his exaggerated response to white religious teaching. He takes it in good faith and brings out its absurdities. That is not his fault. Green Pastures and Father Divine are products of white revivalist teaching; they are not native African creations. They smell of the camp meeting and not of the Heart of Darkness. We have no right to call a Negro a fool when it is our people who have made a fool of him. Julian Huxley insists very definitely on the desirability o1 biology and descriptive geography as the backbone of native African education and on the natural interest and aptitude of the African for such studies. There he would be on his, own ground. But because the African is ready for the right education, it does not follow that the governments in authority over him are. These poor-white schoolmasters can teach him nothing of the sort, because they know none of it themselves.

There is a great conflict of testimony about the abilities of black Africa. His bitterest detractors are unable to deny the Negro an enviable sense of rhythm, natural good-humor and an instinct for civility, a sense of fun, brilliant mimicry, rich artistic aptitudes. And more than that. In the United States, in spite of the severest handicaps, black men have been able to struggle up to do distinguished scientific and literary work, and in South Africa it has been found necessary to protect skilled white labor from the competition of able colored people by discriminating against the apprenticing of natives to skilled trades and restricting "certificates of competency" in various mechanical employments to whites. Obviously you cannot put up barriers to protect yourself from the colored man and at the same time declare that he is incurably your inferior.

The outlook for tropical and sub-tropical Negro life in the coming years is dark and indefinite. An adequate education, that would make a large proportion of that population conscious world-citizens, seems improbable, and the utilization of that great reservoir of ignorant animal vitality as a source of conscript soldiers or conscript laborers is highly probable. It is one of the good marks in the checkered record of British Imperialism that in Nigeria it has stood out against the development of the plantation system and protected the autonomy of the native cultivator—with the most satisfactory consequences to everyone concerned. But against that one has to set the ideas of white-man-mastery associated with Cecil Rhodes and sustained today by General Smuts, which look to an entire and permanent economic, social and political discrimination between the lordly white and his natural serf, the native African, And this in the face of the Zulu and Basuto, the most intelligent and successful of native African peoples. The ethnological fantasies of Nazi Germany find a substantial echo in the resolve of the two and a half million Afrikanders to sustain, from the Cape to Kenya, an axis of white masters (preferably of Dutch origin and speaking Afrikaans) with a special philosophy of great totalitarian possibility called holism, lording it over a subjugated but much more prolific, black population.

That racial antagonism makes the outlook of South Africa quite different from that of most of the other pseudo-British "democracies." Obviously it is not a democracy at all, and plainly it is heading towards a regime of race terrorism on lines parallel and sympathetic with the Nazi ideal. The Afrikander will do his best to be a terrific fellow to the last, and he will see to it that the black insurrection gathering under his heel, is sufficiently under-educated and sufficiently embittered to behave savagely when its day of opportunity comes. He will always be rather afraid, and his fears will brutalize his treatment of his helots until he is intolerable. Slowly but surely a racial self-consciousness, a collective resentment, is being forced upon the Negro, not only in South Africa but throughout the world, and South Africa seems the inevitable theater for its release.

But the fate of South Africa need not concern us now, beyond the plain probability that whether the Dominion follows the fate of Haiti or San Domingo or whether the sjambok holds its own, it is very unlikely to contribute anything of primary value to the reconstruction of human society upon a planetary scale.

And so, too, we cannot consider here the possible survival or disappearance of that little group of human beings, the Australian blackfellows, with their undeniable artistry, their aptitude for mechanical work, and so subtle a sense of form that they invented the boomerang ages before the white man made his first experiments with the much simpler propeller. Nor can we bring in that great festoon of interesting and distinctive human societies which hangs across the subtropical seas from Singapore in the west throughout the Dutch East Indies and New Guinea to Guam in the east. Sixty million brown and yellow peoples they are, illiterate, unawakened, but for the most part excessively polite and subservient.

The problem of all these colored peoples is a vast one, but vast as it is, it is still secondary to greater decisions. If the mind of the world can be pulled together so as to give our species a collective rational guidance, this problem will fall into proportion and be solved deliberately and sanely. The colored man will understand and be understood, he will get his fair chance, so that he will come at last to look the white man in the eye, feeling as equal to him as a musician does to an engineer, with as complete an acceptance of difference and as complete a mutual respect. But if we cannot achieve that intellectual readjustment, then the prospect is fear and more fear, cruelty and more cruelty, trampling suppressions, wild insurrections, massacres and reprisals, atrocities and counter-atrocities, and the ultimate waste of every good possibility in these still largely unbroached reservoirs of human variety.

It is not in their own lands that the destiny of all these people will be determined. It is not on the "illimitable veldt" or in the tropical forest, not in mountain fastnesses or on stormy seas that their hope is to be found. Natural aptitude is not enough. The inherent intellectual quality of a cannibal savage or a coolie laborer, a starving share-cropper or an Abyssinian slave, may be as high or higher than that of a distinguished professor or a brilliant colonial administrator, but the latter is not simply his inherent self; he is that plus an education. The one is like a photographic plate that has been casually exposed to the light, it is an accidental blur; it means little or nothing. The other is a plate that has been exposed in a carefully focused camera. It means. It is related. The education and habits of behavior it imposes are the greater part of the civilized man. The better and fuller his education, the better the knowledge organization of his life, the higher he stands over the bare human being, and the more he and his kind control him and are responsible for human destiny. The only salvation of these threatened millions lies through the patient, incessant ordering of the collective human mind. A man working in a study at Harvard or a student sitting, as Marx and Lenin sat in their time, in the Reading Room of the British Museum, may be linking ideas and devising phrases that will open the way of escape for all these menaced and benighted peoples to equal participation in a reconstructed world.

And here is the place to apply the same line of reasoning to that great miscellany of peoples and cultures which is India. They seem destined to play only a secondary and supporting role in any unification of human affairs that is achieved, not by reason of any inherent inferiority, but because they are debarred by their complicated mental barriers and divisions from any collective understanding of modern constructive ideas. These hundreds of millions also I see as people struggling in a net. At present none of their cultural movements displays an original line of its own that amounts even to a slight contribution to world reorganization. Vague aspirations to an obviously fictitious nationalism of an imitative parliamentary kind, sustained by non-co-operation, preferential trading and the fasts of Mr. Gandhi, point to anything but the coming city of mankind. Starving on the doorsteps of the ruler in the Gandhi fashion is a curiously unfair appeal to the ruler's decency. Directly it is used against anyone tough enough to say "Starve then, and be damned to you," it becomes ineffective.

There would be much to be said for an Indian nationalism based upon the idea of human brotherhood and the common future of mankind. If all these peoples can be fused, 'the whole world can be fused. But speaking generally Indian nationalism is no sort of synthesis; it is based on a common, understandable resentment at the British Imperial Government and on very little else. You cannot build a nation on a vanishing grievance. The old Raj is not going to last forever, and when it fades out the Hindu will still be wearing his caste marks and the Moslem slaughtering cattle at him in a derisive spirit.

A culture which said "We are ignorant and divided and condemned to a collective sterility by our ignorance, and we mean to reorganize our mental energy and stock our minds to play our proper part in human unity," would be a culture to respect. But even the Brahmo Sumaj, most liberal of Indian cultures, does not say that. It is universalist religiously, but it is not acutely educational. In India there are numerous rich men, great industrialists, wealthy maharajas and the like, but it has still to dawn upon any of them that a great, growing, liberating mass of knowledge exists in the world beyond the present reach of any Indian, and that there must be scores and hundreds of thousands of fine brains, which need only educational emancipation and opportunity, laboratories, colleges, publication facilities, discussion with the rest of the world, to add a continually increasing Indian contribution to the ever-learning, ever-growing World Brain. In India now there must be a score of potential unrealized Royal Societies, so to speak, running about in loin-cloths and significant turbans and Gandhi caps and what not, running about at that lowly partisan level, and so running to waste.

The British ruling class has been unable to impose modern ideas upon India for the simple reason that it does not possess them itself. The indebtedness is the other way round. The British picked up the idea of caste from the Brahmins and gave very little in return. And other things they picked up. I do not know if anyone has ever made an estimate of the number of elderly gentlemen who return to Great Britain with gurus in tow, mysterious dodges for breathing down their spinal canals, Yoga and all that. They seem to be quite numerous. Man for man when it comes down to that sort of thing the Hindu is master.

What modernization may come into Indian thought and life is much more likely to arrive tediously and belatedly from the north as an adapted communist propaganda, a propaganda modified perhaps by contact with whatever modern Western science may have come in by, through and in spite of British influence from the south.

55

21. — COMMUNISM AND RUSSIA

IT is difficult to say whether on the whole dogmatic communism is to be regarded as a disaster that has happened to the growing discovery of the rational world state or an unavoidable phase in that discovery. In the earlier half of the nineteenth century and especially in the years of recovery from that embolism called Napoleon, there was a great bandying about of creative and pseudo-creative ideas, humanisms, varieties of socialisms, hand-specimen Socialist experiments, New Lanarks, Oneidas, Brook Farms. In all of them there was a subconscious feeling that something was still wanting, the ideas were incomplete. Such a phase of the collective mind is very distressful to impatient intelligences. They feel that nothing is being achieved; they want to "fix something and get on with it." At this pace, they feel, we shall get nowhere.

So they get into the ditch.

Apt to the demands of such eager spirits came Marx. He was a man of vast intellectual ambitions, emulous of Darwin and Adam Smith. He seized upon that economic aspect of life which the political revolution had ignored, and he hung on to that. The "capitalist system," which was his misnomer for privately owned capitalism, had to be abolished and then social justice would ensue. He proclaimed the materialistic conception of history and the class war as the only practicable way to social justice.

Neither Adam Smith nor Darwin, with whom he was obviously disposed to put himself in competition, betrayed any sense of finality in his thought nor any ambition for leadership. They contributed and passed on, according to the new scientific morality. But Marx was of a more primitive and more immediately practical type of intelligence. He was for conclusive formulation, for dogma and an energetic revolutionary effort according to that dogma. He evoked a vigorous, rigid-spirited movement for the destruction of "capitalism" by an insurrectionary class war. He had no ideas, and he was probably incapable of producing ideas, about the peace that should succeed victory in the class war. It never entered his head that a powerful new organization of knowledge and will would be required to direct an emancipated world system. He was, to be plain about it, too lazy-minded. He invented a phantom, more insubstantial than the Holy Ghost, the proletariat. The ever-blessed proletariat would see to it all.

The curious may read about that proletariat, and what is and what is not the dictatorship of the proletariat, and when the Party is the dictatorship and when it is not, and how the peasant comes in, in Joseph Stalin's Leninism. It is the Athanasian Creed of socialism.

But these complications arose later, and at first the proletariat sans phrase sufficed. That the proletariat would solve everything with the hammer of Thor and the sickle of Rhea Cybele was an all too attractive doctrine for eager minds, and the communist movement, in perfect unison, contemned and despised the intricate and difficult business of foresight as "utopianism," and scientific criticism as a sinful want of faith. And so at last when czarism and private ownership of land and capital did collapse in Russia, and that great country was thrown into the hands of the communist leaders, they were totally unprepared with any conceptions of a better organization of affairs.

The released Russia of October 1917 found itself wildly experimental. It had to reorganize a great community fallen into chaos, and it had only scraps of suggestion of how to set about it. Upon Lenin fell the immense task of rationalizing Marxism and getting it to work.

In § 6 the question "What is democracy?" is asked and answered, and it is shown that the life of a human being can be full and free only if it is politically, economically and mentally liberated; that is to say when it is living in a state of political equality, socialism and universal adequate education. Without that much realization, liberty, equality and fraternity are mere words. Marx and his Communist Party never fully grasped the third, the educational condition. How to direct? how to keep direction?: these were questions they never answered. They filled in the gap in their doctrines with that sprawling, muscular divinity with the 'hammer and sickle, who is in truth hardly more real than those symbolic Hindu gods with countless arms and extra parts who puzzle the realistic Western mind. Believe in Him, said they.

In practice the Russian Communists were less elusive than their creed. If they fudged a pseudo-God, in order to get on with their revolution, they were still acutely responsive to modern democratic ideas. They set themselves with considerable energy and success to liquidate the illiteracy of the common people, but unfortunately they did not go on with the harder task of educating themselves. They did not realize the need for that Instead they suppressed disturbing discussion. They are today blinkered and boxed-in to an ideology as definitely restricted, within its wider limits, as that of the orthodox Jews, the British oligarchy, the Roman Catholic hierarchy or the Chinese patriots we have discussed in preceding sections.

The Russian spectacle for the last twenty years has played an immense part in the thought and imagination of the young everywhere. When everything that can be said has been said against it, it still seems to be ahead of the rest of the world in its progress towards the practical realization of the complete democratic idea. Whether it will go on and keep that lead is quite another matter, but the improvement not merely in the material circumstances but in the spirit of the common people is beyond dispute. They were servile and now they are proud. They have a wholesome conceit that the world looks to them. That has been done at a price, yet nowhere else has anything been done to compare with it. America also has advanced in its ideas, as we shall note in the next section, but it started far ahead, five Centuries ahead, of Russia.

But Russia may have achieved this much progress less by virtue of the Communist Party than in spite of it. The Communist Party did no doubt bring the spirit of revolutionary progress to Russia, but it was not in itself the spirit of revolutionary progress. It might well have been better prepared for the task, and it might have produced men of a finer caliber and greater magnanimity. The darkest shadow on the Russian outlook today is its failure to produce a constellation of first-rate men able to evoke its general intelligence and speak for it to the world. Like most countries today, Russia does not seem to be putting her best men foremost She does not know how to find them and use them. She goes on being clumsy. Russia is faltering and losing its imaginative appeal. Her inability to deal with her internal difficulties without a series of trials and executions, so presented as to be extraordinarily repugnant to the Western mind, and the open and undignified bickering of Trotsky and Stalin, have done much to rob her of her once almost magical fascination for the undergraduate intelligence. That intelligence is now shocked and puzzled. It may easily stampede in some new direction, and the real greatness of the new Russia may be forgotten altogether in its superficial littleness.

But how intolerable these ardent young Communists of the last fifteen years have been! What a rawness they have imparted to social and political discussion, all the world over! How unrighteously is the reasonable man tempted to rejoice at this present deflation of noisy, juvenile leftism! It is rare for the normal human being to attain to an adult mental independence before thirty, and it is rare for it to refrain from the vehement expression of opinions after eighteen. Satan finds some mischief still for idle youth to do. Its natural instinct is to rebel against its parents and the parental generation, which has brought it into the world for no end it finds explicable, and, since it is still much too timid intellectually to act alone, its disposition is to go over, lock, stock and barrel, to the organization in flattest repudiation of the flaccid home atmosphere. The good pagan's daughter goes Catholic and the Catholic's son goes Communist. And there they stick. They have made their little act of assertion, but they must still have the comforting feeling of something not themselves, something built up authoritatively, to which they can cling. The boy who runs away from home likes to get on to a ship and give himself up to that. If not, he usually comes home again.

It is one of the primary difficulties of this creature Homo sapiens that it grows up, so far as bodily and willful energy goes, twenty years before its mind has ripened enough for it to think and act alone. The young want to do vigorous and effective things by eighteen, while their mental unripeness obliges them still to seek authority for the things they want to do. They cannot wait. They will respond to nearly anything that lets their energy loose, as a kitten will pursue a cork on a string. There we have the common clue to the storming young Nazi, the Irish patriot, the Spanish Anarchist Syndicalist, the bomb-throwing Zionist, the Shinto militarist, the gangster, the Ku Klux Klansman. They are all forms imposed upon and accepted by that youthful surplus which is the imperative problem of our species, which will overstrain and wreck every social system until its insurgent need to be used is anticipated and satisfied. It has been made clear how this mental exuberance has been allayed in the past by wars and migrations, and why it is that these natural reliefs are no longer sufficient for the magnified destructive forces of the new time.

In the last three years in Britain there have been three magnetic movements with an unaccountable attraction for unemployed vitality. Fascism, a fourth possibility, was happily made repellently ridiculous for our sons in the person of Sir Oswald Mosley, but the impressionable young men who did not succumb to the God-guided woosh of Buchmanism or the high-toned Anglo-Catholicism of T.S. Eliot, fell very readily to the worship of the heroic Hammer-and-Sickle-God. They joined the Party, surrendered themselves to tasks and disciplines and strategies. They felt they had the revolution and all Russia behind them. How they maddened their serious elders, those undergraduates holding on without thought or question to the Party and being as rude as they knew how to critical liberalism, for all the world like naughty children holding on to nurse's apron strings and putting out their tongues at the grown-up passers-by!

That particular adhesion seems to be drawing to an end after the political and intellectual waste of a generation of silly, gallant young lives. They exaggerated the perfection and finality of Soviet Russia. Some have died for that faith. Now the drift is all against the present regime, and instead of searching criticism we are likely to have partisan condemnation. Yet there is a strong case for the existing regime in Russia.

There, there has been and there is still a sustained, widespread and honest effort to build up a new social and economic order. It is only necessary to contrast the Russian drive with the relative ineffectiveness of the Kuomintang. In Russia "revolution" still means, for millions of minds, a new human beginning. In no other community is that idea of a new beginning so manifestly at work. It had had to work against bad social traditions and a widespread defensive subtlety and disingenuousness, with a people to whom punctuality and precision were strange ideas. Chekhov lived and died before the war, but his stories are saturated with the distress felt by a man with a modern scientific training, at the all too human indiscipline of the land he loved. The Bolsheviks, planless themselves, as we have seen, had to take over that world, shattered, impoverished, chaotic, invaded from every direction, and make a working system of it, some sort of new order, however rough and clumsy, or perish. And they have made a new order, rough and clumsy still perhaps in many aspects, but holding together, really holding together, and not nearly so rough and clumsy as it might have been.

I have visited Russia thrice, in 1914, in 1920 and in 1934, I have had long talks with Lenin and Stalin, I have some well-informed and variously orientated Russian friends, and I have read a library full of books about Russia, pro and con, Like most of the world, I was amazed at those strange public trials and the killing-off of, among others, a majority of the original revolutionaries. And I think that of all my witnesses, I have learnt most from an American mining engineer, Mr. J.D. Littlepage, who wrote a book called In Search Of Soviet Gold.

There never was a writer so free from the taint of political prepossessions. He is no sort of ist or crat at all. But he likes mining to be done properly and shipshape, no fudging, no shirking, no waste, no stealing, no trickery. You have to come down heavily on that sort of thing. He thinks vigorously within his blinkers (excellent blinkers) of honesty and high efficiency. And he tells the story of how he was engaged to revive and reorganize the Siberian mines, copper and other minerals as well as gold. He tells pretty convincingly—and it is illuminating—how Stalin was moved to start this revival, and of all the difficulties and complications of the task. At the Littlepage touch the vast, sinister phantoms of Trotskyite conspiracies and organized capitalist sabotage vanish from the scene, the confessions of the accused join the confessions of sorcerers during the witch mania, and we see the human reality of incompetent men trying to cover up the mess they are making of things, of wrongfully-appointed men holding on to their jobs by trick and subterfuge, of hates and jealousies, of elaborate misrepresentations to save the face of groups involved in a common failure, of the manufacture of countervailing evidence, counter-accusations, resort to influence in high quarters. These are the ways of imperfect, inadequately watched men everywhere. The allied generals on the western front during the great war behaved similarly, though unhappily there was nobody to shoot them. And at the last come the confessions, to put a consistent face on the untellable tale of fudging and muddle-headness. Better persuade yourself you are a consistent conspirator than a self-protective fumbler, a snake rather than a worm.

Littlepage makes you understand not only the slackness of the country and the disappointing output, but also the perplexity at the head of things, the inability to get sound information and to discriminate between merit and speciousness. The head does not know whom to believe, grows suspicious and incalculable. The impulse of most of us when we cannot hit accurately is to hit hard. The shootings become understandable; take on the quality of necessity. After Little-page you can re-read the reports of those trials and begin to understand them. The wonder of Russia is that nevertheless so much has been done.

I write with prejudice about communism, but it is not prejudice on its behalf. I have made it clear, I think, how intensely I detest Karl Marx and how greatly my mind has been irritated by the narrowly dogmatic communism of the young. Yet I am forced to a recognition of the real advance Russia has made since the revolution, not merely in material things. Will it go on? What for us is the significance of the new phase into which Russia is now passing?

The mass of the new Russia still seems in its crude way to be revolutionary, in the best, the creative sense of the word. The great raw organism is still moving forward. But there is manifestly something wrong about the head of it. A great number of disillusioned young men in the Western world are saying now that it is Stalin who is to blame and proclaiming themselves Trotskyites. But the matter goes deeper than that. It is not really a personal matter. The organization at the head of things must be radically wrong to be put out of gear by a mere personal feud. It must be so framed as to eliminate good types of mind and promote mediocrities. Lenin was a first-quality man, Litvinov is a much abler man than the run of diplomatists; apart from that the personalities directing Russian affairs vary from honest ordinary to intricately mean. It is preposterous to suppose that they are the pick of that Russian intelligence which has produced men like Mendeleev, Mechnikov, Pavlov, Pushkin, Maxim Gorky....

The headquarters organization upon the shoulders of the Russian giant is, to be plain about it, a head without a forehead; it has a brain that lacks anything more than a rudimentary cerebrum. Russia, with an area of over eight million square miles and a gross population of one hundred and sixty-six million people, is being run by a directorate as antique and rudimentary in its nature as some small pronunciamento South American Republic or the tyranny of an ancient Greek city state. It has no knowledge organization at all. It has no powers of reflection. It has only the Communist Party—which is dogmatic ignorance. It is a giant—I speak of social structure and not of persons—with the head of a newt.

That is the absurd situation of Russia. Only, unhappily, nobody seems to consider it absurd. The country is still living on the mental impetus of Lenin and the democratic socialism of the nineteenth century. When that impetus is spent it will have nothing to fall back upon but die preposterous pretensions of personal government.

It is this absence of a collective cerebrum that has made the present feud of the Stalinists and the Trotskyites possible. Trotsky I have never met, but he seems to have a considerable personal vanity; Stalin I liked when I talked to him; I did not think he had an overwhelming intelligence, but I thought he was honest and strong and human. I have been disillusioned about him mainly by those foolish films of personal propaganda he has allowed to be made, Lenin In October, for example. Therein Trotsky is elaborately belittled and Stalin made the all-wise hero of the story. He stands over Lenin. Modestly but firmly he indicates the strategic points in the map and tells him what to do. Apparently he is trying to distort the whole history of the revolution for his personal glorification.

Why do these two men behave in this way? Apparently they are posing for posterity. That was something Lenin never did. He was a man of the new order. Both Trotsky and Stalin are middle-aged and have very few years left now in which to do anything more for the world, and this is how they dissipate them. They are behaving as absurdly as Mussolini. Few human beings are adult before thirty-five and most remain puerile to the end. Do they not understand that even if they are remembered they are—in the busy world ahead—certain to be misjudged? Nobody will have time to read whole books about them. One or another thing awaits these legends they are cherishing. If the world fails to readjust itself now, they will pass, with everything else that is human, into oblivion; and if it does readjust itself to its new occasions, then so far as they are remembered at all, they will be taken in hand by a more adult and motherly Clio and spanked and put in their places.

I am amazed at these egotisms and astonished at the complete inability of the Communist rank and file, out of Russia at any rate, to avoid taking sides. Either they take sides or they wander away from the idea of creative revolution altogether, so completely are they dependent on the behavior of their Great Men. This is infantile. The man of the new world order, if ever it is to be attained, must learn to go right on without leaders, just as he must learn to go right on without God.

What is happening to the body of Russia, obscured by this scuffle? The scuffle has so narrowed-down to personalities that a great deal may be happening outside it. It may be that in this matter my wish is father to my thought, but at any rate I believe that a more or less complete restoration of intellectual liberty in Russia in the next few years is a quite possible thing. The Russian, who, like the Englishman or the American, has grown up in an atmosphere of less immediate militant stress, is not nearly so docile as the German. There is an ineradicable disposition to humor and laughter in these less controlled peoples. They are earlier adult. I cannot suppose that the Nazi regime would tolerate for a moment those popular stories by Michael Zoshchenko, which hold up the weaknesses and discomforts of the Soviet regime to the gayest ridicule. Laughter can dissolve prison bars; it can outflank prohibitions. Russian writers are beginning to take liberties.

The Russian mind is an insubordinate mind and an untidy one. This virtue and this vice may be two aspects of one quality. Russian thought lacks and needs the restraint of the more disciplined Western intelligence. It has that courage and irresponsibility which we associate with genius. A release of intellectual energy in Russia, corresponding with and responding to the appearance of a reorganization of knowledge and collective purpose and judgment in the West, would have a vastly stimulating effect upon the thought and will of the entire world. It would be an event of major importance in the mental reorganization of mankind. And in the brightness of this new beginning it would hardly be observed that the Communist Party, the Comintern, too narrow, too insincerely dogmatic and "too clever by half," had unobtrusively disappeared, as I suppose that sooner or later it must do.*

* See R. Borkenau's The Communist International (1938), a history which is also an analysis.

56

22. — AMERICAN MENTALITY

FINALLY, in this stocktaking of human forces, we come to the countries more directly affected by the American and French revolutions at the end of the eighteenth century, the countries in which, beyond the shadow of the British oligarchy, radical and liberal and democratic ideas have had a maximum freedom of expression. Chief of these, and charged now, it would seem, with the main burthen of their common destiny, is that third great mass of human beings with any sort of solidarity, the United States of America, China, Russia, North America; these vast countries make more than a third and nearly a half of humanity; they occupy most of the north temperate zone, which is the zone of maximum human energy, and with the British Empire they constitute the greater part of mankind. They are all fermenting with change. And the most freespoken, active, perplexing and various of all these great vats of destiny is the United States.

The United States is of primary significance in world affairs for a number of reasons. In the first place its population is almost entirely literate, that is to say, it can read. How it reads and what it reads is another matter. There are no cheap books in America such as there are in Great Britain and France; most books worth reading can be got in England for sixpence, while in America they cost from ten times as much upward; and outside a limited world even prosperous people hear very little of any but those best sellers which follow each other like epidemics across the continent. But the newspaper Sunday supplements and the public libraries largely compensate for these present imperfections of the book supply. So the American public as a whole, over the vast areas it covers, is simultaneously accessible, if need be, to new ideas, and that accessibility is greatly enhanced by the nation-wide distribution of the cinema and the radio. And next it has a tradition of free discussion. The American says what he thinks, and even when he doesn't think he is apt to say it. You can always contradict him, and there is no handicap to help any opinion to win.

Education is in the hands of the forty-eight state governments of the Union, and varies widely in its standards and organization from state to state; schools, colleges and universities are scattered abundantly over the land; they range from sheer imposture upward, and the best of them are as good as or better than anything else in the world. There are great endowments for education and for educational enterprises. There are probably more highly educated people in the United States than in any other single country whatever, and when it comes to what we may call the half-educated, people whose minds, already loosely furnished, could easily be quickened, there is no comparison. In one or two backward states, modern scientific teaching—of evolution, for examples—is prohibited in the state schools, and discriminatory obstacles are put in the way of the education of colored people. These are exceptions to a general freedom. The intellectual possibilities of this vast country are unlikely to be seriously threatened by invasion, extreme war stresses or civil convulsions for some time. They are threatened just enough to stimulate them and prevent their becoming lethargic.

Like all the rest of the world, the Union has felt the impact of the new conditions of human life, the progressive abolition of distance, the immense increase of material power and the ensuing dislocations of economic and social order, but less confusedly and with more time and elbow-room for consideration than any other country. It has been able to look and see; it has been able to think more plainly about the change that has come upon us all. It has only realized in the last decade that it has an accumulating surplus of unemployed.

There is a vast elementariness about the past hundred and fifty years in America. It is as if social and political life in the United States was simplified and made plain for demonstration purposes to all the rest of the world. We have there in unqualified contrast the East and the West, the North and the South, White and Black; no petty nationalisms, no traditional hatreds, no language difficulties, no localized religions obscure the broad issues. The War of Independence left the country a democracy, democracy at its first stage, the state of political equality and individual liberty. The extension of the democratic idea to include socialism, educational equality and universally accessible information, which we have traced in § 6, scarcely affected America until the close of the nineteenth century. Throughout all that century she worked out the possibilities for good and evil of a hard individualistic democracy. The Civil War, though it arose out of a number of economic and political stresses, simplified out at last, to a logical completion of the equalitarian idea by the abolition of slavery and the enfranchisement of the liberated slaves.

Life throughout that period resolved itself into a scramble for wealth. The whole nation thought dollars, talked dollars. For several generations it was a distinctly exhilarating scramble. There were so much unexploited land, such reserves of natural wealth available, that it was possible to accumulate vast fortunes and still find fresh employment for everyone who chose to work. After the civil war came a great development and organization of industry. American invention, American enterprise, soon led the world in the expansion of big business and the mechanization of life. For a time it was not realized that this march of Triumphant Democracy* was essentially the rape of virgin resources that could never be replaced. Triumphant Democracy poured across the continent, destroying the forests and so changing the climate for the worse, ploughing up pasture that presently became sandy desert, exterminating animal species, using up coal, oil, mineral wealth as though there was no end to any of these things.

* Andrew Carnegie, Triumphant Democracy (1886).

It was only as the "Wonderful Century" drew to its end, that the immensity and the menace of Waste dawned upon people's minds. Everyone was so keen to get dollars that many of them forgot to get children, but the supply of labor for all that vast ploughing-up, cutting-down and tearing-out was sustained by a tremendous immigration. In 1906 a million immigrants poured into

America, mostly people who knew no English and had a far lower standard of life than the native worker. They were divided among themselves at first by their special ignorances; they supplied a far more manageable type of labor from the point of view of the exploiting employer.*

* See my The Future In America (1906); "Two Studies in Disappointment."

The home-grown strain hoped to save money, get on, escape from employment, and so it was slow to develop any class solidarity until it realized that every door to hopeful competition was being closed upon it. Labor legislation in America therefore fell far behind that of Great Britain. Not only was the immediate real wealth of America being turned to dollars; a rapid deterioration of the common life was also going on. Very reluctantly would America admit that the great uprush was over. Theodore Roosevelt's campaign for Conservation was the first practical recognition in America that Americanism had gone too far.

This is not a history, but a survey of existing possibilities, and we will say nothing here of the events that exalted and depressed American life for the next third of a century, the war, the boom, the collapse, until we come to that nationwide realization of crisis and panic that brought Franklin Roosevelt in as the savior of a staggering social system.

Sometimes a work of art can do more to present reality than a whole library of reports and statistics, and that tremendous genius, John Steinbeck, in his Grapes Of Wrath (1939), has given an unforgettable picture of the last stage in that process of material and moral destruction and disillusionment with which the story of sturdy individualism in America concludes. He gives it all, from the exhausted soil dribbling down to dust, to the broken pride, the hopeless revolt and the black despair of the human victims, without rhetoric, without argument, but with an irresistible effect of fundamental truth.

The crisis discovered a great man in Franklin Roosevelt. As I have written elsewhere,* he is a "patrician" rather in the vein of Lord Grey and Arthur Balfour than a typical American politician. He is rich and his peculiar health makes him float rather above the level of everyday temptations.

* Experiment in Autobiography, Chapter IX, § 9, and World Brain, The Fall in America, 1937.

He has the boldness of imagination needed to meet the challenges of the time, but he has the great gentleman's disposition to look to subordinates for the detailed execution of his designs. None too soon he has carried America forward to the second stage of democratic realization. His New Deal involves such collective controls of the national business that it would be absurd to call it anything but socialism, were it not for a prejudice lingering on from the old individualist days against that word.

At the beginning there was much talk of the Brain Trust, which he had gathered about him to realize the vast changeover of American affairs he had in hand. I was tremendously excited by this Brain Trust idea, and I went off to America, as my Experiment In Autobiography relates, to have a good look at it. He had imagined that the universities could and would give him men of exhaustive knowledge and capacity in sufficient amount to create, on the spur of the moment, a civil service competent to meet the huge demands of this great transition he was so gallantly attempting. These Brain Trusters were what the universities produced for him. My wits were not quick enough to size them up at once. They seemed to be an extremely interesting and miscellaneous set of men, but I had a feeling from the outset that they were not going to justify the President's expectations. He was under an easy delusion about the American universities. He thought they were untapped reservoirs of wisdom. They are not. They were quite unable to give him the knowledge, understanding and responsive imaginations necessary to convert his magnificent gestures of social and economic reconstruction into a working reality.

I went, a traveling note of interrogation, from him to Stalin, because I realized that the same insufficiency of mental resources and support which was baffling the American President, the lack of any adequate mass and structure of administrative knowledge in the state, must also be crippling the socialist thrust in Russia. Was Russia meeting or attempting to meet that difficulty? In some way of its own? And in Russia I found Gorky in a dream of Russia's greatness, unfolding the plans of non-existent universities to my incredulous eyes, and nothing else but intolerant dogmatists and intriguing commissars.

Both Roosevelt and Stalin were attempting to produce a huge, modern, scientifically organized, socialist state, the one out of a warning crisis and the other out of a chaos, and the lack of a brain organization to give that state consciousness and coherence was a difference not in nature, but degree.

The brain organization of the United States is not up to its new job. It needs to be revised, expanded, turned round to face the future. I have compared the head structure of the Russian giant to the brain of a newt. To carry on the biological analogy, the knowledge and will structures of the United States seem, to be somewhere about the level of a horse. It has a cerebrum all right; it remembers almost too well within a limited range, it shies at shadows, stampedes very readily, and has no particular zeal for learning new things. Something very much better than that is demanded.

For the great, closely-organized, human community that socialism contemplates, a World Brain is essential The third aspect of a complete democracy is a tremendous educational expansion, that not only opens the way to the White House to Everyman but gives him the necessary mental equipment, if he can use it, to get there. Such an educational organization has been latent in America for a century and a half. The fathers of the Republic were not unmindful of it. In every state, land was set aside to supply the endowment for a state university, and sometimes that turned out well, and sometimes it did not. In addition, there were older endowments of the British type, and fresh benefactions expanded these and added to their number. The whole community was concentrated upon that fascinating dollar hunt, but when one of the winners felt public-spirited and generous, it seemed a fine thing to him to get some more knowledge and education for the people. And being essentially a business man, he went and bought the stuff; he bought the best in the market; and it did not occur to him—and why should it?—that America might be in need of something at least as new and distinctive of her as the great business plants and concentrations that he and his fellow-magnates were, with such vivid immediate success and such ultimate bad consequences, making. So that the extensive and complicated university system of America remained essentially European, first upon the British pattern and then with an increasing German influence. To this day it clings to the medieval cap and gown, the degree-giving and medieval lecturing of the old world.

Dollar preoccupation was almost as effective in leaving unchallenged the ascendancy of Europe and European patterns in the world of thought and artistic creation. Boston, which had played a vigorous part in British intellectual life in colonial days, resented this acceptance of inferiority, but until well into the latter quarter of the nineteenth century the European ascendancy was tacitly admitted in the rest of America. Lowell might complain of a "certain air of condescension" in the visiting English of his time. This air of condescension had this much justification that in many strata of the American world it was accepted. There were insurgent spirits and many protests indeed, but the War of Independence only reached the realm of literary criticism towards the turn of the century, and then it came as a great shock to the British writers of my generation, who had taken the American tribute for granted. Today no young American writer would dream of sedulously imitating or indeed resembling a British model. And in many fields of thought, the new history and sociological speculation for example, individual minds broke into distinctive American methods. Some thirty odd years ago the American climate, by way of a protest, killed all the cherished ivy on those red-bricked colleges, but it did nothing further in the matter. To this day the shape of the knowledge organization and education, and particularly of the higher education, remains in precisely the same state of picturesque headlessness and material ineffectiveness as the older, natural-grown, European disorder of institutions. The erection of facsimile buildings, Magdalen Tower in Chicago, for example, is merely the extreme expression of this reverential attitude.

The United States, let alone the world, cannot carry on now with an unorganized mentality, a scattered higher education that has no power over the press or the common schools or political consciences. It produces no adequate civil service, no well-informed and easily co-operative administrators. It cannot compass any of the major problems before the nation. The resort of the undergraduate world to the realities of the playing fields is a sure indication of the un-attractiveness of its array of subjects. They yell. Every university has a yell. And well may they yell and go wild and frantic in their stadiums, for their lives and their powers are being largely wasted.

Yet it is in America now that the clearest hope for a beginning of that World Brain resides. A country habituated to the rapid development of vast commercial and industrial enterprises must surely be capable of attempting an intellectual and educational enterprise beyond the imagination of men bred in smaller and more tradition-ridden communities. So far it has been impossible to awaken any influential and resourceful people to this patent, if unprecedented necessity. It is unhappily so novel that they seem afraid to realize how obvious it is and unavoidable. There is no time to lose about it. It is hard to guess what may happen when this abnormal phase of personal government by one inspired, insufficiently able man of genius comes to an end. There is no one to replace him and nothing to replace him. Nothing is being prepared. America may relapse in quite a little time into something as acephalous and incalculable as Russia.

And so I return to my refrain: "We need a World Brain," and to my insistence that the creation of a greater mental superstructure to reorient the mind of the world is an entirely practicable proposal.

At this point I imagine an angry critic interrupts. He has been skimming through this book—he wouldn't deign to read it or mark the course of its argument—looking for occasion for offense. And now he cries: "Who are you, Mr. Know-all, to tell us that all these splendid institutions. Harvard, Yale, Princeton, Columbia, Chicago, Johns Hopkins and a multitude of others, and abroad Oxford, Cambridge, Paris, London, Coimbra, Upsala, Tokio—one could count a thousand galaxies of clustering colleges and dreaming spires—and all these wise and good men, thousands of them, men of eminent learning, men of distinguished character, doctors, teachers, investigators, scholars, not one who is not in every respect a far better man than yourself, that all together they amount to nothing! that this great constellation, this veritable shining skyful of gifts and powers is not sufficient for the needs of the world today! that altogether it amounts to no more, scale for scale—what did you say?—than the brain of a horse! that it needs something far more powerful, some far vaster embodiment of knowledge and purpose—some queer fad of yours?"

To which I answer: What are they doing now? So far from lighting the world, the skies are so overcast that these starry constellations seem scarcely to be shining.

And far from being "Mr. Know-all," I am in helpless ignorance, in a sea of unconscious ignorance. There is one thing, and one thing only, I know, that you do not seem to know, and that is this—that neither you nor I know enough nor know the little that we do know well enough, to meet the needs of the world's occasions. Unless we do something about this ignorance of ours, this universal blinkered ignorance, we shall be overwhelmed, we shall destroy one another.

If only some small fraction of the still considerable wealth and energy of America could be turned not merely to a campaign against the ignorance of others but against its own far more dangerous ignorance; if only this absolute necessity for an organized World Brain, a gigantic but still possible super-university, set above all these admirable but ineffective scattered foundations to utilize and consolidate them, if only that could fire the imagination of a few energetic spirits; then the whole outlook of the human species might still be changed.

There is a last possibility to consider in this survey. Some such appeal as I am making may presently gather force, attract a measure, but an insufficient measure, of support and not enough critical attention. The thing may be tried, the effort may be made, and, as people say, it may fall into the wrong hands. Instead of a living World Brain we may have a sham World Brain. The effort may be made. Money may be forthcoming; the demand may grow. Something to look like a world encyclopaedic organization may be brought into being, good enough to pacify most of the clamor, good enough for those people who say you cannot have everything at once—you must have a beginning. When embryonic tissue cannot build an organ it can still produce a cancer. We may have some large and plausible organization of platitudes, irrelevances and compromises, as adequate as an organization of knowledge as the old League of Nations was of world peace. There may be great academic comings and goings, ceremonies and solemn consecrations.

And at last something in the nature of Dr. Nicholas Murray Butler and President Grover Whalen will appear enthroned, side by side, organizers of the World Brain triumphant, the World Brain of Tomorrow, brooding profoundly over the unmitigated destiny of mankind.*

* Cf. The Columbia Encyclopedia.

That may be. The history of most religions supports this possibility. There is nothing whatever between the stars and the atoms to show why the end of Homo sapiens should not be absurd as well as tragic. The price of human salvation is eternal vigilance, incessant fearless criticism and unrestricted wit. How can one tell beforehand whether that price will be forthcoming? Without unrestrained free speech and irreverence, how can we defeat the universal human tendency to be satisfied with and tolerant towards plausible, pretentious things? There can be no rest, no tactful acquiescences, no mental toleration, no enfeebling politeness, in the Kulturkampf ahead, if man is to escape the evils that close in upon him.

In the design of this book three primary themes interlace and pursue and develop each other. There is first, that invention and science have completely altered the material environment of human life. Next, that the disruptive driving-force of an excess of bored and unemployed young men, which must in some manner find relief, will probably shatter human life altogether under the new conditions. And thirdly, that the existing mental organization of our species is entirely insufficient to control the present situation, which nevertheless might, with an adequate effort, be controlled. These are the Change of Scale theme, the Youth Pressure theme and the World Brain theme. The first two create the problem to which the third indicates the only possible solution.

About the role of those young men; its cardinal importance is still not recognized plainly by sociologists, historians and writers of contemporary history. In practice, however, it is plainly apprehended, and a very considerable amount of propaganda to capture the imagination of this vital stratum is carried on, and particularly by the more aggressive contemporary states. They pursue their co-nationals abroad, and make strenuous efforts to win over opinion in neutral states and bring local conditions into parallelism with their own. Nazi patterns are being studied in South Africa, for example, and we have noted the Fascist disposition of General Chiang Kai Shek. There is a great totalitarian propaganda, and now, awakening and responding to it, there is counter-propaganda.

On the whole the totalitarians make the more exciting and attractive promises and give the brooding young man the most immediate prospect of authorized masterful activities. Official Great Britain pays the dole and encourages no presumptuous hopes. But in America and elsewhere there is a definitely anti-Fascist organization called the World Youth movement. This is a brotherhood and fundamentally a pacifist organization, a combination of a great number of more specialized associations, which attempts to bring the opinions and demands of the young for security from massacre and for employment, training, adult education, health culture and so forth, to bear upon governing and administrative bodies, and exert a critical, helpful and mediatory influence upon their social welfare work. It has the open support of both the President and his wife, more particularly of Mrs. Roosevelt, and it extends its liaison work into most of the so-called democracies—and Russia. Its activities vary with the country and occasion, but its general objective is to keep its young people busy with work of public importance, developing their capacity with use and experience. This World Youth movement claims to represent and affect the politico-social activities of a grand total of forty million adherents—under the age of thirty. Of these, twelve million are credited to Russia, though I cannot imagine how these figures are checked. It includes also a number of War Resisters whose ideas stop short at a repudiation of war. They will have nothing to do with war, but how human affairs are to be carried on in a warless world they do not trouble to think. Anyone else can bother about that, it seems, not they. They carry passive resistance to the pitch of know-nothingness. With a certain disapproval they offer us their bodies to be protected and their mouths to be fed.

I mention the World Youth Movement here, but I am quite unable to estimate its possibilities. It may fade out It may play an important and increasing role in the consolidation of a new world order.

The President and Mrs. Roosevelt, though they seem acutely aware that a developing Youth Movement may play an important part in the political drama of tomorrow, have neither of them betrayed any consciousness of the immense intellectual reorientation of which the world is now in such urgent need. Their circumstances have never directed their attention to that. I doubt if these two fine, active minds have ever inquired how it is they know what they know and think as they do. Nor have they ever thought of what they might have been if they had grown up in an entirely different culture. They have the disposition of all politicians the world over to deal only with made opinion. They have never inquired how it is that opinion is made.

The only representative of Youth I have ever met who seemed to be aware that they were under-educated and improperly educated were some Burmans I met in Rangoon. "We are taught to be clerks in European-owned factories," they complained. "What we want is technical knowledge and the science of our own country and circumstances so as to give us a clear conception of our role in the world...."

Now that was saying something.*

* For a fuller factual and more hopeful analysis of the American process see C.A. and Mary R. Beard's The Rise Of American Civilization and America In Midpassage. A characteristic statement of American notions is Speaking Of Change, giving the ideas, attitudes and limitations of the late Edward A. Filene.

57

23. — THREE FACTORS IN EVERYONE

WE have now exposed, in stripped outline, the primary factors in world affairs at the present time. In all these matters I have written with the complete freedom of a biologically trained and uncontrolled observer. Sir Arthur Salter, for example, in his Security. Can We Retrieve It? (1939), writes with all the discretions and reserves of a responsible politician who has to think and speak within the conventions that I, in my entire irresponsibility, can repudiate and kick aside. His thoughts are capped and gowned and mine are stark. He has an air of scarcely recognizing the realities I assemble. Nevertheless, his intelligence and integrity are manifestly forcing him towards a conception of public policy and the human future essentially the same as those I have stated concisely and brutally here.*

* See Note 23A for a quotation from his Epilogue.

The cultural summaries made in the preceding sections from § 11 onward may be offensive to many readers, if only because of their plainness, but they have been made with deliberation, they have been sustained when necessary by citation, and they will be much easier to run away from than to disprove. The political map is imposed upon these primary factors and more or less conditioned by them, very much as it is imposed upon a contoured physical map of the world. It entirely distorts the truth to attempt to reduce this complex struggle for existence to any left and right antagonism. At the maximum simplification we have still to distinguish three absolutely divergent trends in ourselves and in the world about us. Each of these trends has its variations, but these variations can be put very easily as species under one or other of these three genera. The divergence of the three main trends remains complete.

The first of these trends embodies the inveterate disposition of the normal man to accept his immediate circumstances as he finds them and make the best of them for himself. He sticks to the creed he is born to or to the alternative culture that gives him greater comfort. One might write, indeed, not merely the inveterate disposition of the normal man but the inveterate disposition of every normal living thing. For the ordinary animal the loss of the sense of security releases panic, flight, violence—vehement and usually quite unintelligent efforts to recover the confidence that has slipped away. It is only in the human animal, and probably it is only in the last two or three thousand years that there has been any disposition to look forward, even during a fairly prosperous social phase, beyond the prescribed social round, not only to anticipate and arrest danger but also to enlarge, enrich and alter life. There is a faint uneasiness. "Man looks before and after." For the first time in mental history the quality of reality is shifted from the present or from a past-present system to the future. Already in this book (§ 9) the idea of a rotation of values in time has been developed in reference to European thought in the past half-century and with an auto-vivisection of one particular sample. Now we are able to envisage that forced rotation of the mind as a world phenomenon.

Everywhere we note a natural, retrospective conservatism, and everywhere we have minds reluctantly and inadequately coming about and taking up the constructive challenge of the age. Such are the two main antagonistic trends in the mental life of the world today. The third trend goes neither backward nor forward; it is moral abandon. It is equally regardless of the reactionary passive peace desire and of the creative peace impulse. The manifest relapse of the world towards lawless warfare and recklessly destructive violence is due to the successful blocking of the road to the latter peace by the resistance of those who desire the continuance of the former. The deadlock between conservative instinct" and creative readjustment releases the suppressed beast, the unqualified egotist in the species, from control. It can only be recalled to discipline for good and all by the complete triumph of the new peace over the old.

This triangular struggle is going on now not only in the human species as a whole but in every intelligent individual among us. It is the essential religious struggle of the time. In every one of us there is the disposition to acquiesce in the dear, familiar values, faith, creed, patriotism, culture, amidst which we began. In every one there stirs the protest against, a fatuous surrender to things plainly unstable and unsound; the protest and the creative desire even at the price of personal loss and injury. Moments come when we feel that we "must speak out." And there is the ever-recalcitrant egotism which lies in wait for every phase of perplexity, inducing us to abuse every confidence put in us, to snatch the profit and pleasure and personal glorification that offer themselves, so that even leadership turns insensibly into a clamor for precedence, a jealous tyranny and the betrayal of all it set out to serve.

So it is we are all constituted. "Let him who thinketh he stand, take heed lest he fall."

58

24. — SUMMARY

THERE is no creed, no way of living left in the world at all, that really meets the needs of the time.

When we come to look at them coolly and dispassionately, all the main religions, patriotic, moral and customary systems in which human beings are sheltering today, appear to be in a state of jostling and mutually destructive movement, like the houses and palaces and other buildings of some vast, sprawling city overtaken by a landslide. To the very last moment, in spite of falling rafters and bulging walls, men and women cling to the houses in which they were born and to the ways to which they have grown accustomed. At the most they scuttle into the house opposite or the house next door. They accuse each other of straining the partitions, overtaxing the material; they attack the people over the way for secret mining operations. They cannot believe such stresses can continue. The city is still sound enough, they say, if it is not too severely tried. At any pause in the wreckage they say "What did I tell you? It's all over. Now we can feel safe again," and when at last they realize the inevitability and universality of disaster, most of them have become too frantic to entertain the bare possibility of one supreme engineering effort that might yet intercept those seeping waters that have released the whole mountainside to destruction.

Such a salvaging of the species is still just possible. That is as much as the most hopeful mind can say.

59

25. — IMPOSSIBILITY OF UTOPIANISM

IN a previous section (§ 10) I have given my reasons for and against believing that this creative world peace I have shown to be possible, will be achieved in time to save our species from disaster. I fluctuate, I admit, between at the best a cautious and qualified optimism and my persuasion of swiftly advancing, irretrievable disaster. Now let me assemble the probable experiences before our children in the event of such a conclusive frustration of democratic and progressive hope.

This is a much easier task than an attempt to forecast a progressive triumph. Upon that it would be possible to speculate only in the most general terms. What the human intelligence, no longer hag-rid, released from that abject fear of change that has restrained it through the ages, what the released and implemented creative imagination of thousands of millions of free and happily active individuals might achieve, is beyond any anticipating. At the utmost we can produce words like vacant frames and empty showcases, to indicate that undelivered wealth. We can talk of unhampered and unhurrying swiftness of realization, of universal variety, of abundance and balanced beauty. We are forced to take refuge as St. Paul did, when he evaded the greedy materialism of those who demanded a bodily resurrection from him, in "eye hath not seen nor ear heard, nor hath it entered into the heart of man to conceive"....

It is impossible to foretell what the liberated human mind may produce, but at least we can foretell one certain reaction to what is given here. There are those who cling with an obstinate willfulness to the persuasion that a unified world must be a uniform and stagnating world. It is ridiculous, but they manage to believe it. "Horrible monotony," they say, "stress and servitude. Bolshevik tyranny. Prigs' Paradise," and nothing will dissuade them.*

* See, for example, Aldous Huxley's Brave New World.

Many, I am persuaded, feel an intense jealousy of the possibility of a state of affairs better and happier than their own. It is an intolerable thought for the greedier sort of mind that there should be any possible life finer than the one they live, a finer life that they will never share and which indeed they would be incapable of sharing. Their reaction to all forecasts and Utopias, possible or impossible, is self-protective hatred. They interrupt; they leap out with "That wouldn't suit me!"

As indeed it would not. How inevitable is that uncomfortable, protesting laugh: "I'm glad I shan't have to live in this dreadful, tidied-up, drab, ordered world of yours."

The congratulations are mutual. I won't even ask you, Madam, to read in your newspaper between the social and the sporting columns and mark how brightly and swiftly you and your kind drive down towards your destiny.

On the other hand, mankind in defeat and decadence involves no great probabilities of mental novelty. There is nothing to alarm your self- complacency in that. It is the world we live in now, only a little farther on and a little more so. We need not speculate outside the traditional, limited, human stuff, that dear old "unchanging human nature" of the past twenty or thirty thousand years. And to that we will now apply ourselves.

60

26. — DECADENT WORLD

IT was becoming evident to everyone that the present state of affairs could not continue. The greater part of mankind was living in the immediate fear of sudden, undeclared war. At any time, by night or day, with less than an hour's notice, the screaming sirens and the high explosive and incendiary bombs were expected to burst about us. Every other occupation was subordinated to the ill-conceived exigencies of air-raid precautions, and an ever-increasing proportion of our human and material resources was pouring into military preparations. Almost every intelligent human being and every township and community in Eurasia was in a state of mental tension which was rapidly approaching the breaking-point. Suicides were increasing. Lucid thinking became offensive and intolerable. People attacked and persecuted one another on flimsy excuses. Because of the limited and distorted idea systems in which they are living, they were, as we have seen in §§ 11 to 22, incapable of setting about the necessary readjustments of relationship. We have dismissed any such outbreak of sanity, therefore, as improbable. There is no basis on which it can start. There will be no world unification, because our species is too distraught and divided for anything of the sort.

What seems much more likely is a lapse into actual warfare, red war, on a planetary scale. This will not be a clearly conceived war carried out with the intention of establishing a world peace. Governments will pretend it is that, but fundamentally it will be a fit of frantic violence with no rational objective whatever. The first offensive was just as likely to come from the so-called "democratic" as from the "dictator" side.

As we have shown quite clearly by an appeal to manifest facts, the threefold forces making for conflict are to be found busily active in every existing human community—the evil patriotic and religious traditions, the horribly magnified weapons, the relative excess of unemployed young men—but the states where the pressure of these forces, because they were most pent up, has produced its maximum effect in menace and belligerent gestures, will be marked as the aggressor states. They will be assailed by a loose alliance of incongruous countries animated by the diverse motive systems we have scrutinized, and agreed only upon the need of suppressing these desperado nations. The ensuing war is likely to be briefer but far more violently destructive than the previous world war, because while that war began at a level of equipment which permitted a steady increase in the supply of munitions almost to the end when the losers collapsed through material and moral exhaustion, the combatants this time start from the beginning at something like a maximum of armament, and will reach the breaking-point much earlier. Staying power will decide the formal victory, which is less likely to be decisive even than the surrender of the eleventh of November, 1918.

The material and moral destruction of the actual warfare will certainly be enormous. The population stratum of military age will be largely killed, mutilated, poisoned or mentally unbalanced, and after it, will come a generation or so, which has been more and more undernourished, under-educated, demoralized and mentally distorted, as the concentration upon preparation (guns for butter) and the actual stress, noise and disorder of the conflict, have made a normal growth impossible for them. Vast resources of power will have been wasted for good and all, and the land and the sea bottom will be littered with smashed-up aeroplanes, shattered tanks, twisted railway trucks, burnt-out aerodromes and a great abundance of sunken ships and stores. Exoduses of population hardly less frightful than battle routs will have dislocated all sanitary balances, and famine and its follower, pestilence, will have swept the world. Even the influenza epidemic which followed the previous Great War killed more people than were actually slain in battle. This time the sanitary disorganization will certainly be much greater and the possibilities of morbid infections far more various. Probably there will be a deliberate spraying of disease germs to assist this, more natural mischief. There will have been much gratuitous bombing of cities. There will have been a great burning and smashing-up of human habitations which no one will have had energy to replace, and such a destruction of beautiful buildings, works of art and irreplaceable loveliness of all sorts, as will make the feats of the Huns and Vandals seem mere boyish mischief. All that lies plainly ahead.

And when at last one side admits defeat, and peace is proclaimed upon the world battlefield, what will be the situation? The defeated will be treated as the incurably guilty parties. If that were so, if there were incurably malignant peoples, then the wholesome thing to do would be to massacre them carefully and completely. Mankind will balk at that.

Instead of any such biologically conclusive settlement, there will be, once again, a punitive peace. The victors, to the best of their ability, will make the losers pay. The losers will be quite unable to pay. Further punitive measures will then become necessary. Modern war is a very impartial process, and the victors will probably have suffered quite as much and even more material and social devastation than the vanquished. They will be in no mind for generosity. No country in the world, even those that have preserved a technical neutrality, alert under arms, will emerge from the storm at anything like the level of civilization at which it stands today. There will be less freedom of speech, less opportunity to speak freely, far more fear and far more danger of frantic mass impulses.

In §§ 11 to 22 there has been an attempt to estimate the general trend of the main idea systems of the world. Here we may recapitulate the conclusions to which that survey points. What is going on now?

A very considerable festering of minds is no doubt occurring. People arc reading and thinking feverishly but they are often thinking wrong and with an assisted wrong-headedness. Patriotic and religious teachings surround them, and subtle and insidiously mischievous suggestions. The arts of propaganda in enemy countries improve rapidly. There is no country in the world where enemies are not sowing tares with constantly increasing effectiveness. Every form of discontent is fomented with a skill and energy worthy of a better cause. The suggestions of desperate and destructive revolt that men may fear to whisper to their neighbors, will come to them from abroad.

We have seen that the break-up of the British Imperial system in face of a complex of insurrectionary movements, troubles on which the sun will never set, has a high degree of probability. The conflict of the new Nazi religion with Catholicism is plain and open, we have studied it in the ingenuous speculations of Mr. Teeling, and beneath the surface of most of the established systems of today, some queer development of social dissent is latent. The present ebb of communism is no end to insurrectionary class war. It is muttering vaguely, it may be unorganized and criminal, but it will be none the less socially destructive. We have noted the waning charm of the Italian dictatorship and the lamentable tendency of original sin to emerge as murder and fanatical cruelty under the very shadow of obscurantist Christian teaching. Where Spanish and Portuguese are spoken the pronunciamento flourishes with undiminished vitality.

America has a transitory unity and stability under the protean aspects of the New Deal, but no one knows what will follow when the extremely personal direction of Franklin Roosevelt ceases. There may be a heavily financed drive to put back the New Deal and return to a hard-faced business individualism. Big business has used some rough methods in the past and may resort to still rougher methods again—in an atmosphere that has become much less tolerant of the old forms of firmness. Not without reason do Americans talk of their Bourbons. That once unorganized alien labor has become assimilated and unified and more capable of meeting pseudo-legal violence with extra-legal violence. The country that produced Franklin Roosevelt also produced at the same time Huey Long and an unprecedented regime of gangster terrorism. And in the same period came the revival and the suppression of the intimidations of the Ku Klux Klan. Things have a way of beginning in America, running large and rank, and then coming suddenly to an end. This applies to evil and hopeful things alike. Everything may occur in some part of the United States or another, and the country may still retain an apparent unity. With a strong personality the White House may concentrate the nation, as it were, into one mind; with a less vigorous head that federal unification relaxes and the continental expanse is revealed as a miscellany of divergent issues. War and Roosevelt might impose a temporary national personality upon the United States that would vanish again in a subsequent reaction, giving place to a state of affairs as incoherent and variegated as Europe. The apparent solidarity of the United States may be as personal as any dictatorship; it may be accidental and not essential.

The question of what will come after Roosevelt opens a vista of localized possibilities varying between dull conflict, boss rule and chaotic violence, and the corresponding question of what will come after Stalin opens up not a vista but darkness. We have weighed up the uncertainties of China and Japan, and there too there is no assurance of stability and many intimations of degenerative revolution. A Japanese collapse would probably disintegrate China again, for nothing but patriotism holds China together.

So we have left as the main factors in the settlement after the second world war, a patchwork of staggering governments ruling over a welter of steadily increasing social disorganization. The settlement after the next world war will be only a prelude to further conflict. Informal warfare will succeed the formal struggle. What else can happen? Victors and vanquished will go to pieces and rearrange themselves. There is no body of ideas in existence, no tradition or frame of a world law to which an appeal can be made, that can carry on the shattered, mentally and morally overstrained, but still heavily armed combatants to any sort of world synthesis. The seizures and pronunciamentos that followed the Treaty of Versailles will recur more abundantly and on a more sustained and uncontrollable scale.

Since any new synthesis is improbable, the names of the existing main political systems are likely to continue long after they have lost any real authority, just as the idea of the Empire prevailed among the barbarians in the Dark Ages. The Union Jack, the Swastika, the Cross, or the Stars and Stripes may still float over a thousand dissociated gangs and tribes, claiming its authority, just as the Roman Eagle survived as a legally dominating reality in man's imaginations, side by side with the Church, long after Rome was sacked.

Now it may be thought that so much political and social dissolution may mean an ebb of invention and a break-up of the industrial organizations that supply the destructive apparatus which is smashing up the existing order so rapidly and uncontrollably. The human process will go back, it may be fancied, to a mechanically feeble barbarism, and a new system of expanding states may finally reconstruct civilization. It will be the Dark Ages over again, a planetary instead of a merely European Dark Ages. Homo sapiens will be given a second opportunity. There will be a return to primitive home-made weapons, non-mechanical transport, a new age if not of innocence yet of illiteracy, and slow, feeble and less lethal mischiefs will return to the world. But history never repeats itself, ecological processes are irreversible, and there are many considerations that make it improbable that the new barbarism which is coming upon us will have even a material resemblance to the barbarism of sixteen centuries ago. It will be much tougher, with a livelier and wickeder intelligence, and it will retain a far more destructive equipment.

Because it is proving impossible to assemble and organize knowledge and sane ideas for the establishment of a world civilization, it does not follow that knowledge already scattered about the earth will be destroyed. It may become generally inaccessible and secret, but it may continue available in workable fragments to a number of enterprising people, A vast store of metallurgical and industrial technique was completely lost with the downfall of the Roman Empire,* but then the record of principles and processes was very flimsy and vulnerable.

* Rendered rather vividly in George Gissing's Veranilda.

Many technical secrets were never written at all and none were printed. Even down to the past century that sort of thing went on; a number of the processes in Wedgwood's china factory, for example, were transmitted verbally from one worker to another. Some of the older men carried secrets with them to the grave, and an analytical chemist had to be called in and the processes laboriously rediscovered before the firm could go on producing its characteristic wares. That was a survival of old-world methods. Under such conditions the old techniques disappeared in a generation or so. But nowadays scientific and technical knowledge is embodied in so huge a number of printed and widely distributed publications, the body of people in contact with those records is so large and varied, that even in a world of deepening and extensive disorder, it will still be possible to assemble knots and groups of men capable of carrying on the production of most of the lethal devices now in use. Postal and railway organization may go to pieces, newspapers disappear, roads become impassable and gas supply, drainage, and public lighting cease, because such things depend upon a widespread social co-operation, and still there may be radio transmission, aeroplanes and high explosives, which do not demand anything like the same general participation.

It does not follow that mechanisms and contrivances will disappear in reverse order to that in which they appeared. It may have taken long years of research and the contribution of thousands of scientific workers to discover an explosive or a poison, but when that has been attained only a recipe and material are needed for its production. It has become a part of "our human heritage."

This is evident for example in the steady increase of bomb-making and bomb-throwing in the world. It is a growing feature of the normal social life. Every morning now we read in our newspapers of the young braves of the Irish Republican Army throwing their cheap but effective bombs in Great Britain, the Jew boys and the Arab boys bomb each other with ever-increasing zeal and bloodier results, bomb outrages comment on the new regime in Spain, they multiply in India, in the occupied areas of China. In a world of deepening misunderstandings and grievances, there is no reason to doubt that they will become as common as road accidents and as little thought of, a part of the normal give and take of politics. People will harden their hearts to their consequences until the bomb comes to themselves, and then their enlightenment will be too late.

The world emerging from the next great war, then, will be a tougher world, more disunited than ever, abounding still more in concealed aims and secret preparations and the fears and suspicions they engender. What else can it be? The open forum of the scientific world will have disappeared and the suggestion of any cosmopolitan ideas will have been suppressed, as a weakening of combatant morale. In every country. For the neutral powers, if any remain, will still have had to be mentally as well as materially "prepared-" Human beings who can do nothing else to gratify their craving to exercise power, love to suppress and help suppression.

No doubt great numbers of people will have felt the irrational evil of all this shrinking of thought into strategic holes and corners, but they will have had less and less, opportunity of getting together, or even clearing up their own minds sufficiently to take effective action. Many of them, under the stress of their conscious helplessness, will lapse into mystical religiosity, will refuse to bear children, will resort to suicide or the quasi-suicide of non-resistance. Many will take refuge in opiates. The Japanese are doing their utmost to spread the use of opium and heroin among the Chinese, and they will probably succeed in affecting their own troops also. The ideas and expedients of birth control, now they have spread about the earth, will not be easily forgotten.

More and more will the world be for the tough, for the secretive, the treacherous and ruthless. Cities will be dangerous labyrinths and the countryside an exposure to attack. Ever and again some group or some individual by luck or cunning may achieve a certain width of conquest and establish a peace of terror. Subservient millions may rejoice then for awhile that at last strong government has come back to the world. They will accept an imposed religion, a last revival of Christianity à la Franco perhaps, or of that "clean" Nazi creed, or something on the evangelical lines General Chiang Kai Shek seems to favor; they will observe a dictated morality and a mutual censorship. Any intellectual revival is improbable. This light of free science will have sunken and gone out long since; what remains of technical knowledge will be in the safe hands of properly ordained men. The first thing a youth attracted to mechanical or medical knowledge will do, will be to take orders and put himself under safe direction. History will have shriveled down to the Creator myth again, but the popular imagination will be titillated and appalled by a dim and dying tradition of a former age, our age, of sinful knowledge, of lawless indulgence, of unconsecrated loves, of a terrible disrespect for customs and taboos and sacrifices and priests, that brought great misfortunes upon mankind. A new "World before the Flood" it will be.

A few secret doubters may exist, bookish, silent, hinting and whispering men— men, for a more "wholesome" use of womankind will leave women little time for reading—who will pore guiltily over the unfulfilled promises of a golden age to come, in the old books which men wrote when they still had pride and hope. There may be some wistful whisperings, some weak attempts at a new Freemasonry. But the necessary adaptation of human thought to turn the tide of decadence is something too wide and open in its nature to be brought about by any sort of secret organization. What can be done by timid men who are forced to squeak and scamper like mice behind the arras?

Art may have an Indian summer. The dictator may even build some fine buildings—for most of them build—monasteries, cathedrals, palaces, before he passes. There may be portrait painting and portrait pieces of an ennobling type, glorified history, an effort at a technically lower level to recall the Venetian bravura of Titian, Tintoretto and Paul Veronese. At any rate we shall not live to see that last Art Age. Then, because there will be no correction for the material stresses of a static system, the darkness will close in again. There will be peasant revolts, an exhausting war or dynastic trouble. So human affairs have gone in the past, and so, without any fundamental change in human mentality, they must continue to go, so long as they go on at all.

The coming barbarism will differ from the former barbarism by its greater powers of terror, urgency and destruction, and by its greater rapidity of wastage. What other difference can there be without a mental renascence? The average life will be steadily diminishing, health will be deteriorating. The viruses and pestilential germs will resume their experiments in variation, and new blotches and infections will give scope for pious resignation and turn men's hearts again towards a better world beyond the stars. There will be a last crop of saints and devotees. Mankind which began in a cave and behind a windbreak will end in the disease-soaked ruins of a slum. What else can happen? What other turn can destiny take?

If Homo sapiens is such a fool that he cannot realize what is before him now and set himself urgently to save the situation while there is still some light, some freedom of thought and speech, some freedom of movement and action left in the world, can there be the slightest hope that in fifty or a hundred years hence, after he has been through two or three generations of accentuated fear, cruelty and relentless individual frustration, with ever diminishing opportunity of apprehending the real nature of his troubles, he will be collectively any less of a fool? Why should he undergo a magic change when all the forces, within him as without, are plainly set against it?

There is no reason whatever to believe that the order of nature has any greater bias in favor of man than it had in favor of the icthyosaur or the pterodactyl. In spite of all my disposition to a brave looking optimism, I perceive that now the universe is bored with him, in turning a hard face to him, and I see him being carried less and less intelligently and more and more rapidly, suffering as every ill-adapted creature must suffer in gross and detail, along the stream of fate to degradation, suffering and death.

That, compactly, is the human outlook, the only possible alternative to the willful and strenuous adaptation by re-education of our species now—forthwith—that I am urging in this book. Adapt or perish, that is and always has been the implacable law of life for all its children. Either the human imagination and the human will to live, rises to the plain necessity of our case, and a renascent Homo sapiens struggles on to a new, a harder and a happier world dominion, or he blunders down the slopes of failure through a series of unhappy phases, in the wake of all the monster reptiles and beasts that have flourished and lorded it on the earth before him, to his ultimate extinction. Either life is just beginning for him or it is drawing very rapidly to its close. This is no guess that is put before you, no fantasy; it is a plain and reasoned assembling of known facts in their natural order and relationship. It faces you. Meet it or shirk it, this is the present outlook for mankind.

61

NOTES

Note 4A. A shrinkage of the gross population, one may note, under the new conditions, though it foreshadows an ultimate biological defeat, does not in itself compensate for that superfluity of unemployed and dangerously restless young men stressed in the preceding paragraphs. It does nothing to stabilize the community. Not merely increased productivity per head due to technical progress but also the prolonged activity of skilled older people will still be diminishing employment and the young man's prospects of normal assuagement. A falling birth rate or for that matter a rising one is no relief for that primary social tension, which is essentially a matter of proportion and not of scale. An island community of a few hundred people will still be unstable if it includes a few dozen young men with nothing definite to do.

Note 4B. Semaphore signaling systems seem only to have been invented in the Napoleonic period, though it is remarkable they were not attempted in the great Empires of Egypt, Persia, China and Rome.

Note 6A. It is true that in Great Britain there are certain organizations, the Plebs League, for instance, and the Workers' Educational Association, which owe their existence to the realization that the traditional education, meeting as it does the requirements for upper and middle class survival, may not be entirely adequate for the needs of an awakening democracy. But in practice there is little of the interrogative and creative spirit of science in the work of these quasi-rebel bodies. A rash conceit of finality pervades them. One need only turn over the pages of Plebs to realize the glib, trite omniscience of its attitude. The aim throughout is not knowledge but equipment for the political class war; it is to assemble and supply predigested controversial material for the Labor politician (research!), prepare and train "speakers" for the Labor cause, and sustain the profound satisfaction of its clientele in such education as they have already derived from the general atmosphere of their upbringing. At a Royal Society Dinner one can stand up and say "We are all self-confessed ignorant men, our common aim is inquiry and better knowledge; we want to know, and that is why we are here together." But that sort of thing would provoke either indignation or derision in the Little Bethel of a workers' educational gathering. They have the Gospel; they know. Labor is going to take over things and the millennium will ensue. The Plebs League, it seems, has a doctrinal feud with the kindred Communist Party; I cannot understand why. It preaches practically the same stuff. No seminary for the missionaries of some eccentric sect was ever more specialized and narrow-minded.

Note 7A. There is a very full and well-illustrated Italian (Fascist) Encyclopaedia—one of the many evidences of the higher mental level of the Fascist as compared with the Nazi regime—but I have never seen any competent examination of this work in any English, American or French review. I have no idea of what this attractive-looking publication gives, what it conceals, what it may suggest or misrepresent, and short of learning Italian and reading it through I do not see how I can find out. No university professor anywhere in the world seems to have bothered yet to put a research student or so on to this task. But why should he care? Why on earth should he care? It would be infringing on journalism. It would be vulgar. There is always something more to be done in the best academic tradition about the probable sex life of Leonardo da Vinci or the personal resentments of Dante, which will touch no current controversial issue and still satisfy the highest standards of academic erudition.

Note 9A. See Lord David Davies, The Problem Of The Twentieth Century (1930), Suicide Or Sanity (1932) and various publications of the New Commonwealth Society.

Note 9B. Dr. John Beattie Crozier, 1849-1921. Author of The Religion Of The Future (1880) and A History Of Intellectual Development (1897-1901).

Note 9C. "The world-wide English language is destined, I think, to serve as the primary medium in this renascence of the human spirit. Unquestionably that renascence must ultimately be cosmopolitan, but to begin with it is likely to find its fullest and most lucid expression in one or the other, or maybe one or two, of the existing thought and language systems in the world. What are they? What other systems are there? There is the Latin cultural group expressing itself in French, Italian and Spanish. In the past French has been the common medium, but it is by no means certain that it will remain so as intellectual suppression progresses in Italy and Spain. Then there is the great Slavonic sprawl whose medium of expression is Russian. There is the German system and, last and most widespread and convenient of all, there is the English-speaking network. I want to point out to you that for the next few decades at any rate, the burthen and responsibility for human mental progress or human mental failure will rest principally upon the series of communities using the English tongue either as a mother tongue or as a cultural language. It is becoming the lingua franca of the so-called "democracies." Matters may change later, but that is the present state of affairs. These communities are far more free to discuss, learn and publish than any other people in the world.

Germany as an organized country has, for a time at least, withdrawn herself from any claim to a share in the moral or intellectual leadership of the world. The burning of the books by the Nazis was a symbolical act of detachment from the free mentality of mankind. The expulsion of such men of science as Einstein and Freud, and the assertion of the racial hallucinations of Hitler in place of established ethnology, were practical demonstrations of the same withdrawal. Dogmatic nationalism has stamped upon science and free thought and the German mind and retired into itself. And so too has the Russian. Before the Great War, the Russian language and literature were the medium for civilized thought not only throughout Russia but all over the Slavonic-speaking world of southwest Europe. In the summer of 1938, just before the destruction of Czechoslovakia,

I took part in a small conference upon Slavonic culture in Prague. It was attended by representatives of all the Slav-speaking countries except Poland, and I found that everyone in that meeting spoke and liked speaking Russian. But the present Russian government has seen fit to sterilize this Russian influence by a systematic suppression of free speech, free discussion and free publication. For all practical purposes this leaves only the French-and English-speaking systems. The French intelligence at its best is lucid, brave and enterprising, still finer I think in its quality than any other in the world,, but it works upon a much narrower base than the English. The very precision of French deprives it of an amplitude of expression of which English is capable. So we come to the conclusion that if the human race is not to go on slipping down towards a bottomless pit of wars, conquests and exterminations, it must be through the rapid and zealous expansion and reorganization of the intellectual and education organizations of the English-speaking communities.

But let me make it clear that when I say English-speaking, I say it without any shadow of political propaganda, Anglo-Saxon radicalism, dear-old- Englandism, British imperialism or any shallow-wilted stuff of that sort-1 am thinking of the things our language carries, and can carry, and not of our contemporary "culture." And I think of a flexible language expanding to meet every fresh need. English is a very adaptable language; it borrows and assimilates words and idioms very freely; and when I speak of the English of the future, I have in mind something much more copious and powerful than the "correct English" of the academic scholars. It can already narrow down to Basic or expand to express a thousand delicate shades of meaning. I think of it as stripped of any remaining idiomatic complications with a reformed spelling and a continually expanding vocabulary.

Even now English brings together into one creative fermentation a vast diversity of peoples, from the Maori to the Eskimos; it enables an educated Indian to talk to an educated Norwegian or an educated West African Negro. It can bring all the thought and learning of the world within their understanding, as no other language can do. It translates everything of importance in every other language under the sun. Its center of gravity is now the United States of America, but every several community which participates in its free exchanges contributes its distinctive experiences. See, for example, how the mental world of Australasia receives practically everything that America or Britain can give it, and in return produces great men of science, brilliant artists, writers, thinkers... (Adapted from the Canberra lecture on The Role Of English In The Development Of The World Mind.)

Note 10A. While I was working on this chapter a little friend of mine who draws rather cleverly sent me a card to wish me a Happy Easter. Below that she had drawn two chicks emerging from their eggs with their little heads in gas masks over the legend "Be Prepared." I find my little niece's jest rather a grim one. But maybe there is an idea in that, a topical touch, for the Nativities they will be setting up next Christmas in bomb-devastated Madrid, now that Catholicism has waded through blood to its own again. It would be a halfhearted incarnation that did not fully share the anxieties and precautions of our distressful life.

Note 10B. Since the § 10 was first drafted, a very revolutionary device has come to hand in Major Muir's invention of the "air mine." This is a balloon-sustained mine which can be set adrift in the air at any level, and which will drift before the wind until it contacts with a plane and destroys it. It is too small to be seen and avoided. It can be timed to keep the air for a definite time, a day or a week or so, and then explode and come down. These air mines are cheap to produce and they could be made quickly and released in enormous quantities. So long a.s they were up they would make the air impossible for any sort of air transport, civil or military; they would in fact for the time being eliminate the air altogether. I have consulted several authorities in this matter, and they agree upon its entire practicability. But obviously there are considerable obstacles to its being properly tried out. The combatant air forces detest the idea. Still there we have the possibility of putting the air completely out of action whenever we wish it, and of restoring war to its ancient and slower two dimensions.

Note 11A. It is the practice of those who find the results of scientific inquiry unpalatable, to stigmatize such statements as we have assembled here as "cocksure" and declare them as dogmatic as any other dogmas. They will make it a personal matter if possible, as though I individually had made it all up, or got it wrong, and was being rather absurd about it. And then "Yah!", and they think no more about these uncongenial things. But I am no more responsible for the facts in this book than a telegraph messenger is for the cable he brings, I have been simply gathering up undisputed statements, and they remain intact, however brilliantly I can be discredited personally.
Alternatively these recalcitrant spirits will have it that it is science which is "cocksure." That is a flat misrepresentation of the scientific spirit. Experimental science, natural science—which is what everyone understands by "science" nowadays,—is never assured and final. That is where it differs from all other established systems of belief, and that is why I speak of it throughout this book as a new thing in the development of human mentality, new within the past century or so. The true symbol of natural science is a note of interrogation. A better name would be research. It questions until some false assumption is laid bare or destroyed. It tries out and rejects or accepts. And still it questions. It is rare that it reverses its carefully tested conclusions—it is another defensive invention that "Science is always contradicting itself"—but continually it advances beyond these conclusions and restates with increasing precision and enrichment. The utmost the man of science says to the religious dogmatist is "In view of this and that, your general statement is unsound," or, "In view of this and that it must be untrue."

Note 11B. "The number of one's ancestors increases as we look back in time. Disregarding the chances of intermarriage, each one of us had two parents, four grandparents, eight great-grandparents, and so on backward, until very soon, in less than fifty generations, we should find that, but for the qualification introduced, we should have all the earth's inhabitants of that time as our progenitors. For a hundred generations it must hold absolutely true, that everyone of that time who has issue living now is ancestral to all of us. That brings the thing quite within the historical period. There is not a palaeolithic or neolithic relic that is not a family relic for every soul alive. The blood in our veins has handled it." (From H. G. Wells. First and Last Things, "The Being of Mankind.")
There are, however, certain qualifications to be made to this statement of our common ancestry if it is to pass unchallenged. In every generation there is an elimination of half the genetic elements. The individual is not a mixture of the total ancestry of his four grandparents. He is a compound of a quarter of their genes. And in addition he may be a mutation. Genes are transmitted in asso-

ciated groups, but these groups fall infinitely short of carrying a complete personality. They carry traits, but the traits are carried separately. In so-and-so we may remark this and that trait of his Grandfather William but they are mixed with traits from other progenitors; the practical reappearance of Grandfather William is a mathematical improbability verging on the impossible. Of all this and how there are recessive characteristics masked by dominant ones, but capable of reappearing in offspring, the reader will find a dear and full account in The Science of Life.

A common ancestry does not therefore involve a common physiognomy, and at any time an individual or a type may turn up in which some once prevalent type virtually reappears. Mr. George Bernard Shaw, for example, is a very exceptional person today, but Etruscan tombs and potsherds reveal a departed world of quasi-George Bernard Shaws. There are quasi-Cromagnards in La Dordogne and the Canary Isles today. Certain regions, certain climates, seem to attract and favor their own special types and tend to revive them. That all English people are descended from William the Conqueror and most of the population of the earth from Abraham, implies brotherhood indeed, but not uniformity. The fact that if humanity survives so long, everyone alive will be the descendant of every fertile individual among us today exposes the absurdities of family and national pride, but it does not mean that the dance of the genes will not give us an incessantly restored human variety, in which every individual will be consciously or unconsciously seeking the region, the occupation and the associates most congenial to his make-up.

Note 12A. Some of those who, in spite of much subsequent enlightenment, still cling, out of natural affection and association, to traditions of their home and upbringing that have become a dear and necessary part of themselves, take refuge, I know, in the plea that the idea of the Chosen People has become altogether spiritualized, that they are now segregated not for an ultimate conquest but for a mission. Their mission is to serve and exalt all mankind.

There is moreover another line of sublimation with a bolder appeal, and that is the line taken by that great neglected genius, David Lubin, the founder of the International Institute of Agriculture in Rome. His Israel was indeed an Israel with a mission, but then he claimed everyone who participated in constructive work as one of the elect. To Lubin I was an honorary Israelite.

"But why then call it Israel?" I protested.

This sort of transfiguration of the objectives of the Chosen People is all very well in apologetic discussion, but there is nothing to sustain it in the normal ceremony and practice and teaching of the cult, which remains a narrow and troublesome nationalism. Let these sublimators repudiate the Bible and the Promise and say what they mean plainly. Then we shall be better able to believe in their assertions of an exalted inaggressive modernization.

Note 12B. Louis Golding (in The Jewish Problem) argues that anti-Judaism is due to the fact that the Jews cried "Crucify him," when Jesus came before Pilate. Jesus, as everybody knows, was crucified (a particularly Roman method of execution) not by the Jews but by the Roman Pontius Pilate. Countless people who criticize the Jews today are extremely impartial about the Crucifixion, and I find it difficult to believe that Mr. Golding, who, I presume, is himself a product of orthodox Jewish education, is so entirely unaware of the effect of this Chosen People cult upon the outside world as he seems to be. He ignores it absolutely.

Browne also, refusing to face that primary issue, accounts for the unpopularity of the Jewish community in an entirely different manner. He theorizes brilliantly about Jews being urban while non-Jews are rustic. Certainly the Semitic-speakers were prevalently urban in the first century B.C. The balance, says he, must be corrected and all will be well. So the Jew, he decides (1935) had better go to Palestine and dig himself out of his troubles. Both writers then launch out into an account of the great intellectual superiority of Jews to Gentiles, wholesome rather than ingratiating reading for a puffed up Gentile, and cite a, string of names, Sigmund Freud, for instance, and Einstein and so on, who are as a matter of fact no more orthodox Jews than I am. They are citizens of the world, they work for all mankind. Even now Freud is busy, he tells me, in a patient analysis of the legend of Moses. Moses, he concludes, was an Egyptian! His monotheism was Akhnaton's sun worship. (Moses and Monotheism.)

Both Golding and Browne are typical of a vast literature on the Jewish question. There is no need to multiply instances. Neither, I think, realizes quite clearly what it is that encompasses them, because they are themselves enveloped in it. They accept this taught and cultivated idea system, this ex- religious bias, this artificial solidarity I am arraigning, as though it was in the nature of things and could not be prevented, and thence they wander off into a limitless jungle of controversial irrelevances, of the rights and wrongs of ancient hates, misunderstandings, persecutions and reprisals, to which there can be no conclusion.

But the eloquent and emotional Mr. Josef Kastein, who dedicates his History And Destiny Of The Jews quite incongruously to the entirely unorthodox Einstein, concludes his Jews in Germany with the real irreconcilable note:

"...we were once in Egypt. Already we have compelled a Pharaoh to set us free. We have outlasted the Pyramids. We shall outlast the denials of all those who surround us."

As a matter of fact the Pyramids were there a long time before the Jews.

I reiterate that the whole scheme and purport of this book is to insist upon the supreme decisive importance of what in § 4 I have called the mental superstructure of the human animal. The reconstruction of its idea system is its only practicable method of adaptation, and here is an. idea system that resists and evades reconstruction very obstinately. In §§ 8 and 9 I have assembled and summarized the nature of the great intellectual effort which is needed if our species is to adjust itself to the terrific new conditions that have risen about it. The Jewish conflict disregards this, cuts athwart it, arrests and prevents it, like a noisy quarrel in a laboratory. All the countervailing evil in the world cannot make a bad tradition a good one. Killing or ill-treating a man does not put him in the wrong, but also, we have to remember, and that is not so easy for the liberal-minded, it does not put him in the right The idea of the solidarity of the Chosen People, evade it or not, remains the fundamental Jewish idea, and this fundamental Jewish idea, like any other nationalism, is an offense against the unity of mankind.

Note 12C. Persecution mania is a well-known form of insanity. With certain variations of phrase and form, due to the current ideas of the period, it presents an almost stereotyped pattern through the ages. Formerly it was usually witches and warlocks who were supposed to be at the root of the matter. Anyone odd, anyone different, came under suspicion, old crones and afflicted and odd-looking men were distrusted, and very often the suspects caught a touch of the infection and tried doing the things they learnt were so potent. Multitudes of sorcerers have confessed, under no great duress, to impossible crimes. They brewed potions, stuck pins in wax images, cast spells, sent familiar spirits to gibber and creep and whisper in the night.

Madness like everything else moves with the times; it clothes itself in new fashions while remaining essentially the same. Nowadays the witches have become "Occult Powers." They use hypnotism, electricity, infections (Pah!), they radio voices making threats and evil suggestions. Every prominent publicist continually gets letters from sufferers with this type of obsession. Such delusions may easily make the patient a danger to himself and others, and then he is "certified" and taken care of. But in times of social movement and stress this disorder may become contagious, witness the witch mania of the early seventeenth century. It is then more difficult to deal with.

Like a dark shadow to the rational objections that can be made to the in-and- out double nationalism of the Jews, there is a sustained campaign of sinister suggestion with a considerable literature of its own. Some years ago four or five books written by Mrs. Nesta Webster attracted considerable attention. She is a very competent writer and so sound a Christian, of a faith so uncritical, that she is quite unable to understand that many honest people find a vast amount of Christian doctrine impossible. How impossible, I have sought to show in §§ 13 and 14. To her there is nothing good except in Christianity, and this is so obvious to her that any objection to the faith seems necessarily part of some diabolically hatched conspiracy. She has set herself with the greatest industry to trace and link together the long-drawn succession of Cabalists, Gnostics, Manichaeans, the Old Man of the Mountains, Knight Templars, Satanists, Rosicrucians, Illuminati, Freemasons, Rousseau, Voltaire, Cagliostro, Madame Blavatsky, Mrs. Besant, Trade Unions, Anarchists, Socialists, Theosophists, Communists, Those Bolsheviks, a frightful horde all plotting and getting hold of power and handing it on and doing down Christianity and the Christian life. Her books are written with-conviction enough to make one look under the bed at nights. She has never quite committed herself to those famous forged Protocols Of The Elders Of Zion which were published as the articles of association so to speak of that world conspiracy, but she stoutly maintains that though that book may not be genuine, it nevertheless shows the sort of thing of which the Jews are capable. Her book Secret Societies And Subversive Movements concludes: "For behind the concrete forces of revolution—whether Pan-German, Judaic or Illuminist—beyond that invisible secret circle which perhaps directs them all, is there not yet another force, still more potent, that must be taken into account? In looking back over the centuries at the dark episodes that have marked the history of the human race from its earliest origins—strange and horrible cults, waves of witchcraft, blasphemies and desecrations—how is it possible to ignore the existence of an Occult Power at work in the world? Individuals, sects, or races fired with the desire of world domination, have provided the fighting forces of destruction, but behind them are the veritable powers of darkness in eternal conflict with the powers of light."

I should describe Mrs. Nesta Webster as a perfectly sane and capable person with insane ideas, so widely do I disagree with her. I believe her influence has spread far beyond the circle of her actual readers. Milder forms of the same intellectual malaise at any rate are now very prevalent throughout the more prosperous classes in Great Britain and America. It is the only way to account for the behavior of Mr. Neville Chamberlain, for example, or Lord Rothermere, the British newspaper proprietor, towards the Jews, towards Russia, during the past two or three years. Mr. William

Teeling again, to whom I refer in § 13, is another case. A tepid passive Christianity is becoming an aggressive pro-Christianity tinder the stresses of the time.

Note 12D. Sir Norman Angell and Mrs. Dorothy Frances Buxton, in a very clear and almost pressingly persuasive book, You And The Refugee (Penguin Books, 1939), argue for a practically unrestrained admission of these outcasts. They show in particular how beneficial a large refugee immigration might be to the British Empire. It would bring in new trades, new skill, find fresh work for the unemployed, and in Great Britain arrest the approaching decline in population—if that is desirable. Their plea for a more generous treatment of refugees, so far as assimilable individuals are concerned, is unanswerable.

But our authors' arguments for an inassimilable immigration en bloc are less convincing. That would only renew the trouble at a later, date. There is no time to begin that old history again in new regions and among fresh difficulties. Disaster is advancing too rapidly upon our entire species. Jewish nationalism like every other nationalism must end and end soon. And even though the plea of existing unemployment is an irrational social barrier to assimilable immigrants, it is, in a country where the sense of social insecurity is growing, where confidence in the intelligence and good faith of the government is diminishing, and where large masses of the population, and especially the accumulation of untrained and unemployed young men, see no dear prospect of a tolerable life ahead, none the less a barrier. Implicitly the British authorities admit: "We do not know how to handle our own people, we are getting more and more bothered—by everything—and if these people come into our muddle, there is bound to be serious trouble." And so in effect they give them up to destruction, not outrageously and openly as the Germans do, but by looking in the opposite direction, and delaying action.

In a scientifically organized, forward-looking social order, there will be no people unemployed and there will be no difficulty whatever in the movement of population from point to point. The whole world will be everyman's and the fullness thereof. The bare possibility of such a rational order sustains whatever hope there is for mankind in this present survey of the human outlook. But this world we are living in is not a rational world and the harsh reality we have to face when we cast the Jewish horoscope is this dosing-up of the avenues of escape.

Already in the past year or so, a multitude, scores and possibly hundreds of thousands, must have been done to death. And still it goes on....

In You And The Refugee, however, I came upon one passage that affected me very disagreeably and I think I ought to say a word about it here. It is too germane to this discussion to omit:

"Not all Jews are Zionists, but all Jews will resent the letting down of Zionists, the surrender of Zionists to Arab terrorism. And their resentment will be world-wide. We do not perhaps realize the possible repercussions.

"The power of world Jewry is moral—the power of journalists, writers, dramatists, scientists. It is worth while for an Empire as gravely menaced as the British to have that power on its side."...

That is a threat and a very evil and embittering threat. Happily it is not made by Jews but by two overofficious Gentile champions on their behalf, I do not see things from the Imperialist standpoint .. of these authors. I think the British Empire has outlived its usefulness. But the consolidation of the English-speaking people as the vehicle of a world civilization is quite another matter, and a matter of great urgency. Yet unless the British government does what it is told in Palestine, the Chosen People, we are told, will devote themselves to preventing that consolidation. I think that is a very unhappy suggestion indeed. It does no justice to the intellectual quality of Israel. I doubt if any representative Jewish writer could be quoted in support of it. But it is exactly what the Jews are accused of doing by their worst enemies. My first reaction to it, until I realized that this dream of vindictive sabotage was a purely Gentile invention, was acute resentment and anger. I believe these two authors would be wise to take that tactless and unjustifiable passage out of any further editions of their well-intentioned book.

Note 13A. "We Catholics acknowledge readily, without any shame, nay with pride, that Catholicism cannot be identified simply and wholly with primitive Christianity, nor even with the Gospel of Christ, in the same way that the great oak cannot be identified with the tiny acorn. There is no mechanical identity, but an organic identity. And we go further and say that thousands of years hence Catholicism will probably be even richer, more luxuriant, more manifold in dogma, morals, law and worship, than the Catholicism of the present day. A religious historian of the fifth millennium A.D. will without difficulty discover in Catholicism conceptions and forms and practices which derive from India, China and Japan, and he will have to recognize a far more obvious 'complex of opposites.' It is quite true, Catholicism is a union of contraries. But 'contraries are not contradictories'.... The Gospel of Christ would have been no living gospel, and the seed which He scattered no living seed, if it had remained ever the tiny seed of A.D. 33, and not struck root, and had not assimilated foreign matter, and had not by the help of this foreign matter grown up into a tree, so that the birds of the air dwell in its branches." Professor Karl Adam, The Spirit of Catholicism (1938).
For reasons I have made perfectly clear in this book, I do not believe there will be any Roman Catholic Church at all in the fifth millennium »A.D., but (see § 18) it is amusing to speculate how the successors of Professor Karl Adam, long before then, would have plaited into the Trinity that God of Male Sex Appeal from whose left eye sprang the Sun Goddess, while he blew Susa-no-o, the dragon-slaying Susa-no-o, from his nose. It is, I agree, not at all improbable, given the survival and continual growth of the Church. Morgan Young, in the book I have cited in the text, tells that the great assimilation prophesied by Professor Karl Adam has already begun. The crude early Christians, still in the "acorn" phase, preferred martyrdom to burning a pinch of incense to the Roman God-Emperors, but the more catholic-spirited Church of today has already established friendly relations with the Shinto faith, Japan and Rome have exchanged envoys, and the Japanese Catholic bows in the Shinto temples in acquiescence to the local supremacy of the Emperor-Divinity over the Vatican.

Note 23A. Sir Arthur's Epilogue begins: "Shall we never pluck the best from fate and find the Golden Mean? Must we ever choose freedom without order, or order without freedom? Must justice and mercy bring always weakness in their train, and strength bring tyranny?
"Shall Peace be never made between equals, but imposed always by victor upon vanquished? Must every peace treaty sow the seeds of future war? Shall the strong never be magnanimous and the weak never secure justice? Must success always sap the will, and the humiliation of defeat incite only to revenge? Shall wars with changing victors be for ever the dire fate of men?

"We, the free democracies of the world, have the virtues bred and nursed in the pursuits of peace. That is not enough. We need also the sterner virtues—fortitude, daemonic energy, the will to act—and to act together." (p. 385.)

"...willing cooperation and the endurance which is only possible to an instructed people who understand the purpose of their effort and approve it." (p. 384.) Sir Arthur Salter, Security. Can We Retrieve It? (1939).

THE END

World Brain

World Brain

Published in 1938, World Brain is one of H.G. Wells' most forward-thinking works, outlining his vision for a centralized global information system that would serve as the foundation for a unified world. Wells proposed a permanent, organized knowledge network, accessible to all, that would reshape education, politics, and governance by ensuring that the public had access to accurate, unbiased information.

In many ways, World Brain was a precursor to the internet, Wikipedia, and artificial intelligence-driven knowledge systems—but with a strong emphasis on centralized control and intellectual oversight.

Key Themes & Arguments

The Creation of a Global Encyclopedia – Wells believed that the future of civilization depended on a universally accessible, constantly updated repository of human knowledge, available to people of all nations and backgrounds. This World Brain would act as a single, authoritative source of truth, preventing misinformation and ignorance.

Information as the Foundation of Global Governance – Wells argued that proper education and access to knowledge were essential for world peace and stability. He believed that an informed public could be guided toward rational decision-making, paving the way for a more structured and organized world order.

A Scientific Approach to Learning and Thought Control – Unlike traditional libraries or schools, the World Brain would be a scientifically managed institution, ensuring that information was properly curated, fact-checked, and presented in a way that aligned with the needs of a progressive, unified society.

The Decline of Nationalism Through Shared Knowledge – By giving all people access to the same universal education system, Wells hoped to eliminate nationalist and ideological divisions, creating a global population that thought collectively rather than tribally.

The Role of Universities and Media in Shaping Public Thought – Wells saw educational institutions and the press as key tools for distributing and maintaining the World Brain, ensuring that people received only reliable and constructive knowledge that would serve the goals of a peaceful and productive global society.

A Vision That Predicted the Digital Age

Wells' idea of a World Brain bears striking similarities to modern global information systems, including:

The Internet & Wikipedia – A universally accessible repository of knowledge, continually updated and available to all.

Big Tech & AI-driven Knowledge Curation – Centralized information platforms, such as Google, that prioritize and filter knowledge through algorithms, much like Wells envisioned.

Fact-Checking and Information Control – The growing role of governments, corporations, and media in regulating and verifying information aligns with Wells' belief that only experts should manage public knowledge.

Why World Brain Matters Today

Wells saw information as the ultimate tool for shaping human society. His vision of a scientifically controlled knowledge system may have been meant to unite and uplift humanity, but it also raises concerns about who controls information, what perspectives are allowed, and whether centralized knowledge leads to enlightenment or manipulation.

As the modern world debates misinformation, censorship, and AI-driven thought control, World Brain remains one of Wells' most prophetic—and controversial—works.

62

PREFACE

THE papers and addresses I have collected in this little book are submitted as contributions, however informal, to what is essentially a scientific research. But it is a research in a field to which scientific standing is not generally accorded and where peculiar methods have to be employed. It is in the field of constructive sociology, the science of social organisation. This is a special sub-section of human ecology, which is a branch of general ecology, which again is a stem in the great and growing cluster of biological sciences. It stands with palaeontology at the opposite pole to experimental biology; hardly any verificatory experiment is possible and no controls. It is a science of pure observation, therefore, of analysis and of search for confirmatory instances. On the one hand it passes, without crossing any definite boundaries, into historical science proper, into the analysis of historical fact, that is, and on the other into the examination of such matters as geographical (and geological) conditions and the social consequences of industrial processes.

Human ecology surveys the species Homo sapiens as a whole in space and time; sociology is that part of the survey which concerns itself with the interaction and interdependence of human groups and individuals. It is hardly to be distinguished from social psychology. There has been an enormous increase in the intensity and scope of human interaction and interdependence during the past half-million years or more. Communities and what one may call ranges of reaction, have enlarged and continue to enlarge more and more rapidly towards a planetary limit. The human intelligence is involved in this enlargement and it is too deeply concerned with its role in the process, to observe it with the detachment it can maintain towards the facts, for example, of astronomy or crystallography. Constructive sociology has to bring not only the study of conduct but an irresistible element of purpose into its problems. Human beings are not simply born or thrown together into association like a swarm of herrings. They keep together with a sense of collective activities and common ends, even if these ends are little more than mutual aid, protection and defence.

Throughout the whole range of ecology we study the adaptation of living species to changing environments, but outside the human experience these adaptations are generally made unconsciously by the natural selection of mutations and variations. These adaptations are inherited. They are either successful and the species is modified and survives, or it perishes. In the cerebral animals, however, natural selection is supplemented by very considerable individual adaptability.

Memories and habits are established in each generation which fit individuals to the special circumstances of their own generation. They are adaptations which perish with the individual. Such creatures learn; they are educable creatures; dogs, cats, seals, elephants for example learn and the next generation has, if necessary, to learn the old lesson all over again or a different lesson. In the human being there is an unprecedented extension of educability; not only is learning developed to relatively immense proportions, but it is further supplemented by curiosity, precept and tradition. In such a slow-breeding creature as man educational adaptation is, beyond all comparison, a swifter process than genetic adaptation. His social life, his habits, have changed completely, have even undergone reversion and reversal, while his heredity seems to have changed very little if at all, since the late Stone Age. Possibly he is more educable now and with a more prolonged physical and mental adolescence.

The human individual is born now to live in a society for which his fundamental instincts are altogether inadequate. He has to be educated systematically for his social role. The social man is a manufactured product of which the natural man is the raw nucleus. In a world of fluctuating and generally expanding communities and ranges of reaction, the science of constructive sociology seeks to detect and give definition to the trends and requirements of man's social circumstances and to study the possibilities and methods of adapting the natural man to them. It is the science of current adaptations. It has therefore two reciprocal aspects; on the one hand it has to deal with social organisations, laws, customs and regulations, which may either be actually operative or merely projected and potential, and on the other hand it has to examine the education these real or proposed social organisations require. These two aspects are inseparable, they need to fit like hand and glove. Plans and theories of social structure and plans and theories of education are the outer and inner aspects of the same thing. Each necessitates the other. Every social order must have its own distinctive process of education.

In the past this imperative association of education and social structure was not recognised so clearly as it is at the present time. Communities would grow up and not change their mental clothes until they burst out of them. Ideas would change and disorganise institutions. For the past twenty-six centuries, and particularly, and much more definitely, during the last three, there has been a very great expenditure of mental energy upon the statement in various terms and metaphors, as theologies, as religions, socialisms, communisms, devotions, loyalties, codes of behaviour and so on, of the desirable and necessary form of human adaptation to new conditions of association. From the point of view of constructive sociology, or to coin a hideous phrase, human adaptology, all these efforts, although not deliberately made as experiments, are so much experience and working material, and though almost all of them have involved special teachings (doctrines) the need for a close interlocking of training and teaching with the social order sought, though always fairly obvious, has never been so fully realised as it is today. The new doctrines were often only subconsciously linked to the new needs. The idea, for instance, of a universal God replacing local gods ensued upon the growth of great empires, but it was not explicitly related to the growth of great empires. The connection was not plainly apparent to men's minds. In the looser, easier past of our species, there has never been such a close interweaving of current usage and practices with instruction and precept as we are now beginning to feel desirable. The reference of one to the other was not direct. Now education becomes more and more definitely political and economic. It must penetrate deeper and deeper into life as life ceases to be customary and grows more and more deliberately planned and adjusted. The need for lively and continuous invention in constructive sociology and for an animated and animating progressive education correlated with these innovations, has hardly more than dawned on the world. The urgency of adaptation has still to be grasped.

Throughout the nineteenth century certain systems of adaptive ideas spread throughout the world to meet the requirements of what was recognised with increasing understanding as a new age. Mechanism was altering both the fundamental need for toil and the essential nature of war. The practical and cynically accepted need for labouring classes and subject-peoples, was dissolving quietly out of human thought—though it still exists in the minds of those who employ personal servants. Means of intercommunication and mutual help and injury have developed amazingly. A mechanical unification of the world has been demanding (and still demands) profound moral and ideological readjustments. It is, for example, being realised, slowly but steadily, that the fragmentary control of production and trade through irresponsible individual ownership gives quite lamentably inadequate results, that the whole property-money system needs revision very urgently, and that the belated recrudescence of sentimental nationalism largely through misguided school-teaching and newspaper propaganda, is becoming an increasing menace to world welfare. The old ideological equipments throughout the world are misfits everywhere. Mental and moral adaptation is lagging dreadfully behind the change in our conditions. A great and menacing gulf opens which only an immense expansion of teaching and instruction can fill.

In the field of sociology it is impossible to disentangle social analysis from literature, and the criticism of the social order by Ruskin, William Morris and so forth was at least as much a contribution to social science as Herbert Spencer's quasi-scientific defence of individualism and the abstractions and dogmas of the political economists. The biological sciences did not spread very easily into this undeveloped region. It was a hinterland of novel problems and possibilities. Even today proper methods of study in this field have still to be fully worked out and brought into association. It has had to be explored by moral and religious appeals, by utopias and speculative writings of a quality and texture. very unsatisfying to scientific workers in more definite fields. It is still subject to irruptions of a type that the normal scientist of today finds highly questionable. Poets even and seers have their role in this experimentation. But economics and sociology can only be made hard sciences by eliminating much of their living content. Knowledge has to be attained by any available means. Inquirers cannot be limited to passable imitations of the methods followed in other fields. It may be doubted if constructive sociology and educational science can ever be freed from a certain literary, aesthetic and ethical flavouring. We have to assume certain desiderata before we can get down to effective, applicable work. Yet it does seem possible to state the problem of adaptation in practical scientific terms.

It was not realised at first, and it is still not fully realised, how vague and unsuitable for immediate application the generous propositions of Socialism and World Peace remain, until further intensive and continuous research and elaboration have been undertaken. It is widely assumed that to profess Socialism or Pacifism implies the immediate undertaking of vehement political activities unencumbered by further thought. But the profession of Socialism or World Peace should commit a man to nothing of the sort. Socialism and World Peace are hardly more than sketches of the general frame of adaptation of which our species stands in need. "We are all socialists nowadays," but all the same there is very little really efficient working socialism.

"All men are brothers "—we have echoed that since the days of Buddha and Christ—but Spain and China are poor evidence of that fraternity. We know we want these things quite clearly, but we have still to learn how they are to be got.

Man reflects before he acts, but not very much; he is still by nature intellectually impatient. No sooner does he apprehend, in whole or in part, the need of a new world, than, without further plans or estimates, he gem into a state of passionate aggressiveness and suspicion and sets about trying to change the present order. There and then, he sets about it, with anything that comes handy, violently, disastrously, making the discordances worse instead of better, and quarrelling bitterly with any one who is not in complete accordance with his particular spasmodic conception of the change needful. He is unable to realise that when the time comes I to act, that also is the time to think fast and hard. He will not think enough.

There has been, therefore, an enormous waste of human mental, moral and physical resources in premature revolutionary thrusts, ill-planned, dogmatic, essentially unscientific reconstructions and restorations of the social order, during the past hundred years. This was the inevitable first result of the discrediting of those old and superseded mental adaptations which were embodied in the institutions and education of the past. They discredited themselves and left the world full of problems. The idea of expropriating the owners of land and industrial plant, for instance (Socialism), long preceded any deliberate attempt to create a Competent Receiver. Hysterical objection to further research, to any sustained criticism, has been, and is still characteristic of nearly all the pseudo-constructive movements of our time, culminating in projects for a "seizure of power" by some presumptuous oaf or other. The meanest thing in human natures is the fear of responsibility and the craving for leadership. "Right" dictators there are and "Left" dictators, and in effect there is hardly a pin to choose between them. The important thing about them from our present point of view, is that fear-saturated impatience for guidance, which renders dictatorships possible. First there comes a terrifying realisation of the limitless uncontrolled changes now in progress, then wild stampedes, suspicions, mass murders and finally mus ridiculus the Hero emerges, a poor single, silly, little human cranium held high and adorned usually with something preposterous in the way of hats. "He knows," they cry. "Hail the Leader!" He acts his part; he may even believe in it. And for quite a long time the crowd will refuse to realise that not only is nothing better than it was before, but that change is still marching on and marching at it—as inexorably as though there were no Leaders on the scene at all. Between the extremes of Right and Left hysteria, there remains a great under-developed region in the world of political thought and will, that we may characterise as "do-nothing democracy ". Out of the sudden realisation of its do-nothingness arise these psychological storms which give gangster dictators their opportunities. It is only gradually that people have come to realise that current democratic institutions are a very poor, slow and slack method of conducting human affairs which need an exhaustive revision, and that when one has declared oneself Anti-Fascist, Anti-Communist or both, one has still said precisely nothing about the government of the world. One is brought back to the unsolved problem of the Competent Receiver. It exercised Plato. It has been intermittently revived and neglected ever since.

It is an intricate and difficult problem. To that I can testify because for more than half my life it has been my main preoccupation. The attack on this problem is, to begin with, a task to be done in the study and in the unhurried and irresponsible spirit of pure inquiry. As the attack gathers confidence a taint of propaganda may easily infect it, but the less that constructive sociology is propagandist, the higher will be its scientific standing and the greater its ultimate usefulness to mankind. The application of the results of its researches is another business altogether, the business of the statesman, organiser and practical administrator. And in spite of the paucity of disinterested explorers in this region of speculation and analysis, and in spite of the lack of effective discussion and interchange in this field (due mainly, I think, to the inadequate recognition of its immense scientific importance which forces its workers so often into a hampering association with politically active bodies) there does seem to be a growing and spreading clarification of the realities of the human situation. It is becoming apparent that the real clue to that reconciliation of freedom and sustained initiative with the more elaborate social organisation which is being demanded from us, lies in raising and unifying, and so implementing and making more effective, the general intelligence services of the world. That at least is the argument in this book. The missing factor in human airs, it is suggested here, is a gigantic and many-sided educational renascence. The highly educated section, the finer minds of the human race are so dispersed, so ineffectively related to the common man, that they are powerless in the face of political and social adventurers of the coarsest sort. We want a reconditioned and more powerful Public Opinion. In a universal organisation and clarification of knowledge and ideas, in a closer synthesis of university and educational activities, in the evocation, that is, of what I have here called a World Brain, operating by an enhanced educational system through the whole body of mankind, a World Brain which will replace our multitude of unco-ordinated ganglia, our powerless miscellany of universities, research institutions, literatures with a purpose, national educational systems and the like; in that and in that alone, it is maintained, is there any clear hope of a really Competent Receiver for world affairs, any hope of an adequate directive control of the present destructive drift of world affairs. We do not want dictators, we do not want oligarchic parties or class rule, we want a widespread world intelligence conscious of itself To work out a way to that World Brain organisation is therefore our primary need in this age of imperative construction.

It is an immense undertaking but not an impossible undertaking. I do not think there is any insurmountable obstacle in the way to the production of such a ruling World Brain. There are favourable conditions for it, encouraging precedents and a plainly evident need. The various lectures, addresses and papers, collected here, few, thin and sketchy though they may seem, are all in their scope and measure contributions to this urgent research.

H.G. Wells

63

I. — WORLD ENCYCLOPAEDIA

Lecture delivered at the weekly evening meeting of the Royal Institution of Great Britain, November 20th, 1936

MOST of the lectures that are given in this place to this audience are delivered by men of very special knowledge. They come here to tell you something you did not know before. But tonight I doubt if I shall tell you anything that is not already quite familiar to you. I am here not to impart facts but to make certain suggestions. And there is no other audience in the world to which I would make these suggestions more willingly and more hopefully than I do to you.

My particular line of country has always been generalisation and synthesis. I dislike isolated events and disconnected details. I really hate statements, views, prejudices and beliefs that jump at you suddenly out of mid-air. I like my world as coherent and consistent as possible. So far at any rate my temperament is that of a scientific man. And that is why I have spent a few score thousand hours of my particular allotment of vitality in making outlines of history, short histories of the world, general accounts of the science of life, attempts to bring economic, financial and social life into one conspectus and even, still more desperate, struggles to estimate the possible consequences of this or that set of operating causes upon the future of mankind. All these attempts had profound and conspicuous faults and weaknesses; even my friends are apt to mention them with an apologetic smile; presumptuous and preposterous they were, I admit, but I look back upon them, completely unabashed. Somebody had to break the ice. Somebody had to try out such summaries on the general mind. My reply to the superior critic has always been—forgive me—"Damn you, do it better".

The least satisfactory thing about these experiments of mine, so far as I am concerned, is that they did not at once provoke the learned and competent to produce superior substitutes. And in view of the number of able and distinguished people we have in the world professing and teaching economic, sociological, financial science, and the admittedly unsatisfactory nature of the world's financial, economic and political affairs, it is to me an immensely disconcerting fact that the Work, Wealth and Happiness of Mankind which was first published in 1932 remains—practically uncriticised, unstudied and largely unread—the only attempt to bring human ecology into one correlated survey.

Well, I mention this experimental work now in order that you should not think I am throwing casually formed ideas before you tonight. I am bringing you my best. The thoughts I am setting out here have troubled my mind for years, and my ideas have been slowly gathering definition throughout these experiments and experiences. They have interwoven more and more intimately with other solicitudes of a more general nature in which I feel fairly certain of meeting your understanding and sympathy.

I doubt if there is anybody here tonight who has not given a certain amount of anxious thought to the conspicuous ineffectiveness of modern knowledge and—how do I call it?—trained and studied thought in contemporary affairs. And I think that it is mainly in the troubled years since 1914 that the world of cultivated, learned and scientific people of which you are so representative, has become conscious of this ineffectiveness. Before that time, or to be more precise before 1909 or 1910, the world, our world as we older ones recall it, was living in a state of confidence, of established values, of assured security, which is already becoming now almost incredible. We had no suspicion then how much that apparent security had been undermined by science, invention and sceptical inquiry. Most of us carried on into the War, and even right through the War, under the inertia of the accepted beliefs to which we had been born. We felt that the sort of history that we were used to was still going on, and we hardly realised at all that the war was a new sort of thing, not like the old wars, that the old traditions of strategy were disastrously out of date, and that the old pattern of settling up after a war could only lead to such a thickening tangle of evil consequences as we contemplate today. We know better now.

Wiser after the events as we all are, few of us now fail to appreciate the stupendous ignorance, the almost total lack of grasp of social and economic realities, the short views, the shallowness of mind, that characterised the treaty-making of 1919 and 1920. I suppose Mr. Maynard Keynes was one of the first to open our eyes to this worldwide intellectual insufficiency. What his book, The Economic Consequences of the Peace, practically said to the world was this: These people, these politicians, these statesmen, these directive people who are in authority over us, know scarcely anything about the business they have in hand. Nobody knows very much, but the important thing to realise is that they do not even know what is to he known. They arrange so and so, and so and so must ensue and they cannot or will not see that so and so must ensue. They are so unaccustomed to competent thought, so ignorant that there is knowledge and of what knowledge is, that they do not understand that it matters.

The same terrifying sense of insufficient mental equipment was dawning upon some of us who watched the birth of the League of Nations. Reluctantly and with something like horror, we realised that these people who were, they imagined, turning over a new page and beginning a fresh chapter in human history, knew collectively hardly anything about the formative forces of history. Collectively, I say. Altogether they had a very considerable amount of knowledge, unco-ordinated bits of quite good knowledge, some about this period and some about that, but they had no common understanding whatever of the processes in which they were obliged to mingle and interfere. Possibly all the knowledge and all the directive ideas needed to establish a wise and stable settlement of the world's affairs in 1919 existed in bits and fragments, here and there, but practically nothing had been assembled, practically nothing had been thought out, nothing practically had been done to draw that knowledge and these ideas together into a comprehensive conception of the world. I Put it to you that the Peace Conference at Versailles did not use anything but a very small fraction of the political and economic wisdom that already existed in human brains at that time. And I put it to you as rational creatures that if usage had not chilled our apprehension to this state of affairs, we should regard this as fantastically absurd.

And if I might attempt a sweeping generalisation about the general course of human history in the eighteen years that have followed the War, I believe I should have you with me if I described it as a series of flounderings, violent ill-directed mass-movements, slack here and convulsive action there. We talk about the dignity of history. It is a bookish phrase for which I have the extremest disrespect. There is no dignity yet in human history. It would be pure comedy, if it were not so often tragic, so frequently dismal, generally dishonourable and occasionally quite horrible. And it is so largely tragic because the creature really is intelligent, can feel finely and acutely, expresses itself poignantly in art, music and literature, and—this is what I am driving at—impotently knows better.

Consider only the case of America during this recent period. America when all is said and done, is one of the most intelligently aware communities in the world. Quite a number of people over there seem almost to know what is happening to them. Remember first the phase of fatuous self-sufficiency, the period of unprecedented prosperity, the boom, the crisis, the slump and the dismay. And then appeared the new President, Franklin Roosevelt, and from the point of view of the present discussion he is one of the most interesting figures in all history. Because he really did make an appeal for such knowledge and understanding as existed to come to his aid. America in an astounding state of meekness was ready to be told and shown. There were the universities, great schools, galaxies of authorities, learned men, experts, teachers, gowned, adorned and splendid. Out of this knowledge mass there have since come many very trenchant criticisms of the President's mistakes. But at the time this—what shall I call it—this higher brain, this cerebrum, this grey matter of America was so entirely unco-ordinated that it had nothing really comprehensive, searching, thought-out and trustworthy for him to go upon. The President had to experiment and attempt this and that, he fumed from one promising adviser to another, because there was nothing ready for him. He did not pretend to be a divinity. He was a politician of exceptional good-will. He was none of your dictator gods. He showed himself extremely open and receptive for the organised information and guidance... that wasn't there.

And it isn't there now.

Some years ago there was a considerable fuss in the world about preparedness and unpreparedness. Most of that clamour concerned the possibility of war. But this was a case of a most fantastic unpreparedness on the part of hundreds of eminent men, who were supposed to have studied them, for the normal developments of a community in times of peace. There had been no attempt to assemble that mechanism of knowledge of which America stood in need.

I repeat that if usage had not drilled us into a sort of acquiescence, we should think our species collectively insane to go about its business in this haphazard, planless, negligent fashion.

I think I have said enough to recall to any one here, who may have lapsed from the keen apprehension of his first realisation, this wide gap between what I may call the at present unassembled and unexploited best thought and knowledge in the world, and the ideas and acts not simply of the masses of common people, but of those who direct public affairs, the dictators, the leaders, the politicians, the newspaper directors and the spiritual guides and teachers. We live in a world of unused and misapplied knowledge and skill. That is my ease. Knowledge and thought are ineffective. The human species as a whole is extraordinarily like a man of the best order of brain, who through some lesions or defects or insufficiencies of his lower centres, suffers from the wildest unco-ordinations; St. Vitus's dance, agraphobia, aphonia, and suffers dreadfully (knowing better all the time) from the silly and disastrous gestures he makes and the foolish things he says and does.

I don't think this has ever been so evident as it is now. I doubt if in the past the gap was so wide as it is now between the occasions that confront us, and the knowledge we have assembled to meet them. But because of a certain run of luck in the late nineteenth century, the existence of that widening gap and the menace of that widening gap, was not thrust upon our attention as it has been since the war.

At first that realisation of the ineffectiveness of our best thought and knowledge struck only a few people, like Mr. Maynard Keynes for example, who were in what I may call salient positions, but gradually I have noted the realisation spreading and growing. It takes various forms. Prominent men of science speak more and more frequently of the responsibility of science for the disorder of the world. And if you are familiar with that most admirable of all newspapers, Nature, and if you care to turn over the files of that very representative weekly for the past quarter of a century or so and sample the articles, you will observe a very remarkable change of note and scope in what it has to say to its readers. Time was when Nature was almost pedantically special and scientific. Its detachment from politics and general affairs was complete. But latterly the concussions of the social earthquake and the vibration of the guns have become increasingly perceptible in the laboratories. Nature from being specialist has become world—conscious, so that now it is almost haunted week by week by the question: "What are we to do before it is too late, to make what we know and our way of thinking effective in world affairs?" In that I think it is expressing a change which is happening in the minds of—if I may presume to class myself with you—nearly all people of the sort which fills this theatre tonight.

And consider again the topics that have been dealt with at the latest gathering of the British Association. The very title of the Presidential Address: "The Impact of Science upon Society." Sir Josiah Stamp, as you will remember, stressed the need of extending endowment and multiplying workers in the social sciences. Professor Philip dealt with "The Training of the Chemist for the Service of the Community." Professor Cramp talked of "The Engineer and the Nation," and there was an important discussion of "The Cultural and Social Values of Science" in which Sir Richard Gregory, Professor Hogben and Sir Daniel Hall said some memorable things. There can be no doubt of the reality of this awakening of the scientific worker to the necessity of his becoming a definitely organised factor in the social scheme of the years before us.

Well, so far I have been merely opening up my subject and stating the problem for consideration. We want the intellectual worker to become a more definitely organised factor in the human scheme. How is that factor to be organised? Is there any way of implementing knowledge for ready and universal effect? I ask you to examine the question whether this great and growing gap of which we are becoming so acutely aware, between special knowledge and thought and the common ideas and motives of mankind can be bridged, and if so how it can be bridged. Can scientific knowledge and specialised thought be brought into more effective relation to general affairs?

Q:— Let us consider first what is actually going on. I find among my uneasy scientific and specialist friends a certain disposition—and I think it is a mistaken disposition—for direct political action and special political representation. The scientific and literary workers of the days when I was a young man were either indifferent or conservative in politics, nowadays quite a large proportion of them are inclined to active participation in extremist movements; many are leftish and revolutionary, some accept the strange pseudo-scientific dogmas of the Communist party, though that does no credit to their critical training, and even those who are not out on the left are restless for some way of intervening, definitely as a class, in the general happenings of the community. Their ideas of possible action vary from important-looking signed pronouncements and protests to a sort of strike against war, the withholding of services and the refusal I to assist in technical developments that may be misapplied. Some favour the idea of a gradual supersession of the political forms and methods of mass democracy by government through some sort of elite, in which the man of science and the technician will play a dominating part. There are very large vague patches upon this ¤ idea, but the general projection is in the form of a sort of modern priesthood, an oligarchy of professors and exceptionally competent people. Like Plato they would make the philosopher king. This project involves certain assumptions about the general quality and superiority of the intellectual worker that I am afraid will not stand scrutiny.

I submit that sort of thing—political activities, party intervention and dreams of an authoritative élite—is not the way in which specialists, artists and specialised thinkers and workers who constitute the vital feeling and understanding of the body politic can be brought into a conscious, effective, guiding and directive relationship to the control of human affairs. Because—I hope you will acquit me of any disrespect for science and) philosophy when I say this—we have to face the fact that from the point of view of general living, men of science, artists, philosophers, specialised intelligences of any sort, do not constitute an elite that can be mobilised for collective action. They are an extraordinarily miscellaneous assembly, and their most remarkable common quality is the quality of concentration in comparative retirement, each along his own line. They have none of the solidarity, the customary savoir faire, the habits arising out of practices, activities and interests in common that lawyers, doctors or any of the really socially organised professions for instance display. A professor-ridden world might prove as unsatisfactory under the stress of modern life and fluctuating conditions as a theologian-ridden world. A distinguished specialist is precious because of his cultivated gift. It does not follow at all that by the standards of all-round necessity he is a superior person. Indeed by the very fact of his specialisation he may be less practised and competent than the average man. He probably does not read his newspaper so earnestly, he finds much of the common round a bother and a distraction and he puts it out of his mind. I think we should get the very gist of this problem if we could compare twelve miscellaneous men of science and special skill, with twelve unspecialised men taken—let us say—from the head clerk's morning train to the city. We should probably find that for commonplace team-work and the ordinary demands and sudden urgencies of life, the 2nd dozen was individually quite as good as, if not better than, the first dozen. In a burning hotel or cast away on a desert island they would probably do quite as well. And yet collectively they would be limited men; the whole dozen of them would have nothing much more to tell you than any one of them. On the other hand our dozen specialists would each have something distinctive to tell you. The former group would be almost as uniform in their knowledge and ability as tiles on a roof; the latter would be like pieces from a complicated jig-saw puzzle. The more you got them together the more they would signify. Twelve clerks or a hundred clerks; it wouldn't matter; you would get nothing but dull repetitions and a flat acquiescent suggestible outlook upon life. But every specialised man we added would be adding something to the directive pattern of life. I think that consideration takes us a step further in defining our problem tonight.

It is science and not men of science that we want to enlighten and animate our politics and rule the world. And now I will take rather a stride forward in my argument. I will introduce a phrase New Encyclopaedism which I shall spend most of the rest of my time defining. I want to suggest that something—a new social organ, a new institution—which for a time I shall call World Encyclopaedia, is the means whereby we can solve the problem of that jig-saw puzzle and bring all the scattered and ineffective mental wealth of our world into something like a common understanding, and into effective reaction upon our vulgar everyday political, social and economic life. I warn you that I am flinging moderation to the winds in the suggestions I am about to put before you. They are immense suggestions. I am sketching what is really a scheme for the reorganisation and reorientation of education and information throughout the world. No less. We are so accustomed to the existing schools, colleges, universities, research organisations of the world; they have so moulded and made us and trained us from our earliest years to respect and believe in them; that it is with a real feeling of temerity, of a matricidal impiety, so to speak, that I have allowed my mind to explore their merits and question whether they are not now altogether an extraordinarily loose, weak and out-of-date miscellany. Yet I do not see how we can admit, and I am disposed to think you have admitted with me, the existence of this terrifying gap between available knowledge and current social and political events, and not go on to something like an indictment of this whole great world of academic erudition, training and instruction from China to Peru—an indictment for, at least, inadequacy and unco- ordination if not for actual negligence. It may be only a temporary inadequacy, a pause in development before renascence, but inadequate altogether they are. Universities have multiplied greatly, yes, but they have failed to participate in the general advance in power, scope and efficiency that has occurred in the past century.

In transport we have progressed from coaches and horses by way of trains to electric traction, motor-cars and aeroplanes. In mental organisation we have simply multiplied our coaches and horses and livery stables. Let me now try to picture for you this missing element in the modern human social mechanism, this needed connection between the percipient and informative parts and the power organisation for which I am using this phrase, World Encyclopaedia. And I will take it first from the point of view of the ordinary educated citizen—for in a completely modernised state every ordinary man will be an educated citizen. I will ask you to imagine how this World Encyclopaedia organisation would enter into his life and how it would affect him. From his point of view the World Encyclopaedia would be a row of volumes in his own home or in some neighbouring house or in a convenient public library or in any school or college, and in this row of volumes he would, without any great toil or difficulty, find in clear understandable language, and kept up to date, the ruling concepts of our social order, the outlines and main particulars in all fields of knowledge, an exact and reasonably detailed picture of our universe, a general history of the world, and if by any chance he wanted to pursue a question into its ultimate detail, a trustworthy and complete system of reference to primary sources of knowledge. In fields where wide varieties of method and opinion existed, he would find, not casual summaries of opinions, hut very carefully chosen and correlated statements and arguments. I do not imagine the major subjects as being dealt with in special articles rather hastily written, in what has been the tradition of Encyclopaedias since the days of Diderot's heroic effort. Our present circumstances are altogether different from his. Nowadays there is an immense literature of statement and explanation scattered through tens of thousands of books, pamphlets and papers, and it is not necessary, it is undesirable, to trust to such hurried summaries as the old tradition was obliged to make for its use. The day when an energetic journalist could gather together a few star contributors and a miscellany of compilers of very uneven quality to scribble him special articles, often tainted with propaganda and advertisement, and call it an Encyclopaedia, is past. The modern World Encyclopaedia should consist of selections, extracts, quotations, very carefully assembled with the approval of outstanding authorities in each subject, carefully collated and edited and critically presented. It would be not a miscellany, but a concentration, a clarification and a synthesis. This World Encyclopaedia would be the mental background of every intelligent man in the world. It would be alive and growing and changing continually under revision, extension and replacement from the original thinkers in the world everywhere. Every university and research institution should be feeding it. Every fresh mind should be brought into contact with its standing editorial organisation. And on the other hand its contents would be the standard source of material for the instructional side of school and college work, for the verification of facts and the testing of statements—everywhere in the world. Even journalists would deign to use it; even newspaper proprietors might be made to respect it.

Such an Encyclopaedia would play the role of an undogmatic Bible to a world culture. It would do just what our scattered and disoriented intellectual organisations of today fall short of doing. It would hold the world together mentally.

It may be objected that this is a Utopian dream. This is something too great to achieve, too good to be true. I won't deal with that for a few minutes. Flying was a Utopian dream a third of a century ago. What I am putting before you is a perfectly sane, sound and practicable proposal.

But first I will notice briefly two objections—obstructions rather than objections—that one will certainly encounter at this point.

One of these is not likely to appear in any great force in this gathering. You have all heard and you have all probably been irritated or bored by the assertion that no two people think alike, "quot homines, tot sententiae", that science is always contradicting itself, that theologians and economists can never agree. It is largely mental laziness on the defensive that makes people say this kind of thing. They don't want their intimate convictions turned over and examined and it is unfortunate that the emphasis put upon minor differences by men of science and belief in their strenuous search for the completest truth and the exactest expression sometimes gives colour to this sort of misunderstanding. But I am inclined to think that most people overrate the apparent differences in the world of opinion today. Even in theology a psychological analysis reduces many flat contradictions to differences in terminology. My impression is that human brains are very much of a pattern, that under the same conditions they react in the same way, and that were it not for tradition, upbringing, accidents of circumstance and particularly of accidental individual obsessions, we should find ourselves—since we all face the same universe—much more in agreement than is superficially apparent. We speak different languages and dialects of thought and can even at times catch ourselves flatly contradicting each other in words while we are doing our utmost to express the same idea. And self-love and personal vanity are not excluded from the intellectual life. How often do we sec men misrepresenting each other in order to exaggerate a difference and secure the gratification of an argumentative victory! A World Encyclopaedia as I conceive it would bring together into close juxtaposition and under critical scrutiny many apparently conflicting systems of statement. It might act not merely as an assembly of fact and statement, but as an organ of adjustment and adjudication, a clearing house of misunderstandings; it would be deliberately a synthesis, and so act as a [test] and a filter for a very great quantity of human misapprehension. It would compel men to come to terms with one another. I think it would relegate "quot homines, tot sententiae" back to the Latin comedy from which it emerged.

The second type of obstruction that this idea of a World Encyclopaedia will encounter is even less likely to find many representatives in the present gathering and I will give it only the briefest of attention. (You know that kind of neuralgic expression, the high protesting voice, the fluttering gesture of the hands.) But you want to stereotype people. What a dreadful, dreadful world it will be when everybody thinks alike "—and so they go on. Most of these elegant people who want the world picturesquely at sixes and sevens are hopeless cases, but for the milder instances it may be worth while remarking that it really does not enhance the natural variety and beauty of life to have all the clocks in a town keeping individual times of their own, no charts of the sea, no timetables, but trains starting secretly to unspecified destinations, infectious diseases without notification and postmen calling occasionally when they can get by the picturesque footpads at the corner. I like order in the place of vermin, I prefer a garden to a swamp and the whole various world to a hole-and-corner life in some obscure community, and tonight I like to imagine I am making my appeal to hearers of a kindred disposition to my own. And next let us take this World Encyclopaedia from the point of view of the specialist and the super-intellectual. To him even more than to the common intelligent man World Encyclopaedia is going to be of value because it is going to afford him an intelligible statement of what is being done by workers parallel with himself. And further it will be giving him the general statement of 4 his own subject that is being made to the world at large. He can watch that closely. On the assumption that the World Encyclopaedia is based on a world-wide organisation he will be—if he is a worker of any standing—a corresponding associate of the Encyclopaedia organisation. He will be able to criticise the presentation of his subject, to suggest amendments and re-statements. For a World Encyclopaedia that was kept alive and up to date by the frequent re-issue of its volumes, could be made the basis of much fundamental discussion and controversy. It might breed swarms of pamphlets, and very wholesome swarms. It would give the specialist just that contact with the world at large which at present is merely caricatured by more or less elementary class teaching, amateurish examination work and college administrations. In my dream of a World Encyclopaedia I have a feeling that part of the scheme would be the replacement of the latter group of professional activities, the college business, tutoring, normal lecturing work and so on, by a new set of activities, the encyclopaedic work, the watching brief to prevent the corruption of the popular mind. In enlightening the general mind the specialist will broaden himself. He will be redeemed from oddity, from shy preciousness and practical futility. Well, you begin to see the shape of this project. And you will realise that it is far away from anything like the valiant enterprise of Denis Diderot and his associates a century and a half ago, except in so far as the nature of its reaction upon the world's affairs is concerned. That extraordinary adventure in intellectual synthesis makes this dream credible. That is our chief connection with it. And here I have to make an incidental disavowal. I want to make it clear how little I have to do with what I am now discussing. In order to get some talk going upon this idea of an Encyclopaedia, I have been circulating a short memorandum upon the subject among a number of friends. I did not think to mark it Private, and unhappily one copy seems to have fallen into the hands of one of those minor pests of our time, a personal journalist, who at once rushed into print with the announcement that I was proposing to write a brand new Encyclopaedia, all with my own little hand out of my own little head. At the age of seventy l Once a thing of this sort is started there is no stopping it—and I admit that announcement put me in my place in a pleasantly ridiculous light. But I think after what I have put before you now that you will acquit me of any such colossal ambition. I implore you not to let that touch of personal absurdity belittle the greatness and urgency of the cause I am pleading. This Encyclopaedia I am thinking of is something in which manifestly I have neither the equipment nor the quality to play any but an infinitesimal part. I am asking for it in the role of a common intelligent man who needs it and understands the need for it, both for himself and his world. After that you can leave me out of it. It is just because in the past I have had some experience in the assembling of outlines of knowledge for popular use that I realise, perhaps better than most people, the ineffectiveness of this sort of effort on the part of individuals or small groups. It is something that must be taken up and taken up very seriously—by the universities, the learned societies, the responsible educational organisations if it is to be brought into effective being. It is a super university I am thinking of a world brain; no less. It is nothing in the nature of a supplementary enterprise. I; is a completion necessary to modernise the university. And that brings me to the last part of this speculation. Can such an Encyclopaedia as I have been suggesting to you be a possible thing? How can it be set going? How can it be organised and paid for?

I agree I have now to show it is a possible thing. For I am going to make the large assumption that you think that it is a possible thing it is a desirable thing. How are we to set about it?

I think something in this way: To begin with we want a Promotion Organisation. We want, shall I call it, an Encyclopaedia Society to ask for an Encyclopaedia and get as many people as possible asking for an Encyclopaedia. Directly that Society asks for an Encyclopaedia it will probably have to resort to precautionary measures against any enterprising publisher who may see in that demand a chance for selling some sort of vamped-up miscellany as the thing required, and who may even trust to the unworldliness of learned men for some sort of countenance for his raid.

And next this society of promoters will have to survey the available material. For most of the material for a modern Encyclopaedia exists already—though in a state of impotent diffusion. In all the various departments with which an Encyclopaedia should deal, groups of authoritative men might be induced to prepare a comprehensive list of primary and leading books, articles, statements which taken together would give the best, clearest and most quintessential renderings of what is known and thought within their departments. This would make a sort of key bibliography to the thoughts and knowledge of the world. My friend Sir Richard Gregory has suggested that such a key bibliography for a World Encyclopaedia would in itself. be a worthwhile thing to evoke. I agree with him. I haven't an idea what we should get. I imagine something on the scale of ten or twenty thousand items. I don't know.

Possibly our Encyclopaedia Society would find that such a key bibliography was in itself a not unprofitable publication, but that is a comment by the way. The next step from this key bibliography would be the organisation of a general editorial board and of departmental boards. These would be permanent bodies—for a World Encyclopaedia must have a perennial life. We should have to secure premises, engage a literary staff and, with the constant co-operation of the departmental groups, set about the task of making our great synthesis and abstract. I must repeat that for the purposes of a World Encyclopaedia probably we would not want much original writing. If a thing has been stated clearly and compactly once for all, why paraphrase it or ask some inferior hand to restate it? Our job may be rather to secure the use of copyrights, and induce leading exponents of this or that field of science or criticism to co-operate in the selection, condensation, expansion or simplification of what they have already said so well.

And now I will ask you to take another step forward and imagine our World Encyclopaedia has been assembled and digested and that the first edition is through the press. So far we shall have been spending money on this great enterprise and receiving nothing; we shall have been spending capital, for which I have at present not accounted. I will merely say that I see no reason why the capital needed for these promotion activities should not be forthcoming. This is no gainful enterprise, but you have to remember that the values we should create would be far more stable than the ephemeral encyclopaedias representing sums round about a million pounds or so which have hitherto been the high-water of Encyclopaedic enterprise. These were essentially book-selling enterprises made to exploit a demand. But this World Encyclopaedia as I conceive it, if only because it will have roped in the larger part of the original sources of exposition, discussion and information, will be in effect a world monopoly, and it will be able to levy and distribute direct and indirect revenue, on a scale quite beyond the resources of any private publishing enterprise. I do not see that the financial aspects of this huge enterprise, big though the sums involved may be, present any insurmountable difficulties in the way of its realisation. The major difficulty will be to persuade the extremely various preoccupied, impatient and individualistic scholars, thinkers, scientific workers and merely distinguished but unavoidable men on whose participation its success depends, of its practicability, convenience and desirability. And so far as the promotion of it goes I am reasonably hopeful. Quite a few convinced, energetic and resourceful people could set this ball rolling towards realisation. To begin with it is not necessary to convert the whole world of learning, research and teaching. I see no reason why at any stage it should encounter such positive opposition. Negative opposition—the refusal to have anything to do with it and so forth-can be worn down by persistence and the gathering promise of success. It has not to fight adversaries or win majorities before it gets going. And once this ball is fairly set rolling it will be very hard to stop. A greater danger, as I have already suggested, will come from attempts at the private mercenary exploitation of this world-wide need—the raids of popular publishers and heavily financed salesmen, and in particular attempts to create copyright difficulties and so to corner the services and prestige of this or that unwary eminent person by anticipatory agreements.

Vis-à-vis with salesmanship the man of science, the man of the intellectual élite, is a t to show himself a very Simple Simon indeed. And) of course from the very start, various opinionated cults and propagandists will be doing their best to capture or buy the movement. Well, we mustn't be captured or bought, and in particular our silence must not be bought or captured. That danger may in the end prove to be a stimulus. It may be possible in some cases to digest and assimilate special cults to their own and the general advantage.

And there will be a constant danger that some of the early promoters may feel and attempt to realise a sort of proprietorship in the organisation, to make a group or a gang of it. But to recognise that danger is half-way to averting it.

I have said nothing so far about the language in which the Encyclopaedia should appear. It is a question I have not worked out. But I think that the main text should be in one single language, from which translations in whole or part could be made. Catholic Christianity during the years of its greatest influence was held together by Latin, and I do not think I am giving way to any patriotic bias when I suggest that unless we contemplate a polyglot publication—and never yet have I heard of a successful polyglot publication—English because it has a wider range than German, a greater abundance and greater subtlety of expression than French and more precision than Russian, is the language in which the original text of a World Encyclopaedia ought to stand. And moreover it is in the English-speaking communities that such an enterprise as this is likely to find the broadest basis for operations, the frankest criticism and the greatest freedom from oflicial interference and government propaganda. But that must not hinder us from drawing help and contributions from, and contemplating a use in every community in the world.

And so far I have laid no stress upon the immense advantage this enterprise would have in its detachment from immediate politics, Ultimately if our dream is realised it must exert a very great influence upon everyone who controls administrations, makes wars, directs mass behaviour, feeds, moves, starves and kills populations. But it does not immediately challenge these active people. It is not the sort of thing to which they would be directly antagonistic. It is not ostensibly anti-them. It would have a terrible and ultimately destructive aloofness. They would not easily realise its significance for all that they do and are. The prowling beast will right savagely if it is pursued and challenged upon the jungle path in the darkness, but it goes home automatically as the day breaks.

You see how such an Encyclopaedic organisation could spread like a nervous network, a system of mental control about the globe, knitting all the intellectual workers of the world through a common interest and a common medium of expression into a more and more conscious co-operating unity and a growing sense of their own dignity, informing without pressure or propaganda, directing without tyranny. It could be developed wherever conditions were favourable; it could make inessential concessions and bide its time in regions of exceptional violence, grow vigorously again with every return to liberalism and reason.

So I sketch my suggestion for a rehabilitation of thought and learning that ultimately may release a new form of power in the world, recalling indeed the power and influence of the churches and religions of the past but with a progressive, adaptable and recuperative quality that none of these possessed. I believe that in some such way as I have sketched tonight the mental forces now largely and regrettably scattered and immobilised in the universities, the learned societies, research institutions and technical workers of the world could be drawn together in a real directive world intelligence, and by that mere linking and implementing of what is known, human life as a whole could be made much surer, stronger, bolder and happier than it has ever been up to the present time. And until something of this sort is done, I do not see how the common life can ever be raised except occasionally, locally and by a conspiracy of happy chances, above its present level of impulsiveness, insincerity, insecurity, general under-vitality, under-nourishment and aimlessness. For that reason I think the promotion of an organisation for a World Encyclopaedia may prove in the long run to be a better investment for the time and energy of intelligent men and women than any definite revolutionary movement, Socialism, Communism, Fascism, Imperialism, Pacifism or any other of the current isms into which we pour ourselves and our resources so freely. None of these movements have anything like the intellectual comprehensiveness needed to construct the world anew.

Let me be very clear upon one point.

I am not saying that a World Encyclopaedia will in itself solve any single one of the vast problems that must be solved if man is to escape from his present dangers and distresses and enter upon a more hopeful phase of history; what I am saying—and saying with the utmost conviction—is this, that without a World Encyclopaedia to hold men's minds together in something like a common interpretation of reality, there is no hope whatever of anything but an accidental and transitory alleviation of any of our world troubles. As mankind is, so it will I remain, until it pulls its mind together. And if it does . not pull its mind together then I do not see how it can help but decline. Never was a living species more perilously poised than ours at the present time. If it does not take thought to end its present mental indecisiveness catastrophe lies ahead. Our species may yet end its strange eventful history as just the last, the cleverest of the great apes. The great ape that was clever—but not clever enough. It could escape from most things but not from its own mental confusion.

64

II. — THE BRAIN ORGANIZATION OF THE MODERN WORLD

Lecture delivered in America, October and November, 1937

FOR half a century I have resisted temptations to lecture in America—if for no other reason than the insufficiency of my voice. But the microphone is a great leveller and here I am at last on terms of practical equality with your most audible speakers and very glad indeed of this belated opportunity of talking to you. I want to talk to you about an idea which seems to me to be a very important one indeed. I want to interest you in it, and if possible find out what you think of it. I call that idea for reasons I shall try to make clear as I proceed, The New Encyclopaedism, and the gist of it is that the time is ripe for a very extensive revision and modernisation of the intellectual organisation of the world. Can I put it more plainly than that? Perhaps I can.

Our world is changing and it is changing with an ever-increasing violence. An old world dies about us. A new world struggles into existence. But it is not developing the brain and the sensitiveness and delicacy necessary for its new life. That is the essence of what I have to say.

To put my argument squarely on its feet I must begin by telling you things that you know quite as well or better than I do. I will just remind you of them. It is, so to speak, a matter of current observation that in the past century and a half there has been an enormous increase in the speed and facility of communications between men in every part of the world. Two hundred years ago Oliver Goldsmith said that if every time a man fired a gun in England, someone was killed in China, we should never hear of it and no one would bother very much about it. All that is changed. We should hear about that murdered Chinaman almost at once. Today we can go all round the world in the time it took a man to travel from New York to Washington in 1800, we can speak to any one anywhere so soon as the proper connections have been made and in a little while we shall be able to look one another in the face from the ends of the earth. In a very few years now we shall be able to fly in the stratosphere across the Atlantic in a few hours with a cargo of passengers, or bombs or other commodities. There has in fact been a complete revolution in our relation to distances. And the practical consequences of these immense approximations are only beginning to be realised. Everybody knows these facts now, but round about 1900 we were only beginning to take notice of this abolition of distance. Even in 1919 the good gentlemen who settled the world for ever at Versailles had not observed this strange new thing in human affairs. They had not observed that it was no longer possible to live in little horse-and-foot communities because of this change of scale. We know better now. Now the consequences of this change of scale force themselves upon our attention everywhere. Often in the rudest fashion. Our interests and our activities interpenetrate more and more. We are all consciously or unconsciously adapting ourselves to a single common world. For a time North America and the great sprawl of Russia and Siberia are for obvious reasons feeling less restriction than let us say japan or Germany, but, as my glancing allusion to the stratosphere was intended to remind you, this relative isolation of yours is also a diminishing isolation. The Abolition of Distance is making novel political and economic arrangements more and more imperative if the populations of the earth are not to grind against each other to their mutual destruction.

That imperative expansion of the scale of the community in which we have to live is the first truism I want to recall to you and bring into the foreground of our discussion. The second truism is the immense increase in our available power that has been going on. I do not know if any precise estimate of the physical energy at the disposal of mankind now and at any previous age, has ever been made, but the disproportion between what we have and what our great-grand-parents had, is stupendous and continually increasing. I am told that two or three power stations in the United States are today pouring out more energy night and day than could be produced by the sustained muscular effort of the entire United States population, and that the Roman empire at its mightiest could not—even by one vast unanimous thrust, not a single soul doing anything but push and push—have kept the street and road transport of New York State moving as it moves today. You are almost sick of being told it, in this form or that, over and over again. But we all know about this sort of thing. Man was slower and feebler beyond comparison a century or so ago than he is today. He has become a new animal incredibly swift and strong—except in his head. We all know—in theory at least—how this increase of power affects the nature of war. None of our new powers in this world of increasing power, have been so rapidly applied as our powers of mutual injury. A child of five with a bomb no bigger than my hand, can kill as many men in a moment as any paladin of antiquity hacking and hewing and bashing through a long and tiring battle. Both these two realities, these two portentous realities, the change of scale in human affairs and the monstrous increase of destructive power, haunt every intelligent mind today. One needs an exceptional stupidity even to question the urgency we are under to establish some effective World Pax, before gathering disaster overwhelms us. The problem of reshaping human affairs on a world-scale, this World problem, is drawing together an ever-increasing multitude of minds. It is becoming the common solicitude of all sane and civilised men. We must do it—or knock ourselves to pieces. I think it would be profitable if a group of history students were to trace how this World Problem has dawned upon the popular mind from, let us say, 1900 up to the present time. To begin with it was hardly felt to be important. Our apprehension of what it really amounts to has grown in breadth and subtlety during all these past seven-and-thirty years. We have been learning hard in the past third of a century. And particularly since 1919. In 1900 the general sense of the historical process, of what was going on in the world, was altogether shallower than ours today. People were extraordinarily ignorant of the operating causes of political events. It was quite possible then for them to agree that it was not at all a nice or desirable thing I and that it ought to be put an end to, and to imagine that setting up a nice little international court at the Hague to which states could bring their grievances and get a decision without going to the trouble and expense of hostilities would end this obsolescent scandal. Then we should have peace for ever—and everything else would go on as before. But now even the boy picking cotton or working the elevator, knows that nothing will go as before. The fear of change has reached them. You will remember that Mr. Andrew Carnegie set aside quite a respectable fraction of his savings to buy us world peace for ever and have done with it. The Great War was an enlightening disappointment to this earlier school of peacemakers, and it released a relatively immense flow of thought about the World Problem. But even at Versailles the people most immediately powerful, were still evidently under the impression that world peace was simply a legal and political business. They thought the Great War had happened, but they were busy politicians, and had not remarked that vastly greater things were happening. They did not realise even that elementary point about the unsuitable size of contemporary states to which I have recalled your attention. Still less did they think about the new economic stresses that were revolutionising every material circumstance of litre. They saw the issue as a simple aiirair upon the lines of old-fashioned history. So far as their ideas went it was just Carthage and Rome over again. The central Powers were naughty naughty nations and had to be punished. Their greatest novelty was the League of Nations, which indeed was all very well as a gesture and an experiment but which as an irremovable and irreplaceable reality in the path of world adjustment has proved anything but a blessing. It had been a brilliant idea in the reign of Francis I of France. Still we have to recognise that in 1919 the Geneva League was about as far as anyone's realisation of the gravity of the World Problem had gone. It is our common quality to be wise after the event and still quite unprepared for the next change ahead. It is an almost universal human failing to believe that now we know everything, that nothing more than we know can be known about human relations, and that in our limitless wisdom we can fix up our descendants for evermore, by constitutions, treaties, boundaries and leagues. So my poor generation built this insufficient League. For a time a number of well-meaning people did consider that the League of Nations settled the World Problem for good and all, and that they need not bother their heads about it any more. There were we felt, no further grounds for anxiety, and we all sat down within our nice little national boundaries to resume business . according to the old ways, securing each of us the largest possible share of the good things the new Era of Peace and Prosperity was to bring—at least to the good countries to whom victory had been accorded. Wlten later the history of our own times comes to be written, I imagine this period between 1919 and 1929 will be called the Fatuous Twenties.

We all know better now. Now that we are living in what no doubt the historian will some day call the Frightened Thirties. Versailles was no settlement. There is still no settlement. The World Problem still pursues us. And it seems now vastly nearer, uglier and more formidable than it ever did before. It emerges through all our settlements like a dangerous rhinoceros coming through a reed fence. Our mood changes now from one in which off-hand legal solutions were acceptable, to an almost feverish abundance of mental activity. From saying "There is the Hague Court and what more do you want?" or "There is the League of Nations, what more can you want?" or "There is the British Peace Ballot and please don't bother me further," we are beginning to apprehend something of the full complexity and vastness of the situation that faces mankind, that is to say all of us, as a living species. Our minds are beginning to grasp the vastness of these grim imperatives. That change of scale, that enhancement of power has altered the fundamental conditions of human life—of all our lives. The traditions of the old world, the comparatively easy traditions in which we have grown up and in which we have shaped our lives, are bankrupt. They are outworn. They are outgrown. They are too decayed for much more patching. They are as untrustworthy and dangerous as a very old car whose engine has become explosive, which has lost its brake lining and has a loose steering-wheel. What I am saying now is gradually becoming as plain in men's minds as the roundness of the earth. New World or nothing. We have to make a new world for ourselves or we shall sufier and perish amidst the downfall of the decaying old. This is a business of fundamentals in which we are all called upon to take part, and through which the lives of all of us are bound to be changed essentially and irrevocably.

With this realisation of the true immensity and penetration of the World Problem we are passing out of the period of panaceas—of simple solutions. As We grow wiser we realise more and more that the World Problem is not a thing like a locked door for which it is only necessary to End a single key. It is infinitely more complex. It is a battle all along the line and every man is a combatant or a deserter. Popular discussion is thick with competing simple remedies, these [sometimes] needful proposals, each of which has its factor of truth and each of which in itself is entirely inadequate. Consider some of them. Arbitration, League of Nations, I have spoken of World Socialism. The Socialist very rightly points out the evils and destructive stresses that arise from the free play of the acquisitive impulse in production and business affairs, but his solution, which is to take the control of things out of the hands of the acquisitive in order to put it into the hands of the inexperienced, plainly leaves the bulk of the world's troubles unsolved. The Communist and Fascist have theorised about and experimented with the seizure and concentration of Power, but they produce no sound schemes for its beneficial use. Seizing power by itself is a gangster's game. You can do nothing with power except plunder and destroy—unless you know exactly what to do with it. People tell us that Christianity, the Spirit of Christianity, holds a key to all our difficulties. Christianity, they say, has never yet been tried. We have all heard that. The trouble is that Christianity in all its various forms never does try. Ask it to work out practical problems and it immediately floats off into other-worldliness. Plainly there is much that is wrong in our property-money arrangements, but there again prescriptions for a certain juggling with currency and credit, seem unlikely in themselves to solve the World Problem. A multitude of such suggestions are bandied about with increasing passion. In comparison with any preceding age, we are in a state of extreme mental fermentation. This is, I suggest, an inevitable phase in the development of our apprehension of the real magnitude and complexity of the World Problem which faces us. Except for the faddists and fanatics we all feel a sort of despairing inadequacy amidst this wild storm of suggestions and rash beginnings. We want to know more, we want digested facts to go upon. Our minds are not equipped for the job.

And shaking a finger at you to mark the point we have reached, I repeat, our minds are not equipped for the job.

We are ships in uncharted seas. We are big-game hunters without weapons of precision.

This present uproar of incomplete ideas was as inevitable as the Imperialist Optimism of 1900, the Futile Amazement of the Great War, and the self-complacency of the Fatuous Twenties. These were all phases, necessary phases, in the march of our race through disillusionment to understanding. After the phase of panaceas there comes now, I hope, a phase of intelligent co-ordination of creative movements, a balanced treatment of our complex difficulties. We are going to think again. We are all beginning to realise that the World Problem, the universal world problem of adapting our life to its new scale and its new powers, has to be approached on a broad front, along many paths and in many fashions. In my opening remarks I stressed our spreading realisation of the possibility of a great catastrophe in world affairs. One immediate consequence of our full realisation of what this World Problem before us means is dismay. We lose heart. We feel that anyhow we cannot adjust that much. We throw up the sponge. We say, let us go on as long as possible anyhow, and after us, let what will happen. A considerable and a growing number of people are persuaded that a drift towards a monstrously destructive war cycle which may practically obliterate our present civilisation is inevitable. I have, I suppose, puzzled over such possibilities rather more than most people. I do not agree with that inevitability of another real war. But I agree with its possibility. I think such a collapse so possible that I have played with it imaginatively in a book or so and a film. It is so much a possibility that it is wholesome to bear it constantly in mind. But all the same I do not believe that world disaster is unavoidable. It is extraordinarily difficult to estimate the relative strength of the driving forces in human affairs today. We are not dealing with measurable quantities. We are easily the prey of our moods, and our latest vivid impression is sure to count for far too much. Values in my own mind, I find, shift about from hour to hour. I guess it is about the same with most of you. Just as in a battle, so here, our moods are factors in the situation. When we feel depressed, the world is going to the devil and we meet defeat half-way; when we are elated, the world is all right and we win. And I think that most of us are inclined to overestimate the menace of violence, the threats of nationalist aggression and the suppression of free discussion in many parts of the world at the present time. I admit the darkness and grimness on the face of things. Indisputably vehement State-ism now dominates affairs over large regions of the civilised world. Everywhere liberty is threatened or outraged. Here again, I merely repeat, what the whole intelligent world is saying.

Well....I do not want to seem smug amidst such immunities as we English- speaking people still enjoy, nevertheless I must confess I think it possible to overrate the intensity and staying power of this present nationalist phase. I think that the present vehemence of nationalism in the world may be due not to the strength of these tyrannies but to their weakness. This change of scale, this increment of power that has come into human affairs, has strained every boundary, every institution and every tradition in the world. It is an age of confusion, an age of gangster opportunity. After the gangsters the Vigilantes. Both the dying old and the vamped-up new are on the defensive. They build up their barriers and increase their repression because they feel the broad flood of change towards a vastly greater new order is rising. Every old government, every hasty new government that has leapt into power, is made crazy by the threat of a wider and greater order, and its struggle to survive becomes desperate. It tries still to carry onto deny that it is an experiment—even if it survives crippled and monstrous. The dogmatic Russian Revolution has not held power for a score of years and yet it, too, is now as much on the defensive as any other upstart dictatorship. A lot of what looks to us now like triumphant reaction may in the end prove to be no more than doomed, dwarfed and decaying dogmas and traditions at bay. None of the utterances of these militant figures that most threaten the peace of the world today have the serene assurance of men conscious that they are creating something that marches with the ruling forces of life. For the most part they are shouts—screams—of defiance. They scold and rant and threaten. That is the rebel note and not the note of mastery. We hear very much about the suppression of thought in the world. is there really—even at the present time—in spite of all this current violence, any real diminution of creative thought in the world—as compared with 1500 or 1850—or 1900, or 1914 or 1924? You have to remember that the suppression of free discussion in such countries as Germany, Italy and Russia does not mean an end to original thought in these countries. Thought, like gunpowder, may be all the more effective for being confined. I know that beneath the surface Germany is thinking intensely, and Russia is thinking more clearly if less discursively than ever before. Maybe we overestimate the value of that idle and safe, slack, do-as-you-please discussion that we English-speaking folk enjoy under our democratic regime. The concentration camps of today may prove after all to be the austere training grounds of a new freedom.

Let us glance for a moment at the chief forces that are driving against all that would keep the world in its ancient tradition of small national governments, warring and planning perpetually against each other, of a perpetual struggle not only of nations but individuals for a mere cramped possessiveness.

Consider now the drives towards release, abundance, one World Pax, one world control of violence, that are going on today. They seem to me very much like those forces that drove the United States to the Pacific coast and prevented the break-up of the Union. No doubt, many a heart failed in the covered waggons as they toiled westward, face to face with the Red Indian and every sort of lawless violence. Yet the drive persisted and prevailed. The Vigilantes prepared the way for the reign of law. The railway, the telegraph and so on followed the covered waggon and knitted this new-scale community of America together. In the middle nineteenth century all Europe thought that the United States must break up into a lawless confusion. The railway, the printing press, saved that. The greater unity conquered because of its immense appeal to common-sense in the face of the new conditions. And because it was able to appeal to common sense through these media.

The United States could spread gigantically and keep a common mind. And today I believe in many ways, in a variety of fashions and using many weapons and devices, the Vigilantes of World Peace, under the stimulus of still wider necessities, are finding themselves and each other and getting together to ride. That is to say their minds are getting together. One great line of development must be towards a Common Control of the Air. The great spans of the Atlantic and Pacific may prevent this from beginning as a world-wide Air Control, but that, I think, is just a passing phase of the problem. I submit to you that a state of affairs in which vast populations are under an ever- increasing threat of aerial bombardment with explosives, incendiary bombs and poison gas at barely an hour's notice, is intolerable to human reason. Maybe there will be terrible wars first. Quite possibly not. It may after all prove unnecessary to have very many great cities destroyed and very many millions of people burnt, suffocated, blown limb from limb, before men see what stares them in the face and accept the obvious. Men are, after all, partly reasonable creatures, they have at least spasmodic moral impulses. There is already in action—a movement—for World Air Control. But you can't have a thing like that by itself. Who or what will control the air?

This is a political question. None of us quite know the answer, but the answer has to be found, and hundreds of thousands of the best brains on earth are busy at the riddle of that adjustment. We can rule out any of the pat, ready-made answers of yesterday, League of Nations or what not. None the less that implacable necessity for World Air Control insists upon something, something with at least the authority of a World Federal Government in these matters, and that trails with it, you will find, a revelation of other vast collateral necessities. I cannot now develop these at any great length. But in the end I believe we are led to the conviction that the elemental forces of human progress, the stars in their courses, are fighting to evoke at least this much world community as involves a control of communications throughout the whole world, a common federal protection of everyone in the world from private, sectarian or national violence, a common federal protection of the natural resources of the planet from national, class or individual appropriation, and a world system of money and credit. The obstinacy of man is great, but the forces that grip him are greater and in the end, after I know not what wars, struggles and afflictions, this is the road along which he will go. He has to see it first—and then he will do it. I am sure of the ultimate necessity of this federal world state—and at the backs of your minds at least, I believe most of you are too—as I am sure that, whatever clouds may obscure it, the sun will rise to-morrow.

And now having recapitulated and brought together this general conception of human progress towards unity which is forming in most of our minds, as an answer to the ever-more insistent World Problem, I propose to devote the rest of my time with you to the discussion of one particular aspect of this march towards a world community, the necessity it brings with it, for a correlated educational expansion. This has not so far been given anything like the attention it may demand in the near future. We have been gradually brought to the pitch of imagining and framing our preliminary ideas of a federal world control of such things as communications, health, money, economic adjustments, and the suppression of crime. In all these material things we have begun to foresee the possibility of a world-wide network being woven between all men about the earth. So much of the World Peace has been brought into the range of—what shall I call it?—the general imagination. But I do not think we have yet given sufficient attention to the prior necessity, of linking together its mental organisations into a much closer accord than obtains at the present time. All these ideas of unifying mankind's affairs depend ultimately for their realisation on mankind having a unified mind for the job. The want of such effective mental unification is the key to most of our present frustrations. While men's minds are still confused, their social and political relations will remain in confusion, however great the forces that are grinding them against each other and however tragic and monstrous the consequences.

Now I know of no general history of human education and discussion in existence. We have nowadays—in what is called the New History-books which trace for us in rough outline the growth in size and complexity of organised human communities. But so far no one has attempted to trace the stages through which teaching has developed, how schools began, how discussions grew, how knowledge was acquired and spread, how the human intelligence kept pace with its broadening responsibilities. We know that in the small tribal community and even in the city states of, for example, Greece, there was hardly any need for reading or writing. The youngsters were instructed and initiated by their elders. They could walk all over the small territory of their community and see and hear, how it was fed, guarded, governed. The bright young men gathered for oral instruction in the Porch or the Academy. With the growth of communities into states and kingdoms we know that the medicine man was replaced by an organised priesthood, we know that scribes appeared, written records. There must have been schools for the priests and scribes, but we know very little about it. We know something of the effect of the early writings, the Bible particularly, in consolidating and preserving the Jewish tradition—giving it such a start off that for a long time it dominated the subsequent development of the Gentile world, and we know that the survival and spread of Christianity is largely due to its resort to written records to supplement that oral teaching of disciples with which it began. But the growing thirst for medical, theological and general knowledge that appeared in the Middle Ages and which led to those remarkable gatherings of hungry minds, the Universities, has still to be explained and described. That appearance and that swarming of scholars would make an extraordinary ¤ story. After the lecture room, the book; after that the newspaper, universal education, the cinema, the radio. No one has yet appeared to make an orderly, story of the developments of information and instruction that have occurred in the past hundred years. Age by age the World's Knowledge Apparatus has grown up. Unpremeditated. Without a plan. But enlarging due possible areas of political cooperation at every stage in its growth.

It is a very interesting thing indeed to ask oneself certain questions. How did I come to know what I know about the world and myself? What ought I to know? What would I like to know that I don't know? If I want to know about this or that, where can I get the clearest, best and latest information? And where did these other people about me get their ideas about things?

Which are sometimes so different from mine. Why do we differ so widely? Surely about a great number of things upon which we differ there is in existence exact knowledge? So that we ought not to differ in these things. This is true not merely about small matters in dispute but about vitally important things concerning our business, our money, our political outlook, our health, the general conduct of our lives. We are guessing when we might know. The facts are there, but we don't know them completely. We are inadequately informed. We blunder about in our ignorance and this great ruthless world in which we live, beats upon us and punishes our ignorance like a sin. Not only in our mass-ruled democracies but in the countries where dogmas and dictators rule, tremendous decisions are constantly being made affecting human happiness, root and branch, in complete disregard of realities that are known.

You see we are beginning to realise not only that the formal political structures of the world and many of the methods of our economic life are out of date and out of scale, but also another thing that hampers us hopelessly in every endeavour we make to adjust life to its new conditions—our World Knowledge Apparatus is not up to our necessities. We are neither collecting, arranging nor digesting what knowledge we have at all adequately, and our schools, our instruments of distribution are old-fashioned and ineffective.

We are not being told enough, we are not being told properly, and that is one main reason why we are all at sixes and sevens in our collective life.

The other day my university, the University of London, celebrated its centenary. For some minor reason I was asked to assist at these celebrations. And to do so I had to assume some very remarkable garments—most remarkable if you consider that London University was founded in the year 1836 when gentlemen wore tight trousers with straps, elegantly waisted coats and bell-shaped top hats. Did I dress up like that? No. I found myself retreating from the age of the aeroplane to the age of the horse and mule outfit of the Canterbury Pilgrims. I found myself wearing a hood and gown and carrying a Beret rather like those worn by prosperous citizens of the days of Edward IV, when the University of London was as little anticipated as the continent of America. My modern head peeped out at the top of this get-up and my modern trousers at the bottom. Properly I ought to have been wearing a square beard or have been clean-shaven, but I was forgiven that much. And from all parts of the world representatives of innumerable universities had come with beautifully illuminated addresses to congratulate our Chancellor and ourselves on our hundred years of sham mediaevalism. They came from the ends of the earth, they came up the aisle in an endless process; one ancient name followed another, now it was Tokyo, now Athens, now Upsala, now Cape Town, now the Sorbonne, now Glasgow, now Johns Hopkins, on they came and on and bowed and handed their addresses and passed aside. It was a marvellous, a dazzling array of beautifully coloured robes. It was also a marvellous collection of men and women. I watched the grave and dignified faces of some of the finest minds in the world. Together they presented, they embodied or they were there to represent, the whole body of human knowledge. There it was in effect parading before me. And nine out of ten of them were dressed up in some colourful imitation of a costume worn centuries before their foundations came into existence. It was picturesque, it was imposing—but it was just a little odd of them.

My thoughts drifted away to certain political gatherings I had seen and heard; faces of an altogether inferior type, leather-lunged adventurers bawling and gesticulating, raucous little men screaming plausible nonsense to ignorant crowds, supporters herded like sheep and saluting like trained monkeys, and the incongruity of the contrast came to me—you know how things come to you suddenly at times—so that I almost laughed aloud. Because, when it comes to the direction of human affairs, all these universities, all these nice refined people in their lovely gowns, all this visible body of human knowledge and wisdom, has far less influence upon the conduct of human affairs, than, let us say, an intractable newspaper proprietor, an unscrupulous group of financiers or the leader of a recalcitrant minority.

Some weeks previously I had taken part in a little private conference of scientific men in London. They were very distinguished men indeed, and they were distressed beyond measure at the way in which one scientific invention after another was turned to the injury of human life. What was to be done? What could be done? Our discussion was inconclusive, but it had quickened my sense of the reality of the situation. I put these three separate impressions together before you: First, these anxious scientific specialists, then the unchallenged power and mischief of these bawling war-making politicians and their crowds at the present time, and finally, capping the whole, these hundreds of all-too-decorated learned gentlemen, fine and delicate, bowing, presenting addresses (for the most part in Latin) and conferring further gowns and diplomas on one another. This last lot, I said, this third lot is after all—in spite of its elegant weakness, the organised brain of mankind so far as there is an organised brain of mankind—and it is not doing its proper work. Why? Why are our universities Boating above the general disorder of mankind like a beautiful sunset over a battlefield? Is it not high time that something was done about it? Certain ideas had been stirring in my mind for some time already, but this scene of archaic ceremony just lit up the situation for me. I realised that these mediaeval robes were in the highest degree symptomatic. They clothed an organisation essentially mediaeval, inadequate and out of date. We are living in 1937 and our universities, I suggest, are not half-way out of the fifteenth century. We have made hardly any changes in our conception of university organisation, education, graduation, for a century—for several centuries. The three- or four-years' course of lectures, the bachelor who knows some, the master who knows most, the doctor who knows all, are ideas that have come down unimpaired from the Middle Ages. Nowadays no one should end his learning while he lives and these university degrees are preposterous. It is true that we have multiplied universities greatly in the past hundred years, but we seem to have multiplied them altogether too much upon the old pattern. A new battleship, a new aeroplane, a new radio receiver is always an improvement upon its predecessor. But a new university is just another imitation of all the old universities that have ever been. Educationally we are still for all practical purposes in the coach and horse and galley stage. The new university is just one more mental gilt-coach in which minds take a short ride and get out again. We have done nothing to co-ordinate the work of our universities in the world—or at least we have done very little. What are called the learned societies with correspondents all over the world have been the chief addition to the human knowledge organisation since the Renaissance and most of these societies took their shape and scale in the eighteenth and nineteenth centuries. All the new means of communicating ideas and demonstrating realities that modern invention has given us, have been seised upon by other hands and used for other purposes; these universities which should guide the thought of the world, making no protest. The showmen got the cinema and the governments or the adventurers got the radio. The university teacher and the schoolmaster went on teaching in the class-room and checking his results by a written examination. It is as if one attempted to satisfy the traffic needs of greater New York or London or Western Europe by a monstrous increase in horses and carts and nothing else. The universities go out to meet the tremendous challenges of our social and political life, like men who go out in armour with bows and arrows to meet a bombing aeroplane. They are pushed aside by men like Hitler, Mussolini creates academies in their despite, Stalin sends party commissars to regulate their researches. It is beyond dispute that there has been a great increase in the research work of universities; that pedantry and mere scholarship in spite of an obstinate defence have declined relatively to keen inquiry, but the specialist is by his nature a preoccupied man. He can increase knowledge, but without a modern organisation backing him he cannot put it over. He can increase knowledge which ultimately is power, but he cannot at the same time control and spread this power that he creates. It has to be made generally available if it is not to be monopolised in the wrong hands.

There, I take it, is the gist of the problem of World Knowledge that has to be solved. A great new world is struggling into existence. But its struggle remains catastrophic until it can produce an adequate knowledge organisation. It is a giant birth and it is mentally defective and blind. An immense and ever-increasing wealth of knowledge is scattered about the world today, a wealth of knowledge and suggestion that—systematically ordered and generally disseminated—would probably give this giant vision and direction and suffice to solve all the mighty difficulties of our age, but that knowledge is still dispersed, unorganised, impotent in the face of adventurous violence and mass excitement. In some way we want to modernise our World Knowledge Apparatus so that it may really bring what is thought and known within reach of all active and intelligent men. So that we shall know—with some certainty. So that l we shall not be all at sixes and sevens about matters that have already been thoroughly explored and worked out.

How is that likely to he done?

Not of course in a hurry....

It would be very easy to do a number of stupid things about it—futile or even disastrous things. I can imagine quite a number of obvious preposterous mischievous experiments, a terrible sort of world university consolidation, an improvised knowledge dictatorship. Heaven save us from that! We Want nothing that will in any sense override the autonomy of institutions or the independence of individual intellectual workers, We want nothing that will invade the precious time and attempt to control the resources of the gifted individual specialist. He is too much distracted by elementary teaching and college administration already. We do not want to magnify and stereotype universities. Most of them with their gowns and degrees, their slavish imitation of the past, are too stereotyped already. But here it is that the idea I Want to put before you comes in, this idea of a greater encyclopaedism—with a permanent organism and a definite form and aim. I put forward the development of this new encyclopaedism as a possible method, the only possible method I can imagine, of bringing the universities and research institutions of the world into effective co-operation and creating an intellectual authority sufficient to control and direct our collective life. I imagine it as a permanent institution—untrammelled by precedent, a new institution—something added to the world network of universities, linking and co-ordinating them with one another and with the general intelligence of the world. Manifestly as my title for it shows, it arises out of the experience of the French Encyclopaedia, but the form it is taking in the minds of those who have become interested in the idea, is of something vastly more elaborate, more institutional and far-reaching than Diderot's row of volumes. The immense effect of Diderot's effort in establishing the frame of the progressive world of the nineteenth century, is certainly the inspiration of this new idea. The great role played in stabilising and equipping the general intelligence of the nineteenth-century world by the French, the British and the German and other encyclopaedias that followed it, is what gives confidence and substance to this new conception. But what we want today to hold the modern mind together in common sanity is something far greater and infinitely more substantial than those earlier encyclopaedias. They served their purpose at the time, but they are not equal to our current needs. A World Encyclopaedia no longer presents itself to a modern imagination as a row of volumes printed and published once for all, but as a sort of mental clearing house for the mind, a depot where knowledge and ideas are received, sorted, summarised, digested, clarified and compared. It would be in continual correspondence with every university, every research institution, every competent discussion, every survey, every statistical bureau in the world. It would develop a directorate and a staff of men of its own type, specialised editors and summarists. They would be very important and distinguished men in the new world. This Encyclopaedic organisation need not be concentrated now in one place; it might have the form of a network. It would centralise mentally but perhaps not physically. Quite possibly it might to a large extent be duplicated. It is its files and its conference rooms which would be the core of its being, the essential Encyclopaedia. It would constitute the material beginning of a real World Brain.

Then from this centre of reception and assembly, would proceed what we may call the Standard Encyclopaedia, the primary distributing element, the row of volumes. This would become the common backbone as it were of general human knowledge. It might take the form of twenty or thirty or forty volumes and it would go to libraries, colleges, schools, institutions, newspaper offices, ministries and so on all over the world. It would be undergoing continual revision. Its various volumes would be in process of replacement, more or less frequently according to the permanence or impermanence of their contents. And from this Standard Encyclopaedia would be drawn a series of text-books and shorter reference encyclopaedias and encyclopaedic dictionaries For individual and casual use.

That crudely is the gist of what I am submitting to you. A double-faced organisation, a perpetual digest and conference on the one hand and a system of publication and distribution on the other. It would be a clearing house for universities and research institutions; it would play the role of a cerebral cortex to these essential ganglia. On the one hand this organisation should be in direct touch with all the original thought and research in the world; on the other it should extend its informing tentacles to every intelligent individual in the community—the new world community. In that little world of the eighteenth century, what we may call the mind of the community scarcely extended below the gentlefolk, the clergy and the professions. There was no primary education for the common man at all. He did not even read. He was a mere toiler. It hardly mattered how little he knew—and the less he thought the better for social order. But machinery abolishes mere toil altogether. The new world has to consist of a world community—say of 2,000 million educated individuals—and the influence of the central encyclopaedic organisation, informing, suggesting, directing, unifying, has to extend to every rank of society and to every corner of the world. The new encyclopaedism is merely the central problem of world education.

Perhaps I should explain that when I speak in this connexion of universities, what I have in mind is primarily assemblies of learned men or men rehearsing their ripe scholarship or conducting original research with such advanced students and student helpers as have been attracted by them and are sharing their fresh and inspiring thoughts and methods. This is a return to the original university idea. The original universities were gatherings of eager people who wanted to know—and who clustered round the teachers who did seem to know. They gathered about these teachers because that was the only way in which they could get their learning. I am talking of that sort of university. That is the primary form of a university. I am not talking here of the collegiate side of a contemporary university, the superficial finishing school exercises of sportive young people mostly of the wealthier classes who don't want to know—young people who mean very little and who have been sent to the university to make useful friendships and get pass-degrees that mean hardly anything at all. These mere finishing-school students are a modern addition, a transitory encumbrance of the halls of learning. I suppose that before very long much of this undergraduate life will merge with the general upward extension of educational facilities to all classes of the community. I assume that the tentacles of this Encyclopaedia we are anticipating, with its comprehensive and orderly supply of knowledge, would intervene beneficially between the specialised research and learning which is the living reality in the university and this really quite modern finishing-school side. The time is rapidly returning when men of outstanding mental quality will consent to teach only such students as show themselves capable of and willing to follow up their distinctive work. The mere graduating crowd with their games and their yells and so forth, will go back to the mere teaching institutions where they properly belong. But I will not spend the few minutes remaining to me upon which is after all a side issue in this discussion. University organisation is not now my subject. I am talking of an essentially new organisation—an addition to the intellectual apparatus of the world. The more important thing now is to emphasise this need—a need the world is likely to realise more and more acutely in the coming years—for such a concentration, which will assemble, co-ordinate and distribute accumulated knowledge. It will link, supplement and no doubt modify profoundly, the universities, schools and other educational organisations we possess already, but it will not in itself be a part of them.

Let me make it perfectly clear that for the present it is desirable to leave this project of a World Encyclopaedic organisation vague—in all but its essential form and function. It might prove disastrous to have it crystallise out prematurely. Such premature crystallisation of a thing needed by the world can produce, we now realise, a rigid obstructive reality, just like enough to our actual requirements to cripple every effort to replace it later by a more efficient organisation. Explicit constitutions for social and political institutions, are always dangerous things if these institutions are to live for any length of time. If a thing is really to live it should grow rather than be made. It should never be something cut and dried. It should be the survivor of a series of trials and fresh beginnings—and it should always be amenable to further amendment.

So that while I believe that ultimately the knowledge systems of the world must be concentrated in this world brain, this permanent central Encyclopaedic organisation with a local habitat and a world-wide range—just as I believe that ultimately the advance of aviation must lead, however painfully and tortuously by way of World Air Control, to the political, economic and financial federation of the world—yet nevertheless I suggest that to begin with, the evocation of this World Encyclopaedia may begin at divergent points and will be all the better for beginning at divergent points.

Of the demand for it, and of the readiness for it in our world today, I have no sort of doubt. Ask the book· selling trade. Any books that give or even seem to give, any sort of conspectus of philosophy, of science, of general knowledge, have a sure abundant sale. We have the fullest encouragement for bolder and more strenuous efforts in the same direction. People want this assembling of knowledge and ideas. Our modern community is mind-starved and mind-hungry. It is justifiably uneasy and suspicious of the quality of what it gets. The hungry sheep look up and are not fed—at least they are not fed properly. They want to know, One of the next steps to take, it seems to me, is to concentrate this diffused demand, to set about the definite organisation of a sustained movement, of perhaps a special association or so, to bring a World Encyclopaedia into being. And while on the one hand we have this world-wide receptivity to work upon, on the other hand we have among the men of science in particular a very full realisation of the need for a more effective correlation of their work. It is not only that they cannot communicate their results to the world; they find great difficulty in communicating their results to one another. Among other collateral growths of the League of Nations is a certain Committee of Intellectual Co-operation which has now an official seat in Paris. Its existence shows that even as early as 1919, someone had realised the need for some such synthesis of mental activities as we are now discussing. But in timid, politic and scholarly hands the Committee of Intellectual Co-operation has so far achieved little more than a building, a secretary and a few salaries. The bare idea of a World Encyclopaedia in its present delicate state would give it heart failure. Still there it is, a sort of seed that has still to germinate, waiting for some vitalising influence to stir it to action and growth. And going on at present, among scientific workers, library workers, bibliographers and so forth, there is a very considerable activity for an assembling and indexing of knowledge. An important World Congress of Documentation took place this August in Paris. I was there as an English delegate and I met representatives of forty countries—and my eyes were opened to the very considerable amount of such harvesting and storage that has already been done. From assembling to digesting is only a step—a considerable and difficult step but, none the less, an obvious step. In addition to these indexing activities there has recently been a great deal of experimentation with the microfilm. It seems possible that in the near future, we shall have microscopic libraries of record, in which a photograph of every important book and document in the world will be stowed away and made easily available for the inspection of the student. The British Museum library is making microfilms of the 4,000 books it possesses that were published before 1550 and parallel work is being done here in America. Cheap standardised projectors offer no difficulties. The bearing of this upon the material form of a World Encyclopaedia is obvious. The general public has still to realise how much has been done in this field and how many competent and disinterested men and women are giving themselves to this task. The time is close at hand when any student, in any part of the world, will be able to sit with his projector in his own study at his or her convenience to examine any book, any document, in an exact replica.

Concurrently with this movement towards documentation, we may very possibly have a phase when publishers will be experimenting in the production of larger and better Encyclopaedias, all consciously or unconsciously attempting to realise the final world form. And satisfy a profitable demand. The book salesman from the days of Diderot onward has shown an extraordinary knack for lowering the quality of this sort of enterprise, but I did not see why groups of publishers throughout the world should not presently help very considerably in the beginning of a permanent Encyclopaedic foundation. But such questions of ways and means of distribution belong to a later stage of this great intellectual development which lies ahead of us. I merely glance at them here.

There are certain responses that I have observed crop up almost automatically in people's minds when they are confronted with this project of a worldwide organisation of all that is thought and known. They will say that an Encyclopaedia must always be tendentious and within certain limits—but they are very wide limits— that must be true. A World Encyclopaedia will have by its very nature to be what is called liberal. An Encyclopaedia appealing to all mankind can admit no narrowing dogmas without at the same time admitting corrective criticism. It will have to be guarded editorially and with the utmost jealousy against the incessant invasion of narrowing propaganda. It will have a general flavour of what many people will call scepticism. Myth, however venerated, it must treat as myth and not as a symbolical rendering of some higher truth or any such evasion. Visions and projects and theories it must distinguish from bed-rock fact. It will necessarily press strongly against national delusions of grandeur, and against all sectarian assumptions. It will necessarily be for and not indifferent to that world community of which it must become at last an essential part. If that is what you call bias, bias the world Encyclopaedia will certainly have. It will have, and it cannot help but have, a bias for organisation, comparison, construction and creation. It is an essentially creative project. It has to be the dominant factor in directing the growth of a new world.

Well, there you have my anticipation of the primary institution which has to appear if that world-wide community towards which mankind, willy-nilly, is being impelled, is ever to be effectively attained. The only alternative I can see is social dissolution and either the evolution of a new, more powerful type of man, or the extinction of our species. I sketch roughly—it seems to be my particular role in life to do these broad sketches and outlines and then stand aside—but I do my best to make the picture plain and understandable. And for me at any rate this is no Utopian dream. It is a forecast, however inaccurate and insufficient, of an absolutely essential part of that world community to which I believe we are driving now. I do not believe there is any emergence for mankind from this age of disorder, distress and fear in which we are living, except by way of such a deliberate vast reorganisation of our intellectual life and our educational methods as I have outlined here. I have been talking of real intellectual forces and foreshadowing the emergence of a vital reality. I have been talking of something which may even be recognizably in active operation within a lifetime—or a lifetime or so, from now—this consciously and deliberately organised brain for all mankind. In a few score years there will be thousands of workers at this business of ordering and digesting knowledge where now you have one. There will be a teacher for every dozen children and schools as unlike the schools of to-day as a liner is unlike the Mayflower. There will not be an illiterate left in the world. There will hardly be an uninformed or misinformed person. And the brain of the whole mental network will be the Permanent World Encyclopaedia.

Well, I have designedly put much controversial matter before you, and I have not hesitated to put it in a provocative manner. You will, I know, understand that every new thing is apt to seem crude at first. Forgive my crudities. But my time has been short for what I had to say, and I have said it in the way that seemed most challenging and most likely to produce further discussion.

65

III. — THE IDEA OF A PERMANENT WORLD ENCYCLOPAEDIA

First published in Harper's Magazine, April 1937
Contributed to the new Encyclopédie Française, August 1937

IT is probable that the idea of an encyclopaedia may undergo very considerable extension and elaboration in the near future. Its full possibilities have still to be realised. The encyclopaedias of the past have sufficed for the needs of a cultivated minority. They were written "for gentlemen by gentlemen" in a world wherein universal education was unthought of, and where the institutions of modern democracy with universal suffrage, so necessary in many respects, so difficult and dangerous in their working, had still to appear. Throughout the nineteenth century encyclopaedias followed the eighteenth-century scale and pattern, in spite both of a gigantic increase in recorded knowledge and of a still more gigantic growth in the numbers of human beings requiring accurate and easily accessible information. At first this disproportion was scarcely noted, and its consequences not at all. But many people now are coming to recognise that our contemporary encyclopaedias are still in the coach-and-horses phase of development, rather than in the phase of the automobile and the aeroplane. Encyclopaedic enterprise has not kept pace with material progress. These observers realise that modern facilities of transport, radio, photographic reproduction and so forth are rendering practicable a much more fully succinct and accessible assembly of fact and ideas than was ever possible before.

Concurrently with these realisations there is a growing discontent with the part played by the universities, schools and libraries in the intellectual life of mankind. Universities multiply, schools of every grade and type increase, but they do not enlarge their scope to anything like the urgent demands of this troubled and dangerous age. They do not perform the task nor exercise the authority that might reasonably be attributed to the thought and knowledge organisation of the world. It is not, as it should be, a case of larger and more powerful universities co-operating more and more intimately, but of many more universities of the old type, mostly ill-endowed and uncertainly endowed, keeping at the old educational level.

Both the assembling and the distribution of knowledge in the world at present are extremely ineffective, and thinkers of the forward-looking type whose ideas we are now considering, are beginning to realise that the most hopeful line for the development of our racial intelligence lies rather in the direction of creating a new world organ for the collection, indexing, summarising and release of knowledge, than in any further tinkering with the highly conservative and resistant university system, local, national and traditional in texture, which already exists. These innovators, who may be dreamers today, but who hope to become very active organisers tomorrow, project a unified, if not a centralised, world organ to "pull the mind of the world together", which will be not so much a rival to the universities, as a supplementary and co-ordinating addition to their educational activities on a planetary scale. The phrase "Permanent World Encyclopaedia" conveys the gist of these ideas. As the core of such an institution would be a world synthesis of bibliography and documentation with the indexed archives of the world. A great number of workers would be engaged perpetually in perfecting this index of human knowledge and keeping it up to date. Concurrently, the resources of micro-photography, as yet only in their infancy, will be creating a concentrated visual record. Few people as yet, outside the world of expert librarians and museum curators and so forth, know how manageable well-ordered facts can be made, however multitudinous, and how swiftly and completely even the rarest visions and the most recondite matters can be recalled, once they have been put in place in a well-ordered scheme of reference and reproduction. The American microfilm experts, even now, are making facsimiles of the rarest books, manuscripts, pictures and specimens, which can then be made easily accessible upon the library screen. By means of the microfilm, the rarest and most intricate documents and articles can be studied now at first hand, simultaneously in a score of projection rooms. There is no practical obstacle whatever now to the creation of an efficient index to all human knowledge, ideas and achievements, to the creation, that is, of a complete planetary memory for all mankind. And not simply an index; the direct reproduction of the thing itself can be summoned to any properly prepared spot. A microfilm, coloured where necessary, occupying an inch or so of space and weighing little more than a letter, can be duplicated from the records and sent anywhere, and thrown enlarged upon the screen so that the student may study it in every detail.

This in itself is a fact of tremendous significance. It foreshadows a real intellectual unification of our race. The whole human memory can be, and probably in a short time will be, made accessible to every individual. And what is also of very great importance in this uncertain world where destruction becomes continually more frequent and unpredictable, is this, that photography affords now every facility for multiplying duplicates of this —which we may call?—this new all-human cerebrum. It need not be concentrated in any one single place. It need not be vulnerable as a human head or a human heart is vulnerable. It can be reproduced exactly and fully, in Peru, China, Iceland, Central Africa, or wherever else seems to afford an insurance against danger and interruption. It can have at once, the concentration of a craniate animal and the diffused vitality of an amoeba.

This is no remote dream, no fantasy. It is a plain statement of a contemporary state of affairs. It is on the level of practicable fact. It is a matter of such manifest importance and desirability for science, for the practical needs of mankind, for general education and the like, that it is difficult not to believe that in quite the near future, this Permanent World Encyclopaedia, so compact in its material form and so gigantic in its scope and possible influence, will not come into existence.

Its uses will be multiple and many of them will be fairly obvious. Special sections of it, historical, technical, scientific, artistic, e.g. will easily be reproduced for specific professional use. Based upon it, a series of summaries of greater or less fullness and simplicity, for the homes and studies of ordinary people, for the college and the school, can be continually issued and revised. In the hands of competent editors, educational directors and teachers, these condensations and abstracts incorporated in the world educational system, will supply the humanity of the days before us, with a common understanding and the conception of a common purpose and of a commonweal such as now we hardly dare dream of. And its creation is a way to world peace that can be followed without any very grave risk of collision with the warring political forces and the vested institutional interests of today. Quietly and sanely this new encyclopaedia will, not so much overcome these archaic discords, as deprive them, steadily but imperceptibly, of their present reality. A common ideology based on this Permanent World Encyclopaedia is a possible means, to some it seems the only means, of dissolving human conflict into unity.

This concisely is the sober, practical but essentially colossal objective of those who are seeking to synthesise human mentality today, through this natural and reasonable development of encyclopaedism into a Permanent World Encyclopaedia.

66

IV. — PASSAGE FROM A SPEECH TO THE CONGRÈS MONDIAL

PASSAGE FROM A SPEECH TO THE CONGRÈS MONDIAL DE LA DOCUMENTATION UNIVERSELLE, PARIS AUGUST 20TH, 1937

IT is dawning upon us, we lay observers, that this work of documentation and bibliography, is in fact nothing less than the beginning of a world brain, a common world brain. What you are making me realise is a sort ofcerebrum for humanity, a cerebral cortex which (when it is fully developed) will constitute a memory and a perception of current reality For the entire human race. Plainly we have to make it a centralised and uniform organisation but, as Mr. Watson Davis is here to remind us, it need not have any single local habitation because the continually increasing facilities of photography render reduplication of our indices and records continually easier. In these days of destruction, violence and general insecurity, it is comforting to think that the brain of mankind, the race brain, can exist in numerous replicas throughout the world.

At first our activities are necessarily receptive and we begin most easily with the documentation of concrete facts, and I do not see how this new and great encyclopaedia, this race brain, can develop into anything but a great structure for the comparison, reconciliation and synthesis of common guiding ideas for the whole world. What is gathered will be digested and the results returned through the channels of education, literature and the press to the whole world.

Please do not imagine that I am indulging in any fantasy when I talk of your work and your accumulations as the rudimentary framework of a world brain. I am speaking of a process of mental organisation throughout the world which I believe to be as inevitable as anything can be in human affairs. The world has to pull its mind together, and this is the beginning of its effort. The world is a Phoenix. It perishes in flames and even as it dies it is born again. This synthesis of knowledge is the necessary beginning to the new world.

It is good to be meeting here in Paris where the first encyclopaedia of ideas was made. It is good for representatives from forty countries to be breathing the clear, comprehensive and systematic atmosphere of France, to be recreating themselves in the presence of its sympathetic creative understanding. Again I would thank our hosts for bringing this congress together and enabling a number of widely scattered workers to realise something of the real greatness of the task to which they have devoted themselves.

67

V. — THE INFORMATIVE CONTENT OF EDUCATION

The Presidential Address to the Educational Science Section of the British Association for the Advancement of Science, given on September 2nd, 1937, at Nottingham, as read by Mr, Wells

SECTION L of the British Association is of necessity one of the least specialised of all sections. Its interests spread far beyond professional limitations. It is a section where anyone who is so to speak a citizen at [age may hope to play a part that is not altogether an impertinent intrusion. And it is in the character of a citizen at large that I have accepted the very great honour that you have offered me in making me the President of this Section. I have no other claim whatever upon your attention. Since the remote days when as a needy adventurer I taught as non-resident master in a private school, invigilated at London University examinations, raided the diploma examinations of the College of Preceptors for the money prises offered, and, in the most commercial spirit, crammed candidates for the science examinations of the University, I have spent very few hours indeed in educational institutions. Most of those were spent in the capacity of an inquiring and keenly interested parent at Oundle School. I doubt if there is any member of this section who has not had five times as much teaching experience as I have, and who is not competent to instruct me upon all questions of method and educational organisation and machinery. So I will run no risks by embarking upon questions of that sort. But on the other hand, if I know very little of educational methods and machinery I have had a certain amount of special experience in what those methods produce and what the machinery turns out.

I have been keenly interested for a number of years, and particularly since the War, in public thought and public reactions, in what people know and think and what they are ready to believe. What they know and think and what they are ready to believe impresses me as remarkably poor stuff. A general ignorance—even in respectable quarters—of some of the most elementary realities of the political and social life of the world is, I believe, mainly accountable for much of the discomfort and menace of our times. The uninstructed public intelligence of our community is feeble and convulsive. It is still a herd intelligence. It tyrannises here and yields to tyranny there. What is called elementary education throughout the world does not in fact educate, because it does not properly inform. I realised this very acutely during the later stages of the War and it has been plain in my mind ever since. It led to my taking an active part in the production of various outlines and summaries of contemporary knowledge. Necessarily they had the defects and limitations of a private adventure, but in making them I learnt a great deal about—what shall I say—the contents of the minds our schools are turning out as taught.

And so now I propose to concentrate the attention of this Section for this meeting on the question of what is taught as fact, that is to say upon the informative side of educational work. For this year I suggest we give the questions of drill, skills, art, music, the teaching of languages, mathematics and other symbols, physical, aesthetic, moral and religious training and development, a rest, and that we concentrate on the inquiry: What are we telling young people directly about the world in which they are to live? What is the world picture we are presenting to their minds? What is the framework of conceptions about reality and about obligation into which the rest of their mental existences will have to be fitted? I am proposing in fact a review of the informative side of education, wholly and solely-informative in relation to the needs of modern life.

And here the fact that I am an educational outsider—which in every other relation would be a disqualification—gives me certain very real advantages. I can talk with exceptional frankness. And I am inclined to think that in this matter of the informative side of education frankness has not always been conspicuous. For what I say I am responsible only to the hearer and my own self-respect. I occupy no position from which I can be dismissed as unsound in my ideas. I follow no career that can be affected by anything I say. I follow, indeed, no career. That's all over. I have no party, no colleagues or associates who can be embarrassed by any unorthodox suggestions I make. Every schoolmaster, every teacher, nearly every professor must, by the nature of his calling, be wary, diplomatic, compromising; he has his governors to consider, his college to consider, his parents to consider, the local press to consider; he must not say too much nor say anything that might be misinterpreted and misunderstood. I can. And so I think I can best serve the purposes of the British Association and this section by taking every advantage of my irresponsibility, being as unorthodox and provocative as I can be, and so possibly saying a thing or two which you are not free to say but which some of you at any rate will be more or less willing to have said.

Now when I set myself to review the field of inquiry I have thus defined, I found it was necessary to take a number of very practical preliminary issues into account. As educators we are going to ask what is the subject-matter of a general education? What do we want known? And how do we want it known? What is the essential framework of knowledge that should be established in the normal citizen of our modern community? What is the irreducible minimum of knowledge for a responsible human being today? I say irreducible minimum—and I do so, because I know at least enough of school work to know the grim significance of the school time-table and of the leaving school age. Under contemporary conditions our only prospect of securing a mental accord throughout the community is by laying a common foundation of knowledge and ideas in the school years. No one believes today, as our grandparents—perhaps for most of you it would be better to say great-grandparents—believed, that education had an end somewhen about adolescence. Young people then leave school or college under the imputation that no one could teach them any more. There has been a quiet but complete revolution in people's ideas in this respect and now it is recognised almost universally that people in a modern community must be learners to the end of their days. We shall be giving a considerable amount of attention to continuation, adult and post-graduate studies in this section, this year. It would be wasting our opportunities not to do so. Here in Nottingham University College we have the only Professorship in Adult Education in England, and under Professor Peers the Adult Education Department which is in close touch with the Workers' Educational Association has broadened its scope far beyond the normal range of Adult Education. Our modern ideas seem to be a continuation of learning not only for university graduates and practitioners in the so-called intellectual professions, but for the miner, the plough-boy, the taxi-cab driver, and the out-of-work, throughout life. Our ultimate aim is an entirely educated population.

Nevertheless it is true that what I may call the main beams and girders of the mental framework must be laid down, soundly or unsoundly, before the close of adolescence. We live under conditions where it seems we are still only able to afford for the majority of our young people, freedom from economic exploitation, teachers even of the cheapest sort and some educational equipment, up to the age of 14 or 15, and we have to fit our projects to that. And even if we were free to carry on with unlimited time and unrestrained teaching resources, it would still be in those opening years that the framework of the mind would have to be made.

We have got to see therefore that whatever we propose as this irreducible minimum of knowledge must be imparted between infancy and—at most, the fifteenth or sixteenth year. Roughly, we have to get it into ten years at the outside.

And next let us turn to another relentlessly inelastic-seeming case—and that is, the school time-table. How many hours in the week have we got for this job in hand? The maximum school hours we have available are something round about thirty, but out of this we have to take time for what I may call the non-informative teaching, teaching to read, teaching to write clearly, the native and foreign language teaching, basic mathematical work, drawing, various forms of manual training, music and so forth. A certain amount of information may be mixed in with these subjects but not very much. They are not what I mean by informative subjects. By the time we are through with these non-informative subjects, I doubt if at the most generous estimate we can apportion more than six hours a week to essentially informative work. Then let us, still erring on the side of generosity, assume that there are forty weeks of schooling in the year. That gives us a maximum of 240 hours in the year. And if we take ten years of schooling as an average human being's preparation for life, and if we disregard the ravages made upon our school time by measles, chicken-pox, whooping-cough, coronations and occasions of public rejoicing, we are given 2,400 hours as all that we can hope for as our time allowance for building up a coherent picture of the world, the essential foundation of knowledge and ideas, in the minds of our people. The complete framework of knowledge has to be established in 200 dozen hours. It is plain that a considerable austerity is indicated for us. We have no time to waste, if our schools are not to go on delivering, year by year, fresh hordes of fundamentally ignorant, unbalanced, uncritical minds, at once suspicious and credulous, weakly gregarious, easily baffled and easily misled, into the monstrous responsibilities and dangers of this present world. Mere cannon-fodder and stuff for massacres and stampedes.

Out question becomes therefore: "What should people know—whatever else they don't know? Whatever else we may leave over—for leisure-time reading, for being picked up or studied afterwards—what is the irreducible minimum that we ought to teach as clearly, strongly and conclusively as we know how?"

And now I—and you will remember my role is that of the irresponsible outsider, the citizen at large—I am going to set before you one scheme of instruction for your consideration. For it I demand all those precious 2,400 hours. You will perceive, as I go on, the scheme is explicitly exclusive of several contradictory and discursive subjects that now find a place in most curricula, and you will also find doubts arising in your mind about the supply and competence of teachers, a difficulty about which I hope to say something before my time is up. But teachers are for the world and not the world for teachers. If the teachers we have today are not equal to the task required of them, then we have to recondition our teachers or replace them. We live in an exacting world and a certain minimum of performance is required of us all. If children are not to be given at least this minimum of information about the world into which they have come—through no fault of their own—then I do think it would be better for them and the world if they were not born at all. And to make what I have to say as clear as possible I have had a diagram designed which I will unfold to you as my explanation unfolds. You have already noted I have exposed the opening stage of my diagram. You see I make a three-fold division of the child's impressions and the matters upon which its questions are most lively and natural. I say nothing about the child learning to count, scribble, handle things, talk and learn the alphabet and so forth because all these things are ruled out by my restriction of my address to information only. Never mind now what it wants to do—or wants to feel. This is what it wants to know. In all these educational matters, there is, of course, an element of overlap. As it learns about things and their relationship and interaction its vocabulary increases and its ideas of expression develop. You will make an allowance for that.

[chart]

And now I bring down my diagram to expose the first stage of positive and deliberate teaching. We begin telling true stories of the past and of other lands. We open out the child's mind to a realisation that the sort of life it is living is not the only life that has been lived and that human life in the past has been different from what it is today and on the whole that it has been progressive. We shall have to teach a little about law and robbers, kings and conquests, but I see no need at this stage to afflict the growing mind with dates and dynastic particulars. I hope the time is not Far distant when children even of 8 or 9 will be freed altogether from the persuasion that history is a magic recital beginning "William the Conqueror, 1066". Much has been done in that direction. Much remains to be done. Concurrently, we ought to make the weather and the mud pie our introduction to what Huxley christened long ago Elementary Physiography. We ought to build up simple and clear ideas from natural experience.

We start a study of the states of matter with the boiling, evaporation, freezing and so on of water and go on to elementary physics and chemistry. Local topography can form the basis of geography. We shall have to let our learner into the secret that the world is a globe-and for a time I think that has to be a bit of dogmatic teaching. It is not so easy as many people suppose to prove that the world is spherical and that proof may very well be left to make an exercise in logic later on in education. Then comes biology. Education I rejoice to see is rapidly becoming more natural, more biological. Most young children are ready to learn a great deal more than most teachers can give them about animals. I think we might easily turn the bear, the wolf] the tiger and the ape from holy terrors and nightmare material into sympathetic creatures, if we brought some realisation of how these creatures live, what their real excitements are, how they are sometimes timid, into the teaching. I don't think that descriptive botany is very suitable for young children. Flowers and leaves and berries are bright and attractive, a factor in aesthetic education, but I doubt if, in itself, vegetation can hold the attention of the young. Sometimes I think we bore young children with premature gardens. But directly we begin to deal with plants as hiding-places, homes and food for birds and beasts, the little boy or girl lights up and learns. And with this natural elementary zoology and botany we should begin elementary physiology. How plants and animals live, and what health means for them. There I think you have stuff enough for all the three or four hundred hours we can afford for the foundation stage of knowledge. Outside this substantial teaching of school hours the child will be reading and indulging in imaginative play—and making that clear distinction children do learn to make between truth and fantasy—about fairyland, magic carpets and seven-league boots, and all the rest of it. So far as my convictions go I think that the less young children have either in or out of school I of what has hitherto figured as history, the better. I do not see either the charm or the educational benefit of making an important subject of and throwing a sort of halo of prestige and glory about the criminal history of royalty, the murder of the Princes in the Tower, the wives of Henry VIII, the families of Edward I and James I, the mistresses of Charles II, Sweet Nell of Old Drury, and all the rest of it. I suggest that the sooner we get all that unpleasant stuff out of schools, and the sooner that we forget the border bickerings of England, France, Scotland, Ireland and Wales, Bannockburn, Flodden, Crécy and Agincourt, the nearer our world will be to a sane outlook upon life. In this survey of what a common citizen should know I am doing my best to elbow the scandals and revenges which once passed as English history into an obscure corner or out of the picture altogether. But I am not proposing to eliminate history from education—far from it. Let me bring down my diagram a stage further and you will see how large a proportion of our treasure of 2,400 hours I am proposing to give to history. This next section represents about 800 to 1,000 pre-adolescent hours. It is the schoolboy-schoolgirl stage. And here the history is planned to bring home to the new generation the reality that the world is now one community. I believe that the crazy combative patriotism that plainly threatens to destroy civilisation today is very largely begotten in their school history lessons. Our schools take the growing mind at a naturally barbaric phase and they inflame and fix its barbarism. I think we underrate the formative effect of this perpetual reiteration of how we won, how our Empire grew and how relatively splendid we have been in every department of life. We are blinded by habit and custom to the Way it infects these growing minds with the chronic and nearly incurable disease of national egotism. Equally mischievous is the furtive anti-patriotism of the leftish teacher. I suggest that we take on our history from the simple descriptive anthropology of the elementary stage to the story of the early civilisations.

We are dealing here with material that was not even available for the schoolmasters and mistresses who taught our fathers. It did not exist. But now we have the most lovely stuff to hand, far more exciting and far more valuable than the quarrels of Henry II and à Becket or the peculiar unpleasantnesses of King James or King John. Archaeologists have been piecing together a record of the growth of the primary civilisations and the developing roles of priest, king, farmer, warrior, the succession of stone and copper and iron, the appearance of horse and road and shipping in the expansions of those primordial communities. It is a far finer story to tell a boy or girl and there is no reason why it should not be told. Swinging down upon these early civilisations came first the Semitic-speaking peoples and then the Aryan-speakers, Persian, Macedonian, Roman, followed one another, Christendom inherited from Rome and Islam from Persia, and the world began to assume the shapes we know today. This is great history and also in its broad lines it is a simple history—upon it we can base a lively modern intelligence, and now it can be Put in a form just as comprehensible and exciting for the school phase as the story of our English kings and their territorial, dynastic and sexual entanglements. When at last we focus our attention on the British Isles and France we shall have the affairs of these regions in a proper proportion to the rest of human adventure. And our young people will be thinking less like gossiping court pages and more like horse-riders, seamen, artist-artisans, roadmakers, and city-builders, which I take it is what in spirit we want them to be. Measured by the great current of historical events, English history up to quite recent years is mere hole-and-corner history.

And I have to suggest another exclusion. We are telling our young people about the real past, the majestic expansion of terrestrial events. In these events the little region of Palestine is no more than a part of the highway between Egypt and Mesopotamia. Is there any real reason nowadays for exaggerating its importance in the past? Nothing really began there, nothing was worked out there. All the historical part of the Bible abounds in wild exaggeration of the importance of this little strip of land. We were all brought up to believe in the magnificence of Solomon's temple and it is a startling thing for most of us to read the account of its decorations over again and tum its cubits into feet. It was smaller than most barns. We all know the peculiar delight of devout people when, amidst the endless remains of the great empires of the past, some dubious fragment is found to confirm the existence of the Hebrews. Is it not time that we recognised the relative historical insignificance of the events recorded in Kings and Chronicles, and ceased to throw the historical imagination of our young people out of perspective by an over-emphasised magnification of the national history of Judea; To me this lack of proportion in our contemporary historical teaching seems largely responsible for the present troubles of the world. The political imagination of our times is a hunch-back imagination bent down under an exaggeration. It is becoming a matter of life and death to the world to straighten that backbone and reduce that frightful nationalist hunch.

Look at our time-table and what we have to teach. If we give history four-tenths of all the time we have for imparting knowledge at this stage that still gives us at most something a little short of 400 hours altogether. Even if we think it desirable to perplex another generation with the myths of the Creation, the Flood, the Chosen People and so forth, even if we want to bias it politically with tales of battles and triumphs and ancient grievances, we haven't got the time for it—any more than we have the time for the really quite unedifying records of all the Kings and Queens of England and their claims on this and that. So far as the school time-table goes we are faced with a plain alternative. One thing or the other. Great history and hole-in-corner history? The story of mankind or the narrow, self-righteous, blinkered stories of the British Islands and the Jews? There is a lot more we have to put into the heads of our young people over and above History. It is the main subject of instruction but even so, it is not even half of the informative work that ought to be got through in this school stage. We have to consider the collateral subject of geography and a general survey of the world. We want to sec our world in space as well as our world in time. We may have a little map-making here, but I take it what is needed most are reasonably precise ideas of the various types of country and the distinctive floras and faunas of the main regions of the world. We do not want our budding citizens to chant lists of capes and rivers, but we do want them to have a real picture in their minds of the Amazon forests, the pampas, the various phases in the course of the Nile, the landscape of Labrador mountains, and so on, and also we want something like a realisation of the sort of human life that is led in these regions. We have enormous resources now in cheap photography, in films, and so forth, that even our fathers never dreamt of—to make all this vivid and real. New methods are needed to handle these new instruments, but they need not be overwhelmingly costly. And also our new citizen should know enough of topography to realise why London and Rio and New York and Rome and Suez happen to be where they are and what sort of places they are.

Geography and History run into each other in this respect and, on the other hand, Geography reaches over to Biology. Here again our schools lag some fifty years behind contemporary knowledge. The past half-century has written a fascinating history of the succession of living things in time and made plain all sorts of processes in the prosperity, decline, extinction, and replacement of species. We can sketch the wonderful and inspiring story of life now from its beginning. Moreover, we have a continually more definite account of the sequence of sub-man in the world and the gradual emergence of our kind. This is elementary, essential, interesting and stimulating stuff for the young, and it is impossible to consider anyone a satisfactory citizen who is still ignorant of that great story.

And finally, we have the science of inanimate matter. In a world of machinery, optical instruments, electricity, radio and so forth we want to lay a sound foundation of pure physics and chemistry upon the most modern lines—for everyone. Some of this work will no doubt overlap the mathematical teaching and the manual training and steal a little badly needed time from them. And finally, to meet awakening curiosity and take the morbidity out of it, we shall have to tell our young people and especially our young townspeople, about the working of their bodies, about reproduction and about the chief diseases, enfeeblements and accidents that lie in wait for them in the world.

That, I think, completes my summary of all the information we can hope to give in the lower school stage. And as I make it I am acutely aware of your unspoken comment. With such teachers as we have—teachers trained only to reaction, overworked, underpaid, hampered by uninspiring examinations, without initiative, without proper leisure. Young and inexperienced or old and discouraged. You may do this sort of thing, here and there, under favourable conditions, with the splendid élite of the profession, the 10 per cent who are interested, but not as a general state of affairs. Well, I think that it is a better rule of life, first to make sure of what you want and then set about getting it, rather than to consider what you can easily, safely and meanly get, and then set about reconciling yourself to it. I admit we cannot have a modern education without a modernised type of teacher. A teacher enlarged and released. Many of our teachers—and I am not speaking only of elementary schools—are shockingly illiterate and ignorant. Often they know nothing but school subjects; sometimes they scarcely know them. Even the medical profession does not present such extremes between the discouraged routine worker and the enthusiast. Everything I am saying now implies a demand for more and better teachers-better paid, with better equipment. And these teachers will have to be kept fresh. It is stipulated in most leases that we should paint our houses outside every three years and inside every seven years, but nobody ever thinks of doing up a school teacher. There are teachers at work in this country who haven't been painted inside for fifty years. They must be damp and rotten and very unhealthy for all who come in contact with them. Two-thirds of the teaching profession now is in urgent need of being either reconditioned or superannuated. In this advancing world the reconditioning of both the medical and the scholastic practitioner is becoming a very urgent problem indeed, but it is not one that I can deal with here. Presently this section will be devoting its attention to adult education and then I hope the whole question of professional and technical refreshment will be ventilated.

And there is another matter also closely allied to this question of the rejuvenation of teachers, at which I can only glance now, and that is the bringing of school books up to date. In this informative section of school work there is hardly a subject in which knowledge is not being vigorously revised and added to. But our school work does not follow up the contemporary digesting of knowledge. Still less do our school libraries. They are ten, fifteen years out of date with much of their information. Our prison libraries by the by are even worse. I was told the other day of a virtuous prisoner who wanted to improve his mind about radio. The prison had a collection of technical works made for such an occasion and the latest book on radio was dated 1920. There is, I have been told, an energetic New School Books Association at work in this field, doing what it can to act in concert with those all too potent authorities who frame our examination syllabuses. I am all for burning old school books. Some day perhaps we shall have school books so made that at the end of ten or twelve years, let us say, they will burst into flames and inflict severe burns upon any hands in which they find themselves. But at present that is a little Utopian. It is even more applicable to the next stage of knowledge to which we are now coming.

This stage represents our last 1,000 hours and roughly I will call it the upper form or upper standard stage. It is really the closing phase of the available school period. Some of the matter I have marked for the history of this grade might perhaps be given i.n Grade B and vice versa. We have still a lot to do if we are to provide even a skeleton platform for the mind of our future citizen. He has still much history to learn before his knowledge can make an effective contact with his duties as a voter.

You see I am still reserving four-tenths of the available time, that is to say nearly 400 hours for history. But now we are presenting a more detailed study of such phenomena as the rise and fall of the Ottoman Empire, the rise of Russia, the history of the Baltic, the rise and fall of the Spanish power, the Dutch, the first and second British Empires, the belated unifications of Germany and Italy. Then as I have written we want our modern citizen to have some grasp of the increasing importance of economic changes in history and the search for competent economic direction and also of the leading theories of individualism, socialism, the corporate state, communism.

For the next five-and-twenty years now the ordinary man all over the earth will be continually confronted with these systems of ideas. They are complicated systems with many implications and applications. Indeed they are aspects of life rather than systems of ideas. But we send out our young people absolutely unprepared for the heated and biased interpretations they will encounter. We hush it up until they are in the thick of it. And can we complain of the consequences? The most the poor silly young things seem able to make of it is to be violently and self-righteously Anti- something or other, Anti-Red, Anti-Capitalist, Anti-Fascist. The more ignorant you are the easier it is to be an Anti. To hate something without having something substantial to put against it. Blame something else. A special sub-section of history in this grade should be a course in the history of war, which is always written and talked about by the unwary as though it had always been the same thing, while as a matter of fact—except for its violence—it has changed profoundly with every change in social, political and economic life. Clearly parallel to this history our young people need now a more detailed and explicit acquaintance with world geography, with the different types of population in the world and the developed and undeveloped resources of the globe. The devastation of the world's forests, the replacement of pasture by sand deserts through haphazard cultivation, the waste and exhaustion of natural resources, coal, petrol, water, that is now going on, the massacre of important animals, whales, penguins, seals, food fish, should be matters of universal knowledge and concern.

Then our new citizens have to understand something of the broad elements in our modern social structure. They should be given an account of the present phase of communication and trade, of production and invention and above a.l.l they need whatever plain knowledge is available about the conventions of property and money. Upon these interrelated conventions human society rests, and the efficiency of their working is entirely dependent upon the general state of mind throughout the world. We know now that what used to be called the inexorable laws of political economy and the laws of monetary science, are really no more than rash generalisations about human behaviour, supported by a maximum of pompous verbiage and a minimum of scientific observation. Most of our young people come on to adult life, to employment, business and the rest of it, blankly ignorant even of the way in which money has changed slavery and serfdom into wages employment and of how its fluctuations in value make the industrial windmills spin or flag. They are not even warned of the significance of such words as inflation or deflation, and so the wage-earners are the helpless prey at every turn towards prosperity of the savings-snatching financier. Any plausible monetary charlatan can secure their ignorant votes. They

Informative Content of Education 8 5 know no better. They cannot help themselves. Yet the subject of property and money—together they make one subject because money is only the fluid form of property—is scarcely touched upon in any stage in the education of any class in our community. They know nothing about it; they are as innocent as young lambs and born like them for shearing.

And now here you will see I have a very special panel. This I have called Personal Sociology. Our growing citizen has reached an age of self- consciousness and self-determination. He is on the verge of adolescence. He has to be initiated. Moral training does not fall within the scope of the informative content of teaching. Already the primary habits of truthfulness, frankness, general honesty, communal feeling, helpfulness and generosity will or will not have been fostered and established in the youngster's mind by the example of those about him. A mean atmosphere makes mean people, a too competitive atmosphere makes greedy, self-glorifying people, a cruel atmosphere makes fierce people, but this issue of moral tone does not concern us now here. But it does concern us that by adolescence the time has arrived for general ideas about one's personal relationship to the universe to be faced. The primary propositions of the chief religious and philosophical interpretations of the world should be put as plainly and impartially as possible before our young people. They will be asking those perennial questions of adolescence—whence and why and whither. They will have to face, almost at once, the heated and exciting propagandas of theological and sceptical partisans—pro's and anti's. So far as possible we ought to provide a ring of cleat knowledge for these inevitable fights. And also, as the more practical aspect of the question, What am I to do with my life? I think we ought to link with our general study of social structure a study of social types which will direct attention to the choice of a métier. In what spirit will you face the world and what sort of a job do you feel like? This subject of Personal Sociology as it is projected here is the informative equivalent of a confirmation class. It says to everyone: "There are the conditions under which you face your world." The response to these questions, the determination of the will, is however not within our present scope. That is a matter for the religious teacher, for intimate friends and for the inner impulses of the individual. But our children must have the facts.

Finally, you will see that I have apportioned some time, roughly two-tenths of our 1,000 hours, in this grade to the acquisition of specialised knowledge. Individuality is becoming conscious of itself and specialisation is beginning.

Thus I budget, so to speak, for our 2,400 hours of informative teaching. We have brought our young people to the upper form, the upper standard. Most of them arc now going into employment or special training and so taking on a role in the collective life. But there remain some very essential things which cannot be brought into school teaching, not through any want of time, but because of the immaturity of the growing mind. It we are to build a real modern civilisation we must go on with definite informative instruction into and even beyond adolescence. Children and young people are likely to be less numerous proportionally in the years ahead of us in all the more civilised populations and we cannot afford to consume them in premature employment after the fashion of the preceding centuries. The average age of our population is rising and this involves an upward extension of education. And so you will see I suggest what I call an undergraduate or continuation school, Grade D, the upper adolescent stage, which I presume will extend at last to every class in the population, in which at least half the knowledge acquired will be specialised in relation to interest, aptitude and the social needs of the individual. But the other half will still have to be unspecialised, it will have to be general political education. Here particularly comes in that education for citizenship to which this Educational Section is to give attention later. It seems to me altogether preposterous that nowadays our educational organisation should turn out new citizens who are blankly ignorant of the history of the world during the last twenty-five years, who know nothing of the causes and phases of the Great War and are left to the tender mercies of freakish newspaper proprietors and party organisers for their ideas about the world outlook, upon which their collective wills and actions must play a decisive part.

Social organisation is equally a matter for definite information. "We are all socialists nowadays." Everybody has been repeating that after the late Lord Rosebery for years and years. Each for all and all for each. We are all agreed upon the desirability of the spirit of Christianity and of the spirit of Democracy, and that the general interest of the community should not be sacrificed to Private Profit. Yes—beautiful, but what is not realised is that Socialism in itself is little more than a generalisation about the undesirability of irresponsible ownership and that the major problem before the world is to devise some form of administrative organisation that will work better than the scramble of irresponsible owners. That form of administrative organisation has not yet been devised. You cannot expropriate the private adventurer until you have devised a competent receiver for the expropriated industry or service. This complex problem of the competent receiver is the underlying problem of most of our constructive politics. It is imperative that every voter should have some conception of the experiments in economic control that are in progress in Great Britain, the United States of America, Italy, Germany, Russia, and elsewhere. Such experiments are going to affect the whole of his or her life profoundly. So, too, are the experiments in monetary and financial organisation. Many of the issues involved go further than general principles. They are quantitative issues, questions of balance and more or less. A certain elementary training in statistical method is becoming as necessary for anyone living in this world of today as reading and writing. I am asking for this much contemporary history as the crowning phase, the graduation phase of our knowledge-giving. After that much foundation, the informative side of education may well be left to look after itself.

Speaking as a teacher of sorts myself, to a gathering in which teachers probably predominate, I need scarcely dilate upon the fascination of diagram drawing. You will understand how reluctant I was to finish of at Grade D and how natural it was to extend my diagram to two more grades and make it a diagram of the whole knowledge organisation of a modern community. Here then is Grade E, the adult learning that goes on now right through life, keeping oneself up to date, keeping in touch with the living movements about us. I have given a special line to those reconditioning courses that must somehow be made a normal part in the lives of working professional men. It is astonishing how stale most middle-aged medical men, teachers and solicitors

And beyond Grade E I have put a further ultimate grade for the fully adult human being. He or she is learning now, no longer only from books and newspapers and teachers, though there has still to be a lot of that, but as a worker with initiative, making experiments, learning from new experience, an industrialist, an artist, an original writer, a responsible lawyer, an administrator, a statesman, an explorer, a scientific investigator. Grade F accumulates, rectifies, changes human experience. And here I bring in an obsession of mine with which I have dealt before the Royal Institution and elsewhere. You see, indicated by these arrows, the rich results of the work of Grade F flowing into a central world-encyclopaedic-organisation, where it will be continually summarised, clarified, and whence it will be distributed through the general information channels of the world.

So I complete my general scheme of the knowledge organisation of a modern community and submit it to you for your consideration.

I put it before you in good faith as a statement of my convictions. I do not know how it will impress you and I will not anticipate your criticisms. It may seem impossibly bold and "Utopian." But we are living in a world in which a battleship costs £8,000,000, in which we can raise an extra £400,000,000 for armaments with only a slight Stock Exchange qualm, and which has seen the Zeppelin, the radio, the bombing aeroplane come absolutely out of nothing since 1900. And our schools are going along very much as they were going along thirty-seven years ago.

There is only one thing I would like to say in conclusion. Please do me the justice to remember that this is a project for Knowledge Organisation only and solely. It is not an entire scheme of education I am putting before you. It is only a part and a limited part of education—the factual side of education—I have discussed. There are 168 hours in a week and I am dealing with the use of rather less than six during the school year of less than forty weeks—for ten years. It is no good saying as though it was an objection either to my paper or to me, that I neglect or repudiate spiritual, emotional and aesthetic values. They are not disregarded, but they have no place at all in this particular part of the educational scheme. I have said nothing about music, dancing, drawing, painting, exercise and so on and so forth. Not because I would exclude them from education but because they do not fall into the limits of my subject. You no more want these lovely and elementary things mixed up with a conspectus of knowledge than you want playfulness in an ordnance map or perplexing whimsicality on a clock face. You have the remaining 162 hours a week for all that. But the spiritual, emotional, aesthetic lives our children are likely to lead, will hardly be worth living unless they are sustained by such a clear, full and sufficient backbone of knowledge as I have ventured to put before you here.

68

APPENDIX I. — RUFFLED TEACHERS

Published in the Sunday Chronicle, September 12th, 1937
THE BREEZE AT THE BRITISH ASSOCIATION

I FIND myself in trouble with a number of indignant school inspectors and teachers throughout the country, and I am in the awkward position of a man who is essentially right but who has nevertheless been rather tactless in his phrasing. And also I have suffered from the necessity reporters and editors are under to compress and point what one has said. At times their sense of drama leads them to omit the meat and give only the salt and mustard, and so one's remarks are presented in a state of exaggerated pungency. I find I have wounded more than I intended.

Moreover the reporters at the meeting were supplied with a first draft of my address and this I had already modi6ed in certain respects before I read it. For example, I did not say our schools are "drooling along" much as they did in 1900. "Drooling" was a hard offensive word. Actually I said they were "going along" much as they did in 1900, but the reporters sitting under me with the printed draft before them did not note the change nor did they notice the insertion of a considerable passage upon the underpayment, overwork, limitation upon initiative and so forth that prevent a vigorous teacher from doing himself or herself full justice. But these are subsidiary matters.

I still maintain when all allowances have been made for the progress of education in the past third of a century that elementary teaching throughout the world—even in our own urban elementary schools where progress has been most marked—has not kept pace with the demands of a time in which such things as aviation and radio have leapt out of nothingness into primary importance in our affairs, and in which human power for good or evil has been stupendously increased. Schools as a whole may be going forwards, but nevertheless they are being outrun. In the race between education and catastrophe, catastrophe is winning.

And anxious though I am to salve the feelings of teachers and scholastic authorities in this matter, I am obliged to remark upon one or two characteristics of this storm of protest and repudiation I have provoked. The first is the solidarity of the teachers in their indignation. I say there are teachers who are not up to their job, that some of them have not been done up inside for fifty years. They are as damp and rotten as old houses. And surely every teacher knows that that is true. "Some" is not "all." But will they admit it? Instead they flare up. "You say we are all damp and rotten!" I don't. And when I say two-thirds of the teaching profession is in urgent need of either reconditioning or superannuation, I mean two-thirds and not the whole.

In spite of the anger I have evoked I stick to that rough estimate. The level of qualification is still far too low for modern needs, the amount of reconditioning in brief "holiday" courses and so forth is not enough, and the educational engine in the social apparatus is not up to the stresses it has to meet, We want more and better teachers. We want them urgently. Elementary education lags—throughout the world. I stick to that.

From all the Parts of the country come "retorts" to my address. "Smithstown Director of Education Hits Out", and that sort of thing. Maybe sometimes the journalist barbs the shaft. The more substantial counter-attack is that I am out of date—usually it is "sadly out of date". Poor Mr. Wells! A charming head girl (with photograph) is produced to say that surely I must be thinking of my own school days sixty years ago, and inspectors, masters, head-mistresses and assistants combine in being "amused" at my unawareness of the blinding light in which their pupils live nowadays. They say I have not been in a school for fifty years, which is not exactly true and that lays them open to the obvious remark that some of them seem never to have been out of school all their lives. It is a peculiar atmosphere for I the teacher, that school atmosphere. It seems to beget a peculiar sensitiveness to criticism. One magnificent head-mistress is "disgusted" that I do not know that in 1917 she was teaching exactly what I ask to have taught and taught properly in 1937. Sonic day she may read my address in full, bring herself to study my innocent-looking diagram, and realise with a shock to how much foresight, modernity and religious novelty she had laid claim. Much capital is made of the fact that I hoped some day "1066 and all that" will be altogether forgotten in our schools. My assailants assume this to be an assertion that "1066 and all that" is what they are I teaching today. But is its They should read more carefully. The fact remains that the 1066 stuff is still going on in places now. And even when "1066 and all that" is left behind, it may still be a long long way to the necessary historical basis of a modern mind. A little stuff about "hunter peoples" and "plough peoples" may not settle the matter. I remain unconvinced of this alleged complete modernisation of history teaching. What alarms me most in this outburst of retorts is the tremendous self-satisfaction of so many of these acting educationists. I should hate to think it true that you can teach something to every man (or woman) except a schoolmaster (or schoolmistress). But you should see my mail and press cuttings this week. I remain absolutely sure that no proper treatment of the property-money conventions suitable for teaching has yet been achieved and I deny that any elementary education for the modern world state is possible until that is done. Nothing but twaddle and nonsense about property, money or economic control is being handed out to young people throughout the world. No picture of the economic world is given them. My magnificent schoolmistress, my hitting—out director of education, and all the rest of them, are in a state of self-protective hallucination about that.

I admit the extraordinary difficulty of creating a really modernised universal education, but I insist upon its Urgent necessity. In the course of the remaining discussions of the British Association it did become clear to us that we could not discuss education in vacuo. Education must have an objective and that objective must be the ideal of a community in which the educated person will live. Our Nazi and French visitors, Professor Levy and Mr. F. Horrabin, helped us to realise that. If the activities of the Educational Section of the British Association of this year did nothing else, they serve materially to show how inseparable is education from the general body of social science and theory.

Education and social existence are reciprocal. Its informative side has to be essentially social elucidation. So that the ideal teacher can never be a specialist; he has to have a working conception of the world as a whole into which his teaching fits. When I write or talk to teachers about the real magnitude of their task I am apt to feel like Max Beerbohm's caricature of Walt Whitman urging the American eagle to soar. It remained ruffled and inactive on its perch. Nevertheless for good or ill the future is in the hands of the teachers as it is in the hands of no other men and women, and the more this is recognised the more urgent our criticisms of them will have to be.

69

APPENDIX II. — PALESTINE IN PROPORTION

Published in the Sunday Chronicle, October 3rd, 1937)

THE other day I was talking to an assembly of teachers and scientific workers on the problem of getting the elements of a modern world outlook into the ordinary human mind during its all too brief years of schooling and initiation. I was not persuading nor exhorting; I was exposing my thoughts about one of the primary difficulties in the way of a World Pax which will save mankind from the destruction probable in putting the new wine of mechanical and biological power into the worn bottles of social and moral tradition. I dealt with the swiftness of life, the shortness of time available for learning and the lag and limitations of teaching.

In my survey of the minimum knowledge needed to make an efficient citizen of the world, I laid great stress upon history. It is the core of initiation. History explains the community to the individual, and when the community of interests and vital interaction has expanded to planetary dimensions, then nothing less than a clear and simplified world history is required as the framework of social ideas. The history of man becomes the common adventure of Everyman.

I deprecated the exaggerated importance attached to the national history and to Bible history in western countries. I maintained that the Biblical account of the Creation and the Fall gave a false conception of man's place in this universe. I expressed the opinion that the historical foundation for world citizenship would be better laid if these partial histories were dealt with only in their proper relation to the general development of mankind. In particular I pointed out that Palestine and its people were a very insignificant part of the general picture. It was a side-show in the greater conflicts of Mesopotamia and Egypt. Nothing important, I said, ever began there or worked out there...

In saying that I felt that I was stating plain matter-of-fact to well-informed hearers. But it is not what I should have thought and said, forty years ago. And since the publication of my remarks, there have been a number of retorts and replies to my statement that have made me realise how widely and profoundly and by what imperceptible degrees, my estimate of this Jewish history has been changed since my early years and how many people still remain under my earlier persuasions. Long after I ceased to be a Christian, I was still obsessed by Palestine as a region of primary importance in the history of human development. I ranked it with Greece as a main source in human, moral and intellectual development. Most people still seem to do so. It may be interesting to state compactly why I have grown out Of that conviction.

Very largely it was through rereading the Bible after an i interlude of some years and with a fresh unprejudiced mind, that this change came about in my ideas. My maturer impression of that remarkable and various bale of literature which we call the Old Testament was that it had been patched a lot but very little falsified. Where falsification appeared, as in the number of hosts and slain in the Philistine bickerings, it was very naive, transparent and understandable falsification.

I was not impressed by the general magnificence of the prose, about which one still hears so much. There are some splendidly plain and vivid passages and interludes of great dignity and beauty, but the bulk of the English Bible sounds to me pedestrian translator's English, quite unworthy of the indiscriminate enthusiasm that has been poured out upon it. From their very diverse angles the books of the Bible have an entirely genuine flavour.

It is a collection; it is not a single book written ad hoc like the Koran. And the historical parts have the quality of honest history as well as the writers could tell it. Jewish history before the return from Babylon as the Bible gives it, is the unpretending story of a small barbaric people whose only gleam of prosperity was when Solomon served the purposes of Hiram by providing an alternative route to the Red Sea, and built his poor little temple out of the profits of porterage. Then indeed there comes a note of pride. It is very like the innocent pride of a Gold Coast negro whose chief has bought a motor-car. The prophetic books, it seems to me, reek of the political propaganda of the adjacent paymaster states and discuss issues dead two dozen centuries ago.

One has only to read the books of Ezra and Nehemiah to realise the real quality of the return of that miscellany of settlers from Babylon, a miscellany so dubious in its origins, so difficult to comb out. But a legend grew among these people of a Tremendous Past and of a Tremendous Promise. Solomon became a legend of wealth and wisdom, a proverb of superhuman splendour.

In the New Testament we hear of "Solomon in all his Glory." It was a glory like that of the Kings of Tara. When I remarked upon this essential littleness of Palestine I did not expect any modern churchmen to be shocked. But I brought upon myself the retort from the bishops of Exeter and Gloucester that I was obsessed by "mere size" and that I had no sense of spiritual values. My friend, Mr. Alfred Noyes, reminded me that many pumpkins were larger than men's heads, and what had I to say to that? But I had not talked merely of physical size. I had said that quite apart from size nothing of primary importance in human history was begun and nothing worked out in Palestine. That is I had already said quite definitely that Palestine was not a head but a pumpkin and a small one at that. A number of people protest. But, they say, surely the great network of modern Jewry began in Palestine and Christianity also began in Palestine! To which I answer, "I too thought that." We float in these ideas from our youth up. But have we not all taken the atmosphere of belief about us too uncritically? Are either of these ideas sound? I myself have travelled from a habit of unquestioning acquiescence to entire unbelief. May not others presently do the same? I do not believe that Palestine was the cradle of either Jewry or Christendom.

So far as the origin of the Jews is concerned, the greater probability seems to me that the Jewish idea was shaped mainly in Babylon and that the return to Judea was hardly more of a complete return and concentration than the Zionist return today. From its beginning the Jewish legend was a greater thing than Palestine, and from the first it was diffused among all the defeated communities of the Semitic-speaking world.

The synthesis of Jewry was not, I feel, very much anterior, if at all, to the Christian synthesis. It was a synthesis of Semitic-speaking peoples and not simply of Hebrews. It supplied a rallying idea to the Babylonian, the Carthaginian, the Phoenician, whose trading and financial methods were far in advance of those of the Medes, Persians, Greeks and Romans who had conquered them. It was a diffused trading community from the start.

Jewry was concentrated and given a special character far more by the Talmudic literature that gathered about the Old Testament collection, than by the Old Testament story itself Does anyone claim a Palestinian origin for the Talmud? I doubt if very much of the Bible itself was written in Palestine. I believe that in nine cases out of ten when the modern Jew goes back to wail about his unforgettable wrongs in Palestine he goes back to a country from which most of his ancestors never came.

When Paul started out on his earlier enterprise of purifying and consolidating Jewry before his change of front on the road to Damascus, he was on his way to a Semitic—a Jewish community there, and Semitic communities existed and Semitic controversies were discussed in nearly every centre of his extensive mission journeys. There was indeed a school of teachers in Jerusalem itself; but Gamaliel was of Babylonian origin and Hillel spent the better part of his life and learning in Babylon before he began to teach in Jerusalem. From the Bible itself and from the disappearance of Carthaginian, Phoenician and Babylonian national traditions simultaneously with the appearance of Jewish communities throughout the western world, communities innocent of Palestinian vines and fig trees and very experienced in commerce, I infer this synthetic origin of Jewry, Of course, if the reader is a believing Christian, then I suppose the crucifixion of Jesus of Nazareth at Jerusalem is the cardinal event of history. But evidently that crucifixion had to happen somewhere and just as Christian critics can charge me with being obsessed by mere size in my deprecation of Palestine, so I can charge them with being obsessed by mere locality. If the crucifixion has the importance attached to it by orthodox theologians then, unless my reading of theology is all wrong, it must be a universal and eternal and not a temporal and local event.

Moreover nowadays there is a considerable body of quite respectable atheists, theists and variously qualified Christians who do not find in that practically unquestionable historical event—I throw no doubt upon its actuality —the centre upon which all other events revolve. There has been a steady enlightenment upon the relations of Christian doctrine ceremony and practices to the preceding religions of Egypt, Western Asia and the Mediterranean, to the Egyptian trinity, to the Goddess Isis, to the blood redemption of Mithraism. In this great assembled fabric of symbols and ideas, the simple and subversive teachings of the man Jesus who was crucified for sedition in Jerusalem, play a not very essential part. Christianity, I imagine, or something very like it, would have come into existence, with all its disputes, divisions, heresies, protestantism and dissents, if there had been no Essenes, no Nazarenes and no crucified victim at all. It was a natural outcome of the stresses and confusions that rose from the impact of more barbaric and usually Aryan-speaking conquerors, upon Egypt and upon the mainly Semitic-speaking civilisations, very much as Greek philosophy and art were the outcome of the parallel impact of the Hellenic peoples upon the Aegean cultural life. Old creeds lost their power and old usages their prestige. The temporarily suppressed civilisation sought new outlets. The urgency towards new forms of social and moral statement and adaptation was very great.

It was, I suppose, the advantage of the nexus of Semitic communities throughout the western world, that favoured the spread of Judaism and of the semi-Semitic Christianity that grew side by side with it rather than the diffusion of Persian religious inventions or Greek science and philosophy. It was an unpremeditated advantage. The thing happened so. And on that basis European mentality rests. We are all more or less saturated with this legendary distortion of historical fact. It makes us a little uncomfortable, we feel a slight shock when it is called in question.

Such is the conception of Jewish and Christian origins that has displaced the distortions of my early Low Church upbringing. It has robbed Palestine of every scrap of special significance for me and deprived those gigantic figures of my boyhood, Abraham, Isaac, Jacob and Moses of their cosmic importance altogether. They were local celebrities of a part of the world in which I have no particular interest. Once they towered to the sky. I want to get them and Palestine out of the way so that our children shall start with a better perspective of the world.

70

APPENDIX III. — THE FALL IN AMERICA, 1937

Published in Collier's, January 28th, 1938

I SPENT October and November in America and saw Indian summer at its best, colours such as no other part of the world can boast, russet, glowing reds, keen bright yellows, soft green yellows, grey-blue, black-green, and skies of a serene magnificence. And the white American homes, grey-tiled, nestled brightly in that setting. In Philadelphia it rained, but it always rains in Philadelphia, and New York forgot itself for a day or so and blew and rained. Kansas City looked amazingly fine and handsome and I admired the parklands Henry Ford is laying out by Dearborn and the fine new pile of the Yale library, Gothic with a touch of skyscraper, and 2. great success at that. From the humming plane that took me from Detroit to Boston I looked out and saw Niagara foaming in the sunshine. I spent an instructive day at Flushing while the piledrivers hammered down hundred-foot trees into the mud, like a carpet-layer hammering tacks, preparing for the buildings that are to make New York's World Fair of 1939 the most wonderful ever. Everywhere colour, warmth, movement, vitality-and people talking about the new depression and possible war.

The depression that has struck America this autumn has been the most surprising thing in the world. It has been like the unaccountable failure of an engine. The wheels that had been spinning so busily slowed down until now the spokes are visible, and nobody on earth seems to know when they will pick up again or even whether they will pick up again. I came over to America once in the season of hope and hardship when President Franklin Roosevelt was newly in the White House. I thought then that he and Stalin were the most eventful persons in the world. They are both in their successes, such as they are, and in their human shortcomings, cardinal men. The old private-property money system was showing signs of age and an imminent breakdown. A new order was indicated as plainly in America as Russia. The New Deal, I assumed, was to be a real effective reconstruction of economic relationships and the Brain Trust was to get together and tell us how. I was particularly keen at that time to see and sample what I could of the Brain Trust, that improvised council of informed and constructive men which had to modernise and re-equip a staggering modern community. I found it a trifle incoherent. I went afterwards to Russia to talk to Gorky and Stalin about the absolute necessity for free discussion if a social order is to be effectively reconstituted. But Gorky I found grown old, fame-bitten and under the spell of Stalin, and Stalin, whom I liked, has never breathed free air in his life and did not know what it meant. When I revisited the President in 1935 things were asway and rather confusing. Now they are clearer. The New Deal was a magnificent promise, and it evoked a mighty volume of hope. Now that hope has been dissipated. Mass-hope is the most wonder-working gift that can come into the hands of a popular leader. The mass-hope of world peace at the end of the Great War, the mass-hope of the Russian revolution and the mass-hope of the New Deal were great winds of opportunity. But these great winds of opportunity do not wait for ships to be built or seamen to . learn navigation. They pass; they are not to be recalled. As I flew now over sunlit America and noted the traffics of life ebbing again below, and realised that that great capital of hope was nearly spent, I found the riddle of how people will behave, get past or stand up to, what is coming to them this year, a problem very difficult to contemplate in a sunlit manner. More and more of them will be short of food and shelter this winter—with no end in sight and nothing of the trustfulness that staved of disaster, perhaps only temporarily, in 1934.

Like hundreds of thousands of people I have had some sleepless nights over that riddle. It has been more and more vivid in my mind, since I wrote Anticipation: in 1900, that our world cannot struggle out of its present confusions and insufficiencies without a vigorous re-organisation of its knowledge, thought and will. Its universities, schools, books, newspapers, discussions and so on seem absurdly inadequate for the task of informing and holding together the mind of our modern world community. Something better has to be built up.

Nothing can be improvised now in time to save us from some extremely disagreeable experiences. The Flood is coming anyhow, and the alternative to despair is to build an ark. My other name is Noah, but I am like someone who plans an ark while the rain is actually beginning. This time I have been giving a lecture in a number of great cities about various possible educational expansions. I have been trying to interest influential people in schemes for knowledge organisation and I have been talking to teachers, professors, educationists—in considerable profusion.

I have never lectured before in America and only my real fanaticism about education made me attempt it at all. I liked it much more and it tired me much less, than I had anticipated, and my audiences abounded in pleasant young people who listened intelligently and asked intelligent questions. There were drawbacks—a processional hand-shaking, for example, and a disposition to lure the lecturing visitor by promises of tea and a quiet time, into large unsuspected assemblies where he is pressed to give an uncovenanted address. He is pushed through a door suddenly and there an ambushed audience is unmasked. It is not generally known in Europe—possibly I have been carried away by some misunderstanding—that in every considerable American city large gatherings of mature, prosperous, well-dressed women are in permanent session. They sit in wait, it seems, for any passing notoriety and having caught one insist on "a few words." This year they are all wearing black hats. These hats stick in my mind. Ultimately of the most varied shapes, the original theme seems to have been cylindrical, so that the general effect of an assembly of smart American womankind in 1937 is that of a dump of roughly treated black tin cans. The crazy irrelevance of this headgear on embattled middle-aged womanhood, is as essential a part of my memories of America this year, as the general disposition to discuss the depression and suggest nothing about it, and the still unstanched criticism of the President.

I talked to the President over a lunch tray and I told him how variously he was disapproved of and how incapable the opposition seemed to be of presenting a plausible alternative to him. It was our third meeting. I wrote of him some years ago as floating a little above the level of ordinary life. I find him floating more than ever. He seems to me to belong to the type of Lord Balfour, Lord Grey of Fallodon and Justice Holmes, great independent political figures, personally charming, Olympians detached from most of the urgencies of life, dealing in a large leisurely fashion with human stresses. The President is a skilled politician, as Holmes was a great lawyer, and Grey a bird watcher and fly-fisherman, but the quality their statesmanship has in common is its dignified amateurishness. "Tell me," Balfour used to say, treating the other fellow as a professional whose business it was to know.

At the first convulsive intimations of failure in the economic machinery of America when Franklin Roosevelt came out as the saviour of his country, "Tell me" was in effect what he said and the Brain Trust was the confused response. I recalled his difficulties to him now, because I wanted to see how far he was a disappointed man and what sort of philosophy he had got out of it. The constitution had lain in wait for him, as every written constitution lies in wait for innovators. But his major insufficiency had been the quality of the aid and direction that the American universities and schools had given him. They hadn't told him, and instead of specialists they had yielded him oddities. The Brain Trust had proved very incalculable men. Men whom he had promoted had, he remarked, a trick of coming out against him. I pressed my obsession that America, like all the rest of the world, is in trouble because of its inadequate intellectual organisation. Men and women have been educated as competitive individuals and not as social collaborators and even at that the level of information has been low.

He agreed and began talking of certain experiments that had been made in the cultural development of Poughkeepsie county. It seemed to me an interesting and amiable exploitation of leisure, about as adequate to the urgencies of our contemporary situation, as polishing a brass button would be in a naval battle. I did not think him oblivious to the reality that America has to reconstruct its social life and cannot do so without a modernisation of education from top to bottom, but I got a very clear impression that he did not feel in the least responsible. He was not deeply interested in preparing for the future. That indifference is a common quality of the Olympian type.

The Olympian type assumes a competent civil service, but it cannot be troubled to make one. It takes the world as it finds it, and so the worst thing that can be charged against the President's administration is the continuation of the spoils system in the public services, for which I am told his close association with A. Farley is responsible. You cannot have safe administrators who do not feel safe.

We glanced at the possibility of a successor, but he did not seem to have any particular successor or type of successor in mind. We agreed that the danger of a world-wide war crisis would rise towards a maximum between 1939 and 1940 and he thought that by that time there should be some one younger, quicker, and better equipped to meet the urgencies of possible warfare without delay, in the White House. But he spoke of that rather as his own personal problem than Americas I left this autumnal president, feeling extremely autumnal mysel£ and a day or so after I saw a play in New York, I'd Rather Be Right, in which I found a good-humoured confirmation of my own impression. It was a play about the American future, personified by a young couple who want to marry; the president, sympathetic but inadequate, was the principal character and the cabinet, the supreme court and so forth were presented under their own names. It bore marks of divergent suggestions, cuttings and rearrangements, but the genius and geniality of George M. Cohan made a delightful and sympathetic figure of the chief. The show is saturated with derisive affection. On my previous visits to America I had remarked that President Roosevelt was believed in enormously or hated intensely. The mood has changed. They like him now. They like him more than ever they did, and they believe in his magic no more.

What do they believe in? I varied my old stock question of his critics "What is your alternative?" to "You are in for a bad winter anyhow and what are you doing to prevent an indefinite prolongation of this decline?"

Lots of people just trust to Providence. "I have always come up before," they say as the drowning man said when he went down for the third time. So far as I could find out, that was the attitude of the old Republican guard. Big business in America appears to be completely bankrupt of political and social philosophy. Probably it never had any. It had simply a set of excuses for practices that were for a time extremely profitable and agreeable. It has over-capitalised the world, exhausted the land and stuck. Unhappily it sticks in the way. The only industrial leader who seems to be looking forward is the evergreen Henry Ford. I spent a congenial day with him at Dearborn and found him greatly concerned with growing the soya bean, which fixes free nitrogen and enriches the soil that every one else is exhausting. You can make everything from soup and biscuits to motor-car bodies and electric switches from the soya bean. But Ford, in addition to being a great inventive genius, is an individualist by habit and temperament and he stands outside the American scheme, a system in himself. He is like Science. He projects new things into the world, Ford cars which revolutionise the common roads and the common life of America, Ford tractors which set collectivisation afoot in Russia and now the limitless possibilities of soya. And like Science he has his political and social limitations. In the great American [conglomerate] he is like an island of something else. He does not like acquisitive finance and he does not like trade-unionism, but he does not know how to circumvent these two necessary outgrowths of our present competitive property-money system. He has his prejudice against Jewish particularism and his false estimates about the will for peace, but even in that prejudice and that false estimate there is maybe a gleam of prophetic foresight. A harder-thinking United States might have assimilated instead of isolating this outstanding imaginative genius. On the Left side of American affairs, strikes rather than ideas, increase and multiply. I was as much impressed by the number of pickets on the New York pavements as I was by the multitude of black can hats in the women's societies. I had heard a good deal about john L, Lewis as a coming man who Was going to do great things in politics. I met him and tried to find out how he thought the world was going. It reminded me of the distant past when I tried to get Clynes and Henderson and such-like lights of labour to tell me exactly what they thought they were going to do with the dear old British empire.

Maybe I misjudged him, but the impression I had was of a man, leonine according to the old senatorial model—he would look well in a cage with Senator Borah— and capable, but specialised largely in the purely labour issues of transport and mining. Anthracite and its rights and wrongs have entered into his soul. I aired my lifelong insistence that we and our world are all horribly at sixes and sevens mentally, and that first and foremost the world has to learn and think. He and my host denied hotly that the American Labour Party ignored education.

But I could not satisfy myself that what Labour means by education in America is anything more than an upward extension of the scholastic thing that is, qualified by a certain amount of training for political efficiency. I doubt if in America labour has got even so far as J.F. Horrabin of the British Plebs League or Laski and Strachey of the London Left Book Club, men who have evidently concluded long ago that equipment for an eternal class war is the sole end of human education. I do not believe that any benefit will accrue to America through the development of a special Labour Party in its political life. It is likely to be a heavy drag on intelligent reconstruction. As it has been in Britain. Labour parties have failed to become anything but trade-union parties and trade unionism is nothing more than the defensive organisation of the workers under a private capitalistic system. Its natural tactics are defensive and obstructive. It aims at shorter hours, better pay and a restraint upon dismissals. It is unable to imagine a new system. But a hundred years ago Karl Marx evolved a fantastic notion, partly from an inadequate analysis of British trade unionism and partly out of his inner consciousness, that the worker mass could become a mighty reconstructive force in the world. With no Blue Prints of what it was going to reconstruct. That would be the heresy of Utopianism. That delusion, embodied in communism and labour socialism, has undermined and checked the forces of science and creative liberalism for a century.

The British Labour leaders in power, showed themselves politicians within the containing politics of their time; they had neither the imagination nor the confidence in themselves to lay hands upon the universities, the diplomatic service, the foreign office and the monetary and financial organisations they found in being; they seem never to have heard of the gold standard until it hit them; and put to the test they did not even "nationalise" anything of importance. John L. Lewis may end in the White House as Ramsay Macdonald ended in royal favour, Clynes and Henderson in court costumes and Snowden and Webb in the house of lords. But "end" is the word for what any definitely Labour politician seems likely to do in the way of creative reconstruction.

I question indeed if the United States has sufficient time ahead to go through a phase of class politics at all. It has had all the possibilities of that worked out for it and ready for study—from Great Britain to Russia. It is an unprecedented country in its size, its freedom and its physical opportunities and I think the world has a right to expect something characteristic and original from it. Cannot it cut out that particular phase and get on?

The thing I found most hopeful among the falling equities and the falling leaves of this visit, was my occasional glimpses of the younger people. I saw more of them and I liked them better than I have ever done before. Every country nowadays' shows a contrast between the old and the young—a contrast in more than age; but here the contrast is astonishing. One still has the old boys with their stately, fatherly presences, uttering platitudes with an intensity of conviction unknown in the rest of the world, one is still introduced to a succession of presidential candidates with an irresistible suggestion about them of Tristram Shandy's bull—and THEN you meet the young.

In Henry James's America Revisited he tells of an encounter with a party of pre-war youth, drunken, noisy, coarsely sexual and hilariously irresponsible. I found very little of that, this journey. Instead I found a new generation, alert and interrogative. They have learnt about life in three courses of instruction. The disillusionment of the war made them pacifist. At first in rather a shallow fashion. They just proclaimed they were not to be humbugged into that sort of thing again. Dos Passos, that distinguished writer, has stuck at that stage, he is now a fossil from the first period. He proclaims that the Atlantic is too wide for air-raids, and has not yet discovered Mexico and South America nor the fact that America cannot keep her whole fleet in the Atlantic and the Pacific at the same time. But his juniors have taken these complications into account. Then before they could settle down into a qualified isolationism came the collapse that necessitated the New Deal. There again there was a tendency to think cheaply and there was a rush of uncritical communism, happily arrested—"happily" so far as America goes-by the Moscow trials and the Trotsky controversy, Now they seem to be facing the American problem in something like its real distinctness and complexity. They have to go further and reconstruct more fundamentally than Marx ever dreamt oh making new minds as well as a new world. I talked to a bunch at Harvard and I talked to a bunch at Yale and sampled individuals in the other places I visited. Cheap red paint is at a discount. I suppose that in a world of Tristram Shandy leaders, the phase of resentful insurgent communism was inevitable, but now in America you could put all the organised communists, rich undergraduates and genuine proletarians together, into a third-rate town and still have houses to let.

Reconstruction through socialisation, strenuous educational work to build up a competent receiver for bankrupt and expropriated public utilities, a steady development of a loyal civil service, freed from—"Farleyism" seems to be the word I want—and after the harsh winter that must surely follow this present Fall, a new spring may break upon the world from America. Through its renascent young people.

Two young men—for so I speak of men in the early forties, nowadays—produced a vivid the upon me, the presidents of Harvard and Yale. They are something new in my experience of Americans, something fresh, clear, frank and simple. President Conant of Harvard, for example, is a very distinguished chemist indeed; he has the balanced lucid mind of the research addict, and he is deliberately fuming from physical science to educational and administrative work. Every one speaks well of him. Ever since I met him I have been asking whether there are more like him and why he is not in the running for the White House. "He has been talked of," I was told, "but—"

"Well?"

"You see we've already had one college president there—Wilson."

It seems an inadequate excuse. For Wilson was a professor of history, that is to say, a man trained to be unscientific.

Indian summer still reigned as the Queen Mary with a sort of lazy swiftness pulled out from dock. I watched the great grey and brown and amber masses, cliffs and pinnacles of middle and then of lower New York, soften in the twilight and light up. What a spectacle it is!, Such towering achievement and so little finality. How much more vitally unfinished than the contour of dear old Saint Paul's, brooding like a shapely episcopalian hen over the futile uneasiness of London! America seems to have a limitless capacity for scrapping and beginning again.

71

APPENDIX IV. — TRANSATLANTIC MISUNDERSTANDINGS

Published in Liberty, January 15th, 1938

I HAVE recently been going to and fro in America, talking to all sorts of people and hearing all kinds of opinions. I am one of those realists who refuse to be blinkered by current political institutions. I belong to that great and growing community which has a common literature and a common language in English. There has been a revolution in communications during the past hundred years, a virtual abolition of distance, which makes our old separations preposterous. The English-speaking states and nations scattered about the world are no longer divergent. They are coming together again, in their thoughts, knowledge, interests and purposes. They have a common future.

I believe profoundly in the synthetic power of a common idiom of thought and expression. Given a free movement of books, papers, radio beams and the like, this is a unifying force that will triumph ultimately over every form of particularism, nationalism and imaginative antagonism. It is bringing the Californian into clearer and closer understanding with the Kentishman, the New Yorker, the Scot, the Maori, the Afrikander, the Canadian, the Welshman, the Anglo-Indian and the Eurasian. I doubt if the green barriers of a censorship and an artificial language will suffice to keep the Irish Free State out of our world-wide coalescence for long. Irishmen are not going to live content talking faked Erse in a small damp island when they have for wit and abuse and the whole English-speaking world at their disposal. I refuse to call myself foreign or alien among any people who speak, read and think in English. It is because they are less reasonable today than ever they were, that I find the resistances to this greater fusion, increasingly remarkable. There are such resistances, one must admit. There are still all sorts of queer and out-of-date frictions and obstructions in the confluence of this new world-wide English-speaking community of ours. This is particularly evident between the United States and Britain. Partly this is due to bad tricks of manner and bad habits of mind on the part of the British which irritate many types of Americans excessively; partly it is due to deep-rooted traditions of distrust and antagonism which have long since ceased to have any practical justification.

Almost all English people forget that so far as origins go the population of the United States never was wholly British. They disregard the early Dutch, Swedish, French and other non-British settlers who slowly adopted the English language and traditions before the War of Independence and the immense infusion of the later immigrations, immigrants who had no earthly reason for Anglomania. These people accepted English and the forms of English thought, they amalgamated with the American school of the English-speaking culture, many of them transferred their ancestors to the Mayflower and acquired a kind of pre-natal pride in the Battle of Bunker Hill, yet steadily and particularly since the beginning of this century, their distinctive qualities have manifested themselves in a greater variety, a wider range, in American imaginative literature and a broader, more enterprising quality in American thought. For long Boston remained more English than England, but forty years ago my generation hailed the intellectual revolt against Boston (and refined Anglicanism) first in a sprinkling of isolated writers from Whitman to Stephen Crane, and then in a comprehensive expansion and release, which has now made American intellectual life not so much a continuation as a vast extension and Europeanisation of English culture. The annexations have been enormous. The English element has played the part, not so much of a direction as a flux. These are matters all too frequently ignored by English people. The thing has happened in history before. just as American education has oriented itself to the War of Independence, in which not one in a score of living Americans had an active ancestor, so the great Phoenician, Babylonian and Carthaginian populations acquired and entered into that tradition of Judea which holds together the comity of Judaism today. Probably, too, under the empire, millions of Roman citizens from York to Egypt without a drop of Roman blood in their veins felt a personal pride in Romulus and Remus. Assimilation is far easier and more powerful than inheritance. It is the linguistic link and the progressive development of common ideas and understandings that are destined to hold the English-speaking community together in the future. Britain never was the mother country of the United States, and the first thing an English visitor to America should do is to get rid of that illusion. Long years ago, a century ago, one of the great New England writers of that time—was it Lowell?—wrote a stinging paper on "a certain air of patronage in foreigners." It was an excellent reproof to visiting Europeans and particularly to Englishmen who came over to see America as a new young country, betrayed a sort of upper-form attitude to the new boys, and were quite unable to realise that a man of forty in America is just as old as a man of forty in England, has seen just as much of life and counts as many ancestors between himself and Adam. The political association of Britain and America lasted hardly a couple of centuries. But it set a perennial stamp upon their destinies. From the beginning of their separation there has been a peculiar mutual irritation between Britain and America. It has in it something of the vexation of a divorced couple who still resentfully care for things they had in common. "Think what the Empire would have been if you had stuck to us," is the unspoken accusation of the ordinary Britisher. "Why did you make things so that we had to break?" says the American. "It was your fault," say both of them, "and my side was in the right." Maybe you will think that is now ancient history. It is not. It is as alive today as it was a century ago. The mighty growth of America makes the British none the less regretful for the loss of a common world outlook. They paid too much for clear old George the Third. It was the Hanoverian monarchy, the hungry exploitation of America by the British governing class and the narrow traditions of the Foreign Office that caused that breach. Plebeian Britain was on the side of the colonies in the War of Independence—John Wilkes was very brother to Tom Paine—and from Gibbon's Decline and Fall (1776-88) to Winwood Reade's Martyrdom of Man (1872) you can find the liveliest anticipations in English literature of the role of North America as the hope and refuge of Western culture and freedom. Nothing is forgotten so rapidly as very recent history, and few people nowadays realise how near Britain came a century ago to following the United States along the path to republicanism and to emancipation from an aristocratic ruling class. Joseph Chamberlain, the father of the present Prime Minister, was a republican outright, but nowadays we forget his talk of ransom—his New Deal phase. Both countries are amazingly ignorant of each other's history during the early nineteenth-century period—they were too busy in other directions to observe each other closely—and few Americans seem to realise the struggle that went on in England during their civil war between the ruling class, which looked forward with pleasant resentment to the break up of the Union, and the liberal British, who instinctively realised that the strength and freedom of America were bound up with their own. To this day relics of that old upper-class resentment lingers. The Bourbons of the court and the diplomatic services still betray a lurking patronage, depreciation and a weak vindictiveness towards America. "Society" is in politics in Britain and out of it in America, but the economic, social and political trends in both systems are alike, their massive interests and mental dispositions converge, and however these retrospective elements may falsify our superficial relationships the enduring disposition of the generality in Britain towards America and the drive behind the national policy are, and always have been, co-operative.

But balancing the retrospective resentment of the British ruling class, there is on the other side a whole system of estrangement between these great populations arising primarily out of the too-cherished tradition of the War of Independence. For several generations that great revolt formed the basis of historical instruction in America. The bridge at Concord, the Boston Tea Party were exaggerated gigantically. The new immigrants took them over. The incoming German or Eastern European learnt to boil with indignation at the employment of Hessian troopers by the Hanoverian king. The inevitable misdemeanours on the part of the British were charged up against them in the true spirit of war propaganda. In the war of 1812 they burnt the Capitol. This was not all. All that might have been forgotten. But the newly separated states developed a financial organisation only very slowly. They were not industrialised for nearly a hundred years and they had to be industrialised by foreign capital—which in those days meant British capital. And they developed a diplomatic service belatedly. Because of this an inferiority complex towards the British arose, quite naturally, but one that has long since lost any material justification. Wall Street as it grew seemed to the Americans generally very like a British foothold in their economy. America felt that it was entangled monetarily, sold out to London, mysteriously out-manoeuvred in its foreign relations.

America grew, a unified continental mass. Her population is now two-thirds of the English-speaking world, while the British find themselves responsible for an empire which spreads about the planet, the most vulnerable, the most entangled, the most threatened of all existing political systems. Its foreign policy has become now an almost pathetic self-protective opportunism. But to the American this empire is still a greedy octopus, to be distrusted systematically. It has kept an unguarded frontier to the north of him since the separation, nevertheless it is to be distrusted. Its fleets have never threatened America and for fifty years at least Americans have had no uneasiness on their eastern coasts very largely on account of Great Britain, nevertheless it is to be distrusted. Wherever the Union Jack goes it takes the English-speaking American commercial traveller and a friendly banking system with it, nevertheless it is to be distrusted. Some mysterious undermining process is believed to be going on. The phrase adopted, since the War to express this profound distrust has been "British Propaganda."

Suspicion of British propaganda has become a mania. Old ladies in the middle west look under the bed at nights for British propaganda. At home, I am a persona most distinctly non gram with the court, the church, the public schools, the universities, the whole Anglican system; but when I go to America I am discovered to be a British propagandist. America in her serene path to abundance and happiness, is being lured into another war—for the sake of the British. That is the story. America has no interest in the welfare of China, it seems, because the British have great investments there. But we tempt her in. We invented the Pacific coast on her. It is British propaganda to suggest that America has some slight interest in the destinies of the Spanish and the Portuguese-speaking· worlds. To say that isolation from the rest of the world's affairs is a rather cowardly and altogether impracticable ideal for America nowadays, is British propaganda.

There is a copious literature of propaganda against this imaginary British propaganda. The other day I read a book by Mr. Quincy Howe, England Experts Every American to do his Duty, which is quite typical of the methods of the campaign of distrust and estrangement. The history of Anglo-American relations is combed through to present America as the simpleminded cat's-paw of British cunning. This sort of thing crops up everywhere. I found it in the questions put to me after my lectures; I met it in conversation. "You British" they began. Though I had come to America to talk about educational reorganisation and not about international affairs. A hostile power preparing for a conflict with England solo or America solo could not cultivate a crippling breach of their natural alliance more efficiently than this probably quite spontaneous misinterpretation of the British drift. It may prove a very disastrous thing for the entire English-speaking world.

72

APPENDIX V. — THE ENGLISH-SPEAKING WORLD

"AS I SEE IT"
Broadcast talk delivered December 1st, 1937

I FIND myself on the air for the Empire broadcasting service—free to speak for a quarter of an hour on practically any subject that occurs to me—under this most liberating title of As I See it. I suggest that, As I Think about it, would have been a better title. What I see is a brightly lit desk, a lamp, a microphone in a pleasantly furnished room—and a listener, for I never talk for broadcasting without a real live listener actually in the room with me—but what I am thinking about is a great number of listeners, some alone, some in groups, in all sorts of rooms and places, all round the world. We are, I guess, an extremely various and scattered lot indeed, race, religion, colour, age. We have probably only one thing in common. Which is that we speak, write and understand English.

I want to talk about ourselves and the community to which we belong. I see that as a tremendous world brotherhood full of possibilities and full of promise for the hope, the peace, the common understanding of all mankind.

I have been asked by the Empire Broadcasting Service to make this talk, but it is, you must understand, a quite uncontrolled talk or I would not give it. I hold no brief for the Empire as such; it is a complex of political arrangements, which are constantly changing and will continue to change. Widely as it extends, it does not include the larger part of this English-speaking brotherhood of ours, which is to my mind something infinitely more real, more important and more permanent. I am talking reality—not propaganda.

I spent this autumn in the United States. I was lecturing there about intellectual organisation in schools and universities and I talked with all sorts of people from the President and Mr. Henry Ford downward. We all talked the same language, in the same idiom of thought. We understood each other pretty thoroughly. Yet we are drawn from the most diverse sources. It is a common mistake among English people to suppose that Americans are just English people transplanted.

But from the very beginning the United States were of diverse origin. The Swedes, the Dutch, Germans, the French in Louisiana, the Spanish i.n California, were there as soon as the New Englanders, long before the War of Independence. Afterwards there was an enormous influx of Eastern Europeans. And again in the British Empire itself, there is a great assembly of once alien peoples drawn together into a common interchange—from the Eskimo of the Labrador Coast to the Maori of New Zealand. But the English language has amalgamated—or is amalgamating-all these elements into a great cosmopolis, whose citizens can write to each other, read and understand each other, speak freely and plainly to each other, exchange, acquire and modify ideas with a minimum of difficulty. Once or twice before in history there has been such a synthesis in the Latin-speaking world, in the Semitic-speaking world, but never on such a vast scale as in this English-speaking world in which we live and think today. And English has never been forced upon these multitudes who speak it now, they were never subdued to it or humiliated by it, they have taken it up freely and they use it of their own good-will because it serves them best. Now a thing that impresses me greatly, it seems to me one of the most important things in our present world, is that this English-speaking community is not breaking up and does not look like breaking up, into different languages. In the past that sort of thing did occur. Latin, as you know, broke up into French, Italian, Castilian, Catalan and a multitude of minor dialects. But since then a vast change has occurred in the conditions of human life; the forces of separation have been dwindling, the forces that bring us nearer to one another have been increasing enormously, the printed word, books, newspapers, the talking movie, the radio, increasing travel, increasing trade, now forbid dispersal. History has gone into reverse. Instead of being scattered about the earth and forgetting one another, a thing which happened to the Aryan speakers and the Mongolian speakers of the past, we English speakers are being drawn together and learning more and more about each other. This reversal of the old order of things has been going on ever since the steamship and the railways appeared, a century ago. It goes on faster and faster. In the past new dialects were continually appearing; new dialects are disappearing. The curse of Babel has been lifted from over three hundred million people. This coming together is a new thing in human experience. And having got this unprecedented instrument of thought spread all about the world, a net of understanding, what are we English speakers doing with it to get the best out of it? Are we getting the best out of it?

Are we growing into one mighty community of ideas and sympathies and help and peace as rapidly as we might do? I do not think we are. Something, I admit, is being done to realise the tremendous opportunity of the world-wide spreading of the English language, but nothing like what might be done, if we grasped our possibilities to the full.

Let me tell you as briefly as I can one or two of the things that might be done to make this great gift of a common language better worth while. They are things every one of us in this talk tonight can set about demanding at once. You can write to your representative or member of parliament about them before you go to bed.

First about books. Nothing can pull our minds together as powerfully as books. We all want to read books according to our interests and habits. We find them so dear to buy or so difficult to borrow that most of us cannot read half the books we hear about. And three-quarters of what books there are, we never hear about at all. This is true even here in London. Here I am on the telephone to well-stored book shops and all sorts of people from whom I can get advice. Even so it is true here. But a majority of my listeners tonight may be living in parts of the Empire far away from the centres of book distribution. Mentally many of them must suffer the torments of Tantalus. They perceive there is a great and refreshing flood of ideas, imaginative, informative matter, fantasy, poetical invention flowing through the English world and they Call get only just a splash or so of it to their thirsty lips. In Great Britain in the larger towns you can buy a fair selection of the best books published, even quite new books, for from sixpence to a shilling. But in America there are no really cheap books and the great mass of the workers and poor people there, never read books at all. There are public libraries, of course, where you can wait for books for quite a long time. Most of our 300,000,000 English speakers, through no fault of their own, read nothing better than a few odd books that chance to come their way. They never acquire the habit of systematic book reading. English, which should be the key of all human thought and knowledge, is for them the key to a non-existent door.

The reading, thinking section, the book-reading section, of the Empire probably does not number a million all told. The rest either read newspapers or do not read at all.

Now before you blame the public or the schools or the booksellers for this immense illiteracy, this great mental underdevelopment, consider the difficulties of sending books about. Try sending a book, a good fat book, half-way round the world and see what it costs you. You will realise that a special low postal rate for books and parcels of books, a special preference rate, a rate to encourage the sending of books, is one of the first things necessary before we can begin to realise the full cultural promise of our widespread English tongue. It is a matter that should concern every Ministry of Education. Does it?

Given such rates you'll soon rind every publisher in the world building bigger printing plants and selling books for sixpence—almost as soon as they are issued. But book postage is not considered a public service. It is made a source of revenue and until people like ourselves who read and listen in and want to know begin to make a fuss about it, matters will remain very much as they are.

Cheap good books—and next comes the problem of how to hear of them—so that we may—from the ends of the earth—order the ones we really want and spend our sixpences properly. Well, probably half my hearers have never heard of what is called documentation, and they think bibliography is something remote and scholastic and all that sort of thing. But really it is nothing more or less than indexing all that has been written in the world, so that you can find out quickly and surely what has been done, by whom, and under what title. Don't you want to know that? And do you know it? There are hundreds of clever people working out methods of indexing and in a little while it will be quite possible to print and keep up-to-date bibliographies, lists of all the best books, in every great group of subjects in the world. It would be as easy to keep up such bibliography as it is to keep up the issue of railway time-tables. The cost of producing these book guides need not be very much greater than the cost of producing those time-tables. I doubt if today a hundred thousand of us use any bibliographies at all. What is the good of reading unless you know what books to read? Bibliographies ought to lie about in every educated household.

And another thing which we English speakers have a right to ask for, considering what a vast multitude we are and all that we might be, and that is a general summary of contemporary knowledge and ideas, a real modern, adequate Encyclopaedia, kept up to date and available for the use of any one. That would hold us all together as nothing else would do. We should all be of a mind and nothing on earth would have the strength to stand against our thinking. But is there anything of the sort? No. The latest Encyclopaedia in my study is dated 1929—eight years old—and it is a very imperfect performance at that. Very old-fashioned. Very little better than the Encyclopaedias of a hundred years ago. Discovery and invention have been going on vigorously for the past eight years—but how am I to learn quickly about that new stuff? There is not a sign of a new one in sight. Does any one care—any of our education departments? Not a rap. The French just now—in spite of threats of war, in spite of great financial difficulties are making a new and a very admirably planned Encyclopaedia. You may think an Encyclopaedia is something only rich people can afford to buy. It ought not to be. If you can afford a radio set, if you can afford a motor-car, surely you can afford a summary of human thought and knowledge. Encyclopaedias need not be as dear as they are, any more than books or bibliographies. Cheaper books, handy bibliographies, a great encyclopaedia, our English-speaking world needs all these things. When automobiles first came along, they seemed likely to become a rich man's monopoly. They cost upwards of £1,000. Henry Ford altered all that. He put the poor man on the road. We want a Henry Ford today to modernise the distribution of knowledge, make good knowledge cheap and easy in this still very ignorant, ill-educated, ill-served English-speaking world of ours. Which might be the greatest power on earth for the consolidation of humanity and the establishing of an enduring creative Pax for all mankind.

My quarter of an hour is at an end. I haven't said half of what I would like to say. But if I have made you a little discontented with what we are doing with this precious inheritance of ours—English, I shall not have used this bit of time in vain.

THE END

www.ingramcontent.com/pod-product-compliance
Lightning Source LLC
Chambersburg PA
CBHW081102300726
48976CB00011B/2700

* 9 7 8 1 9 9 8 7 0 4 5 4 5 *